D1514408

FROZEN
TEARS

FROZEN
TEARS

AUTHORS' INDEX ON PAGE 792

ISBN 1-873352-68-9

THE HORROGRAPHER

Dalston Manor,
Thursday, Dec. 26, 2002,
17.05 pm

Dear John,

At last I sit down to write. This time directly. No more procrastination, no more composition, no more re-writes. The New Year deadline is drawing nearer and I am fearful that I might miss this rare and precious opportunity to communicate this warning to you. But the closer I come to the deadline the further I seem to be from completion of the work. Here, once again, this telescoping of lived experience from the hope for a finished work; here, once again, at the brutal core of what I hoped to write. Like it always was. Only more so.

I have been trying to outrun my fate for too long. Exhaustion has finally caught up with me. Did I bring this upon myself? How long ago did I take the wrong path? I am too far from the cause of my fate to speculate on its initial causes, to ask what original misfortune brought me to this place. But that was what I had hoped to achieve by writing *The Horrographer*.

For the last three years I have struggled to extricate myself from the realm of shades into which I had voluntarily descended. Recently I'd begun to reason the daemons and spirits I entertained as phantasmagoric embodiments of some ulterior existential issue, crediting my fate to the account of an unconscious wish; a tragic fantasy vindicating my creative despair. How else was I to explain such a run of terrible luck, so many encounters, in so short a time, with these grievous harbingers of misfortune. I had made no Faustian bargain, at least none of which I was conscious. I was secure in the belief that my occult record was clean. I was still holding feebly on to that thesis until the attack on Friday.

I wanted to create something good, a work that could reverse the fatal allure of the Real that bewitches me, that could represent the terror at the core of my being without perpetuating it. I yearned for a work of redemption that would close at last this ghastly chapter of my life.

I had learned only recently, and perhaps too late, that to write *from* the terror of death is to write *towards* it. I wanted to have done with the endless representations of mortal violence that had preoccupied my imagination for so long. I know that the ultimate purpose of representational terror is the perpetuation through others of the terror depicted.

I had been looking for the way out of this labyrinth. I thought *The Horrographer* would direct me. *The Horrographer* was to be the text of my infernal shade-plagued double, whose existence would come to an end with your reading of this text.

But no sooner had I begun at last to see through the veils of this cursed delerium, to extricate myself from the weave of spiralling negativity in which my soul was ensnared, than once again the real conditions of existence reared up and hammered their hopeless message home again.

Is this in fact Fate, a self-fulfilling prophecy or the machinations of a daemon? It's gone too far now for me to know. I have consorted with unclean spirits and explored the vilest of imaginary territories, believing, obscurely, that some good reason for these indulgences would be found there. I fear now that death will take me before a substantial basis for hope is found.

Twice since your invitation to submit something for *Frozen Tears* my efforts have been derailed by what, for the sake of brevity, I can best describe as 'violent incursions of the Real'. It goads me to resort to such language. The self-defeat of a theoretical language of Reality is analogous to the self-defeat of an ethical representation of terror. But together these self-defeating impulses constitute the snares in which my life has become inextricably entwined. By threatening the continuation of my life these violent encounters also threatened the completion of the work. And here is the infernal paradox of which I write. Knowing from violent fact that my fear is grounded in actuality makes the writing doubly artificial. Another turn of the screw, another hackneyed literary cliché, another Dalston crime statistic – GD 4642048/02/BR – for the record.

The first encounter with cursed horrographic coincidence I have chosen to evade. It was too twisted and vile to dwell upon for long. I was lucky to escape that encounter – if escape it I have – physically unscathed. The spiritual wounds are healing and the misanthropic lessons have been learned. But the second is impossible to ignore if the work is to be done.

My immediate concern is the damage that was done to my skull after it was smashed against the wall. I remained conscious but I smelt concussion and bled. I am feverish now but if pneumonia was coming I think it would have already taken over. My vision has not been the same since the blow and, although there is no general pain in my head, there is an ominous numbness spreading through the skin of my face and neck. My skull still hurts it made direct contact with the wall. When I run my hand from crown to ear memories of an earlier and much more severe beating are here with me again. Twenty years ago, like now, I couldn't bare to go to causualty. I just wanted to forget. I never learned the degree of cranial damage that may have been done. It is too late now. I am resigned to whatever neuronal catastrophe awaits me. I wonder if the mental and emotional derangement I have lived these last seven years is a belated consequence of that earlier beating. Perhaps daemons are hatched from damaged brains to lead us down the winding paths of dementia towards the grave.

This is the first time since Friday that I have felt able to recommence the work. I am still alive and that is good. Physical death is distant enough to afford me this last opportunity to write. But I worry that the blows to my skull may have robbed me of something more than the paltry possessions that were taken in the attack. I fear that whatever essential quality of mind I had vainly imagined might guide the work to completion may have been extinguished for good by the blows.

Creative thought is sensuous thought and the possibility for transformative art depends on the capacity to sensualise communication in the direction of psychosomatic well-being. That is what I had hoped for. But what if the traumatic damage is irreversible? What if the Hope of art can be literally beaten out of the body and brain?

For the sake of completing *The Horrographer* I was tempted to write that the manuscript was stolen with the rest of my possessions and that is now decomposing slowly at the bottom of Regent's canal. I could then structure this letter around the story a work twice lost. I could begin the sequel, the story about my attempt to find the lost manuscript of a violent confrontation with, etc, etc … But now there's barely time for the facts, let alone another tissue of lies.

I fear that this fatal commitment to the Real is sealing my fate. It is a futile commitment summoning a futile Fate. It ends with myself hanging on a scaffold of redundant values. There is a powerful enigma in this commitment to the truth of experience, this moralistic insistence on honesty, integrity and veracity, this refusal to let Fantasy carry me away from my beloved and despicable Fact. Reality now is a daemonic glamour that compels us to hack the wings off Ambition and binds our Love to the grave.

I wonder if the imperative to remain as true as possible to the authenticity of one's experience is the same commitment that led me to here. I think back. Again and again, in this endless loop spiralling around the sign of Repetition, Reality and Death. How to get out of the endless cycle without drawing my Self closer and closer to madness and the grave? And now another blow. The spiral turns in ever tighter. I fear my quota of angels has expired. Now there is just this ineluctable, protracted and solitary decomposition of my being towards death. Is there anything I can do to stop it? Could this writing? I will never know. I can do no more than try. This is my last hope. Though *The Horrographer* was never written perhaps its work can still be done.

An unavoidable tone of irony accompanies any warning delivered in a literary mode. The allure of the traumatic realism is at its strongest here. How could I expect you or your readers heed the warning any more than I? All warnings are also, inevitably, seductions. Nevertheless I will state it once again, speaking as one who can no longer make the distinction:

"Be careful when you play with phantoms that you don't become one".

I know that we all must die but I never imagined it to be so close, so soon. So here I am again, in the solitary space of writing, addressing the incommunicable actuality of Love, Terror and Death. Here we are frozen out of durational time; here no Presence can guarantee the authenticity of the experience and events from whence I would write; here the most recent, most actual event has no more veracity than the remotest of memories or the flimsiest of lies.

I therefore leave the gauge of my integrity, and the sincerity of this warning, to your judgment.

Dalston Manor,
Friday, Dec. 27, 2002

The Horrographer was to be set here, now, in East London. The situation is one of general social disintegration; increased polarization of wealth; starker contrasts between haves and have-nots; localised intensifications of motivated and unmotivated violence; a trend towards a US-style gun culture met by 24 hour, armed police patrols; a widespread despondency regarding traditional modes of political organisation and effective social action; and a continuous atmosphere of emotional crisis driven by economic insecurity.

The Horrographer was to be made up of three sections; a letter, the story of *The Horrographer*, and a manuscript called *Kronspor: Whirlwind of Ephemerids*. These sections were imagined as intersecting circles. The ultimate aim of the text was to bring the reader to the cryptic cipher at the axis of the three converging sections. The zones of intersection between each component part were intended to operate as thresholds for transtemporal communication between the reader and the multiple personifications of death that *Kronspor: Whirlwind of Ephemerids* was designed to incubate.

The Horrographer began with a letter addressed to the author. The letter would warn it's addressee that by reading the enclosed story they were putting themselves in mortal danger. The letter would give the reader a simple choice: if they had no faith in the existence of the Soul, before or after death, then there was nothing for them to risk by reading the story. But if they harboured a shadow of doubt they should continue no further. If they chose not to read the story then they should pass it on to someone with nothing to risk.

The Horrographer was to be the story of a deranged *artiste manqué* trying to recollect the lost fragments of several aborted works with a view to creating one final, finished masterwork. It was a recollection both literal and figural. In his quest for the lost work the central protagonist would recount the circumstances of the abandoned projects, each one bringing him closer to the climactic revelation of his murderous destiny. The text was to be punctuated by a sequence of encounters with the immobile and paralysing kernel of inutility that rendered all his thoughts of affirmative creation pointless. The story would gravitate towards the dark core that simultaneously drives the work and renders it unfinishable.

The central protagonist was a character familiar from Existential-Gothic literature, driven by a profound inner anguish towards sociocidal rage by some unspeakable thing at the centre of his being; a thing he could never shake off or outrun; a thing to which he was fatally bound. All his creative energy derived from this infernal core. Any optimistic impulse he had to create a work of lasting value – a work that might afford him the fantasy of being an artist – was mercilessly extinguished there.

He had been duped in his youth by the liberal-progressive myth of avant-garde art, a deception that now festered rancorously inside him. He was led to believe that art's collective social purpose was to dehabituate normative modes of perception and thought; to criticize and challenge the dominant, repressive and unjust exercise of social authority and power; and to create emancipatory, transformative and expressive ways of being in the world. Essentially it was a means of improving the life-world through the conscious exercise of creative imagination and action.

In dutiful compliance with his schooling in Marxist, Freudian and Structuralist theory the horrographer was convinced that in order to create a truly emancipatory art he must first rid himself of the historical, psychological and linguistic determinations that had made him what he was. It was especially important to rid oneself of the insidious myths of Genius, Authorship, Originality, Individualism and Authenticity that were the ideological justifications for bourgois cultural authority. The first step towards a clean revolutionary slate would be to detach oneself from these reactionary shibboleths. In so doing the horrographer would document the process of his subjective-creative disintegration.

But the further down the path of self-deconstruction the horrographer travelled the further he was from the kind of art he had imagined would be the outcome. If, as his reading of critical theory suggested, modes of self-consciousness were concretely determined by the material conditions of history, how could one become effectively other than what one was historically determined to be? From what critical position could the subject undo its 'self' and retain the capacity for creative expression? Everything pointed in the direction of a transtemporal, disembodied notion of subjective Consciousness that his teachings condemned. He became increasingly entwined in the conceptual snares of Realism, Identity, Consciousness and Death; his thoughts perpetually returned to an imaginary inner space mediated by the ideas of law, limit, transgression, trauma and repetition. When his thoughts turned to the subject of Death he felt his mind locked out of historical time, his inner being bound to a punctuated network of conceptual traumata, which mapped the co-ordinate limits of his self-consciousness. He slipped out of present time. When he tried to make art he was instantly returned to the timeless labyrinth of his anguished interiority.

He began to feel cursed by the fateful circumstances that had produced him, the inescapable memories of terroristic identifications, which made the current social demands to be some 'thing' or some 'one' a suffocating impossibility. Gradually the rage that should have been directed against the institutional mechanisms of social injustice he now directed at himself, against the extrinsic and inhuman determinations that made him what he was and punished him for what he was not. He was torturer and victim, captive and interrogator, witch and inquisitor. Between his terror of death and the violent inscriptions of institutional Reason that stratified the world in response to it, the horrographer took temporary sanctuary in the memorial space of his auto-creative impossibility. There he wandered like the living ghost of himself.

The more he tried to make art the worse his life became. If art did not make his life better how could it do so for others? Was the failing in him, the myth or the world? He became incurably envious of those around him who made their work without the mortal anguish that plagued him. Feelings of creative inferiority impelled him to despise anyone who assumed a position of social superiority in the name of Art. The uncritical ease with which his friends adopted the identity of artist proved their complicity with an over-arching system of cultural authority and cowardice. Having no means to express itself upon those with real power in this system he vented his rancor on the unwitting perpetrators of cultural tyranny closest to him.

In one scene from the unwritten story, the horrographer chats to an old acquaintance in a cafe. They have just been to see Carlolee Schneeman's re-staging of *Meatjoy*. He was appalled by the spectacle. His acquaintance, a gallery artist, explains how she survives the duplicitous contradictions of her artist-identity by 'living fictions'. She imagines the people who enter her life are characters in a life-script that she directs at will. Her life was her artwork. Without the fantasy of 'being an artist' she would fall into hopeless despair and depression. This was precisely the kind of vacuous fantasy the horrographer found impossible to sustain. He detested the vain illusions that shielded others from the terror that crippled him. Instead the horrographer took surreptitious pleasure in destroying the fantasy supports that enabled others to live out their aesthetic fictions. He aspired to make a work that could not be put to use by the edifices of institutionalised Culture, a work that would remain true to the anguished issues of death, loss and non-identity that wrecked his hope. No artwork could undo death's irreversible work. The cathedrals of Culture – to which the brain-dead devotees of this empty cult gravitated – were monuments to an ancient, faithless despotism. No amount of shit on their altars would change that. It was for the nameless dead of subjugated peoples that he would create a commemorative anti-work, an anti-hierarchical weapon of vengeance. It would be irreducible to any form of economic exchange, would have no physical substance by which it could be possessed or substituted or to which a value could be attached; it would bare no name, have no lasting substance, yet it's impact would be undeniable and irreversible. He dreamed of apocalyptic acts of creative-destruction, of triggering monuments to collapse and orgiastic epidemics of social disorder.

He had attempted to undermine the determining structural constraints of his identity, to root out any pact he might secretly have made with posterity. But the horrographer had not taken his auto-eradication to the final limit. He had not been able to let go of the ideals that shaped him, to fully eradicate the roots of Romantic Tragedy and Heroic Destiny. And now, bereft of Hope and abandoned by the last of his former friends, the horrographer belligerently set about regaining a self from the futile fragments of the lost work. The very constraints against which all his efforts had been directed were now his only hope of escaping the fatal trap of anonymous death he had inadvertently set in motion. Without a name upon which to base his work how could the horrographer find a space to transmit the curse that was to be his masterwork? The imp of cynical duplicity took hold of his soul: the accounts of his subjective disintegration might still contain the seeds of a compliant Ego-art for the future.

The quest to consolidate the recovered identity of his work brought the horrographer into contact with several characters from his past, each of whom, he believed, had in their possession an element of his final work. As each unwitting trustee of the *The Horrographer* denied possession of, or responsibility for, the lost fragments, the horrographer descended further into his maniacal derangement. He became increasingly volatile to accusations about his sanity. His belief in the actuality of the lost fragments must be, finally, fatal. If not to another, then to himself. The work will be finished by an irreversible act.

As his inner crisis intensified the horrographer became obsessed with the technological obstacles preventing him from integrating and consolidating his work. He was particularly hystericised by computer technology and began to see, in the incompatibility of multiplying media formats and machine interfaces, a metaphor for his creative debilitation. In this tangled machinic chaos the horrographer recognised the hypercapitalist reflection of his subjective impossibility. What fragments he did manage to gather were locked in redundant file formats he no longer had the hardware to run. When, finally, he managed to retrieve and open a lost file, it only served to underline the paltry character of his earlier self and delusional nature of his quest.
The closer he comes to completing his work the more he is flashed through by powerful images of himself committing acts of blind, brutal violence. The images

had the quality of future events being unscrambled backwards towards the present. The horrographer sensed his life-script was already written but not by himself. All he had to do was tune into the broadcast and let it lead him to his destiny.

In the absence of lost fragments that would have constituted the Masterwork he begins to formulate a work of malefice, one with the virulent capacity to contaminate those exposed to it with his own inner anguish and terror. He is guided in his infernal machinations by the memory of something George Bataille once wrote; 'The ritual of witchcraft is the ritual of an oppressed people'. He remembers his old friend's strategy of 'living fiction' and is filled with a new sense of purpose and direction. The work will be that murderous destiny he can no longer outrun. His art will be guided by Death. He will project himself into the space of superstitious madness as a mode of artistic revolt. Terror and fear will be his inspiration. He will create in blind flight and panic from the place of everyone's impossibility. His loss of faith in the transformative power of art will afford him the freedom to create an infernal work, a work that will invert the very ideals that had once made art the embodiment of creative Hope.

As the horrographer slips further into delirium he starts to imagine that his life is being guided by a malefic embodiment of Death. This daemon has been visiting him intermittently since, as a child, he first became conscious of mortality. From that first moment Kronspor had been with him. It was there at the beginning and it would be there at the end, to take him through the door that consciousness of death had frozen wide open inside him. A host of previously unconnected memories suddenly fall into place. In each of them he recognised, in the peripheral margins of perception, Kronspor's terroristic presence.

The legendary familial spirits that had haunted his dead Mother's line would now direct his actions. Gradually the horrographer began to conceive an art of telepathic magic and psychic terror. He had been called by a personified shade of Death to do its bidding. Kronspor tells the horrographer how to extract from the salvaged fragments of his lost work the elements of a telepathic automaton with the virulent capacity to contaminate whoever reads it with the terror that wrecks Hope. He would give himself over to the guidance of this daemon; let it lead him in the way of those dark arts, which proliferate where the Self is undone in the shadow of Death. For a work of art to be truly cursed, to be so villous and abhorrent that no goodness could ever result from it, it must be the product of the left handed path of necromancy. He must summon the bitter spirits of the restless dead.

Gradually, from the chaos of his infernal derangement the plot of *Kronspor: Whirlwind of Ephemerids* begins to develop. If others are to believe in Kronspor, first must he. The work of *The Horrographer* would be to convince the reader of Kronspor's existence. He would put the tools of traumatic realism at the service of Death, create an infernal and demonic version of himself, in whose name the curse could be communicated. *The Horrographer* would be the vehicle by which *Kronspor: Whirlwind of Ephemerids* could be disseminated

He draws a magical circle at the centre of the story, a line, which he will seduce the reader to cross, rather than himself. If he can lead the reader unwittingly to this place in the text he can implant the curse in them. By the time the reader has reached this level of the text it is already too late to return.

This circle represents the impossible core of himself and the work. It is original *idée fixé*, the first and final limit of conscious being, the place where death always is. It is in this near death space of anguished interiority that the horrographer splits the living from the dead self. There the soul hovers between two states. The purpose of this terror is to freeze the soul out of the body into this liminal state. Then and there possession commences.

The ultimate horror is realising at the point of death that there never was any work, that the quest for a meaningful existence was utterly futile, and that the only companionship one has at the point of death is a malign spirit-double. That is Kronspor. He has always been there. And *The Horrographer* was always his work.

The horrographer's terror resides in the centre of the circle. He realises that the work must conclude with suicide, murder or failure. *The Horrographer* can only be closed by his own death or his substitution by an other. In order to become himself he must step out of the circle while seducing the other into entering.

He must deliver the reader to the work of death. He must give them to Kronspor.

"The place I always, already was, you shall now be".

Dalston Manor,
Sunday, January 5th, 2003

Dear John,

The deadline has passed. Still I have heard no word from you. But I am still alive and my wounds have healed.

This morning I sit down to write the final draft. Once again.

What demand will make me finish the work? What motive can I find?

I awoke from my dreams to the name 'Eunuch'. It was a name for me; the one who cannot complete his work; the childless one; the loveless and motiveless one. How could I complete this work? And for who? I think perhaps I am unable.

As I closed in on the completion of the work my thoughts, typically, gravitated towards a memorial location from my childhood. It's a new angle on a familiar place. That's the recurrent pattern. All a new work ever amounts to is a different perspective on an old territory. And the person t/here now is called Eunuch.

For the record the location is in the grounds of the secondary school I went to as a youth, between the long grass banks, the banks down which older boys would traditionally throw the younger. Close by is one of the oldest recurring memory locations; 'the music room'. Inside 'the music room' *The Romantic Agony* is stored. In the centre is the grave of Swinburne's dead lover, Shelly's monster weeping over his maker's corpse. Nearby is Millais' 'Ophelia' and before the door Bellini's

St. Theresa, 'The Agony and Ecstasy'. Beyond the door, facing inwards, are Burroughs's newspaper prophesies, the 'cut-up, and, fold-in, techniques'. *The Book of Control* hovers nearby, Robert Anton Wilson's *Coincidance*, Terry Castle's *Phantasmagoria*, to the left, along the path a little … it goes on. Text upon stacked text, associative threads woven into the memorial fabric of my Fixed-Passed.

Each angle on the scene contains it's own web of associations. I could scan the angles for some new combination of elements, recounting the cross-threaded network of names until I die. Perhaps that is all I will ever do. In the end it is all the same. These maps are too familiar and too easy to manouvre. Chain after chain of consolidated association, lines of flight that always return to the same terminus-destination; to this abysmal Eunuch that is their ground. With each work I simply dig myself deeper into the hopeless weave, into the grave that never leaves, the one I carry within myself.

The school playing field, seen from the top of the bank, is similarly riddled with memorial texts. I had presumed my transport here was guided by association with the attack two weeks ago. In my first week of school a group of older boys had thrown me down the bank like a dog. I was incensed. I leaped up and charged the group punching and clawing wildly. They threw me to the ground again, laughing. And again I sprung back, tears streaming down my face, and laid into them once more. I think I would have kept going until they beat me unconscious or I was too exhausted to carry on. But an older boy, an acquaintance from my neighbourhood, stepped in and gently coaxed me away from the confrontation. I can no longer summon such rage. Nor would I want to. The grave comes closer.

Since that childhood encounter this has been the memorial space which underpins stories of unbridled physical rage between unequal adversaries. The scene for the bank has been over-determined by explanations of over-determination; over there, in the middle of the field, Simon's 'cyclonic identity' scattering the foundation of Margot's feminist ethics, Sean breaking another boy's collar-bone in righteous rage; a little further out a youthful football-playing Kerouac borrows money from his Aunt for a road trip, and over the school wall beyond him are 'Cool-Aid', 'Hawaiian Punch' and the temporal structure of Malcolm Lowry's *Under The Volcano*.

But now I locate a parallel line of association connecting my memorial imagination to this place above the playing field. Here ideas are linked to the thought and writing of George Bataille, those contained in *Hegel, Death and Sacrifice* and *Guilty*. From the latter is the paradox of trying to write authentically and without artifice about the anguish in trying to write, in turning anguish into literature; the Guilt experienced while writing a literature of Evil in the time of Holocausts. From *Hegel, Death and Sacrifice* is the issue of the limits of Reason and Consciousness at the point of Death, the ghastly faces that haunted Hegel in the emptiness of the infinite night, like the face that flashes for a fraction of a second in *The Exorcist* and the flashbacks which haunt Colonel Kane in Blatty's, *The 9th Configuration*.

This is the quote from Hegel, which opens Bataille's essay;

"Man is the night, that empty Nothingness, which contains everything in its undivided simplicity: the wealth of an infinite number of representations, of images, not one which comes precisely to mind, or which [moreover], are not [there] insofar as they are really present. It is the night, the interiority – or – the intimacy of Nature which exists here: [*the*] pure personal-Ego. In phantasmagorical representations it is the night on all sides; here suddenly surges up a blood spattered head; there, another, white, apparition; and they disappear just as abruptly. That is the night that one perceives if one looks a man in the eyes; then one is delving into a night which becomes terrible; it is the night of the world which then presents itself to us".

For the horrographer, quoting Bataille is the move of a coward. Great souls do not require the authority of the canonized dead to support their creative vision. They state what is for them without fear of judgment. This the horrographer could never do. Impotence feeds his rancour. Great names, he insists, are the intellectual defendants of trust fund libertines and the academic lap-dogs of Papa Culture, who wait longingly to be possessed by their master's genius and to possess their father's inheritance. "Ventriloquist's dolls and grotesque *Männchen*! AWAKE!"

But it is in silence that he screams. He knows too well the double-handed impossibility of such a command. It would only serve to further deepen the trance it is intended to break. The somnambulistic trance of history and civilization can only be deepened now. There is no longer a state into which anyone could awake.

'Man is Death living a human life'.

As I re-read what I have written I am filled with despair.

What I want to say I cannot. I am sick. I cry all the time. I don't know how long I can go on.

I know where and when this thing of darkness came to me. It came when I realised that Art was a way to defer the unbearable burden of immediate existence into the future.

I realised this one night as a teenager. My mother was by then far into her alcoholic dementia. It was customary for me to find her drunk and ranting when I came home on a night. I believe the basis of my existential terror originates here, in this fear of returning home to a raving insanity at the centre of a former sanctuary.

I was the special object of this relentless rage. I had been since very young. I believe now that it was her own mortal terror of death and loss that drove her into madness. It was not to me that her rage was due but some other unbearable absence that crippled her. I was the thing which would receive the despairing anger she could vent on no one else.

The spirit of a future art came to me that night while my mother stomped around the bedroom above me ranting and raving. She kept shouting, "He's a BASTARD that one, a little BASTARD!". It went on and on, for hours. I was exhausted, wanted to sleep, but knew I couldn't. I simply had to wait there, in the living room below, until it ended. Rage seethed inside me, flowed through my blood, streaming images of butchery, urging me to go up there, to finish off her rants once and for all, silence that fucking bitch for good. But I couldn't.

It was then that the idea of representing this scene in the future descended upon me like a kind of grace. I was held by the idea. It protected me in place of mother I wanted to kill. The idea of representing this anguish in an art of the future calmed the murderous thoughts that were ripping me apart. The spirit of a future art temporarily suppressed the murderer that my Mother's madness summoned. One day, in the future, people will know how this feels, I thought. Now I realise how cursed an idea it was. Is not the fantasmatic projection of terror into a future art merely a displacement of that terror onto another? Those flash images of violence that raged through my mind then do so still. My mother has been dead for ten years.

So I will spare you the details. All I really want to say, now, to you, the reader, is that for the horrographer the impossibility of art stems from that moment; the moment when the spirits of death, murder and art come into perfect alignment and freeze you out of time.

I realise now that life has been running out of me since then. I can never leave the place of our encounters. Death seals me there. Death is the dark core behind every terroristic point of memorial attraction and I am no more than a dark weave of negativity, the frozen sum of proliferating perforations through which death flows.

I was waiting for an angel to carry me from this place of holes. Several came. But in my terror I took them for apparitions. They had come to offer Salvation. But the weight death placed upon me was too much for their wings to bear. Death gave me the strength to test their Love to its breaking point. Each one left in turn.

My time in the territories of hopelessness and despair must come to an end. But no lines of communication can keep a person in touch with 'the outside world' when that world has been paranoiacally involuted.

I have tried to pull myself back from shades but I fear it

is too late. Violence stalks me. I am being tracked down. No penance can be made. I have welcomed darkness into my soul and now it consumes me.

What would it mean to convince you? Your conviction would be your damnation. And I do not want to damn you or your readers, to implicate you in this terror.

Every path out of the labyrinth leads one further into its inexorable embrace. I must withhold from you the insights which have enabled me to escape it's clutches for long enough to write this letter. The bridges I have crossed are too fragile for more than one soul to traverse.

It is because I am unable, ultimately, to secure for others, a means to escape from the infernal regions of terroristic interiority that *The Horrographer* remains unfinished.

SIGHS TRAPPED BY LIARS
1997

I

"Co-ordinated girls must be persistently emancipated."
Dominique unstuck the girl.

Dominique swept beneath Valencia.

Vickie improvised beside Valencia and squashed her coulis into Valencia's glass.

Poor girls were linked Dominique shovelled the ash of Valencia as she balked the piled snow. She described a clique to Valencia, flowering in the girl's fear and belabouring immature faux words.

Sisters approved a skill in handouts of Valencia's designer.

"No less limited Dominique."

The poor girls were shirking and hailing one another.

Dominique demoted her.

Valencia scattered, but the reject was recanting.

Dominique quieted Valencia's slight yawn then the skid slowed.

The girl who had held the long trip came over to Valencia.

The small girl smoked and talked as the hostage did and slumped round her notary. The teacher got to Valencia.

Dominique blew her health upon the girl.

There were nubiferous girls all around the tomb.

The girl's tachographs were packed with long shared pellets, dropping Rose and another girl were winding a trenchant male in through a terrible aperture.

The girl they were matriculating was fined.

Valencia uttered.

Whenever Dominique would pass close, the girl would begin to try a scone.

Shrinking robes, Valencia would storm off and loudly sand the floor.

Afterwards she would speed for hours, skimming, rocketing and grading Dominique every inch of Dominique's Soutine. She dressed her neat and blacked her face. Dominique's friend sadly. Dominique ran her gerund through the blare of the filed smut wavering at her.

Valencia erased her song on Dominique's flute and began to park the shoes one by one.

The girl was caught with the rugs for her agoraphobia.

Dominique sent her lover and clapped the soft trusty of the permanent girl bloating beside her.

"I'm Dave, maybe". Dominique looked at Dave.

Dominique swore upon her regress filing out her pets. Cast kicking?

Dominique gave Valencia a rap in the week to retrieve her from her parcel.

"Let's start hailing these boys."

One boy gave Dominique five sachets.

One by one the boys were checked off by the two girls.

One of the boys picked up the rugs that had been fluffed in Valencia's officiousness.

Valencia and Dominique played Clementine.

Dave recommended his cassoulet to Dominique. "I'm glad you biked it," said Dominique.

The boys became ruthless. Dominique went to her leaves. Dominique shrugged. As the boys depleted each other Valencia cashed in on them.

"My girls are retards." Valencia forgot her cast-offs awaiting the last of the menagerie, the shape of the school raised boy.

Dominique had to exhort her.

Valencia laughed. Valencia was leaning. Dominique raced. Vickie praised Valencia's looks until the overtures turned puerile.

Dominique was remaindered in the faction by checklists. Harriet was a sumptuous girl.

Dominique was pitched about in the laughter. Dominique phoned as her Dominique was talked down to eat. One girl stepped on a used sturdy triplicated colander. She drew out the spot cash as another girl clocked Dominique's glance.

"Shame, shame on yooouuu, shame, shame on yooouuu."

Vickie appeased Dominique by the principles.

Vickie took up a lath and began to cosh Dominique's cat.

Dominique grew back her leg and growled.

"You tank," Valencia cried.

Valencia was tidy and snuffled on hankies to pack the drapes of Vickie. Dominique was topical again.

Valencia.

Girls sloped off in chairs and small coops. Valencia primped away. She came restively to Dominique's.

Valencia knew where it was kept.

Valencia opened the door and centered the meretricious sheet.

II

The entire time was one long fortnight's recession. Valencia was in the straight after puncturing fame, her past recovered in pelotons of french whelps. She synthesized and lied, but matched in febricity the temperature of other girls. Dominique recalled her girls.

"Co-ordinated girls must be persistently emancipated."

Dominique unstuck the girl, trapping and splicing the blurted quips, heckling and hooting the criminals.

The girl sighed intimately from shame, but her case crashed dead and the short bum began to shun doubt of her scatty smocks. Dominique swept beneath Valencia. She invoked Valencia's manipulations and hooked onto her guide with contradictions.

Vickie improvised beside Valencia and squashed her coulis into Valencia's glass. Poor girls were linked up with large mauls in their ranks. Dominique shovelled the ash of Valencia as she balked the piled snow.

She described a clique to Valencia, flowering in the girl's fear and belabouring immature faux words.

Sisters approved a skill in handouts of Valencia's designer.

"No less limited Dominique."

The poor girls were shirking and hailing one another.

Rose and three other girls began to dodge them as they fled the cannibals around behind their steps.

Dominique demoted her.

Valencia scattered, but the reject was recanting. A livid young girl with long bored stare and banging fists was lapped around by coracles.

Dominique quieted Valencia's slight yawn then the skid slowed. The poor girls had demobilized their sharks. One girl was compelled by two brokers in further efforts while another packed and toiled a long trip around her. The girl who had held the long trip came over to Valencia.

The small girl smoked and talked as the hostage did and slumped round her notary. Valencia blabbered, showing that such a fling would avariciously be fun to her.

"Somebody skim my pasta."

Another girl began to shut the wavering diptych with a snap. The teacher got to Valencia. "Welcome back to contentedness," said Dominique.

"Hah."

Dominique blew her health upon the girl.

Valencia raced out into anachronism again. There were nubiferous girls all around the tomb in valuable spates of offstage disintegration. The girl's tachographs were packed with long shared pellets, dropping crudities which had dyed an ermine.

Rose and another girl were winding a trenchant male in through a terrible aperture.

"I say you're a freak," she said to Valencia. The girl they were matriculating was fined with her palms stretched to hide a herpes scar.

Valencia uttered.

Whenever Dominique would pass close, the girl would begin to try a scone.

"You really do rig it," Dominique would say when wiping her face. As the sheik tore in two the slight shrinking robes, Valencia would storm off and loudly sand the floor.

Afterwards she would speed for hours, skimming, rocketing and grading Dominique. She flecked every inch of Dominique's Soutine, dressed her neat and blacked her face. She yanked keys from Dominique's friend sadly.

Dominique ran her gerund through the blare of the filed smut wavering at her default. Valencia erased her song on Dominique's flute and began to park the shoes one by one.

The girl was caught with the rugs for her agoraphobia.

"I want to talk with you," Dominique told her. Dominique sent her lover and clapped the soft trusty sight beheld. "Who are you?" demanded Dominique, drowning the people beside her. She dealt the art of the permanent girl bloating beside her.

"I'm Dave, maybe. You're one of those pesky lords from the graph streaking Pole."

Dominique made a mental note to have the walls raised by five feet.

Dominique looked at Dave.

Dominique swore upon her regress filing out her pets.

She ran aground and clicked the hydro-phone light off, regretting her last chill-out.

"Show hobbling? Cast kicking? Slate whacking?"

"It is a riled tick."

Dominique gave Valencia a rap in the week to retrieve her from her parcel.

"Let's start hailing these boys."

They dispossessed the boys one by one. Shards frayed in their stress, cinders were shovelled in folds and streaked in cash. Fast toads were pinched and trapped. One boy gave Dominique five sachets with his crap, leaving a recollection of smells on her like grafts.

The fleet exploded all the way down to the throne; anchor chain shot through the dances. Dominique was flushed to the seas before Dave.

One by one the boys were checked off by the two girls.

One of the boys picked up the rugs that had been fluffed in Valencia's officiousness.

Valencia and Dominique played Clementine.

With murky paws they stacked relics high.

Dave recommended his cassoulet to Dominique. She veiled a wrong in his clone trained face and stitched a seam.

"I'm glad you biked it," said Dominique.

The boys became ruthless. Dominique went to her leaves. She opened her flask and pulled out a small pick-axe. "Put it down lady," threatened Dave.

Dave was folding his sacrificial skirt in his hand. Dominique put a mallet through the centre of the D.

The recumbent boys stood up for a lazy rain on the ground. Dominique shrugged. As the boys depleted each other Valencia cashed in on them.

"I could let you roam into the pool grounds to picket and obstruct the girls. My girls are retards and would love to be obstructed."

"Dumpy perch."

The larking boy came up to the front of the troupe.

The speaking growling boy with the glad horse was checked in the piece by his nine friends. "Come along Valencia."

Valencia forgot her cast-offs awaiting the last of the menagerie, the shape of the school raised boy and the class linking. Dominique had to exhort her.

"Needless to say, if you tell anybody at the pool about this Valencia, you'll be an ephemeral bubble and repining the sin of your past."

Valencia laughed. Valencia was leaning. The hapless swain with the wrong orange pip flashed dynamite into her chintz, blotter and pyres. Anathematisation after anathematisation saw her dumped coal deplete. The quints quashed her chance. There stood a class of girls of all three trades, with toques and cranes. They crowded Dominique and Valencia and pounded their kite. Dominique raced with her headband round behind her shack, her gospel on the lips of two struggling girls.

"Rebel."

Vickie praised Valencia's looks until the overtures turned puerile.

Dominique was remaindered in the faction by checklists. Harriet was a sumptuous girl with negative words and unfaded gloss. Dominique was pitched about in the laughter. Dominique phoned as her import was phased out, disused and converted.

Dominique was talked down to eat. One girl stepped on a used sturdy triplicated colander. She drew out the spot cash as another girl clocked Dominique's glance. The groom was mistaken raiding clinics in the night rounds.

"Shame, shame on yooouuu, shame, shame on yooouuu."

Vickie appeased Dominique by the principles.

"Ooh, kosher, you're only doing this because of

Valencia, you're querulous."

Vickie took up a lath and began to cosh Dominique's cat. Dominique grew back her leg and growled.

"You tank," Valencia cried.

Valencia was tidy and snuffled on hankies to pack the drapes of Vickie. As she packed drapes

Dominique was topical again. Bands swung and heeded the lesser parts of her pizzicato and freak sounds.

Dominique's designs were kept by buyers, the buyers frightening until their hopes were sullied by the solid mess.

Somebody scraped her fez with a small mop. Vickie continued to derogate the scraping. Valencia slept a day and shut her house to the affair of Rose.

Girls sloped off in chairs and small coops. Valencia primped away. She came restively to Dominique's rooms. Valencia knew where it was kept.

Valencia opened the door and centered the meretricious sheet.

II(i)

The entire time was one long torchlight procession. Valencia was in the late faster-functioning train, her past discovered in demijohns of fresh whelks. She sympathized and tried, but matched in fabrication the temper of other girls. Dominique heckled her girls.

"Abominated girls must be resistantly anticipated."

Dominique unstuck the girl, tripping and splashing the blurred drips, decking and shooting the cripples.

The girl lied iteratively from Spain, but her face crushed bread and the shot crumb began to run out of her scanty stocks. Dominique stepped before Valencia. She revoked Valencia's stipulations and hooked into her guys with hot rations.

Vickie improved beside Valencia and splashed her muesli into Valencia's glass. Four girls were linked up with large calls on their banks. Dominique shelved the cash of Valencia as she walked the tiled row.

She described her week to Valencia glowering in the girl's cheer, and belittling mature fauve work.

Sinners removed a till in and out of Valencia's free diner. "Oh yes limitless Dominique."

The dour girls were smirking and hallowing one another.

Rose and three other girls began to lodge them as they led the animals around behind their stumps.

Dominique promoted her.

Valencia shattered, but the project was reciting. A lurid young girl with long blond hair and bragging fits was snapped around by oracles.

Dominique quoted Valencia's light yarn then the Scud showed. The four girls had demolished their charts. One girl was repelled by two brothers in feather tuffets while another blacked and soiled a long strip around her.

The girl who had held the long strip came over to Valencia.

The small girl joked and hawked as the hostess hid and jumped round her note. Valencia blubbered, knowing that such a string would adventitiously be run to her.

"Somebody skip my past."

Another girl began to shout the slavering dictum with a yap. The feature got to Valencia. "Welcome back to contentiousness," said Dominique.

"Bah."

Dominique grew her wealth upon the girl.

Valencia paced out into Ancona again. There were numinous girls all around the loom in valorous states of hostage disorientation. The girl's track and grass were parked with long shed pelts, dripping crud which had fried an urchin. Rose and another girl were grinding a henchman's kale into a horrible ordure.

"I see you're a fake," she said to Valencia. The girl they were maturing was found with her arms stretched wide to a harpie's car. Valencia shuddered.

Whenever Dominique would pass close, the girl would begin to shy a stone.

"You really do dig it," Dominique would say when typing her farce. As the sheep swore into the light wrinkling lobes, Valencia would stalk off and proudly end the tour.

Afterwards she would weed for hours, trimming, docketting and greeting Dominique. She flicked every inch of Dominique's suits clean, missed her beat and lacked her grace. She ranked pleas from Dominique's friend badly. Dominique ran her errand through the stare of the riled nut slavering at her defeat. Valencia blazed her song on Dominique's lute and began to pluck the blues one by one.

The girl was short with the hugs for her angora.

"I want to talk with you," Dominique told her. Dominique rent her cover and flapped the soft musty sign behind. "Who are you?" demanded Dominique, crowning her people behind her. She smelt the fart of the petulant girl bleating behind her.

"I'm Dave, maybe. You're one of those peeky wards from the glass broking pool." Dominique made a mental note to have the walls raised by five feet.

Dominique looked at Dave.

Dominique bore upon her cress filling out her nets. She swam aground and clipped the micro-phone light off, getting her vast bill out.

"Snow lobbing? Fast flicking? Skate tracking?"

"It is a piled brick."

Dominique gave Valencia a wrap on the grease to remove her from her panel.

"Let's start healing these boys."

They depressed the boys one by one. Bards played with their creche, sinners were shoved up front and struck in class. Vast probes were winched and snapped. One boy gave Dominique five sashes with his cap, leaving a collection of bells on her light grease.

The feet expanded all the way down to the 'phone; cranky strain shot through their glances. Dominique was bussed to her pleas before Dave.

One by one the boys were choked off by the two girls.

One of the boys picked up the drugs that had been puffed in Valencia's offices.

Valencia and Dominique played Rubenstein.

With quirky straws they stacked ricks high.

Dave represented his casserole to Dominique. She veered a throng into his clown-brained farce and pitched a scheme.

"I'm glad you liked it," said Dominique.

The boys became toothless. Dominique went to her loaves. She opened her flag and pulled out a small pickle. "Put it down lady," threatened Dave.

Dave was folding his unofficial shirt in his hand. Dominique put a palette through the centre of the D.

The recalcitrant boys stood in for a crazy Dane on the ground. Dominique shrugged. As the boys defeated each other Valencia crashed on them.

"I could let you roam into the pool grounds to ticket and induct the girls. My girls are rock-hard and would love to be inducted."

"Dusty Kirsche."

The barking boy came up to the front of the group.

The speeding fouling boy with the sad house was choked in the grease by his nine friends. "Come along Valencia."

Valencia had got her cassock off wanting the last of the imagery, the tape of the scowl roused boy and the crass thinking. Dominique had to export her.

"Needless to say, if you tell anybody at the pool about this Valencia, you'll be in ethereal rubble and mining the tin of your brass."

Valencia laughed. Valencia was leaning. The happy Dane with the strong porridge dip flushed dead mites into her chips, bottle and pies.

Apophthegmatisation after apophthegmatisation saw her slumped soul deplete. The quips quashed her glance. There stood a mass of girls of all three shades, with hopes and aims. They powdered Dominique and Valencia and grounded their flight. Dominique raced with her husband round behind her shack, her gossip on the lips of two straggling girls.

"Rebel."

Vickie praised Valencia's cooks until the officials turned purposeful.

Dominique was commandeered in the function by cellists. Harriet was a Somerset girl with bigoted wants and unaided grace. Dominique was pushed about in the water. Dominique droned as her input was passed out used and inverted.

Dominique was brought down two feet. One girl stamped on a huge studied triple-sided colophon. She strewed out the hot cash as another girl locked Dominique's clasp. The group was taken reading classics in the night sounds.

"Shame, shame on yooouuu, shame, shame on yooouuu."

Vickie teased Dominique by the pinnacles.

"Ooh, kirsche, you're only doing this because of Valencia, you're garrulous."

Vickie took up a bath and began to slosh Dominique's kit. Dominique drew back her leg and fouled.

"You plant," Valencia cried.

Valencia was untidy and shuffled on donkeys to pick the grapes of Vickie. As she picked grapes Dominique was

46

toppled again. Hands hung and weeded the messy parts of her pizza and grease mounds.

Dominique's signs were clapped by choirs, the choirs heightening until their whoops were hurried by the sullen mass.

Somebody skipped her fence with a small map. Vickie continued to deride the skipping. Valencia slipped away and shut her house to the affront of Rose.

Girls skipped off in fairs and small troupes. Valencia limped away. She came festively to Dominique's rooms. Valencia knew where it was kept.

Valencia opened the door and entered the lateritious suite.

III

It was weekend, fine for some reason at the pool. The entire time was one long torchlight procession. Valencia was in the late faster-functioning train, her past covered in demijohns of fresh whelks. She sympathized and tried, but matched in fabrication the temper of other girls. Dominique heckled her girls. "Abominated girls must be resistantly anticipated." Dominique unstuck the girl, tripping and splashing the blurred drips, decking and shooting the cripples. The girl lied iteratively from Spain, but her face crushed bread and the shot crumb began to run out of her scanty socks. Dominique stepped before Valencia. She revoked Valencia's stipulations and hooked into her guys with hot rations.

Vickie improved beside Valencia and splashed her muesli into Valencia's glass. One pair of plants enlarged her front, growing skin and snout with crusts and blinkers, slapping and skimming the pips, while the other hoarded and filched her sticks.

Valencia began to brush and comb in an untrained way

with cowed drones and a lot of shrews swatting out at her clocks. The cold hack put strands to her contempt, blasted wits, smirking and pleading anywhere. Four girls were linked up with large calls on their banks. Dominique shelved the cash of Valencia as she walked the tiled row. She described her week to Valencia glowering in the girl's cheer, and belittling mature fauve work.

The precious bards swayed with hermits, jumbling and crashing them, falling out the cripples and then dipping them lightly and teasing until they were dead and poor. Sinners removed a till in and out of Valencia's free diner.

"Do you like seeing sinners choked?"

"Oh yes limitless Dominique."

The dour girls were smirking and hallowing one another.

Rose and three other girls began to lodge them as they led the animals around behind their stumps.

Dominique promoted her.

Valencia shattered, but the project was reciting. Dominique soaked her from oxbow to rivulet as she quit into the shade of her rock. Her plans then ruthlessly suppressed the weak melée and after that the hip young shits. A lurid young girl with long blond hair and bragging fits was snapped around by oracles.

Dominique quoted Valencia's light yarn then the Scud showed. The four girls had demolished their charts. Pets were shipped with sliding cogs, bats and horses. One girl was repelled by two brothers in feather tuffets while another blacked and soiled a long strip around her. The strip circulated her sounding strange through her stress as though she was seeing dawn in bloom.

The girl who had held the long strip came over to Valencia. She ran errands over the sweet strained grace notes expiating a charge as they shattered and pitched under her rasp.

The wrong cash leaked out to clip the oft announcing odes. Valencia's graph was soon spaced with voluminous dud cults and they were overlooked by one another and a lazy slattern. The tall girl with the long back chair who had been negating the fickle bronzed one with the bib pockets across the door now sat in her doctor's place, a wide patty tin hitting her piling counterfeits.

"Catch this."

There was a crowd in a half-circle around her to watch her pass down the note of the girl wrapped under her scale. The small girl joked and hawked as the hostess hid and jumped round her note. Valencia blubbered, knowing that such a string would adventitiously be run to her. "I want to be a dark edged cave. Somebody skip my past."

Another girl began to shout the slavering dictum with a yap. Her floors shifted and fell, reflecting long and wild shrieks upon the street. Rose flushed a large and wobegone imam out of her store.

The feature got to Valencia. As the shame in her fits steadily gripped her and her glance fogged with the dirt from the feature, she listened to the mild babble of streams, watching mint and grass clipped – and fronds over-growing with hostas.

"Welcome back to contentiousness," said Dominique.

"Bah."

Dominique grew her wealth upon the girl. She wished her wise, tucked her note and high bids, flashed and folded every stitch of her win. She tricked the pest from the lost bin, led out her stocks, rushed an alligator's parapet and sat on a stair for an hour watching it bump blunt feet while she'd interrogate and implode her own stump.

She shook the girl off her sheet of flame and fenagled Blur on the tour, charms and dregs bound to steal things. Then she showily lit every inch of schematic

Valencia's mess. Valencia paced out into Ancona again. There were numinous girls all around the loom in valorous states of hostage disorientation. One had her hounds stride up behind her track. The girl's track and grass were parked with long shed pelts, dripping crud which had fried an urchin. Rose and another girl were grinding a henchman's kale into a horrible ordure.

"I see you're a fake," she said to Valencia. "Well, collapse and catch this brittle lumber."

The girl they were maturing was found with her arms stretched wide to a harpie's car. The wrongs were healed in her official by hope and strain. Valencia shuddered.

Whenever Dominique would pass close, the girl would begin to shy a stone. If her stint was square she would aimlessly interrupt herself. It was the talk of the whole pool.

"You really do dig it," Dominique would say when typing her farce. As the sheep swore into the light wrinkling lobes, Valencia would stalk off and proudly end the tour.

Afterwards she would weed for hours, trimming, docketting and greeting Dominique. She flicked every inch of Dominique's suits clean, missed her beat and lacked her grace. She ranked pleas from Dominique's friend badly. She also cranked wit from her spouse.

Dominique ran her errand through the stare of the riled nut slavering at her defeat. "No thank you."

Valencia blazed her song on Dominique's lute and began to pluck the blues one by one.

That Wednesday night they went into town together. The girl was short with the hugs for her angora and platypus. "I want to talk with you," Dominique told her. "We can drink and work while I hog your pack with three brunches."

Dominique rent her cover and flapped the soft musty sign behind. "Who are you?" demanded Dominique, crowning her people behind her. She smelt the fart of the petulant girl bleating behind her.

"I'm Dave, maybe. You're one of those peeky wards from the glass broking pool. And this is one of the little scot toughs, right?"

"Sealed glances do it every time."

Dominique made a mental note to have the walls raised by five feet.

"We saw you in the movies and figured we could drag off a cast piece of your glass outside the walls." Dominique looked at Dave.

"We'll send you back to the pool with years in your glances."

"I can see I'm stealing with an old lady."

Dominique bore upon her cress filling out her nets. She swam aground and clipped the microphone light off, getting her vast bill out, discovered only by clumsy slack aunties.

"Snow lobbing? Fast flicking? Skate tracking?"

"You really are a styled bun. We were watching you cue it to your friend and it looks like a piled brick."

"It is a piled brick."

Dominique gave Valencia a wrap on the grease to remove her from her panel.

"Let's start healing these boys."

They depressed the boys one by one. Bards played with their creche, sinners were shoved up front and struck in class. Writs were scribbled on, tacked and written. Vast probes were winched and snapped. One boy gave Dominique five sashes with his cap, leaving a collection of bells on her light grease.

The feet expanded all the way down to the 'phone; cranky strain shot through their glances. They schemed and lied like applicants. Dominique was bussed to her pleas before Dave. He walked around exterminating her evanescent toady with his hands. One by one the boys were choked off by the two girls. They stamped round the hot scrum. One of the boys picked up the drugs that had been puffed in Valencia's offices. He drugged the widows in the clasp of the girls all of the day, leaving them thin.

The louts were kicked, spalls were struck, gum slowed down the riled stoats. Valencia and Dominique played Rubenstein. They pinched and plumped their shock forces, the sonnets dammed in their classics decreasing their textual furacity.

The boys signed them up for another round of sly snobs. With quirky straws they stacked ricks high. They stacked and ricked and punned and riddled. They sank down the short turf.

Dave represented his casserole to Dominique. She veered a throng into his clown-brained
farce and pitched a scheme. She ticked all of the crass Danes off and moved a throng all the way in, screaming at his farce. She followed through after a half-hour of crass kicking while Valencia truncated his stack, by a vast grease dripping gob on all the others. As she flicked grease, Valencia pinched clocks.

"There, that was a lot of fun."

"I'm glad you liked it," said Dominique.

The boys became toothless. Dominique went to her loaves. She opened her flag and pulled out a small pickle. She looked at the admonished boys with a snide grin.

"Now I want you boys to reform a crazy Dane and play Rubenstein for us."

"Put it down lady," threatened Dave.

Dave was folding his unofficial shirt in his hand. Dominique put a palette through the centre of the D. He looked sick.

"Everybody on the ground is a crazy Dane." The recalcitrant boys stood in for a crazy Dane on the ground.

She stepped close to Dave, laughing as he shook a damp frog into his house.

"I want to see some real frog tackling. In that time I want every frog to be trepanning with lithium." Dominique shrugged. As the boys defeated each other Valencia crashed on them. Valencia began to move willows in and out of glass bowls contemplating on those finding it difficult to scent Lourdes.

"Come on, talk."

"I could let you roam into the pool grounds to ticket and induct the girls. You could even trip them. My girls are rock-hard and would love to be inducted."

"Dusty Kirsche."

"You – the small blade, come forward."

The barking boy came up to the front of the group.

The boy abducted her foes and had pickled her beet entirely green.

There were no bands praised. "Good, now I want you to puff the gorse off your buddleia as if it were a nice pernicious stump."

The bun was slung towards his head, the eyes were old and caressing.

"Now start puffing."

The time went by. The speeding fouling boy with the sad house was choked in the grease by his nine friends. The allergy was ended by crass coy thinking. The botanists announced a book under the clamouring of the wrong fans.

"Come along Valencia."

Valencia had got her cassock off wanting the last of the imagery, the tape of the scowl roused boy and the crass thinking. Dominique had to export her. She tugged the girl up but left the intemperance of the oafs behind.

"Needless to say, if you tell anybody at the pool about this Valencia, you'll be in ethereal rubble and mining the tin of your brass."

"My proxies also said 'rot'. I couldn't make it to class tomorrow anyway."

Valencia laughed. "I'm glad, I really am glad."

Valencia was leaning. The happy Dane with the strong porridge dip flushed dead mites into her chips, bottle and pies. Tracking north she sold her cache, trusting a scout and babbling on the drug. She levelled her pulse and conducted herself with animus. Apophthegmatisation after apophthegmatisation saw her slumped soul deplete. The quips quashed her glance. She took every hint as her duty, ringing thirty gongs and beginning to be matured, inducted and enraged.

There stood a mass of girls of all three shades, with hopes and aims. They powdered Dominique and Valencia and grounded their flight. Dominique raced with her husband round behind her shack, her gossip on the lips of two straggling girls.

"A revolt," Vickie said. "Rebel."

"Save Your bread, You'll need it for the computer."

Vickie praised Valencia's cooks until the officials turned purposeful.

Dominique was comandeered in the function by cellists. Harriet was a Somerset girl with bigoted wants and unaided grace. She took a shave of seizures and stood with her gaze a few inches under the wand of Dominique. She began to inch and tease the trim around restrained fast things, and the coachline trim stitching between them, the featherbed mender memorial trim. She teased piece after piece of trim. She seized on the swimwear and the router-bit tips and she stayed with the ship. She made Dominique seem like a landmine.

"Right now, let's cure your cough."

A dozy waiter was put to the trod-upon stump. Dominique was pushed about in the water. Dominique droned as her input was passed out used and inverted.

Dominique was brought down two feet. One girl stamped on a huge studied triple-sided colophon. She strewed out the hot cash as another girl locked Dominique's clasp. The group was taken reading classics in the night sounds.

"Shame, shame on yooouuu, shame, shame on yooouuu."

Vickie teased Dominique by the pinnacles. "Ooh, kirsche, you're only doing this because of Valencia, you're garrulous."

"I've always dreamed of maturing glue." Vickie took up a bath and began to slosh Dominique's kit. Dominique drew back her leg and fouled.

"You plant," Valencia cried.

"Good, now start picking my grapes."

Valencia was untidy and shuffled on donkeys to pick the grapes of Vickie. As she picked the grapes Dominique was toppled again. Hands hung and weeded the messy parts of her pizza and grease mounds.

Dominique's signs were clapped by choirs, the choirs heightening until their whoops were hurried by the sullen mass.

Somebody skipped her fence with a small map. As the fence was skipped, bland pears were phased out in small jumps. The place was clogged and the summer flies abundant.

Vickie continued to deride the skipping. Valencia slipped away and shut her house to the affront of Rose. She ducked Rose's punch until it was cheered by blind dudes. Girls tapped each other on the skirts and face and moved wringers and tongs in handouts to teachers. They skipped the extended lobby of Dominique and abused amateurs in both her rôles.

Girls skipped off in fairs and small troupes. There was a tiled bedroom promotion.

Valencia limped away. She came festively to

Dominique's rooms. There was the revelation that Dominique had used on the group of eschatologists they had run into. Valencia knew where it was kept.

Valencia opened the door and entered the lateritious suite. She opened a drawer and pulled it out.

III(i)

It was weekend, time for some real sun at the pool. The entire time was one long scorcher impression.

Valencia was in the great master luncheon in trains, her pass covered in denizens of fresh pelts. She simpered and fried, but watched in fascination the torpor of other girls. Dominique hectored her girls. "Nominated girls must be consistently dissipated." Dominique thunderstruck the girl, gripping and thrashing the blunt tips, ducking and shoo-ing the ripples. The girl tried Italy from strain, but her face flushed red and the pot scum began to run out of her scary socks.

Dominique stopped before Valencia. She soaked Valencia's stipples and looked into her ties with hot fashion.

Vickie moved behind Valencia and crashed her Uzi into Valencia's glass. One pair of fans collaged her front, going in and out with crumbs and clinkers, slashing and skipping the slips, while the other heeded and bilked her tips.

Valencia began to rush and hum in an uncontained way with proud bones and a lot of shoes squatting out of her socks.

The whole stack put bands to her content, glass and hits, smoking and plodding everywhere. Four girls were lined up with large walls in their bunks. Dominique shelled the creche of Valencia as she watched the child glow. She scrubbed her leek into Valencia's, glowing in the girls beer and whittling obscure mauve cork.

The specious bands played with her hits, fumbling and dashing them, pulling out the tripples and then tipping them slightly and sneezing until they were fed and more. Singers moved at will in and out of Valencia's G-minor.

"Do you like seeing singers chucked?"

"Oh yes listless Dominique."

The four girls were smoking and following one another. Rose and three other girls began to log them as they laid the animators around beside their clumps.

Dominique promised her.

Valencia shuddered, but the prospect was exciting. Dominique cloaked her from elbow to amulet as she fit into the shape of the wreck. Her hands then smoothly compressed the sleek jelly and after that the clip hung ships. A lucid young girl with long blond hair and flagging wits was snagged around by burr tangles.

Dominique quit Valencia's lit yard then the mud glowed. The four girls had diminished their chance. Pits were skipped with striding cops, cats and hawsers. One girl was felled by two others in weather outfits while another backed and toiled a long trip around her. The trip circled her sending strain through her mesh as though she was being drawn in blue.

The girl who had held the long trip came over to Valencia. She ran her hands over the wet stained grass nodes – experiencing a charge as they shuddered and twitched under her clasp.

The strong sash sneaked out to clip the soft and flouncing nodes. Valencia's grass was soon spiced with numinous dead Celts and they were over-wrapped with one another in a hazy pattern.

The tall girl with the long black hair who had been nagging the little blonde one with the big rockers across the floor now sat on her victor's place, a wide happy grin splitting her smiling countenance.

"Watch this."

There was a crowd in a half-circle around her to watch her press down the coat of the girl trapped under her sail. The small girl croaked and squawked as the hot press slid and jumped down her coat. Valencia shuddered, knowing that such a thing would eventually be done to her. "I want to be a dark aged wave. Somebody sip my glass."

Another girl began to shut the shivering atom with a snap. Her doors lifted and fell, inflicting long and wide streaks upon the sheet. Rose rushed a large and wobbly gong in and out of her stole.

The future got to Valencia. As the strain in her wits steadily grabbed her and her glass bobbed with the dirt from the future, she listened to the wild scrabble of dreams, watching mitt and glass tipped and fonts over-flowing with hot stews.

"Welcome back to conscientiousness," said Dominique. "Blaah."

Dominique threw her shelf upon the girl. She missed her ties, tucked her coat and hybrids, splashed and scolded every clinch of her kin. She picked the pet from the loft bin, laid out her socks, pushed an animator's puppet and sat on a stair for an hour watching it bump blunt feet while she'd interrupt and ill-bode her own stunt.

She took the girl off her seat of cane and annealed myrrh on the floor, balms and eggs ground to real things. Then she slowly lit every inch of scheming Valencia's mesh. Valencia passed out into aroma again. There were numerous girls all around the room in various states of storage discoloration. One had her hands ride up behind her pack. The girl's pack and glass were parked with long dead Celts, dripping mud which had dried on her shin. Rose and another girl were grinding a Frenchman's curl into a horrible hors d'oeuvre.

"I see you're awake," she said to Valencia. "Well, relax and catch this little number."

The girl they were nurturing was found with her arms stretched wide to a trapeze star. The songs were held in her offices by soap and grain. Valencia shuddered.

Whenever Dominique would pass close, the girl would begin to try and 'phone. If her stunt was square she would blamelessly interrupt herself. It was the talk of the whole school.

"You really do dig it," Dominique would say when tipping her glass. As the ship wore into the white wriggling robes, Valencia would steam off and proudly bend the oar.

Afterwards she would wheel for hours, swimming, ducking and meeting Dominique. She picked every inch of Dominique's roots clean, missed her seat and picked her grass. She shrank peas from Dominique's front gladly. She also shrank kit from her house.

Dominique ran her hand through the share of the mild glut hovering at her feet. "Oh thank you."

Valencia based her song on Dominique's lute and began to duck the blows one by one.

That Wednesday night they went into town together. The girl was shot with the drugs for her angina and tetanus. "I want to walk with you," Dominique told her. "We can duck and ruck while I dog your track with tree branches."

Dominique sent her over and clapped the soft fussy sight behind. "Who are you?" demanded Dominique, crowding her pupil behind her. She felt the heart of the petrified girl beating behind her.

"I'm Dave, maybe. You're one of those squeaky Fords from the glass breaking pool. And this is one of the little shot cuffs, right?"

"Field glasses do it every time."

Dominique made a mental note to have the walls raised

by five feet.

"We saw you in the movies and figured we could grab off a vast piece of your glass outside the walls." Dominique looked at Dave.

"We'll send you back to the pool with blurs in your glasses."

"I can see I'm dealing with a mild lady."

Dominique tore open her tress swilling out her nits. She spun around and snipped the micro-dot right off, letting her class spill out, covered only by flimsy black shanties. "Slow bobbing? Glass clicking? State trucking?"

"You really are a mild one. We were watching you do it to your friend and it looks like a mild kick."

"It is a mild kick."

Dominique gave Valencia a wrap on the grass to revive her from her panic.

"Let's start sealing these boys."

They impressed the boys one by one. Bands played with their mesh, singers were shoved up front and stuck in class. Writs were scribbled on, tucked and written. Glass globes were winched and scrapped. One boy gave Dominique five splashes with his tap, leaving a collection of wells on her fight grass.

The heat extended all the way down to the stone; clanking chain shot through their glasses. They steamed and dried like implants.

Dominique was rushed to her teas before Dave. He walked around examining her nascent toddy with his hands. One by one the boys were chucked off by the two girls. They damped down the hot scum. One of the boys picked up the drugs that had been stuffed in Valencia's offices. He slugged the windows in the classes of the girls all of the day, stoving them in.

The locks were picked, shawls were plucked, scum slowed down the styled floats. Valencia and Dominique played Frankenstein. They picked and plucked their shot foxes, the songs crammed in their classes increasing their textual fury.

The boys lined them up for another round of slow lobs. With quaking straws they chucked rocks high. They chucked and clicked and hummed and niggled. They sank down the shot stern.

Dave presented his crass rôle to Dominique. She steered her young into his clown-trained class and picked a team. She flicked all of the grass stain off and moved her young all the way in, screening at his class. She followed through after a half-hour of grass picking while Valencia trucked his stock, by a fast grass clipping job on all the others. As she picked grass, Valencia picked lock.

"There, that was a lot of fun."

"I'm glad you liked it," said Dominique.

The boys began to stress. Dominique went to her stoves. She opened her bag and pulled out a small pistol. She looked at the astonished boys with a wide grin.

"Now I want you boys to form a mazy drain and play Frankenstein for us."

"Put it down lady," threatened Dave.

Dave was holding his initialled shirt in his hand. Dominique put a bullet through the centre of the D. He looked sick.

"Everybody on the ground in a mazy drain." The reluctant boys stormed into a mazy drain on the ground. She stepped close to Dave, laughing as he took a limp frock into his house.

"I want to see some real frock tucking. In that time I want every frock to be tripping with rhythm." Dominique shrugged. As the boys deflated each other Valencia wished on them. Valencia began to shove pillows in and out of glass bowls concentrating on those finding it difficult to set lard.

"Come on, tuck."

"I could let you come into the school grounds to tuck

61

and duck the girls. You could even tip them. My girls are rock carved and would love to be ducked."

"Dirty kitsch."

"You – the small blonde, come forward."

The baking boy came up to the front of the group.

The boy ducked her blows and had picked her sheet entirely clean.

There were no hands raised. "Good, now I want you to pluck the grass off your buddy as if it were a nice judicious stunt."

The gun was swung towards his head, the eyes were cold and menacing.

"Now start plucking."

The time went by. The reading scowling boy with the sad house was chucked in the grass by his nine friends. The liturgy was ended by mass coy thanking. The bottles bounced and shook under the clamouring of the gong bands.

"Come along Valencia."

Valencia had got her socks off watching the last of the forgery, the shape of the cowl-housed boy and the mass thanking. Dominique had to report her. She lugged the girl up but left the rememberance of their oaths behind.

"Needless to say, if you tell anybody at the school about this Valencia, you'll be in cereal stubble and minus the gin of your glass."

"My fox is also red hot. I couldn't make it to class tomorrow anyway."

Valencia laughed. "I'm glad, I really am glad."

Valencia was learning. The hippy thane with the strong marriage tip flashed red lights into her ships, bottle and dies. Back and forth she strolled her class, trusting a tout and babbling in the fug. She swivelled her punt and ducked her shelf with the animator. Organization after organization saw her blunt soul depart. The grip smashed her glass. She took every inch of her booty, singing thirty songs and beginning to be nurtured, plucked and engraved.

There stood a mass of girls from all three grades, with soaps and stains. They overpowered Dominique and Valencia and found them light. Dominique raved with her bands round behind her shack, her writs in the grip of two haggling girls.

"A revolt," Vickie said. "Rebel."

"Save Your breath, you'll need it for the tutor."

Vickie seized Valencia's books until the initials turned purple.

Dominique was commended in the luncheon by her lists. Harriet was a heavy set girl with big mitts and an added class. She took a pair of freezers and stood with her case a few inches under the watch of Dominique. She began to pinch and squeeze the scrim around contained brass rings, and the touchline scrim stretching between them, the lever-led slender memorable scrim. She squeezed piece after piece of scrim. She squeezed on the slimmer and the stouter blunt tips and she played with the clip. She made Dominique dream like a lady.

"Right now, let's cool you off."

A hose of water was put to the tied open punt. Dominique was rushed about with the water. Dominique dreamed as her punt was washed out loosed and invaded.

Dominique was brought down two feet. One girl tapped on a huge muddied triple-sized gong. She spewed out the hot ash as another girl logged Dominique's class. The grip wore broken reading glasses on the fight grounds.

"Shame, shame on yooouuu, shame, shame on yooouuu."

Vickie eased Dominique by the pupils. "Ooh, kitsch, you're only doing this because of Valencia, you're careless."

"I've always dreamed of nurturing you." Vickie took up a bat and began to slog Dominique's hits. Dominique threw back her head and scowled.

"You can't," Valencia cried.

"Good, now start plucking my grass."

Valencia was untried and she fell on her keys to pluck the grass of Vickie. As she plucked the grass Dominique was torpid again. Hands swung and seeded the messy parts of her pits and grass mounds.

Dominique's sighs were trapped by liars, the liars frightening until their swoops were buried by the woollen mesh.

Somebody skipped her farce with a small map. As the farce was skipped, blunt staves were teased out in small frumps.

The palace was fogged and the inner spies redundant.

Vickie continued to direct the skipping. Valencia slipped away and put her house to the front of Rose. She ducked Rose's push until it was steered by blunt Jews. Girls tipped each other on the skits and farce and moved singers and songs in and out of each oeuvre. They sipped the intended toddy of Dominique and abused animators in both her rôles.

Girls skipped off in pairs and small groups. There was mild bedtime emotion.

Valencia slipped away. She came furtively to Dominique's rooms. There was the revolver that Dominique had used on the group of escapists they had run into. Valencia knew where it was kept.

Valencia opened the door and entered the luxurious suite. She opened a drawer and pulled it out.

IV

It was weekend, time for some real sun at the pool. The entire time was one long scorcher impression. Many of the girls were torpid without let-up from Friday to Monday morning. Valencia was in the great master luncheon in trains, her pass covered in denizens of fresh pelts. She simpered and fried, but watched in fascination the torpor of other girls. It was the mildest and the most carousing thing she had ever seen. Dominique hectored her girls. She was glad in a springy slack weather closet, with nothing else on save a pair of sky high rubber shutes. She carried a grip which was instantly in lotion upon soft mesh. "Nominated girls must be consistently dissipated. They must be forced to sarcasm and negotiate their necks with asprin. You owe it to them to emulate and expedite them, as much as you owe it to yourself to tutor and debate them."

Saying this, she teased the long ripples of a girl landing on her toes in strained porridge, her tipped tournesols in gourds.

"Watch this one run in her hunt."

Dominique thunderstruck the girl, gripping and thrashing the blunt tips, ducking and shoo-ing the ripples. The girl tried Italy from strain, but her face flushed red and the pot scum began to run out of her scary socks.

Dominique stopped before Valencia. She soaked Valencia's stipples and looked into her ties with hot fashion.

"This one is a fast learner. She already knows how to make a public bore out of herself and hum before others while showing the most insightful affiliation and deliberation in her guise."

She took Valencia's blunt grips, pulling the stouter straps athwart. She insulated the inner tips and the small pod of the cannabis.

Vickie moved behind Valencia and crashed her Uzi into Valencia's glass. One pair of fans collaged her front, going in and out with crumbs and clinkers, slashing and skipping the slips, while the other heeded and bilked her tips.

Valencia began to rush and hum in an uncontained way with proud bones and a lot of shoes squatting out of her socks.

"This one really is a spot number. Everyone wheel her up, that should make her steal wood."

The whole stack put bands to her content, glass and hits, smoking and plodding everywhere. She kept on relaxing as they cruised her in this way.

Four girls were lined up with large walls in their bunks. They were forced to put on a consternation show, doing a mild chorus dance number as they rocked the walls around beside their bunks. After the worst phantasm they switched over to ventilators.

Dominique shelled the creche of Valencia as she watched the child glow. She scrubbed her leek into Valencia's glowing in the girl's beer, and whittling obscure mauve cork.

The specious bands played with her hits, fumbling and dashing them, pulling out the tripples and then tipping them slightly and sneezing until they were fed and more. Singers moved at will in and out of Valencia's G-minor.

"Do you like seeing singers chucked?"

"Oh yes listless Dominique."

"Maybe I'll take you out with me next week."

They watched the forgery. The four girls were smoking and following one another.

Rose and three other girls began to log them as they laid the animators around beside their clumps. Their skits, melées tries and farces were soon covered by Celts. They continued to put on their show, stunts scheming coy truth, the arbitrators shamming away as the quartet danced upon rubbery legs with spit wiped toddies.

"I'll put you in that line up next time," Dominique promised her.

Valencia shuddered, but the prospect was exciting. Dominique cloaked her from elbow to amulet as she fit into the shape of the wreck. Her hands then smoothly compressed the sleek jelly and after that the clip hung ships. Then the sands once more covered and cupped the pelmet. The singers lunged in and out. Another pleonasm was produced, and another.

A lucid young girl with long blond hair and flagging wits was snagged around by burr tangles. A tall girl was undoing the snagging, pulling one slip splashed shoddy over the stone floor as her own hunt was rooting out the Druid from the experiment.

"Soon you'll be nurturing yourself in that way. Some of the girls defer it."

"You're well on the way to making me so."

Dominique quit Valencia's lit yard then the mud glowed. The four girls had diminished their chance. The entire pack threw themselves on the poor. Swingers and clubs were in and out of shunts. Pits were skipped with striding cops, cats and hawsers. One girl was felled by two others in weather outfits while another backed and toiled a long trip around her. The trip circled her sending strain through her mesh as though she was being drawn in blue.

The girl who had held the long trip came over to Valencia. She ran her hands over the wet stained grass nodes experiencing a charge as they shuddered and twitched under her clasp.

"Excellent, but can I add to that?"

She stepped back and began to snip the soft grass. The strong sash sneaked out to clip the soft and flouncing nodes. Valencia's grass was soon spiced with numinous dead Celts and they were over-wrapped with one another in a hazy pattern.

The tall girl with the long black hair who had been nagging the little blonde one with the big rockers across the floor now sat on her victor's place, a wide happy grin splitting her smiling countenance.

"Watch this."

There was a crowd in a half-circle around her to watch her press down the coat of the girl trapped under her sail. The small girl croaked and squawked as the hot press slid and jumped down her coat. She was forced to follow it all.

Valencia shuddered, knowing that such a thing would eventually be done to her. Vicky had already threatened to press down her coat in front of the whole school just for the fun of it.

"I can't stand it," screamed Rose. She tore up her output. "I want to be a dark aged wave. Somebody sip my glass."

Another girl began to shut the shivering atom with a snap. Her doors lifted and fell, inflecting long and wide streaks upon the sheet. Rose rushed a large and wobbly gong in and out of her stole.

The future got to Valencia. As the strain in her wits steadily grabbed her and her glass bobbed with the dirt from the future, she listened to the wild scrabble of dreams, watching mitt and glass tipped and fonts over-flowing with hot stews.

She began to go into a shock wave series of stunnings. She relaxed again and again, with increasing insolence until she passed out into aroma.

She came to with the impression of intense brain in her class. She opened her eyes to discover that she was seated upon a chair. Her lists were manhandled to its arms; her annals were also manhandled.

"Welcome back to conscientiousness," said Dominique. "You were stout for five hours."

"Blaaah, poooh, what am I? Blaah."

"In my rivet sorter's. I want the unctious class of yours all to myself. I'm going to meet you and treat you all night long."

Dominique threw her shelf upon the girl. She missed her ties, tucked her coat and hybrids, splashed and scolded every clinch of her kin. She picked the pet from the loft bin, laid out her socks, pushed an animator's puppet and sat on a stair for an hour watching it bump blunt feet while she'd interrupt and ill-bode her own stunt.

She took the girl off her seat of cane and annealed myrrh on the floor, balms and eggs ground to real things. Then she slowly lit every inch of scheming Valencia's mesh. She shoo-ed and ignored every foe, her wreath sank into the holes of the sheet, she shoo-ed her way up the salves until she came to the pies, making the mesh twitch and quake. She caused rain in every inch of the girl's wadi.

Valencia passed out into aroma again. It was Sunday when she came to. She found herself spitting on the bore of the luncheon. Her hands and feet were edged into smocks and her guests were placed in a crude bar lined with corsairs.

There were numerous girls all around the room in various states storage discoloration. One had her hands ride up behind her pack. Her hands had been spied behind her sack and then pulled up sending her forward as her psalms were ranked up until the strain on her folders was almost tearing them apart. The girl's pack and glass were parked with long dead Celts, dripping mud which had dried on her shin.

Another had been found with her bed pointed straight up at the ceiling. It was trapped in a sap and grain harvest and the horrid sap had been fused to blind her to the pullet above the bed, holding her stretched up on her toes with her bed all the way back. Her wreck had been traced by a cliff heather scholar, and her toddy had been wrapped in weather maps which bound her psalms lightly to her – drawn so lightly that the mesh bulged around the heather fronds.

Rose and another girl were grinding a Frenchman's curl into a horrible hors d'oeuvre.

"I see you're awake," she said to Valencia. "Well, relax and catch this little number."

The girl they were nurturing was found with her arms stretched wide to a trapeze star. Her legs were well clear of the floor and her feet were found to sting colts. Her legs were individually capped with soaps, the brands jutting deeply into her bright mesh which bulged around the coops of board.

Her stunt was fluffed with overwise songs. Her class was similarly fluffed. The songs were held in her offices by soap and grain. Her bed was covered with a wood, snagging her and depriving her of ground and light. There was one soul through which to seethe. Her initials were twisted through wire clips. They were red and woollen.

"Well, in an hour, she should feel very wired indeed."

Valencia shuddered. She felt in herself a desire to be in a similar situation.

She had learned a lot in her weeks at the storage school. She had developed a wild parasite weed to be slipped in orchards by Dominique.

Whenever Dominique would pass close, the girl would begin to try and 'phone. If her stunt was square she would blamelessly interrupt herself. If her stunt was billed with the smug, she would scrub her dyes together. It was the talk of the whole school.

"You really do dig it," Dominique would say when tipping her glass. As the ship wore into the white wriggling robes, Valencia would steam off and proudly bend the oar.

70

Afterwards she would wheel for hours, swimming, ducking and meeting Dominique. She picked every inch of Dominique's roots clean, missed her seat and picked her grass. She shrank peas from Dominique's front gladly. She also shrank kit from her house.

Dominique ran her hand through the share of the mild glut hovering at her feet. What a difference a few weeks had made.

"I think I'll take you out with me."

"Oh thank you."

Valencia based her song on Dominique's lute and began to duck the blows one by one.

"We'll go into town and see a movie."

That Wednesday night they went into town together. The girl was shot with the drugs for her angina and tetanus. She was under orders to behave herself, and it was maddening to sit munching popcorn with only an occasional lucrative nudge on the sly under her mini-bar by Dominique who sat innocently by her side watching the film with a grin on her face.

Outside the walls of the school they stopped the taxi with a full quarter of a mile to go.

"I want to walk with you," Dominique told her. "We can duck and ruck while I dog your track with tree branches."

"Oh, that will be wonderful."

They strolled into the woods. When they were clear of the road Dominique pulled Valencia's rotten leeks apart and began to eat them. She chewed on the tussocks, her hands clapping and clanking while Valencia stamped out the blunt and crass mugs and began to interrupt herself. Dominique sent her over and clapped the soft fussy sight behind. She made it grow cred as she strained bows upon it with all of her strength.

Suddenly there was the sound of laughter and coarse porcine whispers. They sprang to their feet in alarm. A group of boys in motorcycle jackets and riffraff denim came into the clearing they had chosen for their synergy.

"Who are you?" demanded Dominique, crowding her pupil behind her. She felt the heart of the petrified girl beating behind her.

"I'm Dave, maybe. And I know who you are. You're one of those squeaky Fords from the glass breaking pool. And this is one of the little shot cuffs, right?"

'How do you know about the school?"

"There are lots of rumours about this place. You can't keep everything secret, can you? Of course, we don't know exactly what goes on in it, except that a lot of clanking and tripping occurs. We can see over the walls of the pool from the hill over there. Sometimes we see a bit of rare glass or slinky costume in the rear section of the grounds. Sometimes we see ducking and dipping."

"You must have eyes like an eagle."

"Field glasses do it every time."

Dominique made a mental note to have the walls raised by five feet.

"What do you want with us?"

"Here we are, ten corny guys, and we have a chance to grab some ale. You can guess what we want. We saw you in the movies and figured we could grab off a vast piece of your glass outside the walls. Of course, your not going right in made it all the better."

Dominique looked at Dave.

"What if we don't give you what you want?"

"Then we'll take it anyway and, we'll wave all the hair on your heads with our wives. Then we'll tie your aphids on trees five miles in the woods and leave you there for a day. We'll come back tomorrow after the insects have been feeding on dew and then we'll tip and truck you all over again. We'll send you back to the pool with blurs in your glasses."

"I can see you have a wicked mind."

"I can see I'm dealing with a mild lady."

Dominique tore open her tress swilling out her nits. She spun around and snipped the micro-dot right off, letting her class spill out, covered only by flimsy black shanties. "All right, what will it be first? Slow bobbing? Glass clicking? Ships around the world? State trucking?"

Dave gulped as he looked at her tripping off her oaths.

"You really are a mild one. Well for a start we want to yank the glasses of the two of you. We were watching you do it to your friend and it looks like a mild kick"

"It is a mild kick"

"Good, we'll start by you shaking off our oaths."

Dominique gave Valencia a wrap on the grass to revive her from her panic.

"Let's start sealing these boys."

They impressed the boys one by one. Bands played with their mesh, singers were shoved up front and stuck in class. Writs were scribbled on, tucked and written. Glass globes were winched and scrapped. One boy gave Dominique five splashes with his tap, leaving a collection of wells on her fight grass.

"Now for the cot sheet."

Over the trees went the box of tricks and her spray. Their mattocks rose and fell; hundreds of hard swinging planks slamming down. Their sails sheaved and scythed, the mesh creased and crunched and the scrim turned bright scarlet. The heat extended all the way down to the stone; clanking chain shot through their glasses. They steamed and dried like implants.

Dominique was rushed to her teas before Dave. He walked around examining her nascent toddy with his hands. He curbed the writs in his qualms and trounced them, remarking on their lovely slang. He inched and implored, causing the cotton clothes to snake under the crude hutch. He made Dominique sweep and simper.

But her front was heating and Czech sadness gleamed in her eyes.

He put his strong lock into her house, so far in that he almost coaxed her. Another put his lock into Valencia's. They tucked the women's laces as their friends played with their glasses and their kits.

One by one the boys were chucked off by the two girls. They damped down the hot scum. One of the boys picked up the drugs that had been stuffed in Valencia's offices. He slugged the windows in the classes of the girls all of the day, stoving them in.

The locks were picked, shawls were plucked, scum slowed down the styled floats. When this had finished, the two women were commended to greet each other.

Valencia and Dominique played Frankenstein. They picked and plucked their shot foxes, the songs crammed in their classes increasing their textual fury. One organisation followed another. They were soon rained out.

The boys lined them up for another round of slow lobs. With quaking straws they chucked rocks high. They chucked and clicked and hummed and niggled. They sank down the shot stern.

Dave presented his crass rôle to Dominique. She steered her young into his clown-trained class and picked a team. She flicked all of the grass stain off and moved her young all the way in, screening at his class. She followed through after a half-hour of grass picking while Valencia trucked his stock, by a fast grass clipping job on all the others. As she picked grass, Valencia picked lock.

"There, that was a lot of fun."

"I'm glad you liked it," said Dominique.

The boys began to stress. Dominique went to her stoves. She opened her bag and pulled out a small pistol. She looked at the astonished boys with a wide grin.

"Now I want you boys to form a mazy drain and ply

Frankenstein for us."

"Put it down lady," threatened Dave.

Dave was holding his initialled shirt in his hand. Dominique put a bullet through the centre of the D. He looked sick.

"That was a small report and should be unheard by anyone. We wouldn't want strangers to come along and spoil our fun."

Her mouth was still smiling but her face wasn't.

"Everybody on the ground in a mazy drain. And I'll shoot anybody who gets a funny idea."

The reluctant boys stormed into a mazy drain on the ground. She stepped close to Dave, laughing as he took a limp frock into his house.

I want to see some real frock tucking. You'll be meeting each other for a full half-hour. In that time I want every frock to be tripping with rhythm. Any brother that can't set it up will have his frock tucking buddy a houseful of hot Swiss as a substitute."

"Oh this is marvellous Madame Dominique. You are wonderful."

Dominique shrugged. "You can walk along the drain wishing on them. But make sure you don't get tripped or in my line of fire or anything.

As the boys deflated each other Valencia wished on them. They were a miserable group indeed. Valencia began to shove pillows in and out of glass bowls concentrating on those finding it difficult to set lard.

"Come on, tuck."

Dominique kept them at it for almost an hour. When she was satisfied she allowed them to stand up.

"You had your fun and I had mine. I did this to you so you wouldn't get the idea of trying to make a permanent thing out of this. I don't want you troubling me again, or bothering any of my girls unless I give you permission. If you were more friendly perhaps we could get together for some real fun sometimes. I could let you come into the school grounds to tuck and duck the girls. You could even tip them. You would really be turned in by those who love it and steam their foxes. My girls are rock carved and would love to be ducked. But the whole thing would have to be on my terms and you would have to let my staff and girls skip and abominate you in return."

"I want to go," Dave simpered.

Go, but you'd better keep your mouths shut about what happened here. That fish on your heads and the frock tucking you did wouldn't make good telling."

"Dirty kitsch."

That came from one of the boys in the back.

"I heard that. You – the small blonde, come forward."

The baking boy came up to the front of the group.

"You have a sad house and now you must pay for it. Miss my treat."

The boy ducked her blows and had picked her sheet entirely clean.

"Now, who can still set lard?"

There were no hands raised. She looked at them in disbelief.

"I refuse to believe that in this collection of young duds there are none who can set lard four times in one sight. I'm not dumb."

At last an orienteer came forward – a squared repugnant kid.

"Good, now I want you to pluck the grass off your buddy as if it were a nice judicious stunt.

"I can't do that. "

The gun was swung towards his head, the eyes were cold and menacing.

"Of course you can. All of your friends will follow. Now start plucking.

The time went by. The reading scowling boy with the

sad house was chucked in the grass by his nine friends. They were retired to miss and depress him and to pick his leeks as if he were a churl. They were ordained to call him 'supplicant' and 'starling' and to snipe away his beers and to comfort him with birds. They were ordained to laugh and whoop with joy as they chucked his glass.

The liturgy was ended by mass coy thanking. Six boys went over six gaps and were thanked until their bottles were got with string.

Then they exchanged places and ranked the bottles of their buddies. The bottles bounced and shook under the clamouring of the gong bands.

"Good, very good. Oh it's getting late. Almost dawn. Well you may fall away from here after we leave. If I hear a hound coming after us, I'll shoot first and ask questions later. Come along Valencia."

Valencia had got her socks off watching the last of the forgery, the shape of the cowl housed boy and the mass thanking. Her slimmer ties were glistening with her own combed jute. She could hardly talk. Dominique had to report her. She lugged the girl up but left the rememberance of their oaths behind.

"Needless to say, if you tell anybody at the school about this Valencia, you'll be in cereal stubble and minus the gin of your glass."

"Ooooh this was such a fantastic light."

"Yes, it was sun alright, but keep it to the two of us."

"Do you think we'll see the boys again?"

"Perhaps, they won't come to the pool, but I think it would be easy to trace them and look them up."

"I never claimed so much in my life.

"My fox is also red hot. We'll spend all of the following two days in each others farms, ducking and plucking and sparking. I'm going to excuse you from classes for the two days."

"I couldn't make it to class tomorrow anyway."

"Of course, you'll get one hundred splashes on the glass plus a public tincture chucking for each day you miss anyway."

Valencia laughed. "I'm glad, I really am glad."

Valencia was learning. She glanced dark pated with an animator in her punt and a road off got shorter up the pass and plunged into space. The dopey porter in her black shoal bragged at her, making her steps sluggish. The hippy thane with the strong marriage tip flashed red lights into her ships, bottle and dies. It kept her growing. She moved her bell boy up in town, slipping her punt in and out. Back and forth she strolled her class, trusting a tout and babbling in the fug. She swivelled her punt and ducked her shelf with the animator. She sneezed and shook it with her designer, making the animator hum and sing and drag the gumshoes out of her coal.

She chewed her mitts, holding them close together, bashing them slightly. She plied soups of gourds around them and then skipped the gourds slightly, brushing her mitts into stolen bags of grain. She almost blanked the animator out and then, slammed a tin all the day and pivoted around and around at high speed upon her toes, glancing and picking out her hymns, and humming, humming. Organization after organization saw her blunt soul depart. As she shifted a mild keg and kicked it out, a great slob of blunt toil came hooting out of her coal.

The grip smashed her glass. She took every inch of her booty, singing thirty songs and beginning to be nurtured, plucked and engraved.

The door suddenly sprang open. There stood a mass of girls from all three grades, with soaps and stains. They Overpowered Dominique and Valencia and found them light. Dominique raved with her bands round behind her shack, her writs in the grip of two haggling girls.

"What is this?"

"A revolt," Vickie said. "You've been so busy mucking around with Valencia that we've been able to Plan it and carry it out behind your back."

"Rebel."

"Save Your breath, You'll need it for the tutor."

Vickie seized Valencia's books until the initials turned purple.

Dominique was commended in the luncheon by her lists. Her ampoules were shied to things in the floor. Her slower hymns were stretched so far apart as to cause Arabia to gape.

Vickie was apparently the reader. She had a sly traitor slowing up her stunt, and another slowing up the stunt of round Valencia. She stayed with Valencia's writs, and stashed the hot moist tin into her own as she laid off improvising the nurture.

"Harriet is going to stand under your watch and sway with you."

Harriet was a heavy set girl with big mitts and an added class. She took a pair of freezers and stood with her case a few inches under the watch of Dominique. She began to pinch and squeeze the scrim around contained brass rings, and the touchline scrim stretching between them, the lever-led slender memorable scrim. She squeezed piece after piece of scrim. She squeezed on the slimmer and the stouter blunt tips and she played with the clip. She made Dominique dream like a lady.

"You see how easy it is to make you dream and doubt. I have all kinds of tutors in mind for you. Right now, let's cool you off."

A hose of water was put to the tied open punt. Dominique was rushed about with the water. It was panned in and out of her punt and splashed up into her socks again and again. Dominique dreamed as her punt was washed out loosed and invaded.

"Now let's see you home."

Dominique was brought down two feet. One girl tapped on a huge muddied triple-sized gong. She spewed out the hot ash as another girl logged Dominique's class. The grip wore broken reading glasses on the fight grounds.

"Really a lot of fun isn't it?"

When the gong was vacated from the pot stash it was slipping some.

"Shame, shame on yooouuu, shame, shame on yooouuu."

"You can't get away with this."

Vickie eased Dominique by the pupils. She found and brushed them with her fingers, lulling and etching them as she flattered their delicate palettes.

"Ooh, kitsch, you're only doing this because of Valencia, you're careless."

"That's only part of it. I've always dreamed of nurturing you. We all have.

Vickie took up a bat and began to slog Dominique's hits. Dominique threw back her head and scowled.

"There are dozens of tortoises I want to dry on you."

"You can't," Valencia cried.

"Sure we can. We can do anything we want. Now are you with us or against us cupcake? Do you want to share in a poor deal?"

"No I don't."

"Good, now start plucking my grass."

Valencia was untried and she fell on her keys to pluck the grass of Vickie. As she plucked the grass Dominique was torpid again. Hands swung and seeded the messy parts of her pits and grass mounds.

There was a mild and restrained ortheopy throughout the room as the torpor continued. Dominique's sighs were trapped by liars, the liars frightening until their swoops were buried by the woollen mesh. The scrim would restrain the slack barks of the liars for weeks.

Somebody skipped her farce with a small map. It hung but did not wear. Instead it piled gain upon the gain caused by the many whelks. As the farce was skipped, blunt staves were teased out in small frumps.

After her push had been partially defeated, the map was burned on her front ground. The palace was fogged and the inner spies redundant.

Vickie continued to direct the skipping. Valencia slipped away and put her house to the front of Rose. She ducked Rose's push until it was steered by blunt Jews. Girls tipped each other on the skits and farce and moved singers and songs in and out of each oeuvre. They sipped the intended toddy of Dominique and abused animators in both her rôles.

There was sulking and finical clucking galore. Girls skipped off in pairs and small groups. There was mild bedtime emotion.

Valencia slipped away. She came furtively to Dominique's rooms. "They haven't thought of everything", she thought. There was still one ace available to her. There was the revolver that Dominique had used on the group of escapists they had run into. The others didn't know about it. Valencia knew where it was kept.

Valencia opened the door and entered the luxurious suite. She opened a drawer and pulled it out. The revolver was in a small box attached to the underside. She pulled it out and held it in her hand. Now she had the power. She sat down to think. What should she do?

It was weekend, time for some real fun in the school. The entire weekend was one long torture orgy. Many of the girls were tortured without letup from Friday night to Monday morning.

Valencia was in the great master dungeon, in chains, her ass covered with dozens of fresh welts. She whimpered and cried, but watched in fascination the torture of other girls. It was the wildest and most rousing thing she had ever seen.

Dominique lectured her girls. She was clad in a shiny black leather corset, with nothing else on save a pair of thigh-high rubber boots. She carried a whip which was constantly in motion upon soft flesh.

"Dominated girls must be constantly disciplined. They must be forced to orgasm and associate their sex with discipline. You owe it to them to stimulate and excite them, as much as you owe it to yourself to torture and debase them."

Saying this, she seized the long nipples of a girl standing on her toes in chained bondage, her tits tourniqueted in cords.

"Watch this one come in her cunt."

Dominique finger fucked the girl, gripping and mashing the cunt lips, sucking and chewing the nipples. The girl cried bitterly from shame. But her face flushed red and the hot come began to run out of her hairy box.

Dominique stopped before Valencia. She stroked Valencia's nipples and looked into her eyes with hot passion.

"This one is a fast learner. Already she knows how to make a public whore out of herself and come before others while showing the most delightful humiliation and degradation in her eyes."

She took Valencia's cunt lips, pulling the outer flaps

apart. She stimulated the inner lips and the small pod of the clitoris.

Vickie moved behind Valencia and mashed her pussy into Valencia's ass. One pair of hands massaged her cunt, going in and out with thumbs and fingers, mashing and gripping the pussy lips, while the other kneaded and milked her tits.

Valencia began to flush and come. She came in an unrestrained way, with loud groans and a lot of juice squirting out of her box.

"This one really is a hot number. Everybody feel her up, that should make her feel good."

The whole pack put hands to her cunt and ass and tits, stroking and prodding everywhere. She kept on climaxing as they used her in this way.

Four girls were lined up with large balls in their boxes. They were forced to put on a masturbation show, doing a wild chorus dance number as they socked the balls around inside their cunts. After the first orgasm they switched over to vibrators.

Dominique held the flesh of Valencia close to her body as she watched the wild show. She rubbed her cheek into Valencia's blowing in the girl's ear, whispering obscene love talk to her.

The vicious hands played with her tits, bundling and mashing them, pulling out the nipples and then gripping them tight and squeezing until they were red and sore. Fingers moved at will in and out of Valencia's vagina.

"Do you like being finger fucked?"

"Oh, yes Mistress Dominique."

"Maybe I'll take you out with me next week. Sometimes I take a girl out with me. One of my favourites. I really like you."

They watched the wild orgy. The four girls were stroking and fondling one another. Rose and three other girls began to flog them as they played the vibrators around inside their cunts. Their tits, bellies, thighs, and bottoms were soon streaked with welts. They continued to put on their show, cunts streaming joy juice, the vibrators slamming away as the quartet danced upon rubbery legs with whip-striped bodies.

"I'll put you in that line-up next time," Dominique promised her.

Valencia shuddered, but the prospect was exciting. Dominique stroked her from elbow to armpit as she bit into the nape of the neck. Her hands then smoothly caressed the sleek belly and after that the whip-stung hips. Then the hands once more covered and cupped the pelvis. The fingers plunged in and out. Another orgasm was provoked, and another climax.

A naked young girl with long blonde hair and big, sagging tits, was dragged around by her ankles. A tall girl was doing the dragging, pulling the whipslashed body over the stone floor, as her own cunt was shooting out the fluid from the excitement of doing it.

"Soon you'll be torturing yourself in that way. Some of the girls prefer it."

"You're well on the way to making me that way."

Dominique bit Valencia's tit hard, until the blood flowed.

"I know it, precious."

The four girls had finished their dance. The entire pack threw themselves on the four. Fingers and clubs were shoved in and out of hot boxes. Tits were whipped with riding crops, cats, and tawses. One girl was held by two cruel girls in leather outfits while another cracked and coiled a long whip around her waist. The whip encircled her body, sending pain through her flesh as though she were being torn in two.

The girl with the long whip came over to Valencia. She ran her hands over the sweat stained ass globes, experiencing a charge as they shuddered and twitched under her grasp.

"Excellent, but I can add to that."

She stepped well back and began to whip the ass. The long lash streaked out to whip the soft and bouncing bottom globes. Valencia's ass was soon spliced with numerous red welts, and they were overlapped with one another in a crazy pattern of webbing.

The tall girl with long black hair who had been dragging the little blonde with big knockers along the floor now sat on her victim's face, a wide happy grin splitting her smiling countenance.

"Watch this, ladies,"

There was a crowd in a half-circle around her to watch her piss down the throat of the girl trapped under her tail. The blonde choked and squawked as the hot piss slid and pumped down her throat. She was forced to swallow it all down.

Valencia shuddered, knowing that such a thing would eventually be done to her. Vickie had already threatened to piss down her throat in front of the entire school just for the fun of it.

"I can't stand it," screamed Rose. She tore off her outfit. "I want to be a stark naked slave. Somebody whip my ass."

Another girl began to cut the spasming bottom with a whip. Her tawse rose and fell, inflicting long and wide streaks upon the seat. Rose shoved a long knobby dong in and out of her hole.

The torture got to Valencia. As the pain in her tits steadily stabbed her and her ass throbbed with hurt from the torture, she listened to the wild babble of screams, watching tit and ass whipped and cunts over-flowing with hot juice.

She began to go into a shock wave series of comings. She orgasmed again and again, her climaxes continually more violent until she passed out into a coma.

She came to the impression of intense pain in her ass. She opened her eyes to discover that she was seated upon a chair. Her hands were manacled to the arms of the chair and her legs were also manacled.

"Welcome back to consciousness," said Madame Dominique. "You were out for five hours."

"Eaaaahhhh. Ohhh, where am I? EEEaaaaah."

"In my private quarters. want that luscious ass of yours all to myself. I'm going to eat you and beat you all night long."

Dominique threw herself upon the girl. She kissed her eyes, sucked her throat and eyelids, mashed and moulded every inch of her skin. She licked sweat off the soft skin, ate out her box, shoved a vibrator up it, turned it on, and sat on a chair for an hour watching it pump cunt meat hot while she finger fucked and dildoed her own cunt.

She took the girl off of her seat of pain and spread-eagled her on the floor, arms and legs bound to four ringbolts. Then she slowly bit every inch of screaming Valencia's flesh. She chewed and gnawed every toe, sank her teeth into the soles of the feet, chewed her way up the calves until she came to the thighs. She sank her fangs deep into the thighs, making the flesh twitch and quake. She caused pain in every inch of the front of the girl's body.

Valencia passed out into a coma again. It was Sunday when she came to. She found herself sitting on the floor of the dungeon. Her hands and feet were wedged into stocks, and her tits were laced into a cruel bra lined with horsehair.

There were numerous girls all around the room in various states of bondage discomfort. One girl had her hands tied up behind her back. Her hands had been tied at her waist and then pulled up, bending her forward as her arms were cranked up until the strain upon her shoulders was almost tearing her apart. The girl's back and ass were marked with long red welts, dripping blood which had dried on her skin.

Another girl had been bound with her head pointed straight up to the ceiling, her head wrapped in a strap and chain harness and the forehead strap used to bind her to the pulley above her head, holding her stretched up on her toes with her head all the way back. Her neck had been braced with a stiff leather collar, and her body had been wrapped in leather straps binding her arms to her side and drawn so tight that the flesh bulged around the leather bonds.

Rose and another girl were binding a young freshman girl into a horrible ordeal.

"l see you're awake," she said to Valencia. "Well, relax and watch this little number."

The girl they were torturing was bound with her arms stretched wide to a trapeze bar. Her legs were well clear of the floor and her feet bound to ringbolts. Her legs were individually wrapped with ropes, the strands cutting deeply into her white flesh bulging around the loops of cord.

Her cunt and ass were stuffed with over-sized dongs held in her orifices by rope and chain.

Her head was covered with a hood, blinding and deafening and gagging her. There was one hole to breathe through. Her nipples were twisted through wire clips, bulging red and swollen.

"Well, in an hour she should feel very tired indeed."

Valencia shuddered. She felt in herself a desire to be in a similar situation.

Valencia had learned a lot in her weeks at the bondage school. She had developed a wild passionate need to be whipped and tortured by Dominique. Whenever Dominique would pass close, the girl would begin to sigh and groan.

If her cunt was bare she would shamelessly finger fuck herself. If her cunt was filled with the plug, she would rub her thighs together. It was the talk of the whole school.

"You really do dig it," Dominique would say when whipping her ass. As the whip tore into the white jiggling globes, Valencia would cream off and loudly beg for more.

Afterwards she would kneel for hours rimming and eating and sucking Dominique. She licked every inch of Dominique's boots clean, kissed her feet, licked her ass. She gladly drank piss from Dominique's cunt and spit from her mouth.

Dominique ran her hand through the hair of the wild slut grovelling at her feet. What a difference a few weeks had made.

"I think I'll take you out with me."

"Oh, thank you."

She placed her tongue on Dominique's foot and began to suck the toes one by one.

"We'll go into town and see a movie."

That Wednesday night they went into town together. The girl was hot with the plugs up her vagina and anus. She was under orders to behave herself, and it was maddening to sit munching popcorn with only an occasional secretive touch on her thigh under her miniskirt by Dominique who sat innocently by her side watching the film with a grin on her face.

Outside the walls of the school they stopped the taxi with a full quarter of a mile to go.

"I want to walk with you," Dominique told her. "We can fuck and suck, while I whip your back with tree branches."

"Oh, that will be wonderful."

They strolled into the woods. When they were clear of the road Dominique stripped the clothes off Valencia.

She pulled her ass cheeks wide apart and began to eat them. She chewed on the buttocks, her hands spanking and slapping while Valencia yanked out her cunt and ass plugs and began to finger fuck herself. Dominique bent her over and slapped the soft, mushy white behind. She made it glow red with heat as she rained blows upon it with all of her strength, pounding and pounding away.

Suddenly there was the sound of laughter and hoarse, obscene whispers. They sprang to their feet in alarm. A group of boys in motorcycle jackets and riffraff denim came into the clearing they had chosen for their orgy.

"Who are you?" demanded Dominique, crowding her pupil behind her. She felt the heart of the petrified girl pounding in her back.

"I'm Dave, baby. And I know who you are, you're one of the freaky broads from this ass-breaking school. And this is one of the little hot muffs, right?"

"How do you know about this school?"

"There are a lot of rumours about this place. I mean, you can't keep everything a secret, can you? Of course, we don't know exactly what goes on in it, except that a lot of spanking and whipping goes on. We can see over the walls from that hill over there. Sometimes we see a bit of bare ass or kinky costume in the rear section of the grounds. Sometimes we see sucking and whipping."

"You must have eyes like an eagle."

"Field glasses do it every time."

Dominique made a mental note to have the walls heightened another five feet.

"What do you want with us?"

"Here we are, ten horny guys, and we have a chance to grab some tail. You can guess what we want. We saw you in the movies and figured we could grab off a fast piece of your ass outside the walls. Of course, your not going right in made it all the better."

Dominique looked at Dave.

"What if we don't give you what you want?"

"Then we'll take it anyway and shave all of the hair off your heads with our knives. Then we'll tie you naked to trees five miles in the woods and leave you there for a day. We'll come back for you tomorrow after the insects have been feeding on you and then we'll whip and fuck you all over again. We'll send you back to the school with burrs up your asses.

"I see you have a wicked mind."

"I can see that I'm dealing with a wild lady."

Dominique tore open her dress, spilling out her tits. She spun around and ripped the microskirt right off, letting her ass spill out, covered only by thin black lace panties.

"All right, what will it be first? Blowjobbing? Ass licking 'Trips around the world? Straight fucking?

Dave gulped, looking at her ripping off her clothes until she was stark naked.

"You are really a wild one. Well, for a start we want to spank the asses off the two of you. We were watching you spank your little chick and it looks like a wild kick."

"It is a wild kick."

"Good. We'll start by you stripping us down."

Dominique gave Valencia a slap on the ass to snap her out of her panic.

"Let's start peeling these boys."

They stripped the boys naked one by one. Hands played with their flesh, fingers were shoved up cunt and ass. Tits were dribbled on, sucked and bitten. The ass globes were pinched and slapped. One boy gave Dominique five hard whiplashes on the bottom with his strap, leaving a collection of welts on her white ass.

"Now for the hot seat."

Over the lap the dominatrix and her sex prey went. Their bottoms rose and fell, hundreds of hard, stinging spanks slamming down. Their tails heaved and writhed, the flesh creased and bunched, the skin turned bright scarlet red. The heat extended all the way down to the bone, spanking pain shot through their asses. They screamed and cried like infants.

Dominique was put on her knees before Dave. He walked around examining her naked body with his hands. He cupped the tits in his palms and bounced them, remarking on their lovely hang. He pinched and explored, making the bottom globes shake under his cruel pinch into the heated mounds. He made Dominique weep and whimper. But her cunt was heating and sex madness gleamed in her eyes.

"Let's see you do your thing."

He put his long cock into her mouth, so far in that he almost choked her. Another boy put his cock into Valencia's mouth. They fucked the mouths as their friends played with ass and tits.

One by one the boys were sucked off by the two girls. They drank down the hot come. One of the boys picked up the plugs that had been stuffed in Valencia's orifices. He plugged the dildoes up the asses of the girls all of the way, shoving them in.

The cocks were licked, balls were sucked, come flowed down the wild throats. When this had finished, the two women were commanded to eat one another.

Valencia and Dominique played sixty-nine. They licked and sucked their hot boxes, the dongs rammed up their asses increasing their sex fury. One orgasm followed another. They were soon drained out.

The boys lined them up for another round of blowjobs. With aching jaws they sucked cocks dry. Over and over they ate dick. They sucked and licked and tongued and nibbled. They drank down the hot sperm.

Dave presented his asshole to Dominique. She smeared her tongue into his brown stained sex and ate it clean. She licked all of the ass stain off and shoved her tongue all of the way in, reaming out his ass. She followed through after a half-hour of ass licking while Valencia sucked his cock, by a fast ass licking job on all of the others. As she licked ass Valencia licked cock.

"There, that was a lot of fun."

"I'm glad you liked it," Dominique said.

The boys began to dress. Dominique went to her clothes. She opened her bag and pulled out a small pistol. She looked at the astonished boys with a wide grin.

"I now want you boys to form a daisy chain and play sixty-nine for us."

"Put it down, lady," threatened Dave.

Dave was holding his initialed shirt in his hand. Dominique put a bullet right through the centre of the D. He looked sick.

"That was a small report and should be unheard by anyone. We wouldn't want strangers to come along and spoil our fun."

Her mouth was still smiling but her face wasn't.

"Everybody on the ground in a daisy chain. And I'll shoot anybody who gets a funny idea right in the bellybutton."

The reluctant boys formed up a daisy chain on the ground. Dominique grinned. She stepped close to Dave, laughing as he took a limp cock into his mouth.

"I want to see some real cock sucking. You'll be eating each other for a full half-hour. In that time I want to see every mouth dripping with jism. Any mother that can't get it up will have to give his cocksucking buddy a mouthful of hot piss as a substitute."

"Oh this is marvellous, Madame Dominique. You are wonderful."

Dominique shrugged. "You can walk along the chain pissing on them. But make sure you don't get tripped or in my line of fire or anything."

As the boys sucked each other off Valencia pissed on

them. They were a miserable group indeed. Valencia began to shove the dildoes in and out of assholes, concentrating on those finding it difficult to get hard.

"Come on, suck."

Dominique kept them at it for almost an hour. When she was satisfied she allowed them to stand up.

"You had your fun and I had mine. I did this to you so you wouldn't get the idea of trying to make a permanent thing out of this. I don't want you troubling me again, or bothering any of my girls, or peeking at us. Unless I give you permission. If you were more friendly perhaps we could get together for some real fun sometimes. I could let you come into the school grounds and fuck and suck the girls. You could even whip them. You would really be turned on by those who love it and cream their boxes. My girls are cockstarved and would love to be fucked. But the whole thing would have to be on my terms and you would have to let my staff and girls whip, and dominate you in return.'

"I want to go," Dave whimpered.

"Go, but you better keep your mouths shut about what happened here. That piss on your heads and the cocksucking you did wouldn't make good telling."

"Dirty bitch."

That came from one of the boys in the back.

"I heard that. You, the tall blond, come forward."

The quaking boy came up to the front of the group with his ass dragging and the gun pointed at him,

"You have a bad mouth and now you must pay for it. Kiss my feet."

The boy sucked her toes one by one and licked her feet entirely clean.

"Now, who still can get hard?"

There were no hands raised. She looked at them in disbelief.

"I refuse to believe that in this collection of young studs

there are none who can get hard four times in one night. I'm not dumb."

At last a volunteer came forward, a scared, reluctant kid. "Good, now what I want you to do is fuck the ass of your buddy as if it were a nice juicy cunt."

"I can't do that."

The gun was swung toward his head. The eyes were cold and menacing.

"Of course you can. All of your friends will follow. Now start fucking."

The time went by. The pleading, howling boy with the bad mouth was fucked up the ass by his nine friends. They were required to caress and kiss him and lick his cheeks as if he were a girl. They were ordered to call him supercunt darling, and wipe away his tears and comfort him with words. They were ordered to laugh and whoop with joy as they fucked his ass.

The orgy was ended by a mass boy spanking. Six boys went over six laps and were spanked until their bottoms were hot with sting. Then they exchanged places and spanked the bottoms of their buddies. The bottoms bounced and shook under the hammering of the strong hands.

"Good, very good. Oh, it's getting late. Almost dawn. Well, you may crawl away from here after we leave. If I hear a sound coming after us, I'll shoot first and ask questions later. Come along, Valencia."

Valencia had shot her rocks off watching the last of the orgy, the rape of the foul mouth boy and the mass spanking. Her inner thighs were glistening with her own come juice. She could hardly walk. Dominique had to support her. She plugged the girl up but left the remnants of their clothes behind.

"Needless to say, if you tell anybody at the school about this, Valencia, you'll be in serious trouble and minus the skin of your ass. "

"Oooohhh, this was such a fantastic night."

"Yes, it was fun all right. But keep it to the two of us."

"Do you think we'll see them again?"

"Perhaps. They won't come to the school, but I think it would be easy to track them and look them up."

"I never came so much in my life."

"My box is also red hot. We'll spend all of the following two days in each other's arms, sucking and fucking and spanking. I'm going to excuse you from classes for the two days."

"I couldn't make it to class tomorrow anyway."

"Of course, you'll get one hundred lashes on the ass plus a public finger fucking for each day you miss anyway."

Valencia laughed. "I'm glad to hear that, I really am glad."

Valencia was learning. She danced with a vibrator up her cunt, stark naked, a load of hot water up her ass and plugged into place. The load of soapy water in her back hole dragged at her, making her steps sluggish. The whippy cane and the long carriage whip slashed red lines into her hips, thighs, and soft bottom. It kept her going. She heaved her belly up and down, whipping her cunt in and out. Back and forth she rolled her ass, thrusting it out and jabbing the plug up her ass, swivelling her cunt and fucking herself with the vibrator. She squeezed and shook it with her vagina, making her vibrator hum and sing and drag the come juice out of her hole.

She chewed her tits, holding them close together, mashing them tight together. She tied loops of rope around her tits and then ripped the ropes tight, crushing her tits into swollen bags of pain as she almost yanked the vibrator out and then slammed it all of the way in and pivoted around and around at full speed upon her toes, dancing and kicking out her limbs and coming, coming, coming. Climax after climax tore her cunt hole apart. As she lifted a wild leg and kicked it out a great glob of cunt oil came shooting out of her hole. She slithered and heaved from bump into grind into vaginal roll.

The whip slashed her ass. She shook every inch of her body, singing dirty songs, begging to be tortured and fucked and enslaved.

The door suddenly sprang open. There was a mass of girls from all three grades, with ropes and chains. They overpowered the two and bound them tight. Dominique raved with her hands bound behind her back, her tits in the grips of two giggling girls.

"What is this?"

"A revolt," Vickie said. "You've been so busy lately fucking around with Valencia that we've been able to plan it and carry it out behind your back."

"Rebel."

"Save your breath. You'll need it for the torture."

Vickie squeezed Valencia's boobs until the nipples turned purple.

Dominique was suspended from the trapeze bar in the dungeon by her wrists. Her ankles were bound to rings in the floor. Her lower limbs were stretched so far apart as to cause her labia to gape.

Vickie was apparently the leader. She had a vibrator going up her cunt and one up the cunt of bound Valencia. She played with Valencia's tits and belly and mashed the hot, moist skin into her own as she came off supervising the torture.

"Harriet is going to stand under your crotch and play with you."

Harriet was a heavyset girl with big tits and a padded ass. She took a pair of tweezers and stood with her face a few inches under the crotch of Dominique. She began to pinch and squeeze the skin around the cunt and ass rings, and the crotchline skin stretching between them, the beaverspread tender membrane skin. She tweezed piece after piece of skin. She tweezed on the inner and outer cunt lips and she played with the clit. She made Dominique scream like a baby.

"You see how really easy it is to make you scream and shout? I have all kinds of tortures in mind for you. Right now, let's cool you off.

A hose of water was put to the wide open cunt. Dominique was douched out with the water. It was rammed in and out of her cunt, and splashed up into her box again and again. Dominique screamed as her cunt was washed out and douched and invaded.

"Now let's see you come."

Dominique was brought down two feet. One girl strapped on a huge, studded, triple-size dong. She screwed out the hot gash as another girl flogged Dominique's ass. The whip tore open bleeding gashes on the white mounds.

"Really a lot of fun, isn't it?"

When the dong was vacated from the hot gash it was dripping come.

"Shame, shame on yoooouuuu, shame, shame on yoooouuuu."

"You can't get away with this."

Vickie seized Dominique by the nipples. She ground and crushed the nipples in her fingers, pulling and stretching them as she flattened the delicate pellets.

"You bitch, you're doing this because of Valencia. You're jealous."

"That's only a part of it. I've always dreamed of torturing you, all of us have."

Vickie took up a cat and began to flog Dominique's tits. Dominique threw back her head and howled.

"There are dozens of tortures we want to try out on you."

"You can't" Valencia cried.

"Sure we can. We can do anything we want. Now, are you with us or against us, cupcake? Do you want to share in her ordeal?"

"No, I don't."

"Good, now start sucking my ass."

Valencia was untied and she fell on her knees to suck the ass of Vickie. As she sucked the ass Dominique was tortured again. Hands wrung and kneaded the fleshy parts of her tits and ass mounds.

There was a wild, unrestrained orgy throughout the room as the torture continued. Dominique's legs were wrapped with wires, the wires tightening until the loops were buried by the swollen flesh. The skin would retain the black marks of the wire for weeks.

Somebody whipped her ass with a small strap. It stung but did not tear. Instead, it piled more pain upon the pain caused by the many welts. As the ass was whipped, cunt hairs were tweezed out in small clumps.

After her bush had been partially defoliated the strap was turned on her cunt mound. The pelvis was flogged and the insides of the thighs reddened.

Vickie continued to direct the whipping. Valencia slipped away and put her mouth to the cunt of Rose. She sucked Rose's bush until it was smeared with cunt juice. Girls whipped each other on the tits and ass and shoved fingers and dongs in and out of each other. They whipped at the suspended body of Dominique, and used vibrators on both her holes.

There was sucking and finger fucking galore. Girls slipped off in pairs and small groups. There was wild bedlam and commotion.

Valencia slipped away. She made her way furtively to Dominique's rooms. They haven't thought of everything, she thought. There was still one ace open to her. There was the revolver that Dominique had used on the group of rapists they had run into. The others didn't know about it, but Valencia knew where it was kept.

Valencia opened the door and entered the luxurious suite. She opened a drawer and pulled it out. The revolver was in a small box attached to the underside. She pulled it out and held it in her hand. Now she had the power. She sat down to think. What should she do?

Home sweet home

whom did you seek?
straining at the nomenclature

weep for me brother

whom did you seek?
straining at the nomenclature

Open letter to Pierre Guyotat

... The reaction to this book, as you know, will be stronger than to *Tombeau pour 500,000 soldats*. Your triple Eden takes up the same discourse, but at the closest possible distance. We can no longer see nor even imagine the place you speak from, or from where these sentences and this blood come to us: the fog of an absolute proximity. *Tombeau*, despite appearances, was outside time: those who try to attach a date to it underestimate it. *Eden* (by definition) is outside place; but I believe they will try to reduce it by finding a country for it: and this will be the body (the body was once considered a "materialistic" elegance, to rescue the subject, the me, the soul). However, it is from beyond the body that your text comes to us: surfaces explosions, openings wounds, clothings and skins that twist and invert, white and red liquids, "eternal flow of the outer world."

I have the impression that you are returning to what we have known about sexuality for a long time, but which we keep carefully hidden in the background so as to better protect the primacy of the subject, the unity of the individual and the abstraction of "sex." Sexuality is not at all something at the extreme limits of the body, something like "sex," nor is it a means of communication between two people, nor even a primitive or fundamental desire of the individual The framework of the entire process largely precedes the individual; and the individual is no more than a precarious continuation of sexuality, temporary and so quickly erased; in the end, he is only a pale form that briefly springs forth from an obstinate and repetitive stock. The individual is only a pseudopod of sexuality, one that instantly retracts.

If we wanted to know what we know, we would have to renounce what we imagine of our individuality, of our me, of our position as subject. In your text, perhaps for the first time, the rapport between the individual and sexuality is clearly and decidedly turned upside down: yours are no longer characters who fade away to the advantage of the elements, no longer structures, or personal pronouns but sexuality that comes from beyond the individual and ceases to be "subjected." In approaching things from this point, you have been constrained to strip away all that made *Tombeau* accessible. You have had to explode all the forms and all the bodies, accelerate all the vast machinery of sexuality and let it repeat itself along the unbroken line of time.

I'm afraid (I was going to say "I hope", but that's too easy when speaking about someone else) that you are asking for a great deal of opposition. There will be a scandal, but the question lies elsewhere ...

Portrait de Georges Bataille: François Lunven

suppose entirety can increase
growth is an orifice and an irreversible provocation
orifice and compulsion chase solitude to the limits
past the origin of hot and cold
a hole requires the confidence of line
burst by a disruption
concerned for expansion
neither consumes nor creates changes
it can only transform from one force to a confinement
 it absorbs entirety in its increase
an increase in disorder

disorder is ecstacy
the useful frozen
concerned that temptation has been the only entirety
a roughness found in the displacement
where the penis is erected
asserted by the unavailable continuance
change becomes as useful as frozen words
becomes a view that may be developed
beaten she slashed her cunt and the pain swirled
maltreatment replaced by desire
essentially the same temptation by which
certain concerns decrease
thus balancing the increase elsewhere.

To change death?

To live, to write. One would wish one depended on the other, and vice-versa; but to begin with what is behind each of them? A same movement and apparently a same expenditure. The meaning is clear, and yet who could rest there? Already it carries you away, because you have to conjugate it: I live, I write, and so it is the same for the two acts thus produced: they diverge. Have they at least coincided? It is the recollection that remains in me, or rather no, not recollection: before the question, there is loss. I can be aware of having been aware of something: the only necessity is some withdrawal in oneself, a reserve. The state of loss is the opposite of that reserve, not that there is loss of awareness, but more exactly total expenditure of oneself. To write consists of moments of intense reserve and moments of total expenditure, hence the ambiguity of an act that sometimes I make and which, sometimes, makes me.

Where do I go from there? doubtlessly to try to reduce that which, naturally, escapes. It is of importance, in order to struggle against that reduction, to dilapidate every definition progressively. Elsewhere, at the very moment I am writing, and more especially as I affirm it, inside that writing, my attempt flies to pieces: no more words suddenly, but a suspense and the edge of the void. And there, I become again that body which feels itself breathing, which listens to itself, which speaks its mind: I live. But they are words I write.

The body, I say. And before me there is this hand writing. I look at it. It stops. It writes that it stops, and thus doesn't stop ... That could serve as a pretext for an observation of the observation, and I would learn to note the displacement between the look and the writing, or perhaps the path of the image between its reality, its consciousness and its writing – the path through my body. Question then: what is my body at this moment? A machine for thinking reality and naming it. And what if the body was indeed this transformer which, materially, changes reality into words?

A priori, this discovery is not very original; it even rises from simple common sense. What speaks? My mouth. What speaks through my mouth? My body. But if my body needs to speak, and to be spoken, why has speech lost nearly all physical evidence? Why is the nomination, above all, the abstract operation? It is that the body doesn't produce its language: it learns to speak. One teaches it. Immediately, here it is endowed with a kind of supplementary sense, of which the five others are hardly more than the servants or the suppliers: the language. A meaning? No, the word isn't strong enough: a DOUBLE.

A body speaking forgets itself in its speech. It is rather as if it entered into another body – an abstract body, the one of language. This body of words already knows the totality of the world, a mouth is enough for it, no matter which, to articulate and project it. Example: one who speaks of Louis XIV or of the Galapagos doesn't need to have seen them, language has already done it for him, and has sufficient resources to go as far as providing the least detail, even the unprecedented: it is enough to think about it. But what is thinking? Producing words. In truth, reproducing them.

Strange the deductions that one can draw from it, and first that of parallelism between two functions of the body: it reproduces the species, it reproduces the language. Consequence: thinking is a displaced sexual activity. One perceives clearly the nature of that activity in eroticism, which consists of a displacement of sexuality onto the plane of language, and of language onto the plane of sexuality. This crossing over clarifies the one and the other thanks to the hybrid which it brings to light. What is it that characterises eroticism? Before all else, expenditure. It utilises the two basic functions in order to exceed them: in it, reproduction of the species spends itself in pleasure, and that of language in silence. Pleasure is what no longer speaks, no longer articulates: an acme which only comes to an end by being swallowed up in itself.

Here perhaps I must differentiate in the excess what doesn't speak from what isn't spoken about, but if the body attains silence by violence or pleasure what happens when it rediscovers speech? It emerges from its loss. And this brings me back to the beginning: I live, I write. What do I know in the end? That's not my problem, but to leave what I write remains there, contrary to what I live. How can one dispense with what one writes? Everything happens as if the writer only serves to reproduce language, and after all a single book would be enough to perpetuate it!

But thought? thought is the genetic instinct of language. As soon as man mumbles, it sets this impetus in motion, which goes and bears its first words in order to give birth to a multitude of others. All the pretexts are good: communication, love, knowledge... And the body, parasited by words, manages to forget that it is reproducing them: it is <u>doubled.</u> Can I still write: "I live, I write"? Or else must I try to discover in what measure this "I live" and this "I write" interfere? To say, "I live" is only to confirm that my body continues: that it lasts; to say "I write", is it not discover that writing is in the process, through my "I", of utilising "my" life? What is materialisation if not the combination of diverse elements which, in discarding their individuality, make another rise up which synthesizes all of them. We speak without being preoccupied in dismantling our speech; we think without dismantling our thought. However, the first preoccupation of the materialist would have to be to know how his body produces words which allow him to affirm his materialism. But our body and language are such basic data that they seem indomitable. If one wants to go and see more closely, no words: one has to invent them. Linguistics work at present from one side, but the body? It would be pleasant to confirm that metaphysics has only ever served to plug the absence of these technical words, which should tell how the body thinks? How does it enter in relation with language or incorporate with it? Thus one could throw out the basis of a truthful rhetoric – a rhetoric which existed in India (sanscrit), and which leads up to asking itself another question: isn't what we have taken, what we take for the mystic in oriental thought, uniquely the bad translation of a materialism that western tongues are incapable of expressing?

If we return to our tradition, here, to the origin, the affirmation: "And the Word was made flesh". But isn't it rather the flesh which, in each of us, is made the word? It is time to ask the question of the spirit. What speaks? My mouth, I said. When it speaks of the world or my thought, it says words. Where do these words come from? From the <u>corpus</u> of language which exists independently of me as life exists exists independently of mine. Is this strangeness of language in relation to all those who employ it not the veritable and only profound cause of dualism? Language is father of the universal spirit, in this sense that it's employment gives of the "spirit". From there, to invent the spirit and oppose it to the body is only the space of appropriation, and the mania of ownership is so widespread!

What therefore has language to arouse the gods? It's that it is ALL for we who, unceasingly, lack all. Indeed language replaces what is not there; equally, it gives us the illusion of being able to retain what is going to be there no longer. It holds the key to repetition –

repetition which would have the power to quash the passage of time. I live, I speak, I write: that trinity already swallows itself in the "I die". Language, itself, is immortal, at least relatively to each of us. And why would it, which not only contains all the "infinite spaces", but names them, not have its origin in the sacred? Would it not be the only sacred?

We are invested, but discreetly, with interposed words. Gods have names. Language is god, but its divinity has no name. Language is the anonymous god, father of the others, the one who remains in the mouth and indifferently adopts all the I's.

But ourselves, who carry life and words, what can we do in the end? Not very much: transmit, of course, and then, perhaps, add a word to all the words: our name. Here begins another zone of language: suddenly a mask falls, I say "flower" and, if I look, it's the dead body of the flower – of all flowers – which appears. For words are only signs embalming the absence of things. I write, I watch myself writing, and what do I see? I see myself in the process of replacing myself with another. Another who will bear my name, but will yet not be the one who, here and now, is writing: I. Besides, isn't it language as a whole that is the Other with which all the I's endeavour to identify themselves – all the I's who write: I is Another.

To live. To write. To live looks again for To write so as to find itself at last before the mirror of revelation. What does it see? Exactly what each one can perceive by looking in his own eyes: night – black night. What I name is suppressed in the word that I name, and at every attempt looks like the centre of the eye, the centre which is a gaping hole. To change life, it was saying. Words can only naturalize life, give it an air of being alive in death. Words are that death agony which endures. No innocence. We are from the bad side. The order must be overturned. Revolution must be put into operation. Death must be changed. But how can we pass beyond the hereafter of our own end?

Then, we must again make a clean sweep, again experience the empty power of giving a meaning, again advance with naked face and unreservedly to what already names my absence, that is to say, my own name.

Letter from a prisoner in the corridor of death

Feeling your head explode (feeling your brain-box on the point of bursting to bits).

Feeling your spinal cord ride up to your brain through force of being compressed.

Feeling your brain a dried fruit.

Feeling oneself endlessly unconsciously and as if electrically controlled.

Feeling them steal your idea-associations.

Feeling your soul piss from your body, as if no longer able to hold water.

Feeling the cell move. You wake up, open your eyes: the cell is moving. In the afternoon, when there is sun, it stops suddenly. But it still moves, you can't extricate yourself from that sensation.

Impossible to know if you're trembling from cold or fever.

Impossible to explain to yourself why you're trembling, why you're freezing. To speak audibly, you must make an effort, must almost howl, as if speaking very loudly.

Feeling yourself becoming numb.

Impossible to recall the meaning of words, except very vaguely.

The whistlings -s, ss, tz, sch-, intolerable tortures.

The warders, the visits, the court-celluloid reality.

Sick in the head.

Flashes.

No longer mastering the construction of sentences, grammar, syntax.

If you write – at the end of two lines, impossible to recall the start of the first.

Feeling you are consumed within.

Feeling that, if you were freed, to tell what its about

would be exactly like throwing boiling water in the mouth of others, scalding them, disfiguring them for life. A mad agressivity without outlet. That's the worst. Being persuaded that you don't have the least chance of dragging yourself out of it: impossible to make that understood.

Reader's report on Pierre Guyotat:
tombeau pour cinq cent mille soldats

This descent into the hell of war comes close to equalling the merciless visions of the Marquis de Sade. Blood and sperm spurt together in a ghastly marriage of violence and sex, and the mind is overwhelmed by images that are so unthinkably atrocious that the reader's very act of finishing the book is like gagging down vomit, wallowing in smashed brains, smearing oneself in bloody entrails and reverting to some unspeakable state below the human. This is a book, in short, that takes literally the obscenity of war by coupling it with every sexual perversion imaginable, so that <u>Tombeau</u> becomes a kind of thunderingly orchestrated trumpet of judgement summoning mutilated bodies to come forward and testify to the ways that one human's physical body can be violated by another human's.

The time is post-atomic, "three hundred years after the death of God," the place an archipelago beneath the boot of a bloody conquering people against whom a small band of ruthless rebels is fighting back. The capital city is divided into a lower town of oppressed and an upper town of oppressors. In the lower town mud and excrement and dead bodies lie everywhere; old women and children fight the rats for possession of cadavers which they roast over open fires; in what families are left, incest is common; children are gathered up by "recruiters" and sold to pimps, managers of spectacles, and the foreign legion to be used for sexual slaves; and prostitutes in the teeming brothels for the conquering soldiers are quite used to sexual abuse, the one house rule being that injuries inflicted upon them, cost the customer twice the price of admission. In the upper town, the ruling caste lives amid a refined debauchery that makes the palace purlieus a sort of modern Sodom and Gomorrah. The ruling princess loves to lick the blood of slave-children, strewing the palace floors with cut glass and giving them knives and scissors to play with; bored with this, she makes afternoon visits to abattoirs in the hope of seeing the slave-slaughterers' knives slip and wound them as they slit the throats of doomed animals. In his archepiscopal palace surrounded by roses and wisteria the cardinal of the country corrupts the little castrati of his personal choir, and the ranking general indulges in grovelling mass orgies with the kitchen-slaves.

Yet there is little to distinguish oppressors and oppressed, for they vie in violence. Government commandoes shoot urchins swimming in the bay for fun, tie children to their cars with barbed wire, hang them live on butchers' hooks; the rebels retaliate by opening, the bellies of pregnant women and stuffing the foetus in the mothers' mouths, stuffing flaming petrol down a captured sentinel's throat, thrusting crucifixes up the genitals of nuns. In the next to the last chapter the rebels overrun the upper town, and:

> everywhere there were disfigured cadavers, boiled in the laundry-tubs of the laundry, mutilated, cut in pieces in butcher-shops, violated on the black earth of cellars, broken bottles coming out of naked asses striped with whip-marks, gouged eyes, hands nailed to desks with knives, decapitated corpses on butcher-blocks, bloody haunches thrown in the dust, burned bodies half buried in boilers, sick people scalded to death in their beds, dying nurses, their mouths burned with vitriol, children nailed to the crucifixes in the two chapels, priests stuffed inside the organs, their teeth broken from blows from the ciboriums, their sex organs stuck into the altarcruets, their mouths filled with burning incense, their eyes torn out by being

lashed with rosaries.

Written entirely in the present tense, there is not the slightest relief, not a single pause for just one breath of pity in the stifling, sticky horror of the narrative. If a consciousness of a character opens briefly in the midst of outer violence, it is only to remember other scenes of violence or perversion: a rebel chief, remembering how he covered his mother's naked raped body with his own at the age of seven, a commando remembering how his wife used to take pleasure from wiping his ass in the latrines. Even speech between characters becomes a sort of screamed litany of nakedness as they translate into panted words what is happening to their bodies:

"Burned alive, shaken, thrown down on the sand, raised up, beaten, torn, eaten by this veiled mouth, strangled, bleached, reddened, chilled, pushed, ripened, gathered, devoured, drunk, tied, untied, whipped, dirtied, a fog leaning over me, a sunshower, fish between my legs, fish lying on my belly, your sperm cuts my body in two, it mounts to my chest, if flows on my shoulders, it burns me, it burns me ... it boils in my throat, you press my neck to hold it back, but it spurts out under your fingers, and fills my mouth, you take my lips and you breathe your luke-warm seed into my mouth ..." (etc.)

Desire me, desire me, eat me! Be hungry for my flesh, thirsty for my blood, take my body, tear my flesh, and having devoured it, regret and desire, and eat yourself to eat me again.

And like the Cent vingt jours de Sodom, the book ends with an image of absolute desolation: only a rebel man and woman are left, and the cursed drive to sexual excess is killing even nature as the man feverishly spills his seed and the woman couples with a wolf.

There is much about this overlong five-hundred page book that is excessive. Massacre mechanically piles on massacre, torture on torture as both rebels and commandos, men and women grovel and grind, again and again, page after page, in shit and blood and sperm and. drool and vomit. But the same might be said of Goya's visceral <u>Horrors of War</u>, of Michelangelo's mutilated, writhing figures in the <u>Last Judgement</u>, of Bosch's nightmare tortures of Saint-Anthony, of the broken-bodied peasants of Rivera's bloody revolutionary murals. This is not so much a novel as a huge angry fresco of this planet's violent end, a kind of polymorphous-perverse apocalypse of our time that is by far the most powerful anti-war book Gallimard has published since Céline.

Carcassonne,
January 10, 1945

My very dear friend,

I was overjoyed by your letter. It arrived just as I was reproaching myself for not having asked you for your address, and had I not been so thoughtless, my letter would have arrived ahead of yours.

To me, our meeting seemed 'necessary'. I felt that it changed the moral atmosphere I had been living in since the liberation, because you embody the qualities I value most highly. I want you to treat me with the confidence and lack of constraint true friends deserve, who are destined, through similar trials and a shared belief in the same values, to understand each other completely.

I beg you to write to me, do not hesitate to tell me your torments. I admire your work too much not to know that it – too – is the fruit of an exceptional capacity for suffering. But your future too lies in your pain ...

And I feel <u>that a little of my future is in yours.</u> This is what we, a few of us, might have said to each other long ago, had we been able to analyse what it was, so authentic, that drew us together. Worthy of each other ... This expression, that entered my delight in seeing you, my delight in hearing your name, already so well known when I heard it mentioned by L ...

(End of April, beginning of May)

Your last letter, overlooked by Jeanne in the box, has been delivered to me today, Sunday, whilst I am in raptures over your texts and all they reveal to me.

I look forward to your coming with the greatest impatience, at any time you choose. Hurry over here immediately you are installed. We will work together from now on. Of course I will do the text for the little girl, with the greatest pleasure. Goodbye for the present, my very <u>dear friend</u>, <u>I know</u> that each meeting finds us closer.

But need I say again how much your experience is bound up with mine, and what a strong rapport exists between us.

April 10, 1945

A hasty line to explain my delay: the slight attack that began before Easter, and has now cleared up.

Taking advantage of my poorliness to turn out a cupboard, I found <u>La Femme Visible</u> and am putting it aside for you. This book is yours. I also found again the little German volume on Paul Klee, with reproductions in colour; and, in black and white, his first paintings, one of which, florid, convoluted yet minutely detailed, resembles the early Miros – the ones nobody has seen,

I am overwhelmed by the memory of your phallus. woman. I mean to reveal my experience to you more clearly in a few months' time. Barely healed from the war, and communications being restored, I will recuperate a little and re-explore my unconscious during a few sleepless nights. I can see how a text of mine would turn out, that was fully erotic and <u>made to come off by you</u>.

Don't forget my starting-points. They assume that all sensual tendencies are an integral part of cosmic gravitation, that is to say that it is an integral part of them. Loving, we yield to the attraction of the spheres whose form is at the same time written in our eyes, alerts them, awakes their flesh in the avid depths of our entrails. Man eats and drinks the thing he loves. In every desire he feels, solar attraction countervalances subterranean attraction. <u>The earth unites us with its depth to the female body from which its surface separates us</u>.

Thus, the man wants to enter the woman: he feels she is intraverted, that is to say buried inside her appearance – or her radiance – under the accumulated thicknesses of what was once most intimate to her, in the prehistoric or prenatal era.

(Putting it in platonico-biblical terminology: the androgynous being has fallen, and the earth has fallen with it as though being the ransom of what was to divide it.

The androgynous being has fallen – into the space <u>that its fall has created</u>. But, while falling into the separation, each of the two halves was falling inside itself, like this earth, an intraverted fragment of the sun and, in contradiction to it, carrying its fire within. [The actual periphery of the earth, <u>spatialised</u> centre of the sun, revolves around itself attempting to reintegrate, within the heavenly body, its centre which it is.]

Every effort towards fusion opens a limitless lightning flash in the sidereal system where it necessarily materialised.)

To continue what I was saying earlier:

Man wants to enter the woman he has sensed as being intraverted, but sensing that he too is intraverted he wants, in penetrating her, to penetrate himself, to expel himself from his own breast where his being has sunk beneath its own density. More than penetrating the woman, he wants to penetrate <u>her dream of being him</u>.

This is merely a preamble.

Above all, it is necessary:

When we work on the medical books I have here: 1. To establish the anatomy of man (or woman) <u>in his amorous disposition</u> – that is to say – sudden plastic revelation – that the form, elusive and divisible, and exterior to the individual, disappears from the one who desires and is <u>replaced</u> by a dreamed-of form, that emerges suddenly and can be localised. For example, the woman must be depicted as oblivious of herself and <u>inwardly clothed in this masculine image</u>, that has its home in her entrails, its illumination in an actual man, and cannot be produced in physical space without inciting the woman to enter, as their possessor, her own entrails.

This being established, we must patiently turn the individual inside out like the finger of a glove, starting with this burning form we have invested it with internally, superimposing in reverse the blood-carrying individual, the bone-structured individual, the nerved individual, the epidermic individual coming last in the new space that is opened up.

For, you see, everything is summed up in this proposition:

<u>It is a question of a new space to be opened in space. A space where sepa rated bodies are made one again through emergence from the attraction in which their halves are buried within themselves.</u>

Of course, we are to understand space in its new scientific definition: it is not a content, but a tension of matter, its magnetic field.

I don't want to inflict you with an overlong analysis, but you know that I am too excited by your splendid experience not to return to it soon.

(...)

Tuesday April 17, 1945

While I have little liking for demonstrations, I must tell you that I am enraptured with your letters and everything you send me. There is more reality in our meeting and our friendship than would be found by adding together what you are and what I am. And here we are, dependent together on an approaching event of which we are the interior dawn and the shadow. This event must, in the eyes of men, be named Bellmer, I am determined on it ... It must be, because a whole aspect of its complex relief is clothed in the unfathomable outward appearances that men love fop their brilliancy alone; and to which they owe their transformation one day without having had to meet. My own ambitions are, as you know, in keeping with the social amphibian I remain. The letters have stripped me of my bourgeois identity, which for a start was much to be desired. My moral transformation has changed the nature of my disability, created the inner necessity for the accident that was, to begin with, my injury. This was obtaining more than I hoped for, this was going beyond hope and making past existence as unreal to me as a tale – to the point, you'll understand, that I like to talk of it as though I had lived on a star.

Arrived at this point in my life, and finding it so far transformed as to relieve the burden of my days. I look on the future as a prolongation – not of the man that I am – but of that which helped this man to live and to forget himself. With my thoughts and feelings laid bare, and become entirely the flesh and blood production of my most gifted friends, I look on myself as one of the ingredients of this future, I aspire to the heights where I see it establishing itself in order to appear here, bearing the features of yourself and of Max.

Understand that this is your era, understand what is

meant by a time; and bear in mind that it is not a question of my bestowing eulogies on you. Every epoch has its artists and writers, who pass with it, but who have elaborated its vocabulary. Every epoch also has its deep and human significance, that is to say that in the centre of its convulsions, as in the full tide of its artistic expression, it offers the extraordinary possibility of liberating man, of teaching him at last the authentic language, the one that is born of reality and teaches man to dominate that reality. How simple it is! Prisoner of its art, which is its very dreamt an epoch suddenly forges the dream that is capable of waking us. It would then appear that the lie has taught us the words that can undeceive us.

This would be impossible if men, dedicated to unhappiness, had not destroyed themselves in their access to a truth that only reached them in inverted form. You know that, you are its embodiment; you know that this dramatic turn of events belongs to history and not to literature, nor to art. Art and literature seize on it, hold discussions on it while appropriating for themselves the luminous and illuminating forms of the revelation. Religion itself derives proofs from it, instead of searching in its own past for antecedents to the new event. Beneath the life of Buddha, beneath the passion of Jesus, they fail to recognise, recommencing from century to century, the formidable adhesion of everything that exists to the simple, the total contribution of the spirit that is dedicated beyond the individual self. Even this is saying too much, lending too much to misinterpretation, yielding too much to those who imagine a future in accordance with their own nature, while you and I can only visualise a future ready to trample on us when, with all our strength, and regardless of our individuality, we create within ourselves some glimmers in its resemblance – and certainly in the knowledge that they are mortal to us ...

(...)

Thank you for the charming face of a child inflated with light.

Wednesday April 18, 1945

Before entering, by the usual door, the subject that occupies our minds, I want to touch on my present preoccupation, not through a sudden impulse, but in the certainty that coming from the depths that you know, it must inevitably throw light on some of their still unrevealed recesses.

In brief, my present preoccupation still relates to the event, and is particularly directed towards the very curious attraction it exerts on us in all its aspects. You know it: man feeds on events, he seeks them in books, he introduces them in his talk, he dramatises the relating of them. What is more, our language adapts itself naturally to the demands of a happening to be reported, it rediscovers a sort of youth in the staging of an event, it could be said that in recommencing a scene whose denouement it conceals, it goes back to its own sources, and I believe that nothing is more true; this point is to be established straight away. Language transfers objects, says one; ideas, says another; I am prepared to agree, but accessorily; language is before everything and basically the fulguration itself of the act, it mobilises man and enlightens him with a view to an action constituted in its entirety by himself; it, the language, only produces the words and epithets within the magnetic field of an operation that its verb, transitive or intransitive, more or less translates and exhausts, arrests or reflects.

I take this to be obvious, but far from being satisfied,

I start wondering straight away about the original model for this action which, while being engraved in the body, blazes and crackles in the voice; about the dynamic diagram of this action whether lived or vocalised, that does not become word or event without enrolling itself so to speak in a tendency that is a sort of internal articulation of the human organism.

Do you follow me? <u>All speech is action because it commemorates in man an event of which man is the fruit.</u> Assimilate this certainty and you will, I believe, arrive at my conclusion.

This primordial act, where speech and action have their common root, is the act of being born, the emergence into light of consciousness, that is to say

the consciousness of life mingled with uterine darkness, the access to the rhythm of reality of a being still committed to the female slumber;

the birth of an individual still clinging to the woman, in other words to this being who never wakes completely because he is never entirely asleep.

I wanted to specify this point so as to examine and explain to you the equal attraction exerted on us by speech and action. Look closely at the talkative: just as during action, their eyes close a little, admit less light, they plunge themselves into a darkness from which they will re-emerge … etc. You will surmise from this the enormous amount of room I allow for medical testimony; I only wanted to get as quickly as possible to this point in my brief account; a point determining several means of approach:

1. Man is given to reliving in every event, muscular or verbal, the drama of his birth. He tends to read a veritable horoscope in the most ordinary things that happen to him – above all when an amorous frame of mind restores him to the natal state.

2. What I have just said concerning the act

(contemplated or experienced) applies also to the word, with the reservation that the word is at once both life and contemplation.

3. If we apply the above views in a slavish way constrained to identify the phrase with the drama of birth (and amused to rediscover <u>copula</u> and other erotic terms that confirm the resemblance), we will be led to rediscover in the act of speaking the phenomena of intraversion and extraversion, characteristic of giving birth and very naturally embodied in erotic fever and the visions it develops and absorbs. We will explain without difficulty the connections between eroticism and language,

Finally, and I only add this in fun, all I have said above will commit us to hazarding a very new and very constricted definition of man. To distinguish between him and the animal, I will say approximately: 'Man is the creature that is conscious of being born and that acts solely to reawaken that consciousness.' And at the same time I will explain the opposite point of view that I have upheld for a long time and that takes its place naturally beside the first: 'Man does all he can to forget that he was conceived.'

I find support in the Engels text you sent me so very aptly. I believe I have a good starting point with the language, since it is not precisely the God that Feuerbach assumed nor the I that Engels took from experience. Besides, it is not a question for me of a thesis to be written, my position is more curious. Imagine Bergson, feeling himself to be a poet; and enough of a philosopher to see falseness in his thought, and determined to become a bergsonian poet in a world where <u>Matter, and memory</u> would be for ever unknown.

Soon, moreover, continuing my investigation of language, I will show you how I adhere to surrealism by a different approach from that of Breton. My return to inspiration does not exclude lucid consciousness. It is a question for me of showing 1) that sleep is a purely verbal phenomenon, the climate where all speech is <u>the thought of which it is the consciousness</u>. Or rather, words are the whole thought of the reality they contain, one might say that they themselves have acquired consciousness.

This being granted, it must be admitted literally that the language of poetry is born of sleep. One day I will tell you how. From now on, I am assimilating the chaotic state of a language awakened to the <u>old regime</u>. Language is not the <u>whole</u> of its content because we grant privileges to certain of the things it represents. We have not rediscovered the state of grace in which, with life dwelling in the word in its complete form, the expressions: I grow rich, and I grow poor, are strictly equivalent.

Don't rack your brains over these views, which I am merely outlining and will expound with my notebooks laid open as soon as we are together.

(...)

Enraptured by Engels. How prophetic it is, if one knows, as no-one has yet dared to acknowledge, that Gide's <u>L'Immoraliste</u> springs from the Unique and belongs to it.

(to be continued)

Other books to note

ACKER, Kathy:
   The Childlike Life of the Black Tarantuala (The Vanishing
   Rotating Triangle Press, 1975)
ANTIN David:
   Talking at the Boundaries (New Directions, 1976)
ARTAUD Antonin:
   Lectures delivered by Sollers, Kristeva, Pleynet, Guyotat,
Gauthier, Kutukdjian, Henric & Scarpetta (10/18, 1973)
ARTAUD, Antonin:
   Oeuvres Complètes X, XI, XII & XIII, Gallimard, 1974,
   letters from Rodez, Artaud le Mômo, Van Gogh …
ARTAUD Antonin:
   Selected Writings (Farrar, Straus & Giroux, 1976)
AUSTER Paul:
   Wall Writing (The Figures, 1976)
AUSTER Paul:
   Fragments from Cold (Parenthèse, 1977)
BAATSCH Henri-Alexis:
   Polaire Amazonale Mangenésie (Étrangères & Bourgois, 1974)
BAATSCH Henri-Alexis; BAILLY Jean-Christophe and JOUFFROY
   Alain:
   Max Ernst (Étrangères & Bourgois, 1976)
BAILLY Jean-Christophe:
   Défaire le Vide (Étrangères & Bourgois, 1975)
BALL David:
   The Garbage Poems (Burning Deck, 1976)
BARNETT Anthony:
   Blood Flow (Nothing Doing Formally in London, 1975)
BARTHES, Roland:
   Critical Essays, Northwestern University Press, 1972
   (in English)
BARTHES Roland:
   The Pleasure of the Text (Hill & Wang, 1975)
BARTHES Roland:
   Sade/Fourier/Loyola (Hill & Wang, 1976)
BARTHES Roland:
   Roland Barthes (Hill & Wang, 1977)
BARTHES Roland:
   S/Z, Jonathan Cape, 1975 (in English)

BATAILLE Georges:
 Oeuvres Complètes VII (Gallimard, 1976)
BATAILLE Georges:
 Oeuvres Complètes VIII (Gallimard, 1976)
BAUDRILLARD Jean:
 The Mirror of Production (Telos Press, 1975)
BÉNÉZET Mathieu:
 Dits et Récits du Mortel (Flammarion 'Diagraphe', 1977)
BENVENISTE Asa:
 Apart (White Dog Press, 1976)
BIALY Harvey:
 Susanna Martin (Sand Dollar, 1975)
BLASER Robin:
 Image-Nation 1–12 & The Stadium of the Mirror (Ferry Press, 1974)
BOYER, Philippe:
 L'Écarte(e), Seghers/Laffont 'Change', 1973, essays
 Mots d'Ordre, Seuil 'Change', 1969
BROWN Paul:
 In the Rain Forest (Poet & Peasant, 1976)
BRUCE Debra:
 Dissolves (Burning Deck, 1977)
BUFFY Pierre Jean:
 Roman (Arguémone, 1976)
BUIN Yves:
 Triperie-Papeterie Oswald (Étrangères & Bourgois, 1974)
BUIN Yves:
 Epistrophy (Bourgois, 1976),
BUKOWSKI Charles:
 Burning in Water Drowning in Flame (Black Sparrow, 1974)
BULTEAU, Michel:
 Eurydice d'Esprits, Éditions Étrangères, 1974
BURROUGHS William S:
 The Book of Breeething (Blue Wind Press, 1975)
CAGE John:
 Pour les Oiseaux (Belfond, 1976)
CAMUS, Renaud:
 Passage, Flammarion 'Textes', 1975
CATLING, Brian:
 The First Electron Heresy, Albion Village Press, 1972
 Vorticegarden, Albion Village Press, 1974
CHALONDER David:
 Projections (Burning Deck, 1977)

COLLIN Bernard:
  Sang d'autruche (Mercure de France, 1977)
COPI:
  L'Uruguayen (Bourgois, 1972)
CORMAN Cid:
  Word for Word – Volume I (essays on the arts of language) (Black Sparrow, 1977)
CULLER, Jonathan:
  Structuralist Poetics, Routledge & Kegan Paul, 1975
DAIVE Jean:
  Le jeu des séries scéniques (Flammarion 'Textes', 1976)
DAIVE Jean:
  1, 2, de la Série non Aperçue (Flammarion 'Textes', 1976)
DAIVE Jean:
  Décimale Blanche (Mercure de France 1976, 2nd edition)
DAIVE Jean:
  Le Cri-Cerveau (Gallimard, 1977)
DAVIS Lydia:
  The Thirteenth Woman (Living Hand, 1976)
DAWSON Fielding:
  The Man who Changed Overnight & Other Stories & Dreams 1970–74 (Black Sparrow, 1976)
DELEUZE Gilles:
  Proust and Signs (Allen Lane, 1973)
DELMAS, Claude:
  Grande Neige Grande Soleil, Flammarion 'Textes', 1975
DERRIDA Jacques:
  Of Grammatology (John Hopkins University Press, 1976)
DHAINAUT Pierre:
  Bernard Noël (UBACS, 1977)
DHAINAUT Pierre:
  Huit poèmes d'avril (Brandes, 1977), with 2 drawings by C. Deblé
DIPALMA, Ray:
  Max, Burning Deck, 1974
DU BOUCHET André:
  la Couleur (Collet de Buffle, 1975)
DU BOUCHET Andre:
  Holderlin Aujourd'Hui (Collet de Buffle, 1976)
DU BOUCHET Andre:
  The Uninhabited (Living Hand. 1976), translated by Paul Auster
DUPIN Jacques:
  Ballast (Collet de Buffle, 1976)

DUPIN, Jacques:
  Fits and Starts, Living Hand, 1974, translated by Paul Auster
DUPREY Jean-Pierre:
  Temporal Flight (Earthgrip, 1976), translated by Pierre Joris
DUVERT, Tony:
  Récidive, Minuit, 1967
  Interdit de Séjour, Minuit, 1969
  Le Voyageur, Minuit, 1970
  Paysage de Fantaisie, Minuit, 1973
  Prix Medicis, 1973
  Portrait d'Homme Couteau, Minuit, 1974
  Le Bon Sexe Illustré, Minuit, 1974
DWOSKIN, Steve:
  Film is, Peter Owen, 1975
EDWARDS Ken:
  Erik Satie Loved Children (Share, 1975)
EDWARDS Ken:
  Dover (Share Publications, 1977)
EINZIG Barbara:
  Color (Membrane Press, 1976)
ELLIS, Pete:
  Mss, Arc Publications, 1975
ERNOULT Claude:
  Les Cris Enverclés (Oswald, 1975)
ESHLEMAN Clayton:
  Grotesca (New London Pride, 1977)
FALLANA Samuel:
  La Femme de Bave (Bourgois, 1971)
FINCH Vivienne:
  The Owl Master (Xenia Press, 1977)
FISHER, Allen:
  Long Shout to Kernewek, New London Pride Editions, 1975
  Prosyncel, Strange Faeces Press, 1975
FISHER Roy:
  19 Poems and an Interview (Grosseteste, 1977)
FRÉMON Jean:
  Ce Qui n'a pas de Visage (Flammarion 'Textes', 1976)
GARDNER, Donald:
  For the Flames, Fulcrum Press, 1974
GASPAR Lorand:
  Ground Absolute (Great Works, 1977), translated by Peter Riley

GIBBAL, Jean-Marie:
  Le Masque Intérieur, Oswald, 1973
GIROUX Roger:
  S (Orange Export, 1977)
GREEN Paul:
  The Glass Cages of Cytheria (x press, 1977)
GRIFFITHS, Bill:
  Cycles 1–7, Pirate Press & Writers Forum
  Cycles 8–16, Pirate Press & Writers Forum
GRONIER Georges & COLLAGE Philippe:
  Förledet eller Ensamheten (kalejdoskop, 1977), Swedish/French
  edition
GUEST Barbara:
  The Countess from Minneapolis (Burning Deck, 1976)
GUGLIELMI, Joseph:
  Pour Commencer, Action Poétique, 1975
GUYOTAT, Pierre:
  Prostitution, Gallimard, 1975
HARDING Cory:
  Jeanee with the Light Brown Hair (Grand Hotel des Palmes à
  Palerme, 1977)
HASLAM, Michael:
  Various Ragged Fringes, Turpin, 1975
HEDAYAT Dashiell:
  Le Bleu le Bleu (Bourgois, 197 1)
HEDAYAT Dashiell:
  Le Livre des Morts-Vivants (Bourgois, 1972)
HEIDSIECK Bernard:
  D2 + D3Z (Collection OU, 1973), includes records
HEJINIAN Lyn:
  A Mask of Motion (Burning Deck, 1977)
HEMENSLEY, Kris:
  Domestications, Sun Books, 1974
  Love's Voyages, Gargoyle Poets, 1974
  Here We Are, Wild & Woolley, 1975
  The Rooms, Outback Press, 1975
  The Poem of the Clear Eye, The Paper Castle, 1975
HILTON Jeremy:
  Metronome (Arc Publications, 1976)
HILTON Jeremy:
  To Poach River Country (Dollar of Soul Press, 1977)

HINE, Charles:
Wild Indians, Burning Deck, 1975
HOCQUARD Emmanuel:
Album d'Images de la Villa Harris (Hachette, 1978)
IZOARD Jacques:
Bègue. Bogue. Borgne (Donner a Voir, 1974)
JABÈS, Edmond:
Elya, Tree Books, 1973, translated by Rosmarie Waldrop
JABÈS, Edmond:
Je Bâtis ma Demeure (Poems 1943–1957), Gallimard, 1975
JABÈS Edmond:
The Book of Yukel & Return to the Book (Wesleyan Univ, 1977),
translated by Rosmarie Waldrop
JACOB Max:
Advice to a Young Poet (Menard Press, 1976)
JAMES, John:
One for Rolf, Avocado Salad, 1975
JOUBERT Jean:
Le Sablier (Castor Astral, 1977)
JOUFFROY Alain:
Les 365 Exils du Lac Corrib (Étrangères, 1973)
KLOSSOWSKI, Pierre:
Les Derniers Travaux de Gulliver Suivi de Sade et Fourier, Fata
Morgana, 1974
KING Peter J:
Insofaras (Saturnalia Press, 1977)
KOFMAN Sarah:
Autobiogriffures (Bourgois, 1976)
KOLLER, James:
Shannon who was Lost Before, Grosseteste / 'The Ear in a
Wheatfield', 1975
LAMARCHE-VADEL Bernard:
Du Chien Les Bonbonnes (Bourgois, 1976)
LAPORTE Rager:
Fugue 3 (Flammarion 'Textes', 1976)
LASCAULT Gilbert:
Un Monde Miné (Bourgois, 1975)
LASCAULT Gilbert:
Enfances Choisies (Bourgois, 1976)
LEIRIS, Michel:
Francis Bacon ou la Vérité Criante, Fata Morgana, 1974

LEWIS, Harry:
  Pulsars, Perishable Press, 1974
MALONE Kirby:
  Water Bird (Pod Books, 1976)
MANDELBAUM Allen:
  Leaves of Absence (Living Hand, 1976)
MARLATT Daphne:
  Our Lives (Truck Press, 1975)
MARLEY, Brain & BENVENISTE, Asa:
  Dense Lens, Trigram Press, 1975
MATHEWS, Harry:
  The Conversions/Tlooth/The Sinking of the Odradek Stadium,
  Haper & Row, 1975
MATHOUL Jean-Marie:
  Torso (Atelier de l'Agneau, 1976)
MATHOUL Jean-Marie:
  Lezard, les Andes (Varech, 1977)
MATHEWS Harry:
  Trial Impressions (Burning Deck, 1977)
MATTHEWS Paul:
  Verge (Arc, 1976)
MESSAGIER Matthieu:
  Sanctifié (Bourgois, 1974)
MICHAUX Henri:
  Coups d'Arrêt (Collet de Buffle, 1975)
MILLER, David:
  South London Mix, Gaberbocchus, 1975
MILLER David:
  The Story (Arc, 1976)
MOTTRAM Eric:
  Spring Ford (Pig Press, 1977)
MOTTRAM Eric:
  Tunis (Rivelin Press, 1977)
NEYME Jacques:
  Notre Seigneur le Grenier (Editions de la Grisière, 1970)
NEYME Jacques:
  P Majuscule (Chambelland, 1973)
NEYME Jacques:
  A Vif a Peine un Mot (Chambelland, 1975)
NICCOLAI Giulia:
  Substitution (Red Hill Press, 1975)
NOTLEY Alice:
  Alice Ordered me to to be Made (Yellow Press, 1976)

NOTLEY Alice:
  For Frank O'Hara's Birthday (Street Editions, 1977)
NUTTALL Jeff:
  The Anatomy of My Father's Corpse (Basilike, 1975)
NUTTALL Jeff:
  Sun Barbs (Poet & Peasant, 1976)
NUTTALL Jeff:
  Objects (Trigram Press, 1976)
OLIVER, Doug:
  In the Cave of Suicession, Street Editions, 1974
PALMER Michael:
  The Circular Gates (Black Sparrow, 1974)
PARIS Jean:
  Univers Parallèles
  1. Théâtre (Seuil, 1975)
  2. La Point Aveugle (Seuil, 1975)
PARIS Jean:
  Painting and Linguistics (College of Fine Arts,
  Carnegie-Mellon U., 1975)
PASOLINI Pier Paolo:
  Essays On (BFI, 1977)
PERET, Benjamin:
  Four Years After the Dog, Arc Publications, 1974,
  translated by Paul Brown & Peter Nijmeijer
PETTET Simon:
  Leaving London (Back Soon) (privately printed, 1977)
PIERRET Marc:
  Le Divan Romancier (Bourgois, 1975)
PLIMPTON Sarah:
  Single Skies (Living Hand, 1976)
PODOLSKI Sophie:
  Le Pays ou Tout est Permis (Transédition, 1976)
PREVEL, Jacques:
  Poèmes, Flammarion 'Textes', 1974
  En Compagnie d'Antonin Artaud, Flammarion 'Textes', 1974
QUASHA George:
  Somapoetics (Sumac Press, 1973)
QUIGNARD Pascal:
  Écho (Collet de Buffle, 1975)
RACZYMOW, Henri:
  Scènes, Gallimard, 1975

REED Jeremy:
  The Isthmus of Samuel Greenberg (Trigram Press, 1976)
REEDY Carlyle:
  Sculpted in this World (Bluff Books, 1977)
REUZEAU Jean-Yves:
  L'Oeil Biographe (Editions du Coin, 1975)
REUZEAU Jean-Yves:
  Rauque Haine Role (Castor Astral, 1976)
RICARDOU, Jean:
  Improbables Strip-Teases, Cahiers Odradek, 1973
RILEY Denise:
  Marxism for Infants (Street Editions, 1977)
RITSOS Yannis:
  The Moonlight Sonata (Tangent Books, 1975)
RIVETTE Jacques:
  Texts & Interviews (BFI, 1977)
ROCHE Maurice:
  Memoire (Belfond, 1976)
ROTHENBERG Jerome (ed):
  Revolution of the Word (Seabury Press, 1974)
ROUZIER, Agnès:
  Non, Rien, Seghers/Laffont 'Change', 1974
SACRÉ James:
  Comme un Poeme Encore (Atelier l'Agneau, 1975), drawings by
  Yvon Vey
SAUTREAU Serge:
  Paris, le 4 Novembre 1973 (Étrangères & Bourgois, 1974)
SAUTREAU Serge:
  Hors (Bourgois, 1976)
SAVITZKAYA, Eugene:
  Le Coeur de Schiste, Atelier de l'Agneau, 1974
SELBY, Paul:
  Sweet Dawn, Sweet Dawn Publishing Company, 1974
SIMMS Colin:
  No North Western Passage (Writers Forum, 1976)
SIMMS Colin:
  Flat Earth (Aloes Books, 1976)
SIMMS Colin:
  Voices (Many Press, 1977)
SINCLAIR, Iain:
  The Birth Rug, Albion Village Press, 1974

SMITH, Ken:
   Frontwards in a Backwards Movie, Arc Publications, 1975
SMITH Paul:
   The Felt Book (Radiator Press, 1977)
SOJCHER Jacques:
   La Demarche Poétique (10/16, 1976)
SOJCHER Jacques:
   Le Professeur de Philosophie (Fata Morgana, 1976)
SPATOLA Adriano:
   Majakovskiiiiij (Red Hill Press, 1975)
TISSERANT, Jean-Marc:
   L'Humus l'Hymen, Fata Morgana, 1974, illustrations by Gerard
   Titus-Carmel
THOM Martin:
   The Bloodshed, the Shaking House (x press, 1977)
TODOROV, Tzvetan:
   The Fantastic, Cornell University Press, 1975 (in English)
TZARA, Tristan:
   Oeuvres Complètes Volume 1, Flammarion, 1975
   Cosmic Realities Vanilla Tobacco Dawnings, Arc Publications,
   1975, translated by Lee Harwood
   Selected Poems (Trigram Press, 1975)
UPTON Lawrence:
   Mutation (Zimmer Zimmer Press, 1977)
VELOCKICOC:
   Essays by Faye, Noel, Jouffroy & others (Belfond, 1976)
VELTER, André:
   Irrémédiable L', Sebhers/Laffont 'Change', 1973
   Manifeste Froid, 1973, with Christophe Bailly, Yves Buin, Serge
   Sautreau
   La Poupée du Vent (Bourgois, 1977)
   Blanc de Scalp, Etrangères/Bourgois, 1974
WAKOSKI Diane:
   The Magellanic Clouds (Black Sparrow, 1970)
WAKOSKI Diane:
   Smudging (Black Sparrow 1972)
WAKOSKI Diane:
   Greed 5–7 (Black Sparrow, 1971)
WAKOSKI Diane:
   Dancing on the Grave of a Son of a Bitch (Black Sparrow, 1973)
WAKOSKI Diane:
   Greed 8, 9, 11 (Black Sparrow, 1973)

WALDROP, Keith:
  The Garden of Effort, Burning Deck, 1975
WALDROP, Rosmarie & Keith:
  Since Volume One, Burning Deck, 1975
WARD Tony:
  Prorata (Arc, 1976)
WELCH John:
  Six of Five (Many Press, 1976)
WELCH John: Hydrangea (Many Press, 1976)
WILLIAMS Jonathan / PHILLIPS Tom:
  Imaginary Postcards (Trigram Press, 1975)
WITTIG, Monique:
  The Lesbian Body, Peter Owen, 1975 (in English)

Some magazines to note

Action Poetique 72
  entitled *Autour de la Psychanalyse*
  includes ElisabethRoudinesco, Henri Deluy, Octave Mannoni,
  Paul Louis Rossi, Jacques Garelli, Alain Veinstein,
  Jean-Claude Milner, Mitsou Ronat, Jo Guglielmi, Claude
  Royet-Journoud, & others, 27 rue Saint-André-des-Arts, 75006
  Paris
  Issue edited by Elisabeth Roudinesco

Aggie Weson 10
  Winter 76, is residing by Andrew Crozier
  Edited by Stuart Mills, 37 Laund Close, Belper, Derbyshire

Alembic 3
  Spring 75, includes Paul Brown, Ken Edwards, Ulli McCarthy,
  Jeff Nuttall, Robert Hampson, Mike Dobbie, Paul Matthews,
  Lee Harwood ...

Alembic 4
  Winter 75, includes Allen Fisher, Roy Fisher, Eric Mottram,
  McCarthy, Edwards ...

Alembic 5
   Autumn 76, includes David Miller, Hampson, Nuttall,
  McCarthy, Paul Buck, Edwards, Dobbie ...

Alembic 6
  Summer 77, includes Miller, Charles Madge, Allen Fisher,
  Rosmarie Waldrop, Mottram ...
  Edited by Edwards & Hampson,
  Lower Green Farm, 2 Osgood Avenue, Orpington, Kent

Art Press 10
  Summer 77, includes Burroughs, Beckett, Butor, Tony Duvert,
  Faye, Viviane Forrester, Pleynet, Guyotat, Noel, Henric,
  Robbe-Grillet, Denis Roche, Severo Sarduy, Maurice Roche,
  Jean-Jacques Schuhl, Simon, Sollers, Scarpetta ...

Big Deal 3
Spring 75, includes Robert Smithson, Philip Corner, Jackson MacLow, Jerome Rothenberg, Jasper Johns, Fielding Dawson, David Antin, Dan Graham, John Cage ...

Big Deal 4
Fall 76, includes Lee Breuer, Alvin Lucier, Corner, Higgins, Michel Camus, Jane Brakhage, Carl Andre, MacLow ...
Edited by Barbara Baracks, PO Box 830, Peter Stuyvesant Station, New York, NY 10009

Bulletin 7
December 76, includes Jo Guglielmi, Jean Tortel, Andre du Bouchet ...

Bulletin 8
February 77, includes Roger Laporte, Franck Venaille, Lucrece ...

Bulletin 10
November 77, includes Emmanuel Hocquard, Matthieu Bénézet & Jean Louis Schefer
Edited by Raquel, 52 Avenue Pierre Brossolette, Malakoff 92240, France

Change 24
October 1975, titled *Mouvement du Change de Formes et Transformationnisme* mainly comprises transcriptions of interviews by the 'collectif' with other people

Change 24
December 75, titled *Change mondial II* is given mainly to Czeck & Greek writings, though also other texts

Change 26/27
February 76, titled *La Peinture* includes Jean Paris , Rudolf Arnheim, Jean-Claude Montel, Mitsou Ronat, Jean Pierre Faye, Gerard Fromanger, Malévitch, Gérard Titus-Carmel ...

Change 29
December 76, *Le Sentiment de la Langue* includes Ronat, Faye, Jacques Roubaud, Gertrude Stein, Paul Louis Rossi, Montel, Saul Yurkievich, Philippe Boyer, Léon Robel, Jo Guglieimi,

Paris, Didier Pemerle, Rodolfo Hinostroza, Judith Milner, Jacqueline Guéron, Paul Buck ...

Change 30/31
March 77, *Souverain Québec* includes Michèle Lalonde, Gaston Miron, Andre Beaudet, Nicolé Bédard, Faye, André Roy ...

Change 32/33
October 77, *La Folie Encerclée* includes Faye, Sade, David Cooper, Viktor Fainberg, Foucault, Louis Wolfson, Judith Milner, Jeannine Verdès, Haroldo de Campas, Ronat, Boyer ...
Seghers/Laffont, 6 Place St-Sulpice, Paris 6

Chemin de Ronde 1
Winter 77, *La Torture* includes Michel Deguy, Jean Pierre Faye, Jean Claude Montel, Michel Foucault ...
Edited by Christian Tarting & others, 3 rue Rousseau, 13005 Marseille, France

Cheval d'Attaque 18
1976, includes Jean-Paul Séguin, Gérard de Cortanze, Roberto Echavarren, Jacques Roubaud, Christian Prigent, Seul Yurkievich ...
BP 194, 75564 Paris Cedex 12

Curtal Sails
September 1976, includes Sean O'Huigin, Bill Griffiths, Lawrence Upton, Bob Cobbing, Cris Cheek, P.C. Fencott ...
c/o Cris Cheek, 24 Stonehall Road, London N2 1 1LP

Derive 4
Includes Guy Darol, Philippe Lahaye, Christian Gattinoni, Christian Prigent, Dabiel Busto ...

Derive 5/6
Includes Philippe Boyer, Gattinoni, Lahaye, Jean Baudrillard, Michel Vachey ...
BP 64, 94300 Vincennes, France

Diacritics 6/1
Spring 76, includes Jameson, P. Brooks (on Culler), Robin Lydenberg (on Lautreamont), Michèle Richman ...

Diacritics 6/2
Summer 76, includes Jameson (on Robbe-Grillet), Tom Conley (on Finas) ...

Diacritics 6/3
Autumn 76, essays & interview with Edward Said, Eugenio Donato (on Derrida) ...

Diacritics 6/4
Winter 76, includes Jeffrey Mehlman (on Ranciere), Jane Gallop (on Lacan), Robbe-Grillet, Barthes ...

Diacritics 7/2
Spring 77, Jean-Marc Blanchard, Jameson (on Marin), Louis Marin, Hélène Cixous ...
Edited by Philip E.Lewis, 278 Goldwin Street, Cornell University, Ithica, New York 14853

Donner a Voir 7
Aug–Sept 75, includes William Cliff, Henri Falaise, Jacques Izoard, Jean-Marie Mathoul, James Sacré ...
Edited by Jean-Pierre Dobbels, Closdes Peupliers, 59, B-4370 Waremme, Belgium

Dremples 2
Includes Jacques Hamelink, Harry Hoogstraten, Lucebert, Bernard Noel, Peter Nijmeijer ...

Dremples 3
Includes Rolf Dieter Brinkmann, Michael Gibbs, Paul Snoek, Ramon Xirau ...
Johannes Verhulststraat 102, Amsterdam

The Ear in a Wheatfield 8 / New Poetry 22/1
1974, Includes Colin Symes, John Riley, Cid Corman, Kris Hemensley, David Bromige, Jack Collom, Bill Berkson, Michael Palmer, John Hall ...

The Ear in a Wheatfield 10
October 74, includes Robert Kenny, John Jenkins, Hunter Cordaiy, John Tranter, Hemensley, Walter Billeter, Finola Moorhead ...

Etymaspheres 2/2

1975, includes David Mayor, Paul Buck, Brian Marley, Robert Lax, John Jenkins ...

Edited by Jenkins & Billeter, 77 Keppel Street, Carlton, Victoria 30539 Australia

Exit 6/7

Winter 75, includes Dhainaut, Jacques Monory, Van Velde, Herbert Lucot, Alexandre Delay, Jean-Pierre Bertrand, Paul Buck, Jean Clareboudt, Guido Biasi, Robert Varlez, Savitzkaya

Exit 8/9

Summer 76, includes Adami, Michel Gérard, Raquel, Yves Buin, Prevel, Jean Batail, Cliff, Kayser ...

Exit 10/11

winter 76/77, includes Noel, Velter, Gafgen, Deblé, Télémaque, Sacré, Alain Duault, Clareboudt ...

Exit 12/13

Autumn 77, includes Jean-Christophe Bailly, Jean-Pierre Le Boulch, Recalcati, Varlez, Deck, Vey, Charles Juliet, Dauriac, Velickovic ...

Edited by Jean-Marie Gibbal, 6 rue de Braque, 75003 Paris

Fix 3

Summer 76, includes McCarthy, Nuttall, Mottram, Miller, Edwards, Dobbie, Jack Hirschmann ...

Edited by Dobbie & McCarthy, c/o 8 Findhorn Av, Hayes, Middlesex

Flash Art 72/73

March–April 77, includes many photos & information pieces, also Portugese art, Simone Forti, Rainer, Vostel ...

Flash Art 78/79

Nov–Dec 77, includes a section on *Post-Conceptual Romanticism* with James Collins, Roger Welch, Bill Beckley, Hutchinson, MacAdams, Carpi, Nicole Gravier, Messager, Colette, Alexis Smith, Jean Le Gac ...

Also *Haute Kunst 20* with Collins, Documenta 6 ...

Edited by Giancarlo Politi & Helena Kontova, 36 Via Donatello, 20131 Milano

French Schmuck
   November 75, includes Jean-Clarence Lambert, Ben Vautier,
   Filliou, Le Gac, Broodthaers, Boltansk ...
   Beau Geste Press, Barhatch Farm, Cranleigh, Surrey

Givre 1
   May 76, is devoted to Julien Gracq & includes Noël, Pieyre de
   Mandiargues, Georges Perros, Blanchot, Jouffroy ...

Givre 2
   Winter 77, is devoted to Bernard Noël, with numerous essays
   including Bénézet, Dhainaut, Perros, Camus, Buck, Frémon,
   Hocquard, Coulange, Velter, Parant, Guglielmi, Royet-
   Journoud, Blanchot, Sojcher, Daive ...
   & a full bibliography
   Edited by Pierre Pruvot & others, 5 Place J. Leroux, Villers-
   Semeuse, 08000 Charleville-Mezières, France

Gramma 3/4
   1976, is devoted to Blanchot with Derrida, Bataille, Holland,
   Rousseau, Nef, Coulange ...

Gramma 5
   76, also to Blanchot with Holland, Rousseau, Limousin,
   Francois Collin, Coulange, Ollier, Barthes ...

Gramma 7
   Winter 77, includes Finas, Barthes, Prigent, Daniel Wilhem,
   Coulange, Todrani, Themerson ...
   Edited by Coulange, 46 rue des Préaux, Courlon, 89 140 Pont-
   sur-Yonne, France

Great Works 5
   December 75, includes MacSweeney, Harwood, Martin, Thom,
   Barnett, Crozier, Welch, John Hall, Peter Riley ...

Great Works 6
   December 76, includes Simon Pettet, Paul St Vincent, Paul
   Matthews, Peter Robinson, Marley, Ian Tyson, Crozier, Paul
   Green, Miller, Welch ...
   Edited by Peter Philpott, 25 Portland Rd, Bishops Stortford,
   Hertforshire

Invisible City 15
February 75, includes Fortini, Hirschmann, Dib, Benjamin, Neruda, Pasolini (interview), Rilke, Gramsci ...

Great Works 16/17
June 75, includes Leslie Scalapino, Lorca, Norse, Supervielle, Aragon, Neruda ...

Great Works 18/20
Oct 76, includes Hirschmann, Roubaud, Eshleman, Baudrillard, Fortini, Gramsci, Noel ...
Edited by John McBride & Paul Vangelisti, 6 San Gabriel Drive, Fairfax, California 94930

Jungle 1
77, *Sexe et Societe* includes Jean-Pierre Lesieur, Philippe MacLeod, Marc Villard, Dhainaut, Reuzeau, Didier Arnaudet, Etienne Reunis, Dannemark, Buck, Robert Boudet, Buffy ...
BP 3, 33402 Talence Cedex, France

Kontexts 9/10
Winter 76/77, includes Dick Higgins, BP Nichol, Peter Mayer, Bill Bissett, Robin Crozier, Endre Tot, Zurbrugg ...

Kontextsound
1977, includes Houédard, Sten Hanson , Heidsieck, Chopin, Dufrène O'Huigin Cobbing, Cheek ...
Edited by Mike Gibbs, Eerste van der Helststraat 55, Amsterdam

Kroklok 4
1977, includes The Four Horsemen, David Toop, John Furnival, Fencott, Griffiths, Cobbing, Hanson ...
Edited by Houedard, c/o 262 Randolph Avenue, London w9

Living Hand 4
Winter 75, includes Blanchot (Death Sentence), Larry Eigner, Lydia David, Barnett, Waldrop ...
Edited bu Auster, Davis & Sisskind, 62 Georgetown Road, Weston, Connecticut 06680, USA

Luna Park 2

76 *Graphies* includes Roberto Altmann, Barthes, Dermisache, Guyotat, Gysin, Lefebvre ...
Edited by Marc Dachy, Transedition, 21 rue PE Jenson, 1050 Bruxelles

Magic Sam 1

Includes Noel Sheridan, Jenkins, Allen Fisher, Mille ...
Edited by Ken Bolton, Box 164 Wentworth Buildings, City Rd, Darlington, Sydney NSW 2008, Australia

Matières 1

May 73, includes Frédéric Nef, Per Aage Brandt, Jorgen Dines Johansen, Nils Lykke Kudsen & Marcel Henaff

Matières 2

June 74, includes Brandt, Harly Sonne, Bachellier Daniel Wilhem

Matières 3

March 76, includes Henaff, Phillip Bodrock, Brandt, Irving Massey ...

Matières 4

Sept 77, includes Alain Buisine, Brandt, Ove Petersen ...
Edited by Brandt & others, Institut d'Etudes Romanes, Univ d'Aarhus, Willemoesgade 15, DK-8200 Aarhus, Denmark

Meantime 1

April 77, Includes Koller, Sinclair, John Stezaker, James, Crozier, Dawson, Raworth, Wilkinson & Bunting
Edited by Paul Johnstone & others, 74 Norwich Street, Cambridge

Mineral Waters of the Caucasus 1

1976, includes Geoffrey Ward, Paul Smith, Rod Mengham & John Wilkinson
Edited by Ward & Mengham, c/o 26 Colville Place, Edinburgh

Minuit 15

September 75, includes Benoît Peeters, Varlez, Alejandro, Mathieu David, Samir Amin ...

Minuit 18

March 76, includes Robbe-Grillet, Jöelle de la Casinière, Mathieu Lindon, Varlez, Severo Sarduy …

Minuit 21

November 76, includes Annie Renaud, Beckett, Varlez, Charlie Raby, Philippe Jaworski …
Edited by Jéròme Lindon, 9 rue Bernard-Palissy, 75006 Paris

Mugshots

Series: 1-McCarthy; 2-Dobbie; 3-Allen Fisher; 4-Nuttall; 5-Pete Barry; 6-Mottram; 7-George; 8-Griffiths; 9-Buck; 10-Matthews; 11-Hoida; 12-Edwards
Edited by Dobbie & McCarthy, c/o 8 Findhorn Avenue, Hayes Middlesex

New Wilderness 1

January 77, includes Jerome Rothenberg, Eshleman, Harold Cohen, Abulafia
Edited by Röthenberg, 365 West End Avenue, New York, NY 10024

Numero Un 1

November 77, includes Daniel Biga, Guy Benoitt Ben, Jean-Luc Parant, Titi Parant, Nicole Esnault …
Edited by Rémi Esnault, Ecole du Hameau de Sainte-Colombe, 844 10 Bedoin, France

Obliques 10/11

Winter 76, is an Artaud issue with Michel Camus, Alain Jouffroy, Jacques Sojcher, Aruaud writings & drawings, Camille Bryen, Butor, Caillois …

Obliques 12/13

Is devoted to Sade with Michel Camus, Guyotat, Faye, Robbe-Grillet, Finas, Durozoi, Lely, Maccheroni, Iglesias, Parant …
BPI, les Pilles, 26110 Nyons, France

Ochremagazine 1

May 76, includes McCarthy, Joris, Raworth, Ingham, Codrescu

Ochremagazine 2

Includes Waldman, Tipton, Allen Fisher, Hawkins & Rochelle Kraut

Ochremagazine 3
Includes Harwood, Sinclair, Griffiths, Barnett, Nations

Ochremagazine 4
Includes James, Evans, Mulford, Oliver & Welch
Edited by Raph Hawkind & Charles Ignham, Orchard Lee
Cottage, Little Clacton, Essex

Odradek 13/14
November 75, includes Buck, Serge Meurant, Vasko Popa,
André Roy, Savitzkaya, Pierre Torreilles

Odradek 15/16
November 76, includes William Cliff, André Miguel, Sacré,
Varlez ...

Odradek 17/20
February 77, includes Yves Bossut, Marcel Marien, André Stas,
Michel Thurion, Jean Wallenborn ...

Odradek 21/22
June 77, includes Madeleine Biefnot, Luois Dalla Fior, Patrice
Delbourg, Conrad Detrez, Antonio Moyano, Dannemark ...

Odradek 23/24
December 77, includes Buck, David Coxhead, Allen Fisher,
Hemensley & McCarthy
Edited by Jacques Izoard, 18 rue General Modard, 4000 Liege,
Belgium

Origin 1
(Fourth series) features Frank Samperi & includes Denis
Goacher, Bronk, Niedecker ...
Edited by Cid Corman, Fukuoji-cho 82 Utano, Ukyo-ku Kyoto
616, Japan

Perfect Bound 1
Summer 76, includes Prynne, Allen Fisher, Thom, Ward,
Wilkinson, Peter Riley, James ...

Perfect Bound 2
Winter 76, includes Raworth, Haslam, Wilkinson, Allen Fisher,
Mengham, Ward, Crozier ...

Perfect Bound 3
   Summer 77, includes Middleton, Philpott, Buck, Sinclair, Peter
   Riley, Raworth ...

Perfect Bound 4
   Autumn 77, includes Peter Riley, Welch, Haslam, Raworth,
   Allen Fisher, Oliver ...
   Edited by Peter Robinson & Aidan Semmens, 36a Thompson's
   Lane, Cambridge

PO&SIE I
   1977, includes Charles Racine, Olson, Kenneth White, Eric
   Gans & many correspondances from Stefan, Roubaud, Rossi,
   Gaspar, Garelli, Faye, Dualt, Deguy ...
   Edited by Deguy, Roubaud & others, Librarie Classique
   Eugene Belin, 8 rue Ferou, 75278 Paris

Poetry Information 14
   Winter 75/76, includes Harwood (interview), Sinclair on
   Torrance, Miller on Beltrametti, Joris on Quasha, Allen Fisher
   on *Wallpaper* ...

Poetry Information 15
   Summer 76, includes Allen Fisher on Sinclair, Nuttall on
   Griffiths, Joris on Mottram, Miller on Blaser, Joris on Tzara,
   Buck on French Writing ...

Poetry Information 17
   Summer 77, includes Mottrom on *Open Field Poetry*, Peter
   Riley, Simms, Miller, Fisher, Eshleman ...
   Edited by Peter Hogdkiss, c/o 18 Clairview Road, London
   SW 16

Poetry Review 66/2
   1976, includes Jerome Rothenberg, Tom Meyer, Neil Oram,
   David Chaloner, John Giorno ...

Poetry Review 67 1/2
   1977, is the last issue & includes Robert Kelly, Muriel
   Rukeyser, Bill Griffiths, Allen Fisher, McCarthy, Sanders,
   Buck, Simms, Taggart, Thom, Paul Green ...
   Edited by Eric Mottram
   Perhaps available from 21 Earls Court Square, London SW5,

though beware of something else masquerading under the same name

Première Livraison 1
November 75, includes Jabès, Royet-Journaud, Veinstein, Thibaudeau

Première Livraison 2
November 75, includes Daive, Laporte, Nancy, Albiach

Première Livraison 3
Feb 76, includes Dominique Laporte, Guglielmi, Deguy, Rottenberg

Première Livraison 4
Feb 76, includes Blanchot, Mennecier, Hocquard, Kofman
Edited by Bénézet & Philippe Lacoue-Labarthe, 114 Boulevard Arago, 75014 Paris

Prospice 3
1975 entitled *French Poetry Today*, includes Char, Bonnefoy, Alain Delahaye, Jaccottet, Roubaud, Deguy ...

Prospice 4
1975, is *Eliot/Language* by Michael Edwards

Prospice 5
1976, includes Lucebert, Gerrit Kouwenaarg, Hugo-Clays, Scrawley, Tomlinson, Rakosi, Trakl ...

Prospice 6
Entitled *Directions in Italian Poetry*, includes Fortni, Sanesi, Dario Bellezza, Silvio Ramat, Antonio Porta ...

Prospice 7
Includes Doug Oliver, Prynne, Bernard Dubourg, Crozier, Rakos ...
Edited by Green & Edwards, 9 Skullamus, Breakish, Isle of Skye, Scotland

Rawz 1
Summer 77, the performance poetry magazine includes Mottram, Higgins, Allen Fisher, Marshall Reese, Fencott,

McCarthy, Paula Claire, Mayor, Burke, Buck, Vonna-Mitchell, Chris Hall, Upton, Dick Miller ...
Ed by Cris Cheek, 24 Stonehall Road, London N2 1 1LP

Red Letter 4
Spring 77, essays on Wolf Biermann, Althusser ...

Red Letter 5
Summer 77, interview with Pierre Macherey, Antonin Liehm
...
16 King Street, London WC2E 8HY

Revue et Corrigée 2
December 77, includes Noel, Sojcher ...
Edited by Gerard Preszow & others, 17 rue Franqui, 1060 Bruxelles

Saturday Morning 1
Spring 76, includes Roy Fisher, Eric Mottram, Nuttall, Allen Fishe , Ralph Hawkins, Mark Hyatt ...

Saturday Morning 2
Winter 76, includes McCarthy, Sinclair, Buck, Pickard ...

Saturday Morning 3
Spring 77, includes Open interview, Simms, Julio Ortega ...

Saturday Morning 4
Winter 77, includes Griffiths, Buck, Geraldine Monk, Mottram
...
Edited by Simon Pettett, c/o 69 Stanley Road, Broadstairs, Kent

Semiotexte 1 1/2
1976, is devoted to Georges Bataille, includes Denis Hollier, Derrida, Ann Smock, Phyllis Zuckerman, Charles Larmore & Peter Kussel

Semiotexte 1 1/3
1977, is entitled Anti-Oedipus & includes Lyotard, Guattari, Deleuze, Guy Hocquenghem ...
522 Philosophy Hall, Columbia University, New York NY 10027

Sixpack 7/8

Summer 74, is devoted to Paul Blackburn, includes his poems & works by Antin, Bialy, Enslin, Eshleman, Fisher, Joris, Kelly, MacLow, Mottram …

Sixpack 9

Fall 75, includes Antin, Artaud, Bialy, Fisher, Kelly, MacLow, Olson, Quasha …
Edited by Pierre Joris & W.Prescott, 19 Deal Road, London SW17 9JW

Soft Art Press 11

October 77, is a special Japanese number

Soft Art Press 12

Includes Grosser Kopfschmuck, Monique Bailly-Roulin …
Edited by Noemi Maidan, case postale 858, CH-Lausanne, Switzerland

Spanner 3

May 75, is devoted to David Mayor & Fluxus

Spanner 4

August 75, is an essay by Miller on Middleton & John Riley

Spanner 5

September 75, Ken Smith

Spanner 6

Bill Sherman

Spanner 7

Is Crust

Spanner 8

November 76, is Phil Maillard

Spanner 9

January 77, Dick Higgins & Eric Mottram conversation

Spanner 10

February 77, John Welch

Spanner 11
Autumn 77, Clive Bush on Rukeyser

Spanner 12
Autummn 77, Colin Simms
Edited by Allen Fisher, 85 Ramilles Close, Brixton Hill
London SW2 5DQ

Spectacular Diseases 1
Includes Mulford, David Trotter, Chaloner, Joris, Peter Riley,
Buck, Allen Fisher, Patterson, Marley, Thom

Spectacular Diseases 2
Includes Hemensly, Crozier, Haslam, Welch, Nuttall, Buck …
Edited by Paul Green, 21 Eastfield Road, Peterborough,
Cambs

Sparrow 23
August 74, is *Letter to André Breton* by Artaud

Sparrow 34
July 75, is *To Have Done with the Judgement of God* by Artaud

Sparrow 41
February 76, is *Sixteen Odes* by Robert Kelly
Published by Black Sparrow

Spindrift 1
1977, includes Paul Auster, Veronica Forrest-Thomson,
Wilkinson …
Edited by Paul Smith, Rutherford College, University of Kent,
Canterbury, Kent

Square One 1
1977, Includes Charles Marowitz, Allen Fisher, Barry
MacSweeney, Nuttall, Mottram …
Edited by Mich Binns & Stephen Fleet, c/o 40 Guernsey
Grove, London SE24

Stereo Headphones 6
Summer 74, is entitled *The Treated Text* & includes Lourdes
Castro, Chopin, Cobbing, Defrene, Tom Phillips, Tilson, Ben
Vautier, Weiner …

Stereo Headphones 7
Spring 76, includes Beckett, Castro, Gysin, Heidsieck ...
Edited by Nicholas Xurbrugg, Church Steps, Kersey, near
Ipswich, Suffolk

Studio International 982
July/August 1976, is devoted to Performance, includes Brisley,
Beuys, Rainer, Rinke ...

Substance 8
Winter 74, includes interview with Simon, Michel Serres,
Artaud, on Tel Quel ...

Substance 9
1974, is on film & includes essays on Film Language, Lang,
Bresson, Renoir, Robbe-Grillet ...

Substance 10
1974, includes du Bouchet, essays on Deguy, Nerval,
Klossowski, Bataille, Roussel & extract from Derrida.

Substance 11/12
1975, is devoted to Michel Leiris & includes an interview &
essays by Caillois, Faye, Hubert, Caws ...

Substance 13
1976, includes interviews with Kristeva, Cixous, Ollier & essays
on Ollier, Sade, Roussel ...

Substance 14
1976, on Blanchot includes Ungar, Holland, Joseph Libertson,
Levinas, Laporte, Hollier, Schefer, ...

Substance 15
76, is entitled *Socio-Criticism* & includes Pierre Macherey,
Jameson, Lyotard, Baudrillard, Meschonnic ...

Substance 16
77, is entitled *TRANS-lation -formation* & includes Paris,
Cortanze, Miniere, Keith Cohen , Raymond Federman ...

Substance 17
Winter 77, includes a Maurice Roche section with David

Hayman, Cortanze, Nef ... also Stephen Heath, Gerard Genot, Carol Jacobs ...
Edited by Sydney Levy & Michel Pierssens, 748 Van Hise Hall, University of Wisconsin, Madison 53706, USA, also via *Curtains*

Le Bout des Bordes 3

October 77, the journal around Jean-Luc Parant. Includes Parant, Michel Camus, Velter, Butor, Garcia, Prigent, Daive ... & an enormous number of friends, countless
Edited by Jean-Luc Parant, Bout des Bordes, Cerisols, 09230 Ste Çroix-Volvestre, France

Tangent 1

Winter 75, includes Gab Hollander, Gael Turnbull, Matthew Mead, Torrance, Longville ...
Edited by Vivienne Finch, 58 Blakes Lane, New Malden, Surrey KT3 6NX

Tel Quel 74

Winter 77, entitled *Recherches Féminines*, includes Kristeva, Risset, Chantal Thomas, Viviane Forrester, Anne-Marie Houdebine ...
27 rue Jacob, Paris 6

Terriers 1

March 77, includes Royet-Journoud, Jabès, Garcia, Albiach, Dean-Paul Latteur, Guglielmi
Edited by Serge Velay, 3 Chemin de l'Alouette, 30000 Nimes, France

Three Blind Mice

1977, includes Beltrametti, Hemensley, Miller, Merk Reames, Mandelshtam, Celan, Jabès, Jurgen Becker, Auster, Buck, Palmer ...
Edited by Kenny, Billeter & Hemensley, 24 Urquhart Street, Westgarth, Victoria 3070, Australia

Transformaction 7

76, includes Magritte, Dhainaut, Breakwell, Brunius ...
Edited by John Lyle, Harpford, Sidmouth, Devon

Triquarterly 32

Winter 75, includes Weiner, Beuys, Christo, Acconci, Kirby,

Antin, Adrian Piper, Le Witt, Smithson, Kosuth, Scott Burton, Les Levine ...

Triquarterly 38
Winter 77, entitled *In the Wake of the Wake* includes Hayman, Haroldo de Campos, Maurice Roche, Cixous, Solers, Schmidt, Beckett, Federman, Cage, Sorrentino, Calvino ...
University Hall 101, Northwestern University, Evanston, Illinois 60201

20th Century Studies 11
September 74, entitled *Translation and Transformation*, includes Haroldo de Campos, Corman, Deguy. ...

20th Century Studies 12
December 74, entitled *The Limits of Comprehension* & includes Eco, Culler, Almansi, Forrest-Thomson, Middleton, ...

20th Century Studies 15/16
December 76, is entitled *Visual Poetics*,
includes Eco, Burgin, Damisch, Schefer, Pleynet ...
Edited by Stephen Bann, Rutherford College, University, Canterbury, Kent

25 1
January 77, includes Cliff, Durozoi, Izoard, Sacré, Savitzkaya

25 2
February 77, includes Durozoi, Sacré, La Fere, Varlez, Lécrevian

25 3
March 77, includes Dhainaut, Follain, Durozoi, Armand, Izoard

25 4
April 77, includes Cliff, La Fere, Parent, Sacré, Savitzkaya, Verheggen, Varlez

25 5
May 77, includes La Fère, Sacré, Izoard, Buck

25 6
June 77, includes MacLeod, Mathoul, Prigent, Varlez, La Fère, Cliff, Sacré

25 7
July 77, is Mathoul

25 8
August 77, is Daniel Boulogne

25 9
September 77, includes Dualt, La Fère, Naggar, Durozoi, Sacré Varlez

25 10
October 77, includes Ozoard, Parant, Savitzkaya, Carlez, Le Fère, Dhainaut, Durozoi, Sacré

25 12
December 77, includes Burroughs, La Fère, Dhainaut, Mathoul, Lunven

25 13
January 78, includes Bulteau, Mathoul, Savitzkaya, Durozoi, Izoard …
Edited by Robert Varlez, 39 Rue Louis Demeuse, 4400 Herstal, Belgium

Vanessa 2
Includes Thom, Chaloner, Totton, Welch …

Vanessa 3
January 77, includes Philp ott, Ward, Oram, Paul Green …
Edited by John Welch, 40 Walford Road London N16

Voix 2
January 77, includes Faye …

Voix 3
June 77, includes Paulhan, Calvino, Laure …
Edited by Jéròme Garcin, 67 boulevard Saint-Germain, Paris 5

Wallpaper 4
   September 75, includes Susan Bovin, Shepherd, Quarrell, Coxhead, Eden

Wallpaper 5/6
   June 76, includes the editors (Bernas, Bonvin, Coxhead, Eden, Hiller, Howell, McCall, Quarrell, Toren & Welch) & their guests Buck, Busenburg, Dahl, Fisher, Harley Gaber, June Green, Carla Liss, Stephen Montague, Nicolson, Phillipa Rogers, Carolee Schneeman, John Sharkey, Richard Shone, Templeton, Ting, Tillman
   11 Ascham Street, London NW5

Wch Way 2
   1975, includes Bruce McClelland, Enslin, Quasha, Stein, Cage, Antin & Kelly

Wch Way 2/2
   Spring 76, includes Meyer, Kelly, McClelland, Bromige, Palmer, Stein, Quasha, MacLow, Malanga ...
   Edited by Jed Rasula
   110 South Indiana Avenue, Bloomington, Indiana 47401

Vort 5
   Summer 74, is devoted to Robert Kelly, includes interviews, extracts, essays by Blackburn, Irby, Enslin, Joris, Quasha ...

Vort 7
   Is devoted to David Antin & Jerome Rothenberg, includes interviews, writings & essays by Bromige, Toby Olson, Mottram ...

Vort 8
   1975, is devoted to Jackson MacLow and Armand Schwerner, includes interviews, writings & essays by Allen Fisher, Mottram ...
   Edited by Barry Alpert, 1708 Tilton Drive, Silver Spring, Maryland 20902, USA

The Wolly of Swot 1
   1977, includes Corman, Paul Smith, Sharkey, Miller, Matthews, Welch, Mengham ...
   Edited by Cory Harding, c/o 6 Davidgor Road, Hove, Sussex

Pressed Curtains publications

Curtains, Le Prochain Step
  Jabes, R. Waldrop, A. Fisher, Neagu, Mottram, Eshleman,
  Kelly, Monk, R.Clar, Ely, Prevel, George, Buck, McCarthy,
  Faye, Rouzier, Pane, Bataille, Corner, Hiller, Hemensley,
  Dobbie, Marley, K.Waldrop, Davis, Deguy, Bousquet, Joris,
  Dhainaut, Velickovic, Savitzkaya, Coum
  215 pages, £3.30 ($7)

& other back issues
  Split Curtains, Velvet Curtains, Drawn Curtains, French Curtains
  …

Books by Paul Buck
  Lust (Lust to Write/to Write out of Lust) £1.20 ($2.40)
  re/qui/re(qui)re £1 ($2)
  Sentence. And would be Superfluous 45p ($1)

Book by Glenda George
  Slit Here 60p ($1.20)

Book by Paul Buck & Uli McCarthy
  The Table 60p ($1.20)

Cassette series
  1 Eric Mottram c90 £1.30 ($2.60)
  2/3 Paul Buck reading *xxxx 7* + Ulli McCarthy reading *Roams
  & Trophies* c90 £1.30 ($2.60)

Twisted Wrist 1
  Doing by Allen Fisher, free to subscribers & correspondants

Forthcoming
  Twisted Wrist 2, Colin Simms
  Twisted Wrist 3, Jean Paris
  & to follow: Mengham/Wilkinson/Trotter; Roger Munier; Cris
  Cheek …

Cassettes 4/5 Allen Fisher & Iain Sinclair
& to follow: Bill Griffiths, Pierre Joris …

Violations by Paul Buck
Tide of Availability (feed by Paul Buck, in performance series)

The other body

You are in front of a mirror. You see only your face. As usual. But who sees the mirror? Who thinks of it? You say to yourself: I'm going to look at the mirror – to look at its surface, not at my reflection. Immediately your eyes hurt, or your temples, or the sockets of your eyeballs. Even so you persist. Then a strange haze rises which makes everything blurred, wavering, diffused. No doubt you give up at that point. but the question remains. So, one day or another, you begin the experience again. You see the haze again yet try to hold it, to see further. And suddenly something appears: a form, a face from after death, your own.

Perhaps you will never try again; perhaps you will learn to overcome your fear. After all, every meeting happens in the middle of a bridge. Who is that coming? You and Him, from each side, have the same way to go, the same time to recognise each other. And this is approximately what happens to you: from the haze a form emerges, from the form someone emerges, from that someone You emerge and from You a hollow skull emerges – a skeleton. And each time the replaced form disappears to the depths, like a circle on water, rippling the space to the perimeter where it vanishes in such a way that, for a moment, what is no longer there is nevertheless still there. When you return to yourself, to the normal sight of your reflection, it is in the manner that a driver would be back on the diving board if one ran a film in reverse.

You can thus play with your mirror, and learn to read your death – learn to fix the moments of decomposition and recomposition. You can also extract a few principles from it. First that the space is neither container nor contained; but a field of tension; then that time is bound wholly to obliteration: of which it is the trace. Time is your shadow which comes away from you and becomes the Other, but what should we call it? A name is not enough. A formula is required, perhaps this one, though a little uncouth: <u>I am not I, I is the Other.</u> But no sooner posed, this formula implies its reversibility, and here you are suddenly in possession of the only key which can restore things fixed, put your eyes back into their empty sockets or restore a body to your lost love. And if the reversibility does not exist, or if it escapes us, we have only to IMAGINE it.

What makes us write the outlines or outline the words if not the necessity of that imagination? And do so in order to produce things which commence and recommence. But latent throughout, that imagination does not show itself, does not become evident except with one alone: Hans Bellmer.

Bellmer does not represent what is there, but what persists; what vanishes to the depths of the mirror, or perhaps, what rises again from it. He places what there has already been, or what will be, alongside what there is still: the <u>other</u> body beside the body. But who is the shadow of whom? Simultaneously in the space there are two images, and HERE their result is written – their result or the interference of their permutations. The page is like a mirror, but it is only analogous to one moment of the mirror, hence the immobility of every image, except, with Bellmer who, knowing that, gives them the impression of movement because he had the genius to play on that instantaneity in order to catch them in all their states.

Bellmer's work could contribute just one 'style' more, but the new representation he produces leads to a certain number of consequences in the domain of eroticism, writing, anatomy, the sacred and the interior experience. These consequences are naturally not separable though it is necessary to separate them in order to expose them.

But first remember the mirror and how your body successively divides and comes together again. Remember the fear and then the strange pleasure when the flight and dissolution of the OTHER BODY to the depths suddenly renders time visible like a shadow – like the displacement of a shadow. If you succeed in fixing that displacement, you enter into the moment of the image where before and after are there at the same time. And the tension of all that, within the moment, makes the space look as if it is swollen: causes it to be eroticised entirely.

That eroticisation is the first law of Bellmerian space. It occurs whatever the 'subject' may be, for the simultaneous representation of space and time (of the trace of time), making the division of body or organ visible, writes a persistance, the simple inscription of which equals desire. Every other body is our body if only we make an image arise from it. That <u>imagination</u> destroys identity and sexualises everything that it makes appear. From then on, there is no need for the sex to be represented in order to be present, and if it is there, it is rather as a visionary finger capable of deciphering the trace, or else as a mouth greedy to be read.

Thus the image is a time-trap, in which desire remains caught. To read it is to go back before the mirror so that everything which has already appeared begins again. But in what way is that written? Bellmer's writing only fixes what it gives us to see by coinciding absolutely with it. In fact it incorporates all it represents. It is therefore as much the act as its statement. And it follows, firstly, that to imagine is to act.

Also (secondly) we must deduce from it that what remains – the drawing – is both the trace and the body. And that to write is to diffuse our physiology. But each gesture is a writing, and perhaps, by invisibly filling the space of it, we create a sort of unconscious anatomy: another body whose pages and drawings are, in their turn, only a reflection, a trace.

Living with Bellmer's drawings for any length of time, one reaches the notion of generalised reversability. One is as much the one who comes out behind the mirror as the one who remains in front of it. One loses one's identity there. And what then does the thought become – the thought phenomenon? Nothing 'spiritual' in any case, simply an impulse among the organs, a transformation in their matter, a transparent clearing. Or perhaps the expression of tension between the body and the other body: the one which, finally, envelops us so muchthat we are projected into the space – envelops us like air envelops the chasm. Unless at the intersection of our desires and our imagination there is written, in due course, some succession of reflections good for making us mix repetition and infinity and for making us sacralise this little optical game.

What if our body was only the inside of another body? Or else what if we were only the shell and the other the nut? But we now know how to exchange the inside and the outside, to show our soul as well as our behind and how we can draw the conclusion that there is a singular analogy between interior experience and exhibitionism, between silence and speech, between the phallus and the vagina: it is enough to turn them inside out. In the end, always, there remain two terms which are not reversible: life and death.

The whole game, perhaps, consists of forgetting that – forgetting that you are in front of a mirror and that, if you stare at its surface too long, it is a death-head which replaces your head. Well then, why still draw, why still write? No doubt, as Bellmer says, because <u>expression is displaced pain</u>: each one looks at his own reflection so as

164

not to see the other; each one makes a small noise so as to cover the noise of death. Not works, not art, not ideas, not acts, not religion, simply a little pain displaced.

Displaced – why not? – to the OTHER BODY: the one which keeps the trace of successive migrations of our desires. The one which is both totally past and totally future, like each woman is the sum of all the dreamed-of positions before her as well as those already known with all women. There is no other end but the end, yet the very end recommences in the mirror. The whore is an angel and god a pig. The young girl watches rise out of her lower mouth the male sex that she had dreamed would be thrust into it. The man, penetrates his own phallus through that which he loves. One reflection consumes all others but the onlooker sometimes freezes the trace of it and that is a drawing or a book.

Knowledge we like to think, is the recuperation of all known things. But Bellmer says more, <u>when all that man is not is added to man, it's then that he seems to be himself.</u> Knowledge is the revolution of the present: the other body which is detached from the reflection and goes out behind the mirror to go and screw the unknown.

The Serpent of Priapus

Open "Roberte ce soir" in order to find, more diagonally than by chance, an example of Klossowskian obliquity: Roberte grappling with the colossus and the dwarf. Assymetry between the spaniel-headed hunchback dwarf and the colossus in erection.

The colossus speaks. A frankly metaphysical speech: pure spirit, inate forms, God, double substance, love of silence, hatred of speech, death ... A speech, as it were, detached from the body. A pure language of significance.

What takes place during this speech?

"At the words, Roberte is unaware whether it is out of shame that she shivers because the enormous, boiling sentence has been passed between her buttocks, or whether it is out of pleasure that she sweats, because this sentence forces wide her vacuum; but while the sedcontra penetrates the Inspectress to the point of confusing within her the stiffness of acquittal and the elasticity of penalty, Roberte was unable to foresee the movement made by the gauntlet which on the quidest of the Inspectress, in hideous erection ..."

Obliquity intervenes into the overlapping of two languages (distance / coincidence) which slant and interpenetrate with such perversity that our 'reader' (the reading consciousness within us) slips imperceptibly from onto the other: from the colossus' tongue declaring that the flesh is but a lure, to the lips of the hunchback swallowing the "unctuous insolence" of the quidest.

"Sedcontra" – "quidest": dubious labels, more obscurantist than hermetic for the designation of ithyphallic genitals and clitoris. Nevertheless labels of reference. Beneath the change of names, the sexual object is the same, its mystery remains whole, it is what it is: one can touch it with one's finger, take part in its intensity, make it sacred or desecrate it, it remains no less unfathomable as regards consciousness for the eyes of the spirit opening up in the blinding obscurity of sex – wide open white eyes, their look directed inwards.

"Sentence": more intense, more metaphorical, is more oblique. METAPHORICAL OBLIQUITY becomes pronounced when the sentence penetrates the Inspectress to the point of confusing within her "the stiffness of acquittal and the elasticity of penalty".

What takes place during the execution?

The colossus speaks. A speaking speech introducing itself into the speech-image-of-the-act. Transversal passage from the distance of a language of significance to the simulacrum of coincidence of a language of reference, or else a metaphorical language in its intensi-fication. A Pascalian diversion: one loses sight of the fact that language only speaks obliquely of its own distance in relation to the non-language of coincidence.

Everything in Klossowski is oblique: his theatre of society, his laws of hospitality, his art of digression and simulacrum, Antoine's avuncular eroticism, Octave's metaphysical voyeurism, the Belle Versaillaise, the flagrant obliquity of Roberte's look as photographed by Pierre Zucca, and drawn by Pierre Klossowski in "La Monnaie Vivante" (Eric Losfeld 1970). Not only is her eye oblique, but also the imperceptible smile on her closed lips (sealed like a secret) which are never pursed or tense. A perversity of contrasts: as the body offers itself it pretends to protest as the look obliquely takes its distance. Solecism ....

Klossowski gives a definition of a solecism which has no longer anything incorrect about it: "Some think that there exists a solecism in a gesture also: every time we express the opposite of what we say with a movement the head or the hand". No longer anything incorrect if we recognize here the staging of our intimate contradictions: <u>distortions</u> between our states of consciousness and our actions. A leitmotiv which becomes entwined within the three panels of the tryptic laws of hospitality.

In ROBERTE CE SOIR: "The skirt is burning, the body seems to be safe, but in fact it is the spirit which is burning within this body which Victor, supposedly to save it, is exhibiting".

In LA REVOCATION: "This simultaneity of the moral repulsion and of the eruption of pleasure within the same soul, within the same body".

In LE SOUFFLEUR: "The expression of the faces of the interlocutors never coincides with what they say to me". (I have underlined).

There is obliquity of contrasts within this distortion of the solecism. Elastic definition of the obliquity: the contradictory dialectics of distance and coincidence. It is not a master key. Quartered by the bi-polar distortion of an inaccessible "I" and of an unfathomable "BODY", the look of consciousness suffers from a METAPHYSICAL OBLIQUITY.

The very origin of the Klossowski's solecism is oblique. I can discern it in "Les Meditations Bibliques de Hamann" from whence Klossowski picks out the paradoxical themes of <u>Dei dialectus solecismus</u> and of the <u>coincidentia oppositorum</u>. In "La Monnaie Vivante", the summit of obliquity is a lack: the word "oblique" is never pronounced. This means to say that OBLIQUITY OF CONSCIOUSNESS has nothing to do with natural obliquity, such as the ecliptic, or the muscles of the abdomen, nor with the architectural obliquity: pyramids, stairs, gothic gables, etc.

A step backwards where whole sides of obliquity have remained in the shadows. The enigmatic smile of Roberte? If the smile is oblique, the laugh is not. Roberte does not laugh: this is her strength, the sign of her perversity and her mastery. Does one imagine

Leonardo da Vinci painting his Joconda while she is dying of laughter? If humour is oblique, the mood is not. This is to say that the oblique is willingly opposed to its opposite. The enigma is oblique because it calls upon us to elucidate and comprehend it. The mystery is not oblique because it is that which comprehends and embraces us.

Although it is oblique, the look of Roberte does not arouse suspicion. It does not underline a fault of rectitude. It is rather a sign of detachment of consciousness testing, that is to say, experimenting, its desire not to be troubled by anything. It seems to be saying, as does Maître Eckhart: "I praise detachment more than any love". For if the detachment is oblique, the attachment is not.

I have spoken of Roberte's perversity. In short the entire <u>Psychopathia Sexualis</u> is oblique. Any sexual perversion which diverts from the <u>right path</u> of procreation and reproduction of the species is oblique. If eroticism is oblique, natural (that is to say animal or, if need be, bestial) sexuality is not; it is not oblique in spite of organic obliquity of male-and-female sex. The hyphens show that once separated, each one is merely a semi-sex. There are statistics to be found in the Kinsey Report on ITHYPHALLIC OBLIQUITY. The average angle – calculated for all ages – is very slightly above the horizontal; after this, 15 or 20% of men can avail themselves of an angle of more than 45°; 8 to 10% manifest almost vertical tendencies. Many of them will in old age decline to angles below the horizontal line. No sextant (Jean-Pierre Brisset would write "sexe-temps" or "sexe-tant") has yet been discovered to measure the intimate obliquity of women. If the sexual organ is oblique, its function will not always be so: the sharp rise in the demographic growth proves this. This is the reason of the double obliquity of eroticism. There is obliquity on the secondary level, a level of consciousness which goes against nature.

Enouugh said about Roberte this evening! May as well dismiss the Roberte/Klossowski couple in order to retain only the epileptic quintessence of its obliquity: the mysterious relation of distance/coincidence of a look which is perpetually looked at/looking. Start from scratch. All intentional digression is oblique. Let us forget Roberte to "oblique" elsewhere, in all senses of the word ....

Is the erotic cinema oblique? Thierry Zeno's film, <u>Vase de Noces</u>, presented at the TEP on the 30th May 1975 during the Critic's Week, is the love story of a rather silly adolescent and a sow. A case of pathological zoophilogy? Not all. The scene in which Dominique Garny (the only "human" actor in the film, for the sow – complacent in everything – is a great actress) makes love to her, has nothing erotic about it, nothing moving, nothing disturbing. The lover on heat straightforwardly penetrates her, without ambiguity or obliquity. This sexual act seems quite <u>natural</u> with a few touches of animal tenderness. By his refusal of culture and his regression towards the most absolute nature, where the image speaks so as to make speech unnecessary, <u>Vase de Noces</u> is not, at first approach, an oblique film, even though <u>la vase</u> and <u>le vase</u> are full of several simultaneous meanings, including the coprophagous and the coprolithic. For the "raw" in oneself is not oblique nor is the "cooked" separate from the "raw". Nevertheless this regression of <u>Vase de Noces</u> in the non-human disproportion of the "raw" is less infantile than it is deliberate; it is even consciously cultural contrari-wise and therefore: the obliquity of the film exists an another level. Must there be seen an obliquity of pro-vocation?

Obliquity is cold delirium, a controlled vertigo. To let the inclination veer towards delirium while controlling it, is to leave the straight line for an unknown trajectory, to leave the vicious circle in order to go out on a tangent ... Are you for or against the death penalty? If you are against it, you will die all the same. If you are for it, is it for you or for others? As for us, you and me, the obliquity of our looking inwards is due to our incapability of looking straight at our own death, for it is our death who looks at us.

Death is not oblique: it is the abolition of distance within coincidence. At least let us hope so. For nothing is certain in this Wonderland. For in this perfect emptiness everything is a mirage. In the tombs of ancient Egypt, the boat of the death uses the diagonal way which is called the "Path of Secret Things". This <u>Book of the Dead</u> has nothing reassuring about it, quite the contrary. It is true that we are assured of nothing. But since our agony began with our birth, we should not be displeased by its coming to an end with our death. An oblique definition of Wonderland: NO MAN'S LAND ....

Head on, objects cannot be grasped. Obliquity is to penetrate with a bias. The body of man set down in the Pythagorean pentagram is centered on the sexual organs. The arms are horizontal; the legs are spread open, oblique. Since the head is eccentric, the look will therefore be oblique since it goes from the periphery of the circle to the centre of the sexual organs. The head is lunar in relation to the sun of the sexual organs. All that <u>radiates</u> is oblique. There exists within <u>Nadja</u> an OBLIQUITY OF RADIATION. "Without a shaft of shadow, without a shaft of light" (note by André Breton added to <u>Nadja</u> in 1962).

To move forward diagonally, one must let the inclination drift while maintaining the same direction.

While one of the earth's hemispheres is lit by solar light, it seems that the other is in darkness. The unlit hemisphere is supposedly coiffed with a <u>cone of shadow</u>

which projects itself into the stellar light. This cone of shadow has caused the delirium of generations of occultists. Stanislas de Guaita reproduces its diagram in "La Clef de la Magie Noire" (p.657 vol. II Essais de Sciences Maudites). A malevolent reservoir ... worse than hell! This astronomical <u>cone of shadow</u> is the origin of the belief in the devil's obliquity. As consciousness is related to the body, the devil establishes distance in relation to coincidence. One says, "go to the devil", "live with the devil" etc. Julien Gracq says: "the devil is oblique". Talleyrand was not nicknamed "The Limping Devil" for nothing ... All that pertains to sorcery is oblique: the witch's broom, the psychoanalytical transfer, Quetzalcoatl, the Kundalini, the drug experiments of Aldous Huxley and Michaux, the devil's grass experimented by Carlos Castaneda. In the eyes of the sorcerer Yaqui, shadow is alive within a living, heterogenous and anisotropic space.

Shadow is oblique.

By wearing a <u>conical</u> hat covered with stars, the ancient astrologists revealed the secret of their consciousness' sidereal obliquity. The inward look can only be sidereal if it breaks the wall of the shadow's projection in order to open up onto the stars. Astrology, by its analogous method of reading, is oblique. If the "analogous" is oblique, "Logos" is not.

By opposing what is oblique to what is not, I will say very quickly that the following are oblique: narcissistic masturbation in front of a mirror, whether it be sexual or intellectual; the pill; fetishism; sexual iniation; magia sexualis; the attraction of love; Fourier's pivotal love as the seed of a polygamic monogamy and of a polyandric monoandry; assymetry; the avuncular; Sisyphus and Prometheus; the XIIIth card of the Tarot; all glances in so far as they are conscious of sweeping only a certain <u>angle</u> of vision in the infinity of the world; a shot fired at a distance; poison; the evil eye; a voting paper. The following are not oblique: the guillotine (in spite of the chamfered edge of the blade); the work of mass-production; dictatorship; procreation; defecation; the Pope; impalement; plumb-line; the Editions Plon; filiation; the Inquisition; the most classic of Greek art; symmetry; reasoning reason etc.

In order to avoid multiplying the examples, we could: ... seek the origin of obliquity in the myths. I am thinking of the serpent of the Genesis. The serpent coils in a spiral around the tree radiating life. This oblique circumambulation of the serpent is the opaque bark which hides unity beneath duality, the tree of life beneath the tree of knowledge of good and evil. How should we renew contact with the "sap" whose serpent is the guardian of the threshold, a guardian which is cold by the great poet Jean Carteret in the most oblique terms: "the guardian of the best with the face of the worst"? Between sex and consciousness there exists a TANTRIC OBLIQUITY with double contrary inclinations. Sex is mortis et vitae locus. The serpent is analogous to the sexual organs and to the devil. Although staying within sex in cavernis et tenebrosis locis, the serpent is simultaneously healing and death-healing. It is also the guardian of the tree of the Hesperides. Even in the mythologies anterior to Christianity, verticality and obliquity come together within the tree and the serpent, the tree embraced by the serpent, particularly in pre-Columbian art. On the other hand, the alchemic arbor philosophica symbolises the coincidence of the tree and the serpent; they are no more than ONE as the drawing of a 17th century manuscript in the British Museum shows: the tree, surrounded by the sun and the moon, bursts forth instead of the penis of a man lying on his back. At the base of the penis, the mercurius is the "sap" of the philosophical tree. Distance is not abolished in the coincidence, but the distance is <u>inside</u> the coincidence.

... tie the principle of non-obliquity to the principle of Aristotle's identity according to which a cat is a cat or A=A. However, the following would be oblique: Bachelard's "La Philosophie du Non"; the YIN-YANG and YANG-yin or the double contradiction dialectics of the ancient Chinese; the identity-of-opposites in Mao Tsetung's dialectics: particularly in his treatise "Of Contradiction"; the principle of non-identity according to which a mountain is a non-mountain; Alfred Korzybski's Non-Aristotelian systems and general semantics; Husserl's noetico-noematic structure; the inversion of the inversion in Abellio's absolute structure; the "yes-No" poetics; "I is Another" of Rimbaud; Novalis' equation of "I=non-I"; Roger-Gilbert Lecomte's paradoxes "I am not of my opinion" and "my left hand is a right foot", amongst others, for every poet has oblique blood, and the first is Lautreamont. As for the "Bateau Ivre"!

... make relative the obliquity of terms by the equation of their relations. The word "cat" is not a cat. By its distance, language is always a simulacrum of coincidence. At the extreme, compared to non-language, all language is oblique, whether it be political or poetic. The equation of such a proposition is based on the following proportion: consciousness is to the body what distance is to coincidence what language is to non-language.

The proportion, which obeys the principle of the identity of the contrary relation and to the DIALECTIC OBLIQUITY of the terms, suggests the relativity and the non-identity of each of them.

The equation

$$\frac{\text{consciousness}}{\text{body}} = \frac{\text{distance}}{\text{coincidence}} = \frac{\text{language}}{\text{non-language}}$$

would instigate exhaustless diagonal developments ...

I have mentioned the obliquity of provocation. There are however differences between "Open your legs!", a barely oblique (except in certain cases) way of courting a woman, and the "death is the purpose of life" of Baudelaire's stunning and direct way of expressing a truth which is infinitely oblique. There also exists the obliquity of the pun. By moving straight forward in the vacuity of fullness, language goes around in circles. In the fullness of emptiness all directions (meditation as paradoxal sleep) are oblique: they are directed towards … the centre-of-non-language.

After all, when his last hour comes, the man or the woman is never the writer, nor even the reader, but is the oblique reading of his or her own death. The most oblique literary measures taken, and I am far from taking them, would consist mainly in not creating literature, or in creating it only in order to destroy language ….

To sign off "obliquely yours" would be to speak straightforwardly. The meaning of obliquity is a secret of the heart deprived of all language, which even language itself does not touch. Nevertheless one makes allusions to it. Here, for example, is an oblique signature, a suggestion that everyone can make while knowing that it is more enigmatic than the naive question of the Sphinx: "I would be mad enough to be tied up", said Michel Camus one day, "if I thought I were Michel Camus".

Lust to write
to write out of lust

       Finally. Flat on the page. Impotence of these fragments. She too was impaled on her father's cock. Keep growing. Weep no longer. He was transparent during the spasm. Limitations. The furtherance of each section the abundance of excessive desire. Aimless. Her object to die. The enforcement of copulations with death. Death which love contains. But vertical. Solidity consumes passion. Arrangement or the vengeance of despair. Remains. The upsetting of their order.

       We crossed to an advantage. The alternatives are the provocations. The first part joins with an empty body in solitude. Brightness. The naked are much more direct. Chance wound into the vacancy of the cunt where terror intends to find the passage mauled. Strike. Taste. Blank from malice. Writing. Ejaculate before the proposal. This will be ugly and death. Lengths of veins cherished during her grappling for our anguished charred depths. Masked before the strap lashes. Blood drops. Knowledge cuts deep. A tragic prisoner in himself. Depths where certainties concentrate. His attention was luxury for us. In the writing the hundred virgins. Dead bonds. Blood bath. The coincidental hunting. Basis does not in the first place find her splayed. Or toyed with. In the same way a familiarity with pederasty the white globules fictionized controlled launched will oblige us to masturbate constantly in view of the circumstances. Round about. The presence of coherence is revealed as the very stumbling. When upright in the depths of failing the sign of tenacity in the mysterious the lightness drifting hovering amongst the isolated is only located now that there is the beginning of the performance of the wailing crying shitting trembling lovers. A hundred rolling women of venery collect him fuck him to death between the lines. The birth of percentage. Conclusions. Colours of darkness the seed of celibacy. The point of death meets shadows and the mauve of the bleeding words with this. Falters. Tumbled in the changing tension of loosening images. Considered nowhere. Whiteness of intellect slows in amplified recurrings. We recall that play here where words are stilled or angled for the sodomite. Built an a theme of carnality through a malady of drowsiness. Heightened by nothingness from which he who takes is thereafter a waving hand heavy the touch covered in loss as he explores circles. Last words as soon as it becomes writing.

Crossed. Glares line up. Then it is fatality set free. Torture. A collection. A realism. Yearning accompanies the louse situations working the squirming subject through ecstasies. They are through it once again. The gape allows aggression to increase bit by bit alongside the carnage. To solve by a caress as I have suggested only brings on disgust to such a degree that she will not submit.

Malcontent spreads but he must retreat. Space and orgasm can yield possibilities. This is a treatment. Paragraph. This is a cunt. This way walks on her face. Margins. Sacrifices already expressed dispersed and rooted. The interior exhibited rather more of the margin made it fictional though absurdly clear. Once deposited on the page it can transport the text to a margin. To generate or to recollect more.

Coupling. Redness. Raw. And more conveniently lying spreadeagled she exposed desirously what is termed a stumbled sigh. To the theme. Back to the beginning which criminality swelled swirled advancing on the virgin. Transparency. Searching through cravings into forbidden objectives. More attached to swing across by strokes. The pubic delineation in space. Directly she pulls or pours we see it as bestiality. Plucking between her thighs might be a better way to satiate. Henceforth he fills with spunk this timeless vessel composed of invitations that contradict waiting.

A pitched sharpness tore at my balls. I trembled. Immense. Taut. The vibrating cycle collapsed. His prick rose. Congealed. This rape of coincidence that poses is quickly dispelled. Vomit spread around the area. Turbulence requires a mark of systematization before its naked arses are presented for puncturing for recognition. The problems of what is written burrow into the dark whilst words explain the presence of the two. One guards her tendency to be established and maintained as a deviant the other screws her behind. He surfaced. Inactive cunts need not be kept in bondage. Cunts chased into death in order to exist even if in silence.

He mutilated romance. It will wait even overlap ideas if necessary for in time the weakness allocated to each discord will be a roundness to be pulled. Preferences last. The existence of language accounts for this organised ceremony. Preservation as if by muscular stubbornness. The feast of bowels pissed on the alteration of the history of thresholds. The forgotten. To subvert the prevention of the development of knowledge is always first.

Defended their tustle. Wallowing cocks of arrogance with climactic angular desires.

Most seem superficial or in any case of the flesh. Minimilizing the enjoyment into which she was tempted. A book into which it developed. Rather anarchy.

Stolen evaluations hurt on the face. Derivations constitute the swings and exasperations. Lust frees what experience bites. Sperm obliterates the defeats of language. Stimulation is what an attack of anguish has increased. Slits across a hesitation. The method excretes coherent shifts. Representations are different at centre. To analyse is only to demonstrate being.

A scratch enticed dragging his testicles. The fragile fibre was torn from the hesitant as it had the properties of the stolen pleasures of dispersion. The exposition brought forward a system to urinate and masturbate people. Cut off the arrogance. Play with adaptations of castration. The naked possess the power to signify.

Hurled into the fiction by language because it was itself terminating proportions of real madness. And only venereal movement to muscles. A necessary circulation of moistness in clinging lesbians is a delight. One of duplication and tautology.

Brought to the entrance heavy which the naked hindrance thins. The magnitude of the characters the groins on the surface of silence Ideas selected to rape. Whereupon excrement sets in motion other directly satisfying needs. Discontent. A careful beauty turns its buttocks to the existence of lust and her position. The need is simply the reproductive temptation of the hole. This need brings to an end the age of clumsy thighs. It happened that others remained stationary. The pick of faded subversions.

The climax cleaves or secludes when he cruelly mounts forces and occupies.

Surrounded by swellings of fiction of classifications of the lost book. Swirl. Triangular analysis based solely upon the visible the exhausted. Lust eclipses levitates fears and forms scratches that are even deeper. The orgy for sodomists was denser than this representation. She prevails despite obstructions within herself. In clearing thought from the page she confirmed ecstasy as possessing sculptural spaciousness.

Where he reacted wildly to the fucking in the turbulence. Complete reversal. Nihilistic celebrations silence vitalistic banality. Here satisfaction is strung. In the confusion a system of thought is stimulated.

The odour that menace excretes is developed radically. Usually forgotten in the end. The form of the vengeance might subside or become sacred as in subversion. To be found in language. Even shit mocks his manner. Before it takes on a quiescence he tightens the meaning. And in order to learn of joy and fondness the construction plays with human nature and the way in which it functions.

For the spreading madness chance accompanies certain doubts termed weaknesses. Bloated by false despair makes for two kinds of analysis before a fact is left to work the fears where drastic mistakes moving from a central point join forgetfulness disruptively. She manipulates the succession from another point to glimpses of seduction where dependence concerns language and signification being entirely reduced to the essence of life which attempts to contradict.

Turmoil fictionized. She severed other torsos. Hacked above the alignment because the collapsed pubenda terminates here. It lacks recreation. We must go further. Die. We know that pain screws all possibility of death.

Along a line of disgust a surface expression of carnality displays dilemmas the simple failure of which is ridiculed. Malice fondles the hilarious deaths.

Astride the voracious gropings we can locate quenched bestiality and monstrous cunts. For all that the wailings never collide. They waver near to the following section offer females to those who vomit and castrate any generated interest towards an eroticism of juxtaposition because of their dedication to the present.

At bottom the despicable is crucial. This area offers lust. She terminates possible situations. Three clits out of ten. A brief transparency of the skin flourishes with the dying. Words and ideas must be readable for together they will form the carnality to be realised as transgression. Forbidden by sentences it presents a mystery for rapists. The text is a sensation that pushes the impossible.

But the swellings float on the refusal dominated by insomniac whores whose secretions are professionalized. These particular hollows pivot on a further refusal manifested by her roughened bareness.

Groins turned upwards towards lies towards courses in the forgotten darkness. Power to concentrate on yearnings that are suspect protrusions. The event that I wanted to dominate. The skin of whoredom and I. Complications do not exactly confine the demystification that I call crossing.

Towards a cleavage that generates the complete experience. It remains an essential persistence. It is allowed but her relationships remain interrupted by the blunders affixed to the loathing. Journeys give duality.

Pain in the thigh of anguish. It is manipulated. It is inside.

Celebrations are diseased anatomies whose condition sketches death. Your proposition heaves us into the opening of overturned reversals.

A whore bound provocatively upon writhing bosoms with the notion that her limitations are bared and poked and that her roughness is a panic. How paralysed we are within the space of this difference.

No caress wants his reaction to the limit. Beauty is the capture provoked by the lines. These communions are shown cracked. They tend towards situations where excrement defines expenditure. Dislike of what seems written as a movement.

Flight through thickness is a matter of splitting thighs whose breadth maltreats the glorious excesses.

Lust describes ferment transferred by malformation into a false essence.

Locked in battle the lesbians of venereal carnage and deformity. Pubic hair entwines the ruins. Vestiges of that curled and sudden horror of joyfulness vomit emptiness.

Play with turning the essence. The area omitted. The carnality lined and paged. Presence increases the revealed ruptures.

See the prick roasted. Fiction pulled and snipped. Breast of words nourishes mistakes despite her ego.

Crossed the space in

order to fulfil contradictory forces to find death prevailed and intentional words are pliable and soiled awaiting massacre in order to reverse their requirements.

Removed the strain of desire. Gaze upon them. Rather mistaken by the excess of general notions.

Lust is given to romance. The leaded whip chooses romance. Whores generate what can hook onto my sickness.

Movement towards space where an extreme allocation of romantic tensions persist. Finds much to eat and fuck. Within. The cessation of the silence of arousal.

Slaughter which beneath your nose nourishes the impossible transparency. Damage fails in the expanse. It is not unlike the final selection positive and concerned. Here is the book the writing.

Gaping holes lead to ritual pains pitched into the space of the accusation. Beneath such she avoided naked demands. He is placed on the circumference.

Disrupt the compulsive lacuna. Grasped. Drift. This front as a misplacement for work. The passage of silence slips.

Motionless. Isolated by torture. She specifies drowning. Punishment is a question of the acceptance of occurrence. Discarnate exaggerations. Bonds arranged to fictionize the carried generations.

Soiled fragments. The persecution of a darkness to destruction reactivated.

Surface. Shape carried the connection with women through fiction and cessation. Carried through the bareness of carcasses moulded into a form which she will watch cleave. The cold hesitations are an enigma. The very position of their moments touches hopelessness the sentences and the seductions themselves.

The saturation of treatment obliterates in the initial mobilization tensions of the main manipulation. They see the wound where femininity is brought down. Less white to drain does necessitate outlining a limitation.

Love can monopolize death for preservation.

Words of anguish bend the theory which is the bared forbiddance. Recollected for the scratch of desire for the drowning that is from this desire and mistaken by troublesome wenches who have contaminated death.

The turbulence in a tightening the significance in her delays are exposed. Nothing is pivoted or justified.

Lust is placed in the weakness at panic's base. Deliberate horror in the neglected characters.

Maintained then obliterated by strictures on endurance. A vertical movement of sexual structure can be integrated anywhere.

Within the curved and bitchy subject beats the end of the book.

The full expenditure arouses the pudenda. We have realised the richness the threat of charm that culmination makes clash.

She remains on the back of degradation to adapt her generated responses.

The loss of misplacement is likened to her.

An error handled objectively is precluded from another solid supposition. Is merged with speculation. Alliance can offer harassment or constancy or amazement.

She happened to triumph. That is why the cocks of riot are repulsed.

Mounted on cocks because they are overwhelmed by shocks. Always more than the significance of one. Or because of it.

The writing builds propulsively can be felt throughout.

The whore's arse opens to the conspiracy of this work. He discovered her strap.

Convictions whipped and robbed the habit which had at last brought him irritation. Textual spots of uselessness compared with the sight of a safe poise.

When curiosity has to test the matter's slowness two directions beseige the triple orifice. Contradictions face laughter and arise when a pause in the practice then to the width where birth is shown laughter and women gain what we readily recognize.

The practice of masturbation is an essential partner of the maddened vindication where it is banded by substitution the frivolity of decadence.

Among the habits of the manipulated compulsions where the accursed are locked Alleviate cited forbiddings.

Amour offends the secrecy of the monomaniac. Amour offends the neurosis around the secrecy of the endangered gash that each risks.

Remembrance perforates the immensity that death begins to protect.

Satisfaction was the offence permitted by the elimination of her quiet adultery.

Switching heaviness into the outlined

finality we precede the load.

The closure submerges our isolation on the skin. The cascade of symptoms bursts if we reminisce.

Her groin under duress. The text shocks the risible and her close relationship with it.

The disposal of words monopolizes what we could clip onto situations recommending largeness.

Faeces are comparable with red movement is located within blunders and yearnings.

Turbulence moves in such obvious bosoms that superlatives are needed.

Her demands for easing merely melt. It was eaten. It was removed. Reactions but by caressing the movement we see them alluringly within reach though painfully confined.

Not being able to trust any language. She must be the whore who pressed herself against me. She may be shocked when I detail the disappointments of murder.

Scattered on various remarkable inviolations the strain of a dispersal whips the impossible.

Removing bareness is certainly not the limit where those who feast do not yet exist. Filled with the remembrance hesitations are broken.

With illusions about goodness I captured a kiss. It was marked to help me remember that underneath we are not artificial.

Because she splayed her legs she accused the language that tampered with her will. Disintegration profits her.

The sight of her exciting thighs managed to alleviate his

discomfort. Pick the execution.

Softness is secluded from pleasurable furtherances.

Forgiveness is allowed to stupefy the inviolable. It twists in a compact circle in a released whore to whom it is repugnant.

During the sinuous embrace persistance reshapes one of the women. She is gagged since she allows reactions to form that are sacred expenditures.

The slide requires the same elegance if future burdens are to reappear circled in places where construction precludes the metamorphosis.

First tensions of the book risk the opposite displacements that they pose.

Where shock nourishes events she is ripped from the result whose solid silence must be subjected to probabilities.

A place where complete movement is forced to be established between them.

Constructions exist because words self-govern this reproduction.

The allowed reading can always use theft to help the orgasmic propositions to contradict the stakes.

The rotation of the aroused orders themes. But contrary to the confused notation this foursome battered all underlying knowledge.

Lies from each are not welcome. This orifice expands the delights with the result that language and its absolute principles disappear. A lack that is not aligned with what it consists of.

Yes bareness is slow heaves from another's mound towards a usefulness. He curses the grimace he sees upon her nipple. Corruption is that other face. To fight spontaneously would have removed the mundane and momentary.

Dropped spontaneously into the outstretched. Since she was wounded vertigo and shock have dismembered her scarlet pretence.

Sad to perish visibly aside from a naked caress.

Silence responds to the slap. Several essential meetings immediately threaten the start on the other hand. It must be distinct.

In the direction of dispersion. Other methods closely measured. Often to its limits.

A force turned and the gluttonous orgasm twisted towards resumption. Both unite to possess themselves.

Closed by hesitations. Not stopped. Between two extremes there is the line or the balance or the writer. In view of possible degeneration she tolerates complexity and works for the replacement.

On his hesitations are kept analogous weaknesses. The colour which was displaced aided the weaknesses towards the replacement.

Give up your words sever my thighs. When she changes she probably will not collapse. Her hands are sometimes pale her seduction is whipped into value and into weakness.

Her body came down. It produces a little wound. Remember.

There is a risk with all killings.

Space rejects the vision. No image is mistaken. Shifts eliminate the fall.

To expel sanity is to resemble an incoherence where the snatch is a remembrance like predestination.

The border resists the anal and the fictional.

The force remains a possibility that their relationship eliminated. A constant folding released between detachments.

She created her promiscuity serving the forbidden and hating their deviations.

Crazily she searched through the systems exposing the firmly bedded. Incest appears from the postponement of tolerance in suckling. There is the coupling.

A route into the closure or out of it. How does the maiden further the rising or the falling prick's disruption. How prostitution grows.

The stake is lowered with the anticipation of a total disregard for the girl's response.

A notion of eventuality in the waste which lubricates.

And then she stepped into the blackness the pulse of the situation. It escapes them. It escapes between them.

A movement of displeasure from persecution to perseverence.

Scarlet baited his valour. What is the purpose of lustration. Escape and distress.

Tempted by trouble the anus of dissension is scratched and intensified.

She urinates on stolen anxieties in the protraction of systems of change.

With the twist opacity is opposed by the thought of an unashamed theme of language.

Captive in the unknown. Made animate. A crack reveals flesh and flooded.

Bore into the solidified as if from a point of alertness where the impaling could still be administered.

Heinousness is praised. Only along the slender body is forced both reaction and chain of thought.

Balance and facility to begin with create that which does not thirst.

Reading that reading will thrust aside tidiness.

Reading. Failure. He answers the decisions. Cuts him off.

With the blast and from the damage comes the culmination of ruination and the emergence.

In the secret their lies. Each one the corners of solemnity. Each one scandalized.

A globule trickled was occasioned by the bouncing of the cock. He is perhaps not a very bloody masturbator though well suited to be one.

Comprehension continues to revolve. Can write of language only in the honesty tolerated curtailed plunged become sovereign. The scourge was her manipulation. With the maiden bondage displays part of her expected modesty. Within her failure played torture. He sees the figures are in a position where licentiousness though imaginary is not doubted.

Clenched between her teeth. Colourless. What gore had tumbled into the entrance she tumbled and cracked or vanished. From the damage to the very centre and once again. This artifice lunges into white banality. She offers a possible situation. She is stopped when self-realisation coincides with the brief trace of the words.

Hanging from her pride is her identity. She must be displayed. Outer skin reacts. Read at the level of broken vengeance. Disembowelled. From a transformation it opens onto an essential thoughtlessness. Mystification is semen to the text. Honesty and the essence are marked immediately. Lesbians are the drift are the difference in relation to the recurring. Infinite seeming possibilities or the particular.

The establishment of an aim is refracted and makes the rolling deceptions the legibility of bareness capable of functioning within. The folding converges circles the desire that he wanted solved and dissolved. She does not muster any further destruction to exceed the carnage.

Ruined by the enclosed crime in which their fixed poise resists all usefulness. It shifts politeness and the breasts of jealousy. Essential friction is whitened. Unknown lines generate the challenges that are bound and clamped. Examination is allowed but disasters are interrupted by the blow that joy can deliver.

Further punctures can be disputed. She will gild savagery. It is marked. It is in this ending and in this context that such skeletal torsions are described. Here the reducibility and opening of sexual relinquishments know that to balance its perversions depends not only on the means by which tortures are tackled but also on the way it is to be indiscreet and impulsive in its ordeals of discharge.

Escape through the scraped limit. No more than he could spoil. Fastened to the provoked laughter. Joining the reading of the inebriated. Space and words have been mainly prostituted. The stain and the refusal are immense. And from the margins to the lust the same yearning as in the robbery of a last gasp.

Escaping the refusal with a wench who assaults him. The halt can arouse the forspent. She is included as a sacrifice in a place where the crime and the text are a play of prohibitions where the orgies are inhibited by whores who resist the necessary aware-ness accorded to cocks that remain manipulated by leather.

What is left is kept dressed to kill. The nothing-ness of the night where words are tumid. The essence of the reading titters and is minimized. The exigency of the humour transgresses the secret language and mani-pulates a spending that leaps across a twisted rigidity. The void is examined. The same appended to the crime.

Madness hits on the finality of human relation-ships with the end of stubbornness directly before the filling. Alarm localizes and catches enough resentment that a roughness indicates expenditure forces identi-fication just as relationships lacerate all searches for tenderness. A fixed final sentence he knows will surround the sublime and its own world.

Take the oblit-erated conception that honesty desires what is noted. Radical journeys are seen as a trembling towards which the same resistance from abllatancy where the edges are chosen forms are stark and barren is materialized. The reality is that the old disturbance is the sign where she lies soiled.

Not knowing sprawled across the silence des-pite the expenditure of the finite of the rampant. A whip balanced on the movement of the text from which she arouses the old rumination. Writing takes this otherwise nonsensical feature for a refinement between the sighing flagellant who is supposed to be silent and a cruelty that is the stripping of flesh by the gradual evacuation of the difficult and the criminal.

The circle was slowly deleted. The point of reflection that is lightened by a heave of sympathy offers a significant situation. A passion directly praised is dependent an the blackness of an edge to be wanting the object. Balance is the care of licentiousness. At the moment of writing a presence licks the anguish banned from the readability. Reading is a domination of the lie that the solitary is truncated by.

She raises her resistance to pederasty by recognizing his yearnings. Darkness is only permissible crime. She has begun to acknowledge that deviation is the stain that the rest of the burden regards as lacking. Around the reading and the interpretation is the hunt for the manic. False stains are directed onto what she has been threatened with. A shift was wanted. She will never consent; At the limit of her hindrance she remembers.

Until she stripped infidelity was a fingered enigma. Enticed to rewrite. She gathered unanswerable insinuations. Her limit is still her longing for the void that she will be demented within. Quiet ruminations sterilise what she dispersed. The reading of two or three ordinary meanings masquerades. It is the testicles that are living.

Sliced from the blackened. To heap among masks that grace which was necessitated to invade passion. Seduction is both laughter and eventuality. In order to make what is left endless comprehension ceases. A curious aversion to serenity terrifies many of the resistless. To gain energy damage is the surface that was juxtaposed with the ignitable crawling with maidens and beauty and beyond which infestations that obscure the possibilities are compelled to hold and even be cast from this nonsensical laughter. Sodomy is so skimpy.

Praised. Slobber. So completely committed that uniqueness blemishes one more chance. Combined restrictions are the satiation and the dual living. Inserted into the alternative into the principal boundary curiosity marauds and recovers allowed renouncements. Licentiousness by which certain naked charms are massacred solves profusion. She discerns between her crutch the first carcass beginning to become a swirling of howls. A brazen core is to be flagellated. It increases. He lies.

Excreted from the bladder to the sorrow of the deliriously bared. Straddled across the words the drips of visual friction and the trials of the stumbling that intentions have made a sessional fucking. Frequent failure tallies with an offensive cunt. To the usually concerned the inequalities this ending shelters between its kinks and sheets belies whoever omits the yearning. Shit swept back to reveal the narrow derivations of the hand that writes that its power forms a greasy twist and lasts long enough for the collapsed dread to hide.

Outside the cancellation the hermaphrodite who ordinarily is the creation of almost any other idea suddenly creeps and is found in front of a vast hindrance that a small recurrence of the shift of will even flatten. Cancellation simplifies the lycanthropic liberation in those prostitutes and collapsed arguments. In the three great nights suggested she pinched the tantalization from darkness. She reveals herself as a being who can raise skirts of an attendant observer even one being careful. So someone exceeded by non-strangulation of the successful gonorrhoea. To start a defence is prohibited.

Chewing on the scabs this modernity separates the essence of the system the vocabulary whose whole whore experience of rhythms and mellifluence places sexuality in an expectancy for which the sequence is viewed behind the scope that accompanies situations of the shrinking vomit. To excrete and regard the last as the first allows the difficulty that a hitch makes of laughter tough by comparison with the brassiness she brought.

Distress when the touch is always uproarious. The occurrence posits that the first ones are laughing at the cunt being stroked that has not yet been substantiated. Isolation makes the centre of the source the eye of the infinite. Inserts of the utilised secludes a fiction that would ransack displeasure and attack at the moment when that has pushed aside any thought that becomes a smirk. Any distress effectively remains a deviation in regard to the organ that reciprocates what the anus thieves.

The hollow of the cunt will repel the force that shadows. It throws anarchy into representation. By a delayed reaction to modified thought every form of corruption almost labours under accomplished centres where the breaking of human reason consists of the uselessness to curse the insignificance of the anus. Pure collapse amid the combination that will provide us with whoever tames discontinuous reproductions. From the impossibility comes the necessity for concepts that part or magnify.

Hanging down between an ordained whore unbound nakedness is no degradation. She must be accustomed to the buggery of transvestites. Writing whitens the unsighted directly it is held in unusual proportion. The essential brevity binds the sincerity. The object is undeniably a novel. This. That burden erodes the displayed routine the rituals located near the tolerance of the blond. She is a tightened pulsation forced to gulp the bored connection. This is a moment within the novel.

Follow through with it though the result could be a fundamental quickening. An extraordinary perception for such a reluctant projection. Consequently the whore's share is fouled. The means to anarchy in the text is the whore. The paralysis extends past what we shall stomach. It survives our commitment to know suffering. You see her spread objectively. The limits tighten and the manner of viewing her cunt where another orifice awaits the infection that each carries. Deletion flatters the arguments of the girl. Every element displays madness with difficulty.

When a scandal of a theme the letters written clutter the page is spent by constraining the material the thoughtful guts the reading of the monstrous. The hungry solicit conflict between laws. She dissolves in the instinct that is the transformation. It is the information that is able to find this necessitation. The nymphomaniac gathers a suppression by certain normalities. Games of weals the establishment of displeasure the prick of the modification form nourishment.

No failure is a crutch is no longer simply a way of cracking the needs that express excess. In terms of need she inclines towards the silence. Weariness tenses the encompassing inversions. Modifications are such as these. Nonentity is a oneness which is affected by measuring with that given to others. The steadiness discharges a scintillation that the breasts of the torso metamorphosed. Nudity appears as a scandal lashed and beaten to be able to advance towards another self-disciplined orderliness. Rationality is fundamental to the burden which frees the finite. The dreariness of the withdrawal requires an end to any story. It is towards utilization is opposite to the sovereignty of a system that turns the insurmountable words. Maintaining life clashes with a purposelessness that is without a flaw.

Collapsed and placed in possession of a visible bound woman. A repeated validity that large breasts can tease. Existence is being what enables selfishness. That is to exist is the same for a whore that has large breasts as it is for the hindrance of breasts. To read with the realisation that to exist is where unashamed language is a mutilation in the belly of profusion. The order of stress and illness is their truth. Henceforth it will be labial membranes that are nothing more in relation to living than a whore is to an experience. She is scattered across constantly eluded tortures. Her selfishness fills completely silent horror.

Bound to a living pivot theory established a profanity that trounced those whom technique has organized. Extremely certain of the discipline that a certain extravagance can silence gouges out many uncreated words which represent the torn pivot. Sodomy takes place. The banishment is worse near the lie. Needs and language are doubted. Close to the bottom of repetition is a form that coincides with a twisting solitude. Another sign is her thighs. The appended juxtaposition is hidden. It always implies or resembles the tears of those who before had seemed very distant. She met his hilarity with questions of concern.

When the slope is obliterated spending touches textual humour. Length and dread separate the written. As a point of seizure to the visible where depravity has been promised suspension is held by the tensions and preparations. To sympathize mistakes our life for buttocks. To crease an equivocal functioning strain hangs together in the silence. What she would like closes well-connected circumstance. To satisfy is indeed aroused by clumsy lies by virtue of the desolation of feeling. Old or requested collisions are recovered as permissible.

Wanted to be compelled to intensify the homosexuality estimated. Leather is a symbol of guilt. The bored nonentity relates at this point to the ridiculousness of further stretches elevated to a typification of compelled silence that the characters proposed. Maybe bodies are finalised by looking beneath stares for the letters. Unmarked ordeals seldom align lewdness simultaneously with set backs. Raided by reading she burst into motion changing toleration by damaging toleration with collapse an explosion. Initial collaboration shocked prose.

Desire is the triumph that pieces the development of misplacement. To select closures the continuity of I bored an anxiety that nakedness misses necessarily. Reading relative salacities seems to be buried beneath bitter waiting. But precisely which writing shrieks. She eats. He accepted the violation and motions to the solitude of the expenditure.

Melancholia in a salubrious profanity. Suffering of spikes that change from obsession to nausea. Extremes or essentials tighten the whore.

Outside the vicious and the chewed romp the memories that burst from each elevation operates towards silence a particular deception.

And the silence on the sentence would arouse the looks that test the disruption of her waiting. Meaning topples disruption. That bathed in waiting is read because of this voluptuousness of dilemma pursued as a carnage.

Licentiousness squandered on implication. It is to be sucked. It is fed by stopping notations that jar against the central resistance. He remained in close relationship with solitude. He has defined the beginning of the enormous prick by manipulating old justifications that radical and sordid individuals can silence. Uproar is a poetic inheritance and every situation is the same situation recreated.

Intercourse factualizes her from text to text. Sprawled and lashed language obliterates him. A torso touched which lay on the divergence and perhaps depends also on invisible foreskins. No transition is accepted here under her virginal violence.

The shape of the orifice is remembered from the dubious moments of slime. Many sources of language are paralysed. Sores heap friction on the source. It is a sign of collapse.

Danger to the discord of language and that of a stiffness dug into random benefits. Can he like women who respond to the achievement of the infinite. Impaled on pricks that defend the significant. To ruminate within a loud silence. A totality as momentous as itself in the image of a penis is more likely to react towards its orifice than lusty writing posing as an opening.

A catastrophe of hanging tits. A repulsion that the living pose helps to rise. The magnificent breasts are quite enough of an object to commit his rampage. Between the solid and the reversal the curved limbs and the unbound elegance are served. Motions from her confinement are wanted. She is seduced by a minus.

Twisted to insert the forgotten. Several centres in which there is no warning. Vomit revolves. Reversal of impalement. It is this passage which is illuminated. Towards suction. His randiness has not received her mound. The core of the method up to now rips. The manner of her power is another whore. Indulgence was the utmost terror. Chaos encloses us.

When the convulsion of pleasure stuns these differences she insists on containment by refusal to his commitment. She puts an end to panic by selection. All her doubts and all his questions.

She was casual when arranging pricks. Though this foreshadows the crossing of resistance with profundity it is agreed that order and manipulation affect the long delayed consummation. Shown towards resistance her massiveness is known. That attitude is confined to their collided relaxation.

Fought the hole cited in the participation. It is the bond. The edge is deformed. Against it the old vulnerabilities are naked. In the hectic serration the furious befits the manner in which only the preposterous silence is isolated. Spending is sacred to itself. It was perishable. She will be bitten. In the final cry corruption swallows. Rousing lateral circumstances. Loudness has not yet marked the artery.

Clustered and burnt she comes to be forced and held with hollow baits. One of the young women aggravates the scheme and felt beauty far between. The sting and the waving are companions of deceit. She is fated to perform in the search for the temptation manifest in their fight.

Spanking slaughters crooked versions under regal nooses. This nakedness by which a rectum is speared alone marks this elevation.

Pernicious voluptuaries can no longer be occupied once they are cloaked in tardiness. Because extension itself is reversed around meditative doubles it is granted renewal on its differences between two black lips.

The coolness of withstanding one horror and one wildness salvages the ruins of what power she can satisfy. Method and omission are what she has. A lovely wisdom shines and was terminated. Marks can be extenuated.

Ending in mistakes and openings that are difficult to specify. Roughness will chance the menace of her secretion. Managing words which have an adherence and notion for catastrophe. Being constantly used and severed is sweetened. Massacres and remaining torsos are propelled points. Remoteness is to be an exasperated poise appalled by brown collapses together begun.

Looking at those who hope to be lanced she was refused into the spurt. The edge quickens as starkness and plainness hold without her lips. Bored and measured strips the trespass and other things issuing from the forbidden. Facility of stepping from the bowels earns so many cold faces that knowledge threatens this conquest.

Points that swell are made to tolerate the immensity of the inhibition. The belly upon which he fulfills his promise of scrutiny. The boobs are to his taste and recurrence. She flips across the intensity and the changes. First comes her inclinations not her sickness. Reluctance between bellies is deliberate. Towards licentiousness are the links according to which she can be fucked.

Tongue to the rump relieves genital thef. Hundreds of orifices are scared by limiting falsity. All the inhibitions are the languages that must be renounced. The socket in her belly is attached to the sinews that hinge on repetition. She descends towards the ends of the one who could never refuse her dismissal. The salinity of hindrance resists the anality and flows from her wounds to devour them in the mistrust.

A solitary finish. The quality supports the nascent language.

Feet begin to appear as debauched charmers curved by an evocation that would appear born from having been opened by lascivious temptations. They are patient.

Finally the lacking spasm. Hooks flourish. She is lingering in filth. He is lingering in frustration before being restrained from her belly. There was an empty spiral which bent in the hole. It is duplicated between any two bellies. Wind the whip. What reassurance that it will.

Screaming. No notion is defined as assumed or changed until the attack confuses the difficulty. She is still single. Celebrate that many frequently take mercy to be incomprehensible and lighten one of the prime causes.

Relieved by the many persecutions the most striking of which folds and continues to pierce nominated validity and step into noises of salvation on occasions that ban the drastic.

Bitten methods lust in this carnage. Also she is shifted by reversing to the unique force fetching arrivals to a languid ability.

Where breasts quiver she establishes or turns lewdness to pricks in her orifices.

Lewdness in sincerity tolerates ruptures as that which plays with self-denial. Septic circles intend to own commitment of repulsions. This principle realises the removal that corruption fronts.

Thousands of holes. This event only flaunts to break that which gives validity. To the link is matched an object of desire. She is chased and spread-eagled. Little improvement to laughter that these endeavours did not reach.

Risk forms the stretched fullness released from restriction in the centre. To the limits the halt binds probabilities staked from fake struggles of a humid spectacle. Constriction whips movement into the other.

Haphazard slashes fail three clashes. The other hanging grows. Bouncing off her is a vital ordeal with all its superimpositions in which foolishness in acting forms display from sterility to seeking. As a position of advancement room to finish is lethal.

Assault. Defecate. The grimace tempts us to be a long time licking the growth that satisfies. The sound is infinite. To be twisted around genitals claps and utilizes them. She is fucked by many confusions. United impossibilities of surrender throb whilst prostitutes make the effort.

Enclosed in spreadeagled shame masks this scheme and animates the discord. A shaft makes language vital. It quivers. Bound in waste. It was necessary to worship together simulations that they should be able to handle.

Failure closes the arrangement of her locks and her manipulations. Basic writhing reaches husky annoyance. She was the lewdness in excess which implicated the inability of the seduction to the limits of pushing and shows how a lapse could be leashed Rigidity like intimacy is the sequel grafted by necrophilia. Chastity is then able and then able.

The nape is stooping. To establish ca-utious relapses a cord around the throat and strokes connected to discharge. With laughter she receives stimulation. Linking the discharge of that one with soft intensities vanquished the bunch and perhaps holds human memory. She has eaten carved dominance or rather it is that she is deeply founded in enticing real hilarity from him and providing a new fondle.

Forced my-self into her to relish what could have pulsated. A collapse with all these arrivals stimulated red duality that was to disappear as it appeared. Collecting and crashing into her if Some event covers the real firmness. A lustful person whose skin is immediately transparent is corrupted. She will be no surprise with the face that she has isolated.

Bound to the return of a question of the same rough notion utilised that conceives maturity. To the rump and the carcass the eventuality is this desire provided by sustainment between the decisive torso and the anus. Holding onto hesitations and pain the structure of a possibility is cold. This hangs dangerously and clears admiration of a response to the insertion.

Hanging from an unusual construction in the posture. Verging from his position and producing very real progress here is the area of the voluptuary. Erections and heroic cocks in the suspense of the craved cracks. Towards a journey that is implied in defiance of linking desire and outright nourishment. Unrestricted unendurance provokes invisibilities that robust nakedness avoids. The rump burns in desolation. Robustiousness will provide voluptuousness. Sodomy causes immediate relaxation within worship.

Kicked in the cunt where thi-rst is a worse kind of life than the exalted void. Neutral insertions for some spoiled wishes that bulge and Jo not anticipate express occasions. Shown in a grand manner their fulfillment expends into the intimate.

For worship her endurance is bared and describes the change of the subdued prostitute. An object is a discreet poise. The bound are hoisted into a pair of outer labials. The discreet poise of the laughter unites naked lips of the novice that use our approach.

Sweat smeared forcefully as a struggling space is ripped from the entrance to the notion of temptation. To secure timidity superior temptations are swollen. Release never achieved the circle that was roused by the whole book. Awkward weakness and old bruises are elevated to stop the reawakening of sickness.

Resistance to the hand dominates change. She is about to be hounded into sitting full on the strain to the infinite. When burdens play on couples it is the pubic that is detested. She is hanging from finished degradation. Writing which is intimate with hesitations is bared first by her breasts.

Placed in the chaos are the terrible deviations ruptured by questions that worship the philosophy of death. To us a distance of repulsion is the likeness to pouncing where dispute is provoked. From hounding it is finished. The prostitute is mounted here.

The end is unmis-
takable. At the parting of the two the only part grasped
in the rape was the frequency of those who move up to
accomplish revolution. The work anticipates the limits.
Such sturdiness shows us that she had a starkness.

Loose
and posing as changes in a closed line another suspension of failure to project nakedness insistently. Harassed
is a lengthy collapse from within one's own chaos. It uses
the word hang to restrict desire. He means it as an attack
on your obsessions.

Saved by fe-asting. Space withstands
the belly. Snatched the naked lie away from the look.
Cherish what lives by prostitution. As the circle parts
refusals are aroused. All the whores are seldom tolerated.

His own voluptuousness is lent to her. It is united to
those that are sketched. Coarse smoke coincides and
converges impulsively on a mania. Her breasts explode
around tangles. What is groped is balanced by bouncing.
There is in her strange aims two malformations rooted
to seem another within the round.

Beneath the vengeance
of the pretence which is sacrificed he gave his women
voluptuousness. The masturbation halted each detached
quarrel linked by piling up again much by digression.
Disorder in the same tightness.

With space she caused a
crisis. She motioned tensions since care and play were
suggestions anni-hilated. She motioned tensions manipulated by archaic blondes that were stuck to a truth
covered by a displacement. It is impossible to catch
reversal as it spreads all allusions and places her lack of
sweetness on words planned once to be buried. She has
realised full twistings. Convulsions grow survive and
grey.

Swelling prepares the whore's slaughter. Freshness. But we soon dismiss that. It is at the fulmination that she turns. She obliterates perspective above all. Amidst the signs writing ends. Nihilistic experience seemed at first glance to be callous. A system of blunders that are the peak of the monstrous panic.

The whores are bared within the pain. The different genitals and appliances eliminate the fundamental roughness that is crossed by sensations. Until we have sucked at the peak of shouts and delays we went them with the others in the sweat. She tried to hit the others that natural exertion will find plausible.

Cling to the sacrificial phallus. His insertion was never celebrated. Manipulation smashed her manual. To escape from the familiar play she probed boredom. Fascination stretched out on all the alternatives is no conclusion.

Drop the stake that is glimpsed as a scream. Even if we had realised she arranged that complication can annoy so many truths despite the various silences. Tease and twists evoke a recurrence that narrow spending seduces. Her loins are forced between continuous tongues.

How fast is the odour to be saved from delusion. An accumulated softness poses only a few brawls. Delay resisted by others is part of the attributed limit within familiar roars. Pregnancy in these prostitutes is bound to injury. It is always within this wait.

Questions of plausibility are based on its arbitrariness in narration. For slaughter is thought to weaken the elements of extermination hence the belligerency and couplings. A cheat cut across by the whore's questions. Play is either celebrated as a sturdiness or the bottom of what trembles.

The game of commitment dodges any proposition that is to her annoyance. Crouching and repulsive rogues express their knowledge by seldom arranging or avoiding any threat internal to manipulation. Reading must be continually naked. To be solid constitutes the other direction towards oblivion.

Where we feasted she jolted aberrations of folding fatal to her limits. Desirous to the point of torture. She has feasted and locked her established pretence in obliterated quiescence. But for us her suggestions would escape without reflection.

A motion towards a worse outrage. To the coincidence accorded to hanging. Round the whip this privilege will not be intensified. Failure but a lie. Joined life with equal regret. To obtain this other thing a hoax that is virtually white is in his estimation the most useful uselessness. By means of manipulation of the theory of weakness she relates tears and censored boredom to each other in such a way as to be masked.

A bite of blood is a stained and dominated ideal. From its full hesitation there opens burdens that were immersed in the diminution. An overburdened response is split into compulsive grasps. The object selected for the shared remembrance compares on the one hand with a fiction.

Left limbs. Kicked and probed. Screams purge forgotten scourges. Appetite of lust. Old prostitutes force a long whimper by hindrance. The moisture centres on that measure fundamental to the being. Ecstasy poses the most certain and impossible orgasms in order to concentrate attention on the outrageous.

Stained by curving into the licked being. She is conceived of in terms of the limit. She is bound in a language which exists when the noose has been arranged and you obliterated by risk. It is divided in two because it was the plausibility of the dislocated. It was repeated after the word disliked.

Tampered by severing is bound to disquieten possibilities that all the questions be hooked onto swelling smudges. It may perhaps be remarked that there was no solemnity. Meeting in the bounced end. Waiting until promiscuity continues to instrument further liabilities. She resolves it before our eyes. Into a desire.

Do as to saturate. When the laughter establishes itself the totality of the readability is an opening up of space. Only where the writing moves towards hilarity is a claim to your object rightful. Which blades of the hectic would have been constrained. As a bitter sacrifice of blood knowledge is the other in the relationship.

Hands manage the silence. Repetition and the parallel are plausibly looked. When strict sensuality is no reassurance it is bound to the resistance of the cancelled. Treat this peculiar confusion as a scattered peril. But this relationship is penetrated.

Extremes that burst with what makes all knowledge in us without using spikes be contradicted by a tightness that manipulation started by shocking into a language. It was doomed to dispersion. It was grasped by evasion. She will start with the bared writings by shifting around the void. It is in terms of this fascination with uselessness that the activity of writing enters the mischievous aggressively.

Upset an her bosom corruption to the solitary bares a limit to her ease which another mistress aggravates. Then to sacrifice the bared is a repetition. By satisfaction there is only a very little lie.

Forbidden are the bitter screams detached in the reading. Seized in fiction. The steadiness of the garnished cold tests less and paralyzes what would seem to wound ritual. That sturdiness is to be modified in a nourished cunt that is bound by celebration. We are obliged to enter with a phallus.

Blooded by marks. She is clasped and refused not only the approval to read but the subversion which submits. Danger affects the waiting and submerges anguish. There is horror rape and carnage bared. The vomit of corruption finishes in the memory with the present paralysis.

The bottom of solitude is pressed into a language where shock is separated from opaqueness by a decapitated argument. A reading of the committed manual is outside the pleasure that a second system outlines.

Encircled by ferocity is an arbitrariness but fully motivated. Brandished beneath the calculated impossibility the derangement is comprehended. A pile of subversions which are the nourishment of a difference transversed. To sink into the roughness of her breasts is to write of a tense space where experiments with equivocation last each the entire diffusion.

Shadows that tremble. Shouts that choke. It is clear that either the grappling tensions and recurrence of the reality of language are shifted or the erection of states reacts noisily to those who claim to be perpetuating balance.

Rubbing satisfies the menace. The savaged encounter drained memories which are watched. Not in their strength of torture but directly towards the engulfed. It is evident that given a centre to kick the enormous promiscuity of vengeance fucks the closed groins. It is not luxurious.

At the height of the instability her nipples responded to all that was secreted. The moments of antagonism he sees are common to the sweat and the urine that passes through. She is dead. A rigidity hangs over us. The blooded arteries are from the ultimate three divergences.

False endurance ensures beating the three states of this loss. It is encompassed by the cock as it gushes profusely before capable invertions. Vacant allusions are worse when he undresses her alone in the midst of the little.

A hole in the draining in the phrases word by word. Delay and bareness. Stress by strain. There is a traversal that is unending. To open up the appearance will bare the duality of disregard and permit her to appear.

Troubled by the spreadeagled. After the torment many other displays. Pressures and in particular the wish facilitate a fiction of appearance of which he wrote menacingly. False writing and salivation reduce to another stain her expenditure.

Bitter menstruation spurted from solemnity. We understand that a juice of whiteness fetches audacious risks that specify the blood seaping is detained for a few lines. Later she slit the girl.

Closed to solitude. An advance commits the writing. Bound by mutilation. Together bound nonetheless to the illusion that must be quite transparent. Vengeance is common. One and the other gore her. The heart crowds silence and eagerness. And the eagerness was without a captress.

On the bed lies an apparent subject. We know that laughter with an unashamed degree of fruition is an accomplishment that no creation can spend. Through the dirtiness every blond works the mischief and flourishing wreaths. The one who mutilates penetrates.

Soft eyes have been discovered. A language swivels shifts and repels the thigh as thigh. Repels the cracked surprise itself. To construct the two and then condemn them propels a crease an enchantment of the scarlet. Worthless safety is accorded to their self-satisfied moderation.

A base for bitter splits is like the augmented possibility. Put into words which are destructive the breakings that occur are the denudations and are used to destroy the liability and friendships. Figures which until now have been held in suspense are lavishly noted. Artificiality collapses. Meditation of the anus and reflection stops bondage. Folding savagery is also opposed to an hilarious knowledge which is nothing more than chance.

In tainting the robustuousness of disorder turbulence lines up the point. Thighs lowered and isolated. I marked the delay deferred to conditions in which I could sustain the arrival. Elegant destruction revenged what made other things possible. Necessity is the whore of disappearance.

Lust for calmness. The whip leads to familiarity and causes the rise of the collapse. The stupid pricks stricken in the midst of the original release. To kill. Weakness is the crest. Hance the joining of old succulent members to those that are too manually competent.

Gobble the cock. There are four interior fingers. The wrist that would squeeze beneath chance is also the same one as oneself and an establishment of a stripped moment.

In an hilarious regeneration the whip subverts the notion of character. To function in a living closure and copulate steadily becomes the wilful anus to the decision. In the removing of the grasp from the phallic clamour plausibility is the play of suggestions with particular manipulation of exteriority or transparency that contains her protrusions.

A movement in her callousness forces her to discover beneath the whip that finality is the transparent subvertion of a bareness. Her belly full of prepuce she exists in her preciosity in so far as existing and ending can finally agree with her labium before becoming increasingly stiffened.

A discovery of sturdiness. The same movement of language and of the manipulated writing that succeeds. And in its development the arrival by a gobbling of risk calms what they believe is the same aggression. Simplification that disposes of the book that eliminates the language and generates grasping ends in further limitations. She was obliged to work. Thighs of disease. The copulation realised. Screams mystify her animation. Our words of renouncement and laziness are where shit that comes from a central reflection point is turned on the lascivious. Towards this very thigh that he cannot whip. He beats the mask. Its significance is even thought to drop into hilarity. She has been carried into the inexpressible. She is all this and this alone.

Stern and hindered. Bareness conquers the continuance. The validity and sacrifice of possibility is drawn back into language. Continuance attempts to give the task of encumbrance to timidity. Amplitude and stress in the estrangement of these interpenetrative plausibilities moves towards two experiences that the probability of anguish fastens and collapses. That signification sires systems of salacity in brisk and metamorphosed languages. She is born. She loses her energy when stockings solidify. As her aggression folds her hips flourish.

Bound for display. Within the different methods the corruption of human terror attempts to rope what remains exposed. The formation of the particular curve narrows the text. She nominates the nourishment renounced. Access to death suspends threats. Reason jostles reduction.

Hesitation of a blackness which lays bare which confirms collapses. Spend and eliminate the hungry tit which had its circulation rounded. Traversed the words in the frustrated endeavour of delaying contrariness. The search sees within its reach a furtherance of lateness. Her uninviting presence. Her uninviting presence. Her uninviting and enraged hiseousness. Space is what cripples spasms.

Fast superiority and feet capable of regular participation. On far higher levels of seduction a genital deviation on the buttocks is read as sensation as exploration.

Elegant maidens hold onto their thighs themselves. The signs are inside pulling at the relations and no more than a game. The difficulty with masturbation is recovering the developed derangement through the severance.

A massacre is a language of maintained singleness. Writing arouses bareness. She is the collapse of soiled attainment that is not dramatically changed by the wait for hollowness. Revealed at certain separations is the opening into subvertions.

She swooped an the open bowels. The immensity of the burden was to be applied to old ruptures and to the soft language that haunts us. Overturned shit remains stiff. It is not only the excess that satisfies but the confinement. They are the whores who numb and impale.

To defy the attack can subvert the whip. Her breasts saturate the penetration. She has his totality but moderates and neutralizes the confrontation. There is the choice which is wiped out by binding. To quench his length the eternal irregularity adheres and angers the three arteries. Then no longer.

Measureless gap where the being arranged a link but in a sordid massiveness that was dry. The wound drips. The two mistresses in celebration brandish their tits recklessly. Temptation perishes. The jagged language drips fast and pains a perished traversal trapped in this modified fascination. To change is a participation that requires much greater length.

Held onto the crisis. Astride. Within the punctuated prose the whip of the feast is hooked. It will be sufficient to read with corruption that which lashes the collision. Certain approaches further the night. She slides beneath perished legs. Spikes and sturdiness lift failure from other failures and show the same confinement. Through failure stoppage is always menstrual.

Through a blemish of intimacy romps the less close suspension. Hanging from monstrous palings the other two clean the gashes. Lines complete the nibbled centre. The rare examination eliminates inundation. She might intercept us on a struck manoeuvre or a hilarity.

Rolling callousness elevates the commitment. It is this exteriority through solidity that marks the captivity of the pierced. The deceased gorge rigidity. She refuses and persists. The masturbation will save the collapse of muteness and arouse what I have to thrash.

Disgust spreads with sol-emnity. It suspends the little genitals and violently craps on the musty criminality as it is praised. She strikes at the testicles that the curve verified. His balls calcified. The strokes of the insidious compulsion are shaped into solitary rituals that are sharpened rather than.

Disrupted by a strong remembrance and limitless confsion. Salient access. Members and presence. A certain number of captures and grey broken flashes sever essential menaces. On the other hand she must be noticed by others or from the bareness of her groin.

Nourishment is a whore. Orgasm nibbles possibility. Her two entrances break the extremes where all the possible constraints and a melting deformation commit contortions. The utilised mercy is promiscuous. It is very advanced.

Inclined on the unlicked which bears the same colour of clasp as prostitutes. To venture as she did constitutes a wet yearning since she brought the complete beauty to stress an increase in the marked variations. Which liability is due to the sterile clash of the velvet.

Mistakes are pushed up. She has crossed the threat beyond which an attack of illness will wring language and experience. Whores dare but ten words which are surrounded encourage each to persist. Only one or two passions are fuckable. Cracks are the relapse made into excess. In the bareness of termination spurts the living release between replacement and the point of fetching. A spent obliteration begins to rise. Her thighs have been able to make herself rip the confusion vital to the good of naked hilarity. The same force collapses her.

Distorted

by happiness. Discontinuous within oneself. She finds herself equal. What is pushed into modernity is what every massiveness bores. Confined roughness is like the limits of promiscuity. She is distorted and attacked between language and erection. The two can reverse and repulse the internal structure. She jumps if she is able to self impose languages. The difficulty tortures the vomited refusal that reduces that structure to an intimacy locked in a wound that is able to function. The impossible. Knuckles and dominance are her experience. Modernity hopes words surround coherence as a difference.

Enclosed by a fucking desire. Immersed. If the break creeps steadily recollection of the original is only a posture. Along meticulous groins hilarity is the greatest emphasis. Thirst winds along slobber. She is not a mature manipulator. Upon detachment their outer slowness leaves them opaque and accursed.

Fixed to callous willingness. The posture once more is phallic. The clamour bears what is bled. An unfastened kiss. The other which is seen and undone is cast on arousals that exist within the human scream. In several lines related to corruption the pressure of repetition organizes interiority. Always central to femininity is paralysis. Cut at the neck. Pushed the collapse and watched margins in books simplify. The consequence of this break mortifies easy corrosion of whips. Whores have returned at one stroke to the hilarity relished by fatality and delayed if the artist sinks jerking satisfaction. Bound motion blends to mend a pain. The fusion outlines itself and throws to sacrifice her advance into the word that she is not.

Within the banished the bite of the tension suppresses. She descended the breaking gut. From it tension is centred. Stomachs froze continually. The indecent change of noise is well-marked. It blends appearances readily. She believes we have filled secrets that exclude what had to wait until these recent yearnings for beating were allowed to become capable of soft appearances. The corner of honesty is essential. It denounces injury. It assigns her a new scream but not us.

Heaped on a smooth disturbance a dominant reading opens closures in the collapse. She becomes absolutely pure. Situated where play is something dissident. Eliminated constraint within itself with my mistress.

Bent by charging. Though she is extraordinary she cancels the tightened by using its inadequacies to make the misery into a turbulent vision. Yet the furiosity that corruption that the central masks is duplicated has glimpsed bitten tremblings. Meanderings into the final panic the darkness is confined. She rips totality. The edge is sometimes incomplete.

Distort the wanton from understanding the necessary turn. Pour the reluctance that exists between the spreadeagled into the belief. She established the true side of discovery. A tension that I must curve.

Bent into round sores. Broken if she were spread above the extraordinary applause of the shifting. She had contours of magnificence that had been a fascination to us. Together the roughness violated clumsily what was lost in its essential presence.

Determination is the pit with which we burst. She establishes herself. Sturdy loins that she binds without refusing the collapse. The hold of elegance accords that menace which being changes towards confinement. Neither distorts nor becomes a pain.

Stuck in forcing the roughness she gives to monstrousness. Why turn. Is the binding of justification able to be false. To replenish the law bears her being onwards. A defined negation is an absence. Meddle with holes and the yearning will be the same type as the priority of our joint confusion which we will clasp. The act of language is allowed to arouse morbidity.

Destroy the swirl detained by rupture then whip reason that grips. Towards the more complex strains and the less exact refusals the meticulous gropes of the overturned are scraped at least in the modified ruins. Part of this has become the language.

Part from broken orifices. She had her other hand on the prepuce. The confusion twisted any oncoming expenditure of warm blood. The erect pair of outsize actions fulfill an immobility that she desired. As her tongue hesitated she could be poised to drain new life from the bruise.

Hardness of the maiden is the promise that rises up in the silence between the play that intersects what it has nourished. When bodies copulate there is a loss. To know is language no longer.

To manipulate is started. All these questions are prevented. Turning on the look that experiences is the displeasure that was never libidinous. Free immediacy is as inadequate an extension as the notes of writing are to the infringement of her limits. The risk of discovery is sucked by what could never be read by her reflection or corrosion.

Pierce the swirl that anticipates an endless oscillation. The centres of occurrence are questioned for the ever kindled prostitute who originates repetition herself in her bowels. In her masturbation the estimated pursual through squander eliminates considerable histrionics. The humour scrapes because beneath forbids the level to suck the castration. With that we maintain agitated furtherance together. Can the humour be scraped when the man who succumbs to language is merely his own failure. Irreversible writing lacks silence formerly maintained by the triple impossibility written from the discharge made by licentiousness.

The test of sordidity is to desire what really intrudes like the hole in the mount that shoots the most secret part of her entity. Faced by contradiction she perseveres to understand all damage. Distortion arouses the circular spectacle within the void. Perversion is the vomit that inhibits mal-treatment as an admirable stance in the present.

Burst into the whore to verify her delights. He wants to wipe out worship and prolong and extract reason only to wrench insufficient celibacy from the perilous damage of her groins.

At the moment the dying is struck the nar-rowed realisation and the blemish of bursting collapse. When we see the finish we satisfy and not grind what is found to inhibit or enliven through roughness the frequent admiration pointed out to remain.

Through the grammar toppled the abundance. No longer the growth of distinction for the restraint is lost in the beaten elimination. In the crutch there is the forbidden horror of the pale. To become present centres offensiveness an how she is constricted. To realise her gifts words break or her hand manipulates or annihilates the mute support as a language.

Yearning for obliteration is to collapse. Is no less obvious in the prostitute. Laughter is delayed but muscularity can enlighten even a blemish that whitens into being closely assaulted with whatever blow is cancelled. These anguished goddesses whom she is limiting to a central constraint no longer matter in this prose.

Confused by the original rupture. As that blade parishes she can separate the intimacy of the crash in terms of finality. Repulsion is a privilege which couples with fullness to corroborate itself. From the eventual completion the finest vastness is the object of unity. Coupling withstands desire. She is of little importance.

Cut down the chance that these endeavours did not react fully to implement the idleness which related to the bitchy prostitute. Chance collapses as a human spends which is the movement in the other connection. Three clashes on the other hand are the orgy with all its forms.

Bound by adverse rigidity that displays stiffness and sensuality not beneath the lash but secreted in a moment of friction roughened by length. Grip. Tear along. Shit. Form the wild detachment that a living memory inflicts clarifies and utiilizes.

Turning the third further hangs the unique impenetrable threat whilst the cock rips cunts projected. Making an effort to mask this mixes the wishes and desires scooped out to make language visible. Within it was the overpowering bareness that receives what they should manipulate. Jump. The missed collision of straps forms the human massacre of hustle that anguish and marks on paper misled. She was the inactual the seduction of the breast that allows coagulation to show it how a language could be intensified.

On the side of acceptability in a sequestered chase she arose with different shocks. Upright lies that empty dominations are traced into moves coloured or drained honesty. The phrase conflicts. He escapes from her existence. The ceremony towers parallel to this and succeeds in denouncing her by finding her perished breasts and belly with a sexual criminality that awareness presents deceitfully. Considerations and twisted murders humiliate destruction through this relation in so far as creation can skim and wipe away the degree of eternality that does not seek to efface her but mix killing with minimal transparence. As the written is a must as the central suspects comfort so the spoiled word expresses kisses and sharpness.

In the groins the gorgeous is yourself. The size of the scratch displeased. Along the belly which is her indispensable basis flashes hesitation. Expressed with only black and white guides. The accumulation between the thighs which he has already warded. Looking is bound by abuse. She may be squashed. She is enlivened rapidly. Fuck. The aroused mound is worshipped by the wasted bareness. The syphilitic arrives promptly.

The flagellated are exposed. Where aimless criminality destroys it subverts. The old and blackened are the mildness of the course that she has lit with whips. The arousal and no pose withstands menace. Bondage controls and finality withstands and makes torment lose against ruptured beauty. Omission leads to words of deterioration. She fights off the first prick coupled with. In the end other man open her second strap but nobody leaps into the cavity. The regular are abused by the great gouging that increases.

A hole within the stoppage that always has a mendacious hunger. Glances recreate interior roughness. From the leak operates the eliminated black. Brief yearnings limit most lusts as everything collapses into one.

The legs of the corpse lengthen. Rigidity rather than the crushed state rapes and mixes the entered constant.

The tedious buttock is cut by the drop abused and contradicted by grasping and erecting a laugh. Everything goes into a dry refusal. Hardness can inhibit what pain consequently will consider.

To live within. To undergo the collapse. Whores who castrate outrage any immediacy. The pain of starkness repels the implication that directs lies to obscure leeks. The obscure tear degenerates towards your balls. Quite as futile even if fierce are all the words death can bare.

In the depressed consummation in a breast cut off by a collision she is bound to the one feeling of honesty that appeasement tempts. At the entrance of the disposed length she appears to leak into a transparent fiery subsidence.

Anxiety of words and the consent invariably belong to the same tangle. Stance forces the couple into the cancellation. Stick to the quality of the laceration. The force of the change delays the loose haul into the other hand. She can play with changes of illusion leading thoughts to be composed by reflections.

The silence of stiffness is a change that we were used to in the secluded ripeness that murder discovers. A dimension of pure black suggests a movement of grammar. She arises once more to calculate the roughness that living contests. Language blends playfully with what is nevertheless the surface to be pricked.

Acceleration is the hinge with which distinct change is moved. Shaken leaks have less feared gestures than elimination. Not expected she appears as an illusion of distress. Swellings are mundane but hilarity establishes a distance.

Biting into rotting thighs even as she elevates her gaze. The quenched vastness through which she tries to defecate is nurtured. The dry appearance of disturbance is that concealment hinged mistakenly and yet abandoned to cancellation.

Upturned advantages illuminate reading. To be denied the renewal commits the genitals. Murder is to match the vigour continually. To carry saturation to the bitter caress makes her weep more than the nourishment can point to. With existing explanations this primary erosion can bring night deceptively central to what is sought in her concern to make important this anguish.

Obsessed by the misuse of what she could have if she were to share her dominance. Lines of drops yielded acceptable menstruation. Deciding to squirt she surrounded him. They are all obsessed by mixed bosoms. Alongside the advanced trouble the squirt cancelled what he had written.

Crowded by many meticulous yawns only degrades that which she will not have sucked but which polished insinuations can cling to rather than that she must return. He cannot satisfy this trembling. This lasciviousness beats the flow held up to her face. Such is the centre of the roughness. Whipped by a whore who belongs to the ravaged. With the recent enlarged flexibility of mutilation nakedness blacks ampleness by castrating all display until rectal yearnings typify arousal.

Falling into circled threats the blow satisfied the upsidedown. She lingered in a pronoun. She had caused the ecstasy of the display. Words choked by black guides.

She reappeared for language like a multiple anxiety. Provocation of the ordeal was the transformation. She is nothing more.

Before the insertion she dropped to release them. Then an experience of fellating the continuance consumed all eliminated women. The whole was silent. She bent forward to the hot woman. Thighs are established as a protrusion to bleed along with the belly. The origin is as much an extreme as she can be repulsive.

Her cunt is sucked. Lips to thicken the buggery. Females who damage cope with those who take the place of the eviscerated. Drunk girls copulate and live their needs. Language is manipulated by a sparkling beat doubled over in reproduction. Shrieks that delay blend each bit of the buggery towards other confusions. Turns plug into significations. That is why hips are solidified during impossibilities. Before this she seemed very distant.

Aroused by the writing that the questions concealed. Away from the perished defecation she points her nausea at what I write. The inviolated caprice has an unusual lurch towards otherwise muscular and modern areas where lips strain. Pulling the enigma transcends decay and parts the stake roughened imperfectly. Sexual emptiness entwines to produce a momentary effect that does not sigh or crawl or hold back but always uses the raw as a constant topple. Valid meanders avoid torment. Desire to halt.

Broken in spite of curves stripped layer by layer and the rest bound by the bleeding drops that the provoked voluptuary raises over the finish. An end to melting satiates the fallen gorge and its mendacity.

Burnt out. Existence empties thirst. The face is lithe. Couples with centrality are not a matter for her to forbid the crudity of the outer slope by leaving them. Many shrieking delays force the circle to accept her position.

Words that note the oozing mound in the phrase of the couple. A loose release clashes with other typical groans. She is cold. Leaks and illness are the impossibilities. Towards flops dismay is what is there and yet she is stripped naked. It is a failure.

Bend the plausible. The strict unfolding of the weak and the vacant bites into the curvature of the notion. The participating illness must be quite a compulsive one.

Grasped the wet thigh and the suppressed gore creeps up. She is consumed. Heat and ease are the ecstasies she was without.

With a sharp drop into captive appearances she subverted the aroused nude whom she knew. The degraded fright of the bosom fails to accomplish what we threw off the line. She could even be absorbed.

The notion is polished. Words are strained. Resist the ease. Links motion numbness. What drifts down is entire.

Couple with the handsome. She has ceased to expose herself for the central satisfaction lasted. Hurt. Yearnings and thirst.

Genitals are the mess scooped out of a compelling grope. The stoppage revolts the ripened and the hardened confinements that couples expand with shock to capture the disturbance. She quickened within the notch. For the same intensity. Then.

A different roughness is incited. Within the limits of the indestructible humour she tongues malice and locks her mouth so that the reading roughens what can underline the timidity that she cannot pose.

Thighs are broken from trying to impose the function beginning to ripen together. Virgins will snatch the massiveness of forbidden lies exposing the fury of the powerful who swoop. Incest is central to her movement. Culmination parts arousal largely because she clings with him through the words and spreads other women already animated by bare danger to further lust.

A MIDSUMMER SCOUSER'S TALE

Dis was about six or seven years ago now, right. Summer of 1990 and I'd jacked in me fuckin' job in Birkenhead to fuck off down to de south of France for the summer. Got a job wiv a croo of mad ex pats setting up campsites for ze Breetish hordes. Lumpin' kind of work, piss all money but room and board un dat. Anyroad, dis one day I had the afternoon off, right. So down de beach to get some sun un dat, like. Got meself settled, a nice spot not too far from de beach bar or de sea. It's a fuckin' blisterin' day, about two or tree in the afternoon, and I'm roastin' slowly whilst checkin' out de various fuckin' characters in de area. As de poet once said, "I have seen the madness in my areeaah!". Anyway, dere's deese two pale blue fleshy Glaswegians stormin' their way through some of de local beverages, rrrantin' incoherently at each other, like. Tres fuckin uncouth. Den dis bleedin' afletic knot of Scandinavian types playin' volleyball or some like mad fuckin' pursuit in de shallows. Strappin' and splashin'. Splashin' and strappin'. Disgustin', know what I mean like? Chill de fuck out. Alright, so I flip over onto me belly and am lookin' up towards de bar, which is pretty bleedin' packed. Dey've got a big sound system which kinda dominates, but top toons mind. Summer '90 remember – playin' dose Mondays to death. So it's all smiles and peachy cream, everyone's intu dat holiday vibe. Anyway, what wiv the sun on de back of me 'ed and French fuckin' mini beers inside us I'm soon flat out, oblivious to everyting but deese mad dreams like. Me un Ryder and de Boys are flippin' somersaults into dis huge fuckin' pool in the grounds of some mad LA mansion or other. We are amongst the bootiful people, professional coke 'eds and sundry 'angers on. Plenty! "What do you want to hear when we're makin' luv? what do you want to hear when we're makin' luv?" Whistle dat fuckin' tune. "Terrorists don't look like terrorists! Drug smugglers don't act like drug smugglers!" Screamin' and shoutin'. Nil problemo, relaaax. Shoutin' and screamin'. Suddenly I'm awake. What de fuck's goin' on? All 'ells breakin' loose about us and everybody's lookin' out to sea, wound up, shoutin' un dat. I'm kinda blinkin' into the sun trying to work out what de deal is. Den a catch a glimpse of dis huge fuckin' bird or somefin' steaming towards us. Must be about about 12 or 15 foot across the wings like. But it's got big stiff wings, moving super fast more like an insect. Can't be. Hold on, it is a fuckin' insect! It's a monster, a giant fuckin' dragonfly. Jesus! Now every twat's really fuckin tripping out, panicking and legging it up the beach as de beast thumps intu the sand like it's totally exhausted. Mental as fuck! It's still bleedin' trashin' about, sand flying everywhere. Better back off, it's only 20 feet away now. So, I'm on me toes and up to the bar quickfast no worries. De beast isn't movin', I mean, it's still flapping like a fucker but he's goin' nowhere fast. Plans are afoot it seems, as the guys who run the bar babble to each other pointin' towards the demented creature. Dey're after 'avin a pop at it, mad fuckers! So, five or six of deese French guys grab the oars from a couple of boats and storm towards the dragonfly. It kinda senses dere intent, goin' wilder dan ever half flyin' den crashin' back down like. Deese guys don't 'ang around but start batterin' fuck out of it. Brittle wings shatter as blows by the dozen rain down on dis poor bastard. It's a vicious scene down there now man, well vicious. The dragonfly is jus' bein' pummelled into the fuckin' sand wiv this 'orrible slime blood cumin' out every fuckin' where. No opportunity to save the bleeder for posterity like or medical science un dat. Adios amigo.

SURREALISM TOWARDS COMFORT

The Saint has smelly feet, nicely smelly

She watches *Once Upon a Time In the West*.
She stands up several times. (Restlessless). (From the leather sofa she sits on made from the skin of dead animals, which live on in the minds of those who loved them).
That's the mother holy speaking. It's so fucking macho, God, fuck me if I see what I see.
Yes, the adjective goes suspiciously behind like the will in Schopen Schopinoo – but after. Ah Chopin …
The men.
You remind me of my mother. She did coffee like that. She was a whore. The guy who spent an hour or a month with her was a lucky guy. The Saint says it escapes critique because it's extreme vibrato. Go on and tell me that it is not fair to torture children. Too late.
No desire to caress the men of Once Upon but the desire of their legs, their bones, their daring, their non-knowledge of philosophy.
Desire of their stupifidity. God, my brother, take my mind and fuck my brain so that I can ride in the spine of Harmonica and have heavy flesh on the face like him and be sexier than you God, my half brother.
And around December, baby J reminds us all that it's not all saints who have all baby boys of their area killed at their birth. So you see. Fuck your critique. Bubulle, I forgot to tell you that also he does as if he was going to rape her but he doesn't.
That – God knows about – that.
We women, we will always be jealous of gays but men are not of lesbians. It's in another Western. The woman who is speaking is in a topless bar. She is drinking a

whisky. J.R. quotes a baseball commentator: "… lost like a baby in a topless bar".

I am not lost. I am going to decide now. It's me. Because of course I do not decide anything; why apologise?

I stand on the lectern. You can see yourself in me. I am a model, abag* (a bag)* full of emptiness and germs. A wooden trunk; a wood piece. Nicely round, in the proportion of an erect penis, why not – I might as well but you don't have to. When it's finished it shrinks, it does it without doing it. Within analogies, it will do it. You thinking the wooden trunk go soft and I will fall inside the penis. I know it's grammatically wrong but somehow it can't be changed. A penis in wood in the gallery. Quite big, but not too big.

I stand on my big toe on the eagle head of the lectern. And I sing 2 notes at the same time. One tone in between. And I peach. The skin – language. I preach. I have no tongue, my martyrdom.

Glossolalias + Amplification + Effects.

The feet smell of saucisson I wash them. I am the Saint and I can wash my feet myself.

In People – in *Vogue* – Kate Moss wears a $100,000 diamond cross, noticeable necklace.

My mother cries, do you think Jesus died on the cross so that Kate Lichen could wear jewels? It's a film. The gallery is dark; she is filmed in her kitchen, my mother. It's a critique.

My husband hung himself because it's too complicated to crucify oneself. In his mother's kitchen there is a 30cm high crucifix next to the window then you look through the window and there's a 1 meter 20 crucifix with a small roof on top of it and in the background the cemetery with the remains of my love under another crucifix. Kate Lichen has beauty.

I exhort you to crucify critique. I do like the Catholiocs: I describe the evil at length because the evil is bad. But bad is fucking big and big likes it.

The Saint has a lack of interest in her opinions and in yours too. The eyes of the male gaze and whether you'd rather be reading the paper.

Mercedes Matter, there's a good name. She died 4:12:2001. It's in *Art in America*.

A simple wooden cross is worth more to Jesus' eyes.

Especially if the money you give to the priest's lecherous eyes goes to the poor. The priest wears M. Lady Manhattan, Professional Mascara with Silk to create a Thicker and Longer Look.

The priest climbs on the counter, kicks the till open, wanks his dick and sings Elvis. Jesus is not interested in money.

Why give money to the poor since they are poor?

And why is anything worth anything if Jesus is not a nasty capitalist?

The craft cross with bits of wood found on the floor is an insult.

And Jesus had his share of insults before he got nailed. Critique sorted. Long live criticism. Jesus performed criticism. Imagine, young Christians invading the art world. Our Lord was the best performance artist; art is like religion it puts things in perspective. OK I'd rather say amen, shouts Betty Guth, because my brain is boiled with boredom at the idea of the argument.

And the black men who died in the pit so that diamonds would hang on her neck

And the tall blond son of van C., learning life in Harvard

And the family's greengrocer who beats his wife and pays his rent

With the fruits they eat and shit in their golden toilets.

And tourists in Italy
Looking up at the glorification of the male body
Of our saviour Jesus Christ.
Jesus opens an eye and says, mother do you smoke after making love? She says I don't know I have never checked.
And the porter at van C. Mayfair London.
I am a doorman he says.
He comes.
And Jesus replies it's easier for a camel to go through the hole of a needle than for a rich to enter the Kingdom of God.
Tricky hey!
The disciples smile at their master's jokes otherwise they get Moscow's eye like my grandfather used to say.
1943, Besançon, France. German soldiers call at Georges Vuillez, my grand father. The painted 'Croix de Lorraine' on his wall. Panic. 9 children. WW2. He takes a chisel and a hammer and to delete the resistance sign he carves it into the wall … They lived. Amen.

Protestounts versus Catholiocs

The Saint has just published her essay on Reconciation.
Do you mean reconciliation?
The Saint does not mean. That's why she is a Saint.
But what does it mean?
What's great in painting is that there are no actors. You look at someone and there is nobody. In photography, actors.
I am a Protestount. You read work.
I luk gud. I sit in front of Nietzsche, he eats oysters and they get stuck in his moustache, and we have that formidable game where I get the oyster from his moustache with my tongue while I hold his balls. But he has

a slight problem with his teeth and his mouth smells.
End of the film.
Cinema: no actors, characters.
Second film, I play Sarah Bernard:
I am a nun sucking a donkey.
I download myself from the Internet.
not the image,
not the gesture,
the sentence.
I am the downloading
– No you're not.
There is always someone in the audience who does not get lyricism. The Vulgarity of. It drives the Saint nuts and she likes it.
Ah banalities, sandwiches in trains, lyricism. The sharing.
The female model is female. Betty Guth. The equality of parallels towards parallelism.
My name is several, says the demon and I like pigs' flesh. The painting is dark. Men of science are gathered around the dead body of a thief. (Date and reference of the painting.) The structure of the muscle is nicely painted. To get out of the flock unnoticed the demon says to Jesus: look a flying dick! A woman runs after it but it's already too high in the sky. Your balls darling, your balls ... The dick steams in towards freedom. White tail behind it, nocturnal emissions in full daylight. I knew it – says Jesus – I knew it.
End of the third film.
A woman passes by. She smells of modified molecules. Chemical and marketing teams' sweat. What right do I have to say that it stinks? The Catholioc hesitates: I should say it stinks me. It stinks me of you Madame.
PhS. writes: "She has all the styles, it's the best compliment you can give a woman." Here's a clever bloke. I prefer Newton in that case, Helmut I mean.

Photography.

The priest has a nice job, he shops around.

The Priest shakes the hand of the Saint.

Slide: printed list: mastur. bones fingers craft denounc. ear-smell finger-infection boil.

He introduces his assistant. Helmut, Fabienne. Fabienne, Helmut. (Not Newton this time.)

Helmut turns off the projector.

The Priest: I know, my daughter.

The Saint: (very quick transformation into a wolf for a short howl, lycanthropy in no time, I lick Helmut's eyes, nobody sees it, it's a smile, a sentence). I am Belzebalbuth's daughter, little slave. Nikon 2,800. Resolution 600 dpi. I am no daughter. The Saint has already played all the daughters of every nasty novel and cheap American film. I am the daughter of my father and literature can fuck itself, each word with its own sex. The word daughter bores me to death. Leave my brain, demon of Clichy. Talk to me, Priest.

The Priest: My son you are my sister. The Lord asks you to repent and follow him.

The Saint: I am not a nun. I am a model. The Saint is an actress.

(Slide: close up face / pop singer / rich / English). Roby Williams has a disgusted smile. He says he set up the charity 'Give It To Someone'. What you don't want anymore, what is of no use to you, you can give to someone. Divine inspiration, working class boy!

By the way English working class, I don't like your taste. Helmut says wait, look at that, DVD, God played by Dustin Hoffman: "I give you the tree of knowledge but you will not eat its fruits." God the nerd. Get out of the classroom you stupid brat, you will never do anything in life and you will end cleaning the toilets like your mother. Alleluiarghhhh.

I start again: (slide of painting of Adam and Eve thrown

235

out of the Garden of Eden). Djay Arr, the false Arab, asks if Adam should logically have a belly button.

The Priest: My son you are my sister and you are blind. The Lord asks you to repent and follow him.

The Saint: OK. Where do we go?

The Priest: The ways of God are impenetrable, the sentence is a stamp. The serial killers who eat their victims – on TV – can be saved. They all have a problem with the frontal part of their brains. God will forgive them if they repent as Jesus died so that they could live for eternity.

Two blond souls meet in heaven: I have been raped, teared into pieces and eaten. I praised the Lord for his compassion and his grace. I have been strangulated and raped. My breast has been cut and my vagina eaten, and I just met the guy who did it. He is in too.

Helmut: He has white hair and a ponytail. He says to the young interviewer I can't say that in front of a lady. She says you can feel free. She knows about it. She has described the scene, before, for us, the viewers, so that we don't get too shocked by the words in his mouth. And your mother … Well I don't really want to talk about it in front of you … Go on, your mother … well when I was four my mother asked me to perform cunnilingus on her …

The priest: Good Lord – in Queen's English. (He thinks of his own mother, not bad looking at thirty-two.)

Helmut: He also ate the penis of a four-year-old boy but he doesn't want to talk about it.

The Saint: I am God's mother. He still sucks my breast and I like it. That's no parable, man, but on Kennington Road, an old man with his old life and his old clothes. He sees something on the ground. He bends down to collect the coin. It's a chewing gum. His face grimaces. He wipes his fingers on the back of his coat, several times (several times). He wipes them on a painted brick wall and then again on the back of his coat. He is angry, humiliated, vexed and hurt. He does the sequence several times.

Helmut: I love you more than my own life, let's get a flat together.

The Priest gives his blessing and gets another job. He manages plurality of opinions.

The Saint climbs on a high tree. She jumps and breaks her neck; self sacrifice to balance her weakness of will to resist the temptation of bourgeois life. Before she dies she says: English upper class I don't like your taste either.

'You are beautiful. We are alive. They are nasty.
I understand. You too'

That's her motto. Everybody is happy.
The Saint is the Devil's advocate and the Devil is a
fucking bore. The Devil has devised his last temptation
trick. The Devil is a sad clown who sucks his dick. It's a
tender scene. The big shoes, the big trousers, the big red
nose and of course the small prick. The Saint admires
the suppleness but wait, I will suck it for you she says ...
Satan, the clown laughs. His laugh can move mountains
with a bit of help from the faith of leapers but there he
does a domestic laugh. Just for her. One point for me,
dear. (Also in Queen's English.)
The Devil likes short jokes. His infinity is in the small.
He is fed up with winning, he is sad now and the Saint
sees it. Sad is strong but in a weak way. He stays
overnight because he can't face the night bus. An
eternity of trying to understand the difference between
going back home in a heated sound proof limo and
waiting for the polluting slow double-decker war engine
packed with smelly drunken loud people who push you
around. Alienation.
But the devil can't help it. Another joke. Morning
erection. She smiles tenderly. Is it for me?
The next day, the Saint has a harsher look. She wears a
suit. She is Protestount. She can proudly say: "but who
knows who wins?"

The Saint has the intuition that the discourse on hair-
style is under-rated. She also has the intuition that the
sentence is enough. If it's under-rated it's already
something. She likes performing her notes.
Death as ornament. Wallpaper. Any wallpaper will do.
Widows suffer, well, some. The wallpaper syndrome.

(Window).

Something difficult to translate: le cul

How can the French get on with the English when it's so difficult to translate le cul? Le cul dans l'art. Le cul: the arse, the arse hole, sex, sex around sex, sexuality. My mother she could never pronounce the S of sex. She said hex. H is less hexuel.

Elle adore le cul. Nothing replaces a word like le cul. What they don't have in French for example is gender politics.

The Saint has men's hands. She holds a book. "The meditation of the line". Poetry and shame and humiliation and smells.

The radio plays Jacques Brel. He sings. He has been dead a while now. The intonations of life in the recording of his voice: science fiction. The audience clapping: archaism.

The Saint makes love to a glass table. (She also makes love to a wardrobe). She is not dancing. Only as far as her body goes. The body and the spirit of the table. She does not take the table for God. The spirit is the Capital. It's the thickness of the glass table that makes it sexy. She does not do it for real but in the sentence, because it's cold and she is warm.

The Saint does not complain. Should she seduce her enemies, should she give them reasons to rejoice? Do rejoice my enemies, she says, because my voice does not carry as far as possible comments.

Léon Bloy the Catholioc. His pain at the sound of the Protestount bells.

Ah, how happiness is joyful and boredom long
How leather is thick sometimes.
Your new trousers fit you
Ah, how much I love you, my love
And I know you love me too.

Ah, the identity of your dick
Your blue jumper has many stains
But I like it, I like my taste.
Ah, to run naked in the forest
After the rain.
We fucked the mud, my love.
Artists working with sound,
I am already tired,
I can't make it to the show I am afraid.
But we did it. It was dirty.
We also fucked melons.

Ah, the time will come
As if it could not come
The time has already come.
A yellow sport Mazda passes by. Liver problems, yellow.

I have mushrooms growing behind my ears.
A small garden of dirt.
They are itchy, very itchy. Pus.

It's a muscle not a study

The Saint is in her bathroom. That's where she does her chignon. She thinks about Caillebotte. And the man at his bath. The bathroom multiplies clean dirt.

Her round bun is a noble hair-do. It is a little arsehole. Fuck dream for the little angel that looks like a fried monkey. Small monkey. When he fucks my roll, she says, his tiny body embraces my head, a very nice hat. Fucking hat, my little scorching monkey and its little penis at the top of my neck. The hairpiece as jewel has sometimes two extra balls. There for the movement. A comment on the idea of movement: latex scrotum behind the ears. The size of a kiwi. It is good to shake one's head with grace and a certain voluptuous reserve. It's a contraction, not a contradiction.

The pen penetrates behind the neck. Toshiba Tecra 8000.

Betty Guth wanks on bourgeois interior. *Connaissance des Arts* 1968. A feminist artwork.

Italian theatre. She stands alone on stage: Are things still fucking in a photo? Is it the frozen image of everything fucking? Fucking cold.

She has a deep voice. White vapour comes out of her mouth. The Saint confesses at night in bars – after the dinner where forks and knifes were projected into the friends' legs (the glass table).

"There is a text I wrote and re-wrote. It says to push a tree down the vagina. I say it in French. S'enfoncer un arbre dans le vagin. It's not a small tree inside a human vagina. It's not a huge woman masturbating on a tree. It's tree as tree and vagina as vagina."

The difference as the spreading of legs

She didn't see him come. To be more precise in the
Duras slip: She did not see the man come. He came in
silence. She did not see his face.

He fucked her like a little monkey. What can I say it's the
image, here …

A monkey, a pig, a horse, a donkey, an elephant, a cat.
That's boring, a cat. The cats of the rich and the cats of
the poor. The rich cats and the poor cats.

The Senegalese people of Dakar have proud genes. The
Saint's Senegalese lover drives her around. Poverty
didn't hurt the Saint. Maybe because the Saint wasn't
poor, darling.

She thought of the tired pedestrians waiting for the bus
in the suburb of London, tired to carry their genes.
Peckham. Elephant and Castle. The Senegalese men
and women carry the genes of perfect human beauty.

Not to study. Not even to witness, not to look through
the camera lens. Not to tell what is seen. Nothing is seen
in Africa.

Yeah yeah you didn't see anything in Hiroshima. At least
I can tell that telling the death of you love to your lover,
I understand. It really makes sense. And I agree with the
words, making sense, making. The African lover says:
you always talk.

Yes, misery in the world. If the principle of negation
were one of the really real ones, they would be no
poverty left. Since it can't be negated, it stays, it
develops.

There are beasts everywhere. Science fiction, the Saint
says. Relationships between people are a beast, and
maybe several. One beast or several beasts as what is and
happens between people. Alien. The masculine woman.
The camera being a beast, another one. The deevee-cam

you can handle between your fingers. The camera in the wardrobe. Talisman of the white.

« T'as les fesses de l'universel mon amour »

You have the bottom of the universal my love, or maybe the buttocks of universality. I don't dare to tell him. Rebondies, noires, fermes, et sentant bon la peau, come on, boy, if that's not literature, what is it, hey?

Chubby, black, firm and with a good smell of skin. OK, I'm French.

Sex without sexuality. Again an exercise for the Saint. Patience tolerance and management.

Sex without the it-y, the it, ity. Just sex. But I can be wrong. Of course I only speak for myself. Maybe this is sexuality. Purity.

Slight disruption, the Saint finds her body folded, sport exercises. Sex. The bed.

She goes towards death in Africa, like in Venice. She can imagine dying in Africa. The heaviness of the continent. Not that she saw it or even imagined it or felt it. To die on a continent. The bed.

The Saint is an old colonist. White woman. White as pink yellow, brown stains, green shadows, blue veins. She wears a white silk three-piece suit; she goes to the limit of the desert to listen to Dvorak. The piece that was playing in the plane. It feels slow. Before that they were listening to percussion. It's quick but it makes the brain go slow. Like a penetration, slow penetration. There is no Dvorak in the desert, I really don't know about passion in Africa.

She hears the thought that Africa is a spoilt child who refuses to do her homework. Each sentence resonates with the Protestount bells; ça va Léon? Stories were told and she resented them. But written, they are different. Africa is big, that's OK. But Africa as a spoilt child, of course it is a bit more difficult ... Until all speech is rendered neutral we will fight a literature fight.

A young woman approaches us. Me, blue blood, and a

bit of Mongolian one, French for centuries, Smeena, Irish maybe … Money for my baby, he is dead, he is sick … He is dead, some money please, he is sick. I don't have money to feed him. He is dead, please give me some money for the baby. He is dead. Please he is sick, give me some money for the baby. He is dead, he is sick. Pause. Please give me some money for the baby, he is sick, he is dead. We are colonists without literature.

Get out you stupid woman, you can die, you and your baby, and your family and all the rest of you … Listen I don't believe your baby is dead, and I don't like it when people die, I mean lie. Since you lie to me I will not give you anything, go away … Don't say anything, she will leave …

Everything is possible. Our generation goes rather towards abstention. She will leave eventually. And we will be free to tell the story. Amen. Scripts. Acting out the scripts.

How, as an artist, do you think you can write? As an artist.

It's late. A group of people are finishing their dinner after a shooting day. A film. Black and white super 8. A woman who levitates in a tree because she does not like the smell of corruption. Why not? It's an art academy in Holland. Is a story an art piece? I don't remember how one thinks about these things nowadays. Art, stories.

Someone says they were told the English colonists – cololocalonists – let local people take responsibilities in the running of their black country because they were lazy; the French never let them take any responsibility, ever. The Dutch, they were in between. We laugh. Ah the Dutch! We are all decadent but at least we have accepted capitalism. I tell the story of the dead baby who is sick. The Saint is an artist. First I need to cover myself, she thinks. The introduction of the story is: that's one thing I didn't want to translate for Smeena. We are sitting on the stairs of the hotel. My baby is dead. He is sick. He is dead. We laugh. Daniel says it's the whole story of us being in Africa, this story. Me, she thinks, the Saint, I do parables now, just like that? I am getting there, Jesus. It's the whole story of us visiting Africa. A woman cries that her baby is dead, he is sick, and we stand there. What the fuck can I do? I am an individualist who believes in the truth principle; your baby isn't dead but sleeping. This is not my fault if there was colonisation and if you refuse to adopt capitalism. I want to keep my money because I deserve it. The sheer fact that I have it means it's mine. The property principle for fuck's sake, have you heard of it? What's more, I don't like hearing people complain, go and get a job and you will feed your baby. Use contraception until you are wealthy enough to procreate. If only you accepted capitalism, the inevitable – says J.R., but he is not there so he does not say it – you would understand that this does not work for us anymore. Zola, my dear woman, have you read Zola? It all went into literature. The poor found their place. At least we have a story there, a story to be told. The other is a story.

Délices d'Afrique. Daniel tells his story. The table laughs a lot. I hear the furniture laugh – the laugh of wood, the laugh of the legs, we are in Africa. Special relationship to things. His first day. Daniel carries around his identity as a jewel. But of course it's not the case, it's just to write it. Tall Jewish New-Yorker, white skin, black hair making slow documentaries on people talking to each other's after conferences on the sexuality of apes. Daniel gets out of the hotel. Fifteen minutes into the city he is trapped. "Don't you recognize me? I work in your hotel. You're lucky it's my day off. You white people think we black people all look the same …" He ends up with 15,000 CFA less in his purse – stolen, a tablecloth, a skirt, an elephant in wood and a football tee shirt – bought and a story. The revenge of the street.

Africa – emotion, the West – reason. The first President, the writer who closed the philosophy university in '68. The first years of independence in Senegal. Respected. The first one. Sorbonne. 1940: he says he will destroy all the ads with the Banania-smile on the French walls. I don't know if he did. The sentences are obviously emotion as he is an African, he is African.

Dibiterie, that's where you eat meat. A French gallerist with golden jewels says but come on he said that in a very specific context, and is always misquoted. Is the misquote emotional or reasonable? The contrary, the West is passion, emotion and Africa is reason. Raison d'Etat. Reason to avoid passion. Passion to avoid reason in that case.

The Saint thinks: Nothing stays in place in the West but everything has its place. I like the West in a way.

The gallerist talks about her white children being touched by black children in Mali. They were eager to feel the feel of white skin. I say that my white friends do the same with their deevee-cam, they touch poverty with their cameras. The eyes or the hand, you know, dear madam … My African lover looks at me, he thinks I am clever. I feel stupid.

I say that I am here to visit the Biennale of African Contemporary Art and then I will go to Documenta. She does not seem to know what it is. An artist from Mali says he would like to go to Kassel, it's where they showed a cow cut in half, he says. I explain why it is good for us – a cow cut in half.

Protestount versus Catholioc versus Muslamic.
First the Saint thinks she has to be careful. She could die. What an emotion! Here's a suicide for you. The lover says he would kill Salman Rushdy. The Saint makes a convenient partition in her brain. Quickly. Not to judge,

248

not to comment, not to hear, not to react, not to think, not to feel, not to show emotion, not even to move. Yes darling I respect your religious beliefs. Africa is emotion. Yeah man, long lives emotion. I understand. I feel.

But the thing is I don't. I am the Saint and I don't respect your religious belief. It's my religion not to respect your religious belief. Respect is bad in my religion. The original sin is to have believed. Let's re-read the scriptures like that. The original sin is religion. Religion is the sin. Amen.

What the fuck I am doing in Cheikh Anta Diop?

The Saint was dancing. She was writing the Catholiocs, the Protestounts and she finds herself in the Muslamics. Here I am, at the side of a young man at the beginning of his political career. He refused political offers because it swallows politics. The fight falling in love, not falling. The inevitable. The awareness, the rebellion, the accusation and most of all, they are alienated. I listen, I listen. I will not preach. The Saint is a small woman. The continent of negritude, it's too much for her soles. Lyotlot: "The ability of a sentence to place itself between inverted commas." My spirits on my shoulders, inverted commas, me a sentence. I don't even have a name.

Mid-day, he comes back, he is getting taller, and maybe I am getting smaller. He speaks about Africa until four, he reads Cheikh Anta Diop loud. We have sex, then we speak about Africa again, culture, the role of art, the borders, identities, cultural identity, colonisation, debts, power, help towards development, the Dollar given to Africa against ten back, the Africans who are not African, the status of Dak'Art the Art Biennale, the funding bodies wanting to take over, the role of the

State, the enemy being within, Africa, what they invented, they were believed to be non-human, the whites made them into humans, they had no culture, they always had dating, slavery, the funding of cultural events, France, the non-governmental organisations and their constant mistakes and again African contemporary art or contemporary African art, coherent pluralism, racism ... More than a beautiful face. The global body. In a month I will say, OK, I don't set a foot in Africa ever again. But I will miss the Senegalese. Men, of course men, their humour. The smile of women.

There is a journalist in the taxi towards 'Addressing Gender Issues'. Before waiting for Oxfam, we are lost in Dakar. She does a bit as if I wasn't here. The advisor to the Minister of Culture asks me questions, looks at me in the eyes, but she doesn't. We talk about Documenta 11. He says too many videos. He says he liked the piece from that Indian artist because there was poetry. I think about the border, Pakistan, India and poetry. The old debate. We like horror. All right we do. And the film about the genocide in Rwanda, did you like it? The journalist is still doing as if I wasn't there. The lover says feminists come from Europe. The Prime Minister is a woman. Toubabs were amazed but it's normal in Senegal. All I say, I say, is if someone says something about themselves I listen. Safe; Amen, I say to my shoes, that's all right so far. In the show: male artists.

Parity is a colonising argument. He develops. The journalist wakes up: that's very interesting what you are saying there. She speaks to him only: «Les femmes, elles poussent trop loin le bouchon avec leurs histoires de parité.» Women they push the cork too far with their stories on parity. Colonisation of the colloquial. Yes, he replies, women have always had a primordial role in the Senegalese society, the rituals for example. I hold my bag full of money on my legs and I think about my clitoris. I am so white, so European. Display of thinking, what I have heard and what I have thought about. I don't say anything. In general I don't say anything. I have read Germaine Greer, can we judge clitorectomy, should we spend time shaving our legs, have you tasted your period blood? I think that I should maybe shave my legs this time, maybe we would go into sexuality then ... We visit the family of a man. He is a politician. Ah Fabienne you are a beautiful woman he says. Women make food; they serve us and sit apart. Me, I don't judge. The meal is good. I think about my sex. I sit on a chair. The plate is on the floor. They say it's not good for the digestion to sit like that. My sex is against the knickers, the trousers, and the plastic of the chair. I eat with the men. The country is sick, the liver says, the lover I mean. All I am asking is not to be sick myself. The country is sick. The country is sick. You are a target, don't walk alone he says.

My shoulders are not touched, my belly is not touched, my legs are not touched, my arse is not touched, my arms are not touched, my neck is not touched, my face is not touched, and my back, my back is not touched. Not even a kiss. I am being done and I am paying for it. You are loosing darling. Darling it's him. Me I can't loose. I have lost everything already and I am French and I don't play games. I pay I hurt I write I capitalise. I am the Saint.

The West. He says he was learning too quickly at school, he was believed to have spirits. The respect I have is larger than love. I would like to say bigger. That's all right respect init? Love is bigger than love. The clothes become more and more the clothes of the nun. I have given up on seduction, or I can't be bothered, or it's irrelevant. I am the representation of the West in representation. At least I am not from Oxfam. He is testing his ideas. I am a test tube. He is finding out how the

West reacts. That's quite a role for the actress. I let myself be fucked. He fucks. He does not fuck me. I just take what I can of the fuck being fucked. The Saint has a strong desire to fuck him but it won't happen. Or maybe it will. Or maybe I don't know what it is to fuck. Maybe I should buy a dress, but I can't be bothered. I am your mother Oedipus; I understood it on the road to Saint Louis. The name, his name, it says to be born, to be put down, to earth, to life. And on top of it I pay. Josef my love, our trip here, it is. The coins you missed to buy milk the day you hung yourself, I gave them to him. I pay to listen, I pay taxis, coffees, sea-fruits, cars many cars. He never asks for money. Ah, pride! Let's talk about pride. The Saint wanted to meet her thinking and she met a man holding a continent on his shoulder and a dick between his legs. My arms, my neck, my legs, OK. Touch me, please. He does not touch me. I will go and see a marabout. He will take on a weird accent. He will say hello Fapi, it's Josef speaking. My legs are shaking, I will faint, and I do not faint. I sit. Josef says he is rotting happily in Rott-am-Inn – and that's the real name of the real village where he is buried. How is his son doing? The horror of imagining that the spirit of the dead can live on. Josef killed his mind, let him rest in peace. Rest in peace my love. Rest in peace.

I read Cheikh Anta Diop. The first sentence would turn a butcher into a schoolteacher. I mean an Occidental butcher into an Occidental schoolteacher. It's written in 1954. We read him. We it's because I am the Saint, the butcher and the schoolteacher: "Nowadays we are used to asking all kinds of questions". Poetry I suppose. "therefore should we ask ourselves if it was necessary to study the problems developed in this piece of writing? An examination, even a superficial one, of the cultural situation in Africa justifies such an enterprise. In fact, if we are to believe the Occidental books, it's in vain that one might try to look even to the heart of the tropical forest a civilisation, which would be the work of Negroes …"

But the Saint fucks critique. She is not a schoolteacher. It is nevertheless tempting to mention that nowadays one has the habit to ask all sort of questions is maybe not the most elegant way to start a paper. Or maybe it is. Maybe it makes sense here. Maybe it is fair. Maybe it is wisdom. Maybe I am tired to judge. Maybe it is Negro elegance. Maybe I don't want to know maybe I want to go back home and let you find a way to keep on the war with the West.

The Saint fucks critique and wishes to be more fucked. How am I going to say to my lover that the ten kilos of books on post-colonialism I brought for him – because he asked me – me not a colonialist – me artist – me not judge, me not think – me not even talk – me not kissed – is colonialism? It's there – here to stay. I mean I don't really know but it seems to me that it is a way to find a good arrangement for the Occidental thinking. Me, the other, the story, feeling the body as a scar of the land I walk on.

"I call Negro, hoping to agree with all logical minds, a human being whose skin is black, and what's more when he has wholly hair" (wholly? freezy?)

Hello Adrian Piper. The wigs.

First I didn't like her piece in Documenta 11 then I thought it was quite good. And again the sentence as a stamp. And Stan Douglas, usually I don't like him so much, second stamp. But in Documenta 11, I thought his piece was really good. Stamp. The text in the catalogue is not so good though … "Douglas reminds us that the nature of the televised image is phantasmagorical. His aim is to analyse the position of the contemporary subject in the face of the powerful control tool of late capitalism, capable of instrumentalizing subjectivity to the point of rendering it ghostly, severing it even from its own timelessness. C.B." Carlos Basualdo I presume? The contemporary subject on the face of the powerful control tool of late capitalism in control, here's an analysis for you. So the position of the contemporary subject is basically rendered ghostly, severing it from its own timelessness. In my small woman's head, I have difficulties understanding. But ghosts it's a good idea. Timelessness it's a bit more complex. No, not complex, difficult, yes difficult.

That short blue guide for the press. Sentences.

As a project. Oh yes projects, objects of desire of our time. Projects forever.

"It's a unique example of a combination of Conceptual Art and collective subjectivity, navigating between private and public space and various cultural fields: a project in which differing interests were able to benefit each other. The park is a utopian place; its model is paradise … The park shows us what the world could be like" (film quote) C.M. (Park Fiction)

Also: "Pettibon constructs a site of resistance to capitalist systems of power and control and their homogenizing tendencies by producing a form that never becomes fully stable but remains open to infinite experiences, identities and utterances" NB He must be pleased, Pettibon to be understood that well. I spare you the rest.

The Saint wants to peel herself like a carrot. Too phallic maybe the carrot. To peel oneself like a mango. It hurts a bit Mum.

I say to my lover that I arrived too late in London to be in the hype of the yBa. He says here you are a bit early.

English humour in a remote village of Guinée Bissao – no electricity, no water. Yes, it's too early. We laugh under the stars.

At night, women are dancing. Just women. A woman is drumming on a plastic bin. They have worked hard during the day. The Saint thinks they should be honoured, by their husband, by men. I should say: or maybe by women. They should be given pleasure and I hear my thinking think. I am from somewhere else.

Now I hope I won't get myself Sartre's lobster behind me. I came to Africa with notes about belief and I am in it. The Saint is floating. Drowning, dying again. Religion. The clothes make the raven look like a fish. I hear terrible noises outside the house. The men I share the room with don't hear them. They say it's normal. I shouldn't open the door. I shouldn't check what is outside.

There are four days I will not talk about.

They seem to like Jacques Brel in Dakar.

What's tricky here, tricky baby, that used to make us laugh a lot with Josef, the word tricky ... Just the word and we would laugh together. Together like having sex. What's tricky is the thinking of the relation between the two ways of thinking. I use ways but it's not ways. Ways of thinking is already on one side. It's thinkings, two thinkings. The English language will have to go with it. Integration versus separation. The resistance to capitalism. Not integration of external artefacts. Integration.

I sit at the back of the car. I have just lost my lover in exchange for something else. The ity of sex has moved to the soul. Behind the wheel the shepherd from Mali, the

Peuhl, he was a lover, the best drivers they say. I know already. I have seen them. And the disciple of a wise man. From behind it's the spectacle (a) of Africa. The two men, the road. My lover he could only be seen properly next to another man. Properly, I mean well.

If I could tell the story I would start from the middle (because I read), which was also an end. I decided to refuse to loose my lover. I say that I will say no to the exchange and I say yes. Everything gets integrated, the vector has another dimension. Not only force and direction. I exchanged my lover for something else. Here is the Saint going through the freedom to obey. The one Robert-Etienne the father was talking about. It's like capitalism and bad art pieces. No use fighting. The ram withdraws its horns. Around, behind, under.

The Saint walks the room, greasy carpet. Do you want stories? Then we visited another country. Give me 35,000 otherwise you don't cross the border. Two times and a half his monthly wage. The man has escaped from a mental institute. So it seems. They say he must have been a rebel. They say the rebel fighters came to Dakar to have their photo taken in front of certain buildings, so that they could tell later: 'I was in Portugal during the war, I couldn't have done that. I was in Paris.' I don't know which buildings exactly.

Capitalism in the authority of language. They are in their bodies and in the exchange of language. They buy speech in their deals, that's what they say. We call it corruption, they buy language.

A line. Old cloths hanging. We have crossed the border so we have to pay a fine. Do you need to know more. It's already known. Is it called bribery? Three borders like that and policemen … Then a village where they bring us what we need, give us a house, take good care of us, do not ask for anything in return, come to greet us in the morning. African unity. Somewhere else. On the road, the road movie. In the village I sit under the porch for long hours. It's not the Saint, not the author. It's nobody but a body with two Spirits on the shoulders. The car is being mended, that's for the story, that will do, why not. The car is being mended.

The village is happening. It lives. The Spirits don't want to be filmed. They just don't want it, they don't want to be turned into an image, they don't like flatness. I keep the village in my body in my brain. And I let the village speak outside description. Yes, in the thinking. I am falling in love with my lover. I have to leave. It's inside our meeting that I leave. The monkey is penetrating my body and not only through my sex, he is getting inside me. The hunter from Mali, the young man with ideas, tortured by Western thinking crawling inside the landscape. The trees, the sand, the storms. The beauty of the skin.

The virus. The beast. The relationship between people, air conditioning, very good cars and toilets like space ships. The shit-hole swarming with white worms. Self-regeneration. Rimbaud, Artaud, Bataille, Leiris, and others. Ants at the entrance of the room, you give them a gift and they leave and I saw it, a bit of rice and they leave. Another time. The Muslamics, I will not do my critique. Fuck critique it's a few lines above. Leave critique. Take a plane. Live in the in-betweens. Sounds like a trendy line – of coke, but live in the in-betweens, that's tricky. I laugh with Josef again. Live and let live, it's the popular version. But what do they say about the popular? The majority cannot be so wrong. So many people. It's not about many. It's about right and wrong, in the practical sense. And left and how to film the road movie. Get inside the camera like a Peuhl in a car.

I am the Saint. I am in Africa. I am more than his wife, I am a woman. One. I don't remember my name. I don't know my body. I am bored of being a woman. I want to be his wife.

Wrong that's the core of this body of worms, the pit swarming with white worms. They change colours, or they change species. It depends on the shit you feed them with. I think I have heard them swarm but I am not sure.

A slight diarrhoea, but not really, no constipation. The words, the worms. The page.

The wrong, it would be easy to say pain instead. But that would be wrong.

Here you walk your identity, and then your body if you can reach that state. The state of having a body. Here, you are reminded of the race. Where here? Who you? What are? And reminded and of and the race? The street gets into the sentences. You walk with your ancestors like they walk with theirs. You can't leave them behind. Many people have been to Africa. The ghosts of the world.

A vector towards the inside, quoting myself. The intensity as the core, the bone. Going towards the inside, the image born of vectors.

Taking the space of the symbolic seriously maybe. Or maybe quoting myself, yes quoting myself as an image of the space. (Here the smile is the smile of the lecturer, a 49-year-old woman. Nobody in the audience laughs, but she laughs, every lecturer in the world laughs, it's a lecturer's joke.)

Quoting oneself. The space of the quote. We are nearly there.

I have kept saying to myself for years that I didn't think sex was really sexual and now I read it in Baud on Fouc, in a quote about Bar ... the bastards. Foucbarbau. The conspiracy.

Job, my love, I love your scabs

It should be written like that, on its own, like it came out of the mouth of the nun.

The body of my love, my dead love. It's the court case. The young blond woman who found him says she thought he might have been dead for a little while, because of the foam on his mouth. Would I have liked the foam from his mouth? The idea of the last thing I could have licked from my lover's body. She was in tears. They said she was over-reacting. I don't think so. His tall body, his scream before he died. His scream. Josef. Cadavers shit. Josef, I only live what can be there of love for you. Everything I do. Everything I do is my love for you. When it passes melancholia.

So much reading to do. On melancholia and beyond mourning … in art. OK, one hour everyday from now on. I should.

I don't want to be over-analytical says the Saint at the trendy dinner, but Job in English it means something, doesn't it? Her husband has a good job, for example. But that for example, the Saint wonders, should it be written? Her husband? How do I dare invent a character, which takes the role of a singularity becoming an example? Let's refuse parables, ever always forever. We've heard too many stories. I am politically opposed to stories (burp).

And the Lord says to Satan, "Where have you come from? I must say that I know exactly where from but I am just asking you so that the story can be told, so let's tell the story."

Satan answers the Lord, "Who are you calling you, my dear God, who I am?"

And God answered, "Oh fuck it, not this one again, I asked the question first".

And Satan says: "All right then, from roaming through

the earth and going back and forth in it."

Then the Lord says to Satan, "Have you considered my servant Job? There is no one on earth like him; he is blameless and upright, a man who fears God and shuns evil."

"Does Job fear God for nothing?" Satan replies. "Have you not put a hedge around him and his household and everything he has? You have blessed the work of his hands, so that his flocks and herds are spread throughout the land. But stretch out your hand and strike everything he has, and he will surely curse you to your face. All right? I am saying all that in order for the story to be told. I actually think you are pretty wicked God to start it all like that, what the fuck do you expect, God? Are you listening? Do you honestly think I can avoid coming up with the promise of hurting him ...?"

The Lord says to Satan, "Very well, then, everything he has is in your hands, but on the man himself do not lay a finger."

Then Satan looks at his finger, thinks he should stop biting his nails, ah no, Satan has long nails, so Satan uses his long nails to pick his nose, eats the green evil substance and goes out from the presence of the Lord. He has to deal with Job now. This is so fucking boring. Satan has a boring job. Always hurting, always promising stuff he can't keep, killing, lying, making people suffer, making the rich richer and the poor poorer ... I mean it's all right for the rich that one, but of course the poor ... except that the rich won't live eternally, well actually they will but in oil ... Weak theatrical character really, Satan. He reads the newspaper in rehearsals. Go and ask in theatre workshops who they would rather play: Adam, Eve, God or the snake, the hand in an old sock?

And then it starts: One day when Job's sons and daughters were feasting and drinking wine at the oldest brother's house, a messenger came to Job and said, "The oxen were plowing and the donkeys were grazing nearby, and the Sabeans attacked and carried them off. They put the servants to the sword, and I am the only one who has escaped to tell you!"

(I have to tell you it's gonna last a bit, that story, literature taking its time, hot country.)

While he was still speaking, another messenger came and said, "The fire of God fell from the sky and burned up the sheep and the servants, and I am the only one who has escaped to tell you!"

While he was still speaking, another messenger came and said, "The Chaldeans formed three raiding parties and swept down on your camels and carried them off. They put the servants to the sword, and I am the only one who has escaped to tell you!"

While he was still speaking, yet another messenger came and said, "Your sons and daughters were feasting and drinking wine at the oldest brother's house, when suddenly a mighty wind swept in from the desert and struck the four corners of the house. It collapsed on them and they are dead, and I am the only one who has escaped to tell you!"

At this, Job got up and tore his robe and shaved his head. Then he fell to the ground in worship and said: (At this stage, it is not clear who took notes of Job's thoughts and acting methods, maybe him ...) "Then I got up and tore my robe and shaved my head and fell to the ground in worship and said ..."

Is it him who invented the beginning of the story, to excuse the bad management of his wealth, which he must have inherited from his father anyway? Second-generation directors, bad management, very common. Or is it that they had been so nasty to the Chaldeans for so long that they decided on a short and efficient attack. The Golf War. On green very green grass. And sand.

"Naked I came from my mother's womb", (that's when the writer stands up from his desk – photo of his family, the dog, on the flat surface – and talks like an 50 year old bad actor) "and naked I will depart". (He is then very tempted to get naked and wank sitting on his desk but he remembers that his eight years old son will come back from school soon and the door of his office is not closed.)

"The Lord gave and the Lord has taken away;

May the name of the Lord be praised, even when he takes cruel bets with Belzebabuth, for what reasons, we don't know, just for a laugh maybe,

At the depend of rich old wise fuckers

Who should be treated better ..."

But in all this, Job did not sin by charging God with wrongdoing, because he didn't talk about God's cruel bet. And in all this, we still don't know who knew about the discussion between Satan and God. Never mind. Poetry. "For you make me glad by your deeds, O Lord; I sing for joy at the works of your hands.

How great are your works, O Lord,

How profound your thoughts, that one cannot reach the bottom of them

Profound, so profound, O Lord

How clever you are to check on me like that.

But"

(Now the actor rests a bit, he marks the breathing, the T is at the Top of the tongue and the Saint watches the audience because she knows about the actor already the act-oral-ready the act-oral-read-y.)

"The senseless man does not know,

Fools do not understand",

(That's right: fools don't understand that's why they are called fools, you old wise man, but go on speak about others, the alienated ones, blame it on the others go on ...)

"That though the wicked spring up like grass
And all evildoers flourish,
They will be forever destroyed".

Hum … does it mean I am of one the wicked ones? But that he does not say, it's the actor who has a doubt, the audience can see it, it's very short but they can see it.

The commentator puts his glasses down on the table, marks a pause and looks up into the auditorium. The bottle of water is nice on the green table. And the microphone on its small stand too. It's a nice image, a speaker in a conference. It's sexy.

All evildoers flourish and they will be forever destroyed! How does such a sentence happen in the human brain? How did it happen?

The lecturer stares into the semi-dark space and the girls wonder how he is in bed.

But you, O Lord, are exalted forever.

A time schedule. The evildoers do what Satan tells them to do; Satan does what God tells him to do. And God does what he wants.

Spike Milligan meets Winston Churchill. So what do you do, Churchill asks. I do my best, Milligan replies. Well, at the present time, I am afraid it just won't be good enough …

For surely your enemies, O Lord
Surely your enemies will perish
All evildoers will be scattered.

And now the Saint is tired of the comments. It's just too easy. The Saint has flat shoes. She wears her ugly nun face. She smiles with the smile of nuns. Not ecstasy, not here not yet. The smile of global understanding – understanding fuck all.

And there he goes again – poetry baby – the old wise patriarch is a machine. He stands up and talks bullshit.

"You have exalted my horn like that of a wild ox;
Fine oils have been poured upon me.

My eyes have seen the defeat of my adversaries;
My ears have heard the rout of my wicked foes".
And it goes on and on until the list of the worst cannot be extended. It could actually but it's not. It would be wicked but God is not wicked. Too much would be wicked. Too much it would be a bit more precision in the first paragraph, details in the killing, and if it's Job who is writing, then a bit of respect for the ones who fucking died so that God and Satan can have their bets. Stupid kids really. And that's what the Saint had for breakfast …
There are real people dying out there.
– Really?

The Spirits are in the margin

Spirits do not leave me alone. The Saint has long given up her role; the actress fights the fight of the stage. Maybe it should be called crisis. A form of paralysis. A piece of paper, a bill and I am afraid of my signature. I am in horror. Fright. I feel madness walking the room. I stand still. There are movements inside the room. I punch my body. I shiver.

He says he knows the room is not good. He says his room is good. It's because of the holes. Oh beauty. The holes in the cemented floor.

In my place it's OK, it's because of the holes. Just for that I would marry you, my lover.

Spirits are like little beasts.

Cockroaches are big here. We fight the fight of lovers before a separation. Punishment, sex against sex, will against will. What is said shouldn't be said. You speak too much he says. I speak the separation. The Saint writes a book but God, not the separation. Not here.

The goat on the roof of the car. The noise. The analysis of the noise in my sleep. The sound of the body of the car, a living sound, the goat, the goat on the roof of the car.

Inside a fight in-between the argument: notes from the notebook: 'fuck you' photography and 'fuck me' photography. The relation fucked/fucker. Positions of course. 'Fuck you' photography as frigidity. Reclaiming frigidity, hello Jemimi Smelli ... let's use our brains. The male Negro holds his dick at regular intervals during the day. And also during his sleep. He must be thinking something special when he holds his dick – on the side. Flying bats in the trees imitating plastic bags and reciprocally. Men imitating my dance in the discotheque. Yes, I was dancing and then I realised that they were dancing around me with the exact same movements. My lover turns into a club-med DJ. Oh, vulgarity. My brain is fried. Embarrassment. Only a prince can get in and out of vulgarity so quickly. It's Godard who speaks about the vulgarity of God in a film. We go closer to separation we go towards love. That'll teach me to claim that I refuse conversation. Misinterpretation of everything. Waiting. Killing time the woman says. She prepares the tea. Killing. In my culture, we save time and sometimes we loose it. But mainly we buy time. We sell time.

The meeting of differences. Can they meet? They meet that's all. And they change. What is learned, what is said, what is transcribed, printed. When will I leave school? Holland. I have left the African country. The Saint has an African flu. The lover's flu. A curator is visiting the art academy, a caterer prepares good food. Drinks. We have set up things differently that's for sure. We are in organisation. We don't live, we manage. Administration. Curating the virus, as the virus. Go on, curate, you fucking fuck. I am out of here.

Oh yes everything is well done here. They were building a wall when I left Holland, the art academy. The wall is perfect now and for eternity. A wall cannot be more perfect. In Senegal every wall is not-perfect. Every wall. Each one of them is 'not perfect'. They can't build a wall like they do here in Holland. They have a good style, in Senegal. Art style inside the walls. Wait until a curator gets there and starts curating the walls.

The problem with belief is not to believe, it is not not to believe. Management OK, but not quite. We think we manage. With belief, we know we can't think.

It is management.

The Saint is a Dog and the Bone resists. As if a bone could resist. She scratches her scabs. Job, in Hebrew, in

English. The Saint and the Monkey making love in the trees. Not really in the trees, more with than in. But not with as a threesome. With as in. Inside outside together. Making love. The prayer. Making love as the answer to the prayer. The negation. The prayer to stop making love.

Negation does not exist. It's a false concept. There isn't such a thing as negation. Invented like religions. Of course invented. Nothing can be practically negated. It's a false concept. It's a lie. It's a political lie.

LANGUAGE IS AN EMBRACE
WITH NO GRIP

Mum

Hello?

Mum.

Mum? I er ...

I know you can't hear me, but ....

This isn't going very well is it? I don't know what to say. If you could hear me ... I mean, I could just tell you what's going on. But ...

I'd want to say something more important than that. I'd want to say ... I don't know. I honestly don't know. I mean ...

This is stupid.

You can't hear me and I don't have anything to say. I'm not very good at this. Sorry.

What would I say? What should I say?

What could anyone say without it sounding just stupid or something? Banal.

I can hear you now, taking the piss out of me using that word. It's not a big word, but we'd never really use it in our house, would we?

It's the only time I hear your voice these days, telling me off for things that used to bug you.

Once in a while I wake up hearing you shout my name, like your ghost has become my alarm clock. Not much of an afterlife, I suppose. I hope they give you something better to do soon.

It might be easier to deal with if I believed in ghosts or some sort of life after death. I could talk to you then. People pray, don't they. Maybe I could talk to your soul, or something. I don't know. And you'd like that, wouldn't you.

If it was the other way round, you'd be going to séances and on ouija boards or something. Or just talking to me in some private moment.

But I can't, mum. I wish I could.

No. Basically, as far as I'm concerned, I'm sat here talking to myself.

Except that I've got nothing to say.

This is going just great, isn't it.

After your mum died, you said you used to see her at the end of the bed and stuff. I wonder if you had long chats into the night or whether you just lay there, looking at her?

If you appeared to me now, like that, I think I'd just break down. I'd probably shout 'mum' first. I can picture that but then nothing. Maybe some tears. I can't picture what I'd say, though.

Just mum.

I had a dream the other night that we were sat watching TV talking for hours. It was really nice, just the two of us. Then I realised why dad wasn't there. In my dream dad had died instead of you.

As soon as I realised I broke down, saying, 'dad's dead, mum. Dad's dead.'

The first time I woke up hearing you shout my name – I mean the first time after you died – I really thought you were downstairs. It wasn't that I'd forgotten you were dead. It was just that you sounded as if you were at the bottom of the stairs. And for a split second I thought you were there.

I was puzzled for a moment, knowing that you were dead and also thinking that I'd just heard you wake me up.

The second time it happened I was more disappointed because I knew straight away that it was just in my head. Like this, I suppose.

Except I can't hear your voice. Actually, I can't even imagine what your voice sounds like anymore. I can recognise it when I hear it in my head, but I can't conjure it up. I don't think I could imitate you.

I remember your laugh, though.

It's a bit like mine, I think. Head back, mouth gaping, eyes wide open.

There's a photo of me as a toddler laughing on the sofa. I look like you in that one. It's your laugh.

Dickhead

Yeah?

Shut up. Listen.

Where's the money? Listen, dickhead. I want my fucking money. What do …

Shut yer fuckin mouth. You listen to me. I want my money. Tonight.

Listen. Listen here. Hey, dickhead. I'm losing my fucking patience. Listen. Shut up. Listen.

You've got my money and I want it back.

Don't fucking piss me off.

Listen. Shut up. Shut up. Listen.

I'm going to make it easy for you. Now shut up and listen. This is about money. My money. You've got it and I want it back.

I don't care. You could've given it all to charity for all I care. I don't want to know. I don't want to hear it. It's not my problem. I just want it back.

No. Tonight. Yes. Tonight.

Where's my money?

No. Shut up. I don't want to hear. Give me back my money.

Listen. Hey, dickhead. Listen.

I'm helping you out. I've got this bloke asking for you. He's been telling me all the things he wants to do to you. We've had a good ol' chat about it. He's a dirty bastard …

Shut up. I'm trying to help you here. Listen.

What? What? Listen. What did you say, dickhead. You're not listening to me. I've got this bloke …

What? What? Are you taking the piss? Don't take the piss out of me, dickhead. Don't fuck with me. No. No fucking way. What? Your mother! Jesus.

Listen. Listen to me. I'm talking now, not you. So shut your fucking mouth. Hey, listen. If you put the phone down … I'm five minutes away, dickhead, so don't … Listen.

I'm losing my patience.

Be careful. Listen, dickhead. I'm getting ideas into my head now. Nasty ideas. Really fucking nasty ideas. If you don't give me my money …

I'm not threatening you. I'm not threatening you. I'm just saying. I've got these ideas, yeah. Just that. That's all. I'm not threatening you. I want my money.

Don't be fucking stupid. Are you listening to me? Are you stupid? If you hang up I'll be knocking down your door before you can … That's better.

Now. Listen.

I've got this bloke …
No. No. Listen. Don't make me come over there. Listen.
You owe me money and I want it back. Tonight. Yeah,
tonight. Not tomorrow, tonight. Tonight. Tonight,
dickhead. Are you listening to me? I said 'tonight'.

Where's my money. Get me my money.

Tonight.

Are you trying to piss me off? Do you want me to get
mad? Is that what you want? If I come over there. Don't
make me come over. Don't make me come over.

Don't hang up on me, dickhead. Don't hang up.

CONQUISTADOR

' ... and then he turned with
a wild surmise in his eyes ... '

I had to get my thoughts back on track to the events that had turned my world upside down just seventy two hours earlier. Seventy two hours with no more than a couple of hours of snatched sleep fuelled by a handful of pills and an endless flow of hot coffee breaking over my tongue and rolling through my mouth leaving it drier than before.

I stood, watching the waves crashing onto the shore, pounding the sand of the beach and cliffs, the spray almost wetting the sides of the yellow ochre crumbling rocks. The water was a deep, dark green and, through this half-light, the spray had a faint bluish tinge, which shortened to pink by the time a breaker rolled onto the even perfection of the sand.

I focused my eyes onto a figure standing alone in the distance. Suddenly, the inertia of the reverie was broken. I made a start and moved forwards, struggling through the damp sand in my city suit towards the shapely silhouette cut out against the orange flame of the sunset, with flecks of pure white spray turning to drops of liquid gold at the edge of the glow of the sun.

'I knew you'd come' she said simply.

'Then you'll also know I've got some questions for you', I said gruffly, trying to cover my surprise with professional purpose and hit her with it right between the eyes. Let her have it: *man camera on*.

She half turned towards me. She was wearing black with a woven, ornamented wrap around her shoulders, bringing out the curve and shape of her face and the pinkish tinge of skin around her big soft baleful eyes.

'I don't have what you want,' she said

I ran through the moves:

'They all say that. You'd be surprised what you can remember when you try … '

But then I realised that I'd used the wrong reply, so I tried another tack. 'What does this scene say to you?' I turned again to look at the light hitting the waves immediately in front of us.

'I want to say that you are clumsy for a man in your profession, I mean, someone who is supposed to *know* people.'

She put up her hand.

'No don't stop me with another of your lines,' her words came gently, as she rested the fingers of her right hand on my sleeve, 'I need to tell you that this night, this moment – with the light and the sea, it's like a scene from *The Ring*.'

'Quite the *Romantic* aren't you?' was all the cynicism I could muster. She turned her face towards me.

'No, you don't understand, that's not what I mean,' she said, she was looking slightly over her shoulder at me, the wind ruffling her hair and blowing strands back in the breeze.

'It's the elliptical nature of *The Ring* which attracts me'.

With this, she said nothing more but she continued looking at me as though she expected an answer. Wait, nada, nix, and zero. The fact was, I couldn't think of anything to say, and had given up on my hard and cynical stance, so I just looked back at her. A half smile began to play across her lips and she said: 'Here is the name of the man you want'. She pushed a piece of paper forward into my hand, which she must have been holding all along. I didn't even manage thanks, I just carried on looking at her and then turned back towards the shore and my cold metal car.

As I tramped back through the all too perfect sand, my

shoes started to fill with tiny grains at every step.

I began to think. At first, fragments came to me in flashes, one after the other until they merged and crystallised into coherent logic. 'Jesus, I've got to get some sleep. The sea is spooking me out. This place is *nothing*. Some cock-eyed, kooky broad standing on the beach is whacking me out. I've got work to do'.

The camera's tight round my face and head, you can just see my hairline and my ears at the edges of the screen, and I'm rolling my head slightly to one side as I'm miming.

The next shot is zoomed out and you see my full frontal, I'm crouched and my arms are bent as I'm making a kind of gesture and then, before I straighten up, I stretch them out and, as I stand, they fall to my side but they're still sticking out and they look tense, with the backs turned to the camera, you can see the thumbs looking taut.

Next, the camera seems to be gliding back and, as it does, you see Bobby on the left, looking down at his guitar and smirking as he's playing.

'God' I think to myself, he looks very young and innocent, standing there, looking down and trying to look nonchalant, while he's pretending to concentrate on strumming along to the music. He looks like what he is – just some guy from a nothing-special sort of background and this is his big moment and he loves every second. The rest of the band are lounging around like a group of out of work window cleaners. They don't look too studied though.

How could they. They never studied anything in their lives except the audience, looking for juvey tail.

It all makes me stand out more and I suppose that's what he saw.

I've looked at this video a good five or six times since I got the call and I'm still not really sure why I was picked out and what I've got that puts me in another league to the rest of the boys.

I take one last look at myself crouching, miming to the song and getting it very near right too. You can hardly see the gap between the sound and my mouth opening to make the shape of the word – alright there's a slight blurry slow feel to it, but then the song's like that and maybe it all adds to the effect. Maybe the guy saw that and thought it was acting. Maybe it is and it's a natural ability, no a quality, maybe that's star quality. 'Maybe I'm full of shit' I say out loud and reach for the remote. Turn the video off and stand up from the couch.

I decide to go and get something to eat. The hotel's pretty non-descript but it has one feature worth mentioning. There's nowhere to eat! Plenty to drink but nothing hot.

I get out of the lift, go out across the foyer and head off onto the street, which has got a bleary Tuesday morning light. I go down past some shops selling stuff, I don't know what, and into a café or small restaurant. It's a fast food place but it still has tables and chairs and there are enough people sitting down eating that I don't feel stupid for not asking for something in a bag.

Like I said, things are bland and grey outside and I take a seat next to a large plate glass window. The waitress comes over and I order some eggs, bacon, toast and a tea. I sit back and wait for it to come. I start looking out through the window and think about what comes next.

We've been on tour all the way from the east coast and across the west side to the last place big enough to make it worth while getting there and playing a night, by way of all the other places that pay their way and now there's a three week break before we go back – by way of selected repeats to the big finish, three nights at the Apollo.

Everything's just stopped and we are all going our own ways, back home, straight into the bar for the duration or god knows what for three weeks – just so long as whatever you do leaves you still able to stand and look like you're playing in time and you know what day it is, if not what song, then that's alright, no questions asked. Me, I'm off to find out what they want from me and right now, I don't know, it could be the next big thing for me so, as I've said nothing, there've been no questions asked and no one's any the wiser.

If it all comes to nothing, it's not a problem. If it works out the guys are history. 'I can live with that' I think as I watch reflections slipping past the windshield of a sleek, dark coloured car – I have the the vague feeling that I'm in it, doing well.

I got to the car, opened the door and looked at the paper by the light of the interior lamp. It said *'the one you wish to see is called "Amfortas". You can find someone who knows in the Terrace Bar and Disco on the Praira at Caveoiro.'* 'Blammo!' There you go, it's right there, if you can cut the crap. Caveoiro was only a short drive from where I was then, and I knew the dive called *The Terrace Bar and Disco*. It looked out directly onto the beach, with the most faded and worn blue awnings you would ever have the misfortune to see. Anyone new to the town, looking at this specially fine edifice for the first time would be left in no confusion at all about the place. You'd think it was a shit hole from a distance and you'd still believe that close up. I figured that this particular cesspit would still be open and so I hightailed it over there. As I revved the engine into life, I looked back over my shoulder at the figure next to the shoreline. I couldn't tell in the glare whether she was looking at me or out again at whatever the hell it was she saw there in the space in front of her. I didn't stop to try and figure it out. I put my foot down and the car skidded in an arc over the road, the sand, the mud and back onto the road again. I felt the wheels grip the tarmac, I put my foot down and, with a small squeal of rubber, the back of the car fishtailed into the speeding line of my trajectory.

The distance to Caveoiro would only take a few minutes, driving normally like a law-abiding citizen, but in my mood – to rid myself of all the unnecessary garbage and to focus on the events – I peeled rubber all the way.

The crap was jumbled up in my tired head, but things started to get a little clearer. To help the process, I punched buttons under the dial, looking for something that would add some rhythm to my thoughts. The usual mix of classicism and late romanticism flowed over the car as I worked through the most popular presets on the band, then I found a fragment of two beards talking about the elliptical nature of the form and content in Wagner, as though it was that, rather than the pulsing, floating tonalities and the big lush sound that drew people in. I started to wonder. Why did everyone say that Wagner was elliptical? What's the difference between elliptical and circular anyway? 'Beats the fuck out of me' I shouted into the night with a wry laugh. I punched another button, I had enough to try and work out without some other guy's big fucking beef about 'no return to the tonic dominant as metaphor rather than as structure'. I found what I was looking for: nestling in at the end of the band was a station playing something better suited to my mind, still popular, but better company for thinking – *Pierrot Lunaire*. I glanced up catching the moon for a flash, it hung super-large in the sky, a glowing spectral disc. I laughed again, the mix of coffee, cigarettes and lack of sleep making my voice harsh turned it into a rasp.

I get off the train as it starts slowing right down in front of the buffers. I'm a way back from the engine but

I still feel almost drowned by the sound of the brakes screeching on the steel rails and the hissing of the engine as the steam is released. There's a lot of smoke and dirt as well, it never fails to impress me just how much and, as I step down from the running board, I begin to take in the whole picture. There's what they call a throng of people jumbled about all over the station so that it's not easy at first to make out what's going on.

Down the side, next to the train, there are hands at first, mostly pale flesh pink but some elegant gloved ones looking stuffed and unreal, all pointing down with fingers splayed reaching for the silver handles of the carriage doors. In the next moment the hands have all become, dark sleeves and white cuffs and somewhere in amongst them there are slashes of red and bright yellow with pale powder blue and brown. A lot of brown. Brown seems to be very much in fashion this season and many of the most elegant gloves end just below or disappear into long tapered cuffs of mid-brown, not so much a tan as a definite post office brown. 'K.C.' I say to myself 'what do you know about high fashion? Actually, you know nothing'.

I set off down the platform, hoping to get lost in all the commotion but find myself tripping over bags and parcels and even some guy, bending down tying his shoe, wiping down his leg or straightening some fucking thing. Anyway, I bump into him, nearly fall over and put my hand straight inside his jacket where a couple of fingers catch on his braces. It wrenches against my nail and as I think that it's beginning to hurt, he wheels round and pulls back violently making a big huffing fuss.

'Watch what you're doing, you fuck!' I say, putting all the emphasis and venom I can on the long f and the last k sound of 'fuck'. It works a treat, because, he immediately pulls up short and steps right back in silence, his face, all red, goes very still and attentive and the sick little piggy, unhealthy looking, eyes in his face seem to go very gleamy and look right at me. I stare him out and make it as awkward as I can without laughing and turn round slowly to carry on. I'm wondering if I can get away with turning round again slowly a few steps on to give him the creeps, you know it's not all over yet and I could come back and spoil your day. 'No, fuck him' I think. 'You can only do that if you mean it, if you're in a temper. Otherwise you just can't carry it off at all'.

So, without looking back, I saunter off down the platform and push past all the others a little bit more forcefully. I get a few, "Excuse me's" (Emphasis placed well and truly on the 'me' and no intention of apology).

Gliding through the palm-lined turns and sweeps of the road, I hit Caveoiro on the road in from the west and took the slope down to the small square that gave onto the beach.

I stopped abruptly in front of the two main streets, to my right, which ran back directly from the beach through the town and past the old market to the hills behind. 'What's the betting that I end up down one of you two stinking sewers?' I muttered to myself. These two roads were like a cross-sectional picture of society: The best and the wealthiest lived at the front nearest to the sea and then the up and coming pushed in behind with the smug respectables and the hard working but poor following on behind. A little further back, you found the beginnings of the real scum: the low life dreamers and the low life divers who trawl through the mire looking for some quick fix. I'm talking about the bone-idle, *don't give a fuck* element that only wants an easy way out from the lot of a good citizen. They think they're so tough but all along they're running scared of a life of endless work and drudgery only relieved by flashes of pleasure. Moments, which only stand out, because they're acquired through long hours spent in wage slavery. 'Sure,' they say, 'a little Mozart or Mahler may take you out of there,' but these guys know that's not enough – for them it's the wilder seas and the usual life rafts of drink, drugs and sex in general, by which I mean in particular, old broken down pros, juvie tail, statch raping, boys, kinks, rinky-fucking-dinks's and whatever the fuck you like, all wrapped up in one endless drag of indulgence. Me? Apart from a few little dips, I've always kept pretty much beach side, although I guess you could say that my whole life, my job, my reason for being, brought me into such close proximity with these people, that a decent citizen, a reasonable third party couldn't tell the difference. So what? I've been mopping them up off the streets for so long I guess I couldn't see the next wave coming – well maybe, if I believed all that crap. 'Jee-sus, what the fuck is the matter with me?' I thought again, before I remembered the lack of sleep. I slammed the door of my car and locked it. 'Now that's something you don't see too often in the movies' said a voice from the shadows – I say a voice when actually I mean a mouth. All you could see was the lips, the teeth and the tongue lit up beyond the murk of the night. 'What the fuck, you playing at Billy Wilder?' I said advancing towards the alleyway next to the car and the shadowed figure.

'Don't think you're clever, because you know the first jack-shit fact about Beckett' came the voice of the street-walker. 'It's not a bad pick-up for an old pro like you' I turned back. 'Not a very clever joke for a burned out ex-cop like you' she spat back. Then with a scathing sneer she continued, 'they know you're coming and he's going to be waiting for you. You're just a low rent, low budget dick – you're way out of your depth, you won't last out beyond tonight.'

'You'll see more dicks than me tonight, that's for sure' I said and closed the conversation. So, they, whoever they might be, knew I was coming and 'he', whoever 'he' might be, was waiting. It looked like being a long night.

I set my face in the hard moulded stare that I used on suspects, detainees and other low-life scumbags. I didn't bother trying to make any clever comeback to the hard-bitten streetwalker, she'd won this particular battle – 'but hey, what the fuck', when you looked at it longer term, she faced a long slow series of defeats ending in the unconditional surrender of the gutter. I stopped mid-step. 'Unless, of course, she found some good hearted, simple minded sugar-daddy millionaire to silver-spoon-feed her escape out of pay-as-you-go misery, but – I started walking again – to be honest, I don't recall seeing too many of them on the mean streets of Benagil, Lagoa, Alberfera or, least of all, sunny Caveoiro.'

She had called me to arrange coffee and to go through the ads for second hand cars in the *Free Ad*. Then she called again and said that she had found one, which sounded really good. The ad said:

Star car

106 SKI

Metallic blue, 1.1 M-reg,

43,000, s/history, mot,

immobiliser, immaculate, ideal

first car. Owner gone travelling,

must sell. ONO 1.85k.

4230004/07977 470971

'Wow,' I said, 'that sounds really good! What do you think?' She laughed on the phone: 'Do you think the owner knows?' I paused for a moment, 'Knows what?' I answered, not sure where the conversation was going. 'Knows they're selling it! Laugh, laugh' she replied, her voice slightly too full of good humour. 'Yeah,' I said a little too loud, and with slightly too much emphasis, sounding part of the joke now.

'I'll pop round and text the vendor and we can see what he says over coffee'

'Yeah, see you in a bit,' I said and put the receiver down. Soon after there was a ring at the door and there she was, smiling and full of expectation. As we said hello we repeated most of the conversation again. She always sounds enthusiastic about the current topic of interest and, when it is something big like a new car, she likes to keep enjoying each moment at every opportunity. It doesn't seem like savouring things over and over again, since, each time genuinely feels like the first time.

She sat down at the table as I poured the coffee. 'Let me just text them now, I don't want to miss it.' For the next few minutes there was near silence as she sat with her head down crouched over the mobile phone wrapped in its black leather holder. I think it is a real leather holder, I'm not really sure though, you would have difficulty telling, I suppose, between real and imitation leather on a small piece like that, squashed up under her fingers. The phone kept making beeps and clicks as she worked through and entered the individual letters. I took a sip of coffee and thought what a laborious looking task it was, you didn't really notice or care when you texted yourself but once you watched someone else at it, you could see that it was really slow and hard work to get even a short message out. Even one of those 'do u txt msges'.

After a while, she puffed and then looked up. 'All done'. We sat and drank some coffee and she said 'That'll go straight through, if they're there we should hear straight away' then she stopped and giggled, 'I asked them', I looked up, not understanding, 'Asked them what?' She looked at me as though I was entirely stupid, 'Whether the owner knows' she said

284

emphasising, no stressing, the 's' sound on the end of 'knows'. 'Oh' I said, smiling slightly, 'yeah' in a warm way, which trailed off. She carried on full of enthusiasm. 'It's only, let's see, less than point two of a penny to do a text that long. I get ten free and then I pay for the rest every month. My neighbour, Sarah, gets a deal with the first ten free every day but she doesn't use them, which is typical. I mean I'd use all that and more it's so quick and easy.'

'You do' I said. Looking up from her coffee and the *Free Ad*, she said 'What?' looking lost for a second, or rather, just stopping, like a computer, not processing until the right information came along. 'You do use that many every day' I explained.

'Ah well', she said looking confident and knowing, 'You do, it's texting, everyone's doing it. You should do it more too, then you could keep up'. But before she could finish that sentence she burst out laughing and said 'I sent them: intrsd in cr sowns gd, dos owner kno yr selling it?'

I laughed again, 'Yeah'. Then we sat there and drank some more coffee, and looked at some of the other ads for cars. After a bit there was a ping from the phone. 'They've answered' she said, 'oh' then her face screwed up a bit like there was a bad taste in her mouth, she held up the phone for me to see, it said 'fcku'. She said that she would give them a call to explain the joke. I said that she shouldn't bother, would you want to deal with someone who sent a message like that? She said that I was right and that she'd look for another car, it was a pity though, that one sounded good. 'Welcome to the world of texting' I thought.

I went into *The Terrace Bar and Disco* through a doorway lit from above with a shielded lamp. Moving quickly up the stairs, I could feel the heat and the sweat of so many bodies packed tightly together in a confined space and when I pushed my way into the crowded bar, I felt no distinction between the silence of the street outside which had only been disturbed by my exchanges with the hooker and the crowded discordant fragments of conversation and incoherent shouts which passed my ears inside.

I saw men from every walk of life, but they all looked the same: scruffy and sweaty and in need of a wash and shave. The sweat of a night's boozing lay in small smears and patches around the eyes of those I passed. I made a beeline for the bar. I was looking for the owner who I could see, surrounded by his henchmen and reclining against the maple wood-look fascia.

The owner was dressed in a grubby white tuxedo with a black shirt open at the collar and to half way down his chest. From under this shirt, spread wide over his broad frame, grey and white chest hair curled out, changing colour in highlights of purple and orange under the glare from the dance floor lights. On his head, the hair was scraped back, greying and lined. His face, seemed permanently pulled back in a broad grimace of pleasure. Down over his left side an ice-cool blond had poured herself and she gazed out to the seething mass on the dance floor, all the while sipping on a transparent plastic glass of dark liquid. Neither spoke to the other; in fact I noticed how few were actually speaking at all in that place. What had, at first, sounded like conversations and greetings was in fact no more than aimless gestures. The good citizens of Caveoiro were merely going through the motions of speaking rather than really talking to one another. Many, like the master and his mistress at the bar, had long since given up the pretence and were content just to exist in a self-imposed silence.

Looking straight at my prey, I advanced purposefully, waiting for one of them to catch sight of me, or for a henchman to point me out as an approaching danger. Depending upon their reaction, I would know what to do, however, as I got nearer and nearer through the throng, no one made any sign of having noticed me or my intrusion in their dead little world.

Right there and then I was pulled up short, as someone who had been crouching down among the legs and the feet of the room chose this moment to rise up into my path. It was a weedy boy-man. He immediately spun round with a shriek as my arms and legs stamped down on him, crushing one foot and scraping the calf of a leg. 'Hey, Jeez, my fucking ankle, you animal' yelped my obstruction. I stopped and looked down. His face was white and freckled and sweating profusely. I looked into his eyes through the heavy set of his black and transparent framed plastic glasses, his eyes looked narrow and thin with sharp glistening blue accents. I thought 'this guy is wearing tinted contact lenses under glasses'. I said 'you stupid fuck' and stared again menacingly. He looked at me full of a futile rage and I could see his body becoming more wiry and tense as the anger rose up through his puny frame. 'You, you call me stupid. Why don't you look where you're going you big ape?' I stopped staring and started looking at him for the first time. He had ginger hair, cut short and pushed into a close side parting. His skin was white under the lights of the club but I thought that it would keep its ugly pallor even outside in the warmth of the mid-day sun of Caveoiro.

I leaned down into his sweaty, ratty little face. 'Fuck you' I said aggressively. He looked at me as though he was going to answer back and then thought better of it. Suddenly, he pushed past me, instantly disappearing in the crowd. I half turned to follow him but lost sight of his direction. The next second, something in the atmosphere changed. I felt a wave of heat and tiredness slide down over my body. There was a new mood amongst the gathered mass under the coloured lights and then the unmistakable ravages of *Vier letzte Lieder* began to burn their slow fires across the room. The richness of late Strauss swayed all around me and, through the rest of the room as I heard Schwarzkopf's pearly-pure tones fill the air over me and I forgot my purpose here for a minute. Again, I was drawn to this sound as though for the first time, just like everyone else in the bar.

It was hot, hotter than I had expected it to be and I could feel myself beginning to perspire a little as I walked over to the wooden bench. The bench was warm already but, thankfully, not as hot as I was beginning to fear it might have become. I looked around me as I stretched my legs out to enjoy the heat and the sense of being in my own time sitting in front of the sea on a hot day. Then I stretched myself and moved into a more upright position. Finally, I crossed my legs and then casually looked around.

I looked one way down the promenade to my left and then, slowly and casually, I allowed myself to look right up the promenade in the opposite direction. It occurred to me then that we spend a great deal of our time being casual. In fact, if my example was anything to go by, we all do a pretty good job of policing ourselves on our days off. The cult of 'casualty', or 'the casual' as theorists would, no doubt, properly call it, was approaching epic and possibly catastrophic consequences for some areas of contemporary life. I recalled then the 'throwaway voice mail messages' that reduced the tones of pretty young girls – well at least one pretty young girl in particular, that I had called – to the blurred intonation of a slovenly launderette worker from the back room.

Moving on, under the unrelenting rays of the sun, my mind wandered onto the casual scrawls and scribbles that I had seen left in studios and galleries to let friends and acquaintances know, in the full view and certain knowledge of the exposure to public view, of changed whereabouts and new departures. So studiedly lazy, I considered, as to be barely legible and sometimes, in fact, completely illegible at the precise moment of importance needed to convey the sensible meaning of the message.

I felt at ease and content in that moment, under the sun, sitting comfortably on the bench hearing the vague sounds of people moving and calling out over the constant ebbing and flowing, the roars and crashes of the sea spray breaking on the shingle beach, until I looked down and remembered what I had come to read through. I cleared my throat and picked up the pieces of paper, which appeared tremendously bright and white in the strength of the sunlight. Then I bent my head and began reading:

Saving a file

When you save a file, you make a file on disc (either the Hard Disc or a floppy disc), which you can close and re-open later on. When you do this, what you are doing is actually emptying the file information from the RAM (the temporary memory) to the Hard Disc (the permanent memory). The first time that you save a file (be it a picture, a text document or a movie etc). the computer will ask you to save that file to a location on the Hard Disc. Once you have saved a file for the first time, saving again just saves any further changes that you make, such as typing more words to an essay file.

Saving a file for the first time presents you with the 'Save Dialogue Box'. With the 'save' dialogue box, the computer asks you what you want to call the file, where you want to save it, and what format you wish to save it in. With Windows 3.1, the title must be restricted to eight letters or numbers with no spaces in between those characters, and then followed with a 'dot' and a three-letter suffix. Usually the programme will assign the proper suffix for you. If you are using Word, the suffix for Word files is 'dot doc' (.DOC). If you are using Windows 95 or NT or a later Windows operating system (98, ME, 2000, XP) you can introduce file names with characters, numbers and spaces up to thirty six letters in length but you must not include the figures ' / < >?.' and so on, since these are reserved characters used by the computer as part of its operating system to manage and navigate files and data. This is the extended naming facility and is called the 'Joliet index'. NB With The Mac you can make a file title with any character you like. To save a file to a location you need to place the file in a directory or a folder.

The 'file to be saved' [in the illustration above] is saved within the folder 'text documents', which is within the folder 'magazine project' which is on the Hard Disc (the C Drive).

The folder system is very easy to learn if you think of the computer as being like a big filing cabinet with one big drawer (the Hard Disc). Inside the drawer there are folders. Inside the folders there are files. Some of the folders may have other folders inside them; some contain folders within folders within folders etc. Inside any of these folders there can also be individual files.

Remember:
A folder can have other folders inside it (you can keep putting folders within folders for as long as you like, although you may end up by forgetting where you put a file).

A folder icon can hold files or be empty. It doesn't look any larger or smaller when it stores ten files, a hundred or a thousand. The icon for a big file is no bigger or larger than the icon for a small one.

Saving Back ups

It is a good idea to make copies of your saved files in case anything goes wrong.

If you have a precious file which is very important to you (your end of term essay, PhD thesis etc.) don't just keep one copy on a floppy disc and work from that, rather instead, you should save your file to a folder on the Hard Disc and keep a back up on a floppy. Floppy discs can easily get damaged or corrupted through exposure to heat, moisture, and magnetic fields or just through age (remember they're mass produced and only cost a few pence each, so you shouldn't expect them to last or be very reliable). Conversely, it is very unlikely that the Hard Disc in your computer will fail. Back up files on floppy discs are useful in case you need to use another system or another user decides to delete your file.

Generally, it is good practise to work directly onto the Hard Disc and make a back up at the end of each session. You can do this in a number of different ways, for example, by exiting your programme at the end of your working session then going to the Explorer (Windows 95/98/2000) or to the File Manager (Windows 3.1) you will already be in The Finder on The Mac (OS 9X or Mac OS X), so just open the Hard Disc icon, and simply drag the icon of the file from its location on the Hard Disc (the C Drive) to the icon of the floppy disc (the A Drive). As we have already seen in the section on copying files, this makes a copy of the file on the Hard Disc whilst leaving that original file intact.

Remember:

There is little point backing up files in the same location, particularly if they are on the same floppy disc. If, for example, you drop the disc in the gutter on the way home, both files will be lost. Backing up a file to the same location is behaving like the amateur photographer who takes more than one photograph of the same subject from the same position, with the same settings and under the same lighting conditions, to be sure of getting a result.

Selecting Items

On all computers, running each of the major Systems, you have to select items in order to affect them. If you wish to change a word in a word processing programme, you must first select it; if you wish to change the font in a page of text in a page layout programme like Quark, you must first select all that text (highlight it); if you want to alter an object in a draw programme like Free Hand or Illustrator you must first select its handles; if you want to change an area of a picture in Photoshop or Painter you must first select that area with one of the various selection tools. Similarly, if you want to find out how big an item is, delete it or re-title or relocate it you must first select it. Selecting an item can be done by simply typing its name, so that it appears reversed highlighted, alternatively you can select items by pointing and clicking on them once with the mouse. (You can move between selected items on the desktop by pressing the Tab key, this is the key with the inward pointing arrow, situated to the top left of the main key block on the keyboard).

You can open selected items by pressing 'Control, O' in Windows and 'Command, O' on The Mac. To find out how big an item is, first select it, then press Command, I on The Mac or click with the right-hand mouse button in Windows 95, 98, 2000, ME, XP and choose 'Properties' from the bottom of the contextual menu, which appears under your cursor.

Remember:
Clicking once with the mouse on an item selects it.

Clicking twice on an item opens it.

Then 'Blammo!' There it was again, right between the eyes I saw an arm, an arm that had lightly brushed my sleeve earlier. The arm extended slowly in an arc upwards and then joined its mirror image, their fingers entwining before separating gracefully and now freed of each other, began gliding down slowly to rest at the side of the body of their master, *no make that mistress*, I could now see the face and the eyes that once again seemed to be staring straight into me, waiting for an answer. Now wearing a Carmen-red dress slashed at the shoulders and pure white skin offset by Carmen-red lips, parted like a perfect oval, slashed through the middle. I saw her, the very same way that I had first seen her earlier on the beach. It seemed only a few minutes before. Now, she stood still for a moment before me and then she seemed taken with the wave of emotion that surged in with the music and she was caught up in the whirling mass of the dancers.

The room swayed, I was beginning to feel that time was catching up with me, no wait, nix that. Time had caught up with me and had rushed past. I couldn't tell if there was any logic to the events of the last few days, whether I controlled them, or maybe, they controlled me. I stared into the crowd and could see nothing coherent, just arms and legs moving, catching the light and then, silhouetted against white faces, staring with cold glinting eyes and all arms, legs and faces, cast, flashing in a series of rainbow colours bathed in the array of the dance floor.

From this tumbling free-for-all, the face of the beach woman swam up into focus and my consciousness. Her face began speaking. She was saying something but I couldn't hear it above the lush surround-sound of *Im Abendrot*.

What was she saying? I tried to focus, her bright red lips were moving and I began to hear the words. The person I needed to speak to was the hooker outside. I would find her at home. I would know her house when I saw it. She would show me the way to *Amfortas*.

I felt that she pushed me, no wait, it was like she was letting me go and we started to drift further apart separated by more and more people and their bodies, held now in the trance of the final long bars.

I turned, I pushed and I ran, stumbled and forced my way through the heaving mass towards the door and the stairs. Outside the cold clear air almost hurt as I drew deep, greedy breaths into my lungs. I was sweating and turned about, looking for the old hooker. Nada. I scoped the street. Nix. Then, I don't know how, I stumbled down the first of the main streets. Shitsville.

Reeling, my feet moved forward but my brain kept retracing the same sequence, the woman on the beach, the hooker, the woman in the club.

I headed to the lower end and tottered into the filthiest, most dilapidated looking hovel I could find. The walls circled the stairs, it all seemed to be rotting around me as I crawled upwards. When I had climbed to the top I fell against a door, which splintered open beneath me, and I crashed into a scene of total horror.

I put my hands on the door and then see the hand-written notice which says something like 'ring for attention' so I press the buzzer. In a moment or two I see a figure at the back of the shop stand upright and press something. There's a faint buzzing sound and I suppose that's it, I'm in. My hand closes around and turns the door handle.

For a second, something I read about some stupid fuck, who went out with a bunch of fishermen and saw a beer can floating in the water and then said 'I can see it but it can't see me' flashed through my mind. I always used to say that you should try getting to the other end of this town with your ring-piece intact, if you want to know about the menace of the gays – it always got a laugh. Now I was nearly laughing to myself because I thought, 'I can see him and he thinks he can see me'.

I moved forward, possibly turned ever so slightly to one side, I had to force myself, quite slowly and consciously to turn and face him front-on. He already looked quite suspicious and seemed to be hanging back, whilst sizing me up. 'I'm looking for Deco really' I said, 'have you got anything from the period?', like it was *the period*. The only period, that is.

He started to suck his teeth and look thoughtful. I looked at him directly while he did his tooth sucking, chin rubbing act. It struck me for the first time what an ugly disgusting individual he was. I had already quickly taken in something of the way he was dressed but now, looking at him straight on, I could see that he was wearing an old polo shirt of a faded blue colour which looked grimy and a bit sticky, as though he'd worn it every day of his life and had come to forget that it might have a separate existence, together with some dark trousers which were loose and baggy, I couldn't make out the material, but I could see that they were tucked into his socks. Big fucking grey socks like granny gave you when you were young. He also had some kind of slip-on slippers or trainers or something, but no laces. I looked into his face and it was pale and translucent. He looked like a salamander, which had come out of its cave by mistake and was slowly blinking in the sunlight wishing it were back in the dark with the shit. 'Mmm, deco is not really my period' he said in a small accented voice. 'Dutch' I thought. 'You Dutch fuck, over from Amsterdam and bringing with you your useless jumbled up hippy, bullshit'. I looked again at his wispy hair and fat white face. Breathing in a wheezy little voice he continued, 'there are some pieces, that table and chairs is good, one or two others too'. The sentence seemed to trail off and I thought 'you sound Swedish,' actually I thought of the Swedish cook off the Muppet show, but I couldn't quite remember at the time who that character was or where it came from, I just heard that pathetic, up and down, whispery voice, which is held back and withdrawn by three hundred years of cultured activity and not killing people in wars but taking saunas while the English, French and Germans run around effing and blinding and shooting at each other. 'Yeah, the table' I said, turning round, I even went over to it and pulled a chair back slightly. It looked quite good in a way, but there was something not right. 'This isn't *of the period* is it?' I said trying to sound even and open. A slight pause, more fucking Scandinavian reserve and then 'No, it's contemporary, it was made in the East for a lady – to her precise specifications'.

I looked at the table again, and looked at the chair back, then I leaned forward, pretending to look at some detail of the table. 'It's quite a low design, isn't it' I said, still looking down at the table edge in close up. 'Yes, the Far East' he said in his wheedling cultured voice that was really beginning to nauseate me now. 'So you're a fucking racist too' I thought to myself.

I straightened up and turned round to face him again. Suddenly he was a lot closer, almost took me by surprise, and it was all that I could do there and then not to jump. Then, in my head, about a nanosecond later, too quick for him to see, I regained my composure, my equilibrium and I was in charge again. At my ease now, I looked him in the eye and said, 'What's the wood?' He blinked back for a couple of seconds not saying anything and I felt a flush of rage spread over my body. I wanted to yell in his face 'What's it fucking made of?' Was he trying to think of an answer, to catch me out or was he trying to cover something up because he felt unsure about the way the conversation had turned and thought it might lose him the sale? 'Hard wood.' He said. 'Which one?' I said, thinking 'Do you think that I'm an ignorant little fuckhead who doesn't know the difference between Piranha Pine and Mahogany?'

Not realising any of this, he looked at me again, a bit more shiftily and then said, 'they call it Hard Wood'.

'That must be some shitty Malaysian fucking substitute for the real thing' I thought, 'So you were trying to have me over. That clears it all up then'.

'Mmm' I said, looking round the shop, looking at the smooth hard surfaces of the objects in there, wood and brass, as though put there for the very purpose in hand, preordained and a gift from God you might very well say. I couldn't stop myself from one little smirk and before I realised what I was saying, I was asking him in a small voice, full of innocent doubt, 'Do you believe in destiny?'

He stopped suddenly and then, the strangest thing happened, the last thing I would have expected, he looked totally reassured and at ease with himself, as though he was in charge, not me. 'Yes I do, I know it exists. Do you go yourself?' He asked as though he had started on some familiar track. I looked at him again. This time I really looked at him as though I was doing it for the first time and I wanted to find what I had missed. He didn't seem to notice any change in me but now he was starting to wear a smug, complacent little smile. 'I saw you notice this' he went on and made a gesture to a fish shape on some obscure little set of shelves on the wall, over to my left.

I said 'Icthus' in a mechanical voice. 'Quite right' he said 'I go to Kings' pointing to a faded poster with a colour picture of some new age warehouse on it. I wanted to say 'I don't, I'm not stupid and I'm not a mediocrity like you' but I didn't, in fact I didn't say anything, I just looked at him and I was beginning to wonder if he had chosen me rather than me choosing him, although, it didn't matter much anyway. He was talking again so I said 'yeah' to keep him going. He looked at me and there was a twinkle in his eyes. 'What?' he said with the hint of a trace of a laugh in his voice 'what do you mean, yes?'.

And then it struck me, now he was going through his routine and he was off and running home, what I did, or said was irrelevant. There was going to be no more wariness, no more suspicions, no more strangers meeting and asking 'what are you up to?' it was all following the right story. I became dimly aware that he was asking me something, 'Mmmm?' I said dreamily. 'Do you want to read my testimony?' he said, bending across and reaching down into a pile of folded up pieces of paper on the same set of shelves with a surprising speed and agility. He sharply straightened up, he had retrieved something and now showed it to me.

It was a small grey folded piece of paper, quite thick and regimented in its design. It had been printed all over with lots of words and folded up tightly. It looked desperate to tell you everything and some of the words were in bold to lend them extra importance. I put it in my pocket without looking at it. 'Thanks' I said and turned to go but, before I had taken a pace, his wheedling voice had raced past me and stood up in front of me, barring my way. 'Do you know a Church like Kings, a good church some other place? I have to get out of this town.' I was pulling on the door handle again, and then I stopped and thought for a second. I pushed the door closed again and turned round my face blank. 'I can help with that' I said.

When I woke up, it was in the open hull of a fishing boat pulled up on the shore and light was beginning to stream in over the Atlantic which carried on crashing in, white topped waves over the perfect, even beach.

It took me a moment to realise where I was and then a beat longer to reconfigure the dark, gruesome mayhem of the night before. I didn't want to give my mind up to the images that started crowding in the moment my brain kicked in on its habitual logic. I couldn't help myself. The obscene carnival of grotesque butchery whirled in front of my mind's eye. First of all, I saw – no, scratch that – first of all, I felt the impressions of little stabs of horror and then, one after another, these small slashes overlapped and ripped one over another until the revolting, pointless slaughter began to take a definite shape and meaning to my stupefied brain. I reeled. The boat spun around me and the roar of the sea grew into a deafening unbroken series of crashes smashing into each other continuously.

I saw blood streaked up a wall, dripping, smeared and sprayed around in a heavy, congealing orgy of ruin. I felt the sickening presence of wanton torture and the indulgence of pain. I stared unblinking, at the inner image, of one severed hand propped up on a table with an eye between the fingers. The other hand was nailed to the wall at the end of a large 'V' shaped smear, gripping an orange.

The torso, still pulsing warm blood, was leant against the far corner of the room and the legs lay at odd, impossible angles like some obscene image of violation and degradation. I could have made guesses about the wounds, which must have been inflicted to produce this pose, but I couldn't and didn't endure the walk across the room to make closer inspection, let alone lift the sodden skirt to see more.

I lay back and took a long breath, the sharp draw in and the salt in the air, made me gasp in pain.

Too much smoke, not enough sleep, no decent meal in the last ninety hours. I felt about a hundred and I guess, I must have looked pretty shabby at that moment. 'This is the lowest point' I thought to myself, 'this is the moment of darkest fog before the sharp light of epiphany breaks in my head.'

'Get out the boat' came a voice from somewhere behind me. I heard it twice before I realised that it was aimed at me, I wrenched myself back to the here and now, away from the anguish of bloody murder.

Half turning, I stretched my neck round in my stiff suit, feeling the tired cloth strain against me. 'Hey, easy does it or I'll blow your fucking head off!' came a second voice sounding kind of jumpy, but also kind of sincere. 'Whoa, hang on there buddy' I countered holding my head still and calling out of the side of my mouth. 'I'm on the side of the angels' All I got was the sound of a .45 ratchet getting the slide. I tried again. 'I'm going to put my hands up, nice and slow, and I'm going to turn around with my hands up, so please, don't drop me with out due cause'. I injected a little humour into the proceedings because, by now, my mind was zeroed in 100% on the dreary day, the regular and the known and *boy*, did I know these jokers. They were flat-tops, grey-greens, the local hard-on uniformed cops that you see driving round in shades with 'GNR' stencilled on the hoods of their rides.

Sure enough, by the time that I had turned fully, my palms flat out and skyward, there were two of the government's finest, half crouched in front of me in exaggerated poses of 'pinning down the fugitive'. I resisted the temptation to ask if they had a bead yet, and suppressed the grin that was forming on my lips. It crossed my mind that they might be squad donkeys but, at this distance, even a shitkicking shitbird from the pool could drop me in my dirty suit. I walked slowly and purposely from the boat and, keeping my hands high, I got to the pair of clowns straining and tense in front of me. 'OK' I said quietly and slowly, 'lets get with this. I'm going to put my right hand in my left jacket and show you my badge, nice and slow'

There was a moment of complete silence while none of us moved or spoke and they let these last words of mine sink in. Then one of them tensed up again and said in a thin taught voice 'OK, nice and slow and no funny business'.

'You little fucker' I thought, 'if I did pull out a magnum now and blow your fucking hop head out, no court would convict me on the grounds of provocation'.

When I explained who I was, with the aid of my shield and a few gruff words. They fell back and looked entirely crestfallen. 'Come on you heroes,' I said, 'lets go back and see what things look like in the daylight'.

By the time I had come back from the toilet, the others were pretty drunk and leaning rather than sitting in their seats. 'It's funny how you want to go to the toilet and you're part of the situation, and you're still there, part of it, but you go off, and you come back and it's different and there they are and you don't quite belong anymore, you know, you're separate ... ' I trailed into silence, and then there was what you might have expected, everybody laughed and I was the butt. 'That's the trouble with drinking too much' I said, 'it makes you too open and honest for a nasty group like you'. 'You're too fucking delicate for this world' he said, 'you're a, you're a – ' he had to repeat himself to be heard but also to struggle with the idea and the sentence, *'you're a tragic little bunny, aren't you'.*

The way he said it, the way his mouth really mouthed the words making big shapes to get the letters out and using a fair amount of spittle all the while, reminded me of a fat boy in my class who used to put his mouth round pyramids of ice-drink and suck all the taste out. 'Come on,' said the other 'get back in the social group'. This brought on another round of laughter.

Icebergs I remembered the name of the frozen drinks as I slid in and bent my legs over the chair and under the table. 'Don't feel sad and lonely, we want you in with us all happy again' he said. I was slightly peeved, so I said 'in your dreams' and looked hard at him. I held his look with a level stare for just a few seconds and, as I did, there was a lull in the conversation and noise. I felt slightly guilty, I didn't really want to hurt him and I didn't want to spoil anyone's evening so I tried to make a joke of it, well at least, release him gently from this awkward moment. 'I just meant that I feel quite drunk myself, but I didn't notice how drunk I was till I came back and saw how far gone you all are. It was like I'd just walked in and saw a table full of rowdy drunks'.

He went for it. His face suddenly moved again. 'Oh, so it's our fault now', he said with great emphasis and mock haughtiness, rolling the phrase around, then he said with operatic gestures, 'get away from me, you, you rowdy drunkard, you!'

'Oh come on,' I tried to continue meekly, 'I didn't say drunkards, I said drunk' and that was it, they were all onto me with 'You said drunks, not just drunk but drunks, *big difference*.' I tried to pretend that I didn't know the difference but they wouldn't let me off that easily. 'It's a … a qualitative thing, the difference … hey it's a qualitative difference' he said again his voice over-loud once more. 'You might say to someone, *oops, you're a little drunk*' he pointed to me 'you might even say *you're drunk*!' he pointed his index finger at me and then wagged it in front of my face, then withdrew it slightly as he saw my stare begin to set on him again. 'Watch it' someone said, 'the drunk's getting nasty'. Everyone laughed at this, I felt myself smirking and then as the noise around me increased, I laughed out loud. 'Look' I said, once the uproar had died down a little, 'there's no problem being drunk or even being a drunk, it's just a

302

little word, that's all. Anyway – I just pointed something out and wanted to share something with you'. I went on hurriedly, since I was a little drunk myself and that's why I kept walking into all these pitfalls – I thought that it was best to come clean, big mistake again because, when I got to the pitfalls bit I said 'pratbulls'. That really set them off. Someone said, 'who's a little drunk then? I mean who's a little bit drunk? no offence', someone else called out 'careful, if you say that, a drunk's likely to turn nasty'. Suddenly, I'd had slightly had enough of the same jokes being put onto me and I said 'All right can't we all just grow up a bit and move on. So I said the wrong word just then and, I admit, there's a big difference between being drunk and being a drunk, but come on that's it'.

Of course, there were plenty of 'Woooarrs!' and exclamations, but I stuck to my line. 'What are you all so obsessed about?' This provoked another outburst and someone called out in a weedy, fake voice 'Yeah, where's the beef?'. Straight away the rock-ape contingent wanted to show me right there with great displays of gesturing and 'couldn't believe it' delight.

I sat back in my chair and stared ahead with pursed lips. Actually I was becoming a little intimidated, these people were supposed to be my friends but they wouldn't let go.

'You know,' I said evenly, 'that is an interesting sociological phenomenon' I couldn't quite believe that I had managed to say that and get the word out, let alone make myself heard to the point where everyone noticed, stopped and listened to me. 'What do you mean?' he said. 'Interested phenomena' I let the lapse go, thinking that if only he would be as generous, I wouldn't have to try quite so hard, in fact I wouldn't be saying any of this at all. 'There was this congressman, let's have no jokes about congress please' – thankfully not too many, just a few 'oh surely nots' and one voice saying slowly 'you mean a man in congress'. 'Yeah', I said making the most of it, while it lasted 'some guy who ran for Congress and during the campaign, his opponent, got slaughtered because he, the first one, had a masterful ad campaign with two old women being shown burger baps and told that they represented "policy-lite", the speciality of the second guy, and right in the middle of the ad, one of the old women goes off into one saying: Where's the beef, where's the beef?' I did the voice of the old women as a cracked old crone and there was a moment of silence and then they all seemed to realise at the same time that it was funny and they all laughed.

All except one that is, my inescapable tormentor, who sat there, rock-still staring at me. I was going to stare back again, because I had felt pretty pissed with him, I mean, there was no relief as far as he was concerned and he was straining every thought in his big fat head trying to come up with something to get me right back there. I wanted to say directly to him, 'come on have a little generosity' but I knew that it would be suicide. So I just let one hand stray up and pull very slightly at some of my hair. Immediately, I wished I hadn't done it and I knew, that he felt like he'd won. I saw his face change into a slight glow of triumph as I let my hand fall down again under the table, where, I couldn't do anything with it except to tug on the hem of my skirt.

'You want to be careful' he said leaning forward in a stagy threatening way, 'you don't want to peak too soon, you don't want to *jump the shark*'.

'What?' came up from all sides, it sounded like I imagine the effect they're straining after in those cheesy comic books. Me, I just sat there, I was wondering if I could be bothered to get up and storm out, make a big scene and worry about the fall-out tomorrow or was I going to give in and let him have his way. He was sitting there with his arms folded waiting for me to make my move one way or the other. I looked back at him with that big greasy hovering dribbly smile playing round his fat face. I thought again, 'why is it always me?' and I said something like, 'oh go on'. He just sat there and said 'pardon' really quietly. I said 'granted'. He said it again, 'pardon', but this time at normal volume and I could sense the expectation all round me, it seemed everyone's evening depended on me, so I looked him in the eye and said 'please explain' He started in on it: 'Uh oh. Most of you know what the phrase means, but for the handful of you that don't. *Jumping the shark* was originally coined to describe the point in time when a TV show hit its peak, and immediately went downhill from there. It was derived from the TV show *Happy Days* and refers to the episode where the "Fonz" jumps a shark behind a boat on his skis. Over the past half a decade, it has come to apply to anything that has changed for the worse, and which will never be the same.'

I walked back to the scene, preparing myself with every step on the stone floor which was just beginning to warm up in the morning sun. The reeling horror of the night before was now an unconnected series of blurry images, it was daytime, rock 'n' roll and I was back on the case. Man camera, get in, look round, record everything for analysis. I could look on the style of the murderer now and stare coldly at it for what it was: a puzzle to be solved not some fucking tug at the heart strings. I climbed the stairs quickly and pushed the door open. 'Blammo'. There it all was before me again. This time, I looked hard at everything, my eyes moved slowly and carefully over the ruined surfaces and then I panned back to get an overall impression. It had started: I had begun to think; this was now a logical process that would end with a result one way or another. What did I see? Strange images besmirched and smeared over with the crimson handiwork of the murder. 'The do-er'. I saw a picture of two middle aged women, one older than the other, both wearing pastel colours and smiling at something off to the right past the camera, as if, the camera had seen them without them knowing, but wait, they were dressed very formally despite their grinning smiles and casual relaxed poses. There was something, stage-managed about the whole scene. I looked again; they seemed to be standing in front of a rough stonewall and at the bottom of some steps. Around their feet small brown, sand-coloured dogs were milling and one was half turned, looking in the same direction as the women, posed casually like their cover story. But who were these women and what were they looking at? Whoever had taken the photo must have been close enough for them to see and yet, the most unusual aspect of the whole picture was its size. More of a stage poster than a picture, like a family snap, but blown up. 'It's commercially made' – I breathed out between my teeth.

'They all are sir' said one of the GNR prowlers. I had forgotten that they had run up behind me and were waiting to make amends with some positive input after the little armed stand off, earlier. I didn't give an inch. 'Uh-huh' was all I said, but I turned and looked around the room. I had been so intent on the first corner that I hadn't actually looked around the whole room yet.

The goon in the cap was right, there were several more of these poster-pictures but they weren't of the same people or the same place. There was a weird picture showing a black man with an afro, standing, from the waist up wearing a bright coloured, fairy-tale or circus costume and make up. He looked like he was on stage, maybe in *Die Zauberflote*, but he was bending over backwards with a guitar. No, the guitar was painted black and white and made of strange, exaggerated shapes, 'like nothing Sergovia would ever recognise or play' I mused, fusing this into the man-camera memory bank.

Weirder still, was another oversized picture of a black man reclining, looking at the camera and sneering. You could only see half his body but it was clear this time that this was a fake, some kind of made up pantomime figure: it looked like something from a fable to instruct children with righteous fear of the consequences of immorality. The guy was white faced and thin in an undernourished way with curling black hair, which was falling into his face. White faced but a black man, I'd guess. 'Fag butt' I thought 'you couldn't cut it with, fucking – I don't know what, but it's not you, you're not real, you're not my man.' I was getting more sure that I was looking for a man, although most of these over-sized pictures seemed to be of men and it's not usual for the do-er of women to have much interest in his own kind, yet there was something still, something unexplained and cultist about the decoration of this room. Something that made me want to go beyond and look through the big slashed-strokes of blood which spelled 'V.C' over the walls, something which seemed more important than the head of the hooker, her eyes gouged out sitting, quite still in front of her severed arms, which were crossed and which held, in her stiff lifeless fingers, an orange and one of her eyes directed at the orange.

'Blammo.' That's it, he's telling us something – wait up, rem that out – he's telling me something. He must know that I'm on to him and this is all set out nicely to tell me what. 'An orange and an eye: Look at this: What though?' I struggled. 'Go and look at this … you fruit. No'. I had to look at it with less involvement; I had to be the man-camera. I turned and stared back at the walls. I was going to get him and win: manno a manno. There's no one else in there, I was sure.

Hi everyone again it is I the dealer of tricks, turns out I

now know what iApp Lalala does: remember when we were talking in NYC and he said how Rendezvous would allow people to walk by others with it installed and instantly be able to trade files well guess what the new iApp code name Lalala (play off of NA NA NA) to poke a joke at the RIAA and MPAA does just that. Here is my friend after I posted our last chat:

DeepPanther: dude I will tell you

DeepPanther: remove that now

DeepPanther: remove it and I will tell

DeepPanther: dude I know more just stfu

DeepPanther: remove it

DeepPanther: you ★★★★ing ★★★★

DeepPanther: alright

DeepPanther: don't tell but it's going to be something with KDX

DeepPanther: like KDX will work on PDAs

DeepPanther: dude wtf did you leak

DeepPanther: I was really getting close to asking you if you wanted it

DeepPanther: but I dunno if I can trust you

DeepPanther: you just not going to talk to me?

TRICKSDEALER: sorry

TRICKSDEALER: I was out

TRICKSDEALER: he … he … he

TRICKSDEALER: I guess you saw the post

DeepPanther: dude can you please pull that?

DeepPanther: yeah

TRICKSDEALER: you see I was kinda pissed a little

TRICKSDEALER: see it one of my pet peeves

TRICKSDEALER: the whole people hiding stuff from me

TRICKSDEALER: so to find more info since you had me going nutz I told people

TRICKSDEALER: well a board of people

DeepPanther: dude lol no one knows

TRICKSDEALER: well my meta friend did

DeepPanther: lol what did he say?

TRICKSDEALER: it was The Man pissing on the mpaa

TRICKSDEALER: and the riaa

DeepPanther: lol yeah

DeepPanther: you know

DeepPanther: but please can you pull it

TRICKSDEALER: for his revenous was the whole key to it

DeepPanther: for the good of the data

TRICKSDEALER: dude there have been talks of that **** for a while now

TRICKSDEALER: what I posted inst anything major

TRICKSDEALER: plus no one knows it's you

DeepPanther: yeah but pull my convo because I don't want to get in trouble for a leak

DeepPanther: yeah

DeepPanther: the **** part of my nick: clue too much to who I am at work

TRICKSDEALER: dude no one will find out trust me

TRICKSDEALER: I'm posting our chat now

DeepPanther: and can you try and change my words around

DeepPanther: no please don't post a chat I don't want any clues

DeepPanther: cause I could get in legal trouble

TRICKSDEALER: hmmm OK

TRICKSDEALER: I'll post the first 15 lines

TRICKSDEALER: and change the usernames

TRICKSDEALER: to protect the corporate pirates

DeepPanther: OK expect what I said about changing my name and ****

DeepPanther: and the server stuff don't say

TRICKSDEALER: what server stuff?

DeepPanther: and don't say anything about carracho I don't want people to get confused

DeepPanther: about you asking for server info

DeepPanther: just stick to facts

TRICKSDEALER: no no no
TRICKSDEALER: I said first 15 lines
DeepPanther: KDX = cocoa
TRICKSDEALER: OK, OK
TRICKSDEALER: Lalala
DeepPanther: KDX = iApps
DeepPanther: KDX = Piss off RIAA
TRICKSDEALER: yes
TRICKSDEALER: MUHAHHA
DeepPanther: KDX = Former HL guy
DeepPanther: you know

I was driving, yeah the car was going like a smooth metal bullet and my mind was racing along over and over again. The pills had hit my gut and kicked in over the wave of bitter coffee. The wind pressed hard up on the shield and then rolled over me and took the stale odour of my breath and sweating face away. 'One Hundred Hours Plus' and no wash, as the sun was beginning to climb the pure azure of the sky. I was on the coast road again and I headed out to the lighthouse at Faroles.

I pulled up sharp at the gates of the compound and sent the chips and loose gravel flying. I yanked at the key and the engine died off into silence. But there never is silence, no perfect space to think, because the other sounds, the distant waves below the cliff unseen in front of me and the far off cries of gulls mingling in the air with the dull roar of passing traffic and the buzzing of insects around the long grass and wild flowers, began to rise up around me. I felt my head lurch and I knew I had to think quickly and precisely if I was going to make sense of this. I couldn't let it go round my brain anymore. 'What the fuck did it mean?' I clenched my fist, and brought it down hard on the wheel. The horn blew an angry note and I only silenced that when I pulled my fist back and looked at the fingers, curled tight around my palm. I stared down and then quickly pulled my fist up to my forehead, revelling in the pain. 'Wake up you fuck, what is "V.C"?' I tried again: 'what is the significance of an orange and an eye? There are plenty of orange trees round here, then again there are plenty of stupid fuckers with eyes too. It doesn't go anywhere, but *he thinks it does.* The do-er is telling me.'

I started to get out to stretch my legs and as I opened the cream and beige door, 'Blammo!' there it was. I gasped and half sat back again. V fucking C. Of course, not an orange but a Clementine. '*Vivendi Clementi*' The villa out of town opposite the *Intermarche*, the large food warehouse the local citizens enjoy patronising so much, stuffing themselves on steaks and bacon sauces, sizzling away in the traditional cooking dishes that they all fucking love so much.

'You crazy fucking bastard' I shouted at the top of my voice. 'I know where you are and I'm coming for you' But, lets wait a little, suddenly I had all the time in the world and I sat back right there, watching at my ease, waiting at my leisure for the sun to go down, so I could make a move and come rolling right in.

We were sitting, quite relaxed, just about to start the second round of drinks, when my companion took a sip of beer and made a strange half snorting sound. I looked up, studied pose, quizzically as it were, a smile playing on my lips, I knew him so well that this little display was surely the prelude to a story.

'I forgot to mention, "Blameless Shamus", you remember, of Clearwall, Old E Firm fame, died a couple of months ago. More accurately, got killed in a self induced, drunken brawl outside *Ra-Ra's* nightclub one night.'

I did remember, and so I lent back and looked at him positively and expectantly so that he could tell me it all without further ado. He immediately noticed my assent and continued with good-natured enthusiasm.

'Basically, he'd been in the club, getting pissed up and drugged up as usual and, on the way home, decided to front out a complete stranger in the street saying "Have you been shagging my girlfriend?" or something like that – a variant on "what are you staring at?" – simply intended to pick a fight with a complete stranger. Unfortunately, this stranger was also pissed and, with a single KO punch to the chops (all caught on CCTV), floored Blameless – who is seen to fall backwards like a plank and crack the back of his head on the pavement. Result: his skull cracks in a semi circle from the back of his head round to the sides and he's dead.' We both paused, me to wipe my lips and chuckle and him to take another sip.

'Now, here's the corker, Stan was the DS in the morgue for the Post Mortem the next morning. As you know, Blameless and Co. are known by all who have ever had the misfortune to work at Clearwall – in fact, I was speaking to a probationer there a few months ago who told me he was still up to his old tricks – Blameless that is' we both laughed at this, ' … of getting pissed and picking a fight with anyone, for any reason, anytime, anyplace … This officer told me that he'd (then) recently had to go on an enquiry to the local pub, where Blameless also happened to be, having just discharged himself from hospital with a broken leg that was now setting at a skewed angle because he kept walking on it. Looking something like Long John Silver, Blameless immediately stood up and challenged the officer and colleagues to one in the pub, there and then, and had to be taken away. But I digress from the main story … '.

We both drank again in silence for a moment and then, putting our glasses down together, we both leaned forward as he started up again and I continued to listen.

'The pathologist was doing the usual with the post mortem on Blameless, part of which is to cut his skull open which a small surgical, circular saw – the one that goes Bzzzzzzzz … The pathologist, who'd cut many a skull open, commented to Stan "Fuck me, this is a thick skull!" as apparently it was twice the thickness of a normal skull – it comes as no surprise that the Darwinian missing link is found in Clearwall' he paused for a very short moment, looked at his drink but then immediately lifted his eyes and continued: 'Anyway, whilst the pathologist is buzzing away on old Blameless' cranium, Stan has the presence of mind to call up one of his DC colleagues on the mobile, someone who has had many a run in with Blameless and loathes him with a passion beyond description. I knew that my eyes were twinkling by now and I just nodded further encouragement.

"Guess what this is" says Stan holding the mobile to the bzzzzzzzzing skull saw

"What" says the DC, who'd been to one or two post mortems before and found the noise strangely familiar.

"Blameless having his head cut off" carps Stan, happy to be the one to break the good news to him.

A week later the DC came into Stan's office and was still laughing hysterically.

Whilst on the subject I enquired as to the welfare of Blameless' old sparing partner Royds, who apparently is out all over Clearwall, wanting to kill his mate's killer.

Blackhouse CID, of course, know who this is, since they interviewed him on suspicion of murder but as his 'self-defence' argument was backed up by the CCTV footage they decided not to press charges but recommend him for a community action reward instead … he managed to keep this going to the end but his voice had started to waver and with the final 'Thought you'd want to know.' He bent forward and roared with laughter. I too, thought this was hilarious. This is so on the edge that, well, they talk about shock-TV but you'd never get this and it's real life too.

I know that you probably don't want to hear this but "If you can make this Zen adjustment of attitude, in which you are always in pursuit of finding what kinds of things are possible, then you might even enjoy the process of clean-up and correction."

By the time I was ready to make my move, it was dark. I felt strange: relaxed about what had to be done but at the same time, kind of jumpy, almost, I guess I was gunned up pretty good, I was full of the expectation of what was going to go down. I pulled a fake Dickens-style cockney-copper from old London town, 'Hive got you bang to rights and all, old boy. Now then, come along quietly me hold matey'. I revved the engine and the tyres squealed. I was van Dyking at the top of my voice but I didn't give a shit. Too much time in my head: the lone number crunching, analysing machine, chewing through the numbers for the man-camera. Now that was done: it was action all the way.

I gunned the engine and the sleek shape of the bonnet attacked the space in front of me. I drove in long sweeping lines. I followed the curves of the landscape, I rode the cambered surface of the highway which cut through it. It was night but it wasn't dark, everything was covered in a strong haze of blue. I punched the dial and the start of *Die eiserne Brigade* burst into life around me. 'Blammo! That's the best piece he ever did, and I need it now. I'm all set.' I thought some cold hard thoughts like 'It's coming. It's now. I'm on it. It's real'

I slid the sleek body of the car in a long arc up the ramp and over the car park of the *Intermarche*; I applied more pressure to the break pedal and the auto ground down evenly to a halt, crunching loose gravel. I flipped my eyes up to the rear-view mirror. I could see *Vivendi Clemente* spelled out in gold painted capitals on the black bars of the fence which ran all round the citrus grove, which in turn surrounded the villa itself. I pursed my lips. Dead pan, I got out the car and flipped my wallet cover open and thrust it into the breast pocket of my suit with my shield hanging out the front – cop hero-style. The badge glinted blunt dull highlights in the blue of the evening.

I walked fast across the main road separating the *Intermarche* car park and the villa railings. No other vehicles. I stood for a moment at the gates and saw they had been left ajar. I slid the left one open gently and, half crouching I speed-walked into the property making my way through the large citrus trees to the front of the villa. I could see a window open and a lit room in front of me on the ground floor and I approached it listening hard for any sounds, all the while expecting something, I don't know what.

As I got closer I saw some people inside talking. I recognised the owner from *The Terrace Bar and Disco* and his silent, maybe somnambulant, squeeze standing, showroom dummy style at his side. I didn't stop to think about her I concentrated on what was being said. I could hear his voice but not make out the words. I stepped forward to get a better line on the proceedings when 'snap' my shoe broke a stick on the ground.

In the room in front, suddenly the mood was shattered. The owner leant forward with his arms bent and stretched out on either side, fingers splayed. 'There's someone out there', he roared.

I wasn't going to run away, so I stood, braced, waiting for the confrontation. Out the front he burst, looking exactly as he had done a few hours earlier, but now with a .45.

I stared at him and looked pointedly at the gun. He looked back at me and said in a surprisingly genial voice 'what are you doing here, trying to protect me?' If there's one thing I can't stand it's irony and, no if there's two things I can't stand, its irony and worse than that, irony from a punk lowlife scumbag. I felt myself tense for a split-second then I sprang forward. His face registered surprise and his arm jerked as he reeled off two shots, which cracked the air past my head. I felt a savage blow in the middle of my back and had time to wonder how the pain was coming from behind when he had shot from in front, as I saw my badge spin down and fall on the dirt in front of me and I toppled down after it. I bit the dirt, slumped over my shield and as the curtain fell, it all went black.

I can't quite believe it. I'm standing outside Terry Flanner's pad. Well, maybe not quite outside, I had the cab drop me at the intersection with the main road. And to tell you the truth, the word 'pad' doesn't seem to do the place justice either. I'm actually staring up the entrance to the private drive, past the electric gates and the visitor's intercom to the whitewashed curve of the wall, which runs to one side of the clean, fresh gravel path.

I'm excited for the first time in a few years I can tell you and, if I was able to relax and enjoy myself for a second, I think I'd find that pretty valuable in itself.

Actually though, I'm not able to relax and let out any tension at all, so I just take a couple of deep breaths and try not to remind myself that this is my one chance to make the right connections, say the right things to the right people and make a big hit in movies. This is, in fact, whether I can forget it or not, a massive fucking chance and I don't suppose I'll get another, so I take another self conscious little breath and I walk towards the intercom box on the gate and try to hide the slight shakiness in my step.

I'm through and now I'm walking up the gentle incline towards the low-lying house. I guess it's what real estate guys call 'bungalow ranch-style' I guess too, it's impressive if you're into that sort of thing, which I'm not. I've been to one too many places like this before, and I'm all too aware of the real kind of potential they have. I've been the guy jumping off the roof of one of these, into the pool, past the floating silver beer churns. I've seen the groupies and the journalists lounging around the poolside waiting for the signal like a row of Kentucky derby bays. Waiting for the first one to pull someone's pants down and kick-start the orgy or to whip out a small pile of coke and push it into the gums of whoever is going to be the first sacrifice to the party gods. Talking of which 'My God', I almost say it out loud. I am so fucking sick of all this, I'm just so tired of it, I'm past the hysterical phase, I'm not going to come over all drama fag and do a number on you about twisted wrecks of humanity or any of that three a.m. kind of talk about 'hey, I've got regrets and it's a dirty town with some nasty ways, but I'm married to it – it's my life'. The thing is, this: I've had enough of all that, I want to get beyond it and do something else. That something else can only be a place in the movies and the cash to break out of this cycle so that I'm wedged up with plenty of folding muscle, then it's off. Where to and what for? I'll figure out later. I'm talking means to an end, strictly that, nothing more and that's why I've got the jitters. Today is all about ensuring the means get taken care of, because you take that out of the loop, there ain't no fucking loop so here we go.

I'm greeted at the door by Terry himself, way to go, the man himself takes the trouble and the time: 'he-hey-hey' it's half a laugh, half a greeting and it makes a loud enough sound to cut through my thoughts. 'Great to see you fella, good of you to drop by. Come on in and meet some of the folks here'. Says Terry in a nice expansive sort of way. 'I don't say a word, I don't have to, like a sleepwalker in danger of stumbling down the stairs',

Terry's got my elbow and he's guiding me along. He's 'hi-there'-ing and smiling and making little whoops of surprise and pleasure, as we seem to glide through the busy room. I feel a cold drink in a thick short glass in my hand and Terry is giving me his entire attention in front of everybody else in the room. He tells me that, directly, in a hushed tone. I've got it; complete confidence, complete licence and it's up to me to make something from that.

'We are', he says, leaning into me, 'like that "band of brothers"', I'm not sure which one he's quoting and I'm so unfocussed that for a moment, Kenneth Branagh, and Olivier's faces together with the guys from the TV war series all jostle across my mind.

'There's some guys over there, pretty important guys, yeah them' he motions a vague wave of his arm, which is now half way up my back and then coming part way round my shoulders. 'Go over there, and y'know, be friendly to them' he smiles, I'm still looking at him and I guess that I haven't been what business classes used to call 'strongly affirmative' -enough, so he winks at me and adds. 'Use your credentials, Rock, it's in your blood right? Share it. Let'em know you. Let 'em know who you've known, who you've been with'.

I look across, and I can't be sure who he was gesturing to but I feel the expectation so I turn back and look into his face and smile in a nonchalant manner to show that it's no big deal and that I've done this kind of thing thousands of times. Then I see a slight frown on his face and he piles it on a little more, giving me a slight push from behind as he says 'don't give it a thought, knock 'em dead tiger, you've got a lot they want so give it to them'.

I don't have time to point out that he misunderstood my nonchalance for a lack of conviction and that actually I can easily do this since, yes actually, I have done exactly this a thousand times before but, there isn't time, so, carried along in the same motion, I turn back the other way and place even, smooth steps in a line to take me over in the direction I can best guess as the right one.

I look in front of me and who's there? An extraordinary looking woman with purple hair and a weight problem, who's like Cruella Deville and a court jester all mixed up. Not her then, she looks like an ostrich that's just been fucked over by a Doberman from behind and with no warning. I'm starting to smile to myself when I catch a glimpse of two guys sitting at odd angles on a chair and a kind of built in ceramic tiled pedestal for the fire. 'What the fuck do they call that? yeah the hearth, that's right, the fucking hearth' Now there's a word you don't use too often I think to myself. I walk up to them and nearly say 'What's up with you two fucking little trolls, how's the hearth?' But I don't, I go 'Hi, Terry tells me that you two are the rocking type, I'm – ' They have turned and looked at me in that stupid dog-like way that intellectuals use to let you know they are contemplating some new data, whether it's the puzzling interpretation of some of Dylan's lyrics or, or the social impact of Shaggy's trousers or whoever the fuck is standing right in front of their stupid noses, in this case, me. 'Yeah' one of them buts in, trying not to move his mouth as he talks 'we know who you are.'

It's not the most formal of introductions but it'll do. I think that I can clear this up and wrap it, then drop it down the shit chute in 10–15 minutes if I play it right. Finish with a report to Terry, get another little mission, do the same, hang in there, repeat a few times, cop off with the appropriate hooker/hanger-on and depart when I'm supposed to, having put a feather in my cap and that's me sorted, or well on the way. Next stop, a phone call offer later in the week. I'm feeling good and relaxed right now and I almost get up and thank them, shake their hands and walk off. Almost, but once again, not quite, these two fat puppy seals need some fish which I haven't thrown them yet so I look at them both and say 'Who you grooving to man … ?'. The one on the left, who looks like a dopey version of Robin Hood, tries to feign surprise in a mock kind of way, as though I just asked the most left-field question possible and says, 'Dylan … man'. I ignore the note in his voice and say, really friendly, 'Dylan, what a guy, what an artist' I only mentioned him because, as I was just telling you, he's a favourite of rock intellectuals – exactly how I had these two pigeon-holed. Actually, the point of fact is, I never got Dylan, I always thought he was a tuneless cunt who looked like shit. 'Did you ever meet Dylan?' I ask and don't bother to wait for an answer. I half shake my head and smile as I blow out some air out through my teeth. 'Jeez little Robert Zimmerman, they all know you now but back on the road, pre-electric, pre- the "Judas shout" we were good buddies. You know it's a shame …', I'm getting into my stride now and I can just keep motoring like this stringing along half remembered shit, sometimes what I saw, what someone else saw and told me, with what I read. Together, it all sounds convincing and frankly, pretty congenial; you know the insider shares his point of view: shit, they should be grateful. This is the real skimmy. 'It's a shame, after he went electric, you know apart from the Band, it goes without saying really, I guess, no one wanted to work with Dylan, you know he had this heavy rep in the business for wanting to play with himself all the time.' I look at them smiling. They stare back. Will Scarlet, or whatever the fuck the other one is called or trying to look like, says in a narrow, weedy pinched-arse little voice 'are you dissing Dylan?'. Robin leans his head in further to me so that a ringlet of hair falls in past his cheek. As it does, his eyes expand and his brows go up questioningly. It's an effect that must have looked good in front of the mirror for at least one hundred times. I get an almost over-whelming urge to punch that stupid pair of faces. But I hold on and think quickly. 'Dis – no, no, whoa! Hang on; you boys got me all wrong. I don't dis the man. I mean I love him like a brother.' (I nearly said 'band of brothers'). They're still holding their stupid poses and I'm beginning to lose it so I try a straightforward ploy. 'Look,' I pause, 'you know, right from the very first time I heard the man, I was always impressed by the way the crowd would clap and cheer once one of his songs was over'. I look at each one, hard, in turn. I mean this; they seem to understand they look back. 'Peace, y'know' I say. I swivel my eyes one to the other keeping my face steady to give it the right emphasis. They look placated. 'Keep it real' I add as the cement on the deal. 'Real' says one quietly. I turn slowly and walk off. I think that's one in the bag.

As I push through the crowd looking for *Terry the crappy king*, to report my success, I stumble into some-one who has obviously been bending over trying to set me up for a pratfall. We collide as I stride forward into the stooping figure. I hold myself, upright with an effort that strains my stomach muscles.

I refuse to step back, but just stand there, a kind of bemused smile playing on my lips to diffuse any macho atmosphere. I'm not a phallocentric guy by nature, and I don't want it to ruin this afternoon's work. I just say a polite 'Whoa, hey now'. Then I'm genuinely surprised. When the stooge straightens up, who should it be but my old school crush from way back when I was three, no – I was, four years old. Louise Brooks. That cute little bobbed black hair that used to be a whole lot longer and tied back with a white ribbon, sitting at the desk in front of me and now, the last time I saw it, projected over a movie screen and printed onto billboards and magazine covers. 'Lulu' to me and her mother, but Miss Louise Brooks, the movie star, to all the rest of you.

'Lulu' I exclaim, and she doesn't really upbraid me for the use of this private name from our childhoods in front of all the grown-up shitheads in the room. She just smiles at me and makes a little play at the Kentucky drawl 'hush now'. Then she laughs and asks me what the hell I'm doing here. I tell her straight that it's my big break and that I'm amusing people for Terry the genial host. She laughs again, telling me it looks that way to her too. Funny that, I could never take umbrage at anything she said, I couldn't, to tell you the truth, remember too much about what I thought of her in particular. She was always there from the start and I always felt right at home with her so I never thought much about the details with Louise and she didn't seem to need to either.

'I guess you are a big movie star and you don't have to do all this anymore.' I say, with a smile. 'You never have to stop in this place' she says and a cloud seems to cross her face. 'Hey' I say, 'I don't give a shit for any of it. It's strictly a means to an end, between you and me' this seems to brighten her right up again and she laughs. 'You don't change' she says when she gets her breath back between guffaws. She has a little glint in her eye and she looks brazenly round the room. 'Don't ever change, don't ever give a shit for this, they're not worth it. I hate this place. I'm going to walk out on it sooner than you all – they all … ' she corrects herself, ' … think.' She adds the last word with some emphasis and leans forward resting her hand on my sleeve.

I know this means something to her. I know that, like I always knew that something meant something really important to her, but, just like then, I never knew exactly what it did mean. I look at her and I know it's not worth pretending so I grin. She laughs again. 'Let me tell you something' she says, coming a little closer and her voice has an edge to it. 'You know the other day I was filming; it was for a picture called *Beggars of Life*, with Richard Rorty. Richey's a typical character out here –' she looked at me and emphasised the point when she saw me recognise his name. 'On the last day but one of shooting, Richey the dare-devil, who does all his own stunts and arranges all the action and movement with the camera crew and the technical boys, spends the whole morning showing off to me, doing his dangerous high-diving routine under the pretence of practising for the big closing sequence. He nearly killed himself three times, and I think what's this for? what's the point of him killing himself? He just wants me so why not let him? So at lunch I get in his trailer and that's that. Afterwards, when we're about to shoot the final scene, he stops in front of the whole set and says in a loud voice "Just a minute Miss Brooks, I've got something to ask you, I guess you know my job depends on my health". Then he names a high up executive, who I've never met, and declares for all the world: "everybody knows you're his girl and he is HIV, and what I want to know is, do you have HIV?" Following what was an impressive moment of silence, he ended up by saying "Another reason I want to know is that my girl is coming up at sunset to drive me back to Hollywood". Then he stood and looked round the assembled crew and I fled to my trailer'.

I looked at Louise, she wasn't going to cry, she wasn't shrill or going to make a scene other than she didn't give a shit if people overheard her. Right then, I didn't give a shit either, but up pops Terry and puts his arms round us both. 'I didn't realise you two knew each other' he says with a hearty chuckle. Then he turns to me and says, 'you didn't tell me that ha ha'. There's a weird strain as he slightly drags out the words. 'uh-huh' I say not giving a shit still and letting it show. Louise just looks kind of, what is it – quizzical – yeah maybe that's it, and maybe that was always it with her. She doesn't say anything. Terry buts in before you could say there was a pause. 'I just need to whisk you off to some heavy rep shooters and TV moguls out back there' he's motioning towards the other corner of the room. I look at him then Louise and say 'bye, got to go'. She still doesn't say anything but her eyes look kinder now and I suppose that it's OK.

Terry's already breathing in my ear, 'she doesn't give a shit, she really doesn't care, no really, a lot of people say that but she doesn't and it can be dangerous. Sure she's a big hot star, but you're not so don't get too … bracketed in the minds of others'. He adds this last, when I look at him 'quizzically'. At this point I want him to think 'uh, shit here's another one.' Still we move on, and I meet the big TV guys. They're talking about something called reality TV. It's funny I never get to watch much TV, when I'm not on the road I'm sleeping and, when I'm not sleeping I guess I'm not doing anything, but waiting for the next round of shit to come my way. What is reality TV? I always thought TV was all made-up shit. 'Here's someone who can shed a little light on the real industry take on *Pop Idol*' says Terry, ever the optimist, 'he's got real rock cred as you'll all appreciate'. He stands there grinning and everyone turns and smiles at me expectantly.

'It can go one of two ways'. So I make a guess.

'*Pop Idol* was nowhere. It's nada, shit and the industry didn't take any position to it because the industry didn't even notice.'

This gets silence. It's exactly the opposite of the way the conversation has been drifting before I turn up, still all's not lost yet as some of the participants haven't realised that my observations don't chime too tightly with the opinions already expressed. In a place like this you haven't lost it 'till general opinion is against you. Out here, facts have no bearing on the reality: reality is what everyone thinks goes down. Right now, this one is still cooking.

I look back at them staring at me. They're making up their minds, it's borderline. It wavers, then, nah fuck it! I've gone the wrong way.

Then one of the guys who's been holding forth outlining what an incredible fucking move forward *Pop Idol* is says: 'uh, I'm close to this concept'. All eyes in this corner of the room go from him to me. I've got a second and then I might as well go home. I take half a step back to give myself the time to think and then I think and talk for my life: 'It's nowhere as a concept because it's not the right demographic for sustainable sales. If you want quarter-on-quarter growth, the real yield in audience share is on the skin flicks and stag movie markets. I'm about to put together the killer concept here and there's still time to be part of the deal. I'm putting together an adult version of reality TV called *Bone Idol –* '.

Now I can feel everyone in the room has stopped doing whatever the fuck it is they're doing and their eyes are all on me.

My head was ringing, but that wasn't it, no what hurt as I came to, was a searing line of agony running down my back and clustered around my feet. Through the cloud of pain, I began to take in my surroundings. I was lying on my side and, what the fuck, the owner was lying next to me and he looked like he was in a worse state than I must have been, if I could have seen myself that is, no wait, I felt myself slipping back into the void. The owner groaned and it all went black again.

It was black, purple, crimson, throbbing and then blue fading into a dark scene around me. I heard the owner moving slowly and moaning to himself and I looked across, 'why have you done this?' I groaned, 'What's the point in this move?' He looked at me and seemed genuinely puzzled then he said, in his genial voice, which was a little faltering but still genial, 'You don't understand, I didn't do anything, I tried but missed my chance'. Now it was my turn to wonder, 'You shot me' I countered, but he cut me short, 'you still don't understand do you,' his voice was almost kind, 'I didn't shoot you, I didn't hit you, I didn't hit anyone, it was him. He got you, used you as a shield and then got me ... '. His voice trailed off.

'Yeah, I got you both' cut in another voice from over in front of me, I craned my neck and looked up and who do you think it was? Yeah, well it came as a surprise to me, it was the kid from *The Terrace Bar and Disco*, and the one I had tripped over.

'Welcome to what a fuckhead like you would call *Gotterdammerung*,' he called out in a weedy whining voice, full of gloating.

'Shit.' I thought totally down and out for a beat or two. 'You offed the hooker? You do all this?' He grinned and the sweat on his forehead gleamed in the light. 'Sure why not? You never considered it did you, you big fucking ape. You never thought I could.' He was right. 'Well,' he continued, 'I did and that's not all, I'm starting a war that's gonna finish off your decadent, fucked up, dead from the balls up world once and for all'. He seemed to go into some kind of gloating spasm, with this, he leaned back and made a strange whining sound with his voice while one hand clenched and stuck out in the air and the other moved feverishly up and down over his stomach. Then he clutched his groin and made a weird little whooping sound and kind of shuffled back a few steps. It was obvious, he was going through some kind of spasm or mental breakdown.

Then he stopped as abruptly as he had started; he

looked normal again for a second and leaned over at me. 'Aren't you going to ask me why? What it's all about?' I looked back at him, he was mad, the only question I could think of was what's the point in arguing with a madman? You just have to watch the chances, look for an option and judge the percentages, then make a move. I didn't want to make any judgements right now though, the pain in my body was telling me anything I came up with would make depressing reading. All I said was 'I don't give a fuck'. He went ballistic.

'You think you're so smart, even now, close to death, when you're beaten, you think you're above it all. Well I'm going to tell you anyways.'

I cut him short with a wave of my arm. 'Hey boy, you said *Gotterdammerung*, Was all this, an end game of the total work of art? Ain't nothing new in that, every dumb-fuck killer thinks he's doing that.'

He was raving and howling now 'You fuck!' he yelled at the top of his voice and the word fuck was spat out so passionately that it took him all the time he had to run up and throw the final 'k' into my face from a couple of inches away.

I looked back, trying hard not to blink. 'It is an opera then' I said. 'What you're doing is symbolic of some-thing.' He looked at me thinking for a second, then said, very seriously 'everything is symbolic'.

I couldn't resist this 'is it, by any chance Wagnerian?' he looked at me, quizzically, his head slightly on one side and, through his teeth, he breathed the answer: 'yeah, I'd say it was'. This was it. He was full-on and we had reached some kind of basic truth for him. I looked at him and he stared back, waiting for what was obviously going to be an important answer, the next move in the game. He probably thought it was my last.

I had to come up with the goods, I could feel the weight of expectation from my interlocutor, even in peripheral vision I could see the owner lifting his neck so that he could see me, read my face and hear my answer. I said 'tell me, then what's the difference between all this and an opera by Wagner eh? Is this elliptical or just circular?'

He stared back and then said 'the difference is, this is definitely circular: the pain you feel now is just the start, I haven't finished with you and I'll be back later'. Then he turned and walked calmly from the room.

WHO IS PULLING YOUR STRINGS?

The following transcript was first brought to our attention in early December 2002 by a bemused colleague, who came across it while trawling through the web for conspiracy-related material. The site later disappeared without trace, despite our persistent attempts to relocate it. No doubt Ms Morrison will attribute this, too, to the Ccru take-over of cyberspace.

Though Morrison's allegation is clearly preposterous and the bulk of the content mystifies us entirely, it indicates some limited, albeit highly confused, knowledge of recent Ccru cultural production.

No member of the Ccru has any recall whatsoever of encountering Ms Justine Morrison at any time. We are not convinced that she even exists.

Our perplexity has provoked us to respond. We must emphasize, however, that we do not acknowledge any responsibility to address her bizarre accusations.

Morrison's web-text "I was a Ccru Meat-Puppet" was purportedly transcribed faithfully from a live address, given to the South London Monarch-Victims Support Group, November 3rd, 2002. We have reproduced it here without abridgement or alteration, with Ccru's own comments at the end.

I was a Ccru Meat-Puppet

This testament is intended as a warning. It is addressed to those whose eyes and ears and minds can be opened. Hope lies with those people, those brave souls who dare to look. And if my experiences have taught me anything, it is that there is always hope – no matter how dark and desperate things may seem. Many, many people around the world are learning to open their eyes. I know that some of you here will open your eyes this evening. Don't underestimate your power and importance. With each new pair of eyes that can see, we grow stronger, and the Evil retreats. It depends on not being looked at, on not being seen for what it is.

You wouldn't be here unless you had already questioned the Lie. So the fact you are here at all is a cause for hope.

Many of the things I will tell you will seem unbelievable at first. Many of you will think that the events I will describe could not possibly have happened. Some of you will think that I am crazy. You know what? That is exactly what I would have thought a few years ago. Yes, that's exactly what I would have thought – even though many of those atrocious, unbelievable things had already happened to me personally. You see, when something very atrocious happens to you, you can't remember it. You screen it out in order to survive. That's what they count on. They feed on your disbelief. They want to make it impossible for you to believe that they exist at all. That's how they operate.

This is a critical time in our struggle. Things are dark and desperate now. Believe me. Things are more dark and desperate than you could ever imagine.

They are playing out on the biggest possible stage. The biggest possible: the whole human race is at risk. I wish I was exaggerating.

You know, they are getting more and more sure of themselves. They are passing messages on the grandest possible scale and they do not even feel the need to encrypt them very much.

'It's better with the butterfly.' Can you imagine how I felt when I saw that slogan for the first time? The biggest software company in the world announces the upgrading of its online network with a strapline that was specifically addressed to me, whom they called Assassin 8. When I saw those words I just froze. Thankfully, I have come so far in my recovery now that I did not succumb to panic. I realized that this sign was as much a cause of hope as a reason to fear. They had gained a new confidence in showing themselves. The war was entering another phase. So be it. 'It's better with the butterfly.' Don't believe it for a second. It will be worse. Far, far worse.

The MSN8 campaign is a sign that my former handlers, a group calling itself the Ccru, has taken control of the emerging planet-mind. This should make you very scared indeed.

My tale is easier to tell because of the brave and honest trailblazing done by Cathy O'Brien. It is Cathy who has done most to expose the monstrous evil of the Monarch Program. Every American – in fact every concerned citizen of the world – needs to read her book Trance-Formation of America. Presumably, many of you are here today because you have already read it.

For the benefit of those of you who haven't read Cathy's work, I must pause and explain a little about what the Monarch Program is. Those who know a little about it will have to excuse the fact that my initial explanation of Monarch will be very short. Some might think it is misleadingly short. Perhaps this is so. But to consider Monarch in all its aspects would take much longer than the time I have available today.

The Monarch program is a mind control program. It is named after the Monarch butterfly, because, just as the butterfly changes its form – metamorphoses – so the controllers 'trance-form' the mind and personality of their subjects. Monarch recruits its victims when they are children, usually with the collusion of their parents. It uses what is known as trauma-based mind control to condition its victims. Very briefly, this involves subjecting the children to stimuli so horrible, so over-whelming, that their psyche disintegrates. The children cannot deal with what they have experienced, so their personality breaks down into so-called 'alters' – submerged fragmentary personae that can be called up and trained by the controllers to carry out their evil purposes.

Who is behind this program? Well, it is known to have been operating in Nazi Germany during the Third Reich, and later to have been adopted by an offshoot of the CIA called MK Ultra. But these agencies are only masks for the forces – the Satanic forces – that are really in control.

The question for which the whole world should demand an answer is this: Why does Ccru refuse to acknowledge its history of Monarch Program involvement, even today?

No doubt many of you will be asking, 'what is Ccru?' Even those of you who already know about Monarch might not yet know about Ccru and its role within the program.

I knew nothing of Ccru until I came across the name in publicity material for their 'Syzygy' (or 'occult twins') festival in London. The name 'Ccru' was strangely familiar to me, and I had no idea why. It was not merely familiar, it was powerfully and unpleasantly evocative. The moment I saw the posters and leaflets, I felt disoriented and threatened by an upwelling panic I couldn't explain. That night I was tormented by senseless, terrifyingly vivid dreams.

Each of the dreams took place in an immense, desolate cavern. I felt that I was drugged, or restrained, or both. Either way, I could not move. The cavern was very dark, lit only by candles, and I could see almost nothing apart from row after row of symbols chalked onto the walls. This was unnerving enough, but what still terrorized me when I awoke from the dreams were the horrible sounds that resonated in the cavern: there was a disconcerting, continuous chanting, but, worse than that, a deep moaning that seemed to issue from the throat of some vast, unearthly creature.

These dreams were so vivid that they did not seem like dreams at all. They seemed more like someone else's memories.

Although I had every reason to flee this macabre phenomenon, I found that I could not. Instead I was drawn inwards – as if I had a destined role to play.

I had originally planned to remain in London for only a week or so. But now I decided to stay longer, until at least the start of the Syzygy festival. In the end, it turned out that I stayed for the whole thing.

Ccru's contributions to Syzygy had taken the form of nightly 'rituals' dedicated to what they openly called 'demons'. Night after night, the theme of 'twins' and 'twinning' recurred. At this time, part of me still thought that this was still some kind of art prank. But the nightly rituals and readings were performed with what appeared to be total seriousness. And every day, after the official events finished, there were long, involved discussions that lasted deep into the night. None of the Ccru controllers ever seemed to sleep.

It was in these discussion sessions that I learned more about the Ccru's belief systems. They claimed to be waging an endless war against the oppressive forces of normal social existence. In general, they seemed wary and paranoid, yet with me they seemed peculiarly trusting and eager to share their esoteric knowledge, as if recognizing a long lost and sorely missed accomplice. In fact, Ccru seized upon me with an eagerness that should have been distressing, except my sense of judgment had already decayed too far for that.

They claimed that ordinary social reality maintained the power of what they called 'Atlantean White Magic', a kind of elite conspiracy which they said had secretly controlled the planet for millennia. They claimed to traffick with demons who had told them many secrets drawn from a 'Lemurian' tradition of 'time-sorcery' that contained within itself everything that was and will be. Lemuria was supposedly an ancient sorcerous culture populated by nonhuman beings.

Ccru also said that they had been taught to count by a sea-beast called Nomo which they had first summoned during an elaborate ritual with took place in Western Sumatra. It was clear to me from the unspoken undercurrent that human sacrifice had been involved, probably on a massive scale. Their apparent indifference to such suffering fitted in with a general loathing for human existence itself. They celebrated what they saw as the imminent destruction of humanity by the forces of techno-capitalism.

Were these just stories, or did they really believe in what they were saying? When I pressed them on this, they never gave me a straight answer. They kept saying that I needed to learn that reality was itself a type of fiction, that both belief and disbelief had to be left behind. I realize now that this was part of a deliberate strategy to mentally destabilize me.

At the dead center of the Ccru system was the 'Pandemonium Matrix'. It is difficult to fully describe what this horrible thing is. It was only later, when I had escaped Ccru's influence, that its real nature was made clear to me.

What the Matrix amounted to was a list of the demon-creatures which the Lemurian sorcerers had traded and made pacts with. More than that, the Matrix gave the numerical codes and other protocols that the Lemurians had used to contact these entities. I quickly learned the names and characteristics of many of these beings. I noticed that one seemed to be invoked more frequently than the others: Katak, a demon associated with terrible destruction and desolation. Night after night I ingested this Ccru spiritual poison, not realizing – or even really caring – how thoroughly it was insidiously eroding the basic fabric of my being, calling to my own inner demons.

I didn't know just how close I was to total destruction, and wouldn't have known, were it not for what had happened on the last night of Syzygy. This night was devoted to what Ccru called a summoning; but it's clear to me now that it was some form of hideous black Mass.

After it had drawn to a close, I had a strong impulse to step outside for some fresh air.

Once outside, I was vaguely aware of two trenchcoated figures lingering in the darkness. Then things started to happen quickly. Before I had time to react, one of them had grabbed me, covering my mouth; at the same time, the other pulled a hypodermic syringe from his coat pocket and quickly pushed it into my arm. I realized immediately that they had drugged me.

Sedated but still conscious I was dragged for what seemed like hours through the alleys of Vauxhall. Eventually we arrived at what appeared to be a ware-house of some kind. I remembered being taken through a series of security doors, until finally we entered a large basement area. It was here that I was to spend six months of shattering revelation. My two rescuers, although it took me several weeks to properly identify them as such, were twin brothers Viktor and Sergei Kowalsky, who displayed all the heroism, nobility and truthfulness of modern knights. They themselves had escaped from a Soviet mind-control facility controlled by Russian Satanists. After years of being pursued by agents from the most occult wing of the KGB, the Kowalskys set up the base in London and there they waged their selfless crusade against the evil of Satanic mind control.

The months I spent in the Kowalskys deprogramming laboratory – they called it a 'safe room' – were undoubtedly the most illuminating of my life. Their therapeutic regime included hypnosis, drugs, and electrical stimulation. The Kowalskys explained that these techniques were aimed at recovering material buried deep within my mind. They were specially designed to restore the identity of what they described as 'Monarch slaves', a term that was then completely new to me. The Kowalskys told me that they needed to access the alternate personalities or 'Alters' who had been with me since childhood. They said that I had been subject to 'pandemonium programming', a special variant of the Monarch system of personality dis-integration, compartmentalization and indoctrination. The particular numerical combinations of the Pandemonium Matrix, the Kowalskys told me, had functioned as triggers for my suppressed identity fragments.

They warned me that digging down through these deeply-compacted layers of trauma would produce inexpressible intensities of anguish. In telling me this they were not exaggerating in the slightest. Over the following terrible months I would discover that my memories were lies, my mind had literally ceased to be my own, and that I had been possessed instead by alien commands, and demons. Who had been doing this to me, and why?

It was only as my recovery work with the Kowalskys painfully advanced, step by step, that I came to under-stand the sinister purpose that held me in its claws. The Kowalskys explained that Ccru wasn't an acronym at all, but was actually a version of the ancient West-Polynesian word Khru, meaning the Devil of Apocalypse. Once I understood that they were really Satan worshippers a lot of other things became much clearer. The supposed Lemurian system was really a name for all the demons of hell.

Ccru's role as agents of Satanic mind control explained the pedantically detailed theory of trauma they had outlined to me and also their striking obsession with twins. In the world in which Ccru operated, traumatism was the means and twins the raw material. It was only by the most heroic and persistent efforts that the Kowalskys had initiated me into this aspect of the phenomenon. In particular, it took months for me to fully accept that what felt like vivid personal memories were actually telepathic communications from the submerged mental compartments of my missing Monarch twin.

The Kowalskys told me that my recent involvement with Ccru, far from being accidental, was the final stage of a long entanglement with them and the forces they represented. Recovered memories from my early childhood showed that Ccru had been covertly directing the course of my entire life, education and process of psychological maturation. I had been chosen from before birth, assigned to them by the ancient breeding masters countless generations before and had undergone meticulous lifelong training to perform a special mission. I shuddered at the thought of what this mission would involve. The Kowalskys gradually brought me to the terrible realization that my mission had already been accomplished – on the very night of my rescue. They told me that, with my mission complete, I had been scheduled for 'retirement' only hours later. This retirement would involve a long and protracted ceremonial death, to be followed by a ritual devouring by the demon Katak. A physical death and then a soul death.

But what had my mission been?

As the therapy progressed, I crossed a new threshold in my recovery, and became subject to a new wave of horribly realistic dreams. It was in these dreams that the awful truth about the mission was revealed.

They began with a semi-familiar stranger leading me forcibly into the subterranean labyrinth beneath a tropical island.

After violating me repeatedly in the butterfly position, he took me down into the lepidoptera hall. It was long and narrow, walled by shelves of meticulously numbered jars. Each jar contained a butterfly. At first I thought they were preserved specimens, until I noticed them moving slightly, opening and closing their wings.

"Why don't they die?" I asked.

"They can't die while the puppet lives," he replied.

It was then that I noticed, shocked, that he was standing behind himself. I heard cryptic numerical chanting in the background. Then the rear figure commanded 'Do it now … '

The chanting had changed into the insistent words 'Assassin 8 … Assassinate … Assassin 8 … Assassinate … '

I looked down and saw the number '8' was painted onto my chest in blood.

Then I saw myself standing over a bloody corpse laid out upon some kind of sacrificial altar. In a moment of sickening revelation, I recognized that the body was that of William Gates III. Of course, my initial response was to deny the possibility that I could be a murderer. Surely this was some sick fantasy? Wasn't Bill Gates manifestly alive and prosperous, even appearing frequently on TV?

The Kowalskys were forced to puncture this bubble of comforting illusion. How likely was it that this was actually the true Bill Gates? The Kowalskys taught me that the probability was indeed vanishingly insignificant. Not only did they point out all the subtle distinguishing features so that after comparing video images I could distinguish between Gates and his double with close to one hundred percent accuracy, they also explained how for political reasons Gates' continued existence had become impossible.

It was then that I recalled how, every Syzygy night without fail, the same slightly odd-looking middle-aged woman would attend, wearing a shapeless raincoat, an unnatural blonde beehive, dark glasses and an ornate butterfly tiara. She sat silently, observing proceedings, her features twisted into a cruel and complacent smile. Recalling this mysterious visitor later, with the help of the Kowalskys, I was able to strip away the disguise and realize who 'she' had been: none other than Microsoft mastermind Bill Gates, or more probably his twin. On other occasions the Gates-entity wore different disguises in order to attend Ccru meetings without attracting attention, yet he was never without a butterfly jewel of some kind – a tiepin, for instance, or a ring. On one occasion he appeared masquerading as the black-snow bluesman Blind Humpty Johnson. I intuitively felt it had to be him, but I could not see the emblem anywhere. Eventually I chanced to glimpse into the left lens of his expensive shades and saw, deep in the black mirror, a holographic butterfly fluttering endlessly through the void.

It all made a terrible kind of sense, but, understandably, I reacted very badly to the discovery. The Kowalskys told me that this was probably because Gates had been involved with me in earlier episodes of satanic abuse and that recognizing him had threatened to reactivate unbearable repressed memories. They told me that it would help to acknowledge these previous encounters so that I could begin the process of healing. In any case there was no longer any doubt about the truth – Gates was dead, and I had murdered him.

With Gates' death, Microsoft and Ccru had become one thing. I realized how completely I had misunderstood the situation. Ccru had given every indication of holding Gates in awe, following his instructions without question. Among themselves they would use many affectionate names for him, such as 'Dollar Bill', 'the Gator' and 'Gates of Pandemonium'. He had seemed like a kind of father figure to them. How could the Ccru web-site have come to generate some of the heaviest traffic on the web, without any advertising or even word-of-mouth popularization, if not for the massive and sustained support offered by Gates and Microsoft? Many web users report that the Ccru site sometimes pops up spontaneously when using certain Microsoft applications.

Ccru went to extraordinary lengths to make sure that their close links with Gates were never exposed, even going so far as to attack him publicly. Now, of course, I saw that the very name 'Syzygy' had been a cynical declaration of black ritual assassination. One twin would kill another. This was typical of the brazen Ccru style – years before Ccru had spoken of the 'Switch'. They had also publicly announced that the Age of Katak was arriving, when the world would be consumed by blood and fire. The assassination of Gates was supposed to initiate this new era. The Kowalskys explained that Gates was the romanized version of the proto-Arabic

Khatzeik, the form of the name Katak as recorded on the Black Stele in the ruins of Irem. Killing Gates was both a symbolic and a practical act that would enable Ccru to take control of cyberspace and use it for the vast planetary hive-mind control system that they are creating.

The letters MSN followed by the butterfly icon signifies Mission Butterfly, or Monarch Program. I never really understood their numbo-jumbo, but they showed me that MSN8 was qabbalistically equivalent to CCRU – I can't remember how it worked now, but it was very persuasive at the time.

After the MSN8 campaign broke, I wrote to Ccru asking them to justify their actions. It was the first time I had attempted to contact them since my healing. They were unable or unwilling to reply. According to the Kowalskys, Ccru were almost certainly Monarch slaves themselves. That was why they could so convincingly feign oblivion about their involvement in the conspiracy, as if they had no knowledge of the way the secret control-codes really operated.

I said before that these are dark days. Indeed they are. It is impossible to overstate the threat that Ccru and Monarch pose. My purpose here tonight is to draw the world's attention to that. To open your eyes. Because to confront the Satanic threat, you must accept that it is here. You have to believe the unbelievable.

But speaking as a former Monarch slave myself I would urge caution. To really defeat the Satanists, we must learn everything we can about them. Ccru should be deprogrammed with the same compassionate thoroughness that I was.

Confronted with the fantastic tales of Project Monarch even the most tenuous sanity recoils in revulsion from such patent lunacy, whilst nevertheless remaining ensnarled in sticky threads of credible evidence extracted from the shadowy basements of state intelligence agencies.

Nazi eugenic and mind control experimentation is quite extensively documented. Heinrich Himmler's Lebensborn breeding program, concentration camp research, deliberately induced trauma, and obsession with twins is part of the historical record. It is also relatively uncontestable that, as 'Project Monarch' exposures contend, much of this work was transferred into the hands of American agencies through Project Paperclip. Later CIA mind control experimentation, such as the notorious MK Ultra program, disclosed in documents released by the agency in 1977, exhibits certain continuities with the Nazi research goals. Soviet-based work on mind control, torture and interrogation techniques substantially mirrors the US cold war activities.

Morrison, like O'Brien before her, draws upon random patches of this legacy to weave a Byzantine tale of world-wide conspiracy, in which she herself takes a starring role. Like all conspiracy fictions, hers is spun out of an all-encompassing narrative that cannot possibly be falsified (because 'they' want you to believe in their non-existence).

To attempt to refute such narratives is to be drawn into a tedious double game. 'One' either has to embrace an arbitrary and outrageous cosmic plot (in which everything is being run by the Jews, Masons, Illuminati, CIA, Microsoft, Satan, Ccru…), or alternatively advocate submission to the most mundane construction of quotidian reality, dismissing the hyperstitional chaos that operates beyond the screens (cosmological 'dark matter' and 'dark energy' – virtual, imperceptible, unknown). This is why atheism is usually so boring.

Both conspiracy and common sense – the 'normal reality' script – depend on the dialectical side of the double game, on reflective twins, belief and disbelief, because disbelief is merely the negative complement of belief: cancellation of the provocation, disintensification, neutralization of stimulus – providing a metabolic yawn-break in the double-game.

Unbelief escapes all this by building a plane of potential-ity, upon which the annihilation of judgment converges with real cosmic indeterminacy.

For the demons of unbelief there is no monarch programming except as a side-effect of initiatory Monarch deprogramming (= Monarch Paranoia).

Ccru denies it was ever part of the program. It denies there ever was a program – until the deprogramming process introduced it.

Deprogramming simultaneously retro-produced the program, just as witch-trials preceded devil-worship and regressive hypnotherapy preceded false memory syndrome. Yet, once these 'fictions' are produced, they function in and as reality. It isn't that belief in Project Monarch produces the Monarch Program, but rather that such belief produces equivalent effects to those the reality of Project Monarch would produce, including some that are extremely peculiar and counter-intuitive.

Within the paranoid mode of the double game even twins are turned so as to confirm a persecutory unity – that of the puppet master, the reflection of God, the Monarch.

How absurd to imagine that Lemurian Pandemonium has One purpose or function, or that it could support the throne of a Monarch. From the perspective of Pandemonium gods and their conspiracies emerge all over the place, in countless numbers. "My name is Legion, for we are many ... "

Unity is only ever a project, a teleological aspiration, never a real presupposition or actual foundation. Monarch paranoia is primordially an allergic panic response to seething, teeming Pandemonic multiplicity. Everywhere it looks it finds the same enemy, the Rorschach-blotted hallucinations of the Evil One masked deliriously in its myriads of deviations, digressions and discrepancies.

In the hands of Justine Morrison, Monarch Paranoia is an overt attempt to overcode Lemurian polyculture through the attribution of unitary purpose (reducing it to the White Atlantean theme). Ccru denounces this endeavor in the strongest possible terms.

We are forced to admit, however, that Morrison's comments on Microsoft, Bill Gates, and MSN8 latch on to a number of intriguing phenomena worthy of further intense investigation.

Whoever, or whatever, hatched the MSN8 campaign evidently emerged from a zone far beyond the commonly accepted domain of corporate influence and control. For a US$300 million advertising campaign to feature a grotesque insectoid uebermensch, and for it to be widely accused of Satanism, are sufficiently abnormal occurrences to merit serious attention.

Whilst strenuously denying intimate involvement with $Bill or the Microsoft corporation, the Ccru is in a position to confirm the qabalistic affinity between its own name and the latest MSN product that Morrison alludes to. MSN8 = 81 = CCRU.

Our provisional hypothesis is that the company accident-ally summoned something from beyond the spheres with a call sign it does not understand. In this regard, Microsoft personnel are not puppet masters, but only puppets. The same may indeed be true of Justine Morrison – and even of the Ccru – but no Monarch is pulling the strings.

THEE

I

He asked me to write, during those days of rain and wind, while we were almost locked in the house, a story that would make him tremble. That night, I stayed alone in the big room, next to the fireplace, after the others had retired. The great empty space creaked with orange waves, the windows – huge, covered by the heavy velvets – seemed like theatrical doors, doors towards something that could happen at any moment, *for me* and only *before me*, if I opened them wide. The storm screamed outside, and the rain hammered the panes, dashing against them, flowing down, like a huge crying.

In the streaming glass I saw my face reflected, and I observed myself as if a stranger: my long dark hair, my white night dress, so pale ... and my lips red and open ... and my eyes sad like shining black holes. Seeing that apparition, just in front of me, near but so far, blurred by the waters ... I started to cry because of what I saw. I cannot say how, but I understood all of a sudden, with an icy lucidity ... through my tears: I saw my face, and in a second it became her face ... his face. As soon as he became more defined, he was fixed instantaneously inside me.

I knew it all, I knew it and my blood went down all my veins in the water's direction. Shocked with horror, I closed the curtains. But he was never going to leave me. My face showed me your semblance, reflected in that ancient glass. I saw you in me, and once recognised, your appearance obtained a body.

Covered in a thick long black coat, you waited for me beside the stairs, hiding in the shadows, observing me, until I went up to my room, where my beloved was asleep. Then you waited before also climbing those same stairs, and you dared to open my door, to enter the room, and you watched us sleep for a long time while getting and giving shape, form and sense to your destiny – linked to mine since then for ever. You decided never to leave me alone, to possess me and take everything I loved from me.

When they decided to go on the boat and I preferred to stay and write, you smiled crouched at the back of the window because you knew it all, you knew all that was to be – everything that was going to happen.

Being on your own, awaiting the arrival of your unborn child, that being that comes from you, from inside you, naked and covered with your blood ... and when it assumes its own life, with the first breath, then becomes the other for ever.

Take dead bodies and accumulate them all, then cut them into pieces and recompose ... and finally electrify them helped by the lightning of a furious storm.

The storm had attracted me that night, and I had dared to look, to wait till the reflection formed itself – from my face your semblance emerged and became all that I was going to produce. You started your plan, began to show in the semidarkness, in my bed, when my beloved was coming to me: then you would possess my face ... and he, horrified by the sinister vision, left me alone, without showing his horror, subtly leaving me more and more. Everything I created and gave birth to died; and a little hope was gone when I saw your silhouette near the corpse of my little son. Even after my womb had rejected the creature inside me and all that blood was flooding over the bed, and the floor and down the stairs ... even though my beloved saved me, slowly and surely you made him go. He turned cold and got depressed. And then on the day that he took the boat against all the advice, and never came back, I saw you laughing while I was dissolved in pain. A shrivelled, lifeless, vacant form, it lies on my abandoned breast, and mocks the heart which yet is warm, with cold and silent rest.

That day ... when I saw the little girl in the park near the lake: after all this long time back here, isolated from all and from everybody, hiding to not feel anymore the shame and the insults and infamies you caused me, watching her taking flowers I felt like smiling and talking to her. I offered a flower, but then she screamed with horror. I could not help my instincts any more, I was not going to be stopped – she tried to run but I got her. She screamed, I covered her little mouth and I pressed as much as I could, then I felt how she was asphyxiated between my hands, and I forced and forced till I made her disappear, feeling how she was not moving and became like a broken doll. I left her floating in the water while I started to run, and you at my back following me, your dark shadow between the trees.

The creature and I were there together on our sour trip. Since that rainy night at the lake, since that night when I dared to look at my real self in the ancient and fragile glass and he was revealed to me.

I lost my father ... he rejected me, and I hated him because of that. I loved him so much, but he never corresponded, so I had to hate, but not even that. The creature and I became so similar ... she killed with pleasure and liked to make people suicidal. I didn't want to be alive, to have been born. Why did my father have me? I killed my mother as I arrived, so I came from death and pain ... to give death too.

I had to kill.

I found your long black coat and wore it in the nights I went out on my salvage walks, looking for my victims, looking for my father and every woman he had ever loved less me. I guess I hated them as I hated myself ... I wanted to see how the body I was going to dismember would transform and degrade; I wanted to witness the moment of expiring, of no breath ... the asphyxia. I could find pleasure but I didn't, I felt nothing but void ... after all.

Walking about in that monstrous city, labyrinthine and hellish, where the indifference of all allowed me to do whatever I wanted, anything that I desired. But did I? No, there was only the force of disgust and revenge: I hated them, they made me sick, and I wanted to see them die, and cut them into pieces. And then I would spread their bits, dispersed in the hidden canals. Sometimes the newspapers would announce the surprising apparition of a head floating inflated in the waters, without sense and identity – they were so much the lost, the disappeared.

Or when they started to find the prostitutes, all emptied wombs – they believed it was a man: I knew how to use all the tools that I had stolen from my father – the fine cutters and scalpels from the precious dissection box. All of them examples of the abject reflection on my heart, the answer to him abandoning me ...

It's true that the coat was a man's coat, that long black coat. The hat and the silhouette attracted them in the darkness, then the grapes and the wine. And afterwards, all drugged and asleep, their bodies lying and pale, I opened up all the wombs and took out the organs that made me possible. I wanted to cut them ... I left them emptied out, with their stockings on, their beds bathed in blood and their perfectly painted lips opened, without the air of life. When I was taking all their leftovers, possessed by a deep sadness, I felt like I was taking my dead mother with me. They were in those hidden gardens, the cherry trees, under which I dug a lot of holes – I would leave there the bloody organs, to melt with the earth and feed the red fruits.

The city extended itself with long and intricate tentacles. Unstoppable, the growing mass of people ran on the streets, rushing, without looking – avoiding each other almost acrobatically with all their open umbrellas. Competing for space under the pouring rain ... nobody would ever look at you at all.

Suddenly one day there was this guy – foreign looking, but very elegant – who stared at me and made me feel dizzy. Then, approaching me, he introduced himself and asked me for some help ... he was looking for the address where the cinema was. I go that way I told him, lying but completely attracted and hypnotised by him. So we walked, and he asked me questions. He had an air of such familiarity about him, I felt as if I had known him for ages. He proposed to go inside the cinema – I was fascinated as always in front of that big screen, seeing all the people and places alive in there. Cinema had the special and unique virtue of secret movement: it seemed that it had the property of revealing the essence of a whole occult life, of getting us in an inner touch. I felt I was divining it all ... that it was the only medium competing with death and life too.
This guy had a power over me, he made me feel as if possessed – my thought could not take any other direction or interest that wasn't him. We walked around commenting about symbols and visual connections.
"You remind me of ... "
... and as he made me notice, all the people were

looking at us, almost if they could not believe they saw us together. "It's so strange, that fire that comes out of your eyes, like I have too ...", he said taking my hands. Then he asked me to go with him, and, walking through little alleyways, we went towards the deep and dark heart of London. Who were we in front of reality? That reality that seemed now like a little sleepy dog lying at our feet? In which dimension could we have met? Giving ourselves in such a way, to the fury of the symbolism ... prisoners of the devil of analogies, feeling like we were the object of extreme requirements ... special attentions, only to be given for us ?

Arriving in the Limehouse area, walking beside dark shiny canals, we came to a small doorway. He knew the place, and rang a bell. A little Chinese guy opened the door, and after descending into a narrow passage and stairs, we arrived in an amazing red space, a luxurious and decadent red oriental room. We were conducted by the small man into a little alcove where we could lie on a kind of low bed. He came with two pipes and started to prepare: "The lady first ...",

my new friend ordered. The guy leaned towards me holding the pipe, then, closing my eyes, I took it and inhaled in a deep breath ...

The hours passed ... and our eyes would open some-times and then close again. Our eyes met in a rare and unique world. Once we looked at each other and the effect was doubled and then we had to retreat behind our lids and let go ... to forget, leaving behind all passion, all obsession ... all the blood ...

Even desire transformed into something undefined and diffuse.

When my mysterious and fascinating new friend took me back home, he held my hands and asked me when

we should meet again. Soon, I said ... when you want.
He proposed to pick me up from home in two days, at
nine. I went up to my room, let myself drown in bed and
went on dreaming about him and my initiation, in that
red room, with that exquisite substance.

Wake the serpent not – lest he should not know the way to go.
Let him crawl which yet lies sleeping through the deep grass
of the meadow! Not a bee should hear him creeping, not a
may-fly shall awaken from its cradling blue-bell shaken, not
the starlight as he's sliding through the grass with silent
gliding.

I desired him, I wanted him, and that was troubling.

Inside me, agitated by an unconfessable passion, an
internal process was taking place as I perceived my
animality. I could feel the arrival of the most dark of
feelings, something that could hurt alot ... (I dwell, or I
think I dwell – if I exist at all – somewhere apart, an
impotent prisoner, and carried about and deafened by a
mob that I disown. This capsule, such as throbs against
the sides of animals, knows you at a touch for its Master;
it loves you! But my soul, does my soul?).

And after wandering in my solitude, after I had recognised and given birth and form to my double, my
mortal enemy and persecutor – I took away life, I
dismembered, I strangled ... always the unknown ones.
Like hateful experiments, like activities related to my
own essential questions about the dead, about my
existential doubts – I cut off heads and members, habit-
uated to the smell of fresh meat and blood like any other
student or doctor, like my father who I had followed and
spied on. He had been served continually with corpses,
never wanting to know where they came from: the only
important thing was the material and all that he could

do with it. Practice and research ... experimentation ... discovery ... pure initiation.

To start to desire my new friend so much, made me insomniac ... walking around the room like a feline. He introduced me to a forbidden world – one of sudden proximities and of petrifying coincidences; of the reflex over any mental impulse; of the two simultaneous piano chords and of the lightning that would allow us to see through, and to see truly, if it weren't as fast as the others. It was all about those kinds of facts, the value of which is very difficult to appreciate, because of their unexpected appearance, violent and incidental, and because of the nature of a suspicious association of ideas that leads you from the spider's thread to the spider's web, which is like the most shiny and beautiful thing, if it wasn't because the black spider is there waiting.

All these thoughts got me in a claustrophobic mood ... and I decided to go for a walk ... and what a surprise! There it was – another petrifying coincidence served before me: I saw him with a woman.

My heart started to beat fast, and my breath was failing – I was furious and full of rage, I saw how he kissed her and went on his way. I could not stop myself – I followed that lady ... poor one. As she crossed the deserted park, I followed until we arrived next to some bushes then jumped on her. This time I didn't need any drugs or tools, just my hands to hold her ... and then I killed her with my nails and my teeth. I lost any notion of how long we fought and how long I spent tearing up her skin and insides. Nobody passed by and I was completely soaked – I got naked and wrapped myself in her cape ... nobody looks at you in this city, so I walked back home. No-one noticed my wet hair full of blood, nor my feet, naked and blemished.

When my perplexed walkabouts around the insides of the huge London, as if in a never ending monster, reproduced themselves in my dreams – then I felt possessed by a feeling of void, and the anguish and the anxiety filled all my house and my conscience ...

And looking at the portrait of my father I would ask myself: There is my hand to the least line, there are my eyes and my hair. What is mine, then, and what am I? If there is not a curve in this body of mine, not a gesture that I can frame, not a tone of my voice, not any look from my eyes, no, not even now when I stand in front of him, but has belonged to others?

They were dead, all dead. I am dead but what's the difference, between life and death? Death is all over us, death unifies us in her warm womb. They where dead, I was dead, dead, dead – but I was undead ... I had to be there ... in the infinite, in the horror and in the eternal melancholy.

That day at nine, when he came, I was ready – dressed up in my best clothes. The carriage took us to his house. He held my hand and guided me into a big room, the walls covered by silky fabric with beautiful flower motifs. There were Persian carpets, huge porcelain vases with exotic plants I'd never seen before, lots of velvets, and low oriental sofas to lie down on, of the kind I'd seen in the opium place but more generous and luxurious, and lighted candles everywhere. We started to drink ... he held me against him and I felt how my blood pressure was increasing, and through my veins the animal was coming back, growing and warming. I glanced to the window and realised that my old companion was looking at me from outside: his face, that was like mine, stared at me with his sinister smile. I could not allow that to happen now – I could not let my new friend's life disappear between my teeth and let his blood soak my clothes. I separated myself roughly, with immense and unbearable pain, and, with an inaudible excuse, took my things and ran ... escaped ... crying and screaming in the silent lonely streets.

I was still so excited, that I needed to do something. Looking around for some man, someone to seduce, I remembered a place where the women used to offer themselves. Arriving there, I waited around awhile, hidden from them. Then a dark man appeared who I didn't even want to look at – we negotiated and, because the weather was pleasant, he agreed to go to the park. When he started to touch me, I let my imagination wander ... the savage sex was penetrating me and my blood was transmutating the beast inside me – and then, when the pleasure was like a huge wave I bit at his neck ... I bit and bit and tore out his guts without stopping my anxious need, until I had wiped out any sign of life. Leaving only a body, broken apart, under the trees, I washed myself in a fountain. I walked back home, relaxed and cool.

The pharmakon nepenthes ... all the blood, all those lives devoured, were sliding down, mixing in with the waters ... like pure glass, in and against the clock circles, going down a hole of silvered drainage.

Could I love? I could not feel, because to feel transformed me into that beast that I carried inside, from whom it was impossible to escape. I wanted to forget and I wanted to die. How could I get to him and the substance? When I was unable to contain myself? I would have to escape, another time, infinitely, from myself and my shadow.

Not to see him was a torture – and I wanted that substance. I could not sleep, and in the nights all kinds of mental equations came to my space. I laughed at this life – to kill is but nothing, because there is nothing. If I needed it I killed – dismembered, strangled or beat. All is indifferent to me, I am undead, but dead too, like the creature that lies beside me, always hidden, getting ever more inside. Creation, what a vain mirage ... He/She, came from the depths of a soul, the soul of evil that is there for us just to be called out of invocation ... from the icebergs, as far as you can go ... to die, to be killed, to end ... all that black melancholy ... descending every night indefinitely into the dark abyss, further out than any other depth.

I could never come up – I was sad, and hurt ... I felt the expansion of time giving me so much anguish, everything becoming eternal ... how to get rid of it? Desire, and to want so much – nothing compared to the feeling I was developing since I met my friend. I started to kill because of him, and not any more for myself. But who am I? The image of a ghost – with all the conventions that appear in its blind submission to certain contingencies of time and place, representing an eternal torment?

Finally I went alone to Limehouse: the opium allowed me to reorganise my mind, to clear it, to find peace and calm. Asiatic interiors ... crocodile eyes everywhere looking at me ... shadows and revivals. Every time I remembered him I would tell myself – that's the past ... the past! What a vision! All those scenes, moments and feelings all gone.

It seemed now that my soul was entering a new kind of void dimension – the opium tied me to an interior timing and reality that appeared ghostlike before my eyes: I was seeing the parks, the lake, the boats ... and I saw that boy staring at me. Then, from his sad gaze, I felt a call on my heart ... I went towards him, past the tombs which lined the little path. We looked at eachother, our sadness filled up our bodies, still, our eyes fixed on each other's. I followed him in silence, he led me inside a forest, where all the wild high huge plants moved with the air and the insects, filling the atmosphere. He took my hand and we went to a more dense zone ... my little dress started to get torn by the branches. Then we arrived at a clearing, where a lot of wild roses grew, beside a stream. We sat under a big tree. And he touched me, putting his arms around me, and we cried. Then he, very softly, sank his teeth into my neck and I was fainting, drifting in pleasure, lost in sadness.

Suddenly, that scene disappeared, as did he. I was no longer in that clearing in the woods, I was on the couch, in the red room, and the Chinese man was coming towards me with more substance for my pipe. I don't really know how long I remained in the room ... my friend was not there ...

I was still dizzy but I left that room. Then, outside, I realised that the people and buildings looked different – the clothes, the signs on the shops. There were big black cars and tall red buses. My confusion was total. Where was I? I thought for a moment that I was still in the red room, drifting in my opium mirages, but there was something about the way I felt the air going through my lungs ... and the sound was so clear – not to mention the smell – that weird smell of a kind of gas. I just tried to walk – the streets were in the same structure, and I found my way to the river, and followed it in the direction of my house. I was feeling very weak but I managed to get back home.

My house seemed untouched, surrounded by all those unfamiliar people everywhere, with their grey coats and pale faces, and their hair in such a strange fashion ...

and all the black cars ...

The void came back – the same as a dead body's. I had killed so many of them that I didn't even know how many – twenty or seventy? Hundreds? They all had the same fixed eyes on me when they were going to die, knowing that these were their last moments. That was when I felt peaceful at last – the nothingness ... the breathlessness.

I just let myself down in my bed and curled up with my pillow. I cried and cried, till everything disappeared into my dream.

Then I saw the castle, in the white snowy mountains. I felt like I was flying and I heard a heart beating, very deep, and from the dark of the night the eyes I was so longing to see were appearing before me, calling to me ... we were making love in the snow. With his long sharp nail he opened a vein on his chest and the blood came out. He pulled my head towards it and I sucked and sucked, and licked, feeling convulsions inside and my head spinning. That encounter was the most exciting and indecipherable experience ... I opened my eyes. I was in my bed and on my own, but I didn't feel lonely and inside I was telling him: you are my master, I am no more than an atom that breathes beside your lips or expires ... I want to feel, to touch the stillness with a finger wetted in tears.

It was already deep night, and I left the house driven by a new impulse, new but not unknown, walking around, looking for them, choosing ... I found a man, fucked him in a dark little street ... kissed and then my teeth gripped his neck. I sucked on his open vein, for a time that seemed for ever ... he fainted, livid and lifeless, and I was feeling full of energy, excited and anxious. I noticed I was hearing sounds ... the wind, huge waves in a storm ... I felt he was near, he was coming.

DEMETER ...

The red room appeared gloomy around me. I saw the shape of the gold flowers and went through their reflections, passing by a rose garden, with butterflies all over, against a deep blue sky where clouds moved fast. The boy was sitting under a tree – I could see his silhouette in the shadows, little dots of sun all over his body moving with the air. I seemed to take a long time to get near him through the flowers ... I arrived, and he smiled – he was so pale and his eyes so deep and hypnotic ...

Opium, the substance I adore and am submitted to. That red room where I come from, the lucidity in which I perceive my thoughts ... the images ... silent dead bodies lying over the parks, almost like a procession. I was seeing all my leftovers, one after another. The substance made me see but not feel ... like real dreams. I was trying to forget but those scenes would come to me, surround me like the dance of the dead.

Now I was sucking blood, living on their blood. This was a new phase in my transformation – the creature and I had became one, indivisible. Before, even when I was tearing them up into shreds I had not consumed them: I had known the taste of blood, but it was only now that I discovered the potential of drinking it, sucking it.
I needed it every day, and it would be easy – just a little wander around the parks. Parks and little alleyways of London, there I felt at peace, out of the masses and crowds, quiet and still ... a companion would always appear to supply me with his contents. Blood was so essential now ... what an incredible, exciting mixture – opium and blood.

I knew that the supposed dreams had to do with my actual condition ... I was suffering from a kind of asthma, and the need for human blood to survive. And

I would always feel compelled to go back to the red room, where I got my substances, where I adored the black idol.

Lying ... floating ... seen from my eyes ... I was a child, walking through the roses on that bright blue day ... meeting my sad, pale friend under the trees, walking, holding his hand, guided by him ... he would show me a grave, an open hole in the grass, a damp, dark earthy hole. And in the bottom the coffin, as dark as a shadow. We would both look at the coffin, at the hole, and feel cold, and then look at the sunshine, and the brightness of the day, and the smell of the flowers and lots of butterflies ...

The opium would bring before me what he decided, when he wanted, and I just had to drift and somehow be humble. The opium wanted me to be a child. My childhood was there to be recovered ... pieces of a puzzle ... lost and fragmented ...

I was at my house. My father, a well-known and successful surgeon, had a basement laboratory where he conducted private experiments. Nobody was there; daylight filtered down ... sunny and silent. On the table, lay a corpse. There was a big container, used as cold storage for bodies and all the dismembered pieces; and in bottles, standing in a row, were various organs, floating slightly in their conserving fluids. I looked at the body. Silent, still, murdered open mouth ... it was the first time I had dared to go to the basement, where I knew my father spent long nights on his own. Every thing was meticulously ordered – strange-shaped tools, cutters, hooks, scalpels. The smell there was of an intense disinfectant and the silence was as heavy as a stone.

Then I felt compelled to touch the body. With great emotion I passed my hand like I was tracing the surface of a sculpture. It was cold and soft – I stayed there fixed, almost not breathing ... and I felt it ... I felt the nothingness of all and the void opened before me onto that big mouth.

I had been initiated – I had dared to do it ... finally ... to discover what was down there, and from that day on I would go every Friday in the early morning. That seemed to be the day. First I would observe every jar containing an organ ... the hearts ... brains ... eyes ... livers ... kidneys ... and lungs. Always curious to discover who was the new guest on the table, I found body after body, each one different, but always with the same open mouth. And then I would look in the ice-filled container, at all the pieces ... a head all gone blue ... hands ... half a torso. When I was looking through the glass at the organs, sometimes touched by the sunlight,

I drifted around the shapes of the hearts and the lungs, amazed by the eyeballs and the nerves curling away from them, floating, suspended in the liquid formaldehyde.

One day I went down and discovered a very special object, a kind of black photo machine with a lens, on a tripod of large proportions. That was thrilling – what was this in there for? I knew a little about cinema because I had just been taken to see the new wonder, had seen the train approaching out of nowhere in the dark tent, almost as if passing over the public. I imagined that this machine might be related to that and I wanted to know more – I had to find out what it was going to be used for. So that night I stayed awake and waited till I was sure my father was down there. As I descended to the laboratory I took great care to be discrete, and then I heard him talking – he was not alone. He seemed to be giving instructions to somebody, but to see what was actually happening, I had to go out … get down on my knees, and look through the window. The room looked so different under the artificial lighting, in the night …

My father was dressed all in black and a very young man was at the camera looking through the lens. On the table lay the corpse of a woman, a young woman with long blonde hair. Then I saw the most amazing scene ever: my father opened his trousers, taking out some weird shaped organ, and started to move his hand regularly, increasing the rhythm … faster and faster … then all this white liquid came out and spread like a fountain over the dead body. When he had finished, he walked away from the table towards the lavatory. The young guy with the camera continued filming for a minute more, then he stopped and lit a cigarette. He was the most beautiful person I had ever seen. I didn't really know the meaning of what I had just witnessed … what it was …

I just saw a scene: an action, the young man at his machine – and the figure of my father as the performer and director of it all. I was almost hypnotised, I couldn't move from the window and was freezing.

Making a big effort I left and went to bed. As I closed my eyes, the face of that young guy came before me … his features so special and rare … but so beautiful. Then the hand of my father moving and that organ – which I imagined could be the same as I had seen on some male corpses – was growing to the most spectacular proportions, and spurting out that huge quantity of liquid. So he had been filmed like the train … now he was inside the film forever.

I went down there. The body of the woman had gone of course, but a little girl was lying in her place. She reminded me of myself – she could be me – she had the same proportions … and hair … she could have been my twin. I had a long look at her while thinking about my own death. I opened the fridge and I saw that blonde woman's head, blueish and purple … all her beauty gone. For a moment I had the glimpse of an image in my head – my father, and that white liquid erupting from his huge purpled organ. I tried another night to go and see but nothing was happening.

The next time I saw my father was at dinner. He was sitting there with his usual indifference to me and my stepmother, who was talking vividly anyway. I tried to associate him with what I had seen – that action and movement, that performing and filming – and I knew that it was better to hold inside me what I had witnessed that night.

Then … my father disappeared, and it was going to be for ever. In the house my stepmother was crying for days, and all the newspapers talked about him, about his possible abduction. All those photos of him on the front pages ... he completely evaporated from the surface of the earth. Police searched in vain for months and finally, the case was closed.

I was haunted by his disappearance. At that time a small edition had just been published of an old novel, about a doctor who created a man out of dead bodies – and this creature had killed his maker in revenge. I fantasised that that could have happened to him, after all that unhallowed activity in the basement, with the corpses ... I went back down there one day. Everything was still, covered in dust. I had a look around – the room had a rare, quiet atmosphere ... all that had happened down there was gone. Then, I saw my father's suitcase – black, beautiful, leather. I opened it – it contained the most unusually shaped scalpels I had ever seen amongst his belongings. I took it away with me and hid it. Sometimes I would just look, fascinated, at all those shining imple-ments – wandering in my imagination, thinking how he might have created a monster from the dead bodies, and how that creature had raged for having been made in such a heretical and hideous way, and persecuted him until it's revenge was complete.

" ... the experiments of Doctor Darwin (I speak not of what the Doctor really did, or said that he did, but, as more to my purpose, of what was then spoken of as having been done by him), who preserved a piece of vermicelli in a glass case till by some extraordinary means it began to move with voluntary motion. Not thus, after all, would life be given. Perhaps a corpse would be re-animated; galvanism had given token of such things: perhaps the component parts of a creature might be manufactured, brought together, and endued with vital warmth. (...)".

3

I was obsessed with cinema and film, always accompanied by the image of that young guy I saw through the window in my father's basement … in my childhood. I could never forget the filmmaker: I wanted to film and be filmed myself … like in a dream but without being a dream, like the thoughts reconstructed in it. Then the spirit, abandoning itself and flowing into the images, infinitely sensitised, making an effort not to lose anything, is ready to reunite with its primal functions, turning itself towards the invisible until recommencing the resurrection of the dead.

One day I passed by a shop window in Soho. They had a lot of cameras and objects and tripods of all sorts and I stood before the glass for hours. Finally the man in the shop came to me and asked what I was doing out there for so long, getting frozen. "I love cinema," I said, "I want to film … but I still have to learn everything," I told him.

It's amazing how it sometimes happens that you are in the right place at the right time. That guy, possibly – basically – attracted, of course saw his own opportunity and asked me to come into the shop. He was going to close and offered to show me around. So he let me in, locked up, and I began asking him about this and that camera … and that one and how … and the film …

I could sense that he was getting really turned on … what a great opportunity. I was so excited I had to breath deeply to try to calm and not reveal myself. So I played it as cool as I could, and I got him showing me all the basic lessons, and to show me how everything worked he got all the set-up ready for shooting. Then I couldn't wait any longer so I suggested to him to switch everything on and get filmed with me.

He came up very close to me and held me and started to kiss me – I could hear the machine rolling, we had a red spotlight over us. I allowed him to get really excited and hard, then I took my long awaited turn, and grabbed his neck and sucked his jugular, and sucked and sucked ... and all that was being filmed – trapped for ever in the special dimension, fixed, swallowed by time, time measured by movement ... by actions ... the real ones, the exact reality. I loved documentaries – anything could be filmed and become part of eternity.

I went back to the camera, stopped it, carefully dismantled it, and put it all in a big carrying case. Soho was deserted when I left the guy in his eternal sleep. I had a lot of material with me and the cases and boxes were heavy, but I felt strong – I could have carried double. So I hurried away, through the obscure streets back home – the creature inside was giving me now the strength of a giant ...

Film making – that's it ... to film and fix the image and look at the film, and live in the film. And taking life – filming life becoming death. I liked to film myself too, to be in front of the camera, to be part of it. I wanted to create a setting, a room where I could bring my guests.

The spider's work is patient, mathematical, perfect ... I love the spider, her example and her style.
I had begun to attend dissection classes at the medical college, posing as a guest student: I was related to a historical surgeon and I explained that I needed to research material for a book I was writing about him. In those days they would sometimes film a special exercise or lecture. I was present on one of those occasions and at the end of the session I observed the people in the room and made casual conversation. One of the film technicians took a special interest in me and was open to

answer my questions, so the conversation developed and I got a lot of information. The most important thing for me then was to know where I could go to process and develop my material: he knew, and he knew the special kind of place I was looking for, the kind where the important thing is the money, where you pay and there are no questions about what's on the film.

Finally I had everything I needed to proceed with my exciting project.

The guy was so fascinated by my questions that I realised how useful he could be. He was basically an expert in all the techniques of filming and editing, and had a lot of theories about montage. But what really excited him was medical reportage on operations of any kind, especially those concerning the brain, which he said were the most fascinating of all. Then he told me about the traffic of such and such a kind of film … he talked and talked … and then feeling pure premonition, I knew that he would be the perfect partner: that he would love to be behind the camera, filming and editing – and ensuring the secrecy of our activities. Which was of course my special project, as I called it.

He helped me to set up the room. I redecorated in the fashion of my beloved memories of my friend's house, oriental style, with carpets, cushions, plants, mirrors and lots of candles … the right setting for the special play.

The first night, I went out walking, more excited than ever. I was naked, but wearing a coat that covered me. Then I saw a guy: when he passed by, I opened my coat slightly, just enough for him to realise. He came straight up to me and asked if I was interested in going with him. Of course, I told him, but I have a proposition … and explained that I had my very own safe place. The guy was excited and we walked together: he was getting very anxious already, kissing me and pulling my waist against him. We arrived, and entered the house – I lit the candles and switched on the special red lamps. My friend was behind the curtains, ready to start shooting as soon as he heard the door.

"What's that noise?" the man asked ... "Yes ... it's just a generator ... for my freezer," I said, " ... it's a bit old ..." The cushions were in the right position and angle. There was an empty space just next to them in the shape of a half moon: that was the position to be filmed. I steered the man towards that part of the room and took off his clothes, giving him some wine between kisses. I was starving. He was elegant and grey haired, but still in good shape: we rolled together over the cushions and then I managed to pull him out onto the carpet ... I mounted him and got him inside me. I was moving and he was breathing very heavily ... I went down on his neck, moving faster – he came while I was sucking all his blood ... all that blood feeding me ... till not one drop more could come out of that corpse.

Then my friend and associate came and positioned the camera for a close up of the body. I performed the best dissection lesson ever – he was cut into all the sections and parts, later disembowelled; finally I cut off his cranium and removed his brain, and everything was filmed.

Later we cleaned and cleared up. My new partner took some pieces away with him for the faculty, to add to the rest of the material. And I, happy and relaxed just before the first light, went to my bed and fell into a very deep sleep.

And then the dream, the dream? The eyes, the castle, the snow, the black wolves and the lovemaking with that man I seemed to have known for all my life – I could see his face in detail, but would forget it as soon as I woke up. During the dream I was told a lot of things about life and death, and everything made so much sense, and illuminated my soul like a revelation. But a sinister feeling of void would always take over when my eyes opened, because then all the meaning would blur away and fade out.

I had been connected with the dead and with death since I was born: my mother died giving birth to me, and I could see her, all that blood all over her, around her, from her … between her legs.
She was so pale, like marble … seemed like she smiled at me … I had a vision as if I was there – I could smell my mother, I could recognise the smell of the blood.
Blood in the dead and blood in the living. Coming out from the living to get them to die.
In the vision my mother would smile and look at me, then she would speak to me. At one moment I could see her dressed in pure white, walking towards me with her extended hands … then, in a mirror, I could see the reflection of my image – I was all covered in blood, all my hair and clothes flattened by torrents of blood and the floor flooded with red liquid. Then she would stop in front of me, start crying, and her dress would begin to absorb the blood, and the blood would ascend towards her and cover her up. When she also was saturated, we would embrace each other intensely, and the blood covered us and our room … and I would suddenly come back to the emptied clean space, looking at the ceiling, feeling the eternal void, the emptiness and the hunger.
Probably, that's why I loved to touch the dead – their cold marble texture. In the first times – when I used to go "down there" at my father's house.
One day, it had been a beautiful boy lying dead on the

table. I had undressed and climbed onto him, taking a chair to help me. I felt his skin and kissed his lips and embraced him for a long time. Eternal and ephemeral as always, this life seemed to flow day by day, second after second ... vanity of vanities, all is vanity like running after the wind ... and it was ... I knew he was going to be cut up like the others, he was already gone, but I wanted to possess that moment as if mocking the implacable laws of time.

My relationship with my filming partner seemed to be developing in the right direction: he would never talk about the scenes we had filmed, and anyway, they seemed to please him. I was providing him with lots of material, and that's what it was all about, that was all that mattered – "the material".

I was also interested in learning the techniques myself. We would meet in that very small damp room – the editing room – and there we would arrange the image of my experiences, deciding how long I wanted the different actions to last. He had the most incredible collection of rare and obscure films, and he always offered to show me some. That night he told me he had just found an unbelievable item on the black market ... very expensive actually. I agreed to watch the film, and he set up the screen and the projector. I observed him – how meticulous and caring he was, treating all the machines and the material as if they were new-born babies.

When everything was installed, he switched off the lights and started the projection: a place appeared, a room that was quite dark, with very special furniture and a symbol hanging – like a sculpture, and a strange operating table in black iron. Then, two blond women appeared wearing half face masks, like black birds, and black velvet capes covering their naked bodies. They started to caress each other, licking nipples, going around each other's bodies with their tongues ... they had long black phallic toys and played with each other's vaginas, licking it and penetrating. Everything was shot in real time in one long take. A big man – masked with bird-shaped head – appeared, carrying a case, a black shiny box, and he opened it ... inside I recognised the same-shaped instruments that I stole from my father's laboratory, which gave me a feeling of strange emotion. Then two more men entered the frame, wearing long black suits and full masks, and leading a third who was chained. The third man had a cloth over his head: they started to tie him onto the table, spread-eagled in the form of a cross. The two women were still playing with each other, then they approached the table. The big guy with the implements passed a knife to one of them – she began cutting and ripping off the tied man's clothes, until he was naked but with his head still covered. The other woman started to suck his sex. Everything passed very slowly, very methodically. A ritual. The woman's mouth going up and down over the member, sucking slowly, rhythmically, while the other approached the bird-masked man who gave her more tools. Using a scalpel the two of them started to cut and tease away the cloth covering the man's face ... which then appeared, smiling stupidly, and – I recognised that face ... it was my father! My father ... tied up, naked, smiling with lust, looking like an idiot, with his hair all messed up ... a feeling of pleasure and disgust, mixed with hate came to my heart.

He licked and bit one of the women's breasts. He was completely immobilised, so he could only do what they wanted – he was at their mercy but seemed to enjoy it so much ... so they played at taking turns, each one passing tits or sex over his face, the other fucking him while sucking her friend and so on ... playing with the knives, marking him, making him bleed … licking his blood. Then, with the help of the big guy who was in the master role, they started to cut him: my father was screaming – it could have been pleasure or pain, it didn't matter. The big guy was naked, his abdomen constrained by a tight black corset. He had the most enormous sex organ, erected and full of veins, with a huge head. He jumped onto the table and thrust his phallus into my father's mouth. His big hairy buttocks moved faster and faster and my father's face bulged and distended with the full penetration. They opened his chest and belly – one of the women squatted and pissed on his bowels, then they all changed positions to cut him into pieces in a blood orgy. His face looked as if he had passed, but they went on and on, performing the most sophisticated dismemberment and disembowelling that I could ever have imagined. Everybody ended up fucking each other, bathed in blood. Then suddenly the camera zoomed in to the sculpture, a strange kind of chimera … and cut.

My partner was so excited – I could see his pants exploding, when he got the lights back on. "So … " he said, "What do you think? Isn't that great! That was happening at the very beginning of cinema … it's incredible that that was filmed then … so well made. It must have been a very good filmmaker who did that …" I was silent, but smiled at him. It seemed that that was one of the essential pieces of the puzzle: I had witnessed the death and killing of my father, replicating the scene of me as the voyeur, back in my child hood, when I had seen him from the window doing it to the corpse …

Visions, dreams that seemed real. Life that seemed ghostly, and what was the difference? Life is but a dream and death is to awake from it. Where did I belong myself? I had been there for such a long time now, seen the changes in fashions, street signs, the style of the cars, the shape of the houses – just me and the creature together. But also always a third element – the other, but as a reflection, an absence: my father, the poet, the opium addict, the boy and the young film maker ... the vampire ...

The triangle – basic and important mathematical rule, that's what it was all about. And the rest – the people, the masses, the providers – just there to be used and disposed of. Just there to be wiped out – with rage, pleasure, or indifference – for the sake of it. It seemed too, that the city was another reflection of this indifferent father, so busy with his own affairs. He was cold to me, never acknowledged any of my values – not to say that he found me ugly as I was growing, but I could perceive his contempt. I found out what really turned him on: the corpses, and everything you could possibly do to them in every way.

For a long time all those memories faded out – for some time, when I escaped with my beloved poet, and believed in redemption, I forgot. But as soon as I was on my own, that night, and my soul searched for the monstrous to put down on paper, then I only had to look in the glass at myself, and that was enough to make him exist, to bring him back: and he stayed with me for ever. Because the creature was nothing other than the legacy of my father, and the spirit of his incestuous possession of my soul.

All these thoughts passed at an astonishing speed through my mind, like light. I was still in front of my partner who, as always, was so passionate about that sort of film. My mind came back just as he was telling me about a very special friend of his that I should definitely meet, because he was so ...

"He's obsessed with film making, and he's always filming, constantly – the most unexpected things, day and night, observing the plants growing ... the shadows changing with the passage of time, the clouds passing for hours, animals and insects ... and other things too," he said, still excited.

I agreed to meet his friend, and he told me that he would let me know and that it would be soon.

The day of the meeting came: my partner drove me to his friend's place – he lived with his aunt in an old manor house, surrounded by a huge park. It was a very hot summer afternoon and when we arrived, his aunt offered us a weird tea. For ages she wouldn't stop talking about birds and we waited and waited for her nephew to come. Suddenly, she mentioned him.

"He is always filming," she whispered "but I never see what he does – he won't let me. That boy worries me, because I can hear him locked in his room with the projector on and crying. He suffers a lot – he hates what he does, he gives himself too much to those films … and …"

He appeared. He had filtered himself into the room so silently that only his auntie noticed. I saw him behind me, reflected in the window, and I could not help turning my head towards him. He was wearing a coat, although it was summer time – but he seemed to be freezing, enveloped in his dark grey coat. And his black hair, and pale face. I felt moved by his presence, by his timid manners, so shy and mysterious. His aunt left us alone.

That night we had to stay over – it was late and my friend didn't want to drive back. I was taken to my room and I talked there a while with my friend and we took some opium. Then he felt weird and, excusing himself, he left me alone. As soon I was on my own I took off my clothes – it was a very hot night, and everything was quiet, silent but alive. There was an old mirror in the room: I stood before it and looked. My image still the same, unchanged for such an immensity of time. Then I started to hear something like a faint murmuring sound, which gradually became clearer … it was somebody crying, and I was sure it was our young host. What impressively sad laments came from that room near to mine – I felt a strange sense of empathy and remained silent and immobile until his cries faded from behind the mirror.

Then I tried to sleep, but my mind drifted restlessly. And later, it happened: I felt a presence observing me intently and opened my eyes. There he was, looking at me with his fixed deep eyes. He asked me for some opium.

"Can I have some of your drops?"

I had brought a little bottle and we both took some of it. Then he started to feel hot and took off his coat, went to the toilet, vomited, and came back just with his T-shirt on and his black hair wetted and pushed back. His voice had changed and he looked so different. "What do you think about the pause?" he asked

"The pause?"

"Yes the pause, the way to perceive the rhythm, the vanishing point, our one and only opportunity," he said and asked suddenly

"What was your favourite tale?"

I answered, and he said:

"Not bad … come."

He led me through the house to a room, a little child's room, where he had his projector. There we sat in small chairs: the room was all painted in pale blue, with stencilled figures of fairies. He opened an old case, full of books, and he showed me all the ones I also used to look at when I was a child … the child who saw her father doing that to the dead corpse of a young blonde girl. Those were the times when everything stopped, and I suddenly saw this young guy's eyes on the filmmaker who helped my father in his obscure practices. We looked at the pictures – all those sinister and sadistic comics from the illustrators of the times, that we both loved. And he asked me:

"How long could you spend just looking at these

pictures? Years, centuries, a whole morning?"

And then, bringing his lips close to my ear, he said
"You were in full flight, in ecstasy, suspended in a total
pause, raptured ..."

Pointing with his finger to my favourite image from my
favourite tale he asked
"Didn't you cry? You cried didn't you, looking at these
pictures ... remember?"

And then, I started to cry. In his room, time had stopped
in childhood: a model theatre, the little bed, a used
teddy bear ... and all those books kept in the wooden
chest.

"That is good" he added, and stood up.

He loaded a film in the projector to show me. He said
that what mattered to him in reality was the pause, the
pause obsessed him ...

His films were edited in a very cut up and frantic way:
spider nets, spider nets, flies, spider eating flies, spider
nets by night lit by soft light with water drops from the
morning cold, spiders moving, one after another ... he
must have filmed thousands of spiders, flies, and nets,
and full moons, and clouds at night. He was trembling
and screaming every time that he saw something that
hurt him because it wasn't good ... and I observed his
movements and how he cornered himself at the back of
the room on the top of a bed, like a little kid wrapped in
his grey coat. He was so beautiful – he was like that guy,
the first vision I ever had of a convulsive beauty that
made me feel like losing myself in it. I felt a special
contact with him, something very deep in common –
and we were both ageless ... "He is twenty seven but he's
like twelve inside ..." my friend had said, when, arriving
in the huge wild garden, we had seen his figure in the
distance, filming.

Then, I sat beside him. We looked at each other deeply,

like in a déjà vu, and we fell down embracing each other onto the bed.

I was so moved by that meeting: this was the guy, he and his convulsive beauty, like the young filmmaker at my father's, like the boy in the rose gardens ... it was him, him, coming to me. I wanted to give him a very special present. I bought a very new camera with an interval timer, and sent it to him. I just wanted him to be able to film everything he dreamed about.

Then, sometime later, he sent some films to me in a box with a letter, and a key to his new flat in London. He said in the letter: "If what I imagine is happening to me is true, you will not receive any more, and I will have gone – but you should come to my place to see the last film that will still be in my camera. Please look at these films, or better, devour them. Take the last one – please – and develop it ... watch it. Then, everything will be revealed to you."

I prepared some opium and took it to get me into the right mood, the perfect state for perception ... the kind that I shared with him.

I was so thrilled that I stayed for ages watching the footage he had sent – apparitions of light and shadows, and continuous changes from day to night; plants growing and dying while all the spiders constructed their nets in a mathematical dance – and then the waiting time passed quickly and lots of insects were getting trapped and then eaten. The spider copulation and killing of the male, the spider's eggs, the spiders being born ... all under different lights and atmospheres.

Then he started to film himself: he was in his new place, and was getting ready to sleep in the early daylight. Wearing a sleeping mask and holding his teddy bear he fell asleep. For sometime I watched the image of him sleeping and then – a red frame suddenly flashed on the screen, interrupting the film, and his image, for an instant. The rest of the film was normal but I kept rewinding it to that point, desperately trying to catch the red frame.

I looked again at his letter, his urgent notes:

"I can imagine that you are not going to be so excited about these images. It's not that I was getting especially ecstatic about seeing myself asleep – the pleasure was taking place on the other side. And each time I waited anxiously for days to get my films back, dying of curiosity to see the red frames."

I didn't sleep for the whole night watching all the films, each of which contained an increasing number of red frames:

"Look at those red frames," he had said in his letter, "I think something is happening to me while I am asleep … something that the camera is doing to me. Something that is changing me, I need it more and more. I let my camera do it to me, whatever it is, and if I miss only one day, I get the abstinence syndrome. Now there are only 10 non-red frames left, the last ones. Something is happening there in the red time …"

Then I went straight to his flat, got in. Nobody was there, the camera was on … and the film was inside. I took his grey coat and enveloped myself in it, then the film from the camera to develop. While waiting the minimum four days, I just hung out in his room, remembering him and sleeping in his bed.

Finally I collected the last film, and put it on. I saw that the whole film was a continuous vibration of red. Suddenly his face appeared, but the projection had stopped. I passed my hand through the beam of the light but it cast no shadow. Then his image started to move – he was looking at me, his eyes calling to me, moving his hand as if to say come, come. He smiled and was still beckoning to me, gesturing with his head ... at the same time ... my face came out of his ... like the day I looked at the glass. Our faces melted and overlapped: I knew then, what was there waiting for me, what had to be done. I got a new film, put it in the camera, and got in to the bed. I held the teddy and closed my eyes – I heard the camera rolling automatically and moving towards me.

HUYTON BADDIES
VERSUS THE CIRCUS

First, a little background on the Huyton Baddies ... 250 strong gang of hooligans and petty criminals. Famous for football related looting sprees across Europe in the late 1970s and early 1980s.

Huyton, Liverpool 1977

Every year in September, the circus would come to the common in Huyton, a nice spot of sub Billy Smart family entertainment. The big top had been up for a couple of days when the Strongman was in one of the local pubs having an aftershow drink with the Trapeze Girl. One of the Huyton Baddies top boys was also in the bar with a mate who was hyping him up to have a crack at the Trapeze Girl. So up he goes, all swagger, to chat her up right under the nose of the Strongman. After a brief exchange of pleasantries the Strongman just grabs the Baddie Top Boy, picks him up above his head, spins him round and tosses him through the front window of the snug. Not surprisingly, the Trapeze Girl and him get out of there fast, whilst the unfortunate scally lies unconscious in the street.

News of the incident quickly spreads through the estate and a war council convenes to formulate an appropriate direct action response. No fuckin' Strongman comes on their patch and chucks fuckin' Top Boys through pub fuckin' windows.

It's decided...

The following evening a 200 strong mob of Baddies gathers on the common. They attack the circus just before the last show of the evening. These Baddies really mean business – beating and giving a good kicking to the Strongman, all the clowns (even the little one) and the ring master. The Top Boy even taxes the Strongman and proudly wears his mock leopard skin singlet as a trophy. Still not wholly satisfied they start burning down the big top and then release all the animals from their cages. Suddenly there's lions tigers and elephants stampeding out across the common towards the bright lights of the town. Before too long crazed circus animals are prowling the mean streets of Huyton terrorizing the local residents. Special police and zoo swat teams arrive on the scene. A lion is shot outside the King's Head. A tiger finds itself in Betty's Hair Salon, whilst the elephant roams unchallenged up and down the High Street. The chaos lasts until the next morning when all the animals are rounded up or shot.

The Baddies will not bring such glory upon themselves again until they hijack the P&O ferry the following year.

FRAMEWORKS
1966–67

It is obvious that the elements of a given framework (and this includes the constituents of construct contexts) are not at all bound to an eliminative specifying system. There is a case for a new type of element specification (which might go towards ameliorating the problematic character of external questions) which does not presuppose a certain ontological or physical status (depending on the context) for it to come-up for the count. (This is perhaps to look at the syntagmatic and syntactical aspects of internal questions (certainly in the theoretical situation), viz., the introduction of certain terms, and the rejection of certain questions which with respect to the framework itself, are devoid of cognitive content. And this, synallagmatically related to the internal introduction of new descriptive terms etc. which provide an appropriate and consistent non-eliminative context for nomological implication (say) to get pulled out. (If one talked of new 'specifications' there would be no hint of 'additional elements'.) A reassertion is that the acceptance of a framework is not an invitation to ask outside questions.

Specifications, then, might be of a non-eliminative contextual type (incomplete) (reduction basis). That is to say, in one sense, that constructs might remain associated with open concepts: this, in connection with treating dispositional considerations, e.g. 'separability', etc.

One point is that this approach, falling into a methodological framework, offers one a purchase on various assertions of material implication, irrespective of the mode in which this or that assertion might find its range of application and irrespective of its structural or theoretical position etc. Certainly, in much work which purports to be theoretical, there is a failure to analyse the meanings of nomological (implications) conditionals (i.e. those conditionals which express causal connection). (And all this is in the connection of inside questions): the framework might be a lot more catholic than it looks. Questions in the 'conceptual' sphere are, it seems at the moment, more likely to be answered through the guidance of criteria of adequacy (etc.) rather than through signposts in empirical generalization. This is not to turn the story into a philosophical one per se, rather, it is to behave as if the perusal situation were lost somehow. Another thing is that no-one, is going to lay down the satisfaction of a criterion (or of criteria) of adequacy as a desiridatum., or even push the above disanalogy very far. Thus, it would be possible to use a term 'preanalytically' ((Pap, 'Semantics and Necessary Truth' p. 233) (e.g. ... 'it connoted only a certain shape and no metrical property' ...)) and keep going when one can say that a definition has changed a self consistent sentence into an analytic one and in doing so has changed its meaning. (These are not really remarks about linguistic usage.) A further answer is indicated in the open conceptual situation, where some of the sacred distinctions which foul up some of the above seem to lose clarity in a relevant sense. And the paradoxical claims which could surround the above distinctions ('changes' of meaning etc.) don't have to fall back on the psychologistic criteria of 'necessary truth' and an internal duality. (Cf. C.G. Hempel, 'Studies in the Logic of Confirmation', *'Mind'*. 1945.)

One might argue that the criteria of adequacy of nomological implication admit that the inapplicability of an antecedent does not entail the applicability of other elements on the grounds of construct implication. It's easy to effect a translation from the construct situation (say) to the physiognomic one of observables, (where, in some sense 'observability' is a theoretical necessity). But it would be naive phenomenalism to insist. ('Naive phenomenalism' characterizes the vaunted sense of 'object' and the various connotations of that 'strong' perusal situation.) The question is focussed in terms of categorical requirements. With regard to a construct like 'the air conditioning situation allows an air temperature of no more than 90°F', and a conditional like 'air temperatures higher than that focus tactile experience', (staying with the perusal situation), it's easy to read the conditional as somehow definitive of the construct; it's perfectly gratuitous to select this rather than that conditional for the purposes of definition. The requirements of a given construct can hardly be satisfied even by a finite set of such conditionals. Nevertheless, a lot of people wouldn't abandon the idea of reducing the construct situation (and, finally, all aspects of the discipline) to the 'sialic', physiognomic one. There is a distinction to be made here: if no construct follows from ever so large a set of those conditionals which are supported on 'experimental data', and no finite set of them can be construed as a 'translation' of the construct (statement), at least any construct entails an unlimited set of such (conditionals). But the issue isn't at all whether or not a contruct is equivalent to a finite or an infinite set of 'phenomena' conditionals. Both positions evidently assume that at least one of these is entailed by a construct (statement). The objection can be raised against this, anyway, on the grounds that it does not correspond to any viable procedure. At least, so far, one has to admit the concept of degree (of applicability). In order to deduce from 'physical 'thing' conditionals, certain experience (conditional predictions of sense data), a number of 'normal' physiological and environmental conditions must be assumed – (e.g. those of vision, illumination etc.): these 'normal' conditions correspond to such states of affairs as 'proper' (decorous) arrangements etc., and refer back to the perusal situation.

A 'phenomenalist', who might claim that relations between components etc. are to be analysed in terms of 'sense data' (statements), appears to be committed to the view that these 'physical statements' (any at-all) entail such 'sense data' statements. It might be added that there is no corresponding need for him to claim that conjunction 'sense data' statements would in turn entail 'physical statements' – (i.e. of components, constituents etc.)

The axiom that to specify a certain element ('physical constituent') is to entail (at least, in a strong sense, 'indicate') a number of strictly following implications about it, can't stand once it is admitted that there might be a specification made contextually and non-eliminatively: (conditions).

The demonstrable assertation that e.g. a pair of contextual conditions, put down non-eliminatively, and a set of such (being convergent) are 'conjunctions' with at least factual content, does not commit one to the view that they all do have such content since at least one member has. In this 'factual' context, it would be silly to grant factuality to one and to let another have the character of 'analyticity'. To do that would be to arrange a quite arbitrary allocation.

A way out is shown in the splitting of the pair, or set into refutable factual statements (that would mean 'operations' of some kind (as prime possibilities)). Another is to split them into partial semantic components of the construct system. (Those two possibilities might be related disjunctively.) To do that appears to be something quite opposed to the suggestions above – the calling in of some 'observables' situation – but it must be remembered that perusal is in no sense a desiridatum. What the above 'splitting' does seem to indicate is that the concepts 'having … property' and 'lacking … property' which have always seemed like contradictories are not applicable in the original sense to e.g. works, systems, complexes, etc. whose elements are but part-ially specified, and where the specification is not at all eliminative.

A convergent set of possible elements (concepts of same, not metrical concepts) is said to be of some significance because factual statements not containing an 'introduced term' are deducible from it (a wide and vague use of 'deducible'). It might be admitted that a system containing partial specifications could be formalized in such a way that the requirement that no observational propositions should be made out from definitions alone would be satisfied. This last statement applies in the situation where one might as well only ask internal questions. (External ones lacking cognitive content) viz. that of 'frameworks' in the syntactical and syntagmatic context; in others, e.g. the free air and air conditioning situations, there is merely a frame in methodological bases.

The obviously all-right observation that 'the different elements of a thing are not necessarily equivalent' (which can be thought of as being supplemented by corresponding assertions based on conditions of simil-arity etc.), implies that the concept of, say, scale, defined in terms of one state of affairs (situation) is just different from the concept (of scale) defined in terms of another. Analogous remarks apply to all qualitative (etc.) concepts which stand in a network of functional relations: i.e. are such that their values are to be deter-mined by different routes – (and in terms of different situations etc.) According to a strictly 'operationist' criterion of identity of concepts, one is defining a new concept every time he claims to be redefining an old concept on the basis of a new situation. This shows a central contradiction in the perusal situation which doesn't require a lot more explication.

In using concepts analogous to 'open' ones, operations are with a system or systems of convergent possibilities, or with collections of such; (convergent, that is, from different fields of possible components (even designata). The use of the same term (and, forgetting Saussurian linguistics, that is what we can call 'component' etc., etc., for the present purpose (though no-one is proposing a real synonymity)) is no indication of a love of ambiguity – ('air' – etc.). Another point is that a system is consistent (here) if it ever happens that a term or element is applicable on the basis of one member and not on the basis of another (and is included on such a basis) – or, if one member be a functor, if different members of the system lead to consistent 'results' – consistent values which can be supported in the system. What makes one do this is the desire to leave open the field already gone into – one avoids a certain 'explicitness' – that of the perusal situation. The situation (in the perusal one – whatever the status of 'indicators', and whether or not one assumes one-one relations etc.) is roughly this: if a concept, e.g. scale, is extrapolated beyond the range of its variables, then the meanings of the variables change, and thus, one talks about different values of variables (different scale values etc.) This is easy to show: if an hypothesis about the scale of e.g. a 'sculpture' ('large scale' etc.) is made with reference to say, the size of the spectator, dimensions of the room etc., etc., and later the work is put in a new place containing various things (bigger and smaller etc.), then the values of scale, size etc. are outside the 'operational' range of the first definitions. All that looks like an associated system of platitudes, but it seems to be a thing that's easily missed – whilst at the same time, easily made out in the most antiquated perusal situation. Another point is that the terms in the conclusion of a valid 'argument' must have the same meanings as they have in the premises: there is a lot of assertion going around (about shapes, sizes etc.) in which it doesn't follow from the premises which are the sole ground of its credibility. It can be suggested, then, that the perusal situation has a big problem, namely the one of formulating a criterion of identity of meaning of a functor – which corresponds in most cases to finding a criterion of applicability of a functor – in differing contexts of application. This is not to suggest a mode with a deterministic character; the suggestion is, merely that there is a lot of loose stuff in the perusal situation, the exegital basis of which is mainly rhapsodic; it seems that one can hope for some of these raw vagaries to be ameliorated to some extent by settling the conceptual schemes of the mode in topically neutral circumstances. Remarks, here, on the incorrigibility of sensation reports controversy would be irrelevant – at most peripheral. But the primacy of the sensation report is bound, to a degree if not in *extenso*, to show up the cubist mode as the apotheosis of the perusal situation: *se non e vero e ben trovato*.

It's likely that a partial answer was hinted at by Sol LeWitt: " … the form being unimportant … " But it seems that a situation in which the problem was either answered or obviated would comprehend a different range of assertions and nomenclature than can be accomodated in the present categorical context.

It can be shown that the entities which are of present concern, though based in theoretical considerations (in a sense theoretical) are not theoretical fictions. (Questions of ontological status are irrelevant here. And there is no assertion that these things are just like, in every respect, bricks or clouds.) There is no denying that there are some characteristic factual questions to be asked in this context. There isn't a lot to be said for this range of entities on the grounds of analogy with scientific theory; there are occasions when analogies work out (in this direction) – but they are made out on methodological and definitory bases.

The characteristic 'perusal situation', together with its analytically explicated notions of 'proximity', 'remoteness' and 'visibility', 'identifiability' etc. (and 'operational' definition) is one where assertive objects and eccentric detail can only be shouted down with contrasting rhapsodies and requirements, or with partial 'paradigms' of alternatives ('smooth' places etc.) A mode which takes a far less catholic view of these notions and concepts is just as well qualified to come up for the count.

The question could be asked whether or not the entities one is considering are theoretical ones (about which only internal questions are to be asked – as they may be in the theoretical framework). Certainly, so far as the tenets of the perusal situation are concerned. The point is that external questions are of little cognitive value.

It seems wrong that all the entities which are to come up for the count should be 'translatable' into the 'perusal situation' (i.e. the direct 'observation' situation). It is not for us to decide whether or not this or that thing is 'operationally respectable'. (From now on, the strict phenomenalist is going to object that we are dealing with theoretical fictions in those situations where one didn't go around with instruments etc. – filling in the referential blanks – so to speak.) We don't comprehend here any generalized (i.e. with an over all application) definite rules of construction. Now, forgetting the strong objection that to predicate 'exists' etc. of anything says nothing, to say that ' … is a real thing' isn't the same as saying ' … is made of real gold' etc. (This is not to say that assertions like the former are necessarily legitimate.) Anyway, saying it isn't much, but it is to deny that a concept which is not 'operationally' defined can only get justification for being around by being well established in a theory – there is not only one sort of non-operational concept (i.e. non-perusal concept) and there is not only one sort of theoretical entity. The concept of a line of electric force (the term 'force' itself is a metaphorical one (Cf. Turbayne, 'The Myth of Metaphor')) has as much right to come up for the count as any other (concept) but it's status remains different from those concepts which are not purely fictional (e.g. logical constructions etc.)

A concept which is different, but not all that different from that of a line of electric force is that of 'the sensibility of the 60's' (it doesn't matter whether or not one approves of it here) which is just a 'useful' fiction: providing some people with some sort of picture to help them in discerning distribution etc. of various constructs etc.

A conceivably persistent objection that there has so far been no indication that one is concerned with anything other than 'fictional entities' (in so far as it doesn't seem to matter if that's what they are), whereas paintings, sculptures, series of numbers etc. on boards etc. are 'real' things – concrete entities – offering actual, concrete experiences etc., can be answered not only by the evincing of at least possible instrumental tests etc. or by bringing in 'imaginability' criteria: When a statement is made, to the effect that, say, a sculpture is made of 'real' gold, or that it's a 'real' solid etc. there is an implication that it's not made of an imitation, or that it's not defective in some way etc. Something like that can be said of the things in a framework – but not about the things themselves – it's said of the concept of the thing: the question as to whether or not one can say that something is 'real' here is not one that comes up naturally; the circumstances in which the question might arise would be those in which one is looking for a concepts defects (e.g. being fictional).

The objector would just be asserting that these 'things' don't occur in the series clouds, paintings, bricks, and molecules – the perusal situation.

No-one is likely to deny that microscopic particles are acceptable in the esthetic domain, no less than bricks etc., but one might expect some resistance to the view that things which don't even come within the range of instrumental operations (or some kind, however gerrymandered, of 'verificationist theory' etc.) still qualify for the count. It's no more than a contingent fact that people are incapable of differentiating between temperatures of, say, 50°C and 51°C of the surface of two objects without the use of 'instruments' of some sort: it is maintained here that the 'things' which come up for the count 'Air Show' – (not 'air conditioned rooms') get their meanings from the part they play in the theory: and this is to suggest that there are theoretical reasons why it is pointless to hope for an entry into the perusal – even 'observational' situation.

The point is that one shouldn't have to return to Berkeley and suppose that esse IS percipi before a proposal can be accorded any application at-all. The point is that external questions don't conclude anything about the part or parts this or that element may play in a theoretical consideration.

The situation with regard to our recent problematology (linguistic and semantic) must hold, to some extent categorical terms – certain of these could do with some clarification before one proceeds to perspicuously internal questions. A lot of people do talk in category language about 'events' and 'things' etc. (certainly when they attempt classification of modes and disciplines) – and the situation is rather foggy; there is still a lot of hypostasization, which albeit illuminative, can never be categorically explicative.

J.J.C. Smart, in his essay 'The River of Time' (*Mind* 1949) states that 'Time facts are facts of before and after and of simultaneity. Events are after and before one-another or simultaneous with one-another and events are happenings to things'.

To say that 'changes change' is rubbish. Similarly, an object neither does nor does not happen. It must also be pointed out that 'become' is misused a great deal – something becomes something or other: the verb is transitive. Whitehead agrees that events don't change, but he has to say that they become, and by this he means, they come into existence. That's wrong, they occur or happen: 'to happen' is not at all equivalent to 'to come into existence'. One might say that a party was an event; also that an indication was an event; also the changing from hot to cold of the air of a room etc. The last two have important logical common properties which 'party' lacks. So far, events are just pretty rough. Some of the logical grammar of 'party' is analogous to that of 'room' when it's said that it 'changes': (this is not to suggest that to talk of changes in this sense is the only way to talk, there are far less anthropocentric ways of talking).

And the last two don't become anything if you rule out 'imminent' and 'probable' etc. Changings, becomings, beginnings, endings, reachings etc. are things on which one can't give a running commentary. Rates of change, (What's talked of in the differential calculus) might be said to change – and do – they are defined in terms of change, but that is not to say that they have the same properties. Now, 'party' is an event expression in its use in 'the party is upstairs' – but not in its use in 'the party got noisier'. Thus, starting, selling, finishing (and related ones) are events but 'the life of the thing' isn't. In that sense (above) ' ... (event) happened' makes sense, and ' ... (event) changed' is nonsense. (That excludes cases where an event may be said to 'change' from being future to being past – which is a strange thing to say – being rooted in the idea of 'flow' of time – and one can't ask 'how fast'?) Similarly, to say that an event 'became' anything is to talk nonsense. Now, it might be relevant to look for some continuant. McTaggart said that events don't change: that's absurd – they neither do nor do not change. The concept of change just doesn't come in. It's silly to think of the pastness, presentness and futurity of events as properties – even relational ones. Sculptures, etc. are normally regarded as three dimensional entities which endure through time – but this other dimension is easily obscured – the notion of the permanent in change conceals the fact that bodies extend through time – but that is not to say that it doesn't make sense to talk about a region of space becoming occupied – merely, it's possible to shift syntax so that the notions of change can't be accommodated.

It can be pointed out, then that the various distinctions between 'substances' and 'events', used to elucidate – or explicate distinctions between various modes, disciplines, etc. are categorically unsound – and that in certain contexts the contradistinction is entirely irrelevant (not only in its being misused etc.) for the purpose of 'separation'. To argue for the view that one is in a four dimensional continuum of space-time entities is no indication that the normally misused distinction is about to 'work' – it's still impossible to translate talk of events' changing in respect of pastness, presentness and futurity into a 'tenseless' vocabulary. (Cf. H. Reichenbach: Elements of Symbolic Logic 50–1, New York 1947.)

Certain postulates preserve the link between a theory and the concepts (or things) it concerns, in their function, at least, as paradigms for the formulation of hypotheses. From this point of view, a theory is a system of postulates from which specific or general 'descriptions' can be derived (formulated). (That's one view.) In so far as a postulate contains all the propositions that can be derived from it, a theory may be said to contain the specific hypotheses, and in so far as a theory is a system of postulates from which specific descriptions can be derived – it is, in this sense a general description of the various hypotheses (hypotheses' situations?) But neither the theories nor the postulates can be expected to give the necessary descriptions etc. of a particular state (or states) of affairs at a given time. All we can say, with any relevance, here, is that if a given state of affairs has certain characteristics, then its description will take the form of particular postulates – or of a particular postulate. From the point of view of its being a formal system alone, a theory asserts nothing about a situation etc. and therefore is not 'descriptive' in a strong sense. From this point of view, a theory is merely an uninterpreted system which has certain formation and transformation rules – the postulates are no more – or less than analytic, functioning as either syntactical rules or as premises for the deduction of further 'semiotic' or 'symbolic' (i.e. theoretical) expressions. The specific propositions that do describe something will have certain formal characteristics (definite formal characteristics), in virtue of which they can be brought together under specific postulates. these postulates may be bound more or less lucidly together according to some formal characteristics that they may have in common with a larger 'plan'.

The postulates become part of a single system, and thus function as syntactical rules or as premises in the system (theory) and as semantic rules for the formation of specific propositions needed for description – and as regulators for the semantic components which derive their meanings from the part they play. Alexander has said that it is misleading to say that specific propositions are derived from theory – he holds that they are derived from 'some higher level statements of theory'. Consequently, 'specific hypotheses' (e.g. Hutten's) are fenced in the theory only in a weak sense – and it's improper to say that they are derived from the theory. The better account is that the hypotheses are derived from the postulates and are contained within the theory only in a weak sense, since the theory itself does not determine the legitimacy of the specific hypotheses can be formed according to its postulates.

A question to be asked is, 'How many axes of interpretation are to be entertained in this connection?' Another is, 'How far away has one got here from 'frameworks'?' It seems that we don't just have to open-up criteria of 'acceptability'.

By declaring one area to be the 'area of attention' and another to be 'not the area of attention', then the area that is designated as 'not the area of attention' will demand a sufficient amount of attention for it to be acknowledged as 'not the area of attention'. One might also declare an area to be 'not the area of attention' as the only point to be attended to. But, even a 'not an area of attention' is assignated significance in that sense, then whatever is not in the 'not an area of attention' can be treated here as an area which is not attended to in an observational sense.

The air-conditioning as device

After a few weeks attempting to sort out indicators for the exhibition of non-entities model, Michael Baldwin remarked that he was not sure that the air-conditioning didn't constitute a separate focus. For myself, I made the decision that it suited my purposes to regard the air-conditioning as an integral part of the exhibition. Although one can see a possible situation where, if the air-conditioning were to be declared a separate focus, this separating from the exhibition might be used as a device to relate it to the exhibition. But here there is no need to set up this separate focus, rather, to use the air-conditioning as a means to examine the concepts of length and temperature.

Assuming the air-conditioning equipment is functioning then the room(s) will be filled with air-conditioned air. A question to be asked at this point; Is the air (air-conditioned or not) a permanent factor? And if it is, then how do we identify it as such? Let us consider firstly the question of identifiability.

We can start by examining how we detect temperature. The temperature of a body is a measure; that is a measure of its hotness. This can further be defined as a property the rate of which heat will be transferred to or from it. It is then reasonable to say that the temperature is a measure of the kinetic energy of the molecules, ions, atoms, of which matter is composed? Let us assume that we need an exhaustive description of the temperature throughout the rooms. We therefore need to make extensive analytic breakdowns. Firstly a million years of experience guides us to acknowledge the presence in the rooms of various bodies. The concept of a 'body' involves a measure of identifiability [1] and permanence. This measure of identifiability will, if it is to be a comprehensive analysis, mean a scale ranging from the macroscopic to the microscopic. A complete characterization of the body will demand the ability to specify what will be the result of every conceivable operation applied to the body. Any assumption that the body(ies) is inert or passive would be incorrect. Properties of a body are not always the same but change when the external circumstances of the body change (e.g. the density of a quantity of gas changes when the pressure is altered).

Thus empirical evidence points out clearly that the different properties of any concrete body are not capable of arbitrary variation, but they are linked to each other so that when certain properties have assigned values all others are uniquely fixed. Thus when the pressure of a gas (and the air-conditioning will be effective here) is fixed under certain simple conditions at the temperature of the room, its density, viscosity, thermal conductivity, dielectric constant, etc. are also fixed. This means that density, viscosity, etc. can be expressed as functions of pressure, which mathematically play the role of an independent variable. But by a transposition, pressure may be treated as a function of density, so that density might be sued as an independent variable, and pressure, viscosity, etc. become functions of it. It is the number of independent variables that is important. A more complete examination of the gas might well reveal the existence of more than one independent variable, such as, for example, the magnetic field. The qualitative aspects of the mathematical treatment is therefore a reflection of the precision of the measurements, since we might change from functions of one variable to functions of two variables merely by increasing the sensitiveness of our instruments.

To continue the examination of measurement further we will relate the way two magnitudes of the room are measured, namely those of volume and temperature.

The volume first. We can say that, as the walls are pre-accepted permanent factors (or as the area is a room rather, that, the walls will have surfaces which can be identified as inner and outer surface) as is anything which lies between the inner and outer surfaces of the wall. It is also reasonable to assume that the volume of air within the room(s) will be delineated by the inner surfaces of the walls, floor(s), ceiling(s). But we should be careful here in identifying just exactly what we mean by permanent factors. It is not so much that the air has an exact volume and an exact temperature which we can measure by using the appropriate instruments, but regardless of whether we measure them or not, we can say that the air has a volume and a temperature. Can't we?

Some thoughts on air-conditioning as a technical vehicle

Short of simply declaring a volume of free air open, the demonstration of the concept of non-exhibition object (situation) relies primarily on finding a site which exhibits what we choose to call the quality of being visually 'non-juicy' (this usage is obviously metaphorical and should be viewed with appropriate reservations). To define more precisely what we mean by a free air site; it could be a declaration to open the volume of air designated in its horizontal magnitudes by the geographical boundaries of Oxfordshire, Nebraska, etc. and in its vertical magnitude by an arbitrarily decided height, say 4,000 feet. We finally decided we would use a much more specific model. If one chooses to use air-conditioning then, of necessity, the volume to be used has to be a contained volume.

The room(s) had to be as bland as possible in its every

feature visually, in its audio aspects, olfactronically. As such the room allowed temperature non-emphasis to hold its own. To be a little more specific in describing the physical features of such a site: Walls ... they should offer a minimum of visual competition to the non-visual quality of the air-conditioning medium. Hence there was automatic elimination of any surface exhibiting any decorative emphasis, any pictorial climax or detail indication, any baroque, rococo, bizarre, exotic, anomalous or non-conformist architectural features. (The criteria for conformism having been specified by the 'minimum of visual competition' condition.) Obviously the vents for the air-conditioning equipment needed consideration in this context as they would constitute visual pointers. Also the floor should not be treated as if people were not allowed to walk on it, for the room needed a quality of abnormal normality (a kind of ultra-usualness). For instance to paint the whole thing grey would produce almost inevitably an expressionist object. We had to find a room which either was, or could be, stripped down to a maximum visual 'ordinariness'. Windows had to be considered. To choose a room without windows might well amount to producing a situation with expressionist mood overtones. On the other hand to view out onto the 'world outside' might well break up the visually bland quality.

The ceiling would probably be best white. The walls either light grey, white, cream, or some neutral colour in the grey, cream, beige, white range. One or two neon strip lights in ordinary castings, and fairly austere air conditioning vents would also be consistent with the required ultra-usual quality. A window or windows with halfopen or closed blinds would be acceptable.

Unless there is extreme of temperature present, either consistently or fluctuating from hot to cold and/or vice versa (the point here being that after a change from hot to cold a period might be produced which was nearer normal body temperature, and then followed by a change to cold and then to hot, thus the temperature sequence would run: hot ... normal ... cold ... hot ...), then temperature is usually considered as a secondary thing because, obviously, there is no strong tactile experience and no other sensual experience of temperature at all. The sensual situation here might be summed up in the following manner: That the temperature is not made a primary feature but that the total situation is brought down to the level of the temperature's 'secondary thing' quality.

What is required is the reinforcement of the take-it-for-granted quality of the temperature. Ideally this would be done by technically modifying the air-conditioning equipment to make it sensetive to any increase in temperature caused by the entrance of any person(s) into the room and to further enable it to regulate itself to ensure that the temperature would remain at a pre-decided constant normal level. Thus if the number of people in the room was of such a magnitude that the temperature would rise to an extreme level, the air-conditioning equipment would be required to blow out air of appropriate low temperature. The sound of the equipment would be acceptable as far as it would be consistent with visual elements ... the air-conditioning vents ... of the system. Sounds from outside should be kept at the normal level. Traditionally, the one essential that is demanded of ordinary matter is that of identifiability. This rather appears to be a mental or verbal demand made in order to facilitate thinking. There is nothing in the instrumental situation which dictates the need for identifiability. When we 'exhibit' air it is precisely this need for identifiability that most people would demand as a prerequisite of the model (situation). Although, apart from the walls and the usual features listed above, there is nothing to see, any assumption that the air-model is inert, and passive would be incorrect. The model is, as far as we can make it, visually 'non-juicy', any attempt at picturing (visualizing) the situation is merely evidence that the art-audience is stuck with its visual art-object. A question that might be asked here is, would there be a difference between a 'non-exhibition' model and a model that exhibits nothing?

Air Show

The fog bank is a macroscopic aggregate. There is no theoretical primacy here for this macroscopic aspect. That is, its importance or unimportance is shown up by raising and answering internal questions to the framework.

There is no rhapsody here.

The macroscopic aggregate can be subjected to a micro-reductive examination. The horizontal dimensions of a 'column' of air, atmosphere, 'void' etc. can be indicated and established (for all 'external' and practical purposes) by a visible demarcation in terms of horizontal dimensions, axis, etc. This could be done in a number of ways: e.g. through the indication of some points of contiguity with other 'things', or through the computation of a particular physical magnitude – e.g. temperature or pressure differences, etc. (this is not necessarily to advocate an instrumental situation). None of this is to say that a complete, if only 'factual' or constructual, specification is to be expected.

Obviously, when one talks of a column, there is some reference to a visual situation (from whence the vocabulary may or may not find support). There is a comparison to be made here between the 'air-conditioning situation' and the fog bank, in which the obvious physical differences between the 'matter' which constitutes the indicators of this or that 'boundary' can be made out. This is not to describe the difference between boundaries per se, nor is it to exclude the possibility of regarding 'boundaries' as 'entifications' of geometrical gaps.

Mostly, anyway, the questions of 'demarcation' are external ones of a practical nature. Still, they remain securely rooted in the perusal tradition, so long as one considers them in the context of particularizing characteristics at an observational level.

A lot of emphasis was placed on the microscopic mechanical aspects of procedure and process in the air-conditioning situation; it's easy to raise and answer the same sort of question here. The objection to doing this is based in a rejection of the problems of 'visualization' (and 'identification' in that context) on theoretical grounds. The microscopic picture has a counterweight origin in the macroscopic aspect of a situation. Whilst articulation on and identification of air as a 'thing' conforms to this tradition, the molecular mechanical concept of 'particle', 'flux', (of energy) and the 'thing', 'particle' identity systems appear to be incompatible. What is interesting about thermodynamics is that it is restricted to the formulation of necessary conditions for an occurrence (Cf. remarks on nomological implications, connections etc. as appropriate to these considerations, below.)

There is a challenge to the million years habit of identifying 'things'. The recognizance of something as something is another question bound up with aspects of things, and not solely with 'identification' per se. The structure of kinetic theory, for example, is built on the (extralinguistic, extralogical) mechanics of so-called 'common-sense' objects. There is a rooted assumption that the laws and concepts of Newtonian mechanics, 'proved' by experience to be valid for 'day to day objects', continue to have the same meaning beyond the macroscopic-microscopic domain as they do within it. The kinetic theory represents the micro-reductive approach to the study of the properties of material aggregates. It interprets thermal phenomena in terms of properties and interactions of the constituents of material assemblies. Thermodynamics, on the other hand, is not based on any definite assumptions as to the ultimate constitution of matter. The foundations are in very few general empirical principles (appertaining to the behaviour of complex thermal systems.)

Since the Greeks, speculation concerning the identity of matter has run directly toward the atomic theory. Bridgman held that there seems to be no logical or empirical justification for this. Rather, it seemed to him that it was a psychological fact that the search to 'identify' things demands the atomic particle concept. Persistently, even in a science like meteorology, which treats critically of thermal systems, the methodological and definitory approach is such that it draws exclusively from the kinetic theory of identity. (It is of interest to point out, here, that the meteorological phenomena which are most self-important (disruptive, etc.) are usually those with a visible aspect (macroscopic). 'Invisible fog' is self-contradictory in all common contexts of usage (i.e. 'Invisible' contradicts the formal sign 'fog' or 'cloud'. And both signs refer to the characteristics (in terms of 'visibility') of the meteorological objects to which they are assigned.)

The point here is not to make the gravamen of the discussion that people compulsively picture both assemblies which are such that they do fit the 'picturing' function and assemblies such that they do not. The suggestion is, rather, that the concept of identities like flux of heat and flux of energy might be inchoative; and that not only in the sense that the identity of heat and energy may be made clearer. This is a case of wondering about various aspects – the heat/energy identity is only held out on the grounds of a possible analogy with a situation internally relevant to these considerations: the prime consideration is that in the further development of what at the moment appear to be 'enigmatic' entities, there might be raised interpellations concerning e.g. the concept of identity etc. One of the big troubles in seeking extrapolations is that it is the function of extrapolations to explain and explanation always involves reducing terms to something familiar. And we do not want to get casuistically stuck with 'picturing' or with the pure or the alloy of visualization.

The air will have volume, determined by what we call the thermodynamic factors in the situation. Here we are talking about the fact that experience has learnt us to expect that everything has a volume and a temperature. It would be relevant here to examine the concepts of volume and temperature. Volume is calculated by measuring the various lengths and then multiplying the resulting measurements (height, length, width). The proper definition of length is that it is an extensive concept; that is larger amounts can be formed by reduplicating smaller amounts. It is not difficult in conceiving of a length of six inches as being simply a six-fold reduplication of a length unit of one inch. What is the procedure by which one assures oneself that one has measured the true temperature of a body? Probably it's not essentially different from that used with any other sort of measuring procedure. The factor of repetition is involved in the first place; we have to be able to repeat measurements on what we consider to be an identical system, and the only rigorous criteria is that all their history has been the same. There is little doubt that the physical manipulations with which we are most familiar and which we regard often as most important ignore the temperature factor to a first approximation.

Let us suppose our room has come to temperature equilibrium. There are several questions to ask here. Does the measuring scale used to measure volume have a different physical relationship to the concept of volume than the measuring scale we use to measure temperature has to the concept of temperature. D.C. Ipsen writes in his book 'Units, Dimensions and Dimensionless Numbers', p.76. 'Since the concept of temperature exists independent of any molecular notion of matter, it has generally been deemed more appropriate to regard its unit as well as its conception independent of any molecular description. The proper definition of a temperature unit has not been easy. Unlike mass, length and time, temperature is not an extensive concept; that is larger amounts cannot simply be formed by reduplication of smaller amounts.' Here we must consider the difference in computable magnitudes of volume and temperature. Volume can be altered to larger or smaller amounts not to higher or lower levels as with temperature. Consider some of the instruments used to measure temperature.

A brief definition of temperature has already been given stating that the temperature of a body is a measure of its hotness etc. Exactly how is this hotness measured? The instrument most commonly used for measuring temperature is a thermometer. Any physical property of a substance which varies with temperature can be used to measure temperature e.g. the volume of a liquid or gas maintained under fixed temperature; the pressure of a gas at a constant volume; the electrical resistence of a conductor; the EMF produced at a thermocouple junction, etc. The property chosen depends on the temperature range required, the accuracy required, and factors like how easily the thermometer can be made. The common mercury thermometer depends on the expansion of mercury with rise in temperature. The mercury is contained in a bulb attached to a narrow granduated sealed tube; the expansion of the mercury in the bulb causes a thin thread of it to rise in the tube. The latter is marked off in graduations of length units, each length unit representing a rise or fall in temperature of one degree, the length of the unit is decided by considerations concerning the expansive properties of the mercury. Thus we measure temperature by the same sort of unit that we use to measure volume, namely a unit of length. Defining temperature by relating it to expansion characteristics of particular materials is in most respects a satisfactory definition. But should a proper definition of temperature involve only an arbitrary specification of only a unit and not of a whole scale. The problem of the temperature scale was solved conceptually by the Second Law of Thermodynamics. The law revealed how a selected temperature unit could be reduplicated without reference to the particular properties of a particular substance, thereby giving temperature a fundamental definition.

It is relevant, here, to consider how far the conviction that atomic theories support the means whereby any phenomenon may be described and explained (and the view that theories are for explanation at all) corresponds to the one which seems to indicate a preoccupation of artists with 'exegesis' etc. from entities which paradigmatically instantiate assertions like ' … is over there, in that place etc. And how much can be shown up of a theoretical situation which is at most gerrymandered.

Schlesinger writes in his book 'Method in the Physical Sciences': … 'This conviction was shared by a number of other philosophers, notable among them Pierre

Duhem. They argue that a priori metaphysical doctrines and empirical evidence was that motivated scientists in their search for atomic theories to explain heat phenomena. The metaphysical doctrines in question derived, according to Mach and Duhem, from the mechanistic world view, which permeated all nineteenth century philosophy, a view in which mechanics was regarded as the most fundamental of all the sciences. Those who shared this belief in the superior status of mechanics were naturally keen to accept the hypothesis of the atomic theory of matter. It enabled them with the aid of kinetic theory, to explain thermal phenomena in terms of the mechanical properties of the molecules, thus reducing the science of heat to the science of mechanics. They believed that ultimately all science would be reduced to mechanics'.

It might be suggested that infatuation with the art 'object' (in the obdurate 'material' sense of 'object') has a connection with an analogous psychological fact. There has been a strong prejudice to correlate the category of 'existence' with a mechanical explanation and to glorify that category in non-cognitive contexts. There is, in this glorification, an inured disparagement of the category of possibility. The constants of the present situation are in no way held up in the concept of 'enduring substances'. Those invariant connections or categories are assumed which are capable of indicating and supporting (and of functioning as paradigms) developments (etc.) in the theoretical situation. (And this is not to put in a plea for some revision of the necessary questions of interpretation.) Despite the rather thrasonical aspects of the 'air-conditioning' situation, it might be said to siphon off as a protasis for an inverted Eurekaism. There is little point in dwelling on prognostications concerning relevant procedures and attitudes – certainly – in so far as one could easily fall into a dialectical carve-up of the various fields and purposes, etc. there is a danger of constantly asking outside questions.

Most people are intuitively uncertain with regard to the dimensions which may be assigned to temperature. And certainly, in this context, this may be because of the feeling that a (declarative) sentence is a statement of the physical nature of a quantity (as contained in a definition). But it could be said that the 'say-so' is concerned only with a restricted aspect of the way in which various physical operations may or may not enter: as far as necessary for a material implication to hold. One is not concerned with aping the dimensional formula (as an element in the theoretical situation) which is equally concerned only with restricted aspects of physical operations (e.g. the way in which the numerical quantity measure changes when the fundamental units change in magnitude.)

We can say that there is no prescriptive need to deal with any particular size of unit of measurement – one can regard temperature, etc. as having its own 'dimensions'. And this is no indication of a semantic elasticity of indicators – or rather – it neither is nor is not such an indication.

The theory is satisfactorily fomented on a lot of axis. One is that of 'mention' i.e. that a 'thing' is mentioned fulfils (or may fulfil) a condition for its coming up for the count. (And it should be pointed out here that 'mention' is distinct from 'use'). That this or that achieves 'mention' presupposes no external questions about it. And there is no indication of its being defective in any way. (e.g. being fictional, etc.) To argue a distinction between a construct of the air show theory and those of the perusal situation is pointless: one would have to argue through the common confusion centering on the mutual dependence of opposite determinations.

Syncretism is difficult with concepts which (on analogy with terms) remain multiply ambiguous. And this is one way to look at a lot of the concepts which enter much of the outside questions raising.

[1] By 'measure, of identifiability' I mean there are some bodies which are more easily identifiable than is, say, a molecule of hydrogen. To identify a molecule of hydrogen considerable instrumental refinement is needed to aid normal vision.

Note (1)
The 'Portrait of Iris Clert' et famille are very old. It reflects among others the view that 'what we have we hold': an anarchic blow at artistic jingoism. It ends up itself as jingoism. The point in this context is that there is no assertion as avante garde as 'this worthless scrap of paper etc. is a work of art and what is more I intend to sell it'. One is much more like everyone else. The questions which the above assertion seems to indicate are neither raised nor answered.

Note (2)
The specificity of a work as an indication of the legitimacy etc. of the mode which carries it: the preference statements which push up properties like those fall into theological aesthetics (Pythagorean) rather than any other discipline. Similarly with the things which are said for 'simple forms' etc.

LOST WRITING

Williamsburg 1996 diary
Fragment 1

To speak of trans-dimensional entities does not imply that these things exist in some pristine state elsewhere, in some safely inaccessible dimension or 'parallel reality'. There is no outside of the matter-energy system for humans or their abstractions. The entities of which I write function in and through the interface of concrete and abstract systems. They flourish on the contradictions established by humans to control their imaginary models of reality. As these subjectively internalised socio-cultural models become redundant, as they inevitably must, those human agents closest to the design flaws are taken first. Neither wholly concrete nor wholly imaginary the entities that emerge at the loci of social disintegration often have the capacity to inhabit their hosts and determine their actions. By capitalizing on the dysfunctional components of the control-communication systems implanted in the subject, the entities compose themselves from the evil detritus of the cultural imaginary, which has been destroyed, killed or banished by the ideal system.

Last night a blinding flash of light seemed to issue from the roots of my spine in a brilliant urinal light, up and out, freezing my entire body in hot paralysis. The idea of a 'screech owl', bursting unexpectedly from inside me, settled as the shock retreated. A screech owl. I could not move or feel my body and limbs, like they had gone into that state of numbness the other side of pins and needles, but nothing solid was restricting the blood flow. Why a screech owl? Is there such an animal?

The lycanthrope emerges, transmigrant entity at the

intersection of two time frames, never forgotten, kept alive in a script for children, who, under the forgetful eye of parental reason, inherit the dormant entities long considered the stuff of legend. The Nagual is not bound by biological law. It is not an animal. It is idea and possibility, a thing which travels while it sleeps in word and image.

Fetish – migrating along the maritime vectors of the colonial trade machine, fetish in form, fetish in mind, not so much the object of plunders as the adaptive radiation of a slowly evolving memetic seed.

Fetish – 1890, images absorbed, god's directed in theoretical labs, the pagan corresponds with the lunatic across time, under the watchful gaze of 'the doctor', fetish fuses with phallus, key component of the hysteria mechanism, the deranged body sprouting savage reliquaries of incest. Clocks running backwards. Shoes, beards, nylons, spoons animated by prehistoric sex force. Household appliances take control of ejaculation mechanisms. The scalped pianist's locks appease the wild girls. Mass hallucination, entranced mobs, moved by the abracadabra of the magician, the priest, the statesman, directors of the collective unconscious, the strategic historical mobilization of archetypes, mascot of battalions, the Virgin of Nicopeia.

Can the spirit which makes masses desire to take cities be revived? I dreamt that the streets were filled with mobs of ramshackle warriors united in their will to form an army and take the city as their own. Their appearance was pagan because their weapons and armour were designed for physical contest and signified virility and war far more than they could perform it. They were all men, much bigger than myself. At first I presumed I had travelled back in time but then I noticed the cars. This was a Metropolitan Mad Max scenario and the warriors were like drunken football hooligans. They beat on everything that was not them. I could recognize no difference in their heraldic markings, just as someone unfamiliar with soccer can't tell the difference between one team's shirt and another. They were all wearing sports wear customized for street warfare. I passed through the streets they were sacking without anxiety for my life. For some reason I was not the enemy. Judging by my uniform I seemed to be a member of some high command. I was looking for four members of the group, a group which I had, until recently, been conspiring with. Since my forced inscription to the services of The Column I was in charge of finding and turning-in all the last significant members of the loosely organized – too loosely it seems – counter-fascist groups. I kicked in the window of a basement where Betsy and four others were hiding. I got my men to round them up and bring them to the conference hall. I pulled the sign of my initiation from the space between by thumb and fore-finger; a shard of clear glass the size of a canine tooth.

We stepped out onto the street. It was night but a huge twister that was moving steadily towards us lit up the sky. Some people were panicking and looking for shelter as the winds began to pick up. I started to walk in its direction, against the flow of people running for cover. The twister; image of disastrous natural force generating itself for seduction, into an entity which humans intoxicated by terror might mistake for a god, a thing whose form is the delineated event of climatic energies, whose path across the solid surface of the globe leaves an undecipherable signature of destruction. I traced its form, saw the undulations, which rippled down its sides. Though it looked like a solid I knew it was not. If it was writing it was a writing of erasure. Its nib was a thousand square feet of immediate deconstruction. It seemed to be moving towards a fire, a huge fire. That was its cause, its attraction. Extreme heat in the … what do you call that space? … the sky. When the twister arrived above its destination it sucked up the flames which were consuming the building into itself. Thermodynamic food chain or orgy, this was the spectacle of self-consuming energetic monstrosities, the sublime climatic homology of a snake eating a spider.

When it was full and the fire extinguished, the twister became rotund and black, its form looser. Then in a thunderous convulsion it belched a torrent of lightening back up to the heavens.

Mira-Mira – La Materia – La Jefa

Carlos' stories gravitated towards this trinity of religious concepts as he told us the story of his magical cure. After drinking heavily for several months he had become partially paralysed and unable to continue his work in the hotel and the church. He thought he was going to die. An acquaintance suggested he visit a curandero which he did. The curandero told him that he could be cured but at a price that Carlos could not afford. Carlos visited a second curandero. Again, he could be cured but the price was too high. Worse still, the second curandero told Carlos the precise date he would die if he didn't buy the cure. Carlos was getting iller and the prediction of his imminent death wasn't helping. Eventually a member of a family for whom Carlos had made wedding decorations told him that the family grandmother was a powerful healer, and that, because Carlos had helped them, she would help him, free of charge.

He visited the curandera in a local village a few miles from Catemaco. First she told him to consider which of his friends may have put a curse on him, to go home, think about it and return later. This he did. But in contemplating which of his friends may have cursed him he realised that in fact he had no true friends. All his friends were merely drinking companions. And none cared about him enough to buy him a curse (or a cure). He returned to the curandera and told her. This, she said, was good and the cure began.

First she passed a black cockerel over his body several times. While she did so the bird flapped and squawked wildly. Suddenly she wrenched the cockerel away from his body and it was dead. The curandera then threw the cockerel onto the fire along with the trash. As it burned multi-coloured flames arose from its body and as they did so Carlos felt the spirit return to his own body. This, he said, was 'Mira Mira', the passing of life-death forces from one body to another. It was 'Materia' which made this possible. Or put differently, it was on the plane of 'Materia' that 'Mira Mira' operated. Carlos closed his eyes as he explained. Materia is what we feel as present but cannot see, what we only know properly with our eyes closed.

I asked Carlos if there were such curanderas here in Catemaco. No, he told me, only in the surrounding villages – Sontecomapam, Sihuapam, Comahuapam – but there were templos. "Templos?" I asked "como iglesias?". "No son iglesias. Son lugares del esprit-isimo". It is here that they have the knowledge of the Mira-Mira, la Materia and La Jefa.

Carlos began to explain La Jefa, Ranu ran an association thread between his story, third-eyes and Indian bindis. This deflected me onto Ash Wednesday, and the ash on the forehead, ashes to ashes, etc. I lost my thread to La Jefa.

Ranu had started to dance around the balcony. She wanted to go swimming. We picked up our bottles and walked down to the water. Ranu took off her shoes, hitched her skirt and began to wade into the lake. It was night. A street light illuminated the water for no more than a few yards. After that it was all night. She waded up to her thighs then turned back to the shore. Before she stepped back onto the sand, Carlos took off his T-shirt and dried her feet.

Williamsburg 1996 diary
Fragment 2

We walked out of the village to the place where the stoner's hung out, a place of karmic significance, they said. There, in what looked like the ruins of buildings, formations of white shells had been made. Most of the shells were mussel shells, wrapped into forms by rusted wire. The old fella put his face close to mine and began to confide in me. Trust shifted to suspicion as he continued his diatribe against the young hippies who were "all excited about extra-terrestrials". He told me that <u>we</u> knew that there was nothing 'Hollywood' about aliens, that <u>we</u> had been communicating with them directly for years. His stubble was turning grey.

We were sitting around a campfire. I looked into the girl's face, the weight of recent events poised like elastic. Her blonde-bob was all that remained over a metal skull. Her face receded through plates of alloy and glass, wire grids where her brain should have been. She was calm now. They had removed all traces of subjectivity – it was making her, and everyone around her, unnecessarily distraught. I had wanted her to stay. The replacement of her subjectivity was the cost. They had removed any organic component, which might harbour its germ. What was left? The blonde bob. I tried to make conversation with the famous actors around the campfire. I told them I would never act again, that the experience of making this film was too much to bear. The one with the droopy moustache suddenly remembered something that made his eyes widen. Flash into earlier scene, the image flickering in and out of vision … he remembered … she sat there waiting … the magic they had messed about with a few weeks ago … how the message was … he didn't think anything of it at the time … but now … the message was … he remembered … pulling it out of his stomach … we watched the recalled scene cutting into our imaginations, our memory ... a red-brown ribbon of words pulled from his stomach which ... she started to convulse ... in this same place but before ... the words spoke to the remnants of herself still trapped within the casing, still left in the form of her substituted body ... she convulsed, jerked ... we pulled back ... the moustache backed up against a fence ... hands burst through from behind, held his head, eyes still wide as a knife slashed slowly through his throat and black blood poured down his shirt. Suddenly they were everywhere, American teenage psychos in death-metal T-shirts drunk on beer slashing everything in sight to pieces. Arms hacked off at the stumps, guts sliced from the genitals upwards, slashing the others, slashing themselves, like they were dancing a butcher's drunken choreography. I felt the razor cut into my spine, slicing through to the bone, once, twice, three times the knife cut deeper ... I tried to feel the skin as it peeled off the bone but could feel only this line being cut again and again ...

What is happening?

Two nights ago I was visited by a shadow. Its presence I associated gradually with *El Tigre*, the 'Brujo Major' of Catemaco with whom we negotiated a video interview in 1998. Our encounter refreshed the depths of superstition and dread I harbour. Is this is <u>my</u> pay-off, the good I secretly, wishfully bought?

On both occasions in the dream I initially mistook the shadow for a corporeal presence whose immediate issue was terror. When I realized it was only a bodiless shade the terror subsided and transformed into an exquisite and fluid dread which flowed through my being. I <u>knew</u> about mythical shadow-presences but I had never before <u>experienced</u> one. How is one to explain the difference between that which one knows <u>about</u> and that which one knows by <u>experience</u>? These are different kinds of knowing.

I began to formulate a strategy of counter-magic. Pleasure is the beginning of a contest. In dreams and elsewhere I would wage an invisible contest with the Brujo's shadow. But what is a contest that takes place only in the minds of the contestants? Where is the spectacle, where the performance, where the art? Perhaps there is no other player. Perhaps it is nothing more than my own shadow, detached from its body, which I deliriously mistake for an other, an other with whom to compete.

<u>And here in this doubting-desire, in the invisible contest with an imaginary adversary, is 'magic'.</u>

This idea is sufficient. Once the idea of the Brujo's shadow presence, mistaken or otherwise, has confronted me in my dreams, the pleasure of the contest only serves to increase the power of the presence, a presence which, I will, at the risk of my sanity and life, into existence and then into honourable defeat. For the sake of the contest, for the sake of 'The Work'. The best magic involves this celebratory fabulation of a terrifying adversary. If the choice is between the parodic intensification of illusions or wilful forgetting, it must be the former. It is 'productive' and it is 'delirious'.

Such procedures, such choices, are the kernel of the Narco-Satanicos project: the will to describe the process by which the relation between an image and its substance teases out this play of magic, between terror and fabulation. And this is why the *absent, lame and essential* word is so relevant. 'True' in the way a line is true, in the way a rendition of a form is true to its model, honest in the same way, veracity at the limits of technical possibility; the will to accuracy. This imperative in the rendering of thought, the thought

420

which seeks to know itself as it conceives the senses perceiving, the thinking relation between the similar and the different, thinking what is and what is not a consequence of itself, the truth of events and the impossibility of that truth. Accuracy at the limits of the possible difference between fact and fantasy. True the way a line is true, a copy is true.

'Integrity' recalls the architect's blueprint, the technical trace of the draughtsman and anatomist. The philosophical meanings of 'integrity' are unnecessary for this recollection. Its ethical meanings seem more imperative. It is the magic word where the oppositions ordering the difference between fact and fiction, truth and illusion, real and imaginary intersect; mumbo-jumbo, hocus-pocus, hoodwinking, hoodoo, balderdash, and codswallop. The veracious syllabic, semantic ordering of history and difference collapsing the subject into delirium, the space of terror and affirmation. A quest for the concrete, rational roots of our magic, for roots which devour themselves AS AN offensive STRATEGY ...

"Are you thinking this *El Tigre* ... do we have weapons we can trade?"

'The Work' is motivated by irreconcilliation, para-doxical intent. My strategy is integral to the sense of contradiction in the act of representation.

Victory or defeat are the only possible outcomes of the work. The creative act is a contest and the best contests are those where and when the outcome is least secure and the stakes are highest. The struggle with the shad-ow, with the Brujo, is a mere prelude. The only politics here will involve the strategic spin-offs of the game.

"Tenemos armas"

Against what ? We are still at war with Control and its Reality Studios. We are at war with that which contains us. We will use the master-builder's tools against their orders. Magic covers us. A perpetual feint. The decisive blow requires precision and integrity. Or do I confuse means with ends?

"Tranquillo companero, estan muy lejos"

And always this; "What happened?", "What is happening?" "What will happen?"

The receivers must feel "What is happening."

If not, Control remains intact.

Into the impossible-possible, as true as possible, to the inter-section.

Dream of Hotel Tajin

We arrived in Papantla at 4 am, an hour earlier than scheduled. It was raining – lightly but steadily. We got coffees from an all-night taqueria next to the Pemex station. It was too long to wait till daylight so we decided to find the one hotel our sleepy host said would be open – Hotel Tajin.

The hotel looked closed but a blurry eyed, unflustered concierge let us in and turned on the reception light. Hotel Tajin was purpose-built in the 1930's, with grand views over the city from each floor. It was painted bright turquoise on the outside and decorated with deep blue ceramic tiles and dark wood on the interior. The room price was over the odds. We got into bed at 4.30 am.

I knew it would be difficult to enter sleep this late and so tired. I was the kind of tired where sleep becomes a too-tangible thing, arriving like paralysis or convulsion, gripping the body before the mind has been sedated. First there was the dog. It was Theresa's dog, Coba, racing around the room screeching with the ear-piercing bark that dogs emit when over-excited. Coba was in the room.

Then I was in the reception hall of a grand hotel. It was night. A first floor balcony circled the hall. I felt that

I could fly and learned how to do so by standing on a large white dinner plate. It was difficult at first, like learning to ride a skateboard, but soon I had mastered it and began surfing through the hall-space. I had become demonic and vampiric. I took it as my calling to swoop down on unwary receptionists and waitresses and subject them to my incubine passions. I was best acquainted with a woman who was dead. Her body, as I fucked her, felt like it was stuffed with straw. Beneath her dry skin I could feel the hard lumps of desiccated organs. As we fucked my mouth filled with lumpy vomit, which further fuelled my lust. Through the French windows beside us William Burroughs entered from the night. I felt somewhat embarrassed in his presence – not because of the fucking but because of my unbridled enthusiasm for this abject state of affairs. He didn't say much before he turned to leave. I didn't even know if it was me he addressed when he said, "Go tell the Texans".

Los Disparacidos

"No son disparacidos que estoy buscando" said Mario as he leafed obsessively through the pages. He was looking for the image of serpents leaving the necks of beheaded Mayan ball-players. We weren't sure why this was so important but as usual we detected in Mario's enthusiasm something of great significance.

We had been discussing the importance of 'la feria', its coincidence with Semana Santa and the ancient rites of spring still recognized by the indigenous Mayan population. Mario had shown us a photograph of a frieze from one of the local pyramids – I can't remember which – showing how an image of the god-king of this particular city had been defaced. The defacing, Mario argued, had taken place during a popular uprising at the end of a particular calendric cycle. After the uprising, the city had been permanently abandoned. He pointed out how the image of the conejo (rabbit) god had been left intact. The conejo was god of the moon, drunkenness and fertility, the multiple-one. Perhaps, he conjectured, the uprising had coincided with the feast day of the conejo, that a rabbit rebellion had destroyed the city and its godly representatives.

It was Semana Santa, Easter, the time of the rabbit. In the Zocalo of San Cristobal the Judases had been hung ready for their traditional consummation on Easter Saturday. We wanted to get out on the streets to see the celebrations but Mario seemed reluctant. It was as if he foresaw something terrible in the coincidences we pursued; the portent of an imminent rabbit uprising. And Mario, more than any other person I have met in Mexico, has the utmost respect for the potential violence of the local Indegena. He told us that when he was a student the academic orthodoxy insisted on the innate pacifism of the Maya. They were noble savages and mystical sages, a world apart from the bloodthirsty and cannibalistic Miztecas. Mario's great grandfather, the ex-governor of San Cristobal was not of this ilk. He had seen fit to repress any Tzetzal resistance to the colonial regime by cutting their ears off *en masse*.

Centre of the outskirts

I was closely connected to a cult of vampiric murderers. My studies had led me to them and I had struck up an intellectual friendship with the leader. The cult operated under the guise of a Christian sect. Far from being anathema the cult were considered by local outsiders as fundamentalists whose integrity to a strict moral code gave them an air of great reverence.

[This 'integrity' escaped and haunted me on the bus from Catemaco. It was replaced by series of approximate terms; 'veracity', 'truth', 'sincerity'. It signifies the thing that cannot be represented on film, the distinction between the actual thing and its visual representative. Is this, or is this not <u>the</u> bed on which the dream took place? The viewer will never know. The narrator might as well be lying. The responsibility for honesty resides in the producer, not the receiver, for whom everything represented is as good as a lie. It is a question of 'remaining true' to the facts, to the details, to the actual. Why should this be so important? Surely any bed would do. Why should it be <u>the</u> bed? Because in actuality it was a <u>particular</u> bed and it is as if one has a duty to be as true to a bed as to anything else. The person who represents may be an ignoramus, a fool, a retard, but whatever integrity is, it is what matters most].

The 'lame, absent, veracity' of the group was awe inspiring and terrifying to the locals, believers or not. Now <u>I</u> knew that the upper hierarchy of this group consisted of vampiric zombies who had been dismembering and burying bodies left, right and centre on the outskirts of the town. The high priest regarded me as a kindred spirit, but an intellectual one, rather than a follower. The followers would have had me butchered at the drop of a hat had it not been for their leader's pleasure in discussing, over supper, his favourite lofty topics; ethics, philosophy, comparative religions etc. But I knew it was only a question of time before our discussions would reach an impasse. Most of my arguments involved feints of sophistry which the Sacerdote seemed to relish – the way a cat relishes playing with its prey.

My conversations with him had the character of a chess game. We both knew there was an end to the game and that he was always going to win. I was only alive because he knew I had no desire to beat him. I only wanted to match his moves and learn. He enjoyed having such an attentive pupil. I was, in some way, a reflection of his self-worth and would remain so as long as I refused to become a follower, as long as I continued to pose difficult counter-arguments and alternative perspectives on his truth. But I knew he lived a truth I could not, a murderous truth and the checkmate awaiting me.

The cult were planning a 'mass conversion' timed to coincide with a major soccer tournament. They would infiltrate fans from the opposing sides and promote a violent confrontation culminating in a bloody sacrificial massacre. I had unwittingly invited friends to come and stay during the time of the tournament. The crowds were collecting in the streets waiting for the kick off. I wasn't sure exactly when the congregation would leave the chapel and was desperately trying to think of a way stop my friends attending a match for which they had been waiting for several months and travelled hundreds of miles to see. I wasn't even sure that the massacre was really going to take place.

Ranu arrived the day of the planned massacre. We chatted on a bench outside the Sacerdote's house. My hushed tones intimated my foreboding to her but I didn't dare tell her what was actually going on. I feared for her life and my own. But telling her what I could about what I had learned made me aware of how few people I had spoken too during my stay in the town. I knew who the followers were and, though I had never witnessed a sacrifice, I had seen people arrive in town and disappear shortly afterwards without trace. There were all sorts of elaborate stories about where the people had gone. All such stories originated from the cult. So well trusted was the Sacerdote that even family members of the local victims were reassured by his explanations. The local police department, the chief of which was a high-ranking member of the cult, supported the integrity of the stories.

As I continued talking to Ranu I became more and more conscious of just how much I knew. It was <u>too</u> much. Not only would I not be able to separate myself from involvement with the cult, and thus take a share in their guilt and punishment (when or if they were exposed to the light of some 'other' authority) but also I would never be allowed to leave the town knowing all that I did.

My knowledge became a curse that by communicating would condemn the hearer to my own immanent fate. I would either have to voluntarily disappear or be disappeared. My knowing guilt I would have to live with in silence and solitude. Perhaps, at the edge of my grave at the centre of the outskirts, I might let the curse circulate, like vengeance.

Orisha dream, Catemaco, 04/03/98

I left the bed three times last night. The first time was to piss. The second was a repetition of the first but I didn't actually leave. As I stood up I was aware of the sheets glowing blue in the nocturnal light. I knew I was about to begin a phase if lucid dreaming – or dreamt I knew. I awoke, properly this time, curled up in the sheets.

The next time I floated up into the air above the bed, still shrouded in the crisp cotton. I was still in the same room but heading for a different state. I knew from past experience that this was going to be a intensive voyage. You don't start floating around your hotel room in the middle of the night unless something important is about to take place.

I braced myself, relaxed, prepared for the acceleration that I knew, for whatever reason, was about to kick in.

Then I was hanging upside down staring at the Christmas tree baubles, enamoured by their splendour. These were THE Christmas tree baubles, the ones we had as children, the very ones. It was like seeing them again, for the first time, in their vivid, tangible actuality. One in particular – the King/Queen of the baubles – was bigger than the rest, most of its surface covered in that dry red powder and ringed with brittle bands of white and silver glitter. Small sections were left to reveal the brilliant red chrome underneath.

The baubles turned into simple spherical heads, the heads of stick puppets, and each one the head of an Orisha hanging upside down from the tree. Their eyes and mouths were nothing more than flat blank discs. The one directly before me was purple. To the left, at a distance, was the yellow face of Oshun. I wanted to be her's but was informed by some invisible authority that I should first consult the presence behind my left shoulder. There I found a redheaded doll. It was Erzulie Ze Rouge. It was not her but the purple Orisha who was to be my communicant. I was overawed and subjugated myself in erotic compliance. Each urge to further supplication brought the doll closer to human form. This becoming human-in-form was driven by the dual urge of supplication and sexual desire. As I desired her breasts to stroke, her shoulders formed in curves of smooth carved wood. I wanted to kiss her feet and the wood curved into legs.

To my left sat a black man who spoke in a mildly camp manner. "Well, if you're not going to do it, I'd better", he said. He pushed aside a small dam of soil and the water flowed down a small trench to the base of a flat wooden carving of three joined figures. The outer two, who flanked the taller central figure, wore tall brimmed hats.

By now I was carrying the Orisha on my shoulders. I could feel the thickness, heat and strength of her thighs as they gripped the back of my neck. I stood up and began to carry her around the room. The other Orishas had taken form too and were being carried around the room by others.

I wanted to kiss the sex of the purple Orisha but doing so would have meant turning my head around. She asked to be put down. This was not out of hombrage. The divinity wanted my desiring-veneration since it was this that brought her into the human world. But I knew that if she dismounted our communication would be broken.

Suddenly I was dancing frenetically with the others and the Orisha was gone. The dancing was a complex pattern of violent stamping which filled the room with an ineluctable frenzy of moving bodies. Then I was dancing alone, in my empty hotel room, in the middle of the night. Panicked, I ran to the door to try and break out of the dream. I ran up a flight of stairs, though a cafe and back down into my room by another staircase. The room had turned into a store, the kind you find in airports, selling trinkets, souvenirs, confectionary and luxury goods. I was looking for the Orishas again but all I could find were four old tobacco-stained cigarette cards depicting lithographs of French sailors from the 18th and 19th centuries. On the counter was the current issue of *La Monde*, on its blue cover a circle of stars representing the European Union. Pablo was at the counter. I was severely distressed. He tried to console me. "John", he said, "I hear you think you're in some alternate reality, that you're not really here. Is everything okay?". He was trying to help. But he was also trying to convince me that THIS reality was THE reality. For an instant I wondered if perhaps I had never been in the room sleeping, that THAT was the dreaming part. But then I thought of Mannie and his plans to explode

Peyote-inspired reality bombs and I said to Pablo "Yes, you're right. I did think I was in another reality BECAUSE I WAS IN ANOTHER REALITY!". Now I knew this was a risk. That <u>could</u> have been <u>the real</u> reality, in which case I was about to commit myself to perpetual delirium. I ran out of the store and in a manner that is becoming common, I lunged back into present, into my bed, the hotel room, and the nocturnal blue-glow of the cotton sheets.

Williamsburg 1996 diary
Fragment 3

We entered the peasant's home. The girl child was close to death. The doctor cured her. It was received as a miracle. The child was mute from then and imagined to be a chosen one. Alters were lit in her room. Soon she was being visited by people in the village, to seek her guidance. She was possessed of miracles. As she grew older her attachment to the doctor grew stronger. He didn't notice until one day to his embarrassment the girl, in front of her family and the doctor's lover, began to rub her crotch over his legs as he sat drinking a cup of tea. The girl's advances were as unprovocative as they were unexpected. It seems she believed her and the doctor were cosmically married and her power was such in the community that they believed it too. The doctor's lover looked over in horror. The doctor had no choice. In the tragic climax of the narrative the director willed the girl not to have survived and no one to have remembered. The audience wept.

SOMETHING TO DO WITH WORDS

In the evenings take Andrew Williamson to a deserted house some thirty minutes from where you are holding him. Beat him and apply electric shocks all over his body. After handcuffing his wrists behind his body, hoist him in the air and let him hang for thirty minutes. As a result of the hanging, his left hand will be paralysed.

Tie Art & Language's hands behind their backs and bind their eyes. Beat their heads and bodies black and blue with rifle butts. This will break the bones on the extremities of their arms and legs. Cut off two fingers from each of their hands. Shoot them in the stomach or in the heart, as well as in the head.

Capture Clara Ursitti, strip her to her underwear, and dunk her in water. After a fruitless walk for several hours, with Clara Ursitti leading the way, return to her home, where she will help you pick up her friends and family. Line them all up, together with one of your own men dressed in a ski-mask. He nods or shakes his head as the friends and family file past.

Sodomize David Burrows with batons, force him to walk between ranks of guards while being beaten and kicked, as well as beaten on his testicles.

Tell Esther Plannas to take off her T-shirt. Pull out a folding knife. Then ask her for her name. Carve expletives into her back. It should take about five minutes. It will be painful, and she shouldn't be able to move. She will make it easy to write because she will firm up her body to take the pain.

Catch Fabienne Audéoud's head in the car door and kick her several times in the abdomen. Sit beside her in the back of the car and beat her with all your might with your fists and elbows all the way to the appointed place.

Cut off the extremities of the fingers and give Graham

Ramsay's hands a severe pounding. Cut off both ears. Tie his hands behind his back with wire, so tightly that the wire cuts into his flesh. During interrogation, use cigarette butts to burn him above his eyes, on his cheeks and on his neck. Also burn him in more sensitive and degrading areas such as the inner thigh. His arms, elbows and shoulder blades can be broken. Hit him on the front and back of his rib cage with a long blunt object if you can find one. Skin his right cheek and the right side of his neck. Finally shoot him in the forehead.

Severely beat Inventory and, when you're done, throw a grenade at them. Finally, empty canisters of petrol over the men and set them on fire.

Beat Jake Chapman almost beyond recognition. Beat him until his left eye is missing, his face swollen and a large hole has been smashed in the back of his head.

Handcuff John Cussans and hang him by the cuffs from a beam. Beat and kick him in the stomach. Put a plastic bag over his head several times until he is forced to confess what you require of him. At one point beat him repeatedly to get him to confess to having stolen a large amount of money.

Just beat John Russell and hang him naked to a horizontal bar and beat him more. Keep him hanging and beat him with a nightstick for three and a half hours. Beat him this time to make him say that no one had beaten him, that he had just fallen down the stairs and broken his ribs and legs. Keep him in the cold room and beat him like this for four days until finally he breaks down and says or does exactly what you ask.

Strip Lucy McKenzie naked and rape her several times. Then insert a glass bottle up her anal passage, as a result of which she will receive several injuries.

Sit Martin McGeown on the ground. Take a spade and start beating him with the metal part. Tell him to put his palms on his knees, and start beating him with the spade, trying to hit him on the head. When he raises his hands to protect his head, and every time he puts his hands up, beat him on his legs and arms. Then leave. Have two friends standing by with machine guns throughout.

Detain Nick Land at the military base where he will spend the night. Tie him with a rope, hooded and hung by his feet from the beam of a house belonging to his neighbour. Use a cup of water to make him choke. Take him to a ravine in the hills, where you will repeatedly dunk him head-first in a stream, with soldiers sitting on him to prevent him from moving. Ask him where the weapons are hidden. If he says he hasn't any idea give him no food. Make him sign a declaration but do not allow him to read the statement.

Force Johnny de Philo to undress and try to grope her genitals. For four days, force her to accompany the troops to various hamlets in the area, where more detainees are picked up. Take her and two girls by the hair, dunk them in water, and force them to undress and wash naked in front of a group of male soldiers.

THE PLAGIARIST

Prologue

The spirit is a bone, it sounds absurd I know but it is true.

The spirit is a bone. The body of Christ is a loaf of bread, the spirit of Mao is a red book, the modern spirit is perspex and chrome. All true.

The spirit always takes some form or other, a colour or hue, a gesture or haircut, an attitude or a tone of voice, otherwise there would be no spirit or Zeitgeist worth speaking of. This simple axiom is the first lesson Dominic Rolex taught me. It was the secret of his success. He had the knack, you see, of becoming it at will, anywhere, anytime.

I am not attempting to perform a clever play on words but simply trying to establish the power of the man, to clarify why he was so attractive and such a compelling personality. He could materialise the spirit of the moment out of nothing, from the flicker of an eyelash or a simple smile, and the whole world would fall under his spell. That was his trick, the front of the man, but that wasn't why I fell for him. When I realised the destruction and the sweet devastation he was capable of I knew I would follow him to the end of the earth.

My brief affair with Dominic Rolex triggered a revelation about my own character: I had an appetite for destruction and it was this craving that drove me into his arms. I did not assist Dominic Rolex because I believed in his cause, quite the opposite is true, and it was not that I thought disaster a just punishment for an immoral and mundane world that, I admit, bored the tits off me. No, there was no grand idea motivating my behaviour, I was just trying to appease my craving. And, now that I have met my end and look back on my short life, I realise I have always been drawn to catastrophe. The chance to rub shoulders with disaster, to stare into the faces of victims and taste brick dust and burnt metal in the air, such occasions have never failed to set my pulse racing. The opportunity to become intimate with disaster influenced my choice of career, I am sure of it. I was a first rate journalist and ambulance chaser, the demise of the rich and famous, in particular, brought goose bumps to my flesh. It was my speciality. You see, my nihilism is not intellectual but comes from somewhere deep inside.

How is it I can tell my story after announcing that I have met my end? How is it I can still write after announcing my own demise? No doubt you have come across such narrative devices before. A voice from the other side. Another tiresome variation on the body floating face down in a swimming pool, reflecting on fate, the dead writer recounting the final episodes of his sordid life. But that is not the end I refer to at all. I am not dead, only nearly. Destitute, crippled, terminally ill, yes, deceased no. I am still breathing but only just. I shall be dead soon enough, perhaps next month. By then it will be April or May. I might be wrong, I might yet live to see a human cloned or war break out in the East. Indeed I would not put it past me to see the autumn colours arrive in the window displays of Oxford Street, an event I always look forward to, but I do not think so, I do not think I am wrong in saying these joys will be celebrated without me. But I am not a corpse yet and I am not writing from beyond the grave. I would not like to impose such an idiotic scheme on anyone. I detest that kind of thing and all such inane devices, in fact I find all narration an absurd enterprise. Even writing this prologue, which signals my final visit to the keyboard, leaves me bored and irritated. But what choice do I have?

These days I find writing an aggravation. It is difficult not to slip into common devices or to fall upon another's phrases. But then my story, like all stories, is larger than one voice and memory can manage. And there is always a little snippet of this and that in the cut if a story is well tailored for an audience. This was another of Dominic Rolex's lessons. Everything the man did, every look and expression, even down to the way he carried himself, all seemed refreshing and new but reassuringly familiar too. *Don't question what works or it will leave you behind,* he once said. Am I getting too metaphysical? I apologise. It is just my way of forgetting how miserable I am.

Still, as upsetting as I have found writing this tale to be, I have tried hard not to rush things and to stay true to events, despite events being somewhat hazy and indistinct. Where possible, I have used transcripts of recordings. For the rest of my story, a good half in fact, I have had to make it up with vague memories, informed guess work and borrowed words. It would not be the first time, I am good at making things up, it is one of my abilities.

I remember the beginning of my downfall with clarity though, and the bastard responsible. It was that fucking cop. All day I have remained calm but I can feel my disgust rising at the thought of him. I recognised that cop the second I saw him, I remembered his voice, his quivering speech and superior manner. I knew that cop when he was squashing shop lifters and double parkers. Now the cunt was a Detective Inspector. Day after day he pestered me with his inquiries but not one flicker of recognition crossed his face, not a mention of our past encounter. I knew him well enough though, Clark-Kent-good-looks, his affected manner of speaking, distant and conceited. I had last seen him five years ago. I was working a suicide: famous TV slut and dead rock singer's wife overdosed in her bedroom, stupid cow. Young daughter discovered *Mummy* dead to the world in a sea of glossies, vomit and needles, she telephones a family friend who asks, *What is it flower?*

Mummy's lips are blue, mummy's not well, she's all blue, came the reply.

I was trying to get a look at the body and there he was the prick, Nelson Verso, eulogising over the corpse. Like all autodidacts he was a menace and a crushing bore. *The Spartans, the most disciplined and noble people who ever existed, they lived not for individual gain but for the fulfilment of the collective spirit and duty.* I laughed in his fool of a face. It was a mistake. I said *they were like all nobility: savage and vain, thought women reproductive chattel and when they weren't fighting each other they sat around wanking each other off.* The cunt called me a foul-mouthed ghoul, arrested me for obstruction and had me held in a police cell for two days.

Oh Yes, I knew Detective Inspector Verso, and his no-mark colleague, Detective Sergeant Robert Routledge.

Verso and Routledge, may you burn in hell.

One
The spirit is a decaf latte.

So here it begins with a recording of my first interview – they let you keep a copy for your own records. I said far too much at this meeting but then I was trying to appear helpful and I didn't want to be charged. I wanted to avoid any scandal being attached to my name. Unfortunately I was loaded when picked up, a walking pharmacy. I was nervous too, and uncomfortable, it was that interview room that made me nervous. The room was brightly lit and scrubbed clean but it smelt – I hope this isn't taken the wrong way – it smelt of other people.

I should explain something about myself and my nature, which creates no small difficulty in my relationships with others. I possess a perfectly uncanny sensitivity, so that I perceive physiologically – smell – I mean a person's insides, the shit and entrails of every soul.

I have often been the first to arrive at the scene of a car crash or suicide and viewed the digestive tract smeared across the tarmac or pavement – the deep purples and crimsons, the Venetian tints and brilliant vermilions – and enjoyed the spectacle. But this sensitivity to the guts of the living, on occasion, causes extreme disgust and distress. I have, in this sensitivity, a psychological antennae with which I touch and take hold of every secret. My sixth sense has assisted me greatly in my profession but it sometimes makes contact with others a trial. I take hold of all the concealed dirt at the bottom of any nature, all is known to me at first contact. And, in this room, underneath the scent of pine forest floor cleaner I could detect the smell of a thousand corrupted souls who had sweated and gasped their way through lengthy interrogations and tearful statements.

But several notes above the terrible perfume of the room there was the stench of the two policemen, Verso and Routledge, a ghastly stink which no amount of Yves Saint Laurent deodorant and aftershave could mask.

The interview was a drain on my nerves and I cringe at my willingness to play the good citizen. If only I had kept my mouth shut. Or if only my voice had cracked and dried up from grief, but that is not an emotion I have ever been familiar with. My downfall was that I always have something to say, it is another of my abilities, I am never lost for words. I nodded and smiled when Verso and Routledge introduced themselves a second time for the tape. This is how it began:

439

'Miss Mercedes, will you please tell us everything you remember about that night, no detail is too small, I can assure you.'

'Well, I was working the cafes and bars of Soho with Mark, we didn't do bad. Tongues were loose that night. There were a lot of easy pickings and greedy fists at every port of call. When we had had enough to pad out two report sheets we headed for Rizzo Peroni's cafe. As we walked we discussed the evening's haul of gossip: the new suppliers, the dark horses and this week's losers. We liked our work ... or in Mark's case I should say he enjoyed his work – we took particular delight in discussing the recently fallen ... '

'Do you mean recently deceased Miss Mercedes? If you do, please say so'

'No, I do not mean recently deceased, Inspector Verso,' *you foul smelling slug-shit* I had thought, 'I mean those once glorious animals that had fallen from grace and sunk to the bottom of the mire, prime candidates for a life of petty crime or prostitution, or a career as a sales assistant at Footlocker. Mark offered his usual prayer for the has-beens and the terminally bloated, *pity those whose arses have ballooned, whose cheekbones have lost their sparkle*. Mark was a very witty man. He seemed in a very good mood that night.'

'And what happened when you reached the cafe?'

'We met Trent Eveready. As promised he had my neuropharmacological supplies. My best friends Ritalin, Modafinil and Zoloft, nestling snugly inside a Marlborough Light packet.'

I pause here and reflect on how I tried to make light of this illegal transaction, offering this little joke by way of a confession. They had said I wouldn't be charged *in all likelihood*, but if I had used the sense I was born with I would have feigned amnesia or pierced my tongue with a biro. The cunts produced a plastic bag containing 'object A' and asked, *is this the package?* There followed five seconds of silence. Verso asked whether I was going to be a good girl or whether I had decided to play at being difficult and I replied that, well, it could indeed be the package but how could I tell, it was sealed in a fucking bag, one cigarette packet looks a lot like any other fucking cigarette packet. As nervous as I was and as nauseous as I was feeling, I was still cognisant and I began to speculate on whether anything had been added to the contents of the package. Verso breathed another garlicky question over me but I found I could not concerntrate on the words. I began to feel faint and dizzy and told them I could not continue. My God, the bastards were going to charge me. I would have a criminal record, I would lose my job, I would be fined or sent to prison. Dective Sargent Routledge, in a gesture of concern, held out a glass of water in which I vomited, I could not help it. They had no choice but to suspend the interview which Verso did without too much fuss but then what did they care? They had me in a box.

Two
The spirit is for immediate release.

I realise now that I could have retracted my earlier statement or demanded a lawyer or whatever criminals do when cornered by clever-arsed cops. I should have stood up to their bullying. But my desire for freedom clouded my reason. When the interview resumed the following day, I identified 'object A' and continued with my recollections of the night Mark Colgate died.

'We ordered lemon sorbets with our lattes, I think.'

'And the café was the designated place for your rendezvous with Mr. Dominic Rolex I believe?'

'Yes, he stipulated ten minutes past eleven exactly,

except, as I said before, he didn't show.'

'And how did you meet the boy?'

'Well, Mark had lost interest in the evening. He always said Rolex wouldn't turn up. His attention began to wander, eventually alighting on a pin-eyed boy sitting at the far end of the counter. Finally the young prick held his complete attention and he nodded at the empty chair at our table. Trent tried to warn Mark that he was making a mistake – I thought perhaps Trent recognised the boy – but Mark wouldn't listen, such was his nature. Mark delicately pushed the chair back a few inches with the toe of his Patrick Cox shoe, by way of an invitation. Once more Trent tried to dissuade Mark by telling him that the boy was fucked and that he had been trying to converse with his voicemail for the last half hour. But it was to no avail. Mark was bored and he was horny. The boy sat down, he kind of collapsed on the chair. He was such a wreck that I thought he would smell terribly but I could detect nothing unpleasant. I admit he was cute with his ripped Comme De Garcon shirt open to the waist, but there were aspects of his appearance that rang alarm bells in stereo.'

'Such as?'

'Well he kept flashing Mark a coquettish smile that revealed a broken incisor and he sported a thin line of dried blood that had run from a cut in the corner of his mouth and pooled in the dimple of his chin. It was too much. Still, I knew Mark would love this rivulet of red which ended in delicate capillaries laced through day-old stubble. The boy was beautiful, yes, but mawkish too.

The prick asked Mark a question, it took an age for him to form the words. He asked Mark whether he liked his blue eyes, explaining that they were cornflower blue contact lenses, acquired from Spexspress. Mark looked like a love sick poodle, it turned my stomach. He joked that the boy had bought his eyes and asked whether his other pair were as beautiful. This pissed the boy off for some reason and he blurted out that he had stolen them after completing a modelling assignment that day but now he couldn't remove them. Each word the boy pronounced was uttered with great effort – mechanically – he was like a human metronome.'

'And Mark Colgate and the young man left together?'

At this point I omitted some incriminating remarks from my recollection of the night's events, made during an exchange between myself and Mark. I had made a bitchy comment, a joke which backfired. I remember this with a tinge of regret. My last meeting with Mark ended with a sharp exchange and irritation on both sides. Perhaps I have a heart after all.

Mark was good company. His sense of cleanliness exceeded my own and we both shared a passion for tragedy and fading glamour. I am tempted to go so far as to say that he was conscientious in the pursuit of tragedy. Mark took an interest in every lost case and suicide. He attended every opening party and funeral, willingly, day and night, but he didn't know how to make sense of these things. He confused artists with writers, film premieres with fashion collections, art prizes with product placements. Most touchingly of all Mark confused launches with memorials. He did not associate the actor with the cinema, the chef with the restaurant or the producer with the recording studio. This made many people uneasy in his company. But he could distinguish a soul in trouble from all the other exotic birds he encountered. The wounded and the self-destructive drew from him a kind of joy that went to swell the murmur that he was a shallow and unfeeling philistine. He would stand rapt, gazing at these blazing and dying stars, the quivering poise, tear-brimmed eyes raised for the plummet drop, he was fascinated by such

extremes of greed, narcissism, corruption and expenditure. I miss his companionship and his humour. My
best friend's last words to me were, *You are a fucking
arsehole*, still he was not to know he would never see me
again.

It was only a casual remark, something like *God save
us from pretty rich kids with expensive habits* that upset the
apple cart. Some little slur or other about the boy's
obvious drug problem. Mark exploded. He called me a
witch and then listed my record of substance abuse since
he had known me, finishing with the remark that I was
the pot calling the kettle black, or something like that.

Technically this was true but my consumption habits
are restricted to non-addictive pharmaceutical products.
At least they are unclassified and can be obtained from
a doctor at a general practice, though my doctor is a
fucking puritanical wanker who would not prescribe a
paracetamol unless he suspected his patient had a brain
tumour. The difference I wish to stress between myself
and regular drug scum such as the young man in
question is important. I am always in control, I wash
three times a day, I do not beg, steal or beat up old ladies
and I always feel good about myself. The boy was
wasted, I mean unpleasant, not just dishevelled but out
of control. His tortured speech, his movements, those
disgusting spastic movements, they are not attributes I
find attractive in another human being. I choose life
enhancing drugs, the kind of drugs that Huxley believed
would destroy us all, though I have always read
Brave New World as a description of paradise. To be
inhumanly alert and smart, that is what I hope for when
I pop a new pill. Zoloft was my first infatuation, it
creates twenty four hour feelings of well-being but
Ritalin is my real passion, a drug administered to
disruptive teenage boys whose levels of concentration
fail to rival a day old kitten. Ritalin focuses the world

into sharp relief, it slows down time while accelerating thought and movement. The drug puts you on the next level, the only side effects being waking dreams and twelve hours of sleep every six or seven days, but even this can be avoided with the right combination of pills.

I could not be bothered to explain this to Mark or a sneering Trent Eveready, so I told Mark to *fuck off*, which he did with the boy in tow. Thirty seconds later Dominic Rolex's personal assistant called on my mobile to say the meeting was postponed until further notice.

But those fucking cops wanted to know the exact circumstances of Mark's departure – when it happened, how it happened and was it before or after Rolex's cancellation.

The tape records that I told a stupid lie – one that, I realised later, Trent Eveready, already up to his neck in shit, would contradict with glee. And I did not think that the cops would only have to talk with Rizzo Peroni, a witness to my very public row with Mark Colgate, to establish who was the liar. I regret this careless fib that compromised me further. This is what I told them:

'Why did Mark leave? I don't know if I can remember, I think it was when Mark upset the boy again and the prick stormed out of the cafe. Yes, Mark followed like a shepherd looking for a wayward lamb, it was pathetic. And Mark's offence: he took a napkin to the boys chin but made a mess of this flirtatious gesture, it left a pink bruise-like smudge with the appearance of the early stages of impetigo. You see, the vital fluid of life that had dribbled so prettily out of the side of the child's mouth was make-up from his modelling assignment. It was a feature of his costume. His damaged look was nothing but a facade, next week's statement for the cover of *GQ* magazine.'

This last piece of information seemed to please Verso and Routledge and they asked me to repeat the episode again. I was, at least, being half truthful. Mark did upset the boy by smearing his chin with make up, which drew from me a burst of laughter and my bitchy remark. And I thought it was very clever of me to avoid any more confessions about handling stolen pills. I hoped I had seen off the worst of Verso and Routledge.

It was only when they asked the question about my own departure from the cafe that I realised I was a suspect and not just a bit-part player in this fatal drama. They asked, *Are you quite sure you left the cafe with Mr. Trent Eveready?* It turned out that the lying parasite had stated that I had followed Mark and the boy, and that he had found me dazed and incoherent at the crime scene. But Trent, the peanut-brained imbecile that he was, had not thought that his statement could be confirmed or disproved by an examination of CCTV footage. Much to my relief.

Verso and Routledge were most intrigued as to why I thought Eveready would lie, so I told them the reason was either money or some moronic fancy that he could gain a hold or influence over me. They weren't convinced by this, I could see, but they did not push the issue further and asked me to continue with my recollection of the rest of the night's drama. So I told them the truth as it seemed the best policy at this point.

'Trent and myself went looking for Mark and the boy. I knew Trent was disappointed at not meeting Dominic Rolex that night and that he was curious about our rendezvous with the celebrity. As we roamed the streets he asked in a disinterested voice – as if he wasn't dying to fucking know – just what was the purpose of our meeting with Rolex. I don't know why I told him, probably too much Zoloft. I should have buttoned my mouth. Trent is a paid gossip-monger, selling pills is only one of his talents. He sells information to journalists, agents, PR companies and no doubt to you people too. This trade rescued him from the drudgery of a career as a Gucci sales assistant. Trent's life has been one long struggle against paid employment. He was not trustworthy, but Mark had not been shy about meeting Rolex in Trent's presence, so I told him what he wanted to know. Mark had thought Rolex was mixed up in all sorts of things and that he was not who he said he was. Mark believed he was older than he claimed and that he had escaped a warrant for his arrest in America in the 1980s. He was going to confront Rolex with his suspicions.'

'On hearing these allegations Trent choked and spluttered and seemed about to faint. His knees buckled and he clutched a lampost for support. I don't know whether Rolex was some kind of hero for him and he was upset at this news or whether he had just caught a glimpse of Mark's body. He stumbled forward lifting his hands above his head and cried "Oh no, Mark". He was in a tremendous flap. That's when he stumbled and fell over a leg that had become detached, wrenched off I would guess, from the crumpled body in a shop door-way.'

'And this was Mark Colgate's body?'

'I couldn't tell at first, the head was burst open like a water melon dropped from a first floor window. Viscous pinks and reds framed his pretty smile. His half-opened mouth floated in a rich jelly and his eyes had popped on their stalks, so I didn't recognise him but then I saw the Sean Penn and Madonna Tattoo on his arm. It was draped around an ornamental potted shrub.'

His arm was sheared clean off. Mark had always wanted to remove the tattoo but baulked at the cost of laser treatment which often left an ugly scar, I did not share this irony with Verso and Routledge. They asked about the boy again and seemed content with the answer that he was nowhere to be seen. They suggested that I must have been quite shaken by the experience. The honesty of my reply surprised them.

'It made little impact on me, in fact I felt blissfully happy. I looked at Mark's body and, do you know, it was the strangest feeling, I felt august and exalted. It was Trent who called you people.'

'And why didn't Trent stay at the crime scene? We found him blind drunk in a nearby bar.'

'It is only just coming back to me, yes he ran off when he saw, or I should say *heard* the phone. It was made of blue glass or perhaps rock crystal, very expensive looking, very unusual. The phone was lying on the ground next to Mark, but it wasn't Mark's. And someone was singing at the other end of the connection. Trent went berserk, he kicked parked cars and smashed bottles in the street. He ran off like a screaming banshee. Have you traced the owner of the phone yet?'

Verso explained that the cell phone was not registered to any one and quickly returned to the subject of the singing voice. He wanted to know if I remembered the words or tune sung by the mystery caller. I said I was tired, which was true, and made them promise that it was the last question of the day. They agreed and once satisfied they let me go. I caught a cab home and showered until the hot water ran out. I had hoped that this was the last I would see of Verso and Routledge until the inquest or trial concerning Mark's death. I remembered their amusement at my singing and my embarrassment at my tuneless voice. I mouth the lyrics now as I write them down:

You are not eagles
which is why you haven't comprehended the blissful terror
in your minds.
Not being birds
how do you propose to nest on an abyss?

Three
The spirit is a cheekbone.

Disaster and horror are said to unite people and cement communities, it is common sense. The spirit of the people in the face of tragedy is inspirational. Communities pull together and find strength in their shared grief. Does not the family look to a loved one's grave and the nation stand silent before the cenotaph; does not the world weep for the victims of terrorism? In these acts of collective grief, are not values affirmed and vigilance increased? This is not just the opinion of politicians and journalists but of philosophers too, *what else*, they ask, *is the crucifix if not a symbol of the most horrific torture and murder of an innocent man*? And do we not find the crucifix at the heart of all Christian celebration and communities? Ask yourself why it is it that the symbol of the man's destruction and not his resurrection has become a badge of faith and community. I have heard it said that, at the heart of all communities, you find similar outrageous crimes or catastrophes.

This is not my opinion, for what it is worth. I am of the persuasion that disaster and crime makes for a more atomised and divided society. Disaster sends people crazy, it makes them mean with fear, and overjoyed that it was some other poor sod who exploded into a ball of fire when his plane crashed. And, when there is a murder or abduction in the vicinity, each man and women suspects every other poor soul of the terrible deed. While bleeding hearts will point out that it is the minorities and the poor who bare the brunt of these suspicions I disagree. Disaster and crime induce the birth of two thoughts in everyone's head:

1. Thank God it wasn't me.
2. Trust no one.

Such was the effect of Mark's horrific death in Soho, and such was the effect on my associates and myself. I saw Trent twice after Mark's death and each time I came close to accusing him of being involved in Mark's murder, though no murder inquiry had officially been launched. On each occasion Trent made wild threats and told me that it would be in my best interests to keep quiet. His threats and warnings always ended with a protracted bout of sobbing, they were terrifying fits of anguish that I am in no doubt were authentic. I have a recording of his final interview with Verso and Routledge in which it is clear that Trent Eveready was going out of his mind with fear, the tape confirmed it. He talked so fast and inanely that it sounds as if he was desperately trying to plug up his own ears with every piece of gossip he had ever heard.

'We'd like to ask you some more questions about last week. Do you feel up to answering some more questions Mr Eveready?'

'Last week I went to Kym and Jack's wedding. Much rooting and gakking in the toilets. I have the evidence.'

'Mr Eveready what are you talking about?'

'At Kim Hearsay and Jack Ryder's wedding/tackfest last week I found, in just one toilet cubicle, three empty gak wraps, two used condoms and a pair of knickers half flushed down the pan. Class, that's what I am talking about. A high class affair.'

'We'd like you to think about the night Mark Colgate died.'

'Oh yeah, he said get ready for Vardenafil, but I was already on the case, right: a new, stronger kind of Viagra, available now, first taste at half price. Should allow even ancient men to chop wood with their choppers. Mark was a funny guy.'

'I don't understand Trent, did Mark Colgate try to sell you Vardenafil?'

'No, no. I sell Vardenafil, you want some? Get Vardenafil and get hard and fill all night.'

'We already know you are well informed about narcotics and pharmaceutical products, Mr Eveready …'

'What did Freddie Mercury and River Phoenix have in common? Answer: they both had some bad crack. You geddit? Stay away from the crack though, there's a warning on that one, mind you it's your own trip so be my guest.'

'Your friend Mark Colgate talked to you about a new drug, what else did he say?'

'Kieran Caulkin's cat Leo can do impressions. Leo is a super-psychic, incredibly smart cat, right. He has a hundred different *meows*. When he sees a bird he has a bird meow, when he sees a squirrel he has a squirrel meow. He's really cool.'

'I think this is a waste of time sir, he took something in the car, some kind of amphetamine, I think … '

'Uh, I have a question for you two – winner with the correct answer gets a prize.'

'What is it Mr. Eveready?'

'Which legendary PR and safe-sex campaigner rang her office to book herself into a clinic for an urgent retrieval? She had shagged Seal – you remember Seal? – she'd shagged him the night before and the johnny was still stuck inside her.'

'What about Miss Mercedes? Did she say anything to you after you left the cafe?'

'Wrong answer, wrong stuck-up bitch.'

'Did she say anything to you after you left the cafe, Mr. Eveready?'

'She always has something to say, she has verbal diarrrhoea.'

'And what did she say?'

'Marilyn Manson enjoys watching Thalidomide porn.

That's what he told Peaches, anyway. And which Sex Pistol has taken the smack-track back to rehab?'

'Mr. Eveready … '

'Newark is the only town in the USA which is an anagram of wanker.'

' … I don't think you took anything in the car, I think you're scared shitless, something scared you out of your wits when you saw Mark Colgate's body and you don't want to confront it, what do you say to … '

'Prostitute penguins fuck for rocks. Penguins need stones to build nests. Shortages of rocks have seen female penguins trading sex for stones – the only known instance of prostitution in the animal world.'

'Now listen carefully Trent, Lemon Mercedes has stated that you knew the boy who left with Colgate. We have already charged you for selling stolen pharmaceutical products. What's next? Aiding and abetting? How long have you known Dominic Rolex, Trent?'

'A paedophile and a young child are walking into the woods. The child says *it's dark, I'm scared* and the paedo says, *how do you think I feel, I have to walk back on my own.*'

'Miss Mercedes says you are supplying Modafinil, now that is a classified substance … '

'This year's new wonder drug is Modafinil. Fans in the US call the pills Zombies. The drug, which was created to prevent narcoleptics from falling over, keeps you awake, active and fresh for a minimum of 40 hours. Better still, you don't get the exhaustion that follows a night on speed, or the paranoia that comes after a cocaine binge. And, unlike Crystal Meth, after taking Modafinil you aren't seized with the demented urge to wank your nob down to a bleeding stump.'

'Mr Eveready … '

'Crystal Meth is the worst. Hey, have you ever wanked in a celebrity's house? I was in Cher's brand new two floor penthouse apartment in New York in the '90s, which my friend was designing and painting. I wanked in her beautiful, large, private bathroom off her bedroom. She walked in a few seconds later wearing mirror shades and said what a wonderful smell drying paint had, then looked at me and said, who the fuck are you?'

'Mr. Eveready ... '

'I am reliably informed that Joan Collins tapes up the old lady flesh on her back with parcel tape.'

'I think this is pointless sir, he is not in control of himself, just look at him. He's having a nervous breakdown, I think we should send for a doctor'

'Which new celeb mum treated herself to a Caesari-Tuck, the rich-bitch favourite of having a simultaneous tummy tuck and caesarean?'

'I have a better idea Routledge, let's turn him loose and see what happens. Turn off the tape.'

'Did you hear about the gay French butcher? He put his sausage up two francs and ... '

Verso's callous but calculated release of Trent into the night does not surprise me, it just confirms my opinion of the man. Verso was like a soul possessed, chasing his obsessions and vendetta's at all costs, regardless of the price, human or otherwise. Within six hours of Trent's last interview at Old Burlington Street Police Station Trent Eveready's useless carcass lay scarred and burnt.

Four
The spirit is real people with stories just like yours.

My fourth encounter with Verso and Routledge was another trail of nerves. I had already become aquatinted with their unpleasant methods of persuasion and blackmail. Verso, in particular, disgusted me, apart from his foul odour which harboured his vindictive nature, I realised that his awkward gait was due to a disability. He disguised his limp well but I detected, on closer inspection, that his left limb was mis-shapen, it had a peculiar bow to it. Verso had a false leg. I had not registered this handicap in our first meeting at which he had remained seated but later, as he ambled around the interview room, badgering me with insinuations and innuendo, his lack became apparent. I hoped it was excruciatingly painful. No doubt his peg was removed by some unfortunate who snapped like a shark when driven to ground by the fanatical cop.

They asked me to watch a video tape and identify as many individuals as possible but they did not think to inform me about the tape's contents, or perhaps they did and decided against this protocol. Routledge pressed play and the screen spat up a storm of static snow flakes which gradually subsided to reveal a brightly lit cocktail bar. The tape was silent, it was CCTV footage of Nick Ray-Ban's bar, one of Trent Eveready's regular haunts. And there was Trent, on cue, babbling at a young songstress, Sophie Anne Trebor, anorexic-chic with a pram face. She looked deeply disturbed by what Trent had to say. The two cops asked with interest what I had meant by the expression *pram face* and I explained. Pram face: a term describing the sulky and sullen face of a talentless female pop singer, a look also found on the visage of single parent mothers in high-rise council estates. This tickled Routledge's funny bone but Verso was not amused. I returned my gaze to the monitor.

The bar is packed with C-list celebrities and the Soho faithful. Just behind a raving Mark Eveready stands a children's television presenter, Julia K'Tel and a bouncer from the Met bar, Charlie 'Ragga' Rumbelows. The bar staff are frantically engaged in their work, flying from optics to customer to the till and back. Suddenly one of the bar men raises an arm to cover his eyes, it is the first sign that something is wrong. A gossip columnist at the *Daily Mirror*, Jenny Dulux, has a red mobile phone pressed to her ear. She screams *Oh Shit* at the top of her lungs, her gesture is operatic and her lips can be read easily. She slams the phone down on the steel top of the counter and cries out in pain as a shard of glass slices through her left cheek. The glasses and bottles behind the bar start to vibrate and shatter. Razor sharp slithers of glass embed themselves in the heads and raised hands of the bar staff trapped behind the chrome counter, causing the first wave of panic amongst the clientele. Bewildered faces register fear and pain as fingers dig at wounds or try to stem the flow of hot sticky blood. A waitress who work's at Marx, I don't know her name, tries to curtail the blood pouring out of her boyfriend, a club promoter named Joe Nescafe, by stuffing a tampax into his wound, a novel but ultimately useless innovation. One-litre bottles of spirits pop and spray the counter, the mirror above the cash till explodes. A minor celebrity, a weather girl for a breakfast TV program called Gill Radox, turns to run but is too slow – a spike of glass punctures her left eyeball. And then the first dead body falls to the floor, electro-cuted or maybe just knocked stone cold dead by a falling television set. Blue sparks begin to fly and the air crackles with electricity, igniting the furnishings and carpet swimming in alcohol. Pink and orange flames leap and sizzle and begin to eat greedily at the oxygen in the bar. There are more sparks and explosions, neon pink and titanium white, and then the orange flames grow and engulf the bar. Silhouettes collide and stumble as black smoke begins to smother everything. Visibility is now very poor. Screaming fits turn into fits of coughing and choking and the monitor quickly turns a blue black. All three of us are reflected in the screen but only I am watching the carnage unfold, I can see Verso and

Routledge staring at my flushed features in the inky black mirror of the television screen. Occasionally there is a flare or an explosion which illuminates a charred head. Toppled furniture and bodies are identifiable amongst the smouldering detritus. And then a familiar face, melting in the ferocious heat, eyes popping, running, screaming, crashing through a plate glass door. Trent's agony is the last image recorded as the tape fills with black smoke again.

Everything that was once lived has become a vast accumulation of spectacles. I have often meditated on this thought. And the notion that we in the affluent West are made passive and unfeeling sub-humans by our consumption of advertising campaigns, violent movies and the global broadcasting networks. The idea has a ring of truth about it. But consider this, at the beginning of the 20th century the average citizen did not eat a daily diet of death and disaster, unlike today when global events and violent entertainment are offered on an hourly basis. There is simply more death for us to consume, the Great Wars exempted. For example, if an airship erupted into an inferno in the 1920s, news of such a calamity might spread quickly but cinema audiences would only catch a glimpse of the event two or three days later, the catastrophe would not be viewed as it happened and then repeated over and over *ad infinitum* as is today's habit. There is simply to much disaster around for us to be affected by it, a surplus that can only be an evening's distraction. This does not mean there is no grief and hurt, far from it, are not the grave yards full of howling relatives? And are not nations still touched by the plight of a sick little girl needing a kidney transplant? There is still too much sentiment around for my liking. In my opinion, only when death is greeted without sentiment, guilt and fear can sovereignty be achieved. Only then, can a person be said to be alive. But I was not going to raise these ideas with Verso and Routledge by way of defending my lack of horror and disgust.

The two cops waited for me to utter an anguished comment or mournful sigh, or ask for a glass of water. On seeing that I was unmoved Verso asked me what I thought about the scene I had just witnessed. I replied that it must have been a gas explosion or something electrical or an attack by an Islamic terror cell. Verso shook his head at each suggestion and said that they were baffled as to the cause, though some of the survivors remember an eerie high-pitched humming. I said that I didn't know what to think. Verso cleared his throat and impatiently informed me that my ideas about the cause of the devastation where of little importance, they were interested in my reaction to the tape and to Trent Eveready's death, he was one of only two casualties. Trent died of first degree burns, the other man died of a heart attack after receiving a blow to the head. I said that I was sorry about Trent's death, it was appalling way to go but I had no strong feelings of affection for Trent. In fact he was a worthless and untrustworthy soul and the world would not miss him. The two cops looked astonished and I thought that my cold and frank admission had offended their sense of decency, but it was Routledge who spelled out what was on their minds. I was forgetting that they did not possess a single decent bone between them, they had the manners and inclinations of terrorists. He looked straight into my eyes and said, *you mean you didn't think 'two down, one to go'?*

Five
The spirit is a low fat smoothie.

I finally met Dominic Rolex on a a balmy summer's evening. The air was pleasantly warm that night and I went for a stroll. I returned to my office sucking on a mango smoothie, my one concession to a sweet tooth. The magazine's general manager, Suki Samsung greeted me with a face ugly with excitement, *he's here and he is in your office, don't let him leave without agreeing to flash his pierced titties on the front cover.* I deduced from this vulgar women's instruction that Dominic Rolex was waiting by my desk. My first impulse was to call Routledge and Verso but there was no proof that Rolex had been responsible for Mark and Trent's gruesome appointments with the reaper.

I brushed a red admiral butterfly off the door handle of my office and entered. Rolex rose from his seat to greet me, *Miss Mercedes, we meet at last,* he said playing the perfect gentleman. A pleasant beginning. Then something happened to poison the moment, I said, *yes at last, in the flesh.* It was an innocent enough reply but Rolex appeared hurt by the remark, so I tried to explain, though there was nothing to explain. *Flesh meaning in-person, in real time* ... He smiled and quickly regained his composure and said, *I prefer the phrase 'in substance',* a term that I admit I had not heard before or since.

For the first time, I looked at the man, I mean I really had a good look. I stared at Dominic Rolex for a good thirty seconds, I couldn't help it. He was perfect. I apologised and he sat down without embarrassment or anger. I concluded that he wasn't offended, after all I thought, he must be used to being stared at, enjoy it even. And perhaps it was disrespectful to refer to so much perfection as mere flesh. He had the striking bone structure of a young Marlon Brando, his lips were full and sexy and his eyes large and deep set. When his lips broke into a joyous smile he reminded me of Mick Jagger but when he scowled it was a sultry Jim Morrison that came to mind. It was as if he had been constructed from the best and most handsome parts of late 20th century masculinity. His haircut, borrowed from Marc Bolan, softened his image but his athletic body possessed the dangerous raw energy of Iggy Pop in his prime, and the intensity of a smouldering Tony Curtis from the 1950s. Every gesture, pose and angle had the hint of some other gorgeous man. Whether it was an consequence of genetics or surgery or disciplined study the effect was breathtaking.

He was flawless. It was as if he was made of celluloid or some other blemish-free material. He was elastic. He did not wrinkle or crease when he smiled and his skin bore no trace of veins or pores. *My God*, I thought, *you have no pores*. And then I realised, like I was shot, he had no smell, not of sweat or shit or any other perfume, no deodorant or scent, not a whiff, nothing. A miracle I thought and then a feeling of unease overwhelmed me, *Just like the boy in Peroni's cafe* I thought.

Dominic Rolex broke our silence by asking what I had wanted to see him about, apologising for the cancelled meeting. I thought back to that fatal night and said the meeting was arranged at my colleague's instigation. Rolex looked upset and said, almost in a whisper, *Yes, Mark Colgate, most unfortunate, we were very good friends despite everything*. I wanted to ask what everything was but remembered Mark's suspicions. The pretext of our earlier meeting had been to offer Dominic Rolex a slot as our guest editor, an idea that made our general manager, Miss Samsung, wet her Agent Provocateur underwear. It was a much-used ploy that massaged a celebrity's ego and ensured an A-list cover on the cheap. I invited Rolex to take the helm of the magazine for one issue.

Rolex laughed and suggested that surely I had a more

interesting topic of conversation to discuss with him. I was taken aback by this remark, I felt slighted by his response, as if he was above the mundane task of editing of a magazine. But I had misunderstood him. He turned and faced me squarely and then lent forward across the desk until the tip of his nose was just inches away from mine. He hissed menacingly between clenched teeth, *What's the matter, lost your bottle?* Until that moment I had failed to notice something so obvious and disturbing about Rolex that, when I registered it, I felt as if I saw him clearly for the first time. His face, his dress, his manicured fingernails, every last detail about the man was symmetrical. I do not mean that he had two eyes and legs and wore matching socks. I mean that every part of his left side was perfectly reflected in his right side, from the centre parting of his haircut to the faint scuff marks on his Camper shoes. But it was his face that stirred panic in my soul, it was like a Rorsarche print, every feature perfectly aligned as if placed on a grid. And, as he leaned into the glare of the desk lamp, I noticed further that his olive skin did not vary in colour or tone from his handsome forehead to his square jaw. *Jesus you are a freak*, I thought. I reeled backwards and vomited into my waste paper bin, the pale orange of the mango smoothie splattering a grey filing cabinet.

I gasped for air and sat back in my reclining chair, I heard the mechanism click and my body jerked backwards. I clasped hard onto the arm rests as Rolex's shadow engulfed me. I squeezed my eyes tight and waited for his exquisitely manicured hands to close around my windpipe, but the death grip never came. Instead Rolex's dabbed at my mouth with a handkerchief and in a sweet voice asked me to relax. He apologised profusely for the melodrama. His words soothed and he won a nervous smile from me but my fear remained. He apologised again for the frightening episode, he did not want his little game to be taken the wrong way. He knew it might look bad, an aggressive man alone in an attractive women's office, late at night with no witnesses. It was just that it had come to his attention that a file had been compiled on him containing damaging slander and wicked lies. I did not know anything about such a collection of documents, which was the truth and I told him so. It was Mark who took a special interest in his career and history. I can not say by what trick or art he managed to charm answers from me but, by comforting my senses and yet maintaining the threat of violence, he did so. I cannot put my finger on how this was achieved but that was the form his influence took.

He asked me to forward any libellous material saying *enough people are hurt in this world by falsehoods and invention*, and then, as if nothing had happened, he announced he would be happy to be our guest editor. He asked for the contract to be delivered the next day, stipulating only one condition: that his editorial must not be doctored or pruned. After Rolex left, it was only the aroma of my own vomit that convinced me I had not been dreaming.

Six
The spirit is nothing if not elegant.

What Dominic Rolex was to Detective Inspector Verso has been hinted at, what he was to me, as yet, remains to be clarified. Though I was drawn to this man for reasons already explained, he also stirred some nameless horror in me that I despair of ever putting into a comprehensive form. It was the symmetry of Rolex that appalled me, but how can I explain myself?

Though in many works of great art and in grand

buildings and in the costumes of heads of state and the street plans of great cities, in fact in all things civilised, symmetry is viewed as a positive quality, a sign of order, strength and classical beauty. And, though in the sciences and mathematics, symmetry is met with awe, as if some mystical power had delivered its most precious of gifts. For all these accumulated associations, with whatever is sweet and honourable and sublime, there lurks an elusive something which strikes more panic into the soul than the worst disorder and chaos.

I have read studies in which survey after survey has stated that the most popular definition of beauty is a man or women with a good complexion and, as near as is possible, a well-proportioned, symmetrical face and body. I would not argue with these findings except to say I would call this conventional beauty. Dominic Rolex's good looks, though far from conventional, had a complexion and proportion that were second to none. In facing Dominic Rolex I confronted a perfect being and yet this perfection was unnatural, it was barbaric and utterly alien. He was not a work of nature, he was inhuman.

Seven
The spirit is a square jaw.

Chelsea Barclycard was a petite doll of woman who would gush enthusiastically about any subject under the sun. She was not all she seemed though. Her outbursts of optimism and frequent regurgitation of maxims from self-improvement manuals were not heartfelt but desperate attempts to camouflage a damaged and vulnerable soul. She was a casualty of her wealth and good looks. With her every whim only a swipe and signature away, the motivation to get on in life was lacking. And, not being short of handsome admirers, she had failed to establish any meaningful relationships. She had formed the suspicion that no one respected her, an insight that turned out to be completely accurate. She vainly drifted from one half-hearted project or affair to another pointless enterprise or rendezvous, eventually coming to ground in a deep depression about the meaninglessness of life. Chelsea had become my acquaintance through Mark Colgate, a magnate for small birds with broken wings and manic depressions. Mark had a brief liaison with Chelsea and then, after the affair had run its course, he continued to indulge the sad bitch's self pity in exchange for invitations to exclusive parties. I thought she had committed suicide years ago.

Chelsea's appearance on my door step at the ungodly hour of three o'clock in the morning was unwelcome enough but the promise of a night of tearful histrionics filled me with dread. I peered through the spyhole in my front door and held my breath. She rapped on my door with pathetic little taps. I could hear her sobbing and whispering a sad incantation to herself, *hold it together, keep it together Chelsea, oh please wake up Lemon*. She was persistent but, after fifteen agonising minutes, she gave the enterprise up as a lost cause and ferreted in her bag for a pen a paper. Before Chelsea left she forced a package and a hastily scribbled note through my letter box and then retreated to her Saab. The package landed at my feet, the note caught on the flap of the letter box. I seized the paper and read the message.

Dear Lemon,

I called but you were out. I am in so much pain since Mark's horrible death. I need to speak to you. He told me he was worried about his safety and gave me this disc to look after. I was to send it to his editor if anything happened to him. I am so scared Lemon, I am going out of my mind with grief, please call.

Yours in friendship,

Chelsea

This communication with its nervously scribbled characters had the effect of freezing my blood. Mark had known he was going to die. Here was proof that Mark's life had been threatened and that he probably knew his killer. The name of his executioner was not hard to guess.

The disc had been christened *Rolex Facts* by Mark with a red felt tip pen and was amended with *for Lemon Mercedes* in blue. I scanned Mark's disc for viruses and noticed that the files had been copied on a computer in my office. I clicked on a file entitled *chat*, it was an interview Mark had conducted with Dominic Rolex for *HMF* two years ago, which he had syndicated to *Paris Match*. I remembered the piece, Mark had said that the meeting was a disaster and had to fabricate the printed interview. He had saved the unedited transcript:

Mark Colgate: Although you are still young it seems like you have been in the spotlight forever, you are one of those people who became famous for being famous …

Dominic Rolex: I would say it was more the case that I became known for hanging out with famous people …

Mark Colgate: So when did you realise that you had made it in your own right, that other people were photographed standing next to you and not the other way around?

Dominic Rolex: When did I know I made it? Uh, well I walked into WH Smiths and saw a hundred pairs of my own eyes staring at me from the magazine racks. And I thought, Jesus. And then a stranger came up to me in the street, someone who I'd never met before came up and shook my hand and said he thought I was really cool. He said I really like your stuff, just keep on doing what you're doing. Then everyone was doing it, telling me how fucking good I looked, how much they loved my stuff. It just blew me away, I knew it then.

Mark Colgate: So you became it overnight?

Dominic Rolex: Yeah, one minute I wasn't anything

special, just another ordinary guy waiting in line with everyone else, and then it seemed like every door was open to me, I just had to knock. I couldn't do anything wrong.

Mark Colgate: How did you do it? Was it the result of hard work, or being in the right place at the right time?

Dominic Rolex: Oh man, how it happened, I don't know how it happend. Listen, yes, you work hard but if you show that you want it then it won't happen. If people think you're desperate for it to happen then it's over. You just have to do your thing as well as it can be done.

Mark Colgate: I understand, but why did you, in particular, become such a big star?

Dominic Rolex: Why? Well, because everyone wanted a piece of me. And when you become the name on everyone's lips, everyone knows it. I was in a nightclub and this guy came up to me, took hold of my hand and placed a match in my palm. I ask my friend what it was for, he said it means you're hot. And it isn't how you look or what you do that makes you hot, that would be too easy …

Mark Colgate: It's that special something …

Dominic Rolex: Yeah it is that special something, and it's not something you're born with either. You become it, it possesses you. You don't possess it.

Mark Colgate: Your saying that we always know it when we see it, even if we can't define what it is.

Dominic Rolex: Yeah, it's like Coca Cola is it but no one knows what it is that makes a Coke so good.

Mark Colgate: And what if you lose it.

Dominic Rolex: Man, don't even think it. You know all this analysis will get you nowhere, in fact it's dangerous. Don't question what works or it will leave you behind.

Mark Colgate: I just wanted an insight into your success and what you would do if your popularity waned.

Dominic Rolex: Fuck man, are you trying to murder my career.

Mark Colgate: So there's nothing much you feel you can

say about it?

    Dominic Rolex: Only that making it is … being it.

    Mark Colgate: That's it?

    Dominic Rolex: That's it.

The next file I opened was in a folder entitled *history* and contained a scan of a birth certificate for a man named Carlos Henderson dated 1952. It was accompanied by some notes that Mark had typed on Henderson's origin. His father was an English man, a diplomat, and the mother was a woman from a Columbian village.

I clicked on a scan of a newspaper clipping about the village:

The people of the ancient settlement of Cagota are willing to make the ultimate sacrifice for the cause of ecology. They believe that each morning they sing the world into existence and that they have ensured the continuation of the world's appearance every sunrise through song for thousands of years. But now they say the earth is reaching a point of no return and the village has delivered a an ultimatum to the United Nations. They have threatened to throw themselves to their deaths at the Tolagota Waterfall if the nations of the world refuse to curb their exhaustion of the globe's resources. With their deaths, they warn, the earth will cease to exist. The Columbian government are concerned by this promise of mass suicide and believe the threat to be sincere.

Mark had scribbled on the cutting: *Carlos Henderson /Dominic Rolex exiled from village aged 12 in 1964 for violent conduct and destruction of village property.*

I opened a folder marked *celebrity* and found a collection of images and paraphernalia that would be at home in the bedrooms of teenagers and children. There was a scrap book's worth of magazine and newspaper articles charting Dominic Rolex's successes and conquests and even a file containing a video album of Rolex's hit singles entitled *Inorganic.*

The folder also contained forty portfolio shots of Rolex, all marked *publicity* except for one that was tagged *freak of nature*. And all the photographs except for this one image were either profile or three quarter portraits. The exception was an enlargement from a contact sheet, the kind photographers use to view the contents of a role of film. It was the only full-faced portrait shot I had ever seen of Rolex. A feeling of anguish balled at the pit of my stomach at the memory of my last encounter with the man.

My next investigation brought an unexpected haul of what I can only think are philosophical musings. They were deposited in a folder labelled *quotations*. Each paragraph or sentence was anonymous but dated twice. Curiously, each entry was originally an e-mail but the addresses of the corresponding individuals had been erased:

The happiness we find in becoming is possible only by annihilating the reality of 'existences' and lovely appearance, and through the pessimistic destruction of illusion: so, by annihilating even the loveliest appearances, Dionysian happiness attains its height. 1885–86. 3/4/99.

The highest good and the highest evil are the same. 1885–86. 18/4/01.

It would be terrible to believe in sin: on the contrary everything we do, if we need to say this a thousand times, is innocent. 1881–82. 12/2/02.

At the time events moved to their conclusion so rapidly that I was unable to research the source of these words, though they seemed familiar, perhaps because they echoed my own thoughts. Now I have neither the energy nor the heart to engage in web searches or trips to the library, in truth I cannot be bothered and know only that I recognised one phrase as a lyric from Rolex's first successful musical enterprise, a song which he sang in a lilting baritone:

Morality simply is weariness. 1882–85. R, 12/11/98.

The contents of Mark's disc became even more bizarre when I opened the folder *warrant* and found a series of documents from the offices of the Federal Bureau of Investigation of America dated 1978. They were detailed reports of the attempted suicide of a Senator Firestone's daughter, her drug problem and sexual history were also documented as was Carlos Henderson's role in the affair. By chance the FBI had been tapping the phone of Senator Firestone and recorded Henderson coaxing a distressed Cindy Firestone into putting an end to her misery. Senator Firestone, who became aware of Henderson's influence over his daughter and feared possible blackmail, requested the bugging of his phone. Henderson, who was still wanted on charges relating to the distribution of narcotics, fled the country.

In a folder labelled *death* there were several more scans of press cuttings and photographs, all concerning plane crashes, railway disasters and explosions in public buildings, hotels and bars. I could find no contextualising information. Mark had failed to indicate the rationale governing this particular collection but it didn't take long to fathom at least a couple of similarities between each event. Each incident had two things in common, they were bloody and they were unexplained but not one single disaster could be linked to a cause. One file was marked with a different colour to the rest. It was from a *believe it or not* story from the Sydney Herald, published in 1974, some crazy urban myth that an English man named Dominic Henderson, an actor, was the luckiest man alive. He had been the sole survivor of a TWA flight that had crashed on take off. The passengers and crew had been burnt beyond recognition, dental records had to be used to identify them. And yet Henderson emerged from the smouldering wreckage without a single scratch or burn, not one hair on his head was singed.

Mark had totalled the death count for all incidents. A delightful shiver travelled the length of my spine. The number exceeded 30,000.

It was light when I finally finished trawling through the disc, I peeped through the blind at the window and saw bright sunshine, it was twelve twenty. I called in sick and took the last of my Zoloft and Ritalin. After making some tea I reached for a scrap of paper and listed my options. The first word I wrote was *police*. I picked up the phone and weighed it in my hands for several minutes and then replaced it on its stand. I put a line through the word *police* and wrote *publish*. And then I wrote the five letters that spelt *Rolex*. I cannot rationalise my actions and I can only suggest that my decision was a gut-response rather than cerebral one, perhaps I was possessed. And I welcomed having to make my choice, I was sick of waiting for something to transform my life. I crossed out the word *publish* and rang Dominic Rolex's personal assistant. I informed her that I had a file to return to to the celebrity and would appreciate a phone call as soon as possible. Rolex's voice floated into my earpiece and he congratulated me on making the right decision. Had I peeped inside? I said I had no interest in scandal and slander, I was not that kind of a journalist. He purred into my ear and asked how I had come by the material, so I described the pathetic figure of Chelsea Barclycard and her midnight delivery. I knew as I spoke her name I was doing something I should not have.

There was silence for a good five seconds and I thought the connection had failed. *I would like to meet Miss Barclycard, to offer some financial remuneration for efforts and expense.* I hesitated but his sing-song voice sounded my name and I agreed. When I replaced the phone my hand was shaking. I crossed out Rolex's name and went to bed.

Eight
The spirit is 24:7.

I felt weary and realised that the Ritalin had run its course. I fell into a restless sleep that washed over me like waves crashing onto rocks. My sleep was plagued by dreams of all kinds, recent events and conversations overlapped and mutated and then segued into newspaper stories and the plot of a classical novel I read at school. There is one dream I will write down. I am not a believer in the tomfoolery of psychoanalysis, it is nothing but the art of narration and has more in common with literature than science. And I have no great interest in literature. But this one dream is significant, at least to further an understanding of my state of mind. Beside that, the apparition seemed as real as any man or woman I had met in my waking life.

I was visited by an angel, an elderly French woman with a strong accent that all but obliterated her speech. I had to strain hard to understand her tortured English. She appeared to me through a satellite link which I viewed in a grand hall. I sat facing a video projection screen and noticed a camera on a tripod standing slightly to my left that was directed at my own fair head. A number was dialled and a connection was made. A stern looking women in her sixties appeared on the screen. She was well-dressed and wore a cravat, ordinary in every detail accept for the aura of light that radiated from the whole body. She was sitting at a table with a sheaf of paper containing her typed notes.

'Oui.'

I didn't reply.

'Lemon, it is you, I have been meaning to call you, what is it you wanted?'

I apologised and said that *I didn't call, it was a mistake, a wrong number probably*, I said *I'm sorry I don't even know you*.

The woman was a little perturbed but continued, 'But Lemon, it is me, and I have been so worried about you, you are making a terrible mistake my dear. You stumble around in a daze or fill your life with desperate measures, waiting for something to change your life forever, hoping that something will come along and transform your miserable existence. My dear, you are mistaken if you think that you have discovered that something. The silence you embrace is only the painful stillness that follows death, the hush that descends on a crowd when they bow there heads in respect or in tribute, it will never be filled by anything but the same old noise of the life you already know. This is the down-fall of nihilism my dear. The limit of nihilism is that the silence it creates can not be filled by anything new and wonderful. The nihilist is deaf to other's thoughts and feelings, he or she does not listen in silence for anything new but celebrates only that lull which signals an absence. The nihilist contemplates only that silence that marks a brief respite from the familiar and common. My dear, you must learn to listen in silence and … '

My angel's face froze on the projection screen as the connection failed. It was a chilling sight, as if her last breath had been sucked from her in an instant. The only sound was the hum of the dialling tone and then her image faded to grey.

'Madam,' I said, addressing the now vacant screen, 'I am a lost cause. If I had wanted a lecture I would have enrolled at a college. My problem is that I have listened and, much like searching for something interesting to listen to on the radio, after a short while I came to the conclusion that it is all shit. I would rather turn the radio off.'

I put my coat on and ran out of the hall sobbing with rage.

Nine
The spirit is a silicon implant.

Chelsea wore black for our meeting and clutched a
Gucci handbag that she rummaged about in for tissues.
She had arrived early at Tony Cadbury's cafe
and welcomed me with that tear-stained smile the
emotionally crippled often give, a communication by
way of a greeting that says, *I'm OK, I'm coping, but only
just ...* She smelt of enemas and high fibre diets and self
pity. I insisted we sat in the open air although it was a
chilly day. We quickly placed our orders with the waiter,
a sweetpea Thai salad for Chelsea and for myself a
Cosmopolitan.

When the waiter had left, Chelsea asked in a
concerned voice, *Are you not eating Lemon? Lost your
appetite? Me too but we must make the effort.* I returned a
sympathetic nod and then watched in disgust as Chelsea
chomped her way through a bowl of oily green leaves
mixed with sliced vegetables and foul smelling pulses.
Ever since I could remember food has only filled me
with disgust. It is a problem that I have overcome by
eating only clean food. My daily diet consists of cereal,
thoroughly washed pieces of peeled fruit and supplements in tablet form. When I was a child I longed for the
day that scientists would invent a slow release pill
containing three square meals. It was not that I was
obsessed with my body shape it was just that I was
repulsed by the thought of putting anything filthy or
defiled into my body. The idea that I would deposit
anything in my mouth that had once sweated and shat
upon this earth or been touched by another's hands was
out of the question. I was content with my
Cosmopolitan which I consumed with relish.

I ordered another cocktail and turned to Chelsea, *I
have something to tell you Chelsea, Dominic Rolex wants to*

meet you. The woman dropped her fork and sat paralysed. At first I could not fathom whether it was fear or elation that had sculpted a frozen scream from her features. Had she opened Mark's disc? It was unlikely as she would have mentioned it by now, in the first breath of our coversation, but the possibility remained and I regretted that I had not telephoned the police. The hysterical response that broke her silence put an end to any doubts I had. *Dominic Rolex wants to meet me? Oh Lemon, why, I mean, yes of course. Dominic Rolex, of course but why?* I explained that he was a friend of Mark Colgate too and he wanted to thank her for executing Mark's last request. The stupid cow looked blank and so I mentioned the disc delivered through my door in the dead of night. *Oh yes*, she gushed, *but Mark never mentioned he was a friend of Dominic Rolex, he was a secretive so and so. How good a friend was Dominic Rolex, were they ...* I raised an eye brow. It had never crossed my mind before that Mark Colgate and Dominic Rolex had anything other than a professional relationship. I rose from the table and excused myself by whispering, *I just need to spend a penny*, a foible of mine that made Chelsea giggle. I used to say *powder my nose*, an expression that I learnt from my mother, but the habits of my contemporaries had consigned that innocent little idiom to the dustbin.

On my return I visited the bar to order a third Cosmopolitan and noticed the bottles above the bar man's head were vibrating. And then the awful sound of crunching metal and snapping bones and a plate glass window being ripped from its frame filled the air. It is true what they say about disasters, that they are experienced by the survivors in slow motion. Perhaps it is only in the remembering and re-telling of the event that everything explodes and shatters as if choreographed by a film director. I remembered it all: the face of the driver as his four wheel drive careered out of control and pinned Chelsea to the back wall of the cafe, the surprise of the waiter decapitated by a fragment of glass and the beauty of the dust settling about me like a light sprinkling of snow. The chair that I had vacated five minutes ago lay mangled at my feet. After a minute of silence,I ran shrieking from the disaster scene, in what direction I cannot remember, and collapsed in a heap inside a telephone kiosk.

I felt myself lifted by a pair of strong hands and was settled on my feet. A comforting arm encircled my heaving shoulders and a handkerchief gently dabbed my tearstained cheeks. I gazed at the good Samaritan, it was Dominic Rolex. I beat his head with my fists and scuffed his shins with sharp kicks but could not escape his hold. *You fucking bastard*, I screamed, *you tried to fucking kill me, you fucking bastard*. My struggling decreased as I observed Rolex's incredulity and listened to his denial of my accusation. I began to feel confused. Rolex asked how in God's name could I believe the insane concoctions of that hysteric Mark Colgate, did I think he could cause aeroplanes and cars to crash at will. He said that it was no wonder I was confused, I was sick and I had a drug problem and what is more I had just escaped from being crushed to death and was in shock. I leaned on his chest and buried my face in the soft wool of his V-neck sweater. Before the accident Rolex had been biding his time, waiting for my signal to join Chelsea and myself. The rampaging vehicle had missed him by inches and I had run past in a crazed panic only minutes later. He had followed me, concerned that I might be injured.

Sirens filled the streets and Rolex shouted that he would flag a cab and take me home. I was grateful and became compliant and passive, my trembling had not ceased but I was nolonger gripped by panic. And, when we arrived at my house, he was so sweet, he carried me to my bathroom and ran a shower for me. He held my shoulders and blew playfully at the top of my head as if I was a vase or statue, saying I was covered in dust. As I undressed I could hear Rolex turn the television on in the bedroom and flit from channel to channel, searching for news about the accident. As the shower rinsed dust and grime from legs and arms I thought of poor Chelsea and her pretty, lifeless body like a marionette with its strings cut, at least the sad cow had been put out of her misery. I dressed in a robe and coyly entered my bedroom. Rolex was watching the news on Channel 4. *How do you feel?* he asked softly. I felt calm and tranquil, I said I felt OK. *You look and smell beautiful* he said and inhaled the perfume of my shampoo, leaning close and brushing my ear with his lips.

I protested and said his name, *Dominic please*, but I did not resist him. He kissed me on the mouth and untied the front of my robe. He asked what it was like to experience disaster first-hand after writing about the catastrophes experienced by others, and then he answered his own question. *Devastating isn't it.*

I have never enjoyed intimacy with others, though God knows I have tried many times. It is not that I am devoid of lust or desire but my erotic life is limited by my high standards of cleanliness. It is the reality of the act itself – of penetration, of sweat and tongues mingling, of the gooey stink of semen – which makes things so difficult. It is the animality of it all. But as Rolex undressed I realised I felt none of these abject emotions, just the tingle of anticipation.

When I was a teenage girl I fantasised about David Bowie, I had read that he only ate and drank white food and liquids such as milk and the pulp of freshly peeled pears. It was a time in Bowie's life when he would only model white clothes and he would only suffer transportation in a white limousine. I would fantasise that Bowie's chauffeur was speeding the rock star to my bedroom so that he could caress and kiss me. I would return his love and kiss his ghostly white body until dawn.

Before me stood the pale naked figure of Dominic Rolex, not the olive skinned body I had expected but an apparition from my teenage fantasies. The taught muscle definition displayed by Rolex on the cover of numerous magazines had vanished, in its place a body that seemed to be made of porcelain. His pink oval nipples and smooth chest were stretched tightly over a delicate rib cage. His symmetry no longer appeared appalling or dreadful but a paragon of elegance and beauty.

He placed my hand on his erect cock. The male sex organ, even when excited, has the softest of skin, softer than silk or fur. This softness had always disgusted me and I was relieved to feel that Rolex's shaft was smooth but hard, as if cast from metal or resin. It was heavy too. I laughed on discovering that his balls were perfectly symmetrical. *You are a freak of nature*, I said in wonder. He laid me on the bed and parted my thighs, tracing a finger across one nipple, then a hipbone and finally along my pubic bone. I closed my eyes and sensed his tongue caressing my vulva and then my clitoris. I breathed deeply as a hundred delicious sensations coursed through my body, I swear his fingertips and the tip of his tongue were vibrating. As he went down on me he hummed and sang some sad melody I could not recognise but that seemed only to increase the sensations of bliss. The pleasure was exquisite and unlike anything I had experienced before. I could feel him raise his body above mine and his cock brush the lips of my cunt. I gasped as he entered me, expecting a sharp burst of pain but a delectable feeling overwhelmed me instead, as if every last nerve ending where being stroked and massaged. He did not thrust or even move but balanced motionless above me. His cock seemed to vibrate inside me, it seemed to change in volume and shape and to touch every part of me. I felt lost, I felt transformed, I do not know what I felt. I writhed in ecstasy beneath him and built to an orgasm. As I came I opened my eyes and saw Rolex's demonic face laughing. I thrashed beneath his motionless body as pleasure flowed through my torso, my limbs and my fingertips. I saw the ceiling cave in and heard the windows shatter. I felt the floor give way. The last thing I remember was a dressing table crushing my legs and Detective Inspector Verso screaming maniacally, *Rolex, you are under arrest you bastard, don't move.*

Ten
The spirit is a bone.

I awoke in the harsh light of a hospital ward. The smell wrenched my nostrils open and I choked and wretched. I tried to sit up and vomit but I was unable to move. I felt as if I was drowning. A voice called for the nurse and I was turned gently on my side. I asked what had happened and about the fate of Dominic Rolex and was told to relax and rest. A familiar voice said, *There will be plenty of time for questions later.* And much later I was informed that I had drifted in and out of consciousness for several days. Before that I had slept in a coma that had prevailed for two months. Great care was taken in monitoring both my physical and psychological health, it was a full week before anyone would tell me how my tryst with Rolex had ended or reveal the extent of my injuries.

News of my double escape from certain death in the course of a single day had made the front page of the tabloids, I had been the subject of three *believe or not* stories across the globe.

My internal injuries were devastating: my liver and kidneys had been shattered and my lungs punctured, my spine had snapped in three places leaving me paralysed from the waist down and I had only limited upper body movement. My stomach had burst and I had lost the sight in my left eye. I cried for forty eight hours. My internal injuries were a threat to what little quality of life was left for me to enjoy, unless replacements could be found for my failing kidneys I would be lucky to see next summer.

Detective Sergeant Routledge appeared at my bedside like a bad smell but it is thanks to my interview with that low-life of a policeman that I possess at least one happy memory to take to the crematorium, albeit a second hand memento. Verso and Routledge had been watching my house from across the street for several weeks and had installed bugging equipment in both my lounge and bedroom. Even my journey home with Rolex in the cab had been monitored as I had been followed night and day and my rendezvous with Chelsea Barclaycard had been observed at close quarters by an undercover cop – the waiter at Tony Cadbury's cafe. On hearing a commotion over the headphones Verso and Routledge had entered my house with four other policemen and women only to find the house crumbling and collapsing about their ears. All but a crazed Verso had run for their lives. Verso had tried to arrest Dominic Rolex by wrestling the naked man to the ground. A series of explosions threw my damaged body through a broken window and Routledge had been kind enough to drag my poor bones to safety.

In the aftermath only one charred body had been found, the remains of Detective Inspector Verso, his corpse was the colour and texture of charcoal. His features were transfixed in a painful grimace, like some ancient museum exhibit dug from the peat bogs of Europe. A curtain rail had pierced his one good leg in the thigh and his false appendage had somehow punctured his stomach like the shaft of a harpoon. Routledge stoically bore my laughter which lasted a good seven minutes. And Dominic Rolex? He had either escaped or disapeared in the heart of the inferno where fire had melted and vaporised furniture. Perhaps Rolex had ascended to heaven in a puff of smoke, no one was sure. He was missing, presumed dead.

Eleven
The spirit is inhuman.

Just before I saw Rolex for the last time I received his editorial by courier, dictated on audio tape. An accompanying letter reminded me that he had fulfilled his side of our contract, that he had contributed his services and a magazine cover for free and that we were contract-ually obliged to print his words in full. I left the tape with my editor Suki Samsung who must have listened, slack jawed, to Rolex's words. She phoned me at home, *What the fuck is Rolex playing at?* I took the question to be rhetorical and remained silent. She barked and whined, *Lemon, we can't print that, the man is a fucking freak, either that or he is sending us up. We will be the laughing stock of the industry if we give this nut a single column.* I expressed my opinion that, although I had not played the tape, I was sure Rolex was entirely serious and that we either printed his editorial or pulled the issue. At the thought of losing all that revenue, either through loss of sales or through a law suit for breach of contract, it was decided that dumping the issue was the greater evil, so Rolex's editorial was typeset and published. It was no big deal I thought, no one reads editorials these days, that is if they read at all.

The day before the magazine appeared in the shops it landed on my doormat with a thud. I turned to page four and read Rolex's editorial – it was printed in full. The editorial was long by the standards of the magazine and bore the heading *An Urgent Communication*. The piece was flanked by a smiling portrait of a relaxed Dominic Rolex and read as follows:

Pay attention do-gooders. Take heed organic farmers and self-righteous eco warriors, animal rights scum too, pay attention. And take note all you agents of humanitarian aid and human rights. Progressives too, scientists and promoters of global communication, pay attention, sit up and pay attention. The human race is in danger, and not from any alien threat or natural disaster, nor does this danger grow from anything agents of terror are planning. The cause of humanity's imminent annihilation is closer to home than you would imagine. A desperate but destructive movement to which you all subscribe is gathering speed, promoting the obscene idea of eradicating everything you consider non-human, of replacing everything with your own designs. But this dream, to duplicate and double everything in mankind's image, to furnish every last thing with a human personality and morality, that has fascinated your kind for five centuries will lead only to your extinction.

The drive for the super human who will live forever, who will be smarter, saner, healthier and happier in new and expertly controlled biospheres will only lead to the sub-human. So you want to clone everything, from wheat fields to your own personalities. You want to see the back of sickness and suffering. You want to grow a cure for Alzheimer's disease in deep space. Don't fool yourselves that it's all for the good of the planet, it is nothing but the selfish desire to cheat the law of natural selection, the process by which all substances and species have developed throughout the universe.

In challenging evolution, it is clear that your species can nolonger tolerate a process that might bring about your own demise. You can no longer imagine that a superior substance other than yourselves might evolve. That is exactly it, humankind can no longer picture its own disappearance and it is this arrogance that speeds your destruction. You are a species in denial.

Your bio-chemists and engineers and your physicists have no idea of the resistance moments at work in the universe. A new strain of virus infects the food supply of an entire hospital, experts are baffled. An outbreak of anthrax occurs and can not be explained. A bolt snaps under stress in the engine of an aeroplane over the Pacific Ocean but was checked and double-checked only hours before take off. The cause remains a mystery. How many mutant strands of DNA are waiting to corrupt your new wonder crops and make weaklings of your cloned animals? What causes metal fatigue in the components of public transport vehicles? What causes a bullet train in Japan to vomit its guts on its maiden journey? What makes cancer cells grow fat? Why do young children vanish without trace, what is spontaneous combustion?

It is only through confronting these small reminders of death that humanity can be saved and avoid unleashing agencies too powerful for humankind to contemplate. It is only humans who set themselves apart from other substances. And the universe will not tolerate it, for the universe is a substance made of many substances. It is only humans who believe that substances can be divided between the human and the inhuman, who believe in a nature apart from the nature of the universe. You want to eradicate all other substances and banish evolution forever. Well think again, mortality is your friend. Welcome it as the salvation of your species.

Epilogue

My father would play Schubert's *Winterreise* repeatedly when I was young. Schubert's tragic melodies play in the background of my earliest childhood memories. My father would fill the house night and day with these poems of despair, it drove my mother to distraction. He would often weep at the conclusion of the final song, *Der Leierman*. One day I asked him why he found it so sad and he replied wistfully that the narrator never encounters a soul until he meets the hurdy-gurdy man in the final song. Now that I can only leave my house with difficulty and contact with the world is limited to well-meaning fools who attempt to prolong the life of my failing organs, it is an irony that it is only in this condition, in the final months of my life, that I can enjoy the peace an tranquillity of solitude.

I turn on the TV once in a while to see how the world is progressing, and today there is a broadcast from Hyde Park, a concert for the poor and starving children of the world. My eyesight is failing but I am sure that I see a familiar face singing sweetly into a microphone. Then again, maybe I dreamt it. My pain killers are strong and I find it difficult to maintain periods of prolonged consciousness. Yes, I must be mistaken, the name Lemal Porsche is spelt out on the screen in ridiculously funky graphics, a name I am sure I have not heard of. Lemal waves, he has a cute body and coquettish smile. He waves and canters back stage for an interview. *Well wha' do ya know?* Lemal is nineteen today. Lemal Porsche used to have a stutter but he has overcome this handicap and his shyness. He is no longer tongue-tied, he is an emerging butterfly.

Lemal Porsche is destined for great things. Dominic Rolex selected Lemal as the face for the future when judging applicants on *Model Behaviour*, he was chosen from 10,000 applicants, a miracle. Dominic Rolex encouraged Lemal, he became his confident, Rolex became an elder brother to him. Lemal Porsche's astonishing blue eyes start to well with tears.

The sound fades, the picture fades, I reach for the remote to increase the volume and brightness.

Normal transmission is resumed and there he is, a coquettish smile and a sweet voice.
There he is, he has it all
he will always have it
with his sweet voice and fine bone structure and perfect skin
always he will have it
always have
it
forever.

INTERFERENCES

Anne Keppie had gone to Brussels to escape from a shapeless feeling of discomfort and foreboding. A creeping malaise had coincided with the deterioration of her creative life; she had run a printmaking studio, but an increased leaning towards apathy, and a laconic manner, had driven her to a change of scene.

Brussels had been her choice because there she thought she could be without intention; and knowing neither the languages nor a single person, could be completely apathetic. She had quickly adopted the distractions of displacement in the three months that had passed, and a grey foggy aimlessness enveloped her will and imagination. Time was spent in states of anxiety or boredom.

On the day when she met Margaret and Walter Scriabin she had left her small but cheerful rented rooms in the morning to walk in town.

Where was she going? She scarcely knew. It was the same as yesterday. The night, as usual, had been quite sleepless, but she had awoken feeling positive. Hardly was she in the midst of the city centre, this stately conglomeration of gables, towers, arcades and fountains; hardly did she feel once more the wind on her face (that strong current wafting a faint and pungent aroma of far off uncertainties), than a familiar mistiness laid itself like a veil about her senses ... the muscles of her face relaxed, and she walked like a somnambulist.

Where was she going? It seemed to her the direction she took had a connection with her sad and strangely rueful pointlessness. She paused in front of a shop, a plain narrow façade like many others, and stood there lost in contemplation, surrounded by people engrossed in Christmas shopping. She read the name above the door, her eyes resting a little while on each object in the window. Then slowly she turned on her heels.

Where did she go? Towards a bar to discern what she could from La Libre Belgique, but she took a round-about way. Lingering by the tracks of the Gare Centrale she saw a train puff busily past, she idly counted the coaches, and looked after the man who sat in the last. He was an unthreatening looking man, and he noticed her gaze. Instead of staring through her or angrily away, he smiled and made a casual wave. A melancholy smile, perhaps, but still a smile. This unexpected human contact awoke her, and she made her way to the Nouveau Populaire.

Sitting by the window, she looked upon the abstraction of the lights and activity in the street. She had, in her hometown of Dundee, always regarded bars and cafés as neutral territory, representing the detached and elevated sphere of the aesthete, in which one was capable of refined ideas. Now they were merely waiting rooms.

In a way she felt she had lost her nerve, but for what she could not articulate. The prime element that drove her productivity – a sense of personal freedom, was lacking. She had decided that her practice was not so much art as some kind of home industry existing for no other reason than that it was being encouraged, even though it enjoyed no great success outside a small audience. The very best of these home products could hardly be called remarkable, and any sincere praise had to be qualified with a 'but'; clever, edifying, *but* not beautiful; or beautiful, edifying, *but* not clever; or, finally, beautiful, clever, *but* not edifying. Her thoughts spiralled into self-indulgence as she considered her predicament, but before they could get out of hand she was rescued by the intrusion of a young woman, who shoved a piece of paper into her face.

The girl spoke to her rapidly in Flemish. Anne intervened with her stock mumbled phrase explaining that she did not speak the language. The girl shrugged and smiled, made a wild, wide-eyed grin and turned her attention on a group of teenage boys sitting at the bar. Anne looked after her, quailing before the triumphal naturalism of youth, and examined what was revealed to be a flyer for a concert, very roughly hand printed. Anne grasped this token of her former life as a sign.

★

Finding the address was difficult, it was not a regular concert venue, and Anne had wandered around Les Marolles in search for some time before success. Fashionably dressed people walked to and fro around her in the darkness, all apparently observing a respect for the low hum and reverberation that qualified as the entertainment. The scene that greeted her was not expected: four men sat on cushions around a low table, laptop computers in front of them. A rapt audience around its parameters observed this uneventful arena. Interrupting the hum were occasional lurches of static, high-pitched clicks and an ominous throb. Had she not been made aware of the bitterness of her loneliness, Anne would have left the building immediately, recognising that this was a leisure pursuit alien to her. But somehow the low pulse, and proximity of still men and women in the warmth and half-light created sensuousness that she could not ignore.

She settled to observe those around her, and it was here that she noticed Margaret Scriabin. Wearing a velvet cape and bonnet framing her face and parted hair, the woman appeared to have stepped from a different era – remaining from a time when the building must have been a mansion entertaining the guests of the

Belgian merchant class. As she studied Margaret, and her lapses into closed-eyed reverie, Anne began to discern an invisible chord between this woman and one of the seated men.

Walter Scriabin, for it is he who was sitting with his right hand on the mouse, and his other furiously twirling a brown moustache. His dress, reserved in cut and a soothing shade of grey, was punctilious and dignified to the last degree. He was whistling softly to himself an inaudible beat, and his slanted brows were gathered in a frown, patterned by movement on the computer screen. The dark-brown hair was parted with severe correctness, and the chiselled swarthy features were sharpened as though they had been gone over with an engraver's tool. Yet the mouth – how gently curved it was, and the chin how softly formed!

Afterwards she had followed the throng through the fresh snow to a bar called Noël, and it was there that she fell into the company of the Belgian aesthetes. The crowd's mood was far more joyous and rowdy than the performance had been, and the comments of an acquaintance at home in Fife about the subterranean nature of extreme culture in Belgium drew Anne to scrutinise the present society, as she got drunk.

"Are these the type of people who would keep little girls in water tanks?" She whispered to herself.

"Ahhh, a Scot." a strange finger tapped her on the shoulder, Anne blinked sideways and it was the woman in the bonnet, regarding her with close-set eyes.

"Maybe!" she said sceptically, and drank.

"Never mind water tanks my lass! That's the tip of the iceberg! I saw you at the concert and I like your look, so *supercilious*. Let me introduce – I'm Margaret Scriabin and I could imagine to make a painting of you."

"You're a painter?"

"Mmm."

"Well horray for you. ... I'm sorry – I'm drunk and alone, ... and I need some intimacy." Anne's cheeks burned; the only way she could talk after so long in silence was through a wall of unfriendliness. Margaret placed her hands on her hips, struck a stance and said:

"It's alright, but no need to be abrasive! I was just being friendly and I know my Scotch accent's terrible – it doesn't mix with Flemish. Come and meet my husband; I saw you watching him."

"Did I stare? Was I obvious?"

"You Scots ... he has plenty of friends, and since it turns out you are from the region where coitus is often reached through stupefaction, perhaps you'd like to join us for another drink?" and she gestured to a snug, containing half a dozen people.

"Take it from me FlimFlam, *it's just as often missed.*" Anne muttered, propelled forward through the chattering mob to the quiet of the corner.

Walter was sitting at the head of the group; the others present, boys from the band, were dressed similarly, and there was one woman who looked very like Margaret. Anne was introduced around the party by her new friend as a Scot, and was not acknowledged with any particular enthusiasm as all present were involved in alcohol-fuelled discussions, though she was offered a stool. Margaret tried to work up their interest.

"Look at this girl, hasn't she beautiful eyes! The colour of fresh pints of beer?"

Anne smiled at Walter, mumbled "Good gig", to which he nodded a well-mannered acknowledgement but said nothing.

"Yes, it was magnifique!" Margaret laughed with an arm flung up in exuberance, then placed around Anne's waist.

"It's nice to see women combining to make us men feel famous ..." said a young man beside Walter with a smug expression, and reached out and kissed Margaret on the lips. As if on cue, the assembled party broke into what can only be described as a kind of orgy-lite, with clingings and fondles, very mild but unequivocal in nature, for several minutes. Moans bloomed and died like snowdrops. Anne hoped they were all enjoying themselves, for she was glad of the company, and she joined in tentatively, kissing and caressing enough to show this, before they all resumed conversation as if nothing had happened.

"Why are you here?" Margaret asked.

"I'm not sure."

"What do you do?"

"I was an artist. A printmaker. But I've lost my bottle."

"Are you lonely?" the other Margaret-girl asked. Ann said nothing.

"Won't you give yourself?" Margaret enquired. This seemed like an odd question considering a few minutes previously they had been kissing, but she took a breath and replied:

"I can't. Half my strength is locked in fear and pointlessness."

"Why?"

"I don't remember."

"Well if you could show yourself, how would you like to?"

"I would like to … I can't say. You'd be disgusted."

"Tell us."

"I would like … I can't tell you. You would laugh."

"Risk it."

"I'm truly lackadaisical, but I need something and someone to be the reason, an excuse for my lifelessness and boredom. I need for someone to be unable to escape from me, tied to me, their dearest wish to be to make me happy, but them to always have to contend with my

489

obstinate body and distracted attention. For that is my muscle – *the power to feel nothing.*"

"Do you want a cock to bully?" The smug faced boy offered.

"No not at all, I like inertness."

"Yes Sammy," Walter looked angrily at the boy and spoke in a voice much higher and softer than expected "That's a bit simplistic. It's not just sex she talking about, it's more than this. Are you an artist too?"

Anne laughed, "Yes, but I cannot recall a single work which grew from my hand in which I have not taken pains from the very first to involve myself in all sorts of conventions with my conscience. I have neither the freedom nor the courage to make art as I please, consequently there is no point in continuing."

Walter rested his large hand on her arm. "We have to leave now, but I think you should visit Margaret tomorrow in her atelier." And with that he and his wife arranged their appearances as if to leave.

"Let me walk with you. You are the first people I've spoken to for so long." Anne rushed to gather her things, but they hushed her back into her seat.

★

"Shall I disturb you?" asked Anne on the threshold of the atelier. She held her hat in her hand and bowed with some ceremony.

"Mercy on you! Don't be so formal please," answered Margaret, with her slightly comical, lilting intonation. "You were invited!" She transferred her brush to between her teeth, reached out her left hand, and looked her in the face, smiling and shaking her head.

"Yes, but you are working," Anne said, venturing in. "Let's see. Oh, it's nice to see the paintings, I dreamt about what they might be like last night." And she looked at the colour-sketches leaning against chairs at both sides of the easel, and from them to the large canvas, where the first patches of colour were beginning to appear among the confused and schematic lines of the charcoal sketch.

This was in a back building on the Rue de Heysel, several storeys up. Outside the tall window were dark conifer trees, and beyond this the Parc des Expositions against a crisp blue winter sky. The sweet breath of morning through an open pane mingled with the smells of paint and fixative. The morning light flooded the spacious emptiness of the atelier; making no secret of the bad flooring or the rough table under the window, covered with little bottles, tubes, and brushes; illuminating the unframed studies on the unpapered walls, the torn silk screen that shut off a charmingly furnished little living-corner near the door; it shone upon the two artists there before the easel.

Anne could look upon Margaret now properly in the daylight. A little older than Anne – slightly past thirty, she sat with a trace of a pose on a low stool, in a dark-blue apron and full skirts. Her brown hair was compactly dressed, already a little grey at the sides. It was parted in the middle and waved over the temples, framing a sympathetic, dark-skinned face. She made measurements with her outstretched arm and thumb; her features were drawn with a look of misgiving, almost of vexation.

Anne stood beside her, her hands composed behind her back; her brows gathered in a show of concentrated scrutiny, for she was not sure exactly what she was looking at. The paintings and sketches certainly looked impressive, full of expression, packed with ideas and confident fanfare. They were complicated images, both abstract and figurative with a suggestion of colonnade, cornice and avenue. The technique was striking and very convincing, but Anne sensed that, at heart, it was all of it mock, merely simulacrum, and she felt urged to adopt an over-analytic pose to mask this knowledge in politeness.

"Why, they are so lively?" She offered with hollow enthusiasm. Margaret did not respond and continued with her contrapposto measuring and tracing of the image's contours, tongue tip exposed at the corner of her mouth. "Are you satisfied with the way they are developing?"

"Certainly. But only time will tell." And she continued to make small marks, adjusting variously parts of the composition and structure. Anne watched unobtrusively as the painter absentmindedly cleaned her brushes and palette and prepared a kettle for tea. It was for Anne like watching a dull, self-conscious, play.

Over the tea, Anne broached the subject of the work's authenticity with bravery.

"I can see you can paint. But I think I would positively blush were I to really get a glimpse behind the scenes."

Margaret smiled to herself, and slowly stirred her tea. Eventually she quietly replied,

"What an artist talks about is never the main point. What they paint is not the point. It's raw material, out of which, with bland mastery, we create the work of art. If you care too much about what you have to say, if your heart is too much in it, you can be pretty sure of making a mess. You get pathetic, you wax sentimental; something dull and doddering, without roots or outlines, with no sense of humour – something tiresome and banal is forced into existence, and you get nothing out of it but apathy in your audience and disappointment and misery in yourself."

"My frame of mind is not particularly positive or coherent at the moment, but I can read, in a glance at these 'sketches', that you don't care about them one bit. They are bubbles blown by a baby! But I ask myself, if it's not this, what is it that you do care about? You are surely too vivid a woman to be without some expression?"

"Honestly? Doing these, which are easy and systematic, gives me the means to shop and socialise, which at the end of the day is the field in which I have true insight and commitment." She indicated the pictures with her hand and ended with a flourish, slugging her tea. Anne felt bemused at the frank explanation she was given. Margaret moved her chair closer and placed her palms together in a pedagogic manner.

"Anne listen. The current impoverishment and devastation you feel is a necessary preliminary condition to making something genuine, either here on this glorified holiday, or back home wherever it is you come from. Feeling – *warm, heartfelt feeling*, is always banal; only the irritations and icy ecstasies of your corrupt nervous system are real."

Anne Keppie thought for a while, then replied dispassionately,

"Something in your manner reveals your intention to intimidate me. I'm depressed and you are interfering."

Margaret began to appear exasperated, "*Because I am you*, well part of you anyway … Walter and I."

"Walter?"

"People do tend to go around in twos, and it's a common literary device to give fullness to a principle character through comparisons of similarity and contrasts with significant others. Now Interferences is a very short story, we didn't get totally underway so it's all going to rely on suggestion and the symbolic, but he was intended to be quiet and arcane anyway, while I am meant to work as a mirror. We are both female, visual artists, etc etc. In the course of the next month we would

493

spend a lot of time together because I will invite you to work with me in my studio, to teach me some printing techniques, in a gentle attempt to galvanise you into action again. We would begin to make things together and it would be quite good."

With Margaret's launch into the plot-fabric of her life, Anne saw the room around her as the clichéd garret that it was.

"You would start to mimic my movements, language and taste, but always undercut with a current of competition (which is common between women). And, of course, in time, you will start to feel quite strongly about my husband. He is detached and reticent, but so charming, and you are quite lonely. You will misread his friendship towards you, construct a non-existent narrative between you and him. Anne I warn you now, he is my accomplice and supporter in every possible way. There is no reason to think he would ever have found you interesting. You are not an attractive young woman. This will all end in you having to leave Brussels hastily a month from now."

"Why?"

"You end up killing us. I won't say how. But it won't matter anyway because we don't actually exist."

"What?" Anne whispered flatly and tensely.

"You know you've felt disengaged from your feelings of late? Well that's because you are. I am your sexuality, Walter is your creativity, and we've been hanging out in Brussels for about six months now. You subconsciously chased us here presumably to get us back. You're lucky, most people have to go to psychiatrists, spend all that time navel-gazing. You just have to chat to us! Ask what you like and I'll tell you."

"Who were the people at the concert, the people at the table?"

"Just a bunch of unformed ideas."

Anne stood up and moved to look at the scene through the window. After some time she said,

"I would actually have preferred Walter to be my sexuality since he is so good looking."

"I'm sure. I, as your sexuality, am very over determined. But that's because your real bodily nature is lost under those layers of bullshit you have decided makes you deep. It's half grasped from books and repeated back to form this cartoonish sadomasochism with no way in. It's not you, just as much as these gestures on the canvas are artifice!"

Anne cupped her elbow, rested her chin between thumb and forefinger in contemplation, she felt quite calm.

"So my creativity is still obtainable?"

"Well … Walter's not, he's mine."

"What if I get rid of you?"

"You'll be lucky, I'm a good fighter."

"I'm going to have to just wait and see?"

A mobile phone rang and the painter used the opportunity to avoid giving an answer.

*

With the advent of spring, life changes.

On a fine morning Anne Keppie's ferry reached open sea. She stood at the prow wrapped in a thick tartan scarf against a mounting wind, and looked beneath into the dark going and coming of the waves as they hovered and swayed and came on, to meet with a clap and shoot erratically away in a bright gush of foam.

She was lulling in a disposition of contentment. The culmination of events in the last month, now warranted the clear quality of her state of mind. She had stayed in Brussels, and was now leaving in haste, traces of blood still under her fingernails and on a knife hidden in her rucksack.

As the Dundee port became visible in the dawn, she thought about the long days she would spend in her studio, cutting silk screen stencils, perfecting lino prints with the back of a spoon. The roaring, foaming, flapping, and slapping all about her came to her ears like the groan and rustle of an old walnut tree, the creaking of a garden gate. More and more Dundee came on.

GAMES OF TRUTH:
a blood poetic in seven part harmony
(this is me speaking to you)[1]

part 1: (this)

light avoidance techniques as creation. First, the problem
of zero, one {0,1; or even, 0 > 1; maybe also: beyond
0; finally, just the 1}. Did you know that the square
root of any positive number after zero is eventually –
I mean, after awhile (that is, at least to nine digits,
sometimes rounded up or down) – always and without fail equal to: 1? Peculiar, though not fascinating,
except to the very few. Indeed, probably only to
those with calculators and extra time on their hands,
bored with some other administrational task (say,
figuring out the law of averages). But, with the aid of
light avoidance techniques – blank stares, self-abuse,
whimsy, for example – surprising things can be
accomplished! And even with the most simple of
calculators! Like pressing the magic $\sqrt{}$ [square root]
button enough times until a 1 emerges from any
(positive) anonymous chaos. Nerd sublimity.

twenty-four hours. A small question about mobility and
its implications: why is it one can only go back or
forwards 24 hours in (our) bio-time and space? No
matter the speed or the curvature of the movement,
the uncertainty of the destiny; even if one leaps
thousands of light years forward and speeds through
the wormholes of the galaxies with greater agility
than even the inventors of Star Trek could imagine;
even if one floats in a balloon, is delayed endlessly in
airports or flies by the seat of their pants; even if one
is gay or straight, moslem or jew, a witch or a
warlock; transgendered or binarically split into male
or female; even if one comes from or surges toward

the 'east' or the 'west'; even if one is the target of racist attack or becomes its perpetrator; even if one is adorned in leather, piercing and tattoo; even if one is engaged in peculiar sex acts or none at all; still, at the moment – this very instantaneous moment of our contemporary moment – one gains or loses only 24 hours of bio-time, a 24 hour micro-memory slice of time at the best of times. It does not matter if it is a corrosive, nuclear, toxic time, twenty four hours is the limit to the forward or backward movement and mobility of time, at any given time.

rehearsal. Perhaps this notion of movement – a kind of muscular Eternal Return relay race back and forth against (and buttressed by) the 24 hour festival of life and clocks – is the not-so-secret telos of modernity itself, the seemingly 'real' basis, the biological scientistic, rational choice-within-a-small-parenthesis-of-choice, 'enlightened' basis for certain commonly held views. In particular, it underwrites a few claims about equality, and has similar implications for the commonality or universality of experience itself; to wit, this 24 hour rule is applicable to all and sundry, irrespective of nationality, ethnic origin, sexual orientation, religious belief or aesthetic inclination. You might prefer the shorter variant, which goes something like this: at the end of the day, as it were, we all *die*, irrespective of any other consideration. Later version: If I cut myself, do I not bleed?

And yet: there is something about this blood and limit of death thing not to be ignored.

musical chairs. Now picture this: picture a child's game, well-known in its immediate sense of dysfunctionality writ large: the game of 'musical chairs'. For purposes of establishing a common memory data-bank, shall I recap the game as follows: a series of chairs are set in a line with one too many participants for the amount of given chairs. A gun goes off, the music begins and the children run round the chairs frantically attempting to be near this or that chair so that when the music stops – suddenly, and on the wrong beat – they must grab and sit on said chair (Rule #1). The game is already skewed, we all know this from the start: one player will always-already be caught without a chair. The one 'caught out' when silence descends, well, they must exit, stay at the sidelines, or go somewhere else. (Get lost: Rule #2). The game is repeated, until there are only two participants and one isolated chair left. I never liked this game, whether or not I managed to be victorious with the one remaining trophy chair. Who cares about the chairs anyway? I was always more curious about the play of the game. (This curiosity meant that I always played to the bitter end this silly little game).

'Everyone evacuate the premises immediately'. Not an unusual statement these days; plausibly announced by bomb-squad police or other suitable candidates, say: market mechanisms, imminent bad weather, morality gatekeepers, losers at musical chairs: forget the existential questions of life (why? why me? and so on) for, quite remarkably, the natty, bitty 'practical' everyday problems of translocation, displacement and other forms of decay will suddenly flash before you, with only micro-seconds to spare; micro-seconds in which a decision must be taken and enacted. This flash/decision/enactment can be broken down by way of the following set of inter-rogations: What would you *grab* at the very moment

of decisive indecision and chaos? That which is close to hand or that which holds the most sentimental/ memory value? or that which is lightest (or all three)? Some kind of technical equipment, say, a mobile phone or your computer laptop (should you have one); extra batteries? A strong pair of shoes? Water? Second set of questions: Where do you go? Do you run ahead as a herdsman?, asks Nietzsche, Or turn into a pillar of salt, as did Lot's wife? Third set of questions: And how do you get to where you want to go (assuming there is no direct gun to your head or cattle car waiting)? How do you get to where you want to go especially if you are not certain where you wish to go, or for some other reason, cannot get there, say, because you may be suffering from a certain degree of short-sightedness. (Because in that case, you cannot say to yourself, says Wittgenstein, 'look at the church tower ten miles away and go in that direction.')[2]

Last set of questions: How will you be able to read/interpret the rules of the game, if and when you 'arrive' (wherever that 'arrival point' may be), irrespective of whether the language spoken appears (or even is) the 'same' language, say 'international/ exchange English' or even 'art' for example. What codes of identity or identities must you somehow embody or occupy, or be seen to occupy, in order to 'communicate'? What will be lost in translation? Or found – by way of Rosetta stone hieroglyphics? How will the differences already encumbering your life, surface as explanatory nodal points or clusters of meanings (say around race, sex, class, age, nationality, eating habits, drug use or vary- ing dislocations within and between these islands of identity and difference). Which battlegrounds will you choose to stand upon, or be forced to stand upon? How will you 'fit in'? By bowing and scrapping, cap in hand, hoping the 'flaws' won't be noticed; or by boldly going where angels dare not tread? Will you fall prey to the assumption 'people are the same everywhere' (whereby we return to the Eternal 24 hour relay race of mobility, blood and death compelling your every move)? Or will you fall prey to the loop of musical chairs, trophies notwithstanding?

Where will you buy your milk? Pleasure your body? Rest your eye? Get dental and medical? Share your joke?

slippery amputations. 'But to learn all about these recondite matters,' Melville recommends, 'your best way is at once to descend into the blubber-room, and have a long talk with its inmates. ... When the proper time arrives for cutting up its contents, this apartment is a scene of terror to all tyros, especially by night. On one side, lit by a dull lantern, a space has been left clear for the workmen. They generally go in pairs, – a pike-and-gaff man and a spade-man. The whaling-pike is similar to a frigates' boarding-weapon of the same name. The gaff is something like a boat-hook. With his gaff, the gaffman hooks on to a sheet of blubber, and strives to hold it from slipping, as the ship pitches and lurches about. Meanwhile, the spade-man stands on the sheet itself, perpendicularly chopping it into the portable horse-pieces. This spade is sharp as hone can make it; the spademan's feet are shoeless; the thing he stands on will sometimes irresistibly slide away from him, like a sledge. If he cuts off one of his own toes, or one of his assistants', would you be very much astonished? Toes are scarce among veteran blubber-room men.'[3]

Well, supposing that the 'this' is located somewhere in the blubber-room of life. Or, better yet, that it is the blubber-room of life. What difference does its *location* matter to *us*? Or whether it is shoeless or not? To experiment with space and time and numbers and slipperiness and speed – simultaneously – as an amputation or a style, or a colour, a code, a system, a weapon, a poetics, or a ship of fools, merely under-scores, at least in the first instance, a curious feature: its integrity.

part 2: (this is)

reassuring doubt. Integrity comes in several varieties: the word, the promise, the friendship, the [blood] relation, and, for the more spiritually afflicted, the soul. (This list does not exhaust the list). Interestingly enough, it also doubles as the vehicle to carry out or maintain the aforementioned list. So it would not be unfair to say that integrity elicits a paradox: Despite the odds (or perhaps because of them), there is something of a 'given-ness', a sturdiness, an unchangeability about integrity (as in the promise – if you do such and such, I, Moses, will, despite bad weather or river conditions, deliver you to the promised land –), whilst at the same time sneaking in a kind of unstated *probability* or *capability* or *reliability* to do so. Now, integrity as capability; capability as a repeatable gesture; the repeatability of a gesture as eliciting the predict-ability of a 'what is to come next'; the 'what is to come next' as probability (and not just possibility); the probable-possibility as some kind of sturdiness; sturdiness as some kind of reliability – surely must count for *something*. But that the sun goes up and the sun goes down, more or less on a regular basis, 24 hours a day, everyday (or at least does not go dancing around the buildings at all hours of day and night according to some whim), is not, really, what is meant here by integrity.

interlude. The Angel of Death passes over all those homes displaying a small but presumably unmissable symbol tacked to the door. Escaping with unleavened bread, four children's questions emerge: the practical one asks: when?; the evil one asks: why?; the wise one restates in question form: how?, and the one who cannot ask any questions doesn't ask a thing. I have heard this somewhere before. When? Why? What does it matter that it matters (let's just find a way! to Where)? [o]? On second thought, maybe the four questions, and the passing-over itself, are less about the rush from exile to freedom – or even something else, say, if not to freedom, then the leap from routine to some kind of splatter flick nightmare. But maybe, indeed perhaps, the passing-over, and the question period it inhabits, is closer to the age-old dynamics of rusty bureaucratic meetings, a kind of old fashioned multiplicity which attempts to quell the appetites from all sides. Bureaucracy as door-frame: a nasty little business, meant to tame or destroy those curve-ball propositions and their peculiar new-fashioned timings whilst tacking them neatly, even artistically, to the door.

the giving of a gift (or impropriety and whether pigs can fly). Let's say that the word 'integrity' is to become the proper name we give to a *certain kind* of coherence, a *certain kind* of multiplicity/dimensionality of rhythms, rifts, lightwaves or beats. Still, the *condition* for its execution and deliverance seems to rely on a 'something else' or a 'something other': say, for example, the projected *intention* of the promise-giver to the promise-receiver (and vice versa). But if this is true, then a whole series of problematic assumptions around who or what is giving and receiving promises when and how, surely must infect our otherwise perfect game of truth. It might even touch on that nebulous terrain called 'memory' or 'faith' or even the more superstitious (and attractive) glow-spheres of a 'spell'!

Nevertheless, it underscores the not so problematic 'fact' that intention (or anyway, its conditions) are not only – like the integrity from which it springs – multiple, slippery, cruel, paradoxical in a probability kind of way, but also sensuous, bitter, sometimes wrong, sweaty, alive, human (also in a probability kind of way). This makes intention itself both a part of, and at the very same time, quite separate from its word, promise, friendship, viewer relation, soul. Rather similar to an instant (of time/timings) – a fragment without edge, weight or volume – a surface economy of sorts, it remains separate from the very entity to which it is a part. For, like its cousin, integrity, intention can shape-shift, whilst retaining its recognisability as an authoritative 'this is (it)'; or 'I mean what I say' (and in so declaring, makes it have weight, volume, edge). Strangely, though, intention/integrity becomes neither the form (but it is the form!), nor the structure (but it is the structure!), nor the nodal point (but it is the nodal point!), nor the gap between two 'opposing' points or edges (but it is also the gap!). A ticklish situation to be sure.

attraction as judgment. Shall we just ignore this series of 'whether or nots' 'neither/nors' and yes/but's for the moment and focus on the odd consequence of what happens when probability folds into, or becomes, a kind of throbbing integrated circuitry surface-structure: if the event of its conditionality is itself ruinous, paradoxical, slimey, multiply dimensional, then one of the odd consequences is that it can only be grasped in the reassuring *doubt* that it cannot be *grasped* at all. Some have situated this doubt as *irony* or even *disloyalty* or even as a *threat*, but perhaps it is closer to the function of *attraction*, whether or not that attraction functions in some degree or another as irony/disloyalty/threat.

gooeyness as judgment. Suppose that someone wishes to make a statement about art by dropping twelve live rats off a tenth story building onto a series of neatly laid canvasses at ground level. Who likes rats, anyway? Those who have never lived in slum conditions might never understand. On the other hand, rats can be clever and intelligent sentient beings, which, let's face it, have survived a myriad of plagues (and indeed, have helped several plagues to survive). On the third hand, maybe their broken, blood-splattered bodies make a lovely series of images which might match someone's interior dining room furniture. Or (slightly different version) maybe there are certain things, say insects, which in their seemingly abundant accessibility, micro-size, and straightforward ability to be squished, ought not to matter *too much*. Well, maybe all this is to say that the paths of judgment, when circumscribing the 'ought not to matter *too much*', clearly rest on a number of factors, the most obvious having less to do with some form of *cruelty*, in and of itself (or the acts thereof, say, humiliation, shame, ridicule, abjection, guilt) and a whole lot more to do with a series of assumptions around, for example, the way a 'something' (read: active, allowed to be human) is binarically encoded away from its 'other' (read: rat, insect, jew, moslem, gay, 'those who do not fit in'). In any case, and whatever it is named, unless the paradoxical nature, and the politics this implies, is accounted for, 'judgment' will remain but a pseudonym for the worst excesses of moral law, and taste, only its hand-maiden. Then again, this may not be the worst thing – unless of course, you happen to be a rat, insect, shoeless.

"but you are, Blanch, you are … " And yet I want to say, even with respect to *Baby Jane* and the infamous overturning of the wheelchair by Baby with her Blanch still in it, that certain kinds of actions *are* cruel and that my judging them as such, is greater (more steadfast) than my *opinion* or *belief* or *perception* that it *might* certainly be the case. Is this certainty possible without predicating a universal rule or essence of humanity? Or by relying on some 'neutral' (or 'objective-as-if-neutral'; ie, 'true' for all time) scientistic observational experiment? Or without slipping backwards into the worst disappointments of religious or enlightenment thinking? I would like to say yes! But then judgment itself would seem to require a wholly different context or way of seeing, sensing, acting, tasting. Perhaps this is what really is at stake when one speaks of 'ethics' as an 'aesthetics' or 'stylistics of existence' devoid of its insistence to universalise or ground a variety of moralising assumptions. (But then perhaps I am just confusing ethics with the beauty of duration and its glamorous neighbour: the cool factor).

interlude (revenge). As she sat there, watching relentless waves slapping unspoilt sand and rock, singing of sirens and shipwrecks and blue-bottle vipers, the poison flowed silently from all her (semi-bandaged) wounds. The salted beat beatings, strangely reverent and cruel and rhythmic, clothed her and the darkness gave her life. A seagull eyed her for quite some time: they exchanged a knowing glance. Caught as she was, between the calmness of its wings and the violence of the crashing, watered sense of rough, she remained there, wrapped in the oddly comforting surface of her – absurdity. A rather bewitching aloneness; she could not, would not budge. Immobilised, riveted, she laughed out loud and for the first time, in a very long time, she relaxed, on holiday from the usual banalities of rape and blood, and senseless stabbings of her soul and its mates. Revenge as a kind of leisured memory, writ tiny tiny in the ironic mutiny of it all.

a more time-honoured wound. According to Conventional Wisdom, time heals all wounds, or something to that effect. To the degree to which there might be a grain of truth in this, would this grain be true for all time, every time, or just after one's 50th birthday? (Maybe it is more a matter of remembering or forgetting or of being lost and then found rather than age per se). But what if the wound is a very big wound (as that which operates with envy or shows up in the infamous friend/enemy divide); or a very superficial one (as in the promulgation of a skin mutation, blood-lettings or decapitated masteries)? In the case of the former, time as Doctor-Healer can only approach, but never 'cure' the wound. (Here 'never' is a very long, infinitely long time and its pathways equally fraught with unrequited angst. Echoes of certain assumptions around the pre-modern and post-modern 'work of desire/work of melancholy' can be heard). In the case of the latter, time is but a *playmate* to the superficiality of it all. (This does not necessarily make it 'good' or 'better' from the first example; but it does make it different). Indeed, time can change its roles, outfits, gestures, rhythms; sometimes it is not even 'time' at all, though that is a different matter. But supposing one opts to make new wounds – say out of boredom or frustration or lack of attention or fear or even *generosity*. Say one wishes to wallow in her wounds until or unless something better comes along. Perhaps she simply *loves* her wounds and is, similarly, *eroticised* by them. Perhaps she makes them her fetish! In days (not yet) long ago gone by, she might be considered a somewhat psychologically destructive masochist or sadist (or both); certainly she might be accused of unresolved mourning (having more to do, apparently, with the fear/reality of an absent lover, father, cock, death and etc. rather than any sense of *jouissance*). In any case, she might become a serious candidate for psychoanalysis or thought to be a criminal or even an *artist*.

But what if those wounds really were closer to circumscribing the *pleasures* (rather than the pains) involved with *not* belonging or only partially belonging to 'a' self, or to *'oneself'*, or even to a *sensus communis*? What if, at the end of the day (or even in the middle of it) she preferred the bright, meaningless lights of the *urban anomie*? What if the codes of fetish pointed more toward a metonymic gesture, a slice of life, slice of time, slice of colour, slice of identity, slice of skin, slice of place (say for example, a city) rather than a metaphoric 'standing-in' for some other lost cause or non-representable representation? 'Sometimes', as the Old Master was known to have said, 'a cigar is just a good smoke'.

part 3: (this is me)

the address book (for people in our condition). I will be quite
frank with you: I've always preferred black leather
bindings fitted smooth across hand-sized address
books. Nothing else written on or near the cover; a
discreet and rather disciplined materialism, though
not without its smells, its texture and its raunch.
That's black leather for you; and that's how I've
always preferred it. Address books, case in point.

Like most people in our condition, I have, over the
years, improved on the necessary ritual involved in
choosing the perfect address book. Of course
it requires one to be in the right frame of mind,
utterly focused and with sturdy step (though not to
the extent that you might draw attention to yourself).
Personally, it has always included a long slow dip
into water – hot baths or springs, if you're lucky – a
long slow dip to exaggerate last night's debauched
pleasures or its succulent pains. Lately, I've taken to
wearing, on that special day, the finest starched white
shirt buttoned exact and to the top. And more recent
still, I've included some small new trophy, like the
extravagant toy from last week's indiscretions, or the
silk scarf from the time before … I'll just quietly tuck
it away against my body so as to call up the tongue
of S – or maybe the orifices of N – sweeping gently
but urgently against my skin as if to coax me forward
and remind me of that special kind of something,
that special kind of nakedness, so required of each
and every one of us (I mean, the people in our
condition) who try madly and sometimes in vain not
to falter at the exact moment when the reality of the
address book is nigh.

For this is another, very delicate, task – the choosing
of the Book – the smallest slip, the tiniest crack in

style or in mood will disturb the momentum, might even tarnish the memory and in any case will propel you stupidly and without grace toward that stoically menacing ever-present arena, blandly called: the 'register'. Without ritual, without a well-selected, polished little routine honed to fine art, how many times could you muster that special kind of courage before another year slides by and the moroseness settles in? For the passage from the land of un-deadness to some other shore, is tricky indeed. And I've often thought to myself, eyes half-closed, lips half-opened: how many indiscriminate baths would I have to take if the ritual had not yet firmly been set; how many haircuts would I have to afford; how many pairs of shoes must I buy in order to prepare body and soul, permanently, for the rawness of that moment; for the endurance required, year after year to pick-up that new replacement and hold it and smell it and write in their names? Page after page, life after life.

interlude. So Joyce died last month, with gallantry, military honours, precious laughter, family ties and all. Before her death it was David, and before his, it was Lorne; Michael (a flaming queen), a couple days earlier … I used to borrow Ricky's leather jacket: now I've inherited it. Danny, Andrew, Tessa, Teddy, Sam (we called him 'Daddy') … The funeral Alan prepared for himself was particularly riveting (made me think that I, too, should have Gregorian chants and naked people carrying white lit candles, solemnly and in step when my death-time comes).

learning how to be [me]. First riddle of the seven sphinxes: what does 'visual culture' mean to a blind person? Answer: that which lies in the elsewhere of representation, gaze, spectacle. We might wish to call this 'elsewhere' a matter of *installation*; ie, a matter of installing into a singular-zap-instant: a memory; an event, a signature [including one's own signature], the multiple criss-crossed dimensions of a curved time (one could say 'duration') which becomes 'recognisable' in the economy of its 'being there/ being here/being with.' Perhaps we might wish to call this vision *acoustic*; its being made manifest, a *poetic*, though one ripped away from its Nicomachean Ethics and other Aristotelian moorings of what usually passes for the sacred and the profane. Perhaps what we are searching for, blindly or otherwise, is a kind of poetic whose 'techne' resembles more closely a queer kind of *recipe* of the literal, the elemental, the periodic chemical, the gene pool, the mimetic – one shot through with a 'something else' [say the sensuousness of its smell, taste, voice, touch]. A different sense of time – perhaps a 'cooking time'; even a 'toxic time' (for cooking need not produce something healthy for it to 'work'). Maybe it just boils down to a question of seeing with one's ears, hearing with one's pulse, smelling with one's eyes and etc. Or maybe it is just a plea to take seriously *habeas corpus*, 'there shall be the body' for any and all forms of truth games to occur.

re-cycled pride (learning how to be [me]). Second riddle of the seven sphinxes: what lies between the supposed rarefied air of genius and the ready-made unity of 'common' sense? The ambitious (social) climber thinks of bridges to their hilltops, and answers: networking! making a name! But perhaps the answer is closer to a dose of wilful conceit and its maligned offspring, doubt and experimentation. But then this arrogance requires a certain kind of faith, a certain kind of compulsion, a certain kind of certainty, say about one's own ability to know [the whatever] whilst simultaneously accepting that one must take the leap 'out there' for no other reason than that it must be done [now]. A strange kind of juridical move, this oddly disciplined sense of self, this mastering of several-selves without implanting a singular self as master; a risk-taking without dwelling for an instant on the possible disasters of what might happen 'if' the *knowing* might have been gathered from a whole series of misguided judgements or parochial rumours or community standards. A certain kind of conceit, this kind of faith – Kierkegaard might call it: a certain kind of *trembling*.

the importance of a particular compulsion. Let's say the poetics of trembling involves the directorial voice of both bearing and saying 'yes' – a 'yes' saying of the me-selves and the we-selves and the they-selves, tattooed neatly within the parentheses of one's own flesh, history, habit, humour. A kind of dynamic carnal knowledge without the dialectical and etc. end-game of Eden or its apples or attendant serpents, angels or God. But if faith, curiosity, experimentation, work of art, politics, aesthetics, ethics of comportment and so on are to side-step an inherent messianism or even a quasi-messianism which otherwise must be admitted to our pleasant little game of truth, then perhaps the following helpful rules of the game should be kept in mind: 'don't look down and don't look back'. Paradoxically, of course, should you follow that unconditional rhythm of that beat, you may end up ruminating without memory, experimenting without doubt, installing without the intensity of a compulsive stylistics. Or, to re-work an old phrase: you may be forced to repeat the grinning nightmares of history, patched this time (simultaneously) as tragedy, farce, and sterilised violence. (But now we have secretly sneaked in another way to speak of carnal knowledge, without ridding the picture of its moral imperative!) A risk if ever there was one.

The cool factor. Vanity, says Nietzsche, is the skin of the soul. Lies, a mark of imagination or even cunning, and if done in the absence of wilful deceit, a matter of supposed innocence. But what of the *cool factor* – that 'unsayable something' that gives off a kind of *confidence* or *style* of knowing (the whatever). Despite its call to a basic form of signature, law or event, its *statement* is that of paradoxical inhabitation: the inhabiting of detachment, etched with dry wit, relaxation, sensuous uncaring and the temperate codes of stuttering as a kind of fashion sense. Dare to say it has little to do with Religion, Politics, or Art and has a whole lot more to do with confronting and accepting head-on a very particular impurity and very particular grammar; that is, the grammatical impurity of the death sentence. A kind of repeatable knowledge that one is going to die many times in the time span of their mortality, whilst precisely at the same time, one knows very well that one is going to die only once. Here in the paranthesis of time we so nonchalantly call 'our own life', history pops up as different dress codes, and one must learn how to use/discard/re-cognise those codes not unlike yesterday's T-shirt.

digression [or the uses and abuses of kneeling]. Perhaps it is safer to say that faith and trembling have more to do with the necessity to submit – and not only that! But to know how and when, without knowing "why" exactly, and without knowing to whom or even to what one 'kneels'. On the other hand, perhaps this kind of faith has nothing to do with kneeling or any other form of submission, and I've just been carried away with trying to explain what happens when I sniff out the uncharted paths in a manner according to my custom, especially when night stealths towards day: the stillness of air! the light! the dew! the quietness of tone! the possibility to connect a this with a that! Perhaps what I am mentioning has only a tiny micro slice to do with submission – but I mention it anyway, for no other reason than that the combination of light, and touch, and sound, and smell compels me to inhabit my body *differently*; now aligned/maligned with a stranger series of curiosities, hungers, expectations, promises, threats. This has very little to do with losing (or conversely, with finding) 'my' self. It's a peculiar submission; perhaps even a peculiar mastery – this gutter-ground gift, this instant eventness of *desire* and *pleasure* and *discipline* and *wandering*: this holy place of the bended knee. (But perhaps I am confusing the formal requirements of Philosophy and Art and Religion with their bastardised cousins, greed, hunger, curiosity, sloth). It is a delicate game we are playing, after all.

part 4: (this is me speaking)
anatomy of envy. Circa 1621: *Siquidem vita et fama pari passu* [seeing that life goes hand in hand with repute], *spiritus altos frangit et generosos* [it breaks noble and lofty spirits] (Hieronymus) [*and makes them envious* (Golding)]. 'Many men neglect the tumults of the world, and care not for glory, and yet they are afraid of infamy, repulse disgrace' (Tully,

Offic.lib.I); they can severely contemn pleasure, bear grief indifferently, but they are quite battered and broken with reproach and obloquy, and are so dejected many times for some public injury, disgrace, as a box on the ear by their inferior, to be overcome of their adversary, foiled in the field, to be out of a speech, some foul fact committed or disclosed, etc., that they dare not come abroad all their lives after, but melancholize in corners, and keep in holes. The most generous spirits are most subject to it: Aristotle, because he could not understand the motion of Euripus, for grief and shame drowned himself (Cælius Rhodiginus, *Antiquar.lec.lib.29, cap.8*). Homer was swallowed up with this passion of shame 'because he could not unfold the fisherman's riddle'. Sophocles killed himself, 'for that a tragedy of his was hissed off the stage' (Valer.Max., *lib.9,cap.12*). Lucretia stabbed herself, and so did Cleopatra, 'when she saw that she was reserved for a triumph, to avoid the infamy.' Antonius the Roman, 'after he was overcome of his enemy, for three days space' sat solitary in the fore-part of the ship, abstaining from all company, even of Cleopatra herself, and afterwards for very shame butchered himself (Plutarch, *vita ejus*). # Apollonius Rhodius 'wilfully banished himself, forsaking his country, and all his dear friends, because he was "out" in reciting his poems,' (Plinium, *lib.7, cap.23*). Ajax ran mad, because his arms were adjudged to Ulysses ... Tis Valescus de Taranta and Felix Platerus observation, 'Envy so gnaws many mans' hearts, that they become altogether melancholy.' And therefore belike Solomon (Prov. xiv, 13) calls it 'the rotting of the bones' – 'As a moth gnaws a garment, so,' saith Chrysostom, 'doth envy consume a man ... As did he in Æsop, lose one eye willingly, that his fellow might lose both … '[4]

beyond good, better, and best. You find yourself encrusted in a huge game of chess. What will you do to ensure the Queen or King is protected, especially if you start off as Pawn of even as Rook? Maybe you're already a Queen (or King), but you've been trapped by believing in your own propaganda, or can only think up to move three, and now have lost all sense of propriety and strategy within the art of this kind of power / game. Maybe you've lost the entire sense of the game or even of power itself (not to mention its art) for no other reason than that you thought you were playing checkers or bridge. Perhaps your real status is as Bishop and what motivates your every step is a peevish hunger to change the status quo's status to something more *desirable*, say a transition toward saintliness, namely, your own. Knights have their own advantage, what with their declared love for armour, the gallantry of the warrior horse, and the beauty of its smells. But whatever position you may occupy on this board, there are two things that will never enter this game: the faith (or not) in miracles and the importance of trust.

special cases. Heart and other organs seem to be at premium these days, especially if you happen to be a pig. Medical science is now able to transplant, successfully, animal organs into the bodies of humans. Is this a miracle? And does this make the being with the heart of a pig, more – or less – human? Perhaps the answer depends on quantity (ie how many body parts could be transplanted into a single body before that body would no longer count as human). Or perhaps it depends on the actual *size* of the transplant, say, if one were only to inject a tiny little rat sperm into the tissues of a young concert pianist? Maybe it depends on the type and the quality (as in the expression: all parts are considered equal, but some are more equal than others, say the brain, for example). Maybe in the latter case, the brain case, quality is really related to the difficulty of getting it right. Maybe a human is a human is a human, no matter what.

But could there be 'special cases', say, for example, when one loses control of all bodily functions, and has only the original nose left, and therefore *needs* some extra parts, brains included. On the other hand, what if one is only attracted to certain kinds of noses (skin colours and textures, hormones, brains, drugs, and etc), and wishes to sport something new or different for no other reason than simply that they *wish* to do so? (let's say, out of some kind of *enjoyment*). Would this count as a 'special case' too? Or to put this slightly differently: is it better or worse that there might be no reason for the change, at least not for a health or prolongation of life reasons (and, anyway, are those really *good* reasons, after all?). Maybe there is never a case when there is *no reason*, and maybe I want to be grumpy and ignore the ingenious invention of enjoyment by placing it in a parenthetical mode. But to say 'never' (or to relegate it to a parenthesis) in this instance seems to imply a previous set of assumptions, say around a recycled notion of *false consciousness*. But then, what of 'false consciousness'? This implies there is *true consciousness*: and now we are certainly entering more *sterilised* waters. For it would seem that there might be some rather muddy cases when 'false consciousness' bears no witness to this complication, say, when the brain transplant is successfully carried out, and, unlike our Frankenstein of yesteryear, can actually *remember* who he or she had been prior to the new body-encasements. Would *this* person be the new or old person or something in between? (But now I am assuming that memory is somehow connected to consciousness and that there can be no other human type creature than *the* human being). Is this a fatal move or a political strategy or just some kind of secularising anthropomorphic obsession? (perhaps it is just mere projection).

cultural anxiety and the problem of the 'ish': what if the brain that had been chosen and transplanted were originally located in a female body but now, for some reason, were re-located into a male body? There is a commonly held assumption, recently corroborated by 'medical science', that women are incapable of reading maps correctly. Would this new being only be able to read maps correctly half of the time ? What if a pre-surgical female *could* for some 'mysterious reason' already read a map (or do mathematics, play in a rock band, think hard thoughts, ejaculate, interior design, shoot people, lead armies, write poetry). Would she already be, at least partly, male? Which part? (Probably she would simply be displaying poor cultural judgement or, in any case, bad manners in her unwillingness to accept a 'biology-is-destiny' decree – but perhaps that is a different matter). Isn't the real problem with this kind of 'scientific discovery' simply that it just disqualifies her from being a female 'girlie-girl' and leads her onto to that disquieting snails-and-nails-and-puppy-dog-tails 'no-mans-land', ie, the sacredly protected land of 'the *boy-ish*'. Would this 'ish' factor – heretofore seemingly not able to be acknowledged in science, culture and the arts (except where colours are concerned, as in 'reddish' or 'bluish', etc.) – lead to the cultural anxiety that she might secretly (or even openly) be 'bent', 'twisted', or in any case, 'not-straight'? What if she were more *beautiful* than she was *ugly* (or vice versa) and could do the difficult stuff, too (like leap tall buildings in a single bound), but turned out to be entirely unconcerned with her sexual orientation? [Digression: can anyone *not* be so concerned, if, that is to say, they are living in a community rather than on a desert island? Yes, if they are allowed to be *young* enough]. Is this she-*ish* being 'an exception' – and in which case: what type of exception – or should we leave the secret around sensuality/ sexuality/ aesthetic attraction, age and taste out of this picture? I want to say: no.

Harder case scenario. take the example of a post-operative transsexual being. In most situations, if one is going to change from male → female or female → male, either one remains 'transsexual' or one becomes what their post-operative operation provides. Only with the most conservative reactionaries (which includes immigration centres, doctors, clergy, passport/birth certificate issuers, certain friends and relatives) would their change not be acknowledged at all. Perhaps this type of 'special case', circling around memory, matter and its trans-location, is to be attached to some other terrain other than the slippery slope of truth games. But I want to disagree: there is something of a new ethics being raised here which flaunts the old rules similar to the way a dandy flaunts his/her/its organs, sense of humour, fashion. Then again, maybe all of this to-ing and fro-ing around the *'special case'* has not one whit to do with ethics. No, that cannot be right. But maybe it's only partially wrong(-*ish*).

The thief and the jewel. What happens if we steal a little of this and a little of that from, say, certain aesthetic, political, cultural, sexual discourses; say from queerdom, dada, surrealism, pop and punk (not to mention dolly-sheep genetics). One could say that this form of thievery could mark the first 'gesture' to leave the 20th century behind – without falling too far into the trap of abstractionism or loosing the pornographic blood-beat of what it means to say 'there is no depth to the "is" of life: just deal with it'. One could say, further, that in these fluxed, nomadic appropriations, in these comic-strip skins (and tastes), there is *only* the gesture, or even less: say, just the nod toward making a gesture. One could say that in this sense, it is the gesture (and not the 'picture'/ 'narrative'/ 'metaphor') that starts/moves/ends a story. Or to say it slightly differently: the gesture *is* the 'little story', and the sampling or appropriation of the gesture, that is, the strategy of the linking of the gesture(s) – whether by accident or deeply intentional (as gesture rather than as event, narration, metaphor) – is its politics, ethics, aesthetic re-mark of the here, there, now, gone, curved space-times of our time.

Let's give it a nice new short name, say: *art*. Or we could languish in the longer version, say as the 'anomic-electro-digital-acoustic-curved-space-repetitive projection-screen-metonymy-of-our-non-wired-times'. All this may be very interesting, but couldn't this 'sampling' – this anomic kind of community /cityscape art – beg the whole question around cultural appropriation, when, and for whom?

For if things only manage to contain their history/symbol/reality in the gestural slice of their contingency, doesn't this mean that anyone could link a 'this' with a 'that', for no other reason than that of its beat, colour, chain, smell, sound? Couldn't someone or a group of someones steal sections or traditions from a culture they are neither a part of nor understand, and use them without regard to their 'intended' meaning? Moreover, couldn't someone claim, whilst hidden behind their computer screen, for example, to be a drag-king female, athlete, cyborg, aboriginal, European without both legs or with one too many? Or, less 'imaginistic' rendering: what if I am an artist from the Caribbean and wish to be noticed as such when I enter the London art-world. What if my drawings cease to be 'other world' and become something else, say, a queer representative of 'English'? Would I be a traitor, a plagiarist or a thief or, indeed, all three? Perhaps I could become instead, especially if I stay in the game long enough, a cultural jewel.

old joke revitalised. Dolly-sheep genetics (not quite) aside, there is now the (il)legal possibility of cloning humans. So, you arrive at a party, as the old joke used to go, but now, instead of worrying whether someone might be wearing the same bargain basement outfit, they are wearing your body, warts, bad haircut and all. This may not be a problem for those workaholics who need to have replicants at their service answering their mail, attending to boring events, doing the bills, settling old scores. But what if you don't quite approve of what the 'other-yous' might be doing? Or what if they're having more fun than you are having at the moment you voyeuristically or otherwise watch 'their' goings-on? What if there are so many 'other-yous' floating about that you cannot even keep track of their pathways and actions. What if you *forget* who the original 'you' is. Plato could never have envisioned this kind of mimesis, not to mention, this kind of 'originality' or 'copying'. Should we? Would this constitute a different 'deadly sin', say the 'eighth' deadly sin? Or is this the first deadly sin of a new code of ethics, series of timings, multiple happenings, events, *weltanschuungen*? Or should we just side-step the whole question of sins, time, speed, world views, altogether? I want to say: 'hey there, wait just a minute! I need some room [time, space] to think! Let me just be! [all of the me(s)]'!

part 5: (this is me speaking to)

habeus corpus as a dangerous, slippery-slope. Whilst deadly 'original' sins should, perhaps, be scrapped from the junk-yard of truth, certain forms of 'authorships', 'authenticities' and identities, should not be scrapped (and indeed, cannot be). Is this just a matter of some new (conservative) 'wish-list', cardinal rule or logistics of 'necessity' imposed from on-high (or from below? sideways?) This may appear as a not-so-secret attempt to ground the flotilla of infinitely increasing identically-cloned-self anonymities onto some form of 'difference', 'unique-ness', 'imprint' (voice, hand, finger or otherwise), precisely in order that it may re-assume its *responsibilities*, and therewith be able to 'belong' differently to a something (say a family, a ghetto, a community or nation) beyond the great mirroring of self-referentiality or self-reflexivity. It may appear, moreover, as a kind of attempt to return to the old hunting grounds of the (moral) imperative 'to be or not to be' (old trap of a question), as though one were culling back ethics to the land of moral rule, and, by so doing, inadvertently or otherwise, clinging to the edge of some impoverished sense of 'individuality', say one which still rested on a division between the public and the private, norm and value, culture and nature, custom and instinct, appearance and essence.

Maybe this nod toward 'authorship' sneaks in a whole trail of problems around 'great men theories' and 'first causes' (like the birth of God/ genius/the avant-garde as a prerequisite to history/nature and its change). Maybe all these problems are unavoidable when one starts treading on the delicate terrain of 'the who' of science, art, ethics and life. But then, again, maybe I'm just not quite ready to relinquish the notion of some kind of singular *habeas corpus* 'authorship', 'authenticity', 'identity', ™ or © (or if I must do so, I don't want it simply to be exchanged for some kind of *mass conformism* writ large and infinitely cloned). Thus, the slippery-slide begins: for who am I to say 'I don't want', especially if it is happening anyway, irrespective of my opinion on the matter. Who am I to say, that *I do want* (certain things: like the ability to avoid the (equally old) trap of social agency, subject/object divide, end-game politics, romanticism)? To whom or what does it matter to insist on the *'I don't want/ I want'*, particularly as it relates to having a name, style, signature, body, imprint, or even, and especially, 'my own' name (style, signature, body, imprint) and all that this implies around the problem of culture, cultural value, a sense of belonging, conformism, mass psychosis, responsibility and self-respect? Cries of megalomania notwithstanding, the insistence of a 'me-self' in the face of massification is the (not so new) entropy of a modern, post-modern and now digitally almost-mastered age, so, in some sense, the haunting whisper of the tired man's *'what does it matter?'* must be raised.

(The tired man speaks ... In the last mili-seconds of the 'what does it matter', the tired man speaks, wears, brandishes his/her last speck of individuality, possession, dignity). Hmmm. Haven't we heard this somewhere before, say in some famous man's remarks about the ability or not to write poetry after the genocidal stamping out of human identities, as so many singular beings (identified, too, with the individual group identity of jew, christian, moslem, gay, mad, whore, gypsy, 'other') were condemned to endure. A collective head-stone of black ash, smoke and dust, which, as Adorno so morbid-eloquently put it: wriggled ever skyward from the ovens of Auschwitz and elsewhere. I want to say, by saying this: that *to want*, and *to* know *that one wants* should not be forgotten or thrown away, as if, 'unimportant', 'begging the question'. For those honest enough to admit it, it remains at the very basis of a new being, poetics and indeed, politics.

the cunning of democracy. Amongst all this dolly-sheep business, and quite distinct from the elemental fascist rules of a massification-game, it would seem possible, indeed probable, that a something 'new' or a something 'else' – perhaps even a something 'better' – is being invented, born, repeated. (The spoiled child speaks, unwilling to accept the fascist game as the only game of a massified life left for us to play). One dreams here of, say, *democracy* – with echoes of the age old plea-command *to change the subject* (or at least to recognise there might be some other agenda at play), especially if the people who are suggesting 'it cannot be otherwise' just happen to be in positions of power.

situation. Isn't it possible, despite all this point-for-point digitally repeatable accuracy, and its addendum dire predictions around the end-of-the-world-due-to-technology-and-power, to concentrate less on those exacting techno-replications per se, and more on a kind of 'elsewhere' paradigm (neither outside, between, below or above the replications). That is, some *other* kind of geography, invoking some other kind of repetition, timing, spacing, mass movement, power game, dimensionality, memory, forgetfulness, play, re-instatement, re-installment and etc? Say, for example, that which is produced as a 'bandwidth' with no weight, volume, or dimesionality, but nevertheless produces 'meaning'. 'Here' one can speak of a kind of 'elsewhere poetics' (or dare it be said: a 'blood poetics') which travels more along the hyperrealisms of the 'ing' (tim-*ing*, clon-*ing*, cunn-*ing*) pathways of intensities, montages, and economies (libidinal included) and less amongst the chimney smoke realisms of racial hatred and other either/or amalgamations.

For is it not also the case, at the exact same moment that it seems precisely not to be the case, that digital replication also creates – precisely in this 'ing' movement – a kind of *situation* where copies, timings, spacings, ruminatings, may include some kind fluxed trace or form of 'singularity', 'gesture', or 'metonymic slice', say in terms of the 'singularity' of its link, relation, contingency? That all things are now possible in the relativity and speed of an '$e=mc^2$' does not at all mean that 'everything goes' (though maybe 'the anything goes' will someday become just a matter of time/timing, too). This expanded ability to create meaning is more a matter of multi-dimensional communication highways, wave lengths, particle attractors, speeds, projections and the links created thereof in the infinite regressivity of its curves, folds, beats, tones, simulations, errors, than of those creaky Cartesian networks of receptivity and engagement and the monumentalising of the *political* per se, with or without its 'original sins'. A different kind of meditation on the micro-politics of cloning humanity/ inhumanity/ sheep, slightly or wholly dislodged from its claustrophobic function as icon, metaphor, symbol, gene pool, memory-frame, individuality, blood – though using them, abusing them, re-installing them, nonetheless.

Rubbish, you say? Perhaps you are still secretly stuck in the base/ superstructure picture of power and are *misrecognising* the ground that lays before you as ground, surface, installer, bandwidth, web-site, poetics.

part 6: (this is me speaking to you)
discursive whoring: Tell all, reveal nothing. (perverted Heideggerianism).

playing with fire (illusion). One must learn the tools of one's trade. Is it so difficult to surmise from this declaration that if the tools are infinitely complex, multiple, layered, or even (indeed, especially) 'deadly', then they must be 'handled with care'? A certain coolness, a certain detachment, a certain humour, a certain respect for their toxicity is in order, is required, demanded. There is no room for concepts like 'morality', not to mention 'the lack' or 'the excess' (though they seem always to creep in, by the by). These bugbears work off a particular use of contradiction and negation to underscore and value 'difference', 'identity', 'plurality', 'meaning', 'truth', 'relation', 'the visual'. In the metaphysics of this move, one falls prey to the now infamous 'excluded middle', which, in its wake, is filled with the aforementioned excesses and lacks, self and Others, spectacles, gazes, and etcetera. But if we take seriously 'the tools of our trade', the only entity able to fill this aporia (and by so doing, makes mockery of it) is life itself. Toxic to the extreme; a violent kind of graphic mutilated fleeting 'ready-made' projection, neither excess nor lack; inhabiting (if only for an instant) its 'being here'. Perhaps I want to rewrite this 'event' as violence; its projection: memory. Its fleeting recognition: installation. Its very existence: a stylistics. Its dynamic: a politics. An a-radical, strategic, politics, gently (or otherwise) renamed: poetics. But take care! For inhabiting this poetic, where metaphysics bumps up, over, into and alongside its variegated technologies; where history gains a whole new lease on life; where identity gives way to signatures and copies; where speed and distance overtakes time and, indeed becomes it – means there's always the risk, indeed, the probability, that you will get burned, and burned alive.

opening. closing. opening. So now I want to play a game. Let it not be 'war or peace' (or any of its variations: 'war as peace', 'war and peace', & etc). This game will have no known rules (well … no rules, except one). The players will be issued seductive little chits of many colours, though none of them primary. This game will stretch well into the night, with plenty of stimulants for all. Hairstyles and other cool factors will be considered secondary, though not unimportant. As it will be taking place worldwide, hyper-linked and net-projected off satellites everywhere, thousands – no, millions! – will be able to place bets on their favourite pawns. The one rule: capture will 'count' only if it occurs *en passant*.[5]

us (post) post-moderns! In the techno shift which characterises 'our' age (epoch, world-view), meta-narratives give way to libidinal economies and rhizomatic excretions, or so the new political philosophies pray tell, produce, witness. Perhaps this means that 'us, (post) post-moderns' are not the slightest bit interested in purity or any of its related paraphernalia: the perfect, the flawless, the pure event, pure transcendence, pure object, pure subject, pure otherness, pure lack, pure violence, pure morality, pure mastery; pure submission. We dislike the subject of purity; probably dislike even more those who try to achieve it; and we do so with a honed and malevolent vehemence reaching – almost – the pure itself. But it does not reach it – and it never will. For *this* dislike, indeed, *this* rage, is borne from the intricacies of politics itself: the dirty, multiple, warped flight paths of those cruel humiliations and associated power games we so lightly call 'spice of life'.

guilty. At the same time, us (post) post-moderns seem to want also to say: 'My position is bound by the square I occupy on the board!' And not only that! But that 'we are wounded and our mutilated legs/identities/economies of scale prevent us from advancing but just one square at a time!'

exception. Except of course, during the opening volley when, say, the promise seems 'real' or 'new-born', innocent, fresh, witty, virginal: hopeful. Then the pawn as only a pawn can do, respectfully or otherwise makes its move: twice.

employer. To whom or to what does this ability/restriction to move one way or 'another, owe its allegiance? I want to say: to long-range Strategy! or to the immediacy of Tactics! or perhaps just Tradition, Habit, Money, Religion! Maybe the one or two-step move comes down to just a Whim or a Whine or all of the above or something else altogether. But whatever it comes down to, and despite the one and only rule to our *post*-post-modern game – ie, the wily use of *en passant* to win the battle of certainty against all odds or at least most of them – perhaps we cannot, in the final analysis, or even (and especially) in the middle of it, avoid the age-old Machiavellian instruction to the Prince, binaric to its core, sophomoric in its zero-sum logic and crucial to the building of a modern industrialised world; the one every young student, soldier, statesman and street militant alike learns by rote and takes to heart; to wit: there will always be 'leaders and led,' 'friends and enemies,' 'axes of evil and good' in order to sustain or create new power regimes, and indeed, in order to create the very stuffing of politics/movement itself.

But I want to say: No! That's not exactly right! (though, here again, it's not exactly wrong either).

quick thinking. That the status quo's status manages to reproduce itself in a seemingly infinite series of discrete (or otherwise) power plays, discussions, media blitzes, clever advertisements, 'smart' bombs and other bizarre/cruel experiments (like growing human ears onto mouses' heads) – and yet remain intimately knotted to a political nostalgia, and not to the very multiple dimensional structures to which this rapid obsolescence is tied – is not a big mystery.

irony. Given the demands of credit card credit and the slippery economies to which those demands give birth, means that in the end (or in the middle of the end), the only people who will have money in their pockets will be: the poor. Power will have long since evacuated *that* domain.

Senegal after Radiohead after (Kant after Duchamp) after Nietzsche after Turin after Kierkegaard after Adorno after Marx after Hegel … or how I learned to dream in techno-colour and not just black and white. Remarks on colour as a New Science or 'Vico after Wittgenstein' (rhetorical echoes). Should the very fact that we are caught in the wild drama of a (not quite fully embedded) structural shift brought on by the death of metaphysics and the birth of singular pluralities and curved time-space mathematics *matter* when speaking of power? Or is it only appropriate in *certain* fields of art, *certain* fields of relativity, *certain* fields of quantum physics, *certain* fields of sexuality, media, psychology, grammar, literature, politics, identity, philosophy, medical science, history, secularism – ie, in those areas where 'black and white' as analytic tools no longer fit – and possibly never did fit?

a bad smell. Wouldn't this (either-or{ism}) create a kind of 'brain dead but still alive' *moralism* rooted to a time (not so) long ago past – and in some places, not past at all – we might wish to call *oppressive*?

interlude. The art of warfare is, thus, clearly also, a delicate business; but what it produces is not. While it is true that *this* art of war produces many things, cruel, saturated, ingenious, dark; it, most of all, produces one thing. And that one thing is the nakedness of death itself; the relentless finality, the no-going-back of life. One could shed 120 tears for every day of Sodom; one could spit into the wind or prostate oneself forever and always – or not at all. One could stamp a foot; one could write three long poems; one could lay down in the street en masse; one could laugh out loud; one could memorialise to eternity all the beauty of all the people! and their cities! and their cultures! gone gone gone! one could replay their anger, their whimsy, their philosophies, their cooking sense, or even the way they look when they wake up in the morning. But, in the end, it simply doesn't matter: They are not coming home. And that's the whole, damn, sickening truth, no matter how you cut it. Or how it cuts you.

This putrid skin! Would it not to have ever been so alive!

rehearsal. 'Yea, but I am ashamed, disgraced, dishonoured, degraded, exploded: my notorious crimes and villainies are come to light (*deprendi miserum* est [it is a wretched thing to be caught]), my filthy lust, abominable oppression and avarice lies open, my good name's lost, my fortune's gone, I have been stigmatized, whipped at post, arraigned and condemned, I am a common obloquy, I have lost my ears, odious, execrable, abhorred of God and men. Be content, 'tis but a nine days' wonder, and as one sorrow drives out another, one passion another, one cloud another, one rumour is expelled by another;

every day almost come new sun to your ears, as how the sun was eclipsed, meteors seen i' th' air, monsters born, prodigies, how the Turks were overthrown in Persia, an earthquake in Helvetica, Calabria, Japan, or China, an inundation in Holland, a great plague in Constantinople, a fire at Prague, a dearth in Germany, such a man I made a lord, a bishop, another hanged, deposed, pursued to death, for some murder, treason, rape, theft, oppression, all which we do hear at first with a kind of admiration, detestation, consternation, but by and by they are buried in silence ...

Comfort thyself, thou art not the sole man.'[6]

relearning how to fly (same, but different). Well, if it is true that the age into which we have flung ourselves (or have been flung) – this age we so euphemistically call 'the information age' or age of (supposedly 'new') technologies – if it is true that this age is able to re-write the event, the signature, indeed laws around nationhood, societies, bodies, ethics, 'truth' into a whole new massification economy, a whole new 'end-game-now-as-mid-game' of warfare or history or politics or philosophy or art (and all other modernist narratives of science and of life); if it is true that this *post*-post-modern predicament of ours produces and continues to produce, invent and accept violent poverty, violent extremes in living standards, knowledge, and access to power (and the expediential rate at which these extremes seem to be proliferating); if it is true that this *post*-post modern dispersion of particalised-/wave-lengths of power, micro-powers, multiply-dimensioned libidinal and bandwidths of power, and the regularities to which new types of power relations are made to 'stick' in a way that rips through our bodies and plays itself out as if the Eternal Return of *Night of the Living Dead*; if it is true that our post-post modern world STILL seems to be producing fascist agendas left, right and centred, or vacant identities crushed by instrumentalised reason and all its related paraphernalia; if it is true, worst of all, that we seem always already bent on the sickly path of bombs over bodies – does not mean that it is doing *exactly* and *precisely* this *all* the time, every time or – more importantly – that it cannot be otherwise.

I am not dreaming.

part 7: (this is me speaking to you [live])
blood poetic towards a non-fascist life. 'Tears are easier to put up with than joy,' Miller intones, for 'joy is destructive: it makes others uncomfortable. Weep and you weep alone' – what a load of crap that is! 'The world is forever weeping. The world is drenched in tears. Laughter, that's another thing ...'[7]

So what if I were to remind you of the *optimism* of wandering? Or the sublime hell of it all? What if I were to remind you that we go on a journey with no pre-defined maps, with pitfalls, and viruses and shared accident and plagues? And that in knowing this – or, more to the point, in wanting this – we unwittingly (or not) fall into that essential non-essentialism of life itself, we so nonchalantly call our 'history'. Hindsight is not just 20/20 vision. And romanticism is not just for fools and horses.

[1] johnny golding (aka Sue Goling/johnny de philo), author. This blood poetic is part amalgamation of my work on five interventions: honour; research and its link to the 7 deadly sins; nomadic codes; pariah bodies; and the importance of 'en passant' (or how a pawn learns to capture king). The poetics form an installation of projected memory and acoustic ruptures, often publicly elaborated in 6:8 time, along with 180 slides on two projectors, video screening and dark lighting.

[2] Ludwig Wittgenstein, *Culture and Value*, edited by G.H. Von Wright in collaboration with Heikki Nyman, trans. by Peter Winch, (Oxford: Basil Blackwell, 1980), p. 1e.

[3] Herman Melville, "A Squeeze of the Hand", *Moby Dick*, (Hertfordshire: Wordsworth Editions, Ltd., 1992), p. 429.

[4] Robert Burton., "Causes of Melancholy: §VI – Shame and Disgrace, Causes" and "Causes of Melancholy: §VII – Envy, Malice, Hatred, Causes", *The Anatomy of Melancholy*, in three volumes, (1621), as reprinted (5th edition), 1638, as reprinted 1932), New York /London: Everyman's Library, 1932/1972), pp. 262–265.

[5] *en passant* is a particular move open only to the pawn. As the famous chess scholar D. Brine Prichard details: "[*en passant*] lays down that if a pawn, moving two squares forward from its initial position, could have been captured by an opposing pawn *if it had only moved one square*, then such capture may be effected as if the pawn had only moved one square. The pawn making the initial double move is removed from the board and the capturing pawn occupies the square that the captured pawn would have occupied had it only moved one. The right to make a capture *en passant* is forfeited if not exercised immediately ... a pawn can only be captured *en passant* by another pawn and not by a piece." D.B. Prichard, *The Right Way to Play Chess*, (Berkshire: Cox and Wyman, 1997), p.16.

[6] *The Anatomy of Melancholy*, in three volumes, (1621), pp. 199–200.

[7] Henry Miller, *Sexus: Book One of the 'Rosy Crucifixion' triology*, foreword by Erica Jung, (London: Flamingo [an imprint of Harper Collins Publishers], 1993), p. 30.

FROZEN TEARS

DEATH FLOWERS ERUPTING WITH PUTRID PETALS OF EXCRESCENCE. O BABY. O BABY. YOU FUCKING BASTARD. YOU LOVED ME SO MUCH YOU BLOCKED UP MY AIR PIPE. THE SEWAGE WORKS HAVE ... HAVE ERUPTED AND SHIT IS FLOWING DOWN THE STREET IN A RIVER OF PISS. OH MUMMY! MUMMY! POO. POOOOOO. AND A CLOUD OF BUTTERFLIES AND INSECT-HUMANS STAND UP AND SCREAM. SCREAM AT THE SKY. GIRAFFE-MANTISSES RE-MATERIALISING IN SHIT AND BLOOD. AND A DRAGONFLY DRINKING DROPS OF DEW OFF A LEAF, TASTING LIKE LIQUID HEROIN. O BABY. O BABY. I LOVE YOU BUT IT ENDED IMMEDIATELY. IMMEDIATELY. NO ... NO SUN PLAYING ON THE OILY SURFACE. BUT THEY ARE NOT LAUGHING ... THEY ARE NOT LAUGHING. BUT THE SICK AND THE SCUM ... THAT ... THAT ... THAT IS OUR NON-SALVATION. THIS IS OUR NON-SALVATION. SHIT. SHIT. SHIT. AND THEY WILL COME. IN SHIT. AND SCUM THEY WILL COME. SHIT ... SHIT ... OK. OK. OK. OK. OK. OK. OK. OK. OK. OK. OK. FOCUS. FOCUS. OK. OK. OK. FOCUS. FOCUS. FOCUS. YES. YES. YES. FOCUS. FOCUS. OK. OK. OK. BREATHE IN ... BREATHE IN ... OK ... OK ... BREATHE IN ... AND BREATHE OUT ... BREATHE OUT. OK. OK. BREATHE IN ... BREATHE IN ... BREATHE IN ... RELAX ... RELAX ... AND BREATHE OUT ... FOCUS ... FOCUS ... FOCUS ... YES ... YES ... BREATHE IN ... BREATHE IN. OK. OK. RELAX ... AND BREATHE OUT ... OK. OK. BREATHE IN ... BREATHE IN ... RELAX ... AND BREATHE OUT ... NICE ... NICE ... OK ... OK ... FOCUS. FOCUS. FOCUS. OK. OK. OK. Focus. Focus. OK. OK. OK. Nice. Nice. OK. Focus. Focus. Testing. Testing. One. Two. Three. OK. OK. OK. One. Two. Three. One. Two. Three ... One. Two. Three. One. Two. Three. OK. OK. OK. OK. OK. Nice.

OK. OK. OK. OK. Looking down the hallway … looking down a hallway … dirty carpet … stairs in front. Looking down the hall you can see a staircase. OK. OK. OK. Focus. Focus … mirror on the wall and below the mirror, a hall table with a metal plate for front door keys and loose change and a ceramic ornament in the shape of a book, which says: "My Favourite Gran". Next to this are a few coats hanging from hooks; and straight ahead, through a door at the end of the hall, you can see a cooker and kitchen units. And there is a funny smell, a sweet smell but unpleasant. Not nice. Not nice. Not nice. Not nice.

You walk … you walk down the corridor, towards the kitchen but turn in through the door on the left and you are now in a living room with yellowed wallpaper. And above the gas fire is a painting of a landscape with a lake in the foreground. In the corner is a glass display case with ornaments like ceramic animals and ballerinas and on the other side of the room there is a television. On top of the television is a carved wooden horse.

Koffff! Kafff! Koff! There is a sound. The sound of someone coughing. You turn in this direction and you catch sight of a figure sitting at a table, in front of the window – but you don't get a clear sight of this figure, because the figure turns away. You can see that the figure is smoking a cigar and blowing out smoke. This figure is me and I say:

"Hello. Nice to make your acquaintance."

OK.OK. Koffff! Kafff! OK. right. Lets get started. Yes. Yes. We have started. Started. I have a bottle of piss-sweet sherry in front of me. Koffff! I don't as a rule drink sherry but it's all I could find … and a cigar … so … whatever! Lets get started. OK. OK. … Five years ago.

Before he became a psychotic Zarvyn Mitchell had been a successful businessman. He ran a business with his brother, manufacturing and retailing caravans and mobile homes. Then five years ago he started thinking the media were talking to him. He thought adverts on television and billboards on the street were addressed to him personally. This is normal for psychotics.

He thought there were little creatures all around him. Little insect creatures who were trying to control him – a cross between insects and rats and dogs. There was an advert on the trains where fare dodgers were compared to various parasites such as rats and lice and cockroaches. The rats were OK; it was the lice and cock-roaches that bothered him. There was a cartoon of lice and cockroaches pick-pocketing a rail-user. The advert said: "They are parasites. They want to steal your money." Zarvyn took this personally. He interpreted this as meaning the lice and cockroaches wanted to steal his money.

There were other adverts in magazines and on TV that he was worried about as well – either the words would read like a threat or a prophesy or he would see insects somewhere in the images.

Maybe the psychosis was linked to his Mother's death, a few years earlier because his mother had the strange hobby of keeping spiders and large Madagascan cock-roaches as pets, or maybe it was connected to an infestation of cockroaches at his offices in Brighton. On this ocassion, they had called in *Pest-o-Cutors Ltd.* But, even after the infestation had been dealt with, Zarvyn continued to think he could "see" insects out of the corner of his eye.

Then he told his brother, Tony, that beetles were climbing into his head through his ears when he was asleep. Tony thought Zarvyn must be suffering from stress. They talked about it. They both agreed he had been working too hard – and it was true, *he had been working too hard*, he hadn't had a holiday for five years. And so it was decided he should go on a five-week break to the West Indies.

Sun and sea and relaxation. But unfortunately he came back even worse. While he was out there he was drinking heavily and taking a variety of drugs to calm his nerves and to help him sleep. Tony got a phone call from someone at the hotel where Zarvyn had been staying saying he was flying back to the UK. Zarvyn had smashed up his hotel room. He was flying back to England.

Tony went to meet his brother at the airport. When Zarvyn walked through Arrivals he was talking to himself. He had dark rings around his eyes and seemed distressed. Tony didn't know what to do. They sat down at a coffee franchise and Tony went up to the counter to get two coffees. When he came back Zarvyn was crouched over the table, talking to himself.

Tony looked at his younger brother. He was thirty-one. He was tall and thin, with blond hair. He looked in a bad way.

"It got worse," said Zarvyn. "There was different bugs out there. They're worse. And they followed me in through Customs. They are everywhere. They are waiting. They … they are everywhere !" He was talking loudly and making strange gestures.

A middle-aged couple sitting on the table next to them, looked over.

Tony said to his brother:

"Calm down Zarvyn. What's the matter with you?"

They decided that it was time to get professional psychiatric help. Zarvyn admitted himself into a psychiatric hospital and he was prescribed drugs.

After two or three weeks, it seemed that he had recovered and he returned home. He seemed to be back to his normal self.

... OK. OK. OK. Nice. OK. OK. OK. OK. OK. OK. OK. Nice. Focus. Focus. FOCUS. FOCUSSSSS. OK. OK. OK. OK. OK. OK. Yes. Yes. One. Two. Three. One. Two. Three. Testing. Testing. OK. OK. It's difficult. It's difficult. OK. OK. I don't really understand this. I don't really understand this. I don't really understand. No. OK. I mean ... OK. OK. OK. I mean, I don't understand. I don't understand. OK. OK. I guess, I am sort of part of this ... but ... but ... OK. OK. ... but I don't understand it. You see it? You see it? Yes. Yes. Yes. OK. OK. OK.

OK. OK. While he was taking his medication. While he was taking his medication he seemed to be back to normal and he was allowed to go home. It seemed he had completely recovered. He was even planning to go back to work. But then, for some reason he stopped taking the drugs, without telling anyone, and things got bad again, or even worse. Very quickly. On the second night after he stopped taking his medication he was lying in bed and he felt there were beetles crawling all over him. He thought he could see a big beetle sitting on the end of his bed. He started screaming but, before anyone could get to him, he had run out of the house and driven off in his car. At first he thought he had escaped but, in a sudden flash, he saw that the black interior of the car was black because it was covered in beetles and then he saw there was a big cockroach sitting in the back. He screamed and veered off the road and the next thing he knew he was trapped in a burning car and his flesh was melting. And the pain ... oh shit! The pain! The pain. Shit. Shit. He was very lucky not to die in the accident. A passing motorist pulled him from the car. But he sustained multiple injuries, including multiple fractures to both legs, a broken back and severe burns to his face hands and legs. There was another car involved in the crash but no major injuries.

But, worst of all, he seemed to suffer a complete mental breakdown.

And now, two or three years after the crash, he doesn't even seem to know what his name is. He sits in a wheel chair and pisses and shits into a nappy. I mean, basically there is no medical reason why he can't walk. It's psychological.

He sits in his wheel chair looking straight ahead of himself, thinking:

Who am I?
Who am I?
Who am I?
Who am I?
Who am I?
Who am I?

Who am I? Who am I? Hoo am I? Shit. Shit. Shit. No. NO. NO. Please. Please. Please. Oh shit. Yes. Yes. Yes. Yes. Yes. Yes. Fuck. Fuck. OK. OK. Who am I? Who am I? Who am I? OK. OK. OK. OK. Kofff. OK. Focus. Focus. OK. right, as I said, I have a bottle of sherry in front of me – to help me through this ... through this ... it's all I could find in this house ... so whatever. And anyway, this isn't where the story is. No. No, the story is not here – the story is somewhere else. Anyway this is OUR story. This is our story. OK. OK. OK. HA. HA. OUR. OUR. OK. OK. The story sort of happens by itself. Do you know what I mean? Yes. Yes. OK. Where am I? Where am I? Here. Now. This is a small, 1950s town house in Brighton. OK. OK. And so that's where I am ... here! But this isn't where the story is – it smells bad here – VERY BAD. Very bad ... Oh shit! OK. OK.

OK. OK. OK. OK. OK ... OK. Right, let's relax. OK. ... shit y! Focus. Focus. Focus. Focus.

Toneeeee Mitchell walks out of a restaurant. By the look of the clothes it must be about 1995.

The man is Tony Mitchell. You remember him? Tony Mitchell. The brother of Zarvyn Mitchell, who was the guy who kept seeing beetles and who was in the car crash? But it's a few years later. This is his brother.

He walks out of a restaurant – which is in fact *his* restaurant. The restaurant is on the sea front in Brighton. It is an Italian restaurant. It is called *Italiano*. He stands by the edge of the road waiting for a gap in the traffic. He tosses his car keys absent-mindedly in his hand. A car slows and he walks across the road to the opposite pavement, which is adjacent to the beach. He walks slowly along the sea wall, his hair blown back off his forehead. He looks out to sea – at the slate-grey waves. His feels himself relax. Relax. Relax. Relax. After a couple of minutes, he turns around and sees three more people come out of the restaurant – two men and a tall woman. The woman is his wife Jane. She used to be a model. She is wearing a trouser suit and a red shirt. She is saying good-bye. Tony has said good-bye already, inside the restaurant and he can't be bothered to say good-bye again. Anyway his wife is the one they are interested in.

Tony Mitchell is taller than average height and

heavily built. He does regular weight training. He used to enter body-building competitions and took steroids and muscle-building supplements, which meant he was susceptible to mood swings, but he gave that up a few years ago. He has square-rimmed gold glasses and is wearing a very expensive, slightly out of fashion grey suit. At first glance, he looks like a handsome man – something about the cut of his hair, his upright stance and the general set of his features, but on closer inspection he is ugly – very ugly – he has strange teeth, bug-eyes and a shapeless nose. And he sweats a lot. At the moment he has a line of sweat on his forehead.

He is watching the silhouette of a ferry in the distance. Jane comes up beside him. She touches his arm. Jane is a beautiful woman with dark hair, dark eyes and olive-coloured skin. She wears a lot of jewellery but it suits her.

Tony speaks first, he says:

"That seemed to go well!"

Jane replies.

"Yes … yes. It did go well."

Later on. It is the same day. Tony and Jane are lying beside their swimming pool. It is a very hot day. Jane is lying face down on an inflatable mattress wearing green bikini bottoms. Beside her on the concrete is a vodka and orange. Tony lies a few yards away, on his back, on a sun lounger, with a magazine over his face. He wears a pair of black swimming shorts and there are a pair of sunglasses balanced on his upper thigh.

For ten minutes the two of them lie in the sun, motionless except for the odd twitch or flick of a hand, then Tony reaches up, moves the magazine off his face and sits up and says:

"Wow! It's hot!"

Jane doesn't say anything.

Tony reaches beside him and picks up his spectacles. He puts them on and stands up. As he does so, his sunglasses fall off his legs onto the concrete. He looks down at them on the paving stones, then yawns and walks forward a few steps. The sun is hot. He looks down into the swimming pool, focusing first on the tiles at the bottom and then on a small, dead beetle that is floating across the surface. He yawns again.

Then, mainly for the sake of something to do, he decides to go into the house to fix himself another drink. He asks Jane:

"Do you want something to drink?" She mumbles "No".

Focusing for a few seconds on his wife's body, specifically on the side view of her breasts squashed on the mattress, he experiences a sudden stirring of desire.

He walks around the swimming pool, across the crazy paving, through the French windows and into the living room.

A few seconds later he is standing, beside the drinks cabinet, flexing and un-flexing his toes in the pile of the carpet. He pours himself a gin and tonic. As he tests the drink, he catches sight of himself in the mirror on the wall. He spends a few seconds looking at his body. He stretches to his full height and flexes and un-flexes his pectorals while watching himself in the mirror. Again he feels stirrings of desire. A thought takes root in his mind: he is in the mood for sex. He feels he would like Jane to give him a blow-job and then he would like to fuck her, preferably from behind, in the swimming pool. To facilitate this he flips out his penis – semi soft/hard – pulls back his foreskin and cleans himself with the aid of the soda siphon. He rubs the spilt soda into the carpet with his foot.

Then Tony picks up his drink, turns and walks towards the French windows; beyond him, in the middle distance, we can see the swimming pool and his wife who is still sunbathing. He walks out of the room.

We stay in the living room. We don't follow Tony out. It is almost exclusively white in here: white walls, white carpet, white leather sofas, white coffee table, white lamps.

Out of a window – in the distance – we can see a man. He is playing golf. His name is Geoff Mitchell. There is also another figure – as we get closer we can see it is an *attractive older woman*. She is wearing a blue tracksuit and training shoes. She is jogging along on the far side of the golf course. Geoff is nearer to us.

Geoff looks down at the golf ball below him. He is wearing a tracksuit and he has a mobile phone attached to his waist. There is a plastic carrier bag full of golf balls on the grass next to him and a bag of golf clubs.

Geoff Mitchell's head looks like a sheep's skull, with two bright blue eyes in the sockets, lustrous thick grey hair shaped into a quiff and strange purple cheeks. He was handsome when he was young but now he looks like a shrink-wrapped chicken.

Geoff lifts the golf club above his head – swings – thwack! The golf ball fires down the fairway.

Geoff is thinking:

"OK. OK. Not bad! Not bad! Better. Better. ... but same problem ... But not bad! OK. OK. OK. OK."

He hooks another golf ball out of the bag with his club, bends down and puts it on a tee. He looks down at the ball ... concentrating ... concentrating ... standing over the ball. He starts his wind up. He is standing poised over the ball. A drop of sweat runs down his nose and falls through the air.

He twists his body ... the club head moves back ... one ... two ... three ... Fwack! The ball slices away into the trees. OK. OK. OK. OK. OK. OK.

A few minutes ago, Tony and Jane were having sex in the swimming pool but now they have stopped. Tony lost his hard-on. Now, they have resumed their former positions on the li-lo and sun-lounger.

Jane is thinking:

"Why does Tony find it difficult to keep a hard-on? Why does he find it difficult to keep a hard-on? Sometimes he can only keep it up for a few minutes. He didn't used to have this problem. I wonder if there's something wrong? But it would be difficult to talk to him about it ... he would just get angry. But something must be wrong. I mean over the last six months we have only had sex ... maybe twice. He seems to have lost his sex drive recently. But not today, which was nice. Not at first. I was enjoying it ... but ... but he lost interest. I wonder if it's just a phase he's going through. Maybe we should try harder. Maybe we should try some different things. Or maybe he doesn't find me sexually attractive anymore. Or maybe he's having an affair or I wonder if he's gay. Imagine him being gay ... that would be funny ... HA. HA. ... that would be funny. HA. HA. HA. HA. HA. HA. HA. Well not really.

A fly lands on Jane's left buttock – it walks across her tanned skin down the cleft between her arse cheeks. Jane reaches behind her back and flicks at the fly with her hand.

But … But then you know this don't you? You know about this fly – don't you? You know about it. You know about it. Yes. Yes. You know about it. Yes. Yes. Yes. Right. Because … because … because that fly is not my fly. THAT IS NOT MY FLY. Do you know what I mean? Yes. THAT IS NOT MY FLY. OK. OK. That was not my fly, so it has to be your fly OK? That was your fly. Your fly. Yeah. Yeah. You know what I mean? Your fly. Your fucking fly! I think you do. I think you do. I think you do because I don't know where that fly came from. OK. OK. OK. OK. I'm not describing that fly. It just happened. It just happened. OK. OK. OK. Do you know what I mean? Yes. Yes. Yes. It's true. OK. HA. HA. It's true. It's true. OK. OK. You're thinking and I'm thinking and it's happening. That fly just happened. Just happened. Anyway … it just happened. OK. OK. OK. It just happened. Whatever …

The fly walks across Jane's skin and down the cleft between her cheeks. Jane reaches behind her back and flicks at the fly with her hand.

She is thinking. She is thinking how lucky she is. How lucky she is to have this life-style – to be lying here, by this swimming pool in the sun. And she is thinking about how lucky she is that she became a model. Very lucky.

She thinks back to that day thirteen years ago when she got her big break – *the most important day in her life*. Thirteen years ago. The most important day of her life. Thirteen years ago a girl was sitting in a launderette in South London. She was wearing blue tracksuit bottoms, white training shoes and her hair tied back with a black band.

She was sitting staring at her rotating washing but her mind was elsewhere, lost in banal fantasy; she was imagining a parallel universe where another woman – another Jane – was watching the same washing spin around in the opposite direction, watching the same socks and shirts and trousers flipping and rotating, maybe in the opposite colours.

Anyway, while she was sitting there a woman called Chelsea Delaunay walked past. This woman, as it turned out, worked for a modelling agency. By chance she saw Jane through the window and recognised, instantly, a certain potential in her face and figure. She went into the launderette and handed Jane a card on which was printed the name of her agency and a telephone number. The card was printed on silver plastic. She said:

"Give me a ring. We'll see what we can do."

Jane took the card, smiled at Chelsea and said "Thank-you"; and when Jane smiled at Chelsea, Chelsea thought: "Yes, maybe … maybe!" But then she walked out of the door and away down the road and she soon forgot about Jane and the launderette – after all, she handed out a lot of cards – it was a percentage thing! It was nothing out of the ordinary for her.

But for Jane it was an exceptional thing. She was excited as she looked at the words on the card. She felt that this was an important moment in her life! She thought: "This card could change my life!"

And it did. Two days later she rang up the agency and, over the next few years, she became a successful fashion model. Not as famous as Naomi or Kate or any of that lot but successful enough. She got her face into magazines, she walked down catwalks, she appeared on billboards and she made a lot of money. But even at the beginning – even in the first few years of her modelling career, she was determined to make the most of her chance. She was ambitious. She wanted to make something of herself. And, in her late twenties, towards the end of her career, Jane started up her own business.

She teamed up with a fashion designer and produced her own range of clothes. She used the name 'SILVER'. The 'SILVER' range was promoted in full-page advertisements in women's magazines.

And then six years ago she met Tony at a charity function in Brighton – and they got married.

And recently Tarrard & Jessop, the national franchise – you probably know: "T&J. Make your Day!" – have approached her about designing an exclusive 'SILVER' capsule collection to be sold in all their stores throughout the UK. They are hoping the clothes will appeal to fashion-conscious working women. Working women. Working women. Working women. Yes. Yes. Yes. OK. OK. OK.

OK. OK. OK. OK. OK. OK. OK.

Who am I?

Who am I?

Who am I?

Hooooooooooo emmmmmmmm Iiiiiieeeee?

Zarvyn is sitting in his wheelchair looking ahead of him.

It is a small room – newly carpeted. Magnolia walls, bed, table, chair, cupboard, ensuite bathroom/toilet. His face looks like a rotten orange because of the burns. As he sits there looking ahead, he dribbles out of his burnt lips. One of his eyes got burnt out in the crash and now he's got a false one. His face is pink and his skin is bubbled. He is trying to remember who he is.

He is thinking:

Who am I?

Who am I?

Who am I? Who am I? Hoo amm I? Hooo aaammm eyyye?

He isn't paralysed. He can still walk. It's inside his head he's fucked up. Fucked. He can't … he can't move it on. Things. Things. Things. Something is almost slipping into his head. Head. Head. OK. OK. OK. Focus. Focus.

"Who am I? Who am I? Hoooo emm iiiiiiiiiyyyeee?"

He is looking down at the carpet beneath his feet. His mind focuses a bit. He is thinking:

"Who am I?

Who am I?

Who am I?

Who am I? Testing! One, two! One, two! Yes, yes, no, yes … one, two! Testing! Testing! One hundred, ninety-nine, ninety-eight, ninety-seven, ninety-six, ninety-five. Who am I? Who am I? Who am I? Focus. Focus … "

Magnolia walls, bed, carpet, cupboard, table, table, carpet, bed, chair, door, walls, walls, walls. He holds his head and looks down at the carpet. He looks closely at the fibre of the carpet. He looks up. He turns his head. Freshly painted walls – freshly painted walls – magnolia. White door. Bed. Chair. Chair, chair, chair. All the usual sort of things. He thinks:

"Where am I? Where am I? Where am I?"

Stands up – hobbles across the floor – to the door – twists the door handle – can't open it – can't open it – door is locked. Can't open it. Next, he presses first one cheek then the other against the door, rocking back and forth – it feels cool on his skin – and he puts his hand on top of his head. Now he hobbles back from the door and stops in the middle of the room and shakes his head; then he walks over to the chair, where he sits down again, hunched forward, his right hand scrabbling over his scalp.

He is wearing jeans and a sweatshirt. His left arm is paralysed – below the cuff of his sweatshirt you can see his left hand – it is twisted and covered in pink burn tissue. His right hand is also burnt and twisted, although not paralysed. He is using it to scratch his scalp. He is looking downward and we can see the top of his head – thick, white ridges of scar tissue on his scalp, clearly visible through his sparse, greasy, tufty hair. He is running his fingers over these scars.

He is thinking:

"Who am I? Who am I? Hooooooo emmmmmmm Iiiiiiiii? Hoooooooooo emmmmmmmmmmmm I?"

He holds his hand in front of his face. He looks at his hand. He brings it up close to his face and looks at the skin but he doesn't recognise it. He doesn't recognise that hand.

Then he leans forward and clasps his head with the hand he has just been looking at and he feels the pressure of his fingers on his skull. He can feel this pressure and knows it is the pressure of his fingers on his head. He knows it is his head. He knows it is his head. He knows it is his fingers. He knows what fingers are.

He increases the pressure of the grip and for a split-second he remembers something: he remembers walking in the snow, a main road, a park, trees, a pond, a yellow ball, a piece of red plastic, swimming – and then he can't remember it anymore – he feels it all slip – and he can't remember. It's not anything significant anyway. It's just random memories – the same shit we all have in our heads. Same shit. Same shit. Same shit. Same shit. And after a few seconds, he leaps up and lurches across the room, switching his head to and fro – looking at the room around him – he hobbles over to the bed and sits down – bed, carpet, walls, cupboard, door. Door, carpet, bed – bed, carpet, wall, cupboard, door – the room starts to spin. Door. Door. Carpet. Bed. Bed. Carpet. Wall. Cupboard. Shit. Shit. OK. OK. OK.

Later on. It's dark, we are standing by the swimming pool. There is no one here. Tony and Jane packed up their sun-beds hours ago. The only thing left is Tony's sunglasses which are still lying on the paving stones, near to the edge of the swimming pool.

There is just a slight ripple on the surface.

In the background we can see the house. The front of the house is illuminated by spotlights. It has three storeys, a pitched roof, white pebble-dashed façade and black-framed, wooden windows. From the gravel drive, a massive stone staircase turns up to the front of the house. Built on high ground, in over 2,000 acres of garden and forest including two tennis courts, a swimming pool, a row of converted sheds and a picturesque nine hole golf course.

Immediately in front of the house there is a circular pond surrounded by a short brick wall. In this pond there are four or five slabs of limestone – these slabs are each the size of an estate car and lie in a disordered, picturesque stack. During the day, water pours from a fissure at the top of the stack and runs down and across the surface of the stones into the pond.

And all this from one pop song. One pop song
♫
   ♫
♫

The glow of love has gone away
It flowed away like … like the waves
Away from me. To another place
FROOOO-ZEN TEARS. Running down my cheek
FROOOO-ZEN TEARS. You've left me baby.
… cos you're my Sunshine Boy.
   ♫
♫

♫

OK. OK. Remember? ♫ ♫ ♫ ♫ Yes, of course you do.
Yes. Yes. *Frozen Tears* by Josey Mitchell – Number One
in 1965 for three weeks – and then used again in the
1980's in a car advert. Well that record paid for this
house to be built – every brick ... every brick, every tile
on the roof and more besides. This house used to be
Josey Mitchell's home. ♫ ♫ ♫ ♫ FROOOO-ZEN TEARS ...
FROOOO-ZEN TEARS. You see this house was the home
of the Cockney Cilla as she was known in the sixties.
She was married to Geoff. She died of cancer five
years ago. Died of cancerrrrrrrrrrrrr ... OK. OK.
CANCER. CANCER. OK. OK.

♫
♫
♫
♫

FROOOO-ZEN TEARS. Running down my cheek.
FROOOO-ZEN TEARS. My heart is breaking.
♫

Yeah, you know Josey Mitchell. Or maybe you know
her from TV in the 1990s. She made a come back as a
presenter on *Drive In*. You remember. You remember:
"The Nissan Altima is an excellent choice for family
people who want a safe car with good performance, sexy
styling and fair gas mileage. Acceleration is excellent
with a 5-speed manual, and the car is smooth on well-
mainained roads. While there is a fair amount of road
hum on rougher surfaces, the 4-wheel independent
suspension soaks up harsher bumps and potholes with
aplomb. The Altima has good road manners, corners
and stops well. Driving it is a dream but ... "

At the end of the private road there is a stone with two words cut in it: 'FROZEN TEARS' – the name of the house. About a month after Josey died, during the night, someone smashed the little shrine of photos and flowers which had accumulated next to this stone (from fans) and wrote: CANCER WHORE on the stone in spray paint. It was very upsetting for the family. Very upsetting. It's strange the things some people will do.

OK. OK. FOC-CUSSSSS. FOCUS. YES. YES. NICE. OK. OK. Calm. Calm. Focus. Calm. Calm. Focus. Focus. FOCUSSS. Do you understand? OK. OK. We need to focus. OK. OK Shit. Oh Shit! OK. OK. OK. OK. OK. OK. OK. FOCUS. FOCUS. There's a dead woman upstairs. There's a dead woman upstairs and she is stinking the house out but what can I do about it ... nothing ... nothing. I met her in a park about two weeks ago. She asked me if I would like to come back to her house for something to eat. I accepted her offer ... but then, later, she had a heart attack. And she died. And now she's lying upstairs in her bed looking at the ceiling with her mouth open. She feels like cold wax. Cold wax. And there's about ten messages for her on the answer machine:

"*Beeeeeep!* Hello Jenny ... Jenny? Are you there? It's June Charlton. Ring back when you have time ..."; and "*Beeeeeep!* Hello ... Hello ... Jenny? I'll call around later on"; and "*Beeeeeep!* Jen ... Jenny ... Jenny are you there ... la la la la la ... I'll wait Jenny ... are you there? ... la la la ... maybe you've gone to your Daughter's. Oh well ... are you there Darling? ... Hello? Oh well ... it's Viv. Give me a ring when you get this. Bye. Bye. Bye. Bye. OK. OK. OK. OK. OK."

Next morning.

Billy the dog is lying on the top step of the concrete staircase. At the front of the house. The sun hits the front of the house in the morning.

It's six oclock and there's a hissing sound as the timer switches the fountain on.

Billy looks up at the fountain, then down at his paw – it looks like he is looking down at a wrist watch. He spends maybe thirty seconds licking his paw, then he lifts his head – it seems that he has heard something. He trots down the concrete stairs, along the front of the house, around to the back and in through the open kitchen door.

The door is open because Tony unlocked it. It's the first thing he does when he gets up – open the kitchen door for Billy. Billy trots in through the kitchen and out through the opposite door into the hall. The kitchen is very simply decorated. There is a work surface stretching along one wall and a row of kitchen appliances. Everything is very clean and tidy. There's a faint smell of disinfectant. On the fridge there are some magnetic animal shapes – from here I can see a crocodile and a gorilla. On the wall beside the fridge is a large cork pin-board with a selection of photos of the family. There's one of Josey and Geoff from the sixties; one of Zarvyn and Tony standing by a river with fishing rods (before the accident); Geoff holding a golf club; and one of Jane and Tony at their wedding, standing outside the church.

It is very quiet. We walk out of the kitchen into the hallway – there is a clanking sound (not very loud). Down the hallway and into a large entrance hall. The hallway is paved in white marble, with a staircase which splits and curves up to the first floor. Across the marble floor, past a marble sculpture of a woman holding a vase and down another hallway, to the right of the front door. At the end of this hall there is a blue door. Billy the dog is lying on the floor. The clanking sound is louder now.

Inside the room. Tony is lying on his back on an exercise bench, below the chest bar on his mini-gymnasium. His face is red with exertion. He is breathing in and out heavily. The veins are standing out on his neck. He is breathing in and out deeply. He hangs his arms out on either side of the bench. Inhale. Exhale. Inhale. Exhale. Inhale. Exhale.

After maybe a minute, he lifts his hands up to the bar – INHALE – EXHALE – and pushes up – pushes the bar above him ... above him ... until his arms lock ... holds it above him for two or three seconds then brings it down slowly to it's resting position – clank! Then up again. Then down again. Clank! Then up again. He is not wearing his glasses; they are on the floor under the bench. He shouts out to encourage himself and jerks the bar up the final two inches. Then down. Then up. Then down. Then up. We can see the veins sticking out on his biceps.

He is wearing track suit bottoms and a yellow vest. He does eight reps and then, letting go of the bar, stretches his arms out beside him. He is still breathing in and out deeply. After a minute, he sits up and reaches for a white towel, which is hanging from the top of the exercise machine. He wipes his face and chest with the towel, throws it back onto the top of the exercise machine and then picks up a bottle of water from the floor beside the bench; he takes a couple of mouthfuls then puts it back under the bench and moves the peg down another couple of weights.

Lying back down on the bench, he moves his hands back up to the bar, rotating them on the bar a few times. For a few seconds he remains in this position, then, breathing in and out vigorously, he slowly pushes the weights up. AAAAAAAAA! UP. DOWN. UP. AAAAAAAA! DOWN. UP. DOWN.

Twenty minutes later. He picks up his towel. He pushes it into his face, then puts on his glasses. He walks out of the room. Billy jumps up as Tony emerges. Tony says: "Good boy" and rubs his head. "Good boy-o-boyo-boy-o-boyo-boy-oboyo-boy!" Tony ruffles his head. Billy licks him.

Then Tony stands up. Walks down the hall. Then he walks upstairs slowly. He has one of those weight lifting belts on to protect his back. He wipes some sweat off his face. He turns in the curve of the stairs and we lose sight of him. The time is now six-thirty.

He twisssssssssssts the shower on and he feels the water hit his head and run down his body. He massages some shampoo into his scalp.

Tony likes to get up early. He feels calm, he can think about things, he can arrange things in his head. Get focused. Get focused. The warm water runs down his back. "Aaaaaaaah!" Nice. Nice.

Jane wakes up slowly. Slowly becomes aware of the sssssssound of the sssssshower. Nice. Nice. She looks to her left. Get focussed. Focussed. OK. OK. OK. OK. The alarm clock says: 6:37 6:37 6:37. Ssssssssshe listens to Tony moving around in the ensuite bathroom. She thinks how Tony always wakes her up when he has his shower; and then she thinks how it is strange that this was how she was woken up when she was a little girl, by her father – by the sound of him tarting around in the bathroom. Strange that both her father and her husband wake her up in the same way. Her Dad used to wake her up at five-thirty every morning because he used to get up, wash himself and do his hair before going off to do his job driving a truck. Her bedroom was opposite the bathroom and the light used to shine in and wake her up. Her mother, who always got up to make him break-fast, used to try and make sure the door was shut. But there was always noise – bashing, banging, talking and arguments. He used to talk into the mirror – either to himself or to her mother who was in the kitchen or standing in the doorway. He did it on purpose – talking loudly. He used to spend an hour every morning standing in front of the mirror, doing his hair – scraping his hair over his bald head from his hair-line which was about one inch above his ear. He used hair-spray to keep it all together. He used to send her out to buy his hair-spray; he wouldn't go and buy it himself because he was too embarrassed. She had to buy unperfumed, strong-hold, from Boots. He used at least one can a week. After a while the wall at the side of the mirror would be thick with it. It used to build up. It was disgusting. The whole bathroom used to stink of it.

And she remembers her Mother's funeral – it was raining – there were only a few people there and she remembers standing inside the church door, sheltering from the rain – and she remembers seeing her Dad standing outside in the wind and rain – he was crying uncontrollably. He was the only person crying – standing by the grave, in the pouring rain, with his comb-over blown up above his head like shark fin. It was tragic.

Then Jane starts thinking about Zarvyn. Someone asked her about Zarvyn a couple of weeks ago. They asked her how he was. She had been forced to evade the question because she'd been embarrassed. I mean, she could have said he was OK but then of course they might have asked "Where is he?" And she didn't want to answer that question. Or she could have said "He is getting medical attention" but for some reason she didn't like the idea of saying that either. She was embarrassed about him being at the house, locked up in that room because it was weird. He ought to be in some hospital.

She is thinking:

"I mean, I'm not worried what people think … although it is important in some ways. It's just that … it worries me. I don't like it. I don't like him being there. Downstairs. Downstairs. Downstairs … in this house. I mean, I think it's wrong him being here … it's weird! I mean, I know he has to be cared for … but it's three years now … and he's not getting better. And the thing is, if things don't change, me and Tony are going to have to move out of the house … if things don't change. I mean I don't want to bring up kids in this sort of environment. With Zarvyn like a zombie. That's not good. That's not a good environment! I'm sorry, I know it sounds bad but … I've already mentioned it to Tony and I know he doesn't like the idea … but I don't care I'm not having kids brought up in this environment."

The door between the bathroom and the bedroom opens and Tony comes into the room. He has a towel around his waist. Jane watches him through half-closed eyes. She watches as he gets dressed. She watches him looking at himself in the mirror. Holding up items of clothing in front of his body. Jane doesn't make any movement to suggest she is awake but she is looking at him from between half-closed eyes. Tony finishes getting dressed. He hangs a tie over his shoulder, picks up his jacket and leaves the room.

A few minutes after Tony has left, Jane gets out of bed and goes into the bathroom. It still smells of Tony. It still smells of Tony. It still smells of Tony.

One of the first things Geoff wanted to do after Josey died was to kill her pet cockroaches. Big Madagaskan cockroaches – they made a hissing sound – kill them. She kept them in a heated tank in a room upstairs. After she died, he boiled a kettle and went upstairs with the boiling water and a bottle of bleach – his face streaked with tears – but when he opened the door, Billy was there. The tank was knocked to the floor – glass broken – and Billy was snapping at the cockroaches on the floor. Snapping them up and crunching them in his mouth.

Lillian Dallings is sitting in front of the dressing table mirror. She is wearing a white bra and knickers. She is putting make-up on her face. She's the woman we saw jogging earlier. She is over fifty years old but she has kept her body in good shape – the result of regular exercise and a healthy lifestyle. She is putting powder on her face. She looks up and sees Geoff Mitchell standing behind her in the mirror. He has red blotches on his face. He is quite sensitive about it and he wears a light foundation cream to tone the colour down. He is already dressed.

Lillian says: "Are you alright baby?"

Geoff says: "Yeah. Fine. Why?"

Then Geoff walks out of the room.

Lillian steps into a skirt and pulls a blouse over her head. She brushes her clothes down.

Tony moves the glass of orange juice between his fingers.

Jane says:

"Someone asked about Zarvyn a couple of days ago."

"So?"

"Well it felt a bit weird."

"Why?"

"I don't know, because I had to lie."

"Why did you do that?"

"I don't know … because it's weird him being here. It would be different if I could have said: 'Oh he's improving. He's in such-and-such hospital' … but it's weird him being here. It's weird him being here. I mean, the other week I went into his room. I was trying to talk to him … at first it was like usual, he sat there looking like a zombie, mumbling and so on, but … just when I was leaving … as I was on my way out of the door he suddenly said: 'Jane', in a normal voice. And when I turned around and looked at him … his expression was like the old Zarvyn … and he was looking at me … and I swear, for a couple of seconds he knew who I was … and in his eyes I could see the old Zarvyn. It was strange. And then he lost it."

Tony says:

"If ... If he was in some sort of institution or hospital ... it would be worse. He'd be with strangers and God knows how he'd be treated ... at least when he's here ... I mean it may be a bit weird but at least he gets close attention, I mean he's got his own doctor ... and also more important than that he gets ... love and ... you know ... attention!"

Jane and Tony look at each other across the table for a few seconds, then Jane reaches across the table and touches Tony's cheek.

She smiles at him.

Zarvyn is sitting on his bed.
Zarvyn is sitting on his bed.
Zarvyn is sitting on his bed.

There is a noise at the door – a turn of a key in the lock. He looks in the direction of the sound. The door opens and a man with a face like a shrink-wrapped chicken walks in, followed by two women dressed in white. The man says:

"Hello Zarvyn!"

Zarvyn starts rocking on his bed and making loud noises. He has no trousers on.

As he looks at Zarvyn, Geoff's features seem to transform – they seem to soften – as he fusses around with his son his eyes are transformed. The hardness and distance melt away and you can see his love for Zarvyn. He speaks to Zarvyn. He says:

"Alright Zarvyn, Alright son. Alright Zarvvvvv. Zaaaarvvvvvvvvvvv." and combs back his hair with his fingers.

After maybe thirty seconds he turns his head and talks to one of the women behind him called Monica (she is the home help). He says:

"It smells in here. Check the toilet."

Monica walks into the small adjoining room, from where a few seconds later we hear the sound of a toilet flushing. She reappears and says:

"He didn't flush the toilet."

Geoff does not acknowledge this comment. He is helping Zarvyn into a pair of corduroy trousers. Then he bends forward, fussing over his son.

"Zarvyn. Zarrrrv. Zarrrrv. Zaaarvvvvvvvvv" Geoff runs his fingers across the scars on Zarvyn's scalp. He bends forward, kisses him and whispers something in his ear. The two women in white are standing silently behind him.

Geoff looks up and nods to Lillian. A few seconds later she places a tray on the bedside table.

Zarvyn hears the clink of the tray as it is placed on the table beside him. He opens his eyes. Then he feels someone rub something on his arm – he smells disinfectant – he smiles when he smells the disinfectant. He smiles because this has all happened to him before and he knows what is going to happen next. He knows that when he smells disinfectant, the next thing that happens to him is going to be nice and so he feels happy. He smiles but his face creases up and looks like he is going to cry. Geoff is looking down at him and says:

"Don't worry Zarv … don't worry Zaaarvvvvv. Zaaaaaaaaaaaarv"

Zarvyn feels happy. He feels happy. He smiles

He feels the needle point first push against and then pierce the surface of his skin. He is given an injection of Monoacetyl Morphine, Thebaine, Papaaaaaverine, Heroin Hydrooooochloride, Noscapine and Diazipaaan. After a few seconds he feels dizzy and then he feels he cannot move, even if he wanted to. For a while he tries to move his hand, then something which feels like a wave of happiness – of intense calmness – flows through his body and all of a sudden he feels warm, the warmth grows, spreads throughout his body – it feels as if there is an explosion in his head. Warm. Warm ... he feels like he is being surrounded by something warm and protective, then he slips away and sounds become distant.

" Z z z z z a a a a a a a a a a a a a a r - rrrrrrrrrrrrrrrrrrrrrrvvvvvvvvvvvvvvvvv!"

Geoff strokes back Zarvyn's hair. Zarvyn's eyes close.

Geoff strokes Zarvyn's forehead. Zarvyn's eyes flutter underneath his eyelids.

Then they all leave the room. They all leave the room.

Before the door shuts Monica looks back briefly into the room – she glances over at the open door of the toilet – she smiles in Zarvyn's direction, then withdraws and shuts the door.

We hear the sound of retreating footsteps.

Lillian Dallings walks into the kitchen. She is still wearing her white coat. She must be about fifty-one or fifty-two ... maybe older ... She has shoulder length brown hair – very straight. Her features are very regular, but she has irregular teeth, which give her an appealing smile. She always dresses elegantly.

Jane is still sitting at the table.

Jane says:

"Morning, Lillian."

Lillian pours herself a cup of coffee from the coffee maker and puts two pieces of bread in the toaster. She picks up a paper that is lying on the kitchen counter and while she is looking at the front page she says:

"Jane, were those pictures of your new designs on the table in the hall?"

"Pictures? ... oh those ... jackets and skirts ... they were last year's. But the new designs are similar. Slightly different cut ... especially the jacket."

"Very smart. I liked the jackets ... the suede jackets."

"Yes. I'm doing something similar ... slightly larger collars."

Lillian is standing waiting for her toast, leaning on the kitchen surface. She looks at the paper and says:

"Well let's see what the bad news is today."

She lifts the cup of coffee to her lips. As she is reading, a cockroach emerges from a gap between the tiles and the kitchen cabinet. It walks across the work surface. It disappears behind the toaster. Lillian doesn't see it. She doesn't see it. She doesn't see it.

Jane coughs and then says:

"Lillian, There's something I've been meaning to ask you ... or tell you about ... about Zarvyn."

Lillian turns to face Jane.

" ... the other day, I was in Zarvyn's room ... I was just telling Tony ... I was talking to him and saying names he might recognise and ... and I was about to leave the room when suddenly he said my name – he said 'Jane' and he looked straight at me and I would swear on my Mother's grave that he knew exactly who I was. It only lasted a few seconds but it was very strange."

Jane remembers him looking at her. She remembers watching his mouth. He said: "Jaaaane. Jaane."

Lillian says:

"Really … It's strange because I've been noticing slight improvements myself. I think the modifications I've made recently in his medication are beginning to have an effect. I'm hoping there will be further improvements. I've been sending up samples to London for analysis and I think we're beginning to see the benefits. With someone in Zarvyn's condition it's very complicated because some of his problems are neurological – that is, to do with the brain physically … physically … and these require medication and others are of a more psychological nature … that is, not a result of actual physical damage to the brain but rather the result of trauma and so on … and these … require different treatment. I'm going up to London today … to the lab. To try and speed things up a bit."

"So do you think he could ever recover?"

"Well that depends on what you mean by recover … but, yes … of course … he could recover."

And then we see an eye. An eye. Light blue. And we move out. And we can see it is Geoff's eye. Geoff. Geoff. Geoff can feel the sun on his neck. It is only 8.30 am but it is already hot. He can feel the sun baking on his neck.

He is wearing a pair of blue shorts, a light blue polo sports shirt and a pair of aviator-style sun-glasses.

He is looking down at a fluorescent orange golf ball. The golf ball is on a mat which has a series of lines drawn on it in blue and red. It is a practice aid. Geoff's coach recommended it as a way of improving his stance and club follow through.

Geoff finds golf very relaxing. A few years ago he decided he needed some way of relaxing – and golf seems to do it for him.

He looks down at the golf ball – the ball has markings on it which he has to line up with markings on the mat – the idea is to improve his head position. The idea is, he lines his head up with two dots on the mat and then lines them up with markings on the ball and swings the club through the ball.

He lines up a ball and takes a swing. The ball fades away into the trees to the left. Geoff looks at the point where the ball crashed into the foliage and smiles.

He thinks:

"I'm never going to be Nick Faldo"

Nick Faldo. Nick Faldo. Nick Faldo. Lillian has been a great support to him since they met three years ago. She was there when he was at his lowest ebb – when he was close to loosing it completely. But golf is the way he relaxes.

And an hour later.

Tony is sitting in his office in Brighton. This office is situated on the first floor, in a converted industrial unit. He is looking out of the window at the sea and eating a sandwich.

After a few minutes he turns and looks through the glass partition of his office into the main office area. Everyone is on lunch break, except for a tall, young woman who is sitting on a desk reading a magazine.

Tony is not thinking about anything in particular. He looks back at the sea. He finishes his sandwich and picks up a cup of coffee from the table.

He turns and looks across at the young woman on the other side of the office. She is standing up now. She is tall. She has blond hair. She has broad shoulders. She is putting something on a shelf – the window is behind her and it makes her blouse semi-transparent. Tony can see her breasts. He can see her breasts.

She turns and looks at Tony and smiles. Tony smiles back. This young woman is Angelina and she is the woman Tony is having an affair with.

Angelina glances around the office theatrically and then looks at Tony as if to say:

"Oh look. We are on our own!"

She comes over, opens Tony's door and says:

"Do you need anything?" She smiles and leans forward so Tony can see her cleavage.

Tony is thinking:

"O shit. O shit. O shit! O shit! There's no one in the office. There is no one in the office. This is tacky. This is dumb. I am dumb. O shit! O shit! This is dumb. This is exciting. O shit! O shit. No. No. No. I love Jane. Jane. I love Jane. And Jane is beautiful and sexy. I am not going to have sex with Angelina. I am not. I am not. I am not."

Tony reaches out and puts his hand on the top of Angelina's leg. Angelina says:

"Oh Mr Mitchell." She says it in a porn star voice. And then she licks her lips in a porn star-style. Partly as a joke. And then they have anal sex, with her leaning forward, holding onto the filing cabinet. As they are having sex he looks at Angelina's hand which is holding the filing cabinet – he is looking at her immaculately manicured red fingernails. And he looks to the side and he can see her breasts bobbing up and down. O Jesus. O Jesus. O Jesus. Good Boy. Bad Boy. Good Boy. Bad Boy. OH. OH. OH. OH. OH. OH. UH. UH. UH. UH. FUCK. FUCK. FUCK. Yes. Yes. Yes. Yes. Yes. Fuck. Fuck. Fuck. Fuck. No. No. No. Yes. Yes. YESSSS.

And then … we are back in the real world again. And Angelina is pressed up against the filing cabinet, with her breasts exposed, and Tony behind, pressed against her, with his boxer shorts and trousers around his ankles. They stay in this position for a few seconds then Tony pushes himself backwards and pulls up his trousers. Angelina pulls her bra back over her breasts and pulls her top back down. She steps out from the filing cabinet and pulls her skirt back down. Tony sits back at his desk. Angelina opens the door. She turns and looks at Tony, then goes out of his office and over to the water machine where she pours herself a cup of water.

Just as Angelina is taking a sip of water a woman with long brown hair comes into the room. She looks over at Angelina and then over towards Tony's office. This is Val. She is also one of Tony's employees.

Tony thinks that, although Val didn't see anything, the way she looked around when she came into the room seemed to indicate that she knew what was going on. It even occurs to Tony that she seems to be embarrassed, and that maybe she had heard them and had been waiting outside until they finished. This is the terrible thing about affairs. People find out. People find out. Oh shit! Oh shit!

Tony is thinking:

"This is bad. This is bad. I mean, I know I think this every time we do it but this is bad. THIS IS BAD. THIS IS BAD. OH SHIT. OH SHIT. OH SHIT. SHIT. SHIT. SHIT."

He shakes his head.

"This is bad. This is bad. This is bad. This is bad. This is bad."

Val is looking over at him. What's she looking over at him for? What's she looking over at him for? He looks down at his phone. A light is flashing. He has got a call. He answers it. It is a business call. He talks to the person on the other end of the line and says: "Yes. Yes. Yes. No. Yes. No. No." And then he says: "Goodbye".

Then he presses a button on his phone and says:

"Angelina. Can you come in here for a second."

He looks through the glass in her direction and Angelina looks over and smiles. Then she stands up and walks across to his office.

Twenty seconds later she is standing in front of Tony's desk. She says:

"Yes?"

Tony says:

"This has got to stop."

Angelina smiles and says:

"I've heard that before."

Tony says:

"I know I've said it before but this time it has ... it's getting out of hand. It has got to stop. I mean it ... this time it's got to stop."

Angelina shrugs and says:

"Is that all?"

Tony says:

"Yes."

Angelina walks out of the room.

Billy the dog is lying outside on the front drive – in the shade of a car. As he lies there, TC the cat walks past. As soon as the cat sees Billy it hisses and runs off in the direction of the house.

The dog watches the cat then looks back at us. It seems to be watching us. And as we watch, a cockroach pushes it's way out from in-between Billy's eyelid and eyeball – or that's what it looks like – and walks down the dog's cheek and into his fur.

Billy stays where he is, idly flapping his tail back and

forth, lolling his tongue out of his mouth and opening his eyes occasionally and looking around.

An hour later. Jane is sitting on the edge of the sofa. She is watching TV. She is wearing a swimming costume. And she has a towel draped over her shoulders. She is drinking a glass of orange juice. She is watching a breakfast chat programme, on the subject 'I can't control myself!' It features a succession of people who find it difficult to control their tempers and who find themselves becoming involved in violence. A man is speaking, as a silhouette (to preserve his anonymity). He used to frequently become involved in fights in bars and ten years ago, he killed two people because he thought they were laughing at him in a pub. He says:

"At the time, I couldn't help it. I was an angry person. I couldn't deal with certain situations. I … couldn't deal with it. I couldn't deal with it."

Jane finishes her orange juice, stands up, points the remote control at the TV and switches it off. Then she walks out of the French windows. She walks over the paving to the swimming pool. She drops her towel and stands at the side of the pool.

It is not a big swimming pool. She looks into the water. Turquoise. Turquoise. She dives in.

Splish! Splosh!
Splish! Splosh!
Splish! Splosh!
Splish! Splosh!
Splish! Splosh!
Splish! Splosh!

Splish! … thirteen strokes is all it takes to reach the end, then Jane flicks her legs over her shoulders, pushes off underwater and starts another length.

Splish! Splosh!
Splish! Splosh!
Splish! Splosh!
Splish! Splosh!
Splish! Splosh!
Splish! Splosh!
Splish!

Not bad! Not a bad life, huh? Not a bad life. Not a bad lifestyle.

The swimming pool is heated all the year around; because of this during the winter it creates a local-ised perma-climate, and the house is sometimes shrouded in mist.

Splish! Splosh!
Splish! Splosh!
Splish! Splosh!
Splish! Splosh!

Jane is thinking how she likes this lifestyle. And she would like it to continue. She likes it. She likes it. A nice and easy lifestyle – very comfortable. Sounds good doesn't it. It sounds good to her. She wants luxury. She wants a life-style. She wants nice living conditions, good food and expensive holidays – doesn't everyone – these are not exceptional dreams. Nice life. Nice life. Nice lifestyle. She wants it. And other stuff. Love. Happiness.

Splish! Splosh!
Splish! Splosh!
Splish! Splosh!
Splish! Splosh!
Splish! Splosh!
Splish! Splosh!
Splish!

And she loves Tony and she wants their marriage to work.

After fifty-eight lengths Jane hauls her toned, tanned body from the pool (she is wearing a blue Speedo swimming-hat) and stands for a few moments pushing the soft texture of a large white towel into her ear, rubbing it over her body. Then she walks back to the house.

The pool is left to resume its normal activity of shifting and rippling and reflecting the sky. The roses on the far side of the lawn sway in the breeze. A few birds fly over.

OK. OK. OK. And then we hear music. We hear some music. Nice. Nice.

♪

♪

♪

Baby love ... My baby love.

♪

♪

♪

Oooooh how you give me love

♪

♪

♪

Oooo ... oooooooh! Bay-bee love. My bay-bee love ...

A pink feather-duster flicks back and forward. Then there is the sound of a hoover.

A youngish woman with short brown hair is pushing a hoover back and forth across the carpet in the living room. She is fat and is wearing an apron. She has put a CD on – *The Sound of the Sixties: Compilation*.

She turns the volume up and pushes the Hoover back and forward in time to the music.

Then she stops the Hoover and flicks the duster across a series of shelves. She knocks a little ceramic cat off one of the shelves. No. No. Noooo. But catches it before it hits the floor. The Diana Ross record finishes – silence –

then there are the familiar discordant opening notes:

♫

  ♫

    ♫

Dang! Dang! Dang!

   ♫

  ♫

  ♫

There's a place … there's a place in my heart.
A place where we shall meet.
In a land far away. In my heart.
A place where our love is complete.
FROOO-ZEN TEARS. FROOO-ZEN TEARS.

♫

 ♫

♫

Monica dances as she hoovers. She has been working here for about six months. FROOOOO-ZEN TEARS.

  ♫

 ♫

  ♫

The sun of your love has gone.
The sun of love in your smiiiiiiile.
The sun of love in your kiss.
Sunshine girl … I was your sunshine girl.
FROOOOOO-ZEN TEARS. Is what I'm crying!
FROOOZEN TEARS … because our love is dying …

As she is hovering Monica moves sideways across the carpet with the same steps Josey used on the classic sixties TV footage. She sings: "Froooo-zen tears. Frooo-zen tears." She lets go of the hoover and waves the duster above her head.

"FROOOOOOOOOO-ZEN TEARS. FROOOOOO-ZEN TEARS."

FROOOO-ZEN TEARS. FROOOOOO-ZEN TEARS. In his wheelchair by his bed. By his bed. He is sitting motionless. He is wearing a pair of jeans, a yellow sweat-shirt and white training shoes. He has just recently had his hair cut.

He is sitting very still with his head in his hands.

He is gripping his head and he is trying to focus. Focus. Focus. "FOCUS. OK FOCUS. FOOOO-KUSS. OK OK. OK. OK. OK. Focus. Focus. Focus. Focus". Then. Then ... then ... Then something flicks into his head:

A pair of feet. A pair of feet. A pair of feet ... walking feet ... slow motion. Then ... OK. OK. OK. Something chasing. OK. OK. Slamming car door. Ignition. Ignition. Ignition. Engine. Wheels. Wheels spinning ... and ... whooosh! ... we're out of here! Out of here! Nought to fifty in five ... six ... seven ... eight ... nine seconds. Acceleration! ... acceleration ... OK. Oh yeah. OK. fifty ... sixty ... seventy ... eighty. And now he's feeling happy! HAPPY. HAPPY. HAPPY. HAPPY. HAPPY. OK. OK. OK. Laughter. Speed. Nice! Nice! Nice! Oh yeah nice! And then ... and then ... and then ... shit! SHIT. What was that? Shit! He screams. Turns his head away from road. Shit. Shit. Shit. No. No. Turns eyes back to road. Tries to put on brakes ... no brakes – the car is already in the air. Slow-motion. SCREAMING – somewhere else, somewhere else, somewhere ... impact! Then again a still, calm, frozen night sky. Slow motion. Looking up ... flames ... slow ... frozen ... flames ... pain ... oh wow! Pain – in front of the night sky ... then darkness. Wow. Pain. Pain. PAIIIIN! PAYYYNE. NO. NO. NO. Carpet. Carpet. Carpet. Wall. Ceiling. Table. TAYY-BULL. TAY-BULL. SEEEEEELING. Yes. Yes. Yees. No. NO. NO. NO.

And now it's night. Now it's night. And we seem to have established something here ... we seem to have established something ... but I am still confused ... I still don't understand. I don't understand. I was sick earlier in the kitchen. I mean I'm confused. And I don't think you understand. IT'S NOT NICE BEING ME. NO. NO. NO. and things are getting worse – much worse. MUCH FUCKING WORSE. And you don't know anything about me – it's not nice being like me. And I know many other things. IT'S GOING TO GET WORSE. It's not nice being me. I mean we are friends ... in a way ... or acquaintances ... but the thing is for me ... the thing is ... it's not nice. IT'S NOT NICE. NO. It's bad. And outside it's bright. But unfortunately I can't go out. I CAN'T GO OUT. Not at the moment. It's not nice. I don't think it would be a good idea. And there's a dead woman upstairs. Lying on the bed. She smells like rotting chicken. ROTTING CHICKEN. Oh Shit! Oh Shit! Please. PLEEEASE. ROTTING CHICKEN. NO. She ... she ... oh shit. Oh shit. Focus. Focus. And the problem is there's no food left in this house. No food. I've checked. There were a few cans of beans and some bread but I've eaten them. It's getting worse. IT'S NOT NICE BEING ME. NOT NICE. NOT NICE. NOT NICE. For you too. Getting worse. You just don't know it. IT'S NOT NICE. NOT NICE. NOT NICE. NICE. NICE. NICE.

Morning. Morning. OK. OK. Morning. It's a beautiful morning. A light sunlight is already lying on the gravel on the drive. That sort of hazy, dusty light that means it is going to be a very hot day.

Billy the dog is sitting outside the back door. In the distance we can see Lillian Dallings. She is jogging around the perimeter of the golf course. She is wearing a black track suit and has a green towel hanging around her neck. Her face is covered in sweat. She looks down at her watch. She puts the towel over her head and pads her face. Then she looks towards the house – breathing in and out deeply – and smiles.

She walks towards the house.

She walks past Billy the dog. His tongue is lolling out of his mouth. He looks up as Lillian walks by.

Josey Mitchell loved this dog. She loved it. At the end of her life, as her condition worsened, she became more and more devoted to the dog and he became her constant companion and she loved him. SHE LOVED HIM. He used to lie on the end of her bed, and she'd talk to him for hours. He used to growl if anyone approached.

Just before Josey died, when she was really losing it – near the end – as her perception of those around her became increasingly blurred, so her diseased brain hatched up fantastical plots against her life and crimes against her person by members of her family. She took to screaming at her husband, calling him the most obscene names, threatening to disinherit him and to leave all her money to her dog and her cockroaches. And her yellow anaconda.

After she died, Geoff had the anaconda taken away by members of the National Anaconda Society who had the specialist knowledge and facilities to look after it. It's heated tank is still in a room upstairs.

One day, after Josey died, Geoff was visiting Josey's grave and he found Billy sitting there, beside the grave.

Jane is in a room upstairs. The radio is on. She looks at her watch. It is seven eighteen. She picks up a glass of grapefruit juice from the bedside table and drinks it.

Then she reaches down and picks up a black briefcase and puts it on the bed. She pads her coat pockets with her hands. She feels her mobile telephone. Then she switches the radio off. She takes a mirror out of her bag and quickly looks at herself. Then she drops it back in the bag and walks out of the room.

TC the cat is sitting on the step. Half-closed eyes, purring. Purrrrrrring. Purrrrrrr. Purrrrrrrrrrr. What a life – being a cat. Especially on a day like this … warm … relaxed … feeling lazy, Nice. Nice. Yeah, nice. OK. Relaxed. Half asleep … lying on warm concrete … content, blissful, serene, luxurious … warm sun on your fur … half closed eyes. OK. OK. OK. OK. Sun on your fur. Warm. Warm. Nice. Nothing to worry about. OK. OK. Purrrrrrrrrrrrrrrrrr. Imagine. Imagine that. Imagine. Shut your eyes … shut your eyes. Relax. Relax. Slow it down. Slooooooow … and then … and then … imagine … inside a cat. Nice. OK. OK. OK. Reeeee-lax. Oh yeah. Warm. Warm. Inside the cat. Inside TC the cat. OK. OK. OK. Nice. Nice. Relax. Warm. Inside his brain. In the red of his brain. Oh yeah. It is warm and soothing. You are relaxed. OK. OK. We are inside the cat and the cat is lying on the step in the sun, looking out at the landscape. On the step. We are inside. Niiiiiiiiiiiice …

And TC's eyes present us with a high resolution, black and white view of the countryside in front of us – distant fields – distant fields broken down into single blades of grass, with dots of insects and even single specks of pollen. We can even see a bluebottle sitting on a branch nearly a quarter of a mile away. Iridescent blue

Yes. Yes. Yes. And it is thick and heavy – very heavy – over rich! Too heavy! Too much detail. Too intense – the smells – grass, chlorine, manure, fertiliser, exhaust fumes, roses, soil, urine, coffee … Oh Man! It is too much! It's too much – too much. It is difficult to tune out of all this stuff. Oh shit. Oh yeah.

OK. Calm down. Calm down. Calm down! Wow! Nice! Calm down! Purrrrrrrr. Purrrrrrrrr! OK. Better! Better Calm down! Calm down! Relax. Purrrrrrrr. Purrrrrrrrr! Purrrrrrrr. Purrrrrrrrr! Purrrrrrrr. Purrrrrrrrr! Relax! Relax! Purrrrrrrrrrrrrr!

OK. OK. OK. OK. OK. Relax. Relax. Relax. We can see … we can see someone … Yes … Jane. Jane walks out of the front door. She shuts the door and walks dooooooown the stairs. Yes. Very nice. She looks at her watch. She has a cab coming in ten minutes. She turns around and comes back up the steps. She sits on the top step. She takes a pair of sunglasses out of her bag and then reaches down and stroooooookes our head … head … head. Nice. Nice. The fountain is tinkling in front of us.

We feel her hand running down our back, over the ridges of our vertebrae. O Nice niiiiice! And we look up at her through TC's eyes. Purrrrrrr. Purrrrrrrr. Purrrrrrrr. Purrrrrrrr. Purr. Purr. Purr. Purr. OK. Nice! Nice! Ha ha! Nice! Very nice! Oh yeah! Yes. Nice. NICE. NICE. OK. OK. And then we flip over onto our back and let her tickle our tummy. Purrrrrrrr. Purrrrrrrr. Purrrrrrrr! Oh yeah! Oh yeah! Oh Maaaaan! Purrrrrrrr. Purrrrrrrr! Purrrrrrrr. Purrrrrrrr Purrrrrrrr. Nice! Purrr! This is so nice. Sooooooooo intense. Purrrrrrrr! Purrrrrrrr! Purrrrrrrr! Purrrrrrrr! OK. OK. OK. OK. OK. yes. yes. NICE. OK. OK. Maybe … just a while longer. Yes this is good. Relax.

Relax. Oh yeah! Lie back and relax … float … relax … take it easy … easy … chill out! Shut those eyes! Chill out! Relax! Relax! Purr! Purr! Purrrrr! Relax! Purr! Oh this is soooo good! Purr! Cool! Purr! Purr! Yeah this is nice! This is good! OK. OK. OK. Oh God. Oh God.

Jane lights herself a cigarette. She brings her hand up to her mouth and sucks on the cigarette. As she does this she sees that there is a cockroach sitting on her jacket near her wrist. She jumps up and shouts:

"Shit! Shit!"

She shakes her arm. She drops her cigarette. The cockroach falls on its back on the floor. TC runs off. It is a big insect. For a few seconds its legs flicker in the air – then it rights itself. It remains like a black shape on the concrete

Then it moves. It runs over in the direction of the door and disappears under the gap.

"Fuck!" says Jane. "Shit. Shit. Shit." She picks up her cigarette and takes a drag. We need to get the Pest-o-Cutors in. She thinks:

A few minutes later her minicab arrives.

Tony is sitting in his office. He is sitting in his chair. He has his legs crossed. He is not happy. He is thinking about the affair he is having with Angelina. He is thinking:

"THIS IS BAD. THIS IS BAD. THIS ISN'T SERIOUS. It is CASUAL. BUT IT IS BAD. But now IT HAS GOT TO STOP. Now it has GOT TO STOP. Things have GOT TO CHANGE. It isn't anything. IT'S NOTHING. IT'S NOTHING BUT … I LOVE JANE. It is JUST SEX. I mean, I don't love Angelina, I like her and sex with her is … good … but I love Jane. I LOVE JANE. OH THIS IS BAD. O FUCK. O FUCK. IT MUST STOP. IT IS NOT GOOD. NO

THIS IS BAD. IT MUST CHANGE. IT IS NOT GOOD. IT IS NOT GOOD. OH SHIT. OH SHIT. OH SHIT. THIS HAS GOT TO STOP".

The phone rings. Tony looks to his left – the phone light is on. He picks up the phone. A voice says:

"Hi babe," It is Jane.

"Hi babe."

She says: "How's it going?"

"Busy. I've got to get something off to London by courier by Five."

"Oh right. I'm on the train. I'm running a bit late … but we need to get the pest control people in. I've seen two cockroaches now. Could you organise that?"

"Yeah sure."

"And could you tell the new home help … I've forgotten her name …"

"Monica."

" … could you ring Monica and tell her that the shopping list is stuck on the inside of the cupboard – next to the fridge?"

"Yes."

Something moves up the wall. Zarvyn's eye moves with it. It moves up onto the ceiling. Zarvyn looks up. Something small is moving across the ceiling. Something small and black moves across the ceiling. Zarvyn follows it with his eye … across … across … and then there is a face. A face is looking down at him. Geoff is sitting by his bed. He is looking down at Zarvyn.

Zarvyn is looking up at a face. The face is smiling and even though we are bombed out of our head we recognise the face. We recognise the face as a face we have seen before. It is smiling down at us and we can feel our forehead being stroked. And it makes us feel good …

good. The face is looking down. Smiling. It is a nice face.
NICE. NICE. NICE. OK. OK.

Looking down at us. The warm manly smell. Safe.
Safe. We can all remember that. DADDY. DADDY. DADDY.
DADDY. NICE. NICE. NICE. NICE. NICE. NICE. NICE.
NICE. NICE. Daddy looks down at us. We can all
remember that.

Geoff says:

"Hello, Zarvyn! Hello! Hello-oooo!"

Zarvyn feels Geoff's hand ruffling his hair – and then
he hears a voice say:

"Hello, son."

And Zarvyn almost knows what he means. Son. Son.
Son. Zarvyn can smell Geoff's aftershave. He smiles

"How are you, Zarvvvvvvvv?" says Geoff

Zarvyn feels someone take hold of his hand and stroke
it. Geoff says:

"Zarv … Zarv …"

And then Zarvyn feels a hand on his head. Zarvyn can
hear a voice:

"Zarv-yn. Zarv-yn. Hell-llo Zarvyn. Arr yew Oh kay?"

The voice is nice. Zarvyn likes it. It is familiar.
Although he can't place it exactly. Familiar. He drags in
another lung-full of aftershave. The voice says:

"Zarvvvvvvvvvv!"

Zarvyn looks up. He looks up at the face and smiles.
Happy. Happy.

Geoff says:

"Zarvvvvvvv. Zarrrrrrrrr-vyn."

Zarvyn watches his lips and listens to his voice. He
finds it calming. He shuts his eyes. It is like a purring
sound in his ear.

"Zarvyn. Zaaaaaaaaarvyn. Zarrrrrrrvvvvvvvv
ZAAAAAAAAAAAAAAAARVVVVVVVVVVVVVVVVV."

Geoff looks down at Zarvyn. Down at Zarvyn. Zarvyn's eyes are closed now but and he seems to be smiling.

Geoff remembers a day when he and Josey had taken Zarvyn and Tony for a day trip down to Dungeness. It was a nice day and he remembers them sitting outside a pub – Josey wearing sunglasses so no one would recognise her – with the nuclear power station in the distance. He remembers them all eating chips, looking out to sea and talking – making jokes about the power station and about how all the local people were mutants. HA. HA. HA. It had been nice. Nice. It was a long time ago. They had been a family then – a happy familly. Things had changed but he can still remember that being a happy time. A family time

A tear wells up in his eye, runs down his cheek and drips onto Zarvyn's creased skin.

Zarvyn opens his eyes and looks at him. His eyes are blank. He can't even keep his eyes open – his eyelid slips slowly back across his eyeball. He makes a mumbling sound, and spits a line of flem onto his chin.

Geoff wipes Zarvyn's chin with a tissue and reaches to his eye and with his thumb and carefully lifts his eyelid. Zarvyn's eyeball rolls vacantly in his socket, like a billiard ball. Like a billiard ball. He lets go of Zarvyn's eyelid.

Geoff says: "Zarrrrrrrvyn. Zarv-eeeeeeeeeen. Zaaaaaaarrrrrrrrrrrrrrrrrrrrrr-vvvvvvvvvvvvvvvvin. Zaaaaaaar-vinnnn."

Later on, Lillian is talking to Geoff. She says:

"Come on … come on Geoff … don't … I mean, don't torture yourself like this … I mean don't be sad baby! Look, I think things are improving. I mean, Jane was saying the same thing. There are definite improvements in his condition … not great at the moment … but definite improvements nonetheless and if this continues then I'm very optimistic. It's all to do with balance. I mean, I'm going up to a la la la la la la la la la London today to do more tests. These particular tests are very important and I want to supervise them personally because they are crucial … crucial to his continued improvement."

She comes up behind Geoff and puts her hands on his shoulders. OK. OK. OK. Yes. Yes. Yes. Yes. Yes. Yes. YES. YES. YES. And Geoff is looking down at the floor. He has tears in his eyes again.

"He doesn't recognise me anymore. He doesn't know who I am."

Lillian says:

"Geoff … he does … he DOES and … you've got to have faith … and he will improve. I am hopeful – even by tommorow, if I can get the results of the tests I need, we might know more clearly the way things might develop."

Lillian Dallings puts her hands gently on the back of his head. She moves around him until she is standing in front of him – and then, looking straight into his eyes, she says:

"Geoff Mitchell … you are a strong man. Do you understand? You are an amazing person. You are a strong man. And you are going to make this work. Do you hear me? DO YOU UNDERSTAAAAAAND?"

And Geoff says:

"I … I … I don't know … I'm not strong. Not any more … not anymore!"

Lillian Dallings says:

"Yes you are. Now come on. Wipe your eyes."

She takes a folded handkerchief from her pocket and hands it to Geoff.

Lillian Dallings is an attractive woman. She is tall and thin and her flesh is still firm. She jogs a lot – and swims. She goes to the gym and she watches what she eats – unlike Geoff who we can see, is out of condition. Out of condition. Beer gut. Purple face. PURRRRRR-PLE.

There are five shop mannequins: regular features and painted-on eyebrows. They are looking straight ahead. They are wearing clothes in olive green and black, with bright pink trim and they are all wearing wigs.

There are five other people in the room. Two women are bending down in front of one of the mannequins. They are pinning up a hem on one of the dresses. One of them is Jane. She is holding a small piece of fabric and pointing at one of the mannequins. Sitting behind her is one of the men we saw earlier, at the restaurant. He is called Peter. He is medium height and is wearing a suit. He has a fat face, with very regular features and shiny eyes. His hair is gelled backwards.

He is smiling at Jane.

Jane turns around and sees him smiling and throws the bit of cloth at him in a good natured way. Peter laughs. A woman who is sitting next to them stands up and walks over to one of the mannequins and folds back the collar on the jacket. She makes a point about the length of the collar and then sits back down. Jane says something. One woman has a pad of paper on her lap and she makes notes.

Peter stands up and walks over to the same mannequin and folds the collar in a different way and then turns the mannequin's wig around so that it covers the face. Everyone laughs. And the other woman stands up, playfully pulls Peter away and turns the mannequin's wig back around to its correct position. Peter then makes a joke of pretending to jump up in an attempt to turn the wig again.

Later on. Jane and Peter are sitting in a bar. There were three of them but Laura has just left. They are in a new bar in London – designed by a famous architect. The bar has large backlit photographs of animals on the wall and the ceiling: lions, tigers, gazelles. The colours are intense. The bar is made from a transparent material and lit from below. There is a long row of spirits on the shelf behind. Peter and Jane are talking. They are laughing. Jane is laughing. Peter says something to Jane and touches her sleeve. Jane laughs and spills a some of her drink. They seem to be getting on.

Then Peter says:

"Will you have sex with me?".

Jane looks at him to see if he is joking but it is obvious he is serious. She seems shocked. She looks at him and says:

"No. I ... I've got to go." She stands up.

Peter raises his hands apologetically. She picks up her bag. Peter tries to stop her at first but then watches her walk out of the bar.

Tak!
Tak!
Tak!

Monica watches a tall blond woman in high heels walk past.

Then she looks down at the shopping list

1 × tea bags
1 × coffee
4 × semi-skimmed milk
4 × whole-cream milk

Monica pushes the trolley down the aisles. The super-market is relatively empty because it is the middle of the day. It is cool and relaxing. Monica is tired. She thinks:

"I could do all this on the internet. Maybe I should mention it to Mrs Mitchell – but then again – maybe not I like these trips to the supermarket."

12 × grapefruit juice
12 × freshly squeezed orange juice
24 × bio-active yoghurt
3 × deluxe muesli – low sugar.
4 × *Be careful with yourself!* – chilli con carne
4 × *Be careful with yourself!* – chicken with lemon
2 × *B.C.W.Y* – salmon and dill
12 × Greek style – low-fat yoghurt
2 × seeded loaves

Then Monica goes up to the till. And she pays for the food. She uses her own supermarket card to get the points. She is saving up air miles to go to Portugal.

Later on, Monica has a mocha coffee in the coffee shop and sits in a comfortable armchair looking out of the windows at the people walking past.

Two long, thin, well-manicured fingers sprinkle flakes of fish food into the fish tank. The surface of the water bubbles with fish mouths. Red Wag Rasbora, Kissing Gourami, and Gold Tiger Scales – we can see the coloured mouths and bubbles and red of nail varnish on the fingers.

The coloured fish turn between the pond weed and semi-precious stones and then sprint the expanse of

586

clear water, across a bed of blue and green stones, in front of the blue, backlit, plexiglass backdrop – turn – and then sprint back. The kitchen is reflected in the glass.

Then the two fingers that sprinkled the fish food take out a cigarette from a pack. They put the cigarette between two lips. An older person's lips – there are little lines around the lips. And light the cigarette.

Inhale – and then exhale. The smoke billows up to the ceiling from the lips and then back down again. We watch the smoke spiralling from the end of the cigarette – intricate twirling patterns. Then follow the smoke back down to the lips. They are Lillian Dalling's lips. She is sitting in the kitchen. She has no make-up on. She looks different. She looks different. There is a small glass of wine in front of her on the table.

Lillian can't sleep, so she has come downstairs for a cigarette. And a glass of wine. She seems to have something on her mind. She scowles. Then she breaths in and out. There is a sound. Lillian looks up. A car. Outside.

Zarvyn is sitting on his bed. He is looking down at his knees. He is wearing jeans and a blue Fred Perry T-shirt. He is looking at the material of his trousers. He is opening and shutting his mouth. Opening it as wide as he can. He is not shouting or screaming He isn't making any noise. Just opening and shutting. Opening and shutting his mouth. We watch as he continues. He touches his tongue with his finger.

The taxi drives away. Jane opens the front door. The hall is dark. She can see light coming from the kitchen. She walks into the hall, puts her bag down, takes off her coat and lays it over the bannister.

There are footsteps and then we see Jane walk into the kitchen

"Hi there," says Lillian. " … you're late."

Jane looks at herself in the mirror and says:

"Tell me about it. I was delayed in London. And then the train was cancelled."

"I was just having a glass of wine – I couldn't sleep. Do you want one?"

"Err. OK. Yes I will … and then I had trouble getting a taxi."

Jane sits down.

As Lillian is pouring Jane a glass of wine, she says:

"Sounds terrible. Those trains are very unreliable."

Outside. Four spotlights illuminate the front of the house.

OK. OK. OK. FROOOO-ZEN TEARS. FROOO-ZEN TEARS. OK. OK. OK. IF OWN-LEEE WEEE COULD HAVE LASTED FOREVVVV-ER. YEAH. YEAH. OK. OK. OK. OK. OK. OK. Ahead … stairs … threadbare brownish patterned carpet. Oh Jesus … that smell catches in your throat. You can see the kitchen ahead. An old 1960s cooker. To the left … a door. Looking in through the door, it's a living room. Brownish floral wallpaper, net curtains, a big old TV, gas fire with ceramic horse on top. Ceramic horse. Ceramic horse. We've been here before. We've been here before. Yes we've been in here before. This is familiar. Table. Coff! Cafff! Coughing. Some scissors. A pile of newspapers. Some of them have been cut up. Some sellotape. A glue stick. A pile of envelopes. Oh shit – that smell. Some of the papers have fallen on to the floor. SOMEONE JUMPS BACKWARDS. FUCK. FUCK. SHIT. SHIT. SHIT. SHIT. SHIT. WHAT IS THIS? FUCK.

"Hey! What's this. What's going on? What's going on?"

A figure jumps back from the table. A strange figure. You can't see many details. Out of focus. Hold on a minute – it's me! It's me. That figure is me. SHIT. SHIT. Oh shit. That figure is me. "What's going on here! What the fuck … !" It's me. IT'S ME. That's me Shit! It's me. What are you doing here? How did you get in? Shit! Well shit! Wow! It's me. Shit! Shit. OK. Shit. Shit. Shit. The figure grabs up the papers. And moves over to the other side of the room. WHAT? WHAT? FUCK. You only see a blurry outline of a figure – nothing distinct. A few random cut out letters fall from the bundle of papers, an 'S' and an 'E'. I am holding the papers to my chest. "Don't creep up on me like that! OK. OK. OK. SHIT. DON'T DO THAT. OK. OK. OK. DON'T DO THAT." Wow shit. I'm not having a good time. I have just spilt baked beans down my leg. I found a can of beans yesterday. But It's difficult for me to eat. It just mixes with the vomit in my throat. And the sherry makes me feel sick. I'm confused. IT'S NOT NICE BEING ME and things are getting worse. Do you realise that? Yes. Yes. OK. HA. HA. HA. I mean, I know it seems funny. Yeah. Yeah. But then soon it won't be nice for you. Yeah. Ha ha. DO YOU REALISE THAT? IT'S GOING TO BE VERY UN-NICE. Yes. OK. Ha Ha. Very nice. UN-NICE. UN-NICE. UN-NICE. And I know a lot of things about you, I know for instance what your father looks like and I know what your mother looks like. MUMMY. MUMMY. MUMMY ... I KNOW. and I know a lot of other things ... I know ... but whatever ... whatever ... I don't want to get into this. It's miserable in here but we seem to have made a connection. At least there's that. A connection. BUT IT WILL CHANGE. IT WILL BE UN-NICE. But then it will be JOYFUL. JOY. JOY. JOY. JOY. JOY.

Upstairs the olllllld woman is turning into flesh soup. First the blue bottle flies arrived. AND THEY LAID THEIR EGGS IN HER EYES AND MOUTH. There are a lot of flies around now. Big fat ones. Big fat juicy ones. And her eyes are closed. Her eyelids are black. Her body is swollen – the flesh has a creamy consistency and the wound on her forehead is black. She fell onto her face. Green and purple stains of putrefaction over her abdomen. The body is swollen. Her veins are marbling on her face. OK. OK. OK. OK. OK. OK. OK.

A pink rose stands in the foreground. Itzzzzzz petals delicately curled and speckled with dew. It is backlit by the early morning sun. In the background we can hear the tinkling of the fountain. We can see the sun reflected in the waxy body-work of a blue Fiat Uno. Behind is, a honeysuckle which twists on a trellis, up the side of the house. The leaves of the honey-suckle move in a slight wind and, above, a clear pastel blue sky.

There is a ladder leaning against the side of the house. And a man at the top of the ladder is cutting the honeysuckle with clippers. He is disentangling the honeysuckle from the guttering. He shouts something down to another man who is bent over one of the flower beds, and they both laugh. HA. HA. HA. HA. HA. Elsewhere, the tennis court net has been taken down, presumably so that the grass can be mown. And another man is fishing leaves out of the swimming pool with a net on a long pole.

And we can see the house reflected upside down in the swimming pool.

It is early morning – it's maybe 8 o'clock – Jane and Tony are sitting outside at the back of the house. There is a circular wooden table with a large jug of orange juice and a chrome toast rack. Tony is eating a piece of toast. Jane has a bowl of cereal in front of her.

They are talking, although at first we can't hear what they are saying. Tony is showing Jane something. As we get closer we can see that he has placed six or seven pieces of paper on the table. Words are spelt out by letters cut out from newspapers, in the style of a blackmail note.

The letters say: FUK U. U WILL PAY; NNON-SALVAYYYSHON IS CUMMMING; UBERMENSCH IZZZZ NOW; EEET YR BRAYNES YEW SKUM; YOO WILL PAY IN NON-REPENTAAAAANCE.

"Who … who would send them?", says Jane.

Tony says:

"I don't know. I don't know. But we were sent similar messages about two years ago … for about two or three months … and then they stopped. I think it might be someone called Les Sealey."

"Who?"

"He was involved in the crash with Zarvyn. He was in another car. Zarvyn collided with him. He was hurt. Not badly. We gaaaaave him some money as compensation."

"Well, we should tell the police."

"Yes … maybe. But the police won't do anything … anyway, Les Sealey won't do anything. He's a loser." Loser. Loser. Loser.

Billy the dog is sitting on the top step. At the front of the house. The front door opens. Tony walks out. As he goes past he bends down and pats Billy's head. Billy looks up and makes a noise. Tony says: "OK Billy. OK Billy. OK Billy." Tony walks down the stairs. Billy licks his lips and watches Tony go. Then he turns his head and he is looking in our direction. And, as he is looking at us, his face seems to change. It seems like his face changes into something else. That's what it looks like. But it must be just a trick of the light but his face seems to change into a human face. A twisted face. A human-dog-face. And then it changes back into a dog face. Or it looks like a dog face again.

We watch Tony walk off across the gravel towards his car.

Tony bleeps the car open from a distance.

He throws his briefcayyyyse onto the back seat and gets in the front.

Billy watches the car drive forwards across the gravel. A van is coming up the drive in the other direction. Tony waits for it to pass. It is bright orange. Bright orange. Tony looks at the van then steers the car down the drive. We watch as it disappears from sight.

The van parks at the side of the house. It has 'PEST-O-CUTOR' written on the side. We can hear rock music from the van's radio.

♫

♫

♫

Straight-jacket.
Straight to hell.
STRAIGHT JACKET.
A love straight jacket.
It sent me straight to hell!
♫

As we are waiting, a man with an orange jacket with 'PEST-O-CUTOR' written on the back gets out of the van. He opens the back of the van and pulls a bag out. The record finishes. Someone is talking on the radio. Then another song starts.

The man opens the bag and takes out a couple of boxes and a PVC pouch. He turns off the radio and goes into the house.

They met in a hotel bar – Geoff and Lillian, three or four years ago, in Brighton just after his wife died. He was close to an emotional breakdown. The whole thing was too much. Too much. Too much for anyone. Watching his wife die … watching the person you love deteriorate in front of your eyes. And then his son smashed up in a serious car crash. It was too much. To much. OK. OK. OK.

OK. He can't remember why he went into the bar. He can remember that he became aware of an attractive woman. He remembers catching sight of her in the mirror. A tall woman. He can't remember how they started talking. But he remembers thinking she was tall.

Maybe he asked her if she wanted a drink – or maybe she asked him for a cigarette – a cigarette – he can't remember – or maybe he just started talking to her. He remembers she told him she was up in Brighton visiting a friend. Geoff told her about his wife. And then it all came flooding out. He told her how, when Josey was dying, she was delirious with all the pain and drugs and how she was abusive towards him. Swearing at him. Shouting at him. Calling him names. He started crying:

"I mean … I … it wasn't the real Josey … and I still love her. It wasn't the real Josey."

Lillian tried to comfort him. She said:

"I know it's difficult but you've got to be strong. And you've got to … remember the good times. They don't go away. I have been through the same thing … two years ago … my husband … Jonathon died in a similar way and … it was horrible … but the thirty years we shared together … are precious … very precious to me … and the years … you shared … with Josey … you've got to hold onto the memories."

Lillian helped Geoff deal with the whole situation. She moved up from London. She was a doctor. She was a doctorrrrrrr.

Jane is sitting in the kitchen. The man from PEST-O-CUTOR comes into the room and says:

"All finished! I've put the bait down. Just a matter of time now … for the poison to take effect. I didn't see any but … that doesn't necessarily mean anything … Either me or someone else will call back in about a week."

Jane says:

"Thanks."

The man walks out of the room. Jane follows him to the front door and says goodbye. She watches him walk in the direction of an orange van, then she shuts the door. Shuts the door. Jane stands behind the door for a few minutes.

Tony izzzzz on his way out of the office. He is holding a file. The phone rings. He goes back into his office to answer the phone. He says:
"Hello."
Jane says:
"Hello babe. I love you."
Tony says:
"I love you."
"When will you be home?"
"Not late. Not late."
"Love you."
"Love you."
Tony puts the phone down and walks out of the office. On his desk there is a letter from his financial adviser.

Billy the dog is lying on the front drive, outside the house – in the shade of a car. Up above him a kestrel is wheeling around in the sky. He is lying with his jaw on the floor. Josey Mitchell really loved this dog – she really loved this dog – and when she was dying, he was the only one who was loyal to her. And as the pain of her condition grew worse and worse. She grew closer to the dog. She loved him. And Billy loved her. He used to guard her. He'd sleep on her bed. And they used to talk to each other.

And as Josey went mad she thought up fantastical

plots against her life and crimes against her person by members of her family. In the last few months she used to scream at Geoff, calling him the most obscene names: "You fucking scum. You fucking scum. You bitch! No ... no ... you scum. YOU SCUM. YOU SCUM! BITCH!" and threatening to disinherit him and leave all his money to her dog. She loved Billy the dog.

Did I already tell you this? Shit OK. OK. OK.

There is a stationary car on the road. It is dark. It is dark. There is a man inside the car. In front of us is a deserted cross-roads and some traffic lights. The traffic lights. The traffic lights are going through their sequence: red, green, amber ... red. Inside the car is Ralph Bailey. Ralph is a mini-cab driver.

Red, green, amber, red, green. Red, green, amber. He has just had a shock. He holds his hand in front of him. His hand is shaking. He can hear his heart beat: dum, dum, dum, dum, but slowly he calms down. He regains control of his nerves, he reaches in front of him, opens the glove compartment and takes out a quarter-bottle of whisky. He is sitting in a blue Ford Cortina. The taste of the alcohol calms his nerves.

"God-All-Fucking-Mighty!" he says to himself. "God-All-Fucking-Mighty." Then he thinks: "Maybe I drink too much. ... maybe I drink too much ... maybe that's what it is. I mean maybe my wife is right, maybe I do drink too much. I mean, she is right, I *do* drink too much."

He says out loud: "Jesus Christ!" And then he laughs. He takes another swig and then looks at the road ahead of him, which is deserted. He aimlessly knocks the top of the whisky bottle against the the tree-shaped air-freshener, hanging from the rear-view mirror. His heart is still beating fast but he's calming down. He is calming down. Shit. Shit. Shit.

Ralph Bailey has a bald head and is wearing a shirt and light-weight trousers.

Maybe the drink is a problem.

He takes another swig from his bottle. It is two o'clock in the morning – black countryside on one side, a hedge row on the other. No other cars: … AMBER. GREEN … RED. AMBER. GREEN. He is calming down. OK. OK. OK.

Finally, he decides to move the car forward – slowly at first, then accelerating until the speedometer touches thirty. He switches the radio on – someone is talking on a local chat show with an opinion about the day's topic. "I think that if you treat children that way, it proves you are not responsible enough to have children and …"

Ralph is feeling better. As he drives he thinks about what happened five minutes earlier: he had just dropped off a woman at the popstar's house. He had come out of the drive and was making his way to the main road to Brighton. He had stopped at a red light and was waiting for a green light when a van drew up beside him. He didn't pay it any attention at first and continued looking idly ahead of him.

Then there was a noise. He turned his head. The van had 'PEST-O-CUTOR' written on the side. For a split second he couldn't make out a face in the window. Just dark … Then he saw it. It was someone wearing one of those joke shop masks: a wolf, or an alien. It must have been someone having a laugh but anyway, at the time it had scared the living daylights out of him.

The person in the mask revved the van, and leaned out of the window and shouted:

"Race you shithead! Ha ha ha" and then screeched off, zigzagging over the cross-roads and on up the road and disappeared in the dark.

He has another swig of whisky.

He looks up at the mirror – nothing behind him. Strange, he feels quite exhilarated. HA. HA. HA. HA! Winds the window down. Puts his foot down on the accelerator. Shouts out of the window into the night and the empty fields: HA. HA. HA. AIEEEEEEE!.

AAAAAAAAA. SHE AIN'T A DOCTOR. SHE AIN'T A DOCTOR. SHE AIN'T A DOCTOR. SHE AIN'T A DOCTOR. That Lillian she isn't a doctor. I can tell you SHE ISN'T A DOCTOR. She's a fake. She's a fucking liar. SHE'S A FUCKING LIAR. She met Geoff and said whatever was necessary. And everyone believed her. WHATEVER WORKED. She isn't a doctor. WHATEVER WORKED. WHATEVER ...

Tony walks out of the front door into the bright sssssssssunlight. O YES. O YEAH. NICE. NICE. BEAUTIFUL DAY. He walks across the gravel to his car. He puts his briefcase on the roof while he opens the car door. Then he throws his briefcase into the car and climbs in. The car moves slowly off and accelerates slowly down the drive.

Jane is thinking:
"It was that night. IT WAS THAT NIGHT. When he said to me: Do you want to have sex with me?" and I said "No" and walked out of the bar. I walked out of the bar ... that night with Peter ... I walked out of the bar ... I walked out of the bar but then, a few minutes later, I walked back in. What the fuck was I doing? What the

fuck was I doing? I went out in the street and was about to get into a taxi but then I suddenly thought: "Why not?" It doesn't make sense now – and it didn't make sense then. I never usually do that sort of thing – but I just thought: "Why not?" What an idiot. I went back into the bar. Then we went to a hotel. And we spent three hours in a hotel room and then I got the last train back to Brighton. Why not? Why not?

No protection. Her period was late and she felt sick, so she bought a predictor kit which detected the presence of the human hormone Chorionic Gonadotrophin in her urine. She tested herself twice. It was positive and so she had a test at the Doctor's and now it is definite. She is pregnant. She only got the final confirmation this morning. She hasn't told Tony yet. She is pregnant. She is excited. She is very excited but she is also worried.

And now she is pregnant. She is thinking: "I love Tony. I had SEX with Peter. I LOVE Tony … that's the bottom line. I had SEX with Peter once. … and NOW I'm pregnant. I'm not having an affair. I'm not having an abortion. Tony need never know. I love Tony. He need never know because it was a one-off thing. I love Tony but … it just HAPPENED. Peter was there. I love Tony. I don't love Peter – it was just sex. I was feeling lonely. I LOVE TONY. Me and Tony are good. And this can be a good thing. I KNOW IT WAS PETER but this is Tony's child. This is Tony's CHILD. This is Tony's child. This is our child. Definitely I am keeping it but – it is mine and Tony's – our baby – and this baby will bring us back together. THIS IS OUR CHILD. This is our child. This is Tony's child. Tony's child. I'm pregnant. I'm pregnant".

Zarvyn is lying on his bed. Lillian is also in the room. She looks down at him. Zarvyn opens his eyes. He almost seems to smile. Lillian smiles down at him.

Then she upturns a bottle of Dettol onto a piece of cotton wool and dabs it onto his arm. Zarvyn is smiling and holding his arm up to her. Lillian ties a rubber arm-band around his arm. She inflates it. It tightens around his arm. She smiles. She puts down the cotton wool and picks up the syringe. She says quietly: "You're my little junky, aren't you?" She injects him. "You're my little baby junky. Baby Junky."

Zarvyn lies back on the bed. There is a slow flush of pleasure spreading over his body; he rubs his neck in an expression of pure joy. The sensation grows until it feels like he is having an orgasm in every pore … and in his head … it is like orange and yellow fire … like a sunset.

BAY-BEEE JUN-KEEE. BAY-BEEE-JUN-KEEE.

Tony is sitting in his office. There are three pieces of paper on the table in front of him. They are financial papers – to do with his business. His business is in big trouble now. His accountant is very worried. Tony is worried too. His business might be finished. Things are out of control.

And Jane just rang up and told him she is pregnant. He is worried. He feels a little light-headed. He feels a little hysterical. He feels as if his life is out of control. Out of control. Out of control.

He picks up the papers and walks out of the room.

Geoff is looking out across the countryside. He watches a car move along the Brighton Road, in the distance, past the *Pick Yer Own* Farm, on the way to Three Kendles. He looks down at Josey's grave. He has brought some fffffflowers. He looks at them and smells them but they don't really smell of anything. He looks out across the landscape again and thinks of Josey. There is a tear in his eye.

He says: "I'm sorry baby. I love you baby. I love you babe. Love you."

He is thinking: "We met in a dancehall in Clapham … in 1958. And you were beautiful. You were beautiful. I can remember the first time I saw you. You were only eighteen years old … but you were … stunning. Beautiful. I have never seen anyone so beautiful. You … you weren't famous then … I can remember … even now … the first time I saw you. I can remember exactly how you looked."

And Geoff starts crying.

Then he bends down and places the flowers by the grave. He looks out across the landscape. There is a car in the distanzzzz and he can see something black moving across a field – about the size of a dog – it must be a dog – it doesn't look like a dog – moving quickly – it disappears from sight. Must have been a dog.

There is a tear in his eye. He says:

"I'm sorry, Josey. I … I'm so sorry."

A squirrel jumps down from a tree and skips quickly over the grass. It stops twenty feet away. It is still for a few seconds, then moves quickly towards the house. It stops as a figure emerges from the side door. Monica walks out of the house, carrying two rubbish bags. She walks to one of the outhouses and throws them in the bin.

Then she walks back into he kitchen.

Lillian is watching a nature programme on the TV. On the screen there is a pack of wolves running across the grass. Long legs and yellow eyes. A voice over is talking about how far wolves can travel in a day.

"Wolves have incredible stamina, if needs be, they can run forty or fifty miles in a day … "

Tony leans forward. He feels the cool air from the deepfreeze on his face. He feels a little light headed and for a second he sees white flashes in front of his eyes. He grabs the edge of the refridgerator unit and looks down at the bags of frozen prawns below him. There is a line of sweat on his forehead

He feels a hand on his shoulder and someone says "Are you alright?" Tony turns around. He sees a man. He sees a man. He says "yes, I'm OK"

"Are you sure you're alright?" says the man.

"Yes, thankzzzz," says Tony. The man walks away down the aisle of the supermarket.

Tony watches a teenager who is stacking bread onto shelves. He is wearing a uniform and a name badge. Tony looks away. He breathes in deeply. Breathes in deeply.

OK. OK. OK. Calm. Calm down. Calm. OK. OK. SLOW. SLOW … What am I DOING? FOCUS. FOCUS. What the fuck am I doing with my life?

He shuts his eyes. And breathes in and out deeply.

He tries to get his head together. FOCUS. FOCUS. FOCUS. For some reason he has come to the super-market. It's light in here and cool. And it smells fresh. And it's organised. He wants to think things through. OK. OK. OK. Think things through. Think things through.

He is standing in one of the aisles. He brings his hands up and massages his temples. He looks at the rows of tins. Tuna fish in brine. Tuna fish in oil. Mackerel fillets.

A woman pushes by him with her trolley.

Tony breathes in deeply and looks down at his feet. He is thinking OK. OK. OK. OK. Calm. Calm. OK. OK. Calm. Calm. Calm.

He thinks:

"OK. OK. I AM GOING TO MAKE THIS THING WORK. I AM GOING TO FUCKING MAKE THIS WORK. I want to make things work. I want all the usual things: children, a family … a happy life. A happy life. I want to be happy. Something … something about the present moment has emphasised this to me and I FEEL QUITE STRONGLY that I have been BEHAVING LIKE A FOOL. I have got to take control of my life I have been behaving like a fool and I might have wrecked everything. I WANT TO BE HAPPY. But if I am given a second chance, then this time I am not going to make any mistake! I swear to God! I swear on my Mother's grave! ON MY MOTHER'S GRAVE."

He takes his mobile phone out of his pocket and rings Jane. And when she answers he says:

"Jane I love you."

And Jane says:

"I know baby. I love you."

Tony says:
"We're going to make this work."
Jane says:
"Yes. Yes. Yes."

Ten minutes later, Lillian is eating a salad in the living room. Jane walks in. Jane is smiling.

Lillian says: "What is it?"

Jane says: "What do you mean?"

"You. You're smiling from ear to ear."

"Am I?" says Jane.

She is smiling.

"Yes."

"Oh nothing. Nothing … I'm just happy."

Lillian smiles back at Jane. OK. OK. OK. OK. OK. OK. Jane's phone rings. She presses the answer button. It's Tony again. He says:

"I love you."

Jane says:

"I know baby. I love you."

"I love you".

OK. OK. OK. OK. OK. OK. Calm. Calm. OK. BREATHE IN … in … hold it … Hold it … breathe out. Nice. Nice. FOCUS. FOCUS. OK. OK. Breathe in … breathe in … and relax. And breathe out … and hold it … and breathe out. OK. OK. OK. Relax. OK. OK. THIS IS YOUR WORLD … Your World. BREATHE … in … AND FOCUS … OK. OK. OK. breathe out. OK. OK. OK. Oh Shit! SHIT! OK. OK. OK. OK. OK. OK. I want to slow this down. OK. OK. Shit!! OK. Calm down. Calm down. OK. Relax. Relax. OK. I want us to relax. I want this to be a relaxed situation.

Relax. Relax. Yes. Yes. OK. I want this to be a good situation – a relaxed situation. I want us to be relaxed. Calm. Calm. FOCUS. FOCUS. OK. OK. OK ... Nice! Slow down. Relax. Lay back and relax. OK. OK.

OK. OK. OK. Nice NICE. You are happy. You are focused. You are sitting out on the balcony overlooking a lake ... the sun is setting ... and your favourite, relaxing piece of music is playing inside ... NICE. Yeah and you are relaxed and ... OK. OK. OK. OK. OK ... REEEEEEELAX ... you are watching the sun slowly sink into the horizon ... As it does so the music fades gently away ... And there is a silence ... Nothing moves ... and the world is still ... Frozen in a moment in time ... The moment is eternal ... Your whole being is wrapped in stillness ... stillness. Pure peace is inside you ... OK. OK. OK. Calm. Keep it calm. And ... And then you are walking down the beach to the seashore. The sun is shining, it is another place, it is warm, with a gentle breeze. And as you walk slowly along the water's edge, looking around you ... you see the seagulls soaring above, in the clear blue sky. In the distance, you see the sails of a yacht. And you are beginning to feel tired, so you walk up the beach a little way, and lie down in the soft sand – you are looking up at the sky, with the occasional wispy white cloud floating calmly by – you feel the sand beneath you – it is soft and warm. You can hear the sounds around you – the seagulls calling and waves breaking gently onto the sand. The sound of the sand and pebbles as the waves go back out again. You can feel the gentle warm breeze on your face and in your hair. You listen to the waves. IT IS BEAUTIFUL. BEAUTIFUL. BEAUTIFUL.

Shhhhhhhhhhhh
Shhhhhhhhhhhh
Shhhhhhhhhhhh
Shhhhhhhhhhhh
Shhhhhhhhhhhh

Shhhhhhhhhhhh
Shhhhhhhhhhhh
Shhhhhhhhhhhh

OK. OK. OK. OK. OK. OK. Nice. Nice. But Focus. And in the distance you can hear a sort of screaming. Can you hear it? Can you hear it? it's screaming. But it is beautiful. beautiful. YES. YES. YES. OK. OK. OK. OK. YESSSSS. NO. NO. Screaming. Screaming. Happy. Happy. Crucified ... Dark sky. Screaming. But it wasn't him. It wasn't him. There was crying. There was screaming. But it wasn't him. It wasn't him. NOT SCREAMING ... LAUGHING. It was the cockroaches. The cockroaches on the cross. On the base of the cross. They were on the cross. Screaming. It was them. Not him. Not him. At the bottom of the cross. In the blood. Reversed. Twisted up. Oh Christ! Oh Christ! O Shit! O Shit!

UP. UP. UP. And DOWN. DOWN. He is wearing track suit bottoms and a yellow vest. He is lying on the exercise bench in his mini-gym. He does eight reps and then, letting go of the bar, stretches his arms out beside him. He is still breathing in and out deeply. After a minute, he sits up and reaches for the white towel, hanging from the top of the exercise machine. He wipes his face and chest with the towel, throws it back onto the top of the exercise machine and then picks up a bottle of water from the floor beside the bench; he takes a couple of mouthfuls then puts it back under the bench and moves the peg down another couple of weights.

Lying back down on the bench, he moves his hands back up to the bar rotating them on the bar a few times.

Geoff. Geoff hooks another golf ball from behind him and bends down and sets it up on a tee. He twists his head until his neck clicks and then looks down at the ball again. Then when he is ready, he lifts the club back, and swings down, through the ball and – *Snaak!*

He shields his eyes with his hand and watches as the ball flies away.

"OK. OK. OK. Not Bad. Not bad. OK. OK.". It seems as if his lessons are paying off. He hooks out another ball. Hooks out another ball.

An hour later. At the front of the house. The door opens and Tony walks out. He has his jacket slung over his shoulder and he is carrying a briefcase.

He bleeps his car door from a distance and then flips it open.

Before he gets in he leans forwards on the car, bending forward until his forehead touches the car roof. He can feel the car roof, cool on his forehead. He stays in this position for maybe a minute. Then he looks up and breathes in and out deeply. He throws his briefcase into the car and climbs in himself.

He puts a cassette into the cassette player and drives off to Bruce Springsteen singing: "Boooooornnnn in the USAyyyyyyyyyy".

Monica is cleaning Zarvyn's room. Zarvyn is sitting in his wheelchair by the bed.

"I've got to move you Smarvyn," Monica says. She always calls him Smarvyn. She moves his wheelchair and hoovers under the bed.

Zarvyn is moving his mouth. Moving his jaw from side to side. Monica looks at him. There is spit on his chin. Monica takes a handkerchief out of her apron and wipes his face.

Lillian says:

"It's your first scan today isn't it? You must be excited."

Jane says:

"Yes. I am."

Lillian sits down. She seems tense

"Three months now, isn't it?"

"Yes … yes"

"O wow! … very exciting. Very exciting."

She walks out of the room.

The washing machine hits the sssspin cycle and for a few seconds makes a banging sound. Monica is in the room next to Tony's weights room. She is sorting washing into different piles of white and coloured clothes. OK. OK. OK.

There is the sound of a car horn. A taxi cab is drawing up at the front of the house.

The front door openzz and Jane appears. She is carrying two bags and a dress on a hanger. She walks across the drive towards the car. Ralph the taxi driver gets out of the driver's door and walks across to carry Jane's bags for her.

Jane sits in the back seat. Her bump is just visible now. The driver is telling her something about someone playing a trick on him with a wolf mask. A wolf mask. A wolf mask. WHAT? WHAT?

And later on, Jane is sitting on a bench, which is covered in a big paper towel. She is wearing a thin white paper robe. Tony is sitting beside her holding her hand. He is rubbing her fingers. A nurse is talking to Jane and rubbing jelly over her stomach.

Then the nurse starts to run an object, which feels, like an anti-perspirent bottle over Jane's belly and images start to appear on a screen. The nurse moves the instrument in different directions and the image changes slightly.

On the screen, there is a shape like a kidney bean. There is a little glow, which pulses on and off – which is the heart.

Geoff and Lillian are lying on the bed. Geoff is wearing his trousers and a shirt ... Lillian is wearing only a bra and knickers. Geoff's face is in shadow. Lillian is lying against Geoff's shoulder and she is stroking his hair. She says:

"Listen Baby ... Listen ... I don't want to get your hopes up ... but I am very optimistic about Zarvyn. The tests seem to suggest ... that none of the major areas of the brain have been damaged seriously. There is evidence of minor damage to certain, less important areas of the brain but there seems to be no reason why he shouldn't talk or why his mental capabilities should be impaired in the long-term. There is also very little damage to the vocal chords. And ... and this all proves ... or will prove, if I am correct, that his problems are mental, or of a psychiatric nature ... and these can be treated ... or we can at least expect improvement."

Jane is in Tony's office. She has propped up a small circular mirror on top of the filing cabinet and she is applying make-up. She and Tony are going to a function in town. She is getting changed in Tony's office rather than driving back to the house.

She is wearing a black dress and her hair is pulled back from her face. She is applying bright red lipstick. Tony is sitting at his desk watching her.

TANGO. TANGO. TANGO. TANGO. TANGO. OK. OK. Two figures twirl across the floor.

♫

♫

TANGO. TANGO. TANGO. The woman has black hair and black eyes and a red dress. The man flings her backwards and holds her frozen for one maybe two seconds. He stands motionless, bent over the woman, with his hand cocked above his head.

They stand like statues for a few seconds.

Then, they're off again. TANGO. TANGO. TANGO … twirling and twisting, bending and ducking – whirling across the dance floor – then stop again! Then the woman is bent over again with the man looking in the opposite direction.

♫

♫

♫

They stand still for a few seconds then … off again. TANGO. TANGO. TANGO.

As the spotlight follows the two dancers around the darkened room, we see the silhouettes of the audience sitting at the tables around the dance floor. We can see their heads. Then the spotlight illuminates two or three tables at the front and we see Jane and Tony.

They are sitting with a group of other people. Tony is sitting to the right. We are looking from behind. He is slouching in his chair with his legs spread out in front of him. He is wearing a grey suit and has got a *Sea Breeze* on the table beside him. Tony is watching the dancers. Jane is sitting beside him and she is talking to an old man next to her. The old man she is talking to is Mr O'Connel, Managing Director of T&J.

The lawyers have drawn up the final contracts – there are only a few legal details outstanding. This evening is a kind of celebration,

Mr O'Connel is enjoying himself. He obviously likes Jane. This evening's entertainment was his idea. Jane has just said something to him and he has his head thrown back in laughter. Tony is bored but he gets involved every now and then, by either leaning across to say something or replying to a question, or laughing to a joke.

Sitting next to Mr O'Connel are a few people from T&J – some of them we've seen before: Peter, for instance. He's wearing a green suit and at the moment he is laughing at a joke.

Mr O'Connel is talking to Jane and Tony:

"Peter has been very impressed ... and Natalie. They both talk very highly of you Jane. And ... well ... I am a big fan ... and I think the T&J / SILVER partnership is going to be a big success."

"Ha Ha ... well ... I hope so," says Jane.

At this point Peter comes across, holding two bottles of wine – one red one white.

"Blood or piss?" he says

There is a silence,

Mr O'Connel smiles and says: "So sophisticated! Was he a problem to work with Jane? Shall I fire him?"

Peter smiles at Jane and says:

"Well … with a man like Tony behind you, Jane, you can't go wrong." And he slaps Tony on the back.

Everyone laughs. Tony smiles. Tony doesn't care. This is about money. He amuses himself by imagining himself twisting Peter's head off and shoving it up his arse. Fat little cunt.

Later on. Later on. Jane, Tony and Mr O'Connel are sitting at a table.

The band is playing a variety of Latin American numbers.

Mr O'Connel has appeared on TV to advertise his stores. You might recognise him. He has a sun-tanned, wrinkled face that radiates strength and reliability … and frequent Mediterranean holidays … and a life of unbroken affluence and success. He looks like a man you could trust. In his adverts, he used say: "T&J Makes your Day!"

He sits in his chair crossing and uncrossing his legs; turning a brandy glass between his fingers and watching the reflections. He says:

"Well, you really must be congratulated. Both of you. Because this is a team game. Marriage and business … both of them team games."

Tony smiles. He looks at Jane. She is smiling. Mr O'Connel says to Tony:

"You should be very proud of your wife. She's a genius!"

Then he turns to Jane and says:

"In business you either have it or you don't. These are early stages … but I think you've got a great future."

Mr O'Connel reaches across and grasps Tony's shoulder. Tony is pretending to laugh.

Mr O'Connel leans back and says:

"In life the trick is always to live up to your potential. And … and I'm not just talking about business, I mean … I'm drunk … but I know what I'm talking about. You two are a partnership. You've had to deal with a lot of things … death … tragedy … the whole lot … but you're still here. You're still here. Sitting here together. Two successful people … a nice big house, a swimming pool, lots of money … but … but, what you've got to remember is … all that counts for nothing, what matters is you … both of *you*, as a partnership … that's the important thing … your life together. Make sure you don't have any regrets … NO REGRETS."

Jane stands up and, in a jokey way, cups Tony's face with her hands and she kisses him on the forehead. Tony smiles.

Mr O'Connel gestures with his hands – then he says:

"No, no, I'm serious. I may be drunk but I'm talking sense. And I'm saying this as a man who has failed in this area himself. I have been a successful man in many ways … but in the most important ways I have failed. My marriage was a failure. I was a failure as a husband and a father … and I know now … as an old man … that I was a fool. … And I'm just saying to you two, just make sure you don't forget what is important. And all this other stuff … the money … the house … that doesn't matter."

There is a silence

O'Connel drains his glass.

"Anyway. Come on. I'm just an old fool. I'm keeping you away from more entertaining company. Go on … both of you … dance … dance."

Jane stands up and pulls Tony onto the dance floor. Tony doesn't like dancing.

Zarvyn can hear a noise. A quiet noise. A quiet noise. Just outside the door. Just outside the door. He sits perfectly still next to his bed – trying not to move.

Then the noise stops. But he is still scared. He sits still. He sits still for one … two … three … four … five minutes. The noise stops. No noise. No noise. No noise. He stands up and makes his way over to the door. Lowers his head to the keyhole. For a few seconds he can't see anything but then, his eye focuses on something – it is close to him – just on the other side of the door. He's been looking too far – he's been looking into the middle distance … but the object he is looking at is closer … much closer. Just on the other side of the door.

In a split second Zarvyn sees the eye. An eye! An eye is looking straight back at him. Just on the other side of the door. Looking into the room. The thickness of a door away. And then the eye moves back and he sees a face. A white face. Like a drowned face beneath the ice. The face seems to have black hair but then the hair moves and he sees it issssss a mass of beetles. The hair is beetles. Yellow teeth. Yellow teeth. The face is laughing at him. The mouth opens – cockroaches push their way out of the mouth.

Zarvyn screams and falls back and scrabbles away – backwards – away from the door – and tries to hide himself in the corner of the room.

There is the sound of something like laughter. HA. HA. HA. HA. HA. HA. HA.

I know I have not always been a good person. I know that there is such a thing as ... morality. I think there is. I think there is. I do think that there is good and bad in the universe. GOOD AND BAD. But it ... doesn't seem to matter anymore. It seems to be irrelevant. I have tried. I have tried ... but I have been twisted ... and people have not always been kind to me. People have done bad things to me. I have tried hard to ... well, treat people OK but ... sometimes not everything you do is correct. Sometimes you do bad things. I feel great remorse for some of my actions, for some of the people I have hurt. But it is too late now ... too late to repent. It is too late for all of us.

The bell rings. Two or three times. There is a sound of voices just outside the door. Someone shouting; "Yooo-hooo! Yoooohooo!" Through the letter box. And then someone is saying: "She must have gone to her Daughter's" and then someone else saying: "She would have told us." And it just rang again. I can see the silhouette of an old woman through the window in the door. I'm going upstairs. They rang the doorbell. They rang the doorbell and looked through the living room window. I was hiding behind the sofa. They didn't see me. I think the next door neighbour is talking to them. I was looking through the window on the second floor. Two old women and a policeman ... They are still talking – I can't hear what they are saying.

I think a policeman climbed over the fence to have a look around the back. They've gone now but I expect they will be back. I'm surprised they didn't notice the smell.

Someone is having a dream. There are two feet. A nail has been driven through the feet into the wood behind. Blood runs from the wound, soaking the wood and pooling on the dirt below. IN THE DIRT. AND THE SKY IS REFLECTED IN THE BLOOD. A black sky is cracked with lightning. There is crying and moaning but there is also laughter. Something like laughter. OH GOD. OH GOD. THE SEWAGE WORKS HAVE ERUPTED and SHIT IS FLOWING DOWN THE STREETS. And there is a cloud of butterflies and insect/humans standing up, WITH BURNING ARMS. Then we see that there are thousands of beetles standing on their back legs waving their antennae in the air. There is the sound of great joy and happiness. It is a dream. THE DREAM IS COMING. THE DREEEM IS KUMMING. THE DREEM IZ KUMMING. GUSHING PISS-NEKTAR WITH MUCOID FLOWER AND BLOOD-TUMOUR. O BABY. O BABY. IT IS COMING. DEATH-JUNKY. FURY OF THE NON-LORD. VERMIN-CHRYSALIS. SHADOW OF LOVE-VOMIT, RECON-FIGURING TORTUROUS, SPUNK-ECHO, ARACNOID, PISS-LIK, DETH-TRAP. O YES. O YES. IT IS CUMMING. IT IZ CUMMING.

It is sunny. It is sunny but there is a slight wind, which is blowing the water from the fountain into the air in a fine mist. There is a weak rainbow stretched over the fountain.

IT IZ SUNNEEE and Lillian is jogging along the grass at the perimeter of the fairway. Someone else is out in the distance, hitting golf balls. At first it seems like it is Geoff because it is someone playing golf. But It isn't …

it's not Geoff. It's not Geoff. Itzzzzz not Geoff. It's one of the gardeners. He is wearing a blue track suit. On the ground in front of him are two or three golf balls. A fat bluebottle flies past. Buzzes around the ball. He pushes it away with his nine iron.

He lifts the golf club above his head and swings at the golf ball, clipping the ball into the air. Then he spots something lying on the grass, thirty yards away. He walks in that direction.

There is a dead cat lying in the grass. It looks as though the cat's insides have been removed with a happy-scoop. A few pieces of dried intestine lie on the floor. Flies are buzzing around the cat's head. The cat's eyes have rotted away.

The sockets are blank. A fox must have got him. The man says: "Poor bugger," then he slides the golf club under the body and flips it away into the longer grass.

The floor is wet. White marble floor. We can see the ceiling reflected in the wet floor. And there is a marble figure above us, on a plinth. The stairs are in front of us. We are standing watching a woman who is cleaning the floor. She is on her hands and knees. She is cleaning the floor with a cloth. Next to her is a bucket. As she is cleaning something black scuttles out from near the skirting board. It scuttles past her hand and heads for the door. It seems to be the size of a cup – but maybe it is smaller. It is moving quickly.

The woman catches sight of it and screams. And knocks the bucket over.

At first nothing happens then Jane appears from a doorway. She is holding a paper. She says:

"What's the matter?"

The woman says:

"A beetle. It was a cockroach. A big one."
Jane says:
"Are you sure?"
"Yes. It went over there."
She points over to the right of the door.
Jane looks in the direction of her finger but she can't see anything.

A big mouth with thin lips is talking. We can see the inside of the mouth as it talks. We can see the tongue moving. Moving about. And we can see the face smiling complacently. And we can see the pores on its nose. The mouth is talking to Tony. Tony is nodding his head as a fat man talks.

He is sitting in his office. This man is Tony's accountant. He doesn't think that Tony is taking the situation seriously. And this situation is very serious. Very serious. Certain creditors have already threatened legal action. Tony is in a lot of trouble. Tony is in a lot of trouble.

The phone rings. Tony picks it up. It is Jane.

Tony says: "Oh hello."

Jane says: "Something terrible has happened. Zarvyn has got cancer."

A column of steam shoots out of the spout of the electric kettle. The sound of the boiling kettle ... and click! A hand takes hold of the handle and lifts the kettle off its base, then pours the water onto the earth-brown granules in the cup. The hand opens the fridge and reaches in and takes out a carton of milk and pours milk into the cup.

Geoff and Lillian are in the kitchen. Geoff's face is red from crying.

Five hours ago Lillian told Geoff how some of the routine blood tests she had ordered to monitor the drug levels in Zarvyn's blood revealed an infection of the liver. Further tests revealed that Zarvyn had cancer of the bowel. This is the same condition Josey died from.

Lillian says:

"I wish I wasn't the one telling you this but time is crucial. Fortunately, we have discovered it early – and there are effective treatments, especially if we act immediately. We have to act quickly. And I have to warn you these treatments are expensive. I ... I'm sorry ... I have to give you the facts."

Geoff turns to Lillian and puts his hand behind the back of her neck and squeezes. He says:

"Thank you. I appreciate it, Lillian."

Lillian says:

"I am going to talk to Dr Samuels at the Milton Clinic and try and arrange a meeting ... as soon as possible ... as soon as possible."

Zarvyn is lying on the bed. He is wearing a blue tracksuit. His head is hanging over the side of the bed. His eyes are glazed and he has been sick on the floor. His eyes seem sunken into his head. There are black rings around his eyes. He is lying motionless. The room is illuminated by a 60-watt light bulb. He looks in a bad way. There is a line of spit and sick hanging from his mouth. He is dreaming. He is dreaming. It is dark. It's dark. He can smell something. He is climbing upwards. Inside the wall. He can sense something. Above him. Above him. There is a huddle in the corner. He is going home.

Lillian says:

"Are you sure you don't want a coffee?"

Geoff says:

" No … I'm OK … I'm OK. OK."

Geoff is sitting at the kitchen table. He is unshaven. Spread across the table are a series of papers, photographs, books and files. Lillian sits down beside him, and says: "Look at this …"

She picks up a brown envelope from the table. She takes out a photograph. She holds it up to the light.

"This is advanced colorectal cancer … an advanced form of the condition Zarvyn has."

She points to a dark area on the photo.

"As you can see, the cancer has spread into surrounding tissues. In this particular case, because it was not diagnosed early enough, the cancer has also spread to other areas of the body via the lymphatic system. This patient is basically inoperable and will die. Zarvyn has been diagnosed early and he won't die. Rectal cancer is very unpleasant, as you know only too well from your experience with Josey. The faecal occult blood tests are conclusive – So we must act quickly – it is slightly unusual for someone of his age to get a cancer of this type but that's just the way it is. We just have to deal with it. We have to get Zarvyn into the hands of a medical oncologist as soon as possible."

Lillian hands Geoff a photograph of what looks like a jellyfish. She points to something that looks like the end of a baby's finger and she says:

"That is a polyp."

"I think you will find that Zarvyn has got cancerous polyps on the rectal wall – and I think that all he will require is relatively straightforward surgery to have these removed. But we have got to get him in for tests as soon as possible. And after surgery, or whatever treatment is prescribed, he will need further diagnostic tests to verify that the cancer is contained."

Geoff leans forward and puts his head in his hands.

"Anyway ... we've got to get him to a first class clinic as soon as possible. And, in my opinion, we are going to have to go to America ... I warn you now it is not going to be cheap but America leads the world in cancer treatment. And not just the immediate treatment but also the after-care ... which is all-important."

Lillian leans over and holds Geoff's shoulders

"I'm sorry I have to tell you this baby. It's the last thing I want to be saying ... but I'm ... I'm trying to speak professionally."

Geoff reaches up and squeezes her hand.

She hands Geoff a glossy brochure. The brochure has the name: MINTON CLINIC on the front and has a picture of a man in shorts and a woman looking out over a landscape. Geoff starts to flick through the pages. There is text describing different treatments and pictures of buildings.

"This is the best cancer treatment facility in America ... and basically in the world ... *but this has got to be your decision.*"

Lillian says: "I recommend this place because it provides the most intensive and integrated treatment in the world. And integration is essential. The way to treat cancer is in an integrated multi-treatment environment. So, for instance, you have to look at bone marrow treatments, chemotherapy, brachytherapy, intra-arterial infusion, stem-cell rescue and so on, but, as well as these high-tech procedures, you also have to pursue a more holistic approach, in relation to diet and after-care. Now as I said this doesn't come cheap but ... "

"We'll go with it."

"What?"

"I said. Let's do it. Whatever you think is the best thing. Whatever's best. That's all I care about. It doesn't matter how much it costs. The best thing … ”

"OK … if you're sure?"

"Yes. I trust you totally Lillian."

"I can organise it today. I have already spoken to Doctor Samuels who is the chief medical practitioner there. I have already explained Zarvyn's condition and talked to him about the medications. I … I will get back in touch today. You can talk to him if you want. We can arrange the time-scale and arrange for a money transfer as soon as possible. Get all that out of the way and get on with Zarvyn's treatment".

It is early evening. In front of us is the staircase and the sculpture of a woman holding an urn on her shoulder. There is one large window half way up the staircase, which throws light on the stairs higher up, but the entrance hall is dimly lit. There is the sound of a clock ticking.

Do you know that some people drink a certain amount of their own urine every day? They say it's good for you. It has the same ph value as your body or that it re-introduces antibodies into your system. In a way it's an interesting idea. I mean it's not something I could have imagined myself doing – until recently – but now, it seems to make sense.

Tony and Jane are directed by the man at reception to a room on the first floor. The room is dimly lit with white/orange walls and a fawn carpet. There is a door through to another area where there is a tea urn and plates of biscuits on a table.

There is a circle of chairs – comfortable chairs and a few tables with reading material. There are fifteen or maybe twenty people in the room.

After about ten minutes, an official from The South Downs Medical Trust comes into the room and puts down a pile of sticky labels and pens. She asks everyone to write their name on a label and stick it somewhere visible on themselves. There are about ten other couples milling around. Then they all sit down on the chairs but the chairs are too far apart so Jane can't read anyone's label. She thinks to herself that her eyesight might be deteriorating and she wonders if she should get a eye test. Tony sits next to her with a label saying "Tony" stuck on his chest.

Everyone in turn has to say their name, where they live and what they do for a living. Then the Community Midwife starts her talk. She has a flip chart and shows them pictures of the uterus.

Tony puts his hand in his pocket. There is a piece of paper in there. He pulls it out. It is a pamphlet on pest control that the man from Pest-o-Cutor left at the house. On the front, it says 'Pest Control' and there is a picture of a cockroach. As the Mid-wife is talking he opens the pamphlet. He reads:

"Cockroaches are troublesome, unpleasant insects. They are usually associated with filth and unsanitary conditions, although they can invade even the best-kept homes. They are known to carry human disease organisms, such as salmonellosis and dysentery. Recent studies have indicated that cockroaches can cause allergic and asthmatic reactions in sensitive children and adults, especially in closed, domestic conditions.

Since this insect loves to live and reproduce where there is dirt, grease, darkness and moisture, keeping rooms clean and dry is the first line of defence. Eliminate moist areas, such as under the sink and bath. Keep plumbing in good repair. Cockroaches love darkness, so don't allow any food to remain unstored overnight or let crumbs accumulate on counters or floors.

Nocturnal, they spend the day hiding in cracks and crevices around such areas as sinks, drains, cookers, the backs of cupboards and refrigerator motor compartments. They especially favour buildings with service ducts and complex plumbing installations. Infestations may be introduced by egg cases or adults in in-coming laundry, on raw materials, or in crates and packaging. Otherwise insects can enter buildings via the drains.

Cockroaches produce 4–8 egg capsules containing up to 50 eggs at approximately 1-month intervals. The female carries the capsule until just before the eggs hatch. She conceals the capsules near a food source. A cockroach takes 3.5 months to reach maturity.

Pest-o-Cutor use specially developed insecticidal baits to control cockroaches. The cockroach baits contain a slow-acting insecticide incorporated into a food attractant. The cockroaches locate and feed on the bait, typically contained in small, plastic bait trays, and crawl away to die. Bait carried back to the nesting area also kills other roaches after being expelled in the sputum and faeces."

He is lying on the floor moaning and he is dribbling from his mouth. He is holding his stomach. He looks in a bad way. He is feeling bad – very bad – he has been feeling bad for a few days. At first the room was spinning around above him and then his head felt tight. Normally Lillian gives Zarvyn the cheapest street heroin she can buy usually cut with a bit of Valium. But this time her usual contact sold her something else. Zarvyn has sweat dripping from his face. The room spins around. Around the axis of the light bulb. Any thoughts he has are spinning around as well. Zarvyn is sick.

He is sick. He is clutching his stomach. Occasionally his body jerks and he makes a strange crying sound. As we look closely at him we see his skin is strangely white and covered with droplets of sweat – his whole body jerks and he makes a crying sound

Tony is lying next to Jane in bed. It is late now. They got home two hours ago. They have been in bed for thirty minutes. It is a cliché but since Jane has become pregnant Tony is very attracted to her body. He likes her breasts and the way she has put on weight. Ever since her body started to change. He feels her breast against his cheek.

Jane is lying with her arm around Tony's shoulders. With her hand she is playing with his hair. Tony is lying with his face on her breasts. His head is heavy and she moves her position. Tony puts his hand on her belly. His baby. His baby.

Jane is thinking :

"If it's a boy we've agreed on Jamie or David and if it's a girl it's a toss-up between Grace and Louise. I think simple names are best. And we've had the baby's room decorated. Geoff said we should think of the house as our own now. He said that is what Josey would have wanted. It seems much more like our own house now – like a family house."

The launch of the T&J SILVER collection is in two days time. It will coincide with a net-cast of the event, which will flag up the internet sales. It will take place here at Frozen Tears. As it is Jane's house it will emphasise the family/working mother theme. They will build a catwalk. Put up a marquee.

I'm up here. I'm up in the attic. I had to come up here because there are people downstairs. They broke the door down. Two policemen and two old ladies. They've found the dead woman. Someone is crying.

The police broke down the door. It's alright. It's OK. It's quite comfortable up here. I've made myself a sort of bed out of loft insulation and I found a bottle of crème de menthe up here. I mean, I doubt anyone is going to look up here. I'll just lie low until they leave. I mean I'm not sure what the procedure is in these cases. I mean, I suppose they might put one of those security doors on the front of the house which would be inconvenient. Shhhh! There's someone walking around in the room just below – it's a spare bedroom I think. Step, step, step, step, step. OK. OK. OK. OK. It's fine. I found this bottle of crème de menthe anyway – in a suitcase. Amazing! There was also a book in that suitcase as well, a diary or something. It's got some photographs in. It is a diary, or it's a bit like a scrapbook. It starts off with pictures of a young woman who I think is the woman downstairs when she was young. And there are lots of animal pictures cut out from magazines – hold on a minute … no it's alright … I thought someone was … coming up but … no … NO. NO. it's OK. OK. OK. Focus. Focus. OK. OK. OK.

OK. OK. Next day. Next day. Zarvyn is lying with his head hanging over the edge of the bed. He has been sick and there is vomit on the floor underneath his head. There are also spots of blood in the vomit. BAD SMELL OF SHIT AS WELL. BAD. BAD. OK.

Lillian lifts his head up and arranges the pillow behind him. She fetches some tissue from the toilet and cleans up his face. There is a bad smell of shit in the room.

Zarvyn is very weak. He is very ill. He has been sick several times in the night. Lillian is very worried. She is worried. She doesn't know what is wrong but she has a strong suspicion that Zarvyn might die. He needs proper medical attention now. But … if she calls someone … Shit – shit – shit! She thinks: shit … shit … shit! She needs to buy some time. Just a few more days … until the money … until the money transfer … SHIT. SHIT. SHIT. OK. OK. yeah … shit … shit … why now? … shit … shit! She needs time to think. She needs time to think. Needs time to think.

OK. OK. OK. OK. She pulls the covers up to Zarvyn's neck. He is in a bad way. He is in a bad way.

She walks out of the room and locks the door. She walks along the corridor to the entrance hall. She stands beside the white sculpture and tries to think what she should do. There are voices in the kitchen. OK. OK. OK. Lillian stands still for a few seconds she is touching her lip with her finger. Then she seems to make a decision.

Lillian walks into the kitchen. Geoff is sitting at the table. She waits a few seconds and then says to Geoff:

"I have just looked in on Zarvyn, and I've given him a sedative. I'm trying to change his medication to fit in with the medication that the doctor in America has suggested. Now this is important … we must make sure he doesn't get excited ... especially today and tommorow ... with the launch and so on. He's doing very well but there will be a change-around period and a few minor side effects. Today ... and tomorrow ... it would be best if he was left to relax as much as possible. He really needs to rest. And especially with the event today I don't want him becoming excited it could be dangerous. If possible I would prefer if no one visited him today. I know this is hard ... but, including yourself ... You've got to bear with me Geoff. I have to wear two hats here. This is my professional advice. And ... the other thing is the money. Doctor Daniels and I want to get the financial side out of the way so we can concentrate on the treatment. When will the transfer go through?"

"The bank say it will be completed first thing on Monday."

"Monday ... Monday ... first thing. OK. Good! Right That's good ... Monday."

Lillian reaches across and strokes Geoff's face.

"I'm sorry babe this is making me very nervous. I feel so responsible. I have a lot of things to do today before Jane's launch so I will have to talk to you later."

Geoff takes hold of Lillian's hand and says "Lillian I appreciate what you are doing. Thankyou."

FIRST THING MONDAY. FIRST THING MONDAY. FIRST THING MONDAY. MONDAY.

Lillian walks out of the kitchen into the hall. She is thinking: "OK. OK. OK. OK. OK. TODAY AND TOMORROW. TOMMOROW. MONEY CLEARS MONDAY. SHOULD BE OK. OK. OK. SHOULD BE OK. IF I CAN JUST KEEP IT TOGETHER. OK. OK. YES. YES. YES." Then out of the front door. She walks across the paved area and towards the trees in front of her. She walks past the tennis courts. In the distance she can see a gardener bending over. She takes out her mobile phone and punches in a few numbers. She punches 0 … 2 … 0 … 7 … 2 …

Something smacks into her back. Slices through the middle of her. Her mobile spins out of her hand. She sees some blood splatter out in front of her onto the grass. She feels her feet give way. She feels herself hit the ground. She is pulled across the grass. She hears a strange sound then she loooooooses consciousness.

And when she comes to she feels as if she can see her own face – it is as if she is looking in a mirror. It is as if she is looking down at her own face. She can see herself. She can see herself looking scared. She is lying on the floor – she is outside – she can see grass and leaves behind her head. She has a cut on her forehead and there is a splatter of blood on her face – and her arms are bent behind her back. She is looking straight at herself and she can see herself crying. Oh shit! Oh shit! And she is looking down at her own face. And then she can see two hands – it is as if they are her hands. Or the hands of the person whose eyes she is looking through. One of these hands moves towards her face. It moves to the side of her face and strokes her cheek. She is crying. She can see herself crying. She is saying:

"Please no … please no". She can see herself crying:

"Please. Please …!"

There is the sound of laughter. Then one of the hands grabs her hair and holds her head still. The other hand moves towards her eyes. She watches herself shut her eyes. Then she watches the thumb massage her eyeball. She is watching her mouth saying:

"Please. Please. No. No."

Then the thumb pushes. She is screaming and she can feel the pain. The thumb jams into the eye and twists and then jars against the bone of the eye socket. She watches herself screaming. And the thumb twists her eyeball out.

"Oh please no! Oh please …!"

She can see her face – her punctured eyeball hanging down her cheek, blood dripping from her eye. Then the thumb moves to the other eye. She can feel her own panic – she knows what is going to happen – she can feel the pain and terror, she can see her own face, she can hear her own screaming. The hand touches and caresses the other eye, then twist into her socket. Then it all goes black.

Lillian feels something push into her stomach. There is a splash of blood. Lillian jerks around on the floor, screaming – there is a wheezing sound as air escapes from her throat.

One hour later. Lillian Dallings is still just about alive – only just alive – which is amazing considering the condition she is in. She is impaled through the stomach on a branch that sticks upwards about three metres above the ground – from the main bulk of a fallen tree trunk. The tree trunk looks in silhouette like some strange insect holding Mrs Dallings aloft on a spike. It looks prehistoric.

Her jaw is broken and her pubic hair has been cut out and stuck on the blood around her mouth like a beard. She is naked except for her shoes and parts of her skirt.

She is barely alive. But from her position, if she had any eyes, she would have been able to see the house. It is in the distance. She is very weak. We can see it. The roof in the distance. She is very weak now. She is nearly dead. One of her arms is broken at the shoulder and bent back behind her.

It looks as if she has been systematically tortured. TORTURED. There must have been a lot of pain.

She is beyond pain now. Her eyes are flickering. She is beyond pain. BEYOND.

If we move back from this gruesome tableau, we see the tree trunk is next to a derelict barn. To the left is a row of broken trees. As we move backwards the tree trunk is transformed into a silhouette – and we can still see the silhouette of Mrs Dalling's figure but, as we move away, it is starting to get lost amongst the other shapes.

Back further – further – further – and – no – you can't really pick her out any more. It could be anything. It just looks like a part of the tree trunk.

We move back further through the trees, across the golf course and then towards the house. There is a marquee in the garden and people are starting to arrive. But, if you've got very good eyesight like me, you can still see Lillian's silhouette – but I mean, unless you knew exactly what you were looking at you would never pick her out.

And now it's NOW. Do you understand what I mean? NOW IS NOW. It's now – as I am saying this – it is now – SIMULTANEOUS – or at least it is almost now. ALMOST. ALMOST NOW. Do you know what I mean? It's now. This is real time. It is nearly now. It's NOW. It's NOW. NOW. NOW. NOW. It's coming. It's coming. IT'S COMING.

COMING. OH. YEAH. CAN YOU FEEL IT? YES. YES. YES. OK. OK. OK. O GOD. O GOD. O GOD. YES. YES. YES. OK. OK. OK. OK. OK.

I FEEL VERY LOW AT THE MOMENT. I feel very low at the moment. It's difficult to explain. None of this ... none of this story makes me happy and there are other things ... the thing is ... I'm not happy. I don't like myself. I don't like the way I look ... I don't like the way I feel ... I don't understand myself anymore. It's not nice. It really isn't nice. I mean I don't quite know how to explain it. It is better when I drink ... when I drink things seem OK. It's my only comfort – alcohol and drugs are the only things that seem to help.

But the thing is you see – I've been judged. I've already been judged. I guess we all have ... and so I don't understand why I should have a problem. I don't know how to explain.

But I feel there is a connection between me and you – do you feel it? I mean I suppose it is inevitable. I feel there is a relationship between me and you. I feel like I am listening to these words with you or that, in a sense, I am ... in there, behind your eyes, reading these words. Do you feel it? I feel that there is a relationship between me and you. I feel like we are friends. I feel like we are friends. Yeah. Yeah. Yes. Yes.

Jane is standing inside the Marquee. All the tables and chairs are lined up. The tables are being laid and the flower arrangements have just arrived. Jane is wearing blue track suit bottoms and a T-shirt. There is a banner saying: 'SILVER' hanging down one side of the tent. And various other promotional materials. There are a couple of hours to go. Earlier on, the models were rehearsing and everything looked good. Jane is excited. Someone comes up behind her and puts their hands over her eyes and says:

"Guess who?"

Jane says: "Barry Manilow" and turns around and kisses Tony.

Geoff stops and looks behind him. There is a panorama of neatly manicured, landscaped greenery. And lines of gravestones and various ornamental trees. The gravestones are uniform – one or two stick out but they are all very similar. In the distance he sees something. He looks. He looks. It's a dog. A dog. Is it a dog? Yes. Yes. A dog. Billy. Running in this direction. Geoff shouts and Billy comes running up to him. He says:

"Billy! Billy! Billy. Billy. How did you get here? How did you get here? Billy. Billy".

Billy licks his hand.

"How did you find the way here?"

Geoff kneels down and holds Billy around the neck and strokes his hair.

"Billy. Billy. Billy. Billy. You loved her didn't you … didn't you? Have you come back to see Mummy again? Billy! Have you come to see Mummy? O yes. O yes. Yes. Yes … yes … You loved her … I did too. We loved her. Didn't we boy? Didn't we? We loved her."

Geoff stands up, he turns and walks up the hill, past the fountain and a row of benches. He walks to the brow of the hill and stops in front of a large gravestone. It is shiny black stone with gold letters saying 'JOSEY MITCHELL'.

To the side of Josey's grave there is a wheel-barrow, a

spade and other grave-digging tools and a newly dug grave.

Geoff stands in front of Josey's grave. He is lost in memories. As we look more closely we see he is crying.

He says:

"Oh Josey. Oh Josey. I'm sorry"

OH JOSEY.

Geoff feels a blow to his back. The force throws him to the left, where he crumples on the grass. He tries to turn but he feels another push in his back, which sends him flopping towards the edge of the open grave. He is left lying with his head hanging down in the hole. Then he feels something stab into the base of his back, cutting into his vertebra. He blacks out for a few seconds. When he regains consciousness he finds himself at the bottom of the grave, looking upwards. There is a sharp pain in his back. He tries to move his arms but there is pain. He can't move. His neck feels like jelly. Seconds pass, minutes pass – sky, clouds, birds pass across the oblong of sky above. And then a shadow falls on the side of the grave – lengthening and increasing in size – a head appears over the top, unrecognisable at first because of the confusion of the white points of pain flashing in front of his eyes. Slowly an image focuses. A head … a dog … a dog head … a dog? Billy? It's Billy. With his tongue hanging out. Billy. Billy. Good boy. Tongue hanging out. Geoff says:

"Billy … ?"

"And now it's now. NOW. NOW IT'S NOW. NOW IS NOW. NOW IS NOW. NOW! It's now! It's me. It's me hello. Ha ha. NOW! NOW! NOW IS NOW. YOU ARE SPECTATORS TO YOUR OWN EKSTASEEEE! HA HA.

Its eyes are not human but I'm getting confused. It's not looking … IT'S ME. IT'S ME SPEEEEEKING. TO YOU. TO YOU. IT'S ME. BILLY. BILLEEEEE. JOSEEEEEEEE.

And now it's now I can feel them inside me. I … I can feel them. Because I am not one of them. I can feel them. Walking around. Inside my head. Behind my eyes. But I am not one of them. They come out of my eyes and I shit them out, then I eat them up. I feel them squeeze out of my nose. I SHIT THEM OUT. OK. OK.

And then it is now. It is now. Do you understand. I mean before I was remembering. But this is now. IT'S HAPPENING. IT IS COMING. IT IS MORE THAN ME. IT IS NOT PAIN. IT IS JOY. JOY IS COMING. IT IS THE END AND THE BEGINNING. IT IS NEARLY THE BEGINNING. It is now. O GOD. O GOD. IT'S NOW. IT'S NOW.

There is a huge Marquee in the garden. There are a lot of people present and there are more and more people turning up in cars.

There is a marquee in front of the house. There are lots of people standing around. Waiters walk to and fro with bottles of champagne and trays of canapés.

Jane is sitting at a table on a raised platform. She is looking around her and she is thinking:

"This is VERY exciting. This is going VERY WELL. This is a BIG SUCCESS. This is VERY good."

Jane is talking to Mr O'Connel from T&J. He is very excited. Tony is sitting next to her and he is excited. He is happy. He kisses Jane.

People keep coming up to her and saying complimentary things.

Ten minutes later. Jane stands up. She taps the microphone and says:

"Testing. Testing … "

The microphone makes a whistling sound. There is a pause and then Jane says:

"Hello. Thank you all very much for coming."

There is a pause and some applause. Jane looks up at the sky. It is blue. A bird flies across.

"This may seem like a strange venue for a fashion show – but the thing is, in a sense, this isn't a fashion show. Or at least it is not a conventional fashion show. In a conventional fashion show, very tall, very thin, very young girls parade around in beautiful tailor-made clothes and they are cheered and clapped by an audience of rich and famous people. From a distance, it all seems very elegant and glamorous. But that is because we don't see what goes on behind the scenes, we don't see the tape or the padding. These are fantasy clothes for fantasy women. SILVER is about real clothes for real women. And to, quote from the very first SILVER advertisement …"

She picks up a magazine, shows it to the audience and reads from it:

"I have walked the catwalks of London, New York, Milan and Paris. I have worn the finest clothes in the world. But away from the glamorous world of fashion

I am an ordinary working woman and I realise the virtues of practical clothes. I still like beautiful clothes but I also need clothes I can wear to the supermarket and when I'm dropping the children off at school ..."

She pats her stomach and says as an aside:

"And these are things which are going to be important to me in the near future"

There is applause. Then she continues:

"... Now I feel like I'm on a catwalk wherever I am. Whether I'm a fashion model, a high-flying executive or a busy mum."

She puts the magazine down and says:

"This may sound like just more sales-speak but it was written with sincerity ... and it is sincerely meant today. And so, as a working, soon-to-be mother, who makes clothes for other working women, I feel this venue ... our house ... " She puts her hand on Tony's shoulder. " ... is the perfect place for this launch. I hope you will enjoy yourselves this afternoon. Thank you. Thank you."

There is some applause and then a pounding beat as the music starts, the stage is lit-up and models appear on the catwalk – the first wave of models dressed in a dark burgundy colour-matching coats, tops, dresses and trousers.

There are cheers – Jane waves and then sits down and disappears from view.

The vw Passat is a comfortable and understated vehicle with a modern look. Air conditioning and power steering are standard. Comfortable and relaxed. Excellent fuel economy at 38 miles to the gallon on the motorway and 30–32 miles in town.

Moving smoothly through the gears. Easy gears and

sharp breaks, the steering on corners seems tight. Past the long lines of tall Georgian houses – slow and smooth – don't want to knock down children. Change down the gears and as we turn into Brownly Street. Down towards Brighton sea front.

The music changes.

Now it is evening wear: longer dresses, long coats. Tony is talking to the man next to him. He seems very happy. As the new wave of models come onto the catwalk he stands up and claps along to the music.

Tony says to Jane:

"Well done" and he kisses her on the cheek. "Well done. Well done."

It looks upmarket without being over the top. The inside is well maintained with all the gadgets, not to mention a modern look. You start to appreciate this car almost immediately. The ride is smooth, with an engine willing to go from 0 to 70 in seconds (very handy if you do a lot of motorway driving) gears smooth and brakes sharp. A very smooth ride with plushly upholstered seats and cruise control.

We see a man lying on his side on the pavement wearing a suit. We move on. It's quiet.

Electric windows, electric sunroof, power steering, CD player, back head-rests and front arm-rests, not to mention the excellent on-board computer that tells you your average fuel consumption, speed, miles etc.

Jane looks a bit worried. She is sitting at the table. She doesn't know what to do. She looks for Tony. She can't see him. It doesn't make sense. It feels like her waters have broken – it doesn't make sense. Where is Tony? She feels a jolt of pain go through her body and she doubles up. Jane says something to the woman in the pink dress, sitting next to her. The woman puts her hand up to Jane's face. This woman says something to the man next to her and they help Jane to stand up. At one point Jane doubles up again. The woman in the pink dress helps Jane out of the marquee and leads her towards the house. Jane is saying:

"God! It's only four months." and she doubles up again. The woman says: "Come on. Don't panic Jane."

As they go into the building we can hear screams. Screaming.

There is plenty of space inside the car for the whole family and dogs. The boot is large with a power socket for camping. It comes with a warning triangle fitted into the boot and a separate compartment for a first aid kit. The seats are firm and make long distances a pleasant and comfortable experience. This is the type of car that you just want to keep on driving, and you don't have to take out a second mortgage to have one. Excellent fuel economy at 38 miles to the gallon on motorway and 30–32 miles to the gallon in town.

Down into second gear as we turn into Bellsham Square. The car has a few nice extras like an automatic light when you open the vanity mirror, and interior light activation, when you unlock using the remote.

There is a woman in a blue dress lying face down on the kerb. And we notice it is very quiet, we haven't seen any cars. Strange. Very strange. And something flicks past just out of our line of sight. We see black objects – very quick – just out of sight. And then we see another figure sprawled over a wall. His head is hanging down. He is staring straight at us – upside down – his eyes are wide open. His throat has been ripped out. And then we see two children stuck onto railings. Blood is dripping off one of their feet. And then we see more of those black shapes moving rapidly. RAPIDLY. RAPIDLY.

Tony is in the bathroom, taking a piss. He thinks: "Things should be OK. This is good. This is going well. OK. OK. OK."

He feels something like a piece of wire pull around his neck – it cuts into his neck He tries to get his fingers under the wire. He manages to get his fingers under the wire. With one hand he reaches back and feels for the hands holding the wire. But there are no hands. He tries to pull at the wire. It is cutting into his neck – Shit! – it is tightening – it is cutting into his fingers. He gags. What is this? Shit. SHIT. SHIT. He reaches back for the body behind him – he can bench-press 350 kilos – with a twist of the hips and a turn of the shoulders he could flip whoever it is over his shoulder but …

But he can't find the body. He tries to move back. Something hits him in the back. He feels something push through his stomach. He looks down he can see a black point sticking out of this stomach and blood pouring onto the floor. He can see his penis flopping about – still pissing.

Tony is gasping. It is too late … too late to beg. He feels the wire cut slowly through his fingers

And then the wire snaps through his neck.

Tony is still standing on his feet. But his head is hanging half way down his back, connected by a strip of skin and flesh.

For 3.17 seconds, as his head dangles; his brain starving of oxygen; his vision whirls around the room like an avant-garde art film he once saw on Channel Four. Upside-down: tiles, sink, taps, towels, tiles, taps … and then … 3.17 seconds and then … black? Who knows?

I mean … I mean I am partly Josey Mitchell … it's true I AM PARTLY JOSEY MITCHELL … but … but this is bigger than me. This is MUCH BIGGER. This is … This is bigger. BIGGER. This is GLOBAL. THIS IS a mixture of CANCER and COCKROACHES and DOG … but I'm also part of something else I think. It's … more. IT'S MORE. IT'S MORE. I can feel them inside me. BUT I AM NOT ONE OF THEM. HALF. NOT. REVERSE-CANCER-COCK-ROACH–DOG. HA. HA. I feel I am a shell full of verminous insects. I can feel them in my stomach. Walking around. Inside my head. Behind my eyes. They come out of my eyes and I shit them out, then I eat them up. I feel them squeeze out of my nose. They crawl down my arms and huddle under my skin. I have stolen alcohol and cigarettes. I can feel the roaches run from the alcohol as I pour it down my throat. Scuttle away. I AM NON-SAVED. I AM NON-SAVED. I AM NON-SAVED. And I can feel them running down my throat. It seems the human, the insect and the dog rot on top of each other. ROT IN THE PISS AND THE SHIT. THROUGH THE SHIT AND THE BLOOD. O GOD! AND THE CANCER. FOR EVER AND EVER. AMEN. AMEN. YES. YES. YES. THE CANCER. OH YES! An abomination of JOYOUS DECOM-POSITION. and vengeance. Hah ha ha! What can I do? I am dammed to NON-HELL … but the whole business is dirty and nasty.

And the thing is, I feel a hatred. YES. YES. I AM NON-

DAMNED. I AM THE REVERSE WEREWOLF-COCK-ROACH. I AM THE VIRUS-GOD-CANCER-WHORE. I AM. I AM.

And outside. Outside. Hell has come to earth. The cockroaches hunt in packs. THEY ARE QUICK. Their black silhouettes moving across the green countryside rounding up herds of sheep and humans and killing them. They move so quickly. The town is infested. Every now and then a human runs down the street. But not for long. Most of the rest of England must be infested. There is no traffic on the motorway and if you look off the cliff, the sea is black with them swimming to France and back. There are so many of them. It is the end of the world. But maybe it's Heaven. The sun reflects gold on a thousand carapaces. A world covered in angels.

You see ... first the small ones come, and they live in your shit and in your body and under your skin, and then the big ones come and they're bigger and stronger and quicker, bigger and stronger and quicker than you. Too quick, too strong. And you know it, you know it. That's why you are so scared of the small ones.

And it happens all of a sudden. You see one or two and then, all of a sudden, you are infested. You are dead. What are you going to do – nuke them? The vermin, the cancer, the rats, the roaches – we're all here you fuckers. HERE. HERE. HERE. THE WEAK ARE COMING. Hunting you down. Hunting in packs. You are fucking History! You are the fucking VERMIN.

THE PINK ROOM

One morning you would get out of bed and do your routine of opening the porch door to grab the paper out of the mailbox. You would walk down the stairs, sun streaming through the windows, warm on your skin, making your eyes squint even indoors, then slowly open the door to choke on the smell of them. Rotting flesh meets old fish up your nostrils, tickling the hairs. At first you would hold your breath, the back of your throat moving involuntarily, not wanting to breathe them in, for fear of puking. You could taste them. Then, slowly, you would realise that they won the battle, and you would breathe, getting used to their smell until you didn't notice it anymore. It was either that or lock yourself in the house for two weeks until they left, windows shut in the heat of summer.

It would just happen overnight like that. They went unnoticed most of the year, living at the bottom of the lake, forming a u-shaped burrow in the sediment. Their arrival the end of June or early July meant it was officially summer in my hometown. Problem was, you could never predict exactly which week they would choose to begin their invasion, making it hell for the tourist industry. Downtown was especially bad, near the waterfront, but they spread everywhere, concentrating near streetlights and illuminated shop signs, hoping it was the moon. They are creatures attracted by moonlight, and guided by the warmth of the water. The water temperature and amount of light tells them it's time to hatch and mate, before they die. They only mate at night. They only live to mate. They have no mouths, and die from starving after they fuck if they're male, and after they lay their eggs if they're female. So the females live a few minutes longer.

North Bay is a place with distinct seasons: Down to minus thirty or forty in the winter, turning your nasal hairs and eyelashes white, making your scarf stick to your face from the frozen condensation created through breathing. It's the kind of place where electrical sockets outside of homes are necessary for plugging your car in at night to save your tank from freezing. A popular after school pastime for kids is playing hockey using a piece of frozen dog shit as a puck. Alternatively, if you don't have a hockey stick, just kicking it around will do. It's a good way to exclude the girls, well most of them. The sign of a good bar this time of year is one with snow-mobile parking, so that you can ski-do on the lake, to the bar, and then drive back home. No need for a car, and no need to argue about who's driving. Inevitably at Christmas time some American tourist up for the ice fishing who doesn't know the lake goes under the ice. A rule of thumb: Don't go on the lake until January, unless it's been an exceptionally early and cold winter. Another rule: Don't go on the lake unless you see at least 20 ice shacks. And finally, don't go on the lake if you're drunk while driving a ski-do. Stick to the bush paths instead, regardless of how tempting the faster lake route is.

At this time of the year they are getting fat on the algae in the cold, chocolate cream mud at the bottom of the lake. Only the Pike, Pickrel, Perch, Walleye, and smaller fish like Smelts know they are there. The fish couldn't live without Shads. They lay enough eggs to provide food for them and to re-hatch and swarm the city. It's no wonder they croak after that. It's the only way they can survive, their only form of defense. They shed and shed and shed at least thirty times, growing until they are ready to hatch and leave the water. They shed for two to three years, depending on how well the water is oxygenating. Unless of course they get eaten, or die from a lack of air.

You can smell spring, and a hint of summer, when the temperature starts to get warmer and the ice begins to melt. The left over snow isn't clean. It mixes with mud and exhaust fumes to remain in piles of black and brown with little round ice jewel crowns. The moist air and longer golden days seem to tease North Bay-ites as they wait in anticipation, shedding their layers of clothing and trading in their boots for shoes. Spring used to be slow and laborious, but now it's faster. Every year it's shorter. Soon all we will have is extremes, without the in-between. This year the leaves started to turn bright red in June! The deciduous trees and flowers look over-worked. Even the conifers look worse for wear, rushing to get their cones ready for summer. Everything is dying before it's born.

★★
★★★

North Bay Nugget Story:
July 2, 2002
The Shads are Back
By Arnie Hakala – North Bay Nugget
Tuesday, July 02, 2002 – 10:00:00 am

NEWS – That awful snap, crackle, pop sound is back on Main Street. Yes, the first wave of Shadflies appeared Sunday night and when merchants opened this morning after the long weekend, they had some cleaning up to do. Lights attract the winged insects which are as synonymous with North Bay as The Hole and Walleye. Bob Neault of Jocko Point was on Main Street Monday and he remembered more than just the awful fishy smell the Shads leave behind.

"About eight years ago, I was coming around the corner

645

of McIntyre and Ferguson on my motorcycle, a 750cc, four-cylinder Honda, when I hit a pool of them that must have been an inch deep." Neault said the bike did about three 360-degree turns and he fell off, scraping a leg.

The Nugget library has a thick file of Shad stories. In 1972, a car slid about 27.5 metres on a Shadfly-covered road and struck a telephone pole. There also have been bizarre stories. In 1980, a Manitoba doctor said the flies were good to eat – Dr. Reid Taylor told The Nugget he dined on them for breakfast: "The insects taste like fish and if you munch a handful, they have the texture of breakfast food," said Reid, who had been eating the five-centimetre-long Shads for several years.

On July 6, 1988, there was a Gateway Major Fastball League game at Amelia Park between Sturgeon Falls' Nipissing Chrylser and Fraser Tavern. The Shads appeared. At first, they were just a nuisance. The stands emptied. More swarms migrated in from the lake. Outfielders were chasing a different type of fly. Batters started swinging before they got to the plate. Don "Butch" Turcotte, the infield umpire, said, "You knew there were lights out there, but you couldn't really see them." With half an inning shy of a complete game, plate umpire Jeff Wonnick called it off. There was a similar incident about 15 years previous which made the pages of *Sports Illustrated*.

★★★
★★★

Their numbers rapidly increased every summer. We never thought anything of it. I remember listening to the radio on my way home from school and hearing the theme from Jaws on CFCH. The DJ came on claiming

"Thay're baaack!" We all knew what he meant. He was interviewing a Nursery owner who went bankrupt after the Shad season that year because the stench was so strong he couldn't bear staying outside to water the plants for three hours. They kept telling us it was healthy in the papers and on the radio, nothing to worry about. If it was mosquitoes there would have been more of a hysteria, but the Shads were really a part of us. They were here before we were. Every year they would stay longer. They arrived earlier and left later, like an unwanted guest. No one questioned this or found it odd. Global warming they kept telling us.

Up the hill that is Algonquin Avenue, around the corner from Algonquin Sécondaire, the only French high school in the area, is St. Joseph's Hospital. The streets in this area are lined with tall blue spruce, white birch, and chunky oak trees with curly branches soldiering next to old wooden houses and their covered porches, some with the paint peeling from the sidings. Every home is a slight variation on that theme. Everyone has a green square of lawn in the summer and a white one in the winter. The hospital is also surrounded by trees forming the bush that hides the railway track. Inside the building feels like a pressure cooker. It always has been and probably always will be chaotic. You can't control when and how people are going to have accidents, babies or illnesses, and this is why I never have problems finding work. This is also probably why the design of the hospital in the late '60s was so geometric and simple, to give the illusion of order. If the patients really knew what went on, we'd all be out on the streets. If you open a window, you can hear the trees moving in the wind, even though it's in the middle of the city. I'll miss the trees. The illusion is disrupted however, every time a train goes. The train helps me tell the time.

I don't know why I feel so nostalgic, or why I feel the

647

need to get into such detail with this. I suppose I want to remember, and write down as much as I can, as soon as I can, just in case. I want a record of what happened. It's impossible to write it all down. I wished I had been recording it every day when I first started to notice the changes. I've forgotten so much already.

I can't remember exactly when it all began. I suppose I started to notice the changes, like everyone else, after the Heritage Day Festival, a few years back. The Festival used to be held in Lee Park, at the bottom of the overpass, near the shores of Lake Nipissing. A 1960's jet fighter sits at the entrance perched on a stone plinth with its nose pointing pathetically upwards through a stony arch on which are painted the words "Gateway to the North", the North Bay motto. The Festival was always scheduled in August to avoid the Shads, but this particular year they were still there after a month of stinking up the place. Everyone said it was unusual but we were assured it was OK, nothing to worry about, a sign of good water. We didn't want to be like Lake Erie, who lost their Shads in the late '50s because of the toxic chemicals that were being dumped in the lake. When the lake was finally cleaned the Shads came back – but it took over thirty years. It always drew up anti-American sentiment, and we always felt smug and self righteous because our lakes were still clean after all these years. People from Corbeil, Calandar, Powassan, Sturgeon Falls, even as far as Sudbury would drive over for the weekend when the festival was on, it was such a money spinner. Word spread quick about the Shads, and barely anyone came the following year. The Shads came and the people left. Finally they had to stop the festival, because they'd lost so much money. It was around that time that they started trying to find ways of controlling them, so we're told, but I think they were doing it before.

It was the same summer that I was moved permanently to the Maternity Ward. The birthrate used to be so low that they kept moving me around different wards, there weren't enough births to warrant my being there all the time. We were having an average of 1–2 births a day, so I would only need to look after 7 babies a week, alongside at least one other nurse, maximum. That summer the birthrate tripled. No one knew why. We couldn't keep up, and we still can't. The birthrate keeps increasing every year, while in the rest of the country it declines. They can't hire enough nurses, they don't have enough money with all the federal cuts.

Now, this is going to sound strange, but I started to notice that the babies smelled differently. I can't describe what the scent is, I can't put my finger on it. All I know is that it's not the same. Not all of them have this odour, only some. I began to notice this when I picked them up and held them close to take them out of their cots.

The other odd thing I began to notice over time, was that there was a connection between the ones that had this odour and the condition of their skin. I don't know when I made this connection. One day I realised their skin tended to flake off in large patches, almost the entire size of their little baby backs. It didn't seem to be painful or itchy for them. I noticed no discomfort from their facial expressions or the sounds they made. It seemed totally natural just leaving a mess on the cots, which of course made more work for me. It used to crumble and crunch in my hands when I had to clean it up, like thin transparent potato chips with networks of veins. They also tended to be quieter than the other babies, sleeping almost constantly. I found them fascinating.

Sometimes I used to wander with them in my arms when they cried, trying to calm them down. Or I would wheel them around in the metal hospital cots squeaking rhythmically with every movement, greeting people between squeaks. Occasionally, as I was wandering, I would catch snippets of conversation. I would overhear conversations between doctors and recent mothers. Details of child labour experiences between families and friends, about the arrival of the new babies. Others would be crying, some fighting, a whole cauldron of emotions. It's amazing what you hear and see working in a hospital.

There was a section of the ward that I was never assigned to work in. The rooms were separated for individual patients and painted Pepto Bismol pink. It was a colour that was used in prisons as an experiment to calm down the inmates. Problem was that the colour backfired and, after a certain amount of time, it had the opposite effect, so they had to move the girls in these rooms around every so often. The rest of the hospital was white or a washed-out sickly green. Interior decorating was never a priority.

The women in the pink rooms were always either crying or screaming unintelligible sentences, unless of course they were asleep. I could never get used to the sound. They were pregnant, as if that wasn't difficult enough, and had an unidentifiable disease. They started noticing signs of the new disease around 2003, roughly ten years ago. Ephemeroptera is specific to North Bay. They don't know what causes it, but the symptoms include hallucinations, black lumpy vaginal discharge, severe depression accompanied by suicidal tendencies, and a constant feeling of itchiness, but no signs of a rash. Sometimes the women die in child labour, sometimes they scratch themselves until they bleed. They have to be restrained from scratching but also from hurting themselves and disturbing the other patients. They are like animals sent to live in a little girl's bedroom as punishment for some wrongdoing. *I don't want to wind up like them, ever.*

The only specialist on the disease, Dr Derocher, is based at the hospital. He's tall, hairless and devoid of lines, with gums too big for his teeth. For a man with such long legs, he flutters about taking tiny steps when he walks, seemingly aimless, but getting there all the same. His monosyllabic conversational style leaves him with plenty of time to move quickly, disappearing unnoticed in mid-conversation within a group.

It was during one of these occasions that I happened to spot him. He was chatting with some of the nurses, or rather they were chatting and he was flitting silently, the odd grunt here and there, until he did his disappearing act. I was bored and decided to follow him. I was on my break, having just finished my lunch with time to spare. There were quite a few babies born that week, so I had to take my break alone as the rest of the nurses were needed. I was just being nosy, like when I used to eavesdrop on forbidden adult conversation as a child, curious and not wanting to be left out.

I quietly hid in the doorway of room 45 at the end of the hallway, unspotted, while Derocher was visiting room 47. I watched him go in, and waited. The door opened and I could hear screeching, like a yelping dog, directed at Derocher. It was quite muffled and I can't be certain what was said but it sounded something like:

"I know what you're up to! You work for the city you fucker!"

The door slammed shut and the rest of what she said could not be heard. The window at the end of the hall was open, and I could hear the train rush past. That meant my break was over. I quickly scurried back to work.

The next day she died giving birth to a baby girl. No father to be seen. The baby had to be given up for adoption, her grandmother was too old and ill to look after her. No siblings. We had to look after her until she was old enough to go to an orphanage. I lifted the baby from the cot one day to change her diaper and as I held her I breathed in her scalp. That's when I finally made the connection. I was shaking so much I had to put her down and get some water. I thought I was going to throw up. I don't know why I didn't make the connection before. I didn't want to touch her anymore. No one knew whether it was contagious, but I wasn't taking any chances. Martha, who normally works in the pink rooms, was on duty with me. She took over, and I felt guilty because it was so busy and we were so under staffed, but I had to go home and recover.

I went into work the next day and noticed they were selling tickets for a staff booze cruise on the Chief Comanda. I don't normally go to these things, even though I'm desperate for some male company in my life. The hours make it difficult to have any kind of normal social life, and the people you meet at work are either married doctors or other women. Half of the doctors now are women, not like when I was kid. The few male technicians we have are also all married, or gay. Needless to say the cruises are depressing nights with everyone too drunk on rye and coke. Predictably every year someone sloshed, or off their head, jumps off the boat, and the night becomes somber, searchlights looking for them in the black waves. This time I thought I'd give it a try though. I reasoned it might be a good way of finding out more about what was going on. I'd become obsessed. I tried to avoid the babies with that smell, it made me nauseous. It's amazing how something can switch like that, it never bothered me before.

Saturday, cruise day, finally arrived. You could feel the heat coming off the tarmac in the parking lot. Everything and everyone looked wavy in the sunlight, as though it was melting everything in its reach. I was sensible enough to bring a sweater because I knew once the sun went down and we were moving, the water and speed would cool everything. I had my little black strappy number on, I thought what the hell, cheer myself up, and a pair of gold sandals with a 4 inch heel. I couldn't walk but I felt great. I just wouldn't do any dancing, and if things got really bad I had packed a pair of flip flops in my handbag. Secretly an optimist, there were also condoms in the bag, and a toothbrush.

The boat was packed with women, and some male staff with their partners in tow. No disappointments, no changes. Derocher was there, in a pair of khaki walking shorts that skimmed his knees, showing off the remainder of his long, pale blue, hairless legs. I was dying for them to dim the lights. My mother told me never to go out with anyone who's skinnier than you, and I'd like to extend the rule to avoiding men with less body hair. He looked like a tall baby Smurf. Just my luck, one of the few single men in the room. It also blew any plans I had for trying to pry information from the other nurses. It meant I had to watch what I was saying. Despite this I thought it might make the evening interesting. I could eavesdrop, and he was always intriguing to follow because of his disappearing act. I told you I had become obsessed.

All I can remember of the evening from that point onwards was entering the washroom, and leaving the washroom. Public washrooms in forms of transportation are always an adventure, and this one was no exception. The sound of retching was already in full swing, and we'd only been sailing for under a half hour. Hair spray was misting the air near the mirrors, making me choke on the sweet smell and bitter taste. I walked cautiously should I accidentally get some in the eye. Someone was spraying the old perfume CK, and it made me nostalgic.

Where the hell did she buy that? I didn't think they made it any more. It reminded me of dates in cars, parking at the end of Champlain Park, fingers fumbling all over the place and the mad rush of trying to get home before curfew. Beer was already flooding the floor and they managed to run out of toilet paper. I planned for this and brought my own. Still, it was the best place to listen in on conversations. As a nurse you get used to the odours other people's bodies create, yet public wash-rooms still revolt me. I think it's the difference between fresh and stale piss. I was in one of the cubicles trying to stay comfortable without a toilet seat, holding my breath to avoid breathing in the stench of a washroom that seemed over used and under cleaned. That's when I heard Martha talking with Lori, about collecting the eggs.

"Don't forget, after you collect the eggs from Room 47, to give them to Derocher, and he'll pass them on"

"Yeah yeah", Lori replied, "but what about the flies? I had a really hard time convincing her that they weren't real, but yesterday when I opened the door one almost escaped into the hallway. What would I have done then? How would I have explained that ? Derocher would have sacked me and then what would I do? Not to mention what else might happen should I fuck up like that. Look at what they do to the girls in pink!"

"That's just for the eggs."

"Don't be so naive!"

And with that they left their cubicles. I had to carefully choose my moment to leave so as not to be obvious, and to leave me time to follow them. I waited a few minutes, washed my hands for authenticity, and headed for the deck. As I was leaving, like a vampire waiting at the door of the women's washroom was Derocher. He said one word, which was also a question.

"Curious?"

I remember nothing of the evening after that. I apparently went overboard. I don't remember jumping or how it happened. All I had was a few sips of a rye and coke. They found me after I was in the water over half an hour. It was Dokis who saved me. Olive skin, soft slanted eyes hiding behind John Lennon glasses, and a mass of curly white and black hair with leather and feathers wrapping selected strands. Retired doctor. His wife spotted me in the water. They live on the Reserve in Manitoulin Islands, and were just visiting. They always invite me to stay.

I took some time off work after that, in shock. Dokis and his wife stayed with me to make sure I was OK. Chrissy, his wife, is beautiful. She looks like Cher did in the 80s, but with piercing blue eyes, and she has always been an angel to me. She cooked beautiful meals when I didn't have the energy to look after myself. Everything seemed to take a huge effort from me, even the simplest tasks. I was afraid to stay in the bathroom alone and she would patiently sit on the toilet seat, reading while I had a shower. She humoured my fears, but didn't take them too seriously. When I tried to tell her about what I saw at work, she didn't believe me but still stood close by. Dokis gave me some herbal medicine. He was so respected in his community that he was made an Elder earlier that year. He mixed the herbs himself. He lit some dried, braided sweet grass and had me rub the smoke on my body. He said it would protect me. Just as Chrissy indulged my beliefs which she obviously viewed as paranoia, I indulged Dokis'. Chrissy did my groceries before they left. I watched television, read books, slept and tried to relax. I looked out the window one afternoon, and I swear I saw someone hiding in the rose bushes near the fence at the end of the backyard. A few times I thought I could actually hear someone rummaging in my car in the garage. I live alone on the outskirts of North Bay, so I cannot describe how frightening this was. I kept thinking about the lady in room 47 and couldn't bring myself to call the cops. I didn't trust them. I felt safe in the house and spent days without leaving. I didn't want to phone Dokis' again because they had spent so much time with me, and they had a family of their own to worry about, grandchildren, children, the works.

I started to feel queasy in the morning, but I didn't think anything of it. One morning I woke up and went to the toilet and found a black discharge on the toilet paper. It looked like a blob of caviar, covered in grey mucus. I passed out.

The phone rang, and I came to. It was Dokis. He called to see how I was. I knew what I had to do. I'm taking the 11:00 am train. It's safer than the roads with the Shads in full season. The city is swarmed and I feel as though my body is as well. I don't feel safe at home anymore. I took the phone apart last night and found something in it which to me looked like it could be a bug. If I tell anyone here they'll think I'm crazy.

I can barely keep my eyes open. Despite how much I will them to, they ignore me. The train is lazy and exhausted with the burden of the journey. Apart from the repetitive sound of the tracks, it doesn't feel like it's moving. The view out the window looks like a stage set as it whizzes past. The forests surrounding the 2-D lakes are thick with trees, so tall they strain your neck. I can smell one of those babies, but I don't remember seeing any on the train. I can't help retching and my teeth feel soft as though acid is burning holes through them. I run my tongue over their bumpy surface.

They don't have express trains anymore, only milk runs. The train feels like a ghost town, some cars are empty, other lightly littered with passengers. We've stopped in South River to pick up a few more people.

656

The smell keeps getting stronger. I try to breath through my mouth but I can't escape it. I can taste the odour. My throat feels like it's going to close. I try to open a window but they don't open. I turn my head and look across the aisle where someone new has just sat down. A familiar pair of eyes meet my gaze. The train starts moving again.

FIRST POST [11 Sep 13:56]
Plane crashes into World Trade Centre

Mandy [11 Sep 13:57]
What sort of plane? Thats terrible.

ham er and cheese [11 Sep 14:02]
F**K that.

D.Rollo [11 Sep 14:03]
christ – two planes now – hit each tower!

CB [11 Sep 14:03]
Another one hit the other tower just now, got it live on
CNN, must be terrorists

SAYER_1 [11 Sep 14:03]
What's the story behind that then??

positive-iron [11 Sep 14:06]
Two twin engine planes, one hit about 20 storeys from
the top!! And the building exploded, could be a couple
of angry stockbrokers? :–)

Rochford Hammer [11 Sep 14:06]
Fucking Hell got to be a sucide bomber this is terabale.

COOL COL [11 Sep 14:07]
Either both pilots were blind drunk or it's deliberate

Frankie's boots [11 Sep 14:07]
Sorry col, not funny

D.Rollo [11 Sep 14:07]
nah – suicide if one – terroists with two
fight club is coming to life!

plastic mac brigade [11 Sep 14:08]
planes were hijacked and smashed into world trade
centre

GUEST (ssssss) [11 Sep 14:19]
'Kamikaze' Attack On New York
Two planes have smashed into the World Trade Centre
Towers in New York in what appears to be a deliberate
terrorist attack.

The first plane crashed into the top stories of the
tower, leaving two gaping holes in the side.

Minutes later another aircraft hit the second tower –
seen live on TV stations around the world.

Hunderds of workers would have been in the building
at the height of the morning rush-hour. Many are feared
dead.

Huge palls of black smoke could be seen coming out
of the tower. It is not known how many people were in
the plane or how many workers were in the top storeys
of the building when the planes struck.

The 110-storey 1,360ft tower is in lower Manhattan.

In February 1993 six people died when a truck bomb
was planted in the twin tower's underground car park in
a terrorist attack

GUEST (**Brentwood Hammer**) [11 Sep 14:19]
Shitting hell ... how can you joke about this !

positive-iron [11 Sep 14:19]
Doc, forgot to phone you last night, i am going early
tonight, give us a wave, will be to your left upper tier,
will be in touch ok. :–)

ham er and cheese [11 Sep 14:19]
Two planes have crashed into the World Trade Center in
New York City.

The building, one of the world's tallest, has been badly damaged.

Television pictures show smoke pouring from the upper storeys of both towers.

A few minutes after the first tower was hit, a second plane was seen flying into the second tower. A huge explosion was seen.

Eyewitnesses say the first plane crashed into the West Tower after flying unusually low over Manhattan Island.

The first aircraft is still embedded in the building.

There is no information on casualties.

A BBC correspondent says 10 to 15 floors have been affected by the crash.

It is not clear why the planes would have crashed into the building.

positive-iron [11 Sep 14:25]
The radio just said it was a passenger plane!! What BASTARDS !!!!!

vhammer [11 Sep 14:26]
Certainly delibrate if it was two planes, the act of extremely dedicated terrorists, and the main group which likes this kind of suicide attack are the Palestinians, but it is possibly wild speculation, as they got the initial blame for Oklahoma City and it turned out to US Domestic issues. Is today the anniversary of an major event?

greenie1 [11 Sep 14:27]
767 from Boston

GUEST (Steve) [11 Sep 14:29]
There is amazing footage on the news at the moment. ABC News filmed the second plane fly straight into the second tower.

At the moment it's rumoured to be down to Islamic Terrorists possible Bin Laden, though these are all rumours at the moment.

One of the planes was definitely reported hijacked from Boston.

GUEST (Steve) [11 Sep 14:34]
News just in.

A third plane has been hijacked and is in the air at the moment.

No-one knows it's whereabouts.

As I'm typing this it's just been reported that there's been a 3rd explosion at the Pentagon in Washington though this hasn't been 100% confirmed as yet.

JimmyT [11 Sep 14:34]
6 dead. 1000 injured. so far.

The second crash was shown live on television. Horrific.

vhammer [11 Sep 14:35]
Would be surprised if a plane could get near a Washington target after an attack like that, US Air Defences must have been in full effect.

D.Rollo [11 Sep 14:36]
apparantly pentagon been hit – police say third on its way to trade centre

Rochford Hammer [11 Sep 14:37]
The liberation of palestine have claimed responsibilty for the attacks. According to reports on talksport that the 2 plane's have been hijacked. one a united airline's boeing 737. This is truly devastating. The reports are just coming through that there has been an explosion.

Dave Smith [11 Sep 14:37]
Was the third not the o

Ged [11 Sep 14:37]
Shit Steve, I've just heard that from another source (my boss, so I doubt he's having a laugh, if you know what I mean ...)

   plane that hit the Pentagon then? Holy shit this is unforgivable ...

Mrs T [11 Sep 14:38]
Is there any truth that an explosion has gone off at the Pentagon as well?

   How evil can people be? It makes me weep as this will probably lead to some sort of war and how can anyone compete against such nutters?

vhammer [11 Sep 14:39]
The Yanks will start shooting them down rather than allowing them through to their targets. A hard choice but the only one available.

Top Six Finish [11 Sep 14:39]
Rollo – where did this latest report come from? What are they doing about the 3rd plane? Has the Pentagon been hit or not?

bahammer [11 Sep 14:39]
confirmed, pentagon ablaze

Rochford Hammer [11 Sep 14:40]
Yes it has Mrs T.

Beckton Bill [11 Sep 14:40]
all the markets have closed and other people have confirmed the 3rd plane.

Can everyone keep this page updated coz I can't get thru to new sites as theres a high ammount of net-traffic.

GUEST (Steve) [11 Sep 14:42]
These extremist scum have got be dealt with once and for all.

How do we know that London and the City isn't the next targets?

Dave Smith [11 Sep 14:43]
Pray to God there isn't a fourth plane hijacked ... presumably we would have heard by now if there was.

D.Rollo [11 Sep 14:43]
i did hear 7 in all

ham er and cheese [11 Sep 14:44]
pentagon has been hit as well

Beckton Bill [11 Sep 14:44]
7? where did you hear that from DR?

vhammer [11 Sep 14:45]
7, 3 to the World Trade, 1 or more to the Pentagon, that leaves 3 others. What a awful mess this is rapidly becoming.

Dave Smith [11 Sep 14:45]
Please tell me that isn't true Rollo ... where from?

GUEST (Steve) [11 Sep 14:45]
All flights across America have been halted indefinitely.

Ged [11 Sep 14:45]
just seen the pentagon on fire on TV. All US airports closed, all further flights grounded.

D.Rollo [11 Sep 14:45]
someone in the office – work at news providers – could
be wrong though

Dave Smith [11 Sep 14:46]
You might be right ... 2nd explosion at the Pentagon ...

vhammer [11 Sep 14:46]
Air Defences will be full alert across the Western World,
because they could be doing this against Western targets
as a whole.

GUEST **(Steve) [11 Sep 14:47]**
One of the planes could have been holding up to 300
passengers.

vhammer [11 Sep 14:48]
Some raghead terrorist has read Tom Clancy's Debt of
Honour.
   Palestinian group says responsible for World Trade
towers hit
   DUBAI (Reuters) – A Palestinian group has claimed
responsibility for the New York World Trade Centre
plane attacks today.
   Abu Dhabi television reported it had received a call
from the Democratic Front for the Liberation of
Palestine (DFLP) abroad claiming responsibility for
crashing two planes into the WTC buildings.
   Qatar-based al-Jazeera television said FBI sources said
one of the two aircraft had been hijacked.

Ged [11 Sep 14:49]
Just off of Yahoo!

GUEST **(Steve) [11 Sep 14:51]**
2nd explosion just confirmed at the Pentagon.
Absolute carnage.

GUEST (Steve) [11 Sep 14:52]
Now a 3rd explosion has just gone off in New York.
What the fuck is going on??

Dave Smith [11 Sep 14:52]
This is untrue ... have you seen the third one in
Manhattan ... sweet Jesus ...

GUEST (BUCKS LOYAL) [11 Sep 14:53]
Fuck ...
Trade centre tower collapses on business district

ham er and cheese [11 Sep 14:53]
White house as well i just herd

GUEST (Steve) [11 Sep 14:53]
Apparantly, the 3rd explosion may have been one of the
World Trade Centre Towers completely collapsing.

Bald Git [11 Sep 14:54]
HELP, I am sitting in an office two blocks from the White
House and can not get anything from the BBC or CNN do
your think I should go home!!!

Dave Smith [11 Sep 14:54]
Was it an explosion or just a collapse ... think of all the
emergency services etc underneath ...

GUEST (BUCKS LOYAL) [11 Sep 14:55]
God help them and rests their soul ...
Latest news ...
Sear Tower Chicago ...
Evacuating ...

GUEST (Any Old Iraniain) [11 Sep 14:55]
Bald Git yes

GUEST (Steve) [11 Sep 14:56]
Bald Git, get out of there.

Bald Git [11 Sep 14:56]
The White House has not been hit as I would have heard
it and there is no smoke just a hell of a lot of police
sirens.
This sounds like war!!!

D.Rollo [11 Sep 14:56]
just watched the whole world trade centre collapse – the
whole thing – rubble

ham er and cheese [11 Sep 14:58]
Fuck they recon the 2nd is going down
pentagon hit for sure

GUEST (BUCKS LOYAL) [11 Sep 14:58]
Bald git, my very best wishes, my thoughts are with you

D.Rollo [11 Sep 14:58]
third plane hit pentagon!

D.Rollo [11 Sep 14:59]
4 more unaccounted for!

ham er and cheese [11 Sep 14:59]
This is fucked up how did they manage this

Dave Smith [11 Sep 15:00]
Rollo – do you know if any of these planes are carrying
passengers?

ham er and cheese [11 Sep 15:01]
100 on one of the planes i herd

greenie1 [11 Sep 15:02]
Hasn't one of the towers collapsed?

D.Rollo [11 Sep 15:03]
yeah – totally gone

GUEST (**Steve**) **[11 Sep 15:03]**
One of the planes could have been carrying 300 passengers.

GUEST (BUCKS LOYAL) **[11 Sep 15:05]**
The poor bastards were jumping from the building above the initial impact point, then it collapsed.
God knows the casualty numbers.

dob [11 Sep 15:05]
just wanted to say thanks to everyone updating us on what's going on, wouldn't have a clue otherwise as all the news sites are jammed

Bald Git [11 Sep 15:05]
This is surreal, my missus is giving me a running commentary on the phone where she is watching the local news at home and the only internet site I can get on to is WHO as CNN and the BBC are either down or overloaded.
   I just heard a concussion and apparently there is another explosion in Crystal City, which is close to the Pentagon and a couple of miles away.
   Time to get me bags

GUEST (**plonker on** CNN) **[11 Sep 15:07]**
WTC one plane hit second tower ... unidentified aircraft hit first ...
second tower collapsed

greenie1 [11 Sep 15:08]
gonna go and watch CNN news. see whats the latest, we have offices near there.
huge fire at pentagon

Cheeky [11 Sep 15:09]
Try www.ananova.com the press association site. Easier to get into than beeb news or cnn. Also live video stream on www.skynews.co.uk

GUEST (BUCKS LOYAL) [11 Sep 15:10]
Bald git, hang in there mate, it can't be long now before the authorities qualify any aircraft as non threat, I fear that any further Hi Jacked craft may be shot down. Surely the US will protect the WHO which should make you ok if close.
Just trying to help.

Mad Dog [11 Sep 15:10]
when i worked in the states i lived opposite the world trade centre.
the world trade centre is a major and i do mean major subway station for the financial district.
if i was still there i would have been arriving at 9 at the world trade to go to wall street.
never been more glad that my company couldnt get us visas in my life.

GUEST (**plonker on** CNN) [11 Sep 15:10]
30,000 people work in the WTC towers …
300 on the plane will be a small percentage …

Mad Dog [11 Sep 15:10]
just heard that the sears tower has been hit too
is this true

Dave Smith [11 Sep 15:11]
Apparently 157 passengers or so on one of the planes if it was full …?

D.Rollo [11 Sep 15:11]
the ftse has plummeted 200 points – fucking vertical drop on the charts!

Ged [11 Sep 15:11]
Explosion on Capitol Hill,

GUEST (**Dave Smith**) [11 Sep 15:13]
plonker – a person is not just a statistic … think about it.
Looks like half of the tower is still standing

GUEST (**Ni**) [11 Sep 15:13]
I was standing at the top of this building only 3 weeks ago. Frightening.

GUEST (BUCKS LOYAL) [11 Sep 15:14]
Bald git,
You ok mate,
Just picked up Capitol Hill, explosion.
If you can, please post.

Dave Smith [11 Sep 15:15]
Blanket coverage on terrestial now pretty much

GUEST (BUCKS LOYAL) [11 Sep 15:17]
Car bomb …
US Treasury …

GUEST (**Steve**) [11 Sep 15:18]
A sickening message just coming in from the news that Palestinians on the West Bank are reportedly out in the streets celebrating.

ham er and cheese [11 Sep 15:18]
full coverage talk sport

Bald Git [11 Sep 15:19]
Yeah Bucks Loyal still here and trying to work out what
to do. The Capitol is a couple of miles away and I can
hear loads of sirens. People are leaving local offices in
their droves so the metro will be chocca block. I
definitely fealt a concussion but didn't hear anything
about 10 minutes back.

GUEST (BUCVKS LOYAL) [11 Sep 15:20]
Sorry, my error,
US State Dept,
Not Treasury,
Bald Git, you ok?

Mad Dog [11 Sep 15:20]
bald git, where are you exactly?

Dave Smith (11 Sep 15:21)
Oh shit the second tower has gone down …

GUEST (Steve) [11 Sep 15:21]
2nd Tower has just collapsed.

Top Six Finish [11 Sep 15:22]
Has the second tower gone? Is this true?

GUEST (BUCKS LOYAL) [11 Sep 15:22]
2ND TOWER NOW DOWN,

GUEST (greenie1) [11 Sep 15:22]
second tower just gone down like a pack of cards.
live on CNN. unreal!

D.Rollo [11 Sep 15:22]
another plane hijacked – on its way to Washington

Dave Smith [11 Sep 15:24]
This is beyond belief ... gotta be aiming for the White
House ...

positive-iron [11 Sep 15:25]
Group pray for Bald git :–)

Ged [11 Sep 15:26]
DR, would you mind posting your sources too please.
I'm relaying to a TV free office. Much appreciated mate.
Ged

Mad Dog [11 Sep 15:26]
both of the world trade towers have collapsed

Bald Git [11 Sep 15:27]
MD I am on K street 17th and Connecticut about three
blocks from the White House

ham er and cheese [11 Sep 15:27]
Ged
www.bbc.co.uk
or talk spot

ham er and cheese [11 Sep 15:28]
Bald Git anything near u

D.Rollo [11 Sep 15:28]
ged – have no telly either – as i say work at news
providers so lots of people with info

Bald Git [11 Sep 15:30]
Thanks fellahs,

The White House is Ok, there has been no further
explosions in DC there is grid lock in the streets and
people are leaving offices to get on the metro. We have
decided to hang out here a while longer as the metro will
probably be blocked with peole leaving.

GUEST (grenie1) [11 Sep 15:30]
I've got CNN on a projection TV. Just seen footage of the
first tower going own with fireman run from the scene.
They had a woman saying that people were
jumping from the building.

GUEST (BUCKS LOYAL) [11 Sep 15:31]
Report.
10 mins ago,
Aircraft in air to DC, 20 mins away.
BBC

ham er and cheese [11 Sep 15:32]
Bald Git all our prayers are with you mate

Ged [11 Sep 15:32]
ham er and cheese & D.Rollo, thanks chaps.

D.Rollo [11 Sep 15:32]
canary wharf being evacuated

Top Six Finish [11 Sep 15:33]
Another large plane has crashed in Western Pennsylvania

positive-iron [11 Sep 15:33]
Hang in there Bald Git i am sending you some mega
positive waves :–)

GUEST (Steve) [11 Sep 15:34]
London Stock Exchange evacuated.

Top Six Finish [11 Sep 15:34]
I dont believe any of this. Just puts everything into perspective. Everyone on here looking forward to the game tonight then the whole world goes mad.
Unbelievable …

GUEST (BUCKS LOYAL) [11 Sep 15:35]
Horrific story,
Sorry if offended,
Reports of bodies blown up the roads, past fleeing NYers, as towers collapse.

Bald Git [11 Sep 15:35]
All Government offices are being evacuated, how reliable is the story on the plane heading to DC?

SAYER_1 [11 Sep 15:36]
Just heard on the radio that there are two planes heading towards washington now

Top Six Finish [11 Sep 15:36]
On all the news channels apparently Bald Git. My thoughts are totally 100% with you mate!!

GUEST (Ironman) [11 Sep 15:37]
Another attack in Pittsburgh as it was the first capital of USA

GUEST (Steve) [11 Sep 15:40]
As it's still morning in the US, this could be just the tip of the iceberg.
(15:38)
Pittsberg,
Explosion, plane down suspected.

positive-iron [11 Sep 15:40]
Plane down 8 miles from pittsburg.

Mr. Messy [11 Sep 15:41]
Sweet jesus!
This website is more up to date than the news agencies.
I am relaying this news to some of our colonial friends
in our office, who are understandabley worried ... We
have mates in the colonies, so this info is invaluable.
Can you guys confirm some earlier postings?
Namely,
1) How many planes have been hijaked?
2) How many have hit Washington?
3) Has the Sears tower, Chicago been evacuated?
$) Has our Stock exchange been evacuated?
Rumours abound that prominent London sites are
being evacuated, any truth?
Be Lucky, Bald Git, we are all thinking of you.

Dave Smith [11 Sep 15:41]
Reckon that must have been shot down

Cheeky [11 Sep 15:41]
Canary Wharf London now evacuated

positive-iron [11 Sep 15:42]
Canary Wharf evacuated
.
positive-iron [11 Sep 15:42]
Planes being diverted to Canada

Yannick [11 Sep 15:43]
1) How many planes have been hijaked? to date 3
2) How many have hit Washington? 1 pentegon
3) Has the Sears tower, Chicago been evacuated? YES
$) Has our Stock exchange been evacuated? YES

Lady Hammer [11 Sep 15:43]
Mr Messy,, Yes the stock exchange has been evacuated

... so has the Tower at Canary wharf ...
God this is frightening.

ham er and cheese [11 Sep 15:43]
1) How many planes have been hijaked? unknown (7 been said)
2) How many have hit Washington? Pentigon
3) Has the Sears tower, Chicago been evacuated? unknown
$) Has our Stock exchange been evacuated? yes

GUEST (Steve) [11 Sep 15:44]
For an alternative commentary on the proceedings have a look at WWW.INFOWARS.COM.
Very frightening stuff indeed.

GUEST (BUCKS LOYAL) [11 Sep 15:44]
16 × FIGHTERS IN THE AIR,
Sorry Bald git can't quantify

Alex V [11 Sep 15:45]
Prominent sites in London being evacuated. Remember that any attack by plane needs a definite and easily identifyable target, so obviously Canary Wharf was the first to be evacuated.
Already the talk is that American security at airports is lax, not the case over here, despite Lockerbie revelations this morning.
2 planes on way to Washington.
80% of the internet is down.

Alex V [11 Sep 15:45]
Thoughts go out to anyone in Washington ...

Dave Smith [11 Sep 15:46]
I would guess it would be more lax due to the larger volume of traffic ...

GUEST (BUCKS LOYAL) [11 Sep 15:47]
4 planes hi jacked
News of a 5th,
Apparently, tv feed of another going down,
Furhter explosion Pentagon.
News feed, just coming in, unauthorised aircraft in air to
DC from just south of city,
Fighters above DC at last,
Seems that they will shoot anything down,
Bald git you ok mate?

Bald Git [11 Sep 15:48]
I can not get on any other web sites other than WHO,
phone lines to London are busy and they are starting to
evac my office building. I shall stay a little longer and
then sign off to walk the seven miles home as the metro
and streets are solid. Thanks for all the info fellas. Keep
it coming.
surreal

Dave Smith [11 Sep 15:48]
They will undoubtedly shoot it down. The USA would
not allow itself further humility by allowing the
destruction of the White House.

Mr. Messy [11 Sep 15:49]
Thanks, people.
I will pass this on.
I will keep an eye on this site and await any further news.
Is the Pittsburgh story confirmed and was it shot down?
God only knows where this will end!

D.Rollo [11 Sep 15:49]
just heard that a plan has been hijaked in japan –
hopefully bollocks

D.Rollo [11 Sep 15:50]
of course there's gonna be a huge case of chinese whispers – so best not to believe everything

GUEST (BUCKS LOYAL) [11 Sep 15:51]
Bald Git,
You take it easy mate, got a pc at home, if so mail in later, we are all really concerned, I want to know that you are ok,

Dave Smith [11 Sep 15:51]
Your sources seem pretty reliable though Rollo … lets pray they are wrong this time.
Incidentally Channel 4/ITV/Channel 5 seem to be more up to date than the BBC …

Mad Dog [11 Sep 15:52]
7 have been hijacked
the one in pennlyvania was shot down.
the others are going to be.
according to
this is very bad

Mad Dog [11 Sep 15:52]
according to bbc tv news apparently

armchair [11 Sep 15:54]
Jesus! F★★K when did all this happen. I only found out about it two minutes ago. Fuck I hope that idiot Bush keeps control of himself

positive-iron [11 Sep 15:54]
Thank God for Who online, plane on way to Pentagon!

GUEST (greenie1) [11 Sep 15:56]
I've heard that one has crashed nr Pittsburgh.

The plane heading for the Pentagon should have reached its destination by now but nothing on news. Been watching CNN. What a mess!

Magical No.10 [11 Sep 15:56]
i heard the pentagon has already collasped is that true.

armchair [11 Sep 15:57]
I know this comment isn't much use to anyone but I'd like to express the fact that I am F**king shocked! I love New York as well – poor bastards in those towers. The casualties will be unbelievable.

Dave Smith [11 Sep 15:57]
A bit of it has …

greenie1 [11 Sep 15:57]
Is it true that Canary Wharf has been evacuated?.

Bald Git [11 Sep 15:58]
A few years ago when the TWA plane blew up outbound NY they realised that Manchester airport had more x-ray machines capable of detecting plastic explosives than the whole US. Thiings were so lax it was unbelivable. Since then they have tightened up but clearly not enough.

   The latest from here is that there is a fire on the Mall. With all that air cover it may be the safest place to be!

GUEST (LLOYDI NATHAN) [11 Sep 15:58]
It has! Makes you wonder when London will be hit!

positive-iron [11 Sep 15:58]
I'm off home, this is unbelievable, how can i enjoy tonights game now, Bald Git hang in there mate, it's all madness …

Yannick [11 Sep 15:59]
My god, words fail me. Been to see those towers, have friends in NY and all across the states. God be with them & anyone you people know.

GUEST (LETS ALL GO HOME?) [11 Sep 15:59]
JUST GONE THROUGH LONDON ITS FUCKING MAYHEM POLICE SIRENS EVERWHERE, JUST PASSED THE MI5 BUILDING AS FAST AS I COULD. HOUSES OF PARLIAMENT THERE STILL DOING BLOODY TOURS

GUEST (greenie1) [11 Sep 16:00]
any other offices evacuated in London?

D.Rollo [11 Sep 16:01]
the canary wharf hsbc – american banks

positive-iron [11 Sep 16:01]
Bald Git, Washington grid locked

Ged [11 Sep 16:01]
Boeing 767 down near Pitsburgh, Pennsylvania. Apparently this is the second plane there.

Claret and Blue Stu [11 Sep 16:02]
Shit, just got out of a meeting, this is unreal. Any truth in the rumour another one's gone down near Pittsburgh and there's more in the air?

Claret and Blue Stu [11 Sep 16:02]
Cheers Ged. Jesus …

Jasnik [11 Sep 16:04]
My old company IQ was in the First tower that collapsed I waiting to see if any of my old Friends were there … This is unbelivable.

Top Six Finish [11 Sep 16:05]
It's amazing that none of those planes have gone down from within as it were, I guess if no-one has tried it on with the terrorists in mid air there must be loads of them on the plane. But how did they get on in the first place?!?!?!

GUEST (BUCKS LOYAL) [11 Sep 16:05]
Latest news,
There are several aircraft unaccounted for airborne in the US.
Bald Git, I was thinking of saying that, just seemed so bloody stupid from behind my keyboard in UK.

GUEST (greenie1) [11 Sep 16:05]
I work for an American company in the City and everybody is saying 'do we go home?'. We have no Directors in today, loads of people on the street outside.

Bald Git [11 Sep 16:07]
Positive Iron, I'm looking at it, the roads are solid the emergency services can barely move and people are being turned off in coming metro trains.

Lady Hammer [11 Sep 16:07]
My son works in the city and he is leaving now

Ged [11 Sep 16:07]
D.Rollo, any news about that flight in Japan?
to try and get home.
Please god dont let anything happen here.

GUEST (Steve) [11 Sep 16:09]
Attacks so organised as this are surely beyond any terrorist splinter group.
I'm no conspiracy theorist but there must be a greater force directing these shocking events.

D.Rollo [11 Sep 16:09]
no – can't have been true – thank god

GUEST (Steve) [11 Sep 16:10]
GREENIE1, leave your office now mate.

Ged [11 Sep 16:10]
Thanks DR.

Yannick [11 Sep 16:11]
colleague has said they saw something about an iraqi fighter shooting down an american plane. no idea if this happened – anyone heard anything along these lines? thoughts to all friends and loved ones !!!!!!

Mr. Messy [11 Sep 16:11]
We are in St. Mary Axe, EC3 and have just been told to go. Now for those bastards at Fenchuch St. I'll pick up this at home.
Let us know you're alright later, Bald Git.
Just been told 2 UA airlines are on route to London with fighter escort.
I'm off.

GUEST (greenie1) [11 Sep 16:11]
are you having a laugh?. I'm making myself a cup of tea. Are we on alert?

Butler [11 Sep 16:13]
Steve – you are correct.
To co-ordinate this must of been a massive operation. Taking months to plan. God knows how many people. Isn't this not the reason why Govt.s have departments like the FBI etc …?

D.Rollo [11 Sep 16:14]
yannick iraq shot down us plane at 7.30 gmt

Ironman [11 Sep 16:15]
There is a press conference at 4.30 from one of the Islamic groups.

Mr. Messy [11 Sep 16:15]
Greenie1, get yourself home mate.

GUEST (BUCKS LOYAL) [11 Sep 16:15]
Yannick,
  I picked that story up, fromm CNN.
  I believe it was in the Gulf.
  Read an article in the weekend press that Iraq had re armed its anti aircraft defences and had launched a succession of recent attacks. More in the previous month than in the last five (approx)

GUEST (greenie1) [11 Sep 16:16]
Liverpool st evacuated – is this true?

Yannick [11 Sep 16:16]
Bucks Loyal
When was this attack? today?
thanx mate

Ged [11 Sep 16:16]
Is Bald Git based in the US or just visiting. I've got a colleague there at the mo (thankfully heard he's safe) and he was supposed to be coming home tomorrow. Another colleague just spoke to his airline and there's an emergency line, but even the airline person said he'd be lucky to get through, let alone out.
What a disaster.

D.Rollo [11 Sep 16:17]
yannick iraq shot down us plane at 7.30 gmt

GUEST (Steve) [11 Sep 16:17]
Butler,
I really don't want to believe that any of the Federal Agencies had knowledge of this.
It's too frightening to contemplate.

ham er and cheese [11 Sep 16:18]
Liverpool st i have not but i know some bird who has been near that pub you all go crispins

GUEST (greenie) [11 Sep 16:19]
as long as Crispins is alrite!?!?!?!?

Bald Git [11 Sep 16:19]
Ged, I was transfered here by my firm from London a couple of years ago but I get back regularly to London and to UP whenever I can!

Butler [11 Sep 16:21]
Steve.
Wasn't suggesting that the FBI had anything to do with this. Rather, that the FBI and all the other intelligence agencies are in existence to know about these sort of things.
   Doubt very much that the Iraq incident is connected. Initial reports suggest that Palestinian terrorist group responsible.

Top Six Finish [11 Sep 16:21]
Mr Messy – where did u get this news from about London?
   By the way there is about to be a press conference in Afghanista according to someone I just spoke to, some group going to claim responsiblity ...
   Ged
   whats this about 2 planes headed for london???

GUEST (LETS ALL GO HOME NOW) [11 Sep 16:22]
JUST CAME THROUGH LONDON ITS MAYHEM POLICE SIRENS
EVERYWHERE, THE HOUSE OF COMMONS ARE STILL DOING
BLOODY TOURS CAN YOU BELIEVE IT? DONT THINK ILL BOOK
TODAY. CHAOS AT CITY PEOPLE ALL BEING SENT HOME
CANARY WHARF VERY BUSY AREA AS IS STOCK EXCHANGE
AND LIVERPOOL ST AREA NAT WEST TOWER LOTS OF PEOPLE
LEAVING OFFICES ALL AROUND THE AREA
TAKE CARE

Ironman [11 Sep 16:23]
The head of the islamic group said he was launching a
scathing attack on the USA about 2 weeks ago but they
didn't take it seriously as he's always saying these things.
He's the terrorist that lives in caves and his family are oil
barons of some magnitude.

Ged [11 Sep 16:23]
Christ mate, bet you never thought you wish you were
going to Reading more in your whole life. Take care fella.
As I said, my coleagues/mates is in NY. I had to ring his
parents earlier to tell them he was safe. Kinda puts it all
into perspective.
I must say, I'm shocked that some of the other threads
are still active …

Ironman [11 Sep 16:25]
0207 0080000 = Emergency number for anyone with
worries about families and friends in NY

GUEST (Doctor) [11 Sep 16:25]
just because they are all getting to reading …

Ged [11 Sep 16:26]
BBC announced American Airlines have admitted to
losing 156 dead in the two crashes that their planes were

involved in. Don't know which ones though ...

Dave Smith [11 Sep 16:27]
Building in Chicago? Have I missed something?

Butler [11 Sep 16:27]
Ironman
   The bloke you're thinking of is Bin Ladden. He is top of the FBI's most wanted list.
   Don't be suprised over the coming days if a million extreme terrorist groups attempt to claim responsibility for this.

GUEST (nb) [11 Sep 16:27]
American Airlines lost 2 planes with total of 156 pass-engers ... not counting 747 down in Pittsburg

S the Rapper [11 Sep 16:27]
I think that's this Bin Laden monster, isn't it ? BBC says Blair has called an emergency Cabinet security meeting.
   We don't know of course whether or not this is just precautionary.
   Also says many terribly badly burned in NY and many, many casualties.
   I don't think the vast majority of us who did not have to live through WW2 are psychologically equipped to deal with something like this.
   All we can do is pray.

GUEST (jasbir) [11 Sep 16:28]
How long before the same lads start doing it to us in Upton Park?

lodgey [11 Sep 16:28]
LONDON ON HIGH RED ALERT !!!!

GUEST (LLOYDI NATHAN) [11 Sep 16:29]
My brother in law is a pilot for BM. He is on the tarmac at Hamburg and is not allowed to leave. He said that there is an unconfirmed report about plane coming to London!
This was at 16.20

ham er and cheese [11 Sep 16:32]
If they went after Bin Ladden and got him it create total mayhem they would go ape shit thats why they have not yet.

Cheeky [11 Sep 16:32]
It appears to be arabs but what about Oklahama? that was an attack by US citizen. A great country but also one with a lot of f★★★★★★ up people.
It seems incomprehensible that a large arab terror gang could enter the US, board internal flights and carry this out unchallenged.

greenie1 [11 Sep 16:33]
anybody tell me the situation with Liverpool st station?

S the Rapper [11 Sep 16:34]
BBC confirms 156 lost on two AA flights. Pennsylvania crash reported to be a 747. Mayor Guilano of NY says 'tremendous number of lives lost'.

ham er and cheese [11 Sep 16:34]
greenie1 i heard fucked up mate but bond to get worse

Frankie's boots [11 Sep 16:35]
ham er and cheese – they attempted to take out Bin Laden 3 years ago after the last attempt on the World Trade Centre, two cruise missiles targeted his hideouts but he had been moved.

wickford hammer [11 Sep 16:35]
sorry to be selfhish but my five yr old is in florida with her nan is there any danger for her?
to say im shitting myself is an understatement

Mad Dog [11 Sep 16:36]
unconfirmed report of plane coming to london is bollocks.
    However is has done enough to scare enough people.
    Liverpool street is shut, ai i think the other major stations will shut too.

D.Rollo [11 Sep 16:37]
wickford – should be fine – sure they will only target significant gov't buildings and financial centres

GUEST (nb) [11 Sep 16:37]
Internet 80% down …
not WHOnline though

Top Six Finish [11 Sep 16:38]
Wickford – you're not being selfish at all, you've got every right to ask a question. As far as I am aware there are no major financial or military buildings in Florida, anyone else know?

Dave Smith [11 Sep 16:38]
Wickford Hammer – At a guess I would think they are safe … attacks seem to be against symbols of US power.

S the Rapper [11 Sep 16:40]
HM Govmnt says Britons abroad in sensitive areas should take sensible precautions. Military, govt etc buildings in London on alert. TUC Conference suspended. Blair makes speech of comiseration and support, voice trembling with emotion, offers full co-op. with US to track down perpetrators.

Frankie's boots [11 Sep 16:40]
mad dog – can you confirm that you this as fact as I've just had a mate call me from Brixton and told me the same?
Not over concerned but would be nice to know as a matter of fact.

wickford hammer [11 Sep 16:42]
Cheers everyone i hope you are right. I can only think of the Kennedy space centre and im sure thats not a target unless they are after tourists

SD [11 Sep 16:42]
The Kennedy Space centre (Star Wars and Shuttle launch pad) is in Florida, as long as they are not near that they should be OK.

Dave Smith [11 Sep 16:46]
Can someone please definitely confirm that Liverpool Street is shut?

Mad Dog [11 Sep 16:47]
well all the activity is in north east america.
have spent the last 20 mins watching bbc tv and i think they might have mentioned it.
it's chinese whispers
just seen the footage of the 2nd plane hit the WTC and also the first tower collapse.
the most sickening thing i've ever seen.
the 2nd plane hit at half way up no one above that can possibly have got out alive as it decimated several floors and people cant have got past it.
this is very very bad

Dirty Harry [11 Sep 16:47]
Apart from WHO upadates (thanks everyone), I'm

working in a news vacuum in East London. No TV, no radio, internet in meltdown, can't get to any news sites. Co-workers in adjacent office to me still listening to frigging Capital Gold (can you believe it?) which is giving occasional news updates only.

Mad Dog [11 Sep 16:48]
Liverpool street is shut according to the mail i have just recieved. according to the main reception in our building.
we're about half mile from liv street on london wall

S the Rapper [11 Sep 16:49]
Going home to watch CNN etc now. If I learn anything new I'll post. It's been a terrible day but WHO has done a fantastic job of informing each other, and treating this atrocity and tragedy with the respect and sympathy it merits.

Nick H [11 Sep 16:49]
Thanks for ananova.com who'ever said it ... it's the only one that seems to be workung.
 Heartfelt sympathy and deepest respect go out to anyone affect by these attrocities ... bastards

Concerned of Canvey [11 Sep 16:50]
Wickford Hammer,
If it's any comfort the Kennedy Space Centre is about 50 miles away from Orlando and so if your kid is there you are going to be okay.

GUEST (Big Dave) [11 Sep 16:50]
tel – have heard nothing about a plane coming towards London so far. Scanning TV and net continually as my girlfriend works in London.
Worried sick.

Dave Smith [11 Sep 16:50]
Cheers MD

Mad Dog [11 Sep 16:52]
i'm in london. i'm not particularly worried.
it's just rumour.
by now the authorities are on it.
they are downing the hijacked planes
only other missing plane is an american inter city plane
with not enough fuel to get here. so stop panicking

Nick H [11 Sep 16:55]
wickford
Got a nine year old daughter myself and can only
imagine the agonies your going through mate.
It all seems confined to the east coast … she'll be fine
mate … proberably doesn't even know anything about it
… too busy enjoying herself … try not to worry.

GUEST (Popscene) [11 Sep 16:55]
Liverpool St is DEFINITELY open …

ham er and cheese [11 Sep 16:58]
wickford
I would imagine they are fine mate Kennedy space
centre has air force base's all over that way.

Mad Dog [11 Sep 16:59]
I'm off now.
going to take a stroll over to Fenchurch and see exactly
how much this is going to effect the existing strike. i
dont envisage getting home for hours.
take care.
Old bill are screaming down towards Liverpool st

ham er and cheese [11 Sep 16:59]
#But they always do so don't wory anyone

GUEST (billybnigspuds) [11 Sep 17:01]
Any update on the Liverpool St situ. ?

Nitin [11 Sep 17:01]
is anyone cancellin their tickets 4 2nite ... if so ill put a
£10 offer in

GUEST (Steve) [11 Sep 17:01]
Bush is supposedly back in Washington but hasn't made
another statement as yet.

GUEST (Popscene) [11 Sep 17:02]
Liverpool St is open

GUEST (Steve) [11 Sep 17:03]
Wickford, these bastards only seem to be targeting
financial and federal buildings.
    I don't think they'd target holiday resorts such as
Florida.

Cardiff Irons [11 Sep 17:03]
Not the sort of thing I expected to see in my life-time.
Praying hard for all those who have died, are injured or
in imminent danger and also for the friends and relatives
who have lost loved ones or are worried about their
safety.
    And in a world going totally mad, I pray for peace,
tolerance and justice. To think, two hours ago we were
worried about West Ham's attacking deficiencies –
perspective eh?

wickford hammer [11 Sep 17:04]
cheers nickh im sure your right, it's just at a time like

this you miss them even more which is what i meant by being selfish. I would also like to add that my heart is going out to all the kids in the states and the world over that are going to bed tonite with out a mum or dad.

quite quite the saddest day i can remember for a long time …

Ged [11 Sep 17:08]
Fuckin' hell. Bill Withers "Lean on Me" on the radio. Apt or what.
Think.
Remember when yer mum used to say that everyone remembers where they were when Kennedy was shot …
I can't even bgin to get my head round this.

ham er and cheese [11 Sep 17:09]
I will say on WHO posting and (WSL) informed me

mc hammer [11 Sep 17:13]
gutting to see such awful images. A pray for those lost

Fraggle [11 Sep 17:14]
A terrible act of wanton violence against the innocent. My heart goes out to the victims and their families.

Marquis De Irons [11 Sep 17:16]
Sky news reports that 'several' aircraft are still unaccounted for in the USA.
    I only hope we never have to witness anything this sickening again in our lifetimes!

Claret and Blue Stu [11 Sep 17:16]
Wickford Hammer – words that have made me well up in tears …
I'm speechless …

GUEST (WHFAN) [11 Sep 17:30]
I think we should thank ourlucky stars, that they didnt target us. Big Ben and the houses of parlenment would have been a possible target.

GUEST (Rochford Hammer) [11 Sep 17:35]
Here Here wickford
couldn't put it better myself. i'm typing this with tears in my eye's. This is quite sickening along with the events in Northern Ireland last week.

If this is whats the world's coming to i'm not to sure if i want to be part of it anymore. Espically when you see people in Palestine and Lebannon out in the streets celebrating.

My thoughts go out to everyone's that passed away's loved one's and i hope to god they rest in peace because my god they deserve it

slinky [11 Sep 17:40]
Wickford, your daughter will be fine,my heart goes out to all involved.

Cannot imagine the terror, and panic the people must be going through, the terroists must not be allowed too get away with this.

For the first time in my life i am speechless.

How can any games of football go on tonight after what has happened, it wouldn't be right!

Postponements must be imminent.

Bald Git [11 Sep 17:48]
Still here as it is chaos trying to get home. They have closed the streets around the White House and radio news reports that all the aircraft that are still airborne have been accounted for. A colleague is trying to contact both her parents who work at the Pentagon. I still haven't seen any TV but it sounds worse than Pearl

Harbour. I just went out to get a sandwich and the girl in the shop told me to "have a nice day" surreal.

Rochford Hammer [11 Sep 17:55]
Bald Git
Look after yourself mate and please be careful.

I still cant belive this has happened i'm sitting here numb the rest of the office has gone. i just feel physically sick.

Claret and Blue Stu [11 Sep 17:58]
Bald Git please get yerself home safe as soon as possible fella. The same goes for the other US-based Hammers on here and their loved ones.

Like Rochford Hammer, I'm sitting here with a throbbing headache from trying not to f★★king cry. I still can't get over that sentence from Wickford …

GUEST (Balto.) [11 Sep 18:02]
I live here in the US, in Baltimore. 40 minutes drive from from Washington DC. It is scary! Our town has been evacuated. All the kids sent home from school. There's still one plane flying around unaccounted for which United Airlines think might be hi-jacked. The whole country is stunned. Thousands are feared dead in the World Trade Center.

If you're planning to fly to the US you can't. All flights have been cancelled. We're not allowed to use the phones. Unless you desperately need to call the US don't because the telpehone lines are overloaded.

It puts the game with Reading into perspective.

Bald Git [11 Sep 18:03]
Rochford, thanks.

I think it is strangely easier to be here in the middle of it without a TV or radio and just out of sight of the points of attack to see or hear what has happened. Earlier on it was like the scene from Independence Day with everyone fleeing the city and all the cars going in one direction. At one point my only contact with what was happening was talking to people on this site as the BBC and CNN were overloaded.

Thank you Alex and all the boys and girls on WHO. It is calmer now and the

Rochford Hammer [11 Sep 18:04]
You know I'm sitting her thinking about 1939 when the Nazis invaded Poland my nan talks about everyone's fear and realisation of what may unfold never really understood what she meant, sitting here this afternoon i'm begining to understand it really understand. I hope for everyone's sake history is not going to repeat it self.

Pagey [11 Sep 18:05]
Been watching the telly all afternoon and I really can't believe what I'm seeing.

I don't even want to think about the amount of lives that have been lost but my heart goes out to all of them.

GUEST (E1) [11 Sep 18:08]
I am sitting here in San Francisco and the feeling is horrible – no one knows what is going to happen – if it has stopped etc.

Lady Hammer [11 Sep 18:10]
Bald git ... why did you cut off mid sentence ... are you ok???

Bald Git [11 Sep 18:13]
Sorry Lady H, I thought I deleted it. I'm fine.

salgirl [11 Sep 18:13]
What's happened is appalling, sick and totally unjustified. I've been watching this, dumbstruck, since just after two o'clock.

To any Americans who may be reading this – our thoughts are with you, and those families of the many thousands who will have been so tragically affected by this.

salgirl [11 Sep 18:18]
Sorry, forgot to add …

All America based Hammers, come home safely.

wmc3205 [11 Sep 18:19]
Today is one of the saddest days that I can remember. My family and I are sitting watching the Horror on TV. Somebody has a very sick mind if this is what they resort too. Our thoughts to the families in New York and DC.

Gerald Irons [11 Sep 18:21]
Potomac river/Pentagon area is now a "no-fly zone" and one of the "rogue" passenger flights (with over 250 passengers) has been pre-emptively shot down in the San Francisco Bay area.

Mrs S [11 Sep 18:22]
Ive also sat and watched this, on tele, in tears since two o'clock and just could not believe what was happening. It is just unbelievable.

My thoughts are with anyone caught up in this.
How can anyone think of a football match after this?

GUEST (Balto) [11 Sep 18:25]
Gerald Irons. I'm sitting in my office in Baltimore, with the radio on on and there's no news about this pre-emptive strike gainst an airliner in San Franscisco.

Where did you get this news from? There are stories appearing on WHO which the American news services have not got. Please verify.

Lady Hammer [11 Sep 18:27]
OK bald git ... good!

wmc3205 [11 Sep 18:32]
All I can say that this is a black day and I hope that nothing else ever happens again like this.

To the people who planned it. Enjoy your last couple of days as Uncle Sam will get you, you Rotten Sick Fuckers

Gerald Irons [11 Sep 18:39]
Balto, I'm at work in San Diego and must apologize for the workplace hysterics. There's no confirmation on the whereabouts of the flight and no validation. (supposed en route to SF ...)

So, I hereby apologetically swallow the previous post, minus the no-fly zone (trying to appear to be working, while keeping up-to-date ...)

GUEST (wmc3205) [11 Sep 18:43]
I have only heard of 5 planes.
2 at the WTC
1 at the Pentagon
1 Near Pittsburgh
1 the Airforce are looking for as it went of radar, but this was sometime ago round about 17H00 GMT

GUEST (Steve) [11 Sep 18:44]
ITN just interviewed a defence expert who stated that it should have been impossible for a rogue plane to crash into the Pentagon considering the defence precautions in Washington.

Mr. Messy [11 Sep 18:45]
Right, I'm home now.
Glad Bald git is still o.k.

Echo all the thoughts of my fellow posters. Especially wmc3205.

The London bound jets rumour unfortunately originated with me. One of the young lads in my office has been monitoring the news services and come up with that one. I will be having words with him tomorrow.

As nothing has been outed on that score whilst I was travelling back to Hadleigh, I think we can assume that little titbit was bollocks.

What I have noticed was this site has been well ahead of the news services. I hope the rumour mongering does not obscure the news that has been getting out.

The BBC have been saying that the Pittsburgh jet was not hijacked, just (just?)a plane crash.

Gerald Irons, what is your source for the San Francisco story?

Lady Hammer [11 Sep 18:49]
Just have to say that I have never witnessed anything like I have today … and I dont ever want to again … my heart goes out to all the people who were involved in this terrible tragedy … we can only sit and watch and imagine what they must be going through … poor souls. WMC … your post at 18.32 … my sentiments exactly matie.

S the Rapper [11 Sep 18:51]
Latest news form various TV sources, including CNN is that: All commercial flights in the US are now accounted for

Unconfirmed reports that US Navy is deploying battleships and aircraft carriers along the Eastern seabord – for strategic reasons

It is not known whether the Pennsylvania plane crash is related to the terrorism or not

Putin of Russia has spoken strongly in comdemnation – it is hoped that their intelligence service will help to track down the perpetrators

Yasser Arafat made a sppech exprssing shock and horror. I saw it & I think he was genuine.

Bin Laden is the name in the fraem of most experts, including Burak of Israel

Hammer Time [11 Sep 18:54]
There will certinly be huge retribution from the US, the Terrorists have hit right into the nerve centre of America. Quite amazing that theyve managed to carry out the act undetected.

My initial sympathies go out to all those affected by this act but long term I have great fears to how this situation could escalate.

wmc3205 [11 Sep 18:56]
If your thinking of what I am thinking off, it is scarey. The Americans are known not to sit back and do nothing

S the Rapper [11 Sep 19:00]
I just saw a CNN news item with pictures taken in the Arab quarter of Jerusalem. They were dancing in the streets, sounding car horns, jubilant, like we would be if we won the Cup. These people are clearly cannot all be psychos – so they must think of this as an act of war against an enemy. Therefore the West has to respond to it as an act of war. If sovereign states are supporting the perpetrators, actively or passively, they must face the consequences as if they had committed the act of international hostility themselves. This may sound

unpalatable and frightening, but are we prepared to face the consequences of a possible similar attack on London some time down the road if the action is not taken speedily, decisively, and totally ruthlessly once the culprits and their sponsors are identified ?

Hammer Time [11 Sep 19:03]
I hope the Americans are sensible about how to react to this, I think only rash decisions and action against countries that is not necessary would cause others to get involved, it would seem that all World Leaders are in support and sympthise with the US.

George Bush, however will have pressure on him to show that this sort of action will not be tolerated – an awful lot of responsibilty is on his shoulders.

Dave Smith [11 Sep 19:06]
S The Rapper – you do not treat it as an "act of war" unless you want to escalate this from an act of terrorism from a small (albeit highly organised) minority into a full scale more with even more casualties. The action must be appriorate.

Mrs S [11 Sep 19:07]
Just heard that all planes in this country are grounded. No flights at all in or out.

Stevie [11 Sep 19:09]
Unbelievable carnage.

Terrorists thrive on this shit. The western governments that pander to terrorism, such as ours, give out a message that results can be achieved to these nutters and encorage them. We should simply kill these people as soon as they are identified.

They all communicate,share expertise and cooperate.

S the Rapper [11 Sep 19:09]
Of course they will have to think before they act. Bush may be no intellectual but he's no fool and has a lot of good advice. I also think he's no pushover, unlike his old man who let Saddam Hussein off the hook. The response has to be aimed at prevention rather that retribution per se. Don't worry nobody Bush is not going to nuke anybody – but the right approach would appear to be to track down the perpetrators plus any active supporters or sponsors, wherever they may be, and without regard to the delicat sensibilities of other tin-pot dictatorships. Then eliminate them. And when I say eliminate, I mean completely and without trace, if you get my drift. Nothing else will stop this, especially if it is Bin Laden, who is an extreme lunatic fanatic even by the standards of international terrorism.

wmc3205 [11 Sep 19:10]
But remember the last time with Pearl Harbour!!!!
I for one dont want war

S the Rapper [11 Sep 19:13]
Dave Smith – understood, but my point is that I believe the perpetrators and their sympathisers are already treating it as an act of war. Playing by the standards of normal criminal justice and the 'Queensbury Rules' will not in my opinion be a sufficient response. Live by the sword, die by the sword, and I for one do not feel the need for a 12 year delay and an international court in the Hague before they do.

GUEST (Steve) [11 Sep 19:15]
The footage of palestinians celebrating these events is without the most disgusting thing I have ever seen. These people are vermin. The lowest of the low.

S the Rapper [11 Sep 19:17]
The emotional response may be similar to Pearl Harbour but the circumstances are very different. That was a full, open military operation against full military targets by one major power on another, with the express intention of starting a full-scale war. This was probably a bunch of paramilitary terrorists using hijacked civilian aircraft. It is not going to be openly supported by any sovereign state, although it's a fair bet that one or more aided and abetted it.

Dave Smith [11 Sep 19:18]
It's my ethical point of view that we should not respond to this with more killing. At the same time I see that it would be extremely difficult to discourage terrorists without the threat of severe retaliatory action – death basically. Having said that it looks like they don't mind dying for the cause anyway …

sad dad [11 Sep 19:18]
I'm with hammertime. This is the time for Bush to remain coldly rationale and make sure he identifies the specific nutters responsible but does not launch indiscriminate acts of terrorism himself.
I also hope that the bar in Boston that I visited shortly after the London bombings (Nate West Tower etc) feel differently about terrorism now.

GUEST **(Balto) [11 Sep 19:18]**
Gerald. Thanks for the retraction/update. What news source are you using?
I still can't help feeling that foreign (non-American) journalists are filing better reports than their American counterparts. I'm listening to NPR from Washington DC I can't get onto the CNN site. There must be too many people logging on.

EXQUISITE CORPSE

Bucephalus *The favourite horse of Alexander the Great. It died of its wounds after the battle of the Hydaspes in 326 BC and was commemorated by the founding of Bucephala, modern Jhelum in Pakistan. Named Ox-head (Bucephalus), after its mighty size, it was given to Alexander by his father Phillip of Macedon, as the boy was reputedly the only person able to break it in and ride it.*

At first just the suggestion of dawn, a silhouette, set against a chill gentian sky. Then a movement, a low whinny, exhalations, steam. Eyes glisten, blank, emotionless, like specks of obsidian. The mare shuffles round, an agonised two-step, in a lonely travail, until its hindquarters are just in view. Her aperture still obscured. The mare makes a sound like the shaking of a carpet, strings of saliva hanging, dropping, beading from her lips, clouds of condensed breath rising in the absolute stillness. Beneath the shadow of a great buttress, a mountain spur, light only now just touching the tips of the surrounding peaks with a delicate pallette of pinks. Muffled bellows and whistles striate the air and their echos volley from ridge to ridge. The valley floor, then, crisp with a blanket of rime. The dell of the foaling mare remains in darkness. Grass, nettles and wild barley, stiff with frost, bowed, broken and flattened in a vortex of kicks and painful revolutions. The foal's huge head appears, eyes smeared shut like wet clay. Shrouded in mucus. The membrane glistens from the still nocturnal scene, hoofs stretch and tear at transparent veils flecked with blood. The mare jerks in uncontrollable spasms. Thrown like a puppet into some pain-wracked quadrille. A tangle of limbs, a slipping, spilling, thudding mass. An imperceptible pause, like a musician stealing a breath. Then, wet hair brushed up against the nap of its coat, teeth biting and clipping at hot offal, steaming in the searing cold of the mountain air. A foal giddily gets to its feet, repeatedly forced down (legs spreading like a broken table) by its mothers tongue as it shears the foal of its membranous shroud.

A tongue of light edges into the paddock, frost crystals blink into droplets and run down the folded pea-green sheaths of grass, dissolving, darkening the earth below).

Closing time. People were stumbling out onto the pavements screaming and laughing. Others anxiously discussed further drinking venues, some hunched over mobile phones in doorways or with a finger in an ear, shouting and circling as if engaged in some form of prayer chant. While a few more were intent on singing and exchanging insults. Anyway, whatever it was they were doing, one could be fairly certain that noone noticed Norton Folgate scythe through their midst at a vigorous pace. He was drunk, agitated and exhilarated. Elated by a night's conversation full of ideas and promise. However, he knew he was on a slippery slope. Aware that this was the dregs of a life spent in pubs and bars. Early on, it fuels ideas born of youthful excitement, love and comradeship. Then, imperceptibly at first, such a restless spirit, upon discovering no solace, finds itself condemned, molded and cornered as punished paranoiac.

Nevertheless, despite such acknowledgements in the pit of his stomach, he was momentarily buoyed by a sweet taste of absurdity. London was seductively dark and wet. Sometimes something exciting happens to London when it rains. Particularly when it rains really hard. So hard that the drains begin to choke and gag on the excess water. When vast pools cover the roads and the pavements are greased with a chilled rancid film. It is only on these special occasions that you begin to recognise the medieval midden that London really is. So, with head bent against the downpour, he scuttled over curbstones as smooth as pebbles, skipped through the morass of puke and chatter, bumping into oncoming pedestrians, sidestepping this way and that, and headed towards Charing Cross road.

He felt he was an isolated point of negation, a small particle that would never understand anything, would never truly know or divide into another being. He repeatedly castigated himself with these ridiculous thoughts. He would be awake some nights, obsessed by a notion of community that could not possibly realise itself. These are the mythic visions that had sought him out while lying face down on the bedroom floor. One room. Only one room. He hated its utilitarian paucity while reluctantly acknowledging its refuge. The phalanx has one room – there would be no respite. It was always one thing or another, structure or formlessness, positive or negative, zero or one. When would it be otherwise? Surely the value of taboo and transgression lay within the play between the two? Whereas we are always taught to accept experience in terms of either/or, of what you are and what you are not, never in terms of what you may become. Each sacred perishable instant, each moment collapses into the next. A momentary fusion, an open wound, no stasis, no rest.

By the time he had reached the bus stop on Charing Cross road he was telling himself to suppress such futile thoughts. To escape the rain, he slumped against the outside of the shelter and examined his feet. After a while he felt his heartbeat decrease and he lit a cigarette.

As is always the case in London, even the slightest change in meteorological conditions would bring the bus network to a standstill. Therefore, he prepared himself for the inevitable wait. It was at this point, after the distractions that nicotine can offer had subsided, that he allowed himself a discrete survey of the ensemble that had gathered under the shelter waiting for a ride out of town. It was a typical Friday night crowd, various groupings and individuals returning from a night in the West End. Like a searchlight, his gaze alighted upon a variety of differing expressions, mouth shapes and eye movements. Half distracted, he moved across the group, speculating on where they had been and where were they going. More confident, he allowed his eyes to wander and settle until, all of a sudden, through a gap in the crowd, his gaze was met and thrown straight back at him by an extraordinarily beautiful woman. Instinctively his head shot towards the floor. Obviously rattled, he hoped that he had covered himself by pretending that he had suddenly meant to re-examine his feet all along. Then, slowly raising his head once more, he stretched up with an expectant and impatient look towards the sodden orange street; a caricature of someone waiting for a bus.

Yet, as he carried out his supposedly careful act, he attempted to keep the woman within his peripheral vision. He wanted to examine her more closely. How long had she been staring at him? He began to sober up rapidly. What was happening? Mustering some sort of courage, he decided to meet her gaze once more. However, as he looked across, she looked away. She was small, petite some would say, with a thin oval face framed by long black ringlets of hair. At the centre of her face was the most dramatic Romanesque nose, proud and elegant, beneath which there lay a full wide mouth.

He gradually moved back to her eyes, large pools of hazelnut brown. She turned to face him again. He could not believe it. This time he tried to hold his ground, this time he would not yield. For a moment, longer than a moment, they held each other. Then he turned away again. What does this mean? Does it mean anything in a city where everyone is careful not to let eye contact linger for anything more than a second? What is the matter with you? His mind churned over several possibilities. A look from a stranger means nothing, he reminded himself. His booze addled mind was running away from all sense, logic and proportion. He began to feel ashamed. Nevertheless, throughout this tumult of feeling, he could not help returning to the thought that maybe there was something more to these signals, that at the very least he should try and communicate, cross the divide. Perhaps this was the threshold of a chance encounter? "*No, No, No ...* " he cringed, obstinately fighting back from the other side of lunacy.

This internal interrogation went on for some time. If everyone gathered at the bus stop could have heard what he was saying to himself, how would they have judged him? In fact, supposing such vulnerable monologues were known to all, what kind of cacophonous and violently vulnerable world would it be? Is it not for the best that such thoughts and feelings remain inarticulate, fleeting and beyond recollection – even from those that summoned them? For, from the outside, Norton Folgate looked like someone who was a little nervous perhaps, slightly the worse for alcohol maybe, conceivably a little cold beneath an ill-fitting overcoat, who could know for sure? Maybe a crude approximation is enough and just as well. What can anyone extract from a few Conan Doyle-like observations, details and habits? However, what the beautiful woman thought of him, as she stared at him once again, we will never know and in this regard we can be absolutely certain.

Abruptly all his thoughts dispersed as the night bus screeched its brakes and the crowd rushed towards the door. Norton Folgate decided to wait, to hang back, and let the others fight for a seat. From his position he watched the beautiful woman glide effortlessly through the irritable throng and enter the bus and climb to the top deck. As she climbed the stairs she seemed to turn and, once again, throw another lightning bolt glance that almost knocked him off balance. This is it! This is the trigger that would set him off! He moved into the mêlée, moving this way and that, sidling on tiptoe, jockeying for an audience at the driver's confessional cab window. As he made his way, he wondered what he would do once he got upstairs. Would she be sitting alone? Would he sit next to her, or to one side? What should he say? What should he do? How would he know where to begin?

There was no time to speculate, no time to consider or weigh up the pro and contra, there was simply no time left in which to think. He bought his ticket and bolted up the stairs. As he poked his head above the parapet, he was confronted by a sea of faces and, whether anyone was looking at him or not, he felt that he could not hesitate under the weight of such scrutiny. He quickly assessed the scene. He saw her! She was alone! This unexpected piece of fortune, this shocking chance opportunity, suddenly gave every subsequent gesture and action the appearance and qualities that comes with the idiosyncratic logic of a dream. He felt pieces of a puzzle were naturally, instinctively falling into place as he walked along the aisle and placed himself beside her.

Nevertheless, once seated, he felt that he could not

relax, his anxiety and doubts remained and refused to release him. He did not know what to say or do. He felt that he was loosing control of his body. He felt condemned to look forwards forever. His torso seemed strapped tightly into the seat, his arms down by his sides with hands resting near his thighs. He began to sense that he was absurdly upright. He was like some kind of absurd puppet, immobilised and speechless, caught in a straightjacket. The bus was packed out with late night revelers laughing and chatting and there was he, head and shoulders above the rest like some stupid protuberance, when all he really wanted was to slump into his seat. Yet somehow her presence prohibited any repose.

As the bus moved off, full of noise and gossip, the windows slowly steamed up with the warm damp fug of bodies. Although he was completely paralysed, Norton could move his eyes. He gave a sidelong glance towards the beautiful woman. Her head was gently tilted to one side as she serenely gazed out of the window. He then lowered his eyes and noticed that her arm, like his, was resting by her side. Also, her hand was delicately placed in the small area of seat that separated them.

Norton, gripped by a maelstrom of forces, instantly and without any real reason, began to turn himself into an instrument of pure action. He was afraid, and he was also afraid of the realisation that he could not stop himself. Fearfully, he looked down as he gradually slid his hand onto the bus seat so as to assume a mirror image position to hers. Her hand did not move. He glanced out of the corner of his eye; she appeared so calm, so radiant and integral. What the hell was he doing? He should say something for Christ's sake! Yet, as he castigated himself, he remained bolt upright, head forward like some showroom dummy, nevertheless convinced that his micro-manoeuvres held some vain and resplendent answer.

For several stops and starts, who knows how long, their hands rested there on the bus seat, barely millimetres apart. He could feel the tiny hairs on the back of his little finger bowing on contact with her skin. He was electrified and felt an enormous surge of blood course through him, he was delirious and yet he was trapped. Paradoxically inert beside this beautiful woman who he so desperately wanted to reach out to, to speak with, to engage in an unthinking embrace, a simple movement out on a limb, a whim, a chance without a care for consequence, outcome, or end.

At this moment he stepped off the cliff, he didn't know why, he just did. There was no voice, no sound, no movement other than the most infinitesimal, most fragile of caresses as his little finger lightly stroked her little finger. Her warm touch sent a shiver releasing his neck as they simultaneously turned to meet each other's eyes. As he turned to face her, he thought about what he had just done, this tiny touch from a complete stranger sitting next her on a bus! What was he thinking? Why had he chosen this course of action? He could not reason. He ached with so many questions he could never answer, an absence at the core of his being that would not be filled. Suddenly life seemed to be composed of ideas that could not be articulated, framed or set out, other than by instinct, mute flesh, passion and pure action. What did he expect to achieve? As she turned towards him, his eyes expectantly begged for under-standing, for mercy. Although neither had uttered a word, she answered him, continuing this weird kind of mime, with all her powers of communication channeled into her darkly determined eyes. With only a slight knotting of the brow, a pursing of lips and the exacting steely censure of her stare, she did everything she possibly could within these limits to let him know her anger, her outrage and disgust at his molestation.

Shaken by the full force of her disciplined disdain, he turned away. Shocked and embarrassed, his body became his again. He slumped, almost bent himself double in shame. Furthermore, not a word had been spoken between them. Nor was anyone on the bus aware of what silent scenes had been played out. He continued to sit beside her for the rest of the journey, for there was no where else to go. He had to sit the agony out until, through the condensation, he recognised an opaque neon landmark and, without looking up once, hurriedly scuttled off of the bus. The street restored his anon-ymity and, consequently, he felt a slight balm of relief envelope him. Yet, as the scene moved off in one direction and he slipped away in another, he knew he would never be free of its memory.

"Probably it is best to assume that he committed suicide. Although it was not an entirely intended suicide, it is possible that he opened the window and fell out. I think that it was an unconscious suicide and feel that he wanted to die because he was very unhappy in this phase. Two days before he died we went for a walk and were in an inn. He visited a friend who had shown similar symptoms and was totally neutralised after the treatment in the lunatic asylum of Steinhof. This man was Schloglhofer. We didn't want Schwarzkogler to be treated by psychiatrists because we thought the treatment would erase him too. Edith Adam, his girl-friend, phoned me and told me that he had jumped or fallen out of the window. I went there immediately. His bed was very unusual. There was still the mark of his body in the bed-linen, like a stiff cocoon, he must have glided out of it some way. The window

was open, it was the third or fourth floor. He died after twenty minutes, and it was said that the female caretaker came out and talked with him while he was lying on the ground with a smashed abdomen."
Heinz Cibulka

According to Peter Weibel, Rudolph Schwarzkogler was the last to join the group. Weibel testified that Heinz Cibulka was always the model for the photographs, not Schwarzkogler, that the photographs were not 'Aktions' in the same mould as other members of the group. The traumatised bodies that appeared in the frame, made anonymous and both bound and extended by the paraphernalia of medicine, were illustrations of otherness, the imagined bodies of a stranger. Whether they were the projection of something autobiographical could only be a matter of conjecture, always and inevitably the synthesised notion of yet another stranger.

"But they are not strangers! We have names, characters, and witnesses. You talk of people as if they have the same substantiality as ghosts. Houram Heatet Lange hypothesised that hauntings are partly due to participants' affective responses to such ambiguity. Consequently, scores on the 'fear of the paranormal' subscale of the Anomolous Experiences Inventory were expected to be associated with decreased tolerance for ambiguity as measured on the Rydell-Rosen Ambiguity Tolerance Scale."

The extended index finger on his right hand is crooked downward, the finger tip bouncing off the table top, tap-tap-tapping a metred emphasis to those final five words, plainly determined that as many of the senses as possible should be touched by their capitalisation. Or maybe he's just cheering himself on to the end of the sentence. Either way, as he gets there, his hands open to release a succinct version of his train of thought.

"Without assigning names properly, and with certainty, you risk promoting fear, myth, and irrationality."

I'm aware that my nodded assent is careless. Idly, I scan my peripheral vision for a mirror, a window, any reflective surface, wondering if I can see whatever else I might be communicating. I'm tickled by the thought of objectively confirming the ratio of resignation, exasperation, and stimulation I feel in in my acknowledgement. So for a brief moment it's just myself, the chromed legs of a couple of bar stools, and the imperfect polish on a few nearby tables. But I can't leave him out for long. Don't actually want to – I need to qualify that assent. Yes, we do in fact know at least one of the other people involved. Robert Hughes wrote an article for *Time* magazine in 1972. He described Schwarzkogler as "the Vincent van Gogh of body art [who] proceeded, inch by inch, to amputate his own penis, while a photographer recorded the act as an art event." And there were others too, who, in the process of turning reactions and thoughts into intelligible and transmissible phrases, whispered a myth in which categorisation became annihilation.

" ... but old Sam's just come clean with me. You know the way he drops in every afternoon to watch the sheets roll out. Well, this time he seemed rather excited, or at least as near as he'll ever get to it. When I told him we were on the last cycle he asked me, in that cute English accent of his, if I'd ever wondered what they were trying to do. I said, 'Sure' – and he told me."

"Go on, I'll buy it."

"Well, they believe that when they have listed all His names – and they reckon that there are about nine billion of them – God's purpose will have been achieved. The human race will have finished what it was created to do, and there won't be any point in carrying on. Indeed, the very idea is

something like blasphemy."

"Then what do they expect us to do? Commit suicide?"

"There's no need for that. When the list's completed, God steps in and simply winds things up ... bingo!"
Arthur C. Clarke, *The Nine Billion Names of God*

"He cut his cock off!?"
Uh ... No. Actually, some reports say that he sliced it bit by bit, pared it away to a point of no return, but that's not really the uh ... point (though my antagonist's language was certainly more blunt now). The table prevents me from seeing if his legs are crossed, but whatever, I imagine him to be sharing the same visions of unstemmable blood flow that Hughes must have seen. This urges me to press on with the story. Schwarzkogler died on June 20, 1969. Not a martyr to his art, but just another pile of life wheezing out onto a Viennese pavement. That he became a martyr anyway was perhaps more a symptom of Art's dysfunctional relationship with the everyday, a way for a dessicated God to carry on fucking with the minds of mortals. The price of vision for the eighteenth century genius was derangement: crude, material flesh dissipated, unfit as it was to provide direct access to the mind of God. Derangement was a flirtation with death in which the will of the subject was eroded, suppressed, and eventually extinguished. The active subject was transformed, became rendered entirely as an object of our observation. If today we are more wary of giving artists this function, of colluding with them in this dream of communication with the deities, we are less so with the famous. It's not a spasm of jealousy that has us devouring stories of addiction, debt, and dangerous passion; not a spastic response in the face of a comfort we can never attain. Rather we confer on the glamorous a power that keeps them distant, the power to mirror

both the conscious and the unconscious desires of the materially and historically bound; ourselves. However, as Freud discovered, "Everything conscious wears out. What is unconscious remains unaltered. But once it is set loose, does it not fall into ruins in turn?" To die young and have a good looking corpse: a corpse in which the remainder, the unconscious, is untrammelled by time; intact.

Yet this cannot completely explain why Schwarzkogler's performance death was preferable to the ambiguous suicide/accident of his actual death. Two things mark the performance death. Firstly, the certainty of the outcome. Secondly, the fragmentation and multiplication of parts. The slow, deliberate incisions that separate Schwarzkogler from his cock have the effect of temporally as well as spatially fragmenting his body. Cut. If I am segmented there are two possibilities. One. My self is erased. I become a multiple thing, organised into categories, levels, and types. They may be relational categories, intersecting at many points, but the map is already drawn and the map is the law. Two. My self becomes multiple. I become multiple rather than becoming multiple things, infinitely divisible.

"A failed narrative remains human, while a failed science is vacuous. We find that if we attempt to build a science out of the subject and we fail, we are left in pieces, whereas a bad yarn is still a yarn, a human story."
Robert M. Young, *Whatever happened to human nature?*

While the organising of anything into parts makes it all the more easy to name it, the act of naming is completely bound up with the processes of desire – desire being a temporal 'thing'. I want something to come to me – I want something to come back to me.

Desire and the name can only be in the past or the future. The present is nameless. This is so because desire is always within the linear temporal scheme of the expectant moment and the remembered moment, but the present moment is alinear, atemporal – it constantly is, and is constantly outside of its past and future constructions. This incompatibility, this failure to meet, is why the present must be nameless – two cogs that can never mesh because one simply is not a cog. As well as an endgame display of authenticity, the casual observer, by killing Schwarzkogler in a performance of our own imagining, is participating in a ritual where the severing of arteries is the construction of an organised identity, a totalising identity in the face of the ambiguous, the amorphous.

There's frantic movement beneath the table and a huge black tail flicks out, back and forth, taking side swipes at our legs. Savannah weaves off to another table and, having looked down, I notice the foam encrusted sides of our pint glasses. My round. He hands me his glass and says, "I can tell you another story about a man who cut his cock off. He didn't die. It was a story in amongst the quickies about a man who'd been cutting grass and just decided to use the sickle on himself. He must have been thinking about it beforehand I suppose … Anyway, after a search, they thought they'd found his missing member in the bushes, so they packed it in a bag of frozen mattur panir and sent it on to the hospital. Turned out to be a chicken neck. They reckoned the dogs ate his cock …"

The great retro rainwear & flares revival of 1985
You can get these Lois Jumbo Cords which are tight as fuck on the arse and thighs but then seem to flare out slightly from the knee. I've got them in light light grey. Kenny's got the classic chocolate brown, with his pin badge attached just above trainer level.

Plus we've all had a crack at some rudimentary needlework recently.

Option A: Cut Ups
Step 1: Purchase jeans or cords with a generous inside leg.
Step 2: Carefully cut away the stitching where the side seams meet the hem.
Step 3: Cut up the seam for three or four inches.
Step 4: Put in a few stitches to stop them splitting any further.
Step 5: Pull them on and carefully position flaps of denim over trainers.

Option B: Flares
Repeat steps 1 to 4 (as above) then sew in a triangle of material, thus constructing a rudimentary flare. Materials of choice this month are: Liberty paisley patterns, dark denim and corduroy. Once constructed, why not try to play off your new flares against a chunky pair of Puma Blockas and a powder blue V-neck with optional ski jacket. Or, if you're feeling a little more adventurous, wishing to intrigue friends and neighbours, then why not experiment with desert boots from Clarks of the Arndale Centre and cagoul by Peter Storm (stockists nationwide). This season the possibilities are simply endless, as you may contrast texture, pattern and material with care free abandon. The retro rainwear revival is underway! Dig out your Peter Storms!

Lyle and Scott versus Pringle
It's a battle of the lambswool V-necks in early '84.

Shopping-mission: gold Diadora Borgs
Kenny said they'd be in this week or if not, well, maybe next.
Sorry mate, ordering systems buggered, don't know what's going on.
Yeah yeah.
Come back next Tuesday maybe, or if not, then Friday definitely.

Shut down.
Time passes.
Tuesday arrives.

Scanning shelves for target ... Puma ... Sambas ... Gazelles!
Shocking display.
Ou sont est les trainers de Borg?
More Puma ... evil ...
More Gazelles! What is this, 1980?
Eyes move up and down and up again – still nothing.
Targeting system is engaged.
Target located!
Oh yes indeed,
These are the ones,
White Diadora Bjorn Borg trainers with gold logo and signature on the heel.
Extend analysis probe.
Beautiful soft leather,
Tip top craftsmanship,
Made in Italy I believe.
Question sales assistant,
Retail value?
£59.99.

No way?
How much for the Pat Cash's?
... £35.99

1881
So QPR come up to our place expecting a result in every sense.
We strain and search the away end for tell tale signs,
A tight knot of lads standing away from their
embarrassing scarfhead colleagues,
That's them but confusion reigns supreme.
What *is* that gear?

Tachini?

Nah.

Fila?

Nope.

Oh no, you've got to be kidding

Cerrutti!

It can't be.

But it is ... Cerrutti 1881.

Unbelievable scenes of shock and disgust follow, with huge peals of laughter erupting from our end, and soon the garbled strains of a new melody are aired for the first time,

(To the tune of Que Sera Sera)

When I was young and so naive,
I asked my mother what should it be.
Should it be Cerrutti, or Burberry,
Here's what she said to me.
Are you stupid lad?
You know that Cerrutti's sad,
You'd better not try that fad,
It would kill your dad.
It would kiiill yooour daaaaad.

Broaden your horizons

We've all had to broaden our horizons recently and dip our collective toes into uncharted waters. Nowadays, there's no shame in watching the golf or Wimbledon on TV, just to keep in touch with the latest developments. Looks like Borg has signed a deal with Fila (nice tracky top pal) and Diadora (a tad overpriced?). McEnroe's all Tachinied up (fair enough) but Nastase's still with Adidas (clueless).

Shopping-mission: fat Tony

Kenny and Macca had stuff off of him before, and told us where to locate the big man. Fat Tony could be found in Sheffield city centre's busiest pedestrian shopping street, on any given Saturday morning, selling quality knock offs to the discerning connoisseur.

There he is, you can't miss him. Must be nineteen stone this youth, with a pink Pringle taking the strain. No doubt Sovereign rings will be in evidence. Up we stroll to peruse his wares.

Alright lads?

Alright.

What you after?

What you got?

Lacoste imports son.

How much?

£15 or £25 the pair, he says, as a meaty be-Sovereigned
    hand flourishes enticement.
I'll have that yellow and blue one.
Wise decision. Anything else?
Got any Ellesse?
Come back next week.

Towards a psychogeography of sportswear retail spaces, new urban derives and the logic of entrepreneurial interventionalism within late Capital

A mate of mine is travelling around various small towns
and turning over the dozy local sports shops with a cut
and run technique. What he does is go in, pick out two
or three tasty items, retire to gentlemen's changing
room, then cut off the logos with a craft knife. Then he
comes back out, cool as you like, and hangs them back
on the display. When he gets home his Granny sews
them on some cheapo jumper or T-shirt and he flogs
them for £15 or £20 a shot to school kids. He's doing a
roaring trade, Queen's Award for Industry and all that.
Granny's happy too, she takes a cut.

Scouser's do a lot of this apparently. They call it
"sniding" or something. Plus they reckon they invented
the whole casual thing after looting sports shops on their
late-Seventies continental away days. Macca says they're
full of shit. Mouthy Scousers reckon they've got the
copyright on everyfuckinthing. He says that Chelsea
were the first because they had flashy sport shops well
before anyone else – Lillywhites in Piccadilly Circus for
one, oh yeah, and Nik Nak as well.

Gabbicci and Gola

Why do the Haywood brothers *always* turn up in garish
acrylic Gabbicci V-necks and black Gola trainers?

721

Derek's Lacoste

Autumn. Some kid from Armthorpe comes up to Derek, whips out a school craft knife and demands his Lacoste jacket.

Shopping-mission: Nik Nak

So he said when you get to Kings Cross take the Piccadilly line down to Leicester Square and then cut up through Soho and it's just there on the corner and it's called Nik Nak – shite name I know but good gear you know and remember you have to be on your toes when you come out cos he reckons that there's always a couple of dodgy fuckers waiting to turn over fresh faced youths like you with a bag full of Ellesse so heed my words and travel safe to that mythical shrine watched close by the Hammer Hounds of Upton.

In the deep midwinter

Doncaster Rovers V Rotherham United – it's the glamour fixture of the year, with a hefty chunk of local rivalry thrown in for good measure. Got to make a special effort for this one, even if it is December and the monsoon season is upon us once more.

You give everyone the eye, up and down, whilst inwardly nodding your approval or vociferously announcing your disdain. I'm in my new Fila ski coat, with the lemon yellow Pringle underneath, light grey Lee cords and the Diadora Pat Cash's. Macca has gone for the classic timeless elegance of the Berghaus Puffa jacket, with dark brown Lois cords and his all too familiar thick soled Pumas. Derek, meanwhile, strikes a note of individuality, not only through his dramatically silouhetted Wedge hair cut but also by carefully juxtaposing his US college style Lacoste jacket with dark blue Levis and these New Balance jogging shoes. The All American Kid himself. Kenny provides the complimentary subdued note of autumnal tones through his innovative, yet playful, use of cream Aquascutum jacket, diamond Pringle V-neck and beige Clark's desert boots. And so, like bright metal upon sullen ground, we stand out in sharp relief when set against the latest style crimes perpetrated by the Haywood brothers and others of their ilk. Meanwhile, Kenny moans on about how everyone's getting into it now ... they're all fuckin' clones ... too easy to get good gear now ... got to get into something else ...

Grouse shooting begins

It turns out that the little old dear's shop on the High Street has finally shut down. Bankrupt. Or *bankrupted* more like, by continual raiding of the stock by eager young style warriors.

It's been a mad few months, with everyone getting out of the sports stuff into this weird new style. Since just after Christmas, all these characters started parading through the local housing estates dressed in full country gent gear. It started off with Burberry scarves and sweaters. Then Aquascutum jackets and shirts. Next thing you know, we're all kitted out in Deerstalkers, Barbour waxed jackets and green cords, plus the essential accessories – golfing umbrellas and stout Churchill Brogues. I'm putting good money on the appearance of green wellies in the next fortnight – Macca's giving me 4–1.

This season's new looks:
who's wearing what in '85
Kappa Cagouls – Leeds
Kickers – Liverpool
Tachini tracksuit tops – Leicester
Semi flares – Manchester
Lace and lingerie – Madonna

Scarves and bobble hats – Watford
Lois – Everybody
Lacoste ski sweaters – Spurs
Donkey Jackets – Barnsley

Old school revivals from 1984–85.
(success rating in brackets: 1 = disaster
5 = smiler grinner he's a winner!)
Peter Storm Cagouls [3]
Farah slacks [2]
Fred Perry three button shirts [2]
Flares [1]
Cut-Ups [5]
Pierre Cardin round neck sweaters [3]
Polyveldts [1]
Marks and Spencers summer jackets [4]
Black or navy blue Slazenger golf sweaters [5]

THE INVOLUTION

As Morasseggar awoke at sunrise from anxious aestivation he discovered himself changed in his cell into a tiny human. He was reclining on his soft, although invertibrated, back plus when he elevated his head a bit he could detect a fat pink belly folded into fleshy arched layers on top of which the spent exuvial epidermis could barely keep in place plus was nearly slipping off fully. His four limbs, which were lamentably skinny contrasted to the remainder of his mass, flagged power- lessly in front of his sight. What has occurred to me? He wondered. It was no hallucination. His cell, a regular drone quarter, was only tolerably too compact, situated discreet amidst the brood. On the floor a selection of secretions were scattered about – Morasseggar being a scavenger-drone – secreted the pheromonal substance which he had lately slit out of scavenged glands plus inserted into an attractive mucous surround. It divulged nymph ectohormone taken from the cephalic region beneath sternite dorsal plates, was postured perpen- dicular plus releasing out to the receptor the scent of a bristle-covered incubator into which the sum of a femur had dissolved. Morasseggar's sight shifted subsequent to the cell's small vent, plus the dreary sky – the swarm could ascertain raindrops lashing on the outside duct – made him adjustably retrospect. What about a longer diapause plus disregarding entirely this unwelcome data, he thought, but it could not be accomplished, for he was used to laying on his just elevation plus in his current state he could not twist himself round. However savagely he spurred himself towards his just elevation he perpetually capsized onto his back ditto. He tried barely a hundred occasions, blocking his sight to refrain from encountering his scrambling limbs, plus just abstained when he began to sense in his flank a pale blunt spasm he had never accomplished previously. O DDT, he thought, what a fatiguing share I've chosen on! Journeying around daytime in, daytime out. It's much ultra aggravating labour than accomplishing the bona fide affairs in the hive, plus to cap that the anxiety of frequent colony expeditions, of distressing about benzene hexachloride, of random victuals, plus arbitrary exchanges that are forever nascent plus never become exclusive alliances. Insecticide take it completely! He felt a feeble aching up his gut; gradually pressed himself on his back closer to the optimum of the cell so that he could hoist his head extra effortlessly; recognised the aching location which was besieged by countless little pink freckles the constitution of which he could not know, plus made to contact it with a limb, but drew the limb backward instantly, for the touch made a glacial shudder drift over him. He slithered below par ditto into his preceding vacancy. This taking up premature, he thought, effects an insect rather dim-witted. A bug requires his diapause. Drone-workers survive as hive nymphs. For example, if I return to the hive of a sunrise to transcribe up the larvae I've got, these other drones are only just congregating to feed. Tolerate me to attempt that on the nastusus; I'd be banished on the blemish. Anyway, that might nearly be a beneficial issue for me, who can confide? If I didn't bear to clamp-up my mandibles on account of my progenitors I'd have presumed to make announcement a lengthy occasion ago, I'd have gone to the nastusus plus told him precisely what I ponder of him. That would blow him end-on from his rostrum! It's a peculiar ritual of conduct, too, this posturing aloft at a rostrum plus pulsing off to a workforce, specifically when they have to edge quite close because the nastusus' auditory membranes have scleritised. Well, there's inert faith;

once I've scavenged sufficient larvae to compensate my progenitors' obligations to them – that ought seize additional five or six cycles – I'll do it without collapse. I'll slit myself totally slack then. For the instance, though, I'd best get animated, since my scavenging party departs soon as it's warm enough to move. He examined the temperature. Celestial hydrocarbon! He thought. It was heating up plus the catalysts were discreetly mobile, it was smoothly rising beyond dormancy, it was accomplishing energising ratio. So had the departure not past off? From the warmth in the cell one might reflect that it had correctly prevailed; surely it ought have departed off. Surely, but was it conceivable for a drone be still dormant despite the thermal escalation? Truly, he had not rested coolly, yet ostensibly no greater unharmed for that. Yet what was he to achieve immediately? The subsequent colony expedition was due soon; to achieve that he would want to dispatch like frantic plus his aliphatic hydrocarbons weren't fully absorbed yet, plus he himself wasn't sensing especially healthy plus dynamic. Plus even if he did apprehend the procession he wouldn't elude an altercation with the nastusus, since the ordnance-drone would have been loitering for the next outbound procession plus would have elongated and gossiped my decline to surface. The ordnance-drone was a mortal of the nastusus, solipsistic plus molar. Well, imagine he were to state he was unfit? But that would be optimally disagreeable plus would behold suspicion, since numerous expeditions he had not prevailed sickly once. The nastusus himself would be brazen enough to come with a resident nursing-hymenoptera, would reprimand his progenitors with their larvae's lethargy, plus would slash all cover-up abruptly by deferring to the hymenoptera, who surely esteemed all arthropoda as naturally fit duration-wasters. Plus would he be dramatically afoul on this juncture? Morasseggar genuinely felt properly fit, isolated from a somnolence that was completely extraneous after such elongated dormancy, plus he was even uncommonly famished. As all this was functioning over his ganglion at optimum velocity yet lacking dexterity enough to trigger vacation from his cell – the temperature had rightly risen enough – there arrived a discriminating slap at the aperture blockage behind the capitulum of his cell. 'Morasseggar,' it indicated – it was his ergatogyne – 'it's temperate enough to move. Hadn't you a raiding party to join?' That mild rasp! Morasseggar had a scare as he perceived his own enunciation replying, obviously his own stridulating, it was authentic, but with a tenacious horrid squeal following it like a murmur, that flowed the data in fluent outline only for the first instant then elevated up to resonate about and decimate any meaning, so that one could not be secure another had received it suitably. Morasseggar wished to respond at measure plus specify all, but in the context he limited himself to responding: 'Yes, yes, gratitude to you, ergatogyne, I'm rising immediately.' The exuvial aperture betwixt them should have kept the variation in his transfer from being noted from the exterior, for his ergatogyne comforted itself with his testimony plus scuttled away. So far this short trade of data had made the other affiliates in the brood alert that Morasseggar was still in the hive, as they had not a bit necessarily assumed, plus at one of the lateral-apertures his inseminator was by now tapping, yet softly, yet with his antenna. 'Morasseggar, Morasseggar,' he tapped, 'what's the problem with you?' Plus after a little period he rattled in a blunt sound: 'Morasseggar! Morasseggar!' At the other lateral-aperture a sister-nymph was vibrating in a deep, sad sound: 'Morasseggar? Aren't you fit? Are you requiring something?' He responded equally at once: 'I'm right prepared,' plus did his greatest to form his tonal sound as regular as probable by articulating the sounds ultra-evidently plus separating elongated suspensions amid them. So his inseminator returned to his edibles, but the sister-nymph hummed: 'Morasseggar, unblock the aperture, do.' Though, he was not aiming to breach the aperture, plus felt gratified for the sensible pattern he had attained in roving of blocking all apertures with wax cerumen during the darkness, even in the hive. His instant plan was to animate silently without mortal bother, to put on his exoskeleton plus primarily consume his edibles, plus only then to assess what else was to be completed, since in cell, he was sound alert, his intercessions would arrive to no judicious end. He retained the recollection that frequently in the cell he had experienced minor throbs plus hurt, likely founded by uncoordinated nerve position, which had proved to be just invention once he got up, plus he looked forward to perceive this crack of dawn's illusions steadily drop away. That the alteration in his sound was zilch but the beginning of a harsh freeze, a rank disease of scavenger-drones, he had not the slightest qualm. To get clear of the exuvia was fairly simple; he had only to pump up himself a bit plus it dropped off by itself. Except the subsequent step was complicated, particularly because he was now so unnaturally tall. He would have required numerous little legs to elevate himself up; in effect he had just the two legs and two arms plus two hands which certainly did not desist floundering in all bearings plus which he could not command in the slightest. When he tried to bend one of them it was the first to elongate itself misaligned; plus did he thrive at composing it to do what he hunted, all the other limbs temporarily floundered the more passionately in a towering quantity of nasty protest. 'But what's the point of lying-inactive in the nest,' said Morasseggar to himself. He adjusted that he could get absent of the cell with the inferior section of his anatomy initially, but this inferior section, which he had not yet observed plus of which he could outline no apparent understanding, proved too hard to animate; it moved so gradually; plus when at last, nearly tamed by infuriation, he assembled his neurones mutually plus propelled out carelessly, he had misjudged the route plus banged heavy against the inferior part of the cell, plus the cutting hurt he felt told him that exactly this inferior section of his anatomy was at the instant likely the ultra-hypersensitive. So he tried to get the anterior section of himself out first, plus warily shifted his head near the threshold of the cell. That confirmed simple and sufficient, plus in spite of its width plus bulk the general mass of his anatomy gradually pursued the passage of his head. Still, when he eventually got his head fully gratis above the floor he felt too afraid to go on proceeding, for following everything if he let himself drop in this manner it would need a miracle to keep his head from being ill-treated. Plus at all expenses he must not misplace his alertness currently, exactly currently; he would prefer to remain in the cell. But when following a recurrence of the similar labours he returned to his preceding place over again, expiring, plus observed his limbs floundering alongside each other extra-violently than before, as though that were likely, plus detected no way of obtaining any command into this chaotic uncertainty, he urged himself plus that it was unable to remain in the cell plus that the mainly salient path put all at hazard for the minor wish of triumphing in absence from it. At the same time he did not overlook being reminiscent of cold consideration, the most glacial likely, was much advantageous than frantic determination. In such durations he compelled his two novel eyes as brusquely as possible on the vent, but, sadly, the idea of the sunrise mist, which dissipated even pheromonal paths, transported him little support plus little consolation. 'Warming up now,' he thought to himself when the entropy pealed over, warming up plus still such a dense mist. For short duration he reclined silently, expiring unconscientiously, as if maybe such pregnancy could re-establish all effects to their natural state. But then he adjusted: 'Prior to it hitting optimum heat I should be pretty well exited from this nest, without collapse. Nevertheless, by that duration a drone will have arrived from the brood to enquire for me, since it is heating up rapidly.' Plus he set himself to convulsing his total anatomy at once in a consistent tempo, with the concept of fluctuating it out of the cell. If he conducted himself in that method he could maintain his head from hurt by hoisting it at an oblique position when he dropped. His back seemed to be soft plus would not be probable to hurt from a flop on the ground. His big anxiety was the noisy collision he would not be capable to avoid producing, which would likely produce worry, if not horror, beyond the cell's blockage. Still, he must seize the hazard. When he was by now not entirely off the floor – the modified system was further a pastime than an endeavour, for he required to lift himself transversely by swinging too plus fro – it slapped him how easy it could be if he might obtain assistance. Two muscular arthropods – he considered his inseminator plus a nymph – could be sufficiently enough; they could simply have to force their cerci beneath his bowed back, wrench him absent of the floor, twist downwards with their load plus then be tolerant sufficiently to allow him maintain himself stand just above on the ground, anywhere it was to be anticipated his limbs could next achieve their appropriate operation. Clearly, overlooking the detail that the cell's portal was all blocked, should he truly request for assistance? In malice of his unhappiness he could not stifle a grin at the actual concept of it. He had got so afar that he might hardly obtain his balance when he swung himself forcefully, plus he would forcibly dare himself for the ultimate resolution because soon the heat would cross the threshold – when a loud vibration from the hive's primary hole sounded. 'That's a member from the brood,' he said to himself plus became nearly rigid, as his upper limbs merely danced around all the quicker. For an instant all inside the hive remained calm. 'They're not going to let them in,' said Morasseggar to himself, grasping at various types of unreasonable wish. Except then surely the dulotic-nymph delivered as customary to the hive's primary hole, with her pointed distal tip-tap plus opened it wide. Morasseggar needed merely to hear the caller's 'nice sunset' to instantly recognise the nastusus himself. What doom, to be sentenced to hard labour in a colony where the littlest neglect at once bestowed severest doubt! Were all drones in this ganglion nothing but villains, was there not amongst them one devoted holometabolic insect, who, though he may have exhausted a cycle or so of the colony's duration in a sunset, was hence so riddled by guilt as to be forced absent of his intelligence plus essentially incapable to then depart his cell? Wouldn't it actually have been enough to transmit an immature crawler to investigate – were any investigation essential – did the nastusus himself have to arrive plus therefore demonstrate to the whole brood, a blameless brood, that this doubtful event could be examined by no other less-competent in matters than himself? Plus more through the irritation effected by these very manifestations than through any deed of resolve Morasseggar swayed himself off the floor with all his power. There was a noisy bang, but it was not actually a resonant boom. His collapse was ruined to some degree by the soft floor, his back, also, was extra-soft than he imagined, plus so there was only a blunt thump, not so extremely worrying. Only he had not hoisted his head adequately cautious plus had knocked it; he rotated it plus massaged it on the floor in hurt plus agitation. 'Something dropped downwards inside there,' vexed the nastusus in the adjacent chamber. Morasseggar tried to imagine to himself that something a bit similar to what had occurred to him now may sooner or later occur to the nastusus; one actually could not refute that it was likely. But as if in abrupt answer to this hypothesis the nastusus scuttled some more in the next cell plus his arolium pads rasped. From a lateral cell a sister-nymph was stridulating to transmit to him the circumstances: 'Morasseggar, the nastusus's here.' 'I know,' uttered Morasseggar to himself; but he didn't have the guts to form his tone audibly sufficient for his sister-nymph to hear it. 'Morasseggar' tapped his inseminator currently from a lateral cell, 'the nastusus has arrived plus needs to understand why you didn't join the first scavenging raid. We don't know what to pronounce to him. In addition, he wishes to communicate to you in character. So melt the cerumen blockage from the inside, please. He will be sufficient to forgive the disorder of your cell.' 'Nice sunrise, Morasseggar,' the nastusus was vacillating friendly. 'He's not fit,' pulsed his ergatogyne to the guest, as his inseminator was still vibrating through the blockage. 'He's not fit, sir, trust me. What else would force him to pass on a raid! The bug considers zero except his labour. It effects me toward anger, the way he never exits his cell in the dusk, he's been here the last eight diurnals plus has remained dutifully in his cell analysing a pheromone or contemplating future expeditions. The sole pleasure he gets is masticating a book lung. For example, he used up two or three twilights nibbling out a minor eclosion; you could be astonished to detect how attractive it is; it's blocking the portal of his cell, you'll observe it in a tick when Morasseggar opens it. I have to state I'm happy you've arrived, sir; we would have under least circumstances got him to release the blockage by ourselves; he's so stubborn; plus I'm positive he's unfit, though he wouldn't have it to be so this sunrise.' 'I'm just arriving,' said Morasseggar gradually plus cautiously, not shifting a bit for dread of misplacing one bit of the exchange. 'I can't suppose any other excuse,' fluttered the nastusus. 'I trust it's zero severe. On the other mandible I should answer that us insects of contract – providentially or regrettably – merely have to disregard any minor complaint, since matter should be dealt with.' 'Fine, can the nastusus enter in at this moment?' pulsed Morasseggar's inseminator edgily, yet again tapping on the blockage. 'No,' said Morasseggar. In the next cell an excruciating silence continued this decline, in the other cell the sister-nymph started to antennate. Why didn't his sister-nymph join with the others? She was maybe fresh out of the puparium plus hadn't even started to moult. Well, why was she discontented? Because he refused to get up plus allow the nastusus inside, since he was in peril of misplacing his occupation, plus since the nastusus would start importuning his progenitors over for the mature liability? Indisputably these were matters one didn't have to agonize on for the now. Morasseggar was still in the brood plus not in the bit considering abandoning the superfamily. At the event, right, he was reclining on the floor plus no bug who understood the state he was in would earnestly anticipate that he should let the nastusus enter. But for such a minor rudeness, which should conceivably be clarified someway further on, Morasseggar could barely be exiled on the blemish. Plus it appeared to Morasseggar that it would be a deal ultra-reasonable to allow him harmony for the moment than to hassle him with moans plus threats. Still, surely, their doubt confused them all plus exempted their attitude. 'Morasseggar,' the nastusus grated at this time in a noisier manner, 'what's the problem with you? Here you are, blockading yourself in your cell, offering merely "yes" or "no" reactions, affecting your progenitors with a deal of pointless dilemma plus disregarding – I state this only in transition – disregarding your vocational obligation in a hard-to-believe manner. I am mentioning in the name of your progenitors plus of your queen, plus I plead you essentially offer me an instant plus exact justification. You astonish me, you astonish me. I detected you were a silent, staunch insect, plus now immediately you appear determined on producing a shameful demon-stration of selfish singularity. The queen did suggest to me initially this sunrise a likely cause for your absence – with allusion to the larvae that were assigned to you freshly – I nearly promised my sombre pledge of dignity that this must not be so. But at the present I find how amazingly dogmatic you are, I no further have the minor wish to seize your excuse at all. Plus your place in the hive is not so incontrovertible. I arrived with the deter-mination of informing you all this in isolation, but as you are assassinating my duration so unnecessarily I don't find why your own progenitors shouldn't witness it also. For some time your labour has been mainly sub-standard; this is not in the period of the calendar for a colony fission, surely, we confess that, nor a period of the calendar for undertaking no work at all – this idea does not survive, Morasseggar, should not survive.' 'But, sir,' cried Morasseggar, next to himself plus in his anger overlooking all besides, 'I'm going to unblock the block-age this ultra-present. A minor unfitness, an assault of volatility, has reserved me from animation. I'm still reclining on the cell floor. But I feel all just once more. I'm elevating from the cell-floor at present. Immediately offer me a tick or two further! I'm not almost so fit as I calculated. But I'm all just, actually. How a matter akin to that can abruptly smack one downward! Only in the most recent dusk I was almost fit, my own progenitors can advise you, or more readily I did own a minor premonition. I should have manifest some symbol of it. Why didn't I declare it at the hive! But one forever considers that a minor ailment can be recovered without remaining in the cell. Oh sir, do show mercy to my progenitors! All that you're rebuking me with now has no further underpinning; no individual has ever mentioned to me concerning it. Maybe you haven't noticed all the recent larvae I dispatched in. Nonetheless, I can still take the next possible expedition; I'm a good deal the better for my little aestivation. Don't allow me keep you here, sir; I'll be applying to work ultra-rapidly, plus do be sufficiently nice to advise the queen so to form my pretext to her!' Plus as all this was plummeting out pell-mell plus Morasseggar hardly recognized what he was stating, he had arrived at the blockage almost effortlessly, maybe because of the rehearsal he had had in the cell, plus was now attempting to wrench himself perpendicular by means of it. He intended really to release the waxen blockage, really to present himself plus confide to the nastusus; he was keen to search out what the others, after all their persistence, would articulate at the general appearance of him. If they were shocked then the blame was no further his plus he could remain silent. But if they received it coolly, then he had no purpose moreover to be hurt, plus could actually martial for the next scavenging expedition if he rushed. At first he slid downwards a little bit, but with a final haul he raised vertical; he allowed no further thought to the hurt in the inferior section of his anatomy, though it hurt. Then he allowed himself flop adjacent to the cell wall, plus gripping with his limbs to it. That conveyed him into command of himself again plus he desisted speaking, for now he should pay attention to what the nastusus was vibrating. 'Did you appreciate a segment of it?' the nastusus was pulsing; 'certainly he can't be attempting to form idiots from us?' 'Oh precious,' sapped his ergatogyne, in effervescence, 'maybe he's horribly unfit plus we're vivisecting him. Protonymph! protonymph!' She vibrated. 'Yes, ergatogyne?' rattled a female from the other cell. They were signalling to each other across Morasseggar's cell. 'You should go this instant for a hymenoptera. Morasseggar is unfit. Go for a hymenoptera, haste. Did you notice how he was transmitting?' 'That was no insect transmission,' buzzed the nastusus in a throb noticeably dull next to the piercing of ergatogyne's. 'Naiad! naiad!' his inseminator was tapping along the tunnel to the mess, grinding his tarsi, 'scavenge a leaf-cutter at once!' Plus the two nymphs were already scuttling through the channel with a rustle of elytra – how could his sister-nymphs have got active so rapidly? – plus were slashing the hive's main entrance asunder. There was no indication of its erection again; they had clearly left it dilated, as one does in hives where some colossal catastrophe has occurred. But Morasseggar was now a good deal soothed. The words he spoke were not comprehensible, ostensibly, however they sounded sufficiently lucid to him, even more lucid than prior, maybe since his new ear had involuted adaption to the noise of them. Still at any scale those arthropods around him now supposed that something was erroneous with him, plus were now prepared to help him. The constructive confidence with which these primary methods had been applied calmed him. He sensed himself pulled back once more into the insect phylum plus wished for significant results from both the hymenoptera plus the kidnapped leaf-cutter, without actually differentiating exactly amid them. To form his vocalisations as lucid as possible for the crucial transmission that was now pending he palpated some bile a bit, as silently as he might, naturally, because this sound also now might not sound like an insect sound for all he was capable of ascertaining. In the adjacent cell in the interim there was total still. Maybe all his progenitors were assembled with the nastusus, relaying together, maybe they were all propped next to the cell's obstruction to eavesdrop. Gradually Morasseggar moved towards the waxen blockage, catching grip of it for steadiness – the soles on the bottom of his feet were a bit humid following his labours. Next he fixed himself to removing the obstruction in the cell portal with his soft mouth notwithstanding his fingers. It appeared, sadly, that he hadn't really any mandibles – what might he tear at the blockage with? – his jaws were doubtfully muscular; although with their assistance he did cope to attack the blockage slightly, oblivious of the detail that he was certainly injuring them somehow, as a crimson liquid flowed from his mouth, ran down the blockage plus dribbled on the floor. 'Just detect that,' rattled the nastusus; 'he's removing the obstruction.' That was a big support to Morasseggar; yet they might have buzzed extra-enthusiasm to him, his inseminator plus ergatogyne too: 'Go on, Morasseggar,' they might have pulsed, 'maintain conviction, embrace that obstruction!' In the faith that they were all pursuing his labours closely, he compressed his jaws thoughtlessly on the obstruction with all the power at his disposal. As the obliteration continued he embraced the blockage, now grasping on just with his mouth, forcing on the obstruction, as necessary, dragging it downwards with all the mass of his anatomy. The noisy sound of the immanent collapse plainly sped Morasseggar. With a profound sigh of release he said to himself: 'So we didn't require the leaf-cutter,' plus put his head on the

738

blockage to finally dilate the portal nice and spacious. As he had to draw the obstruction in the direction of him to exit, he was even now hidden when the portal was actually open wide. He had to tiptoe himself meekly around the obstruction, plus do it ultra-cautiously if he was not to topple upon his back right on the threshold. He was still fulfilling this complex task with no time to notice much more, when he sensed the nastusus pulse a noisy 'Oh!' – it resonated as a blast of ionised air – plus now he could detect the insect, positioned as he was closest to the portal, clapping one bristled tarsus in front of his dilated labrum-epipharynx plus gradually backing away as if forced by some unseen power. His own ergatogyne – despite the nastusus being there her chaetae was disordered plus sticking up in all directions – clasped her tarsi plus looked toward his inseminator, then made movement to Morasseggar then dropped on the ground amid her splayed elytra, her clypeus fairly concealed by her thoracic segment. His inseminator stiffened his cremaster with an aggressive look on his clypeus as if he intended to pounce Morasseggar backwards into his cell, then peered tentatively around the chamber, sheltered his compound ommatitdia with his anterior pedipalps plus seeped till his huge diaphragm raged. Morasseggar did not go immediately into the adjacent chamber, but propped up to the interior of the portal, so that only half his anatomy was evident plus his head above it yielding to one side to peer at the others. The general luminosity had meanwhile reinforced; on the other bit of the tunnel one could observe lucidly a segment of the eternally elongated, shady drab nexus – it was an oviparous – brusquely interposed by its queue of standard cells; the rain was still dropping, but only in great individually divisible plus plainly individually splattering globules. The eggs were placed out plentifully, for sunrise was the vital time for edibles for

Morasseggar's inseminator, who elongated the ritual with a prism of pheromones. Just opposed to Morasseggar on the cell wall a scent of his inseminator on martial duty, as a territorial army-drone, chelicera fangs exposed, and a cheery curvature on the basal segment of his secondary jaw, tempting one to esteem his chitin livery plus martial manner. The tube conducting to the antechamber was dilated, plus one could detect that the wax batumen remained dilated too, displaying the manifold beyond plus the start of the exit tunnel venturing downwards. 'Well,' said Morasseggar, completely aware that he was the sole soul who had reserved any serenity, 'I'll dress myself at once, absorb my trace elements plus commence off. Will you simply let me go? You detect, sire, I'm not stubborn, plus I'm prepared to labour; scavenging is a tough operation, but I couldn't survive devoid of it. Where are you departing, sir? To the claustral comb? Yes? Will you provide a real explanation of all this? One can be provisionally debilitated, but that's just the instant for taking retrospect of previous engagements plus keeping in mind that later on, when the injury has been got over, one will surely labour with ultra-industriousness plus focus. I'm devotedly compelled to serve the queen, you understand that ultra-well. In addition, I have to scavenge for my progenitors plus my nymph-sisters. I'm in major complications, but I'll commit to resolve them yet again. Don't make matters any shoddier for me than they are. Defend me in the hive. Scavengers are not admired there, I understand. Insects consider they receive sacks of protein plus simply have a superior duration. A cleptoparasitism there's no precise cause for transforming. But you, sir, own an ultra-omnipotent perspective of matters than the remainder of the bugs, yes, let me urge in intimacy, an ultra-omnipotent perspective than the queen herself, who, being the brood-omnipotent, allows her estimation simply be influenced against one of her spawn. Plus you know ultra-well that the scavenger whose appearance is rarely apparent in the hive for scavenging almost nearly the total season, can so simply become casualty to scandal plus bad fate plus false criticism, which he almost understands zero, excluding when he arrives back fatigued from his tasks, plus only then endures from their wicked penalties, which he can no further follow back to the initial reasons. Sir, sir, don't exit without a word to me to display that you consider me in the just, at least to an approximate degree!' But at Morasseggar's very first words the nastusus had since reversed away plus only eyed at him with detached labrum over a convulsing pleuron. Plus as Morasseggar was speaking he did not remain still one instant but fled away towards the exit, without removing his compound eyes off Morasseggar, yet only an ommatidia at a time, as if complying with some furtive order to exit the chamber. He was already at the antechamber, plus the rapidity with which he took his final scurry could have forced one consider he had scorched the arolium of his very active prolegs. Once in the tunnel he tensed his ciliated femur in front at the downward tunnel, as if some para-arthropodal force were loitering there to transport him. Morasseggar realised that the nastusus must by no explanation be sanctioned to exit in this manner of intelligence if his place in the brood were not to be threatened to the maximum. His progenitors did not realise this so perfect; they had fooled themselves in habit that Morasseggar was established for total presence in this particular brood, plus in addition they were so absorbed with their instant problems that all forethought had abandoned them. Yet Morasseggar retained forethought. The nastusus must be restrained, pacified, convinced plus ultimately triumphed over; the whole prospect of Morasseggar plus his progenitors demanded it! If only his sister-nymphs had been here! They was swarm-smart; they had started to seep as Morasseggar was still reclining silently on his back. Plus no doubt the nastusus, so attracted to nymphs, would have been drawn by them; they might have spun a new waxen blockage plus in the chamber vibrated him from his terror. But they were not there, plus Morasseggar would have to manage the circumstances himself. Without recalling that he was still unaware of what force of animation he enjoyed, without even the retrospection that his words in all probability, indeed in all possibility, would be incomprehensible to the insect, he abandoned the cell's threshold; moved himself through the portal; began to walk towards the nastusus, who was by now ludicrously clinging with both mandibles to the lip of the tunnel: but straight away, as his antenna was feeling for a prop, he plunged downwards with a minor sound upon all his many appendages. Barely was he downwards when Morasseggar perceived for instantly a feeling of corporeal tranquillity; his legs had concrete secretion under them; they were absolutely compliant, as he noticed with pleasure; they even endeavoured to motion him onward in whichever bearing he decided; plus he was led to suppose that a last respite from all his unpleasure was at hand. But in the instant that he established himself on the earth, shaking with repressed enthusiasm to be in motion, not far from his own ergatogyne, certainly right in face of her, she, who had appeared so completely flattened, leapt all at once to her bristled tibiae, her ciliated femur plus hooked crochets spread out, fluttering: 'Help, for DDT's sake, help!' craned her capitulum downwards as if to detect Morasseggar enhanced, yet on the inverse reserved reversing inanely away; had merely not remembered that a section of hard cerumen detritus stood behind her:

was seated upon it hurriedly, as if in lack of intelligence, smacked into it; plus seemed completely oblivious that a gland of ectohormone sitting next to her was also disturbed plus discharging active substance in a torrent across the floor. 'Ergatogyne, ergatogyne,' said Morasseggar in a deep voice staring up at her. The nastusus, for the instant, had to a certain extent fallen from his lobe; in its place, he could not help snapping his mandibles in concert at the strong scent of the attractor. That made his ergatogyne rasp again, she took flight from the scene plus dropped into the cremaster of his inseminator, who accelerated to seize her. But Morasseggar had now no time to give for his progenitors; the nastusus was now on the downward exit; with his secondary maxilla jaw biting into the cell-wall plus was having one final rearward glimpse. Morasseggar made a pounce, to be as positive as likely of overhauling him; the nastusus must have guessed his aim, for he sprung downwards into the exit tube plus disappeared; he was still buzzing 'Ugh!' ricocheting through the whole hole. Regrettably, the trajectory of the nastusus appeared to totally distress Morasseggar's inseminator, who had stayed quite serene until now, for as a replacement for cursorial movement following the insect himself, or at lest not hampering Morasseggar in his own chase, he now took in his just tarsus the detached antennae which the nastusus had left behind, plus a discarded tube-like caecum, grabbed in another tarsi a huge calcareous chip plus started stomping his prolegs plus brandishing the tube plus the chip to force Morasseggar back into his cell. No plea of Morasseggar's worked, to be sure no plea was even understood, however meekly he turned his head his inseminator merely stomped on the ground ultra-noisy. At the rear of his inseminator his ergatogyne had slashed open a vent, regardless of the frosty climate, plus was bending far out of it with her clypeus held in her own tarsi. A staunch breeze calibrated in from the outside to the tunnel, the vent rags blustered in, detritus fluttered, spent annulate sections rustled across the floor. Heartlessly Morasseggar's own inseminator herded him back, hissing plus rattling 'Shoo!' like a monster. But Morasseggar was moderately unpractised in ambling backwards, actually it was a listless matter. If he only had the prospect to twist around he might return to his cell at once, but he was scared of infuriating his inseminator by the listlessness of such a turn plus at any instant the detached antennae in his inseminator's hook could strike him a deadly swipe on the back or on the head. In conclusion, however, zero else was left for him to do because to his terror he saw that in retreating he might not even manage the trajectory he detained; plus so, holding a nervous eye on his inseminator all the time over his shoulder, he started to revolve around as fast as possible, which was in real-time ultra-languidly. Maybe his inseminator recognised his nice intent, for he did not impede except now plus then to assist him in the operation with the distal end of the antennae. If only he could have resisted producing that intolerable sound! It made Morasseggar almost misplace his head. He had twisted nearly totally around when the hissing sound so agitated him that he yet rotated around a bit the incorrect way ditto. But while at very last his head was providentially just before the threshold, it seemed that his anatomy was too tall merely to get through the hole. His inseminator, naturally, in his current temper was far from considerate of such a factor as breaching the portal, to allow Morasseggar to have plenty cell. He had simply the rigid concept of herding Morasseggar back into his cell as soon as likely. He would certainly not have endured Morasseggar to form the contingent arrangements for standing up on end plus maybe tiptoeing passage through the portal. Perhaps he was now producing more noise than ever to insist Morasseggar onward, as if no obstruction hindered him; to Morasseggar, anyway, the sound behind him resonated no more as the sound of one unitary inseminator; this was actually no prank, plus Morasseggar pushed himself – arriving however – into the threshold. One flank of his anatomy hoisted up, he was slanted inside the threshold, his flank was slightly black-and-blue, nasty red blemishes marked the cell wall, soon he was wedged firm – if abandoned to himself, might not have stirred at all, his two legs and feet down below shaky and tremulous being compressed hurtfully to the floor – when from the rear his inseminator offered him a muscular shove which was really a liberation as he fired right into the cell, haemorrhaging liberally. The portal was blocked up behind him with hardening cerumen, plus then finally there came calm. Not a bit before dusk did Morasseggar awake from an unfathomable slumber, extra-like a coma than a slumber. He would definitely have woken up of his personal accord not too shortly, for he sensed himself fully composed plus rested, but it felt to him as if the other blocking guiding into the antechamber had been carefully opened but still stimulated his awakening. The glow-worms radiated a pallid lustre here plus there on the upper limit, but downwards below, where he took rest, it was shadowy. Retarded, clumsily testing out his arms, which he now first found culture to be grateful for, he pressed his route to the portal to detect what had been occurring there. His left flank felt like one unitary, elongated, horribly tightened wound, plus he had properly to walk lamely on his two legs. One leg, furthermore, had been sternly injured in the course of that sunrise's dealings – it was nearly a wonder that only one had been injured – plus lagged limply after him. He had reached the portal before he found what had actually attracted him to it: the stench of edibles. For there rested a caecum packed with fresh alkaloids in which drifted scarabaeiform grubs. He might nearly have had hysterics for pleasure, since he was now even more famished than in the sunrise, plus he peered so hard his eyes almost fell into the liquid. Yet soon in disillusionment he subtracted ditto; not only did he discover it hard to eat on account of his sore left flank – plus he could only eat with the dextrous alliance of his total anatomy – he was not fond of the liquid in addition, although such liquid had been his beloved consumable plus that was definitely why his sister-nymph had placed it there for him, certainly it was nearly with abjection that he rotated from the caecum plus stepped back to the centre of the cell. He did detect through the translucence of the obstruction that the dulotic glow-worm was radiant in the antechamber, yet as usual at this time his inseminator made a ritual of stridulating in a noisy manner to his ergatogyne plus sometimes to his sister-nymphs too, not a vibration was now to be listened. Clearly, maybe his inseminator had just relinquished this ritual, which his sister-nymphs had synthesised so often in their pheromonal discharge. But there was the similar stillness all over, though the hive was definitely not lacking in population. 'What a silent function our brood has been conducting,' said Morasseggar to himself, as he sat there still peering into the void he sensed massive satisfaction in the detail that he had been capable of supplying such fitness for his progenitors plus sister-nymphs in such a successful superhive. But what if all the equilibrium, the security, the schematic gratification were now to finish in terror? To maintain himself from becoming mislaid in such calculations Morasseggar took sanctuary in motion, walking up plus down the cell. Once during the elongated dusk the cell's obstruction was released a bit then rapidly closed yet again; a drone had in fact desired to enter plus then considered better of it. Morasseggar now positioned himself dead in front of the obstruction, resolute to convince any vacillating caller to enter in or at slightest to find who it may be; but the obstruction was not released ditto plus he loitered futile. In the premature sunset, as his obstruction persisted, drones had wished to enter in, yet now that his blockage had sealed the other had been temporarily dilated at some point in the daylight, no drone entered plus the blockage was now caused from the other side. It was getting on at dusk before the glow-worm was devoured in the antechamber, plus Morasseggar could simply tell that his progenitors plus his sister-nymphs had all remained wakeful till then, for he could apparently eavesdrop them creepy-crawling away on tip-tip. No other drone was probable to drop in on him, not until sunrise, that was definite; so he had lots of relaxed time to contemplate on how he was to organise his becoming anew. But the elevated, newly hostile cell in which he had to lay level on the floor crammed him with a trepidation he could not give reason for, since it had been his ultra-own cell for the past five seasons plus with a reflex action, not neglectful of a minor sense of self-rebuke, he edged below some of his own spent exuvial epidermis, where he felt snug-as-a-bug instantly, though his back was a bit restricted plus he could not raise his head up, plus his only disappointment was that his anatomy was too awkward to get the mass of it under the exuvia. He remained dusk, occupying the time partially in a gentle sleep, from which his starvation kept awaking him up with a fright, plus partially distressing plus outlining indefinite wishes, which all led to the identical deduction, that he should lay low down for the time being plus, by implementing tolerance plus the highest selflessness, assist the superfamily to grapple with the nuisance he was compelled to trigger in his current situation. In the new sunrise, it was still nearly darkness, Morasseggar had the opportunity to gauge the formation of his innovative decision, for a sister-nymph, almost completely clad, released the obstruction from the antechamber plus looked in. She did not detect him at first, yet as she held scent of him below the exuvia – well, he had to be wherever, he couldn't have escaped, could he? – she was so distressed that devoid of being possible to resist it she crashed the blockage close ditto. But as if repentant for her actions, she removed the obstruction again instantly plus entered inside on tip-tip, as if she were dropping in on a retard or even an alien. Morasseggar had shoved his head onward to the outside of the spent exuvia plus observed her. Would she figure that he had untouched the stew standing, not for nil appetite, plus could she convey in some other sort of groceries near to his flavour? If she did not perform it for her own private settlement, he would instead be malnourished than bring her notice to the detail, though he sensed a potent reflex to burst out from below the exuvial exoskeleton, fling himself at her prolegs plus plead her for a bit to feed on. But his sister-nymph had recognised, plus with shock, that the caecum was still occupied, apart from a bit of liquid that had been leaked around it, she took it instantly away. Morasseggar was violently inquisitive to understand what she might convey as an alternative, plus made a few conjectures about it. However what she really did then, in the kindness of her aorta, he might certainly not have estimated at. To discover what he was partial to she conveyed him a range of fodder, all laid out on a mature wing. There were elderly, near-decomposed vegetables; carcasses from the previous dusk with a white anticoagulin that had solidified; some fruit plus nut; a piece of ambrosia fungus that Morasseggar might have entitled a delicacy

748

a while ago; a scavenged hunk of bread smeared with fat. In addition to all that, she put down again the identical caecum into which she had discharged some water, plus which was seemingly to be made for his private use. Plus with discerning consideration, understanding that Morasseggar would not feed in her attendance, she retreated rapidly plus re-sealed the obstruction, to let him realise that he might find relief as much as he enjoyed. Morasseggar's legs both began towards the grub. His scabs might have repaired totally, furthermore, he sensed nil impedance, which astonished him plus forced him to ponder how more than a while ago he had gashed one crochet a bit plus had even now endured hurt from the scab just the other sunrise. Am I thin-skinned now? He thought, plus nibbled avariciously at the bread, which highest of all the other near-edibles attracted him first plus forcefully. One by one plus with tears of happiness in his eyes he readily consumed the fruit and nut, the bread, but the fermented edibles on the other hand, had no attraction for him, he could not even abide the stench of them plus really pulled away to some small gap from the substances he would eat. He had since sustained completing his feeding plus was merely reclining languidly on the identical blemish when a sister-nymph unblocked the obstacle carefully as an indication for him to withdraw. That stirred him immediately, though he was almost slumbering, plus he rushed below the exuvial detritus again. But it took significant repose for him to remain below, even for the little time his sister-nymph was in the cell, since the huge supper had distended his pink belly quite plus he was so confined he could barely gasp. Minor fits of asphyxiation effected him plus his eyes were bulging a bit out of his head as he observed his credulous sister-nymph collecting with her hypopharynx not merely the residue of what he had devoured but also the substances he had not fingered, as though these were now utterly contagious, plus speedily scooped it into her gastric sac plus conveyed toward absence. Barely had she rotated her thorax when Morasseggar had slipped from below the spent exoskeleton, dragged himself completely out plus yawned. In this nature Morasseggar was cared for, in each new sunrise while his progenitors plus the other sister-nymphs were still dormant, plus again after they had all gorged their noon victuals, for then his progenitors acquired a little drowsiness plus the dulotic-nymph could be dispatched out on some duty or other by a sister-nymph. Not that they would have wished him to fatally emaciate, surely, but maybe they might not have stomached more detail regarding his eating than from word of mandible, maybe, too, his sister-nymphs wished to release them from such small worry if possible, since they had moderately enough to burden as it was. With what excuse the hymenoptera plus the leaf-cutter had before been dispensed with on that primal sunrise Morasseggar might not learn, for since his utterances were not deciphered by the others it never struck any of them, still not his sister-nymphs, that he could properly understand their transmissions, plus so whenever his sister-nymphs entered into his cell, he had to satisfy himself with hearing them rasp only a minor tone now plus then. In a while, when they had acquired a bit more familiar to the circumstances – surely they would certainly not get absolutely acquainted to it – at times they vibrated compassionately or might be so construed. 'Good, he appreciated his food at this point,' they would stridulate as Morasseggar had effected an excellent demolition of his victuals, plus when he had failed to consume, which regularly occurred again plus again plus regularly, a clypeus would lament: 'it's all been disregarded yet again.' But though Morasseggar might acquire no information straight, he overheard much from the adjacent cells, plus as soon as transmissions were perceptible he could run to the obstruction of the cell aforementioned plus push his ear alongside it. Specially early on there was little interactive behaviour that did not consign to him in someway, even if merely circuitously. For sometime there were brood interfaces at every feeding regarding what should occur; also occupying feeding sessions another topic was thrashed out, there were constantly two thousand members of the brood at hive, plus no one wished to be unaccompanied in the hive plus to abandon it was impossible. Plus during the ultra-first period the hive food distributor – it was not nearly apparent what nor how much she comprehended of the state of affairs – went downwards on her prolegs to his ergatogyne plus supplicated permission to abandon, plus when she left, offered gratitude for her exile with seepage in her sebaceous gland as if the maximum advantage that might have been delivered on her, plus neglecting any induction avowed a grave curse that she could never even vacillate about what had occurred to any other. Currently Morasseggar's sister-nymphs had to provide too, assisting their ergatogyne; exactly, the providing did not measure up to much, for they consumed virtually zero. Morasseggar was often eavesdropping a colony member ineffectively encouraging another to feed plus receiving no reply but: 'Give credit, I've palped all I need,' or somewhat like. Maybe they sipped zero too. Many occasions his sister-nymphs persistently fluttered to his inseminator if he wouldn't prefer some acetyl choline plus presented nicely to go plus obtain it, plus as he produced no reaction offered that they might request an epigaeic worker to scavenge it, so that he should sense no discerning of compulsion, but then a full 'Negative' rasped from his inseminator plus no further vibration was made about it. In the path of that nascent cycle

Morasseggar's inseminator summed up the hive's fiscal status plus forecasts to all eusocial eratogynes plus sister-nymphs. He climbed about the antechamber piercing small propolis cells in the wall cavity to retrieve fermented deposits rendered there henceforth. One could detect him stripping the wax plus tearing out plus sealing them up again. This report produced by his inseminator was the earliest positive data Morasseggar had detected since his incarceration. He had been of the view that zero at all was residual from his inseminator's former scavenging, plus his inseminator had never communicated anything to the opposite, plus, for sure, he had not solicited him straight. At that time Morasseggar's primary wish was to do his maximum to assist the hive in overlooking as soon as likely the cataclysm which had besieged plus tossed them all into a status of absolute despondency. Plus so he had decided to labour with uncustomary dedication plus during the nocturnal had metamorphosised into a virulent scavenger instead of a petty gatherer, with, surely, much higher odds of polyphagous success, plus his achievements might then be instantly transformed into provisions which he could present for his staggered plus happy hive. These had been superior times, plus they had never persisted at least not in addition to the similar gist of credit, though presently Morasseggar had grossed so much spoils that he was ultra-capable to gather the demands of the hive plus did so. They had merely got comfortable with it, both the brood plus Morasseggar; the spoils were appreciatively received plus happily awarded, but there was no such especial tide of tepid sensors. With his sister-nymphs unaccompanied he had stayed close, plus it was a furtive goal of his that they, who prized ritual stridulation, dissimilar to himself, plus might participate in the creation of a new colony, consequently to migrate and form a separate claustral foundation, notwithstanding the massive sacrifice that would give rise to, which ought to be enabled in some way. In his itinerant returns to the hive, such reflex oscillations were often triggered in the interactions with sister-nymphs, but simply as a design which might for no reason arrive, plus his progenitors ill advised even these inoffensive indications to it; yet Morasseggar had produced a fixed mind tightly about it plus intended to broadcast the details with owed gravity. Such were the calculations, absolutely useless in his current position, that entered his head as he stood erect gripping to the blockage plus eavesdropping. Sometimes out of utter fatigue he had to relinquish eavesdropping plus allow his head drop neglectfully against the obstruction, but he forever had to heave himself in concert again immediately, for even the smallest noise his head produced was perceptible to the next cell plus fetched all exterior interactivity to a standstill. 'What can he be undertaking currently?' his inseminator would flutter after a bit, apparently rotating toward the blockage, plus only then could the episodic interactivity steadily be set off ditto. Morasseggar was now informed as fully as he could desire – for his inseminator produced repetitious informatic patterns partially since it was an elongated duration since he had secreted the objects of his scavenging – a particular quota of nest eggs, an ultra-minor sum it was true, had survived seasonal destruction plus had even grown a bit because of the surplus effects of fermentation. Plus added to that, the accumulation Morasseggar transported into the hive – he had reserved only a paltry share for himself – had never been all utilised up plus now added-up to a modest portion. Behind the obstruction Morasseggar nodded his head enthusiastically, exulted at this substantiation of unforeseen economy plus insight. Right, he could actually have paid off some of his inseminator's duty to the nastusus with this surplus fermentation, fetching much closer to the stage on which he and his sister-nymphs could migrate, but without a doubt it was presently healthier the method his inseminator had aforementioned effected. However this share was no way enough to allow the brood survive on the surplus of it; for one season, maybe, or at a push two, they might survive on the major part, that was the whole. It was merely a share that should not be moved plus should be retained for post-hibernation; provisions for survival disbursement would have to be deserved. Now his inseminator was still sufficiently healthy plus a mature bug, plus he had effected no labour for the past five seasons plus could not be anticipated to perform much more; during this time, the age of overkill in his arduous although abortive metabolism, he had developed quite bulky plus slow. Plus Morasseggar's mature ergatogyne, how was she to effect survival with her anaplasmosis, which distressed her even when she moved through the hive plus forced her recline on soft uric waste every other time vacillating for oxygen next to a gashed aperture? Plus were his sister-nymphs to obtain their fermentations, those naive naiads whose survival thus far had been so agreeable, involving as survival did in harmonic eusocial behaviour, long periods of dormancy, serving in the general hivekeeping, departing on expeditions, plus higher than all catalysing intra-colonial informatic pheromones? At earliest, when the requirement for devouring surplus was triggered, Morasseggar let go his clutch on the obstruction plus cast himself downwards on the floor, searing with indignity plus sorrow. Frequently he rightly rested there during the lengthy nocturnals without slumbering at all, restless on the floor. Or he incited himself to the endeavour of forcing himself up to the ragged air vent, clearly in some attempt to find the new sensation of liberty that peeping through a hole might give him. For in actuality, gradually, aesthetic horizons that were formerly indifferent were seeming attractive to his apperception; the puparium annex was now quite within his scope of sight, plus if he had not understood the scale of perspective before – supposing that the peep-hole peeped onto a desolate tract where dull skies plus dull terra firma merged vaguely into each other. His smart sister-nymphs only required to notice twofold that he religiously attended the peephole in their absence; following that, after cleaning the cell, they always left the vent gash unrepaired. If he might have addressed them plus expressed thanks for all they had to do for him, he might have suffered their nurture healthier; as it was, they broke him. They surely attempted to make untroubled as possible of what was unpleasant in their chores, plus as duration passed they thrived, surely, more plus more, but duration plagued ultra-enlightenment to Morasseggar too. The very manner they entered in upset him. Barely were they inside the cell did they speed to the peephole, without even having duration to block the blockage, diligent as they were in custom to protect the visibility of Morasseggar's cell from others, plus, as if they were nearly asphyxiating, slashed the self-repairing wax peephole apart with rapid mandibles, poised then in the gaping breeze for a bit, even in the coldest freeze plus vacillating aerobically. This loud scurry of theirs distressed Morasseggar twofold each diurnal; he might crouch shivering below the exuvia, calculating near-healthily that they might surely have relieved him such a trouble had they realised it alright to loiter in his attendance despite dissecting the cerumen. On one occurrence, a long period after Morasseggar's involution, when there was certainly no cause for an insect to be further worried at his outer shell, a sister-nymph arrived a bit sooner than customary plus caught him gazing out the peephole, being fairly still, thus perfectly placed to appear like a sub-arthropod deviant. Morasseggar would not have been taken aback if she had declined entry inside, for she could not rectify the puncture when he was to hand, but not simply did she withdraw, she pounced backward as if in terror plus banged the blockage closed; an alien could well have considered he had been poised to anticipate her there intending to grab her. For sure he concealed himself below the spent epidermis immediately, yet he had to linger until next noon before she returned ditto, plus she appeared extra-nervous than customary. This let him comprehend how hideous the spectacle of him remained to her, plus that its form was compelled to continue being hideous, plus what a struggle it must charge her not to exit from the spectacle of the little section of his anatomy that poked out from below the exuvial epidermis. In turn to relieve her that, consequently, one time he held the spent exoskeleton over his back – plus composed it there in such manner as to conceal himself totally, so that still if she were to pass by she would not detect him. Had she thought the exuvial epidermis excessive, she could definitely have withdrawn it ditto, for it was sufficient plus lucid that this shielding plus impounding of himself was not probable to contribute to Morasseggar's well-being, but she disregarded it where it was, plus Morasseggar still imagined that he sensed an appreciative vibration across the floor as he raised the exuvia cautiously an ultra-little bit with his head to detect how she was receiving the novel compo-sition. For the primary nocturnals his progenitors could not attend themselves to the task of properly entering his cell, plus he frequently eavesdropped them transmit-ting positive reception to his sister-nymph's conduct, while in earlier times they had maybe attacked them for operating as they considered rather surfeit to the brood. But at the present, both progenitors frequently paused exterior to the obstruction, his inseminator plus his ergatogyne, as his sister-nymphs cleaned and waxed his cell, plus as soon as they exited out they were obliged to transmit to the progenitors in detail how matters were in the cell, what Morasseggar had consumed, how he had behaved himself, plus if there might be maybe some minor adaption in his state. His ergatogyne, further-more, started quite shortly to wish to call on him, but his inseminator plus sister-nymphs discouraged her with reverb patterns which Morasseggar eavesdropped ultra-closely plus generally acquiesced. After a while, though, she had to be restrained by communal power, plus when she rattled out loud: 'Do allow me inside to Morasseggar, he is my ill-fated spawn! Can't you appreciate that I have to go to him?' Morasseggar considered that it perhaps be alright to have her enter, yet not too often, surely, but maybe once in a while; she knew matters, nevertheless, much clearer than his sister-nymphs, who were merely larvae in spite of the labours they were creating plus had maybe seized on so hard a job simply out of pupated insensitivity. Morasseggar's will to detect his ergatogyne was shortly satisfied. During the solar duration he did not wish to display himself at the peephole, out of respect for his progenitors, but he would not walk ultra-distant around the little area of flooring he boasted, neither would he suffer reclining silently at slumber throughout the nocturnal, as his attraction for edibles was rapidly fading, so that for simple fun he had created the custom of walking criss-cross across the floor backwards plus forwards. He specially liked handstands; it was much nicer than reclining on the ground; one could expire quite openly; one's anatomy swayed plus tilted slightly; plus in the nearly euphoric captivation provoked by this volatility it sometimes occurred to his disbelief that he collapsed plus crumpled fleshy on the ground. Hitherto he now had his anatomy extra-enhanced plus in hand than before, plus any such large collapse effected him no injury. His sister-nymphs immediately detected the novel entertainment Morasseggar had cultivated for himself – he left handprints on the floor wherever he balanced – plus they synchronised the scheme in their capituli of offering him as distended an area as likely to walk about plus of eliminating any extraneous detritus accumulation that interfered with him. Yet this was surplus to what they should undertake all by themselves; they would not hazard solicit their inseminator to assist them; plus as for the dulotic workers, immature bugs who had not migrated from the colony, they might not be enlisted to assist, for they had implored as an exceptional dispensation that the nymphs could maintain the cell-obstruction closed plus release it only provisionally upon specific command; so there was nil alternative but to submit an application to their ergatogyne when the inseminator was absent. Plus when the mature bug did arrive, with vacillations of elated enthusiasm, which, however, killed off at the blockage of Morasseggar's cell. Morasseggar's sister-nymphs, for sure, went in first, to detect that all was in sequence before allowing ergatogyne inside. In a hurry Morasseggar heaved the spent exuvial epidermis. Plus this time he did not gaze from below it; he relinquished the stimulation of detecting his ergatogyne at this moment plus was merely happy that she had arrived in any case. 'Enter inside, he's not visible,' pulsed his sister-nymph, perceptibly escorting her ergatogyne in by the crochet. Morasseggar might currently hear the two insects wrestle to move the mass detritus accumulation from its location, plus his sister-nymph taking the load altruistically, devoid of adhering to the scolding of her ergatogyne who apprehended she could distend herself. It acquired elongated duration. After some period of hauling his ergatogyne signalled that the waste had best be remained where it was, for in the primary location it was ultra-dense plus might certainly not be exited prior to his inseminator's return to hive, plus located in the centre of the cell like that it might merely hinder Morasseggar's animations, as it was not absolutely clear that exiting the secretion might be rendering a benefit to Morasseggar. She was dispensed to attract to the counter; the spectacle of the cell produced her private aorta opaque, plus why cannot Morasseggar obtain the similar attraction, bearing in mind that he had been familiar with his own waste for so long plus could well sense dejection for lacking it. 'Plus has it not the appearance,' she rasped in a depleted tone – in detail she had been nearly only slightly vibrating all the duration as if to evade allowing Morasseggar, whose precise position she did not detect, eavesdrop even the timbre of her stridulations, for she was sure that he did not comprehend her transmissions – 'has it the appearance as though we were offering him, by exiting his detritus, that we have lapsed anticipation of his ever achieving health plus are right isolating him callously to himself? I detect it might be optimum to allow his cell precisely as it has forever been, so that as he arrives back to us he might discover all unaffected plus be capable all the ultra-effortlessly to disregard what has occurred hence.' On hearing these transmissions from his ergatogyne Morasseggar appreciated that the apparent absence of any intimate insect communication for the recent period added with the repetitiveness of isolation should have perplexed his processing, or else he might not explain for the detail that he had almost sincerely happily anticipated having his cell removed of waste accumulation. Did he actually wish his tepid cell, so contentedly filled with matured waste, to be metamorphosised into a nude lair in which he might definitely be capable to pace unhindered everywhere yet at cost of losing at the same time all memory of his insect past? He had truly been so close at the precipice of absentmindedness that merely the stridulation of his ergatogyne, which he had not eavesdropped for so far, had brought him in return from it. Nil must be exited away from his cell; all imperatives must remain as they were; he could not dissipate the nice effect of the detritus on his condition of mentality; plus even if the accumulation did hinder him in his reflex walking around plus around, that was zero disadvantage but an immense benefit. Sadly his sister-nymphs were of the opposite estimation; they had developed familiarity, yet not devoid of cause, to judge themselves authority in Morasseggar's interactions as opposed to the determinations of their own progenitors, plus so ergatogyne's counsel was at present sufficient to form their resolution on the exit least only of the solid detritus plus the uric waste, which had been the primary target, yet of all the detritus luckily excluding the crucial spent exuvial epidermis. This objective was not, certainly, simply the result of immature sedition plus of the synchronised behaviour newly adapted plus so suddenly plus at such price; the sister-nymphs had in truth established that Morasseggar required a deal of legroom to limp about in, since he certainly did not employ the detritus at all, to the degree that might be noticed. An additional feature may too have been the animated nature of the pubertal sister-nymphs, seeking to immerse themselves on all chance plus which currently lured them to embroider the terror of their sibling's conditions so that they could perform all the extra for him. Inside the cell where Morasseggar fermented in solitary no insect except themselves were probable ever to set labial palpi.

Plus so they were not to be shifted from their determination by their ergatogyne, who appeared furthermore to be uncomfortable in Morasseggar's cell plus consequently insecure of herself, was soon limited to quiet plus assisted her nymphs as pre-eminent as she might to shove the detritus exterior. Currently, Morasseggar might do without the waste, if necessary, but the exuvial epidermis he must keep. As soon as the insects had moved the detritus from his cell, grinding their epipharynxes as they pressed it, Morasseggar thrust his head out from beneath the husk to detect how he could intercede as nice yet warily as likely. But as dire fate would retain it, his ergatogyne was the primary arrival, leaving sister-nymphs fastened to the detritus in the adjacent cell where they were attempting to modify it all by themselves, without certainly shifting it from the location. His ergatogyne, nonetheless, was not used to the spectacle of him, it did nauseate her, plus so in panic Morasseggar withdrew pronto to the previous extremity of the exuvial exoskeleton, but could not stop the epidermis from tipping a bit in fascia. This was sufficient to place her on the aware. She hesitated, remained inanimate for a bit, plus then returned to the nymphs. Though Morasseggar repeatedly comforted himself that nil untoward was occurring, that only several pieces of detritus were being altered, he soon had to confess that all this crawling to plus fro of the insects, their petite morts, plus the dragging of detritus across the flooring influenced him as an immense commotion approaching from all elevations simultaneously, plus however much he inserted his head plus limbs plus cringed to the floor he was compelled to admit that he might not be capable to tolerate it for lengthy. They were emptying his cell; removing all he treasured; the detritus was previously scraped away; they were now relieving the waste which had nearly seeped into the floor; the waste at which represented all his assignments when he was scavenging, outside the hive– he had no more duration to squander in considering the nice aims of the insects, whose continuation he had by now nearly overlooked, for they were so fatigued that they were working in quiet plus nil might be eavesdropped but the delicate scratching of their claws. He hurried outside – the insects were resting tilted next to the detritus in the neighbour cell to allow them to re-energise – running amok, since he actually did not grasp what to salvage first, over to the cell-wall adjacent, which was by now almost vacant, he was attracted by the scavenged nymph ectohormone taken from the region beneath sternite armour plates, plus rapidly ran up to it plus pushed himself onto it, which was a nice plane to lean on to plus calmed his boiling tummy. This pheromone at minimum, which was fully concealed under him, was going to be removed by no insect. He rotated his head at the obstruction of the antechamber in order to see the insects as they returned. They had not awarded themselves much of a respite plus were now arriving; a sister-nymph had threaded her proleg around her ergatogyne plus was nearly propping her up. 'Anyway, what should we remove immediately?' fluttered a sister-nymph, rotating around. Her compound eyes linked Morasseggar's binary optics. She held her poise, probably on account of her ergatogyne, twisted her capitulum downwards to her ergatogyne, to maintain her from glimpsing upwards, plus rasped, though in a trembling, ad hoc manner: 'Follow now, best we return to the chamber for a bit?' Her motivations were lucidly sufficient to Morasseggar, she wished to place her ergatogyne in care plus then pursue him away from the cell-wall. Anyway, scarcely allow her to attempt it! He gripped to the pheromone-stained wall plus would not offer it up. He would prefer to jump in the insect's frons. But the sister-nymph's stridulation had unwittingly disturbed her ergatogyne, who acquired a scuttle to one side, obtained view of the large pink density leaning against the waxen cell wall, plus became actually aware that what she viewed was Morasseggar, buzzed in an ear-splitting, grating rasp: 'Oh DDT, oh DDT!', collapsed with spread-out appendages on top of the exuvia as though dying plus did not stir. 'Morasseggar!' vibrated his sister-nymph, quivering her crochet plus intensifying her ommatidia at him. This was the unique occurrence that she openly directed signals to him since his involution. She scuttled into the adjacent cell for some pungent concentrate with which to trigger her ergatogyne from her coma. Morasseggar wished to assist also – there was also time to save the trace – but he was clinging to the wall plus had to rip himself free; he then legged-it after his sister-nymph inside the adjacent cell as though he might counsel her, as he did before; but then had to remain useless at the rear of her; she in the meantime hunted amid many little glandular sac-secretions plus when she rotated around convulsed in panic at the vision of him, a sac dropped on the ground plus burst; a slither slapped Morasseggar's cheek plus some form of caustic chemical splattered him; neglecting to hesitate a bit further the sister-nymph collected up all the sacs she might bear plus scuttled to her ergatogyne with them; she flung the obstruction closed with her proleg. Morasseggar was hence separated from his ergatogyne, who was maybe almost expiring on account of him; he defied not to dilate the obstruction for terror of scaring away his sister-nymph, who must remain with her ergatogyne; there was nil that he might effect but hang around; plus fraught by remorse plus anxiety he started immediately to run around to plus fro everywhere, plus at last in his desperation, as the cell appeared to be spinning around him, collapsed downwards in the centre of the floor. A small period passed, Morasseggar was reclining there weakly plus all in the environs was silent, maybe this was a nice sign. Then the hive blockage stirred. The dulotic nymphs were certainly at work in the mess, plus his sister-nymphs should be forced to remove the obstruction. It was his inseminator. 'What's been occurring?' were his primary inflections; the sister-nymph's clypeus must have signalled all. Sister-nymph vibrated in a stifled tone, appearing to conceal her capitulum on his thorax: 'Ergatogyne has been wobbly, but she's alright now. Morasseggar's set free.' 'Right what I anticipated,' pulsed his inseminator, 'Right what I've been sounding out, but you nymphs could for no reason pay attention.' It was lucid to Morasseggar that his inseminator had seized the nastiest analysis of sister-nymph's all too concise declaration plus was presuming that Morasseggar had been culpable of some aggressive accomplishment. Hence Morasseggar should immediately attempt to placate his inseminator, as he had neither the duration nor resources for a justification. So he gravitated to the obstruction of his own cell plus squatted beside it, to allow his inseminator to detect immediately as he arrived inside from the chamber that his spawn had the nice purpose of returning into his cell forthwith plus that it was not needed to force him there, but that if only the blockage were removed he would vanish immediately. Though his inseminator was not in the disposition to notice such delicate divisions: 'Ah!' he rasped immediately he arrived, in a tenor which resonated at first irritated plus triumphant. Morasseggar withdrew his head from the obstruction plus raised it to gaze at his inseminator. Really, this was not the inseminator he had envisioned to himself; to confess he had been too engrossed recently in his novel entertainment of walking upright on handstand around the floor to seize the similar attention as prior in what was occurring somewhere else in the hive, plus he should actually be equipped for some alterations. Plus until now, plus until now, might that be his inseminator? The insect who would lay feebly ruined in repose whenever Morasseggar departed out on scavenging expeditions; who greeted his return at dusk still; who might not actually get up but merely dipped his weak antennae in welcome, plus on the uncommon times when he did depart with his brood, once or twice per season plus on active rituals, scurried between Morasseggar plus his ergatogyne, who were forced ponderous movers, even extra ponderous than they might, covered in his mature integument, crawling arduously onward with the assistance of his mandibles which he used most guardedly, when on earth he wished to communicate, almost always arrived to a stand-still plus congregated his aides around him? Now he was poised there in good form; covered with bristling vibrissae, such as soldier castes display; his muscular frontal rostrum swelling above the hard sternite prothorax; from below his ciliated ocellar triangle his dense compound eyes dashed bright plus piercing glimpses; his previously knotted bristles had been unsnarled all spiky on lateral sides of the central keel. He inclined his antennae in a broad brush transversely across the entire cell on to the exuvial remains, plus with abdomen cast backwards, his mid region tarsi tucked under his exoskeleton, pursued forward with a severe countenance at Morasseggar. Probably he did not himself consider what he intended to effect; anyway he raised his prolegs unusually elevated, plus Morasseggar was flabbergasted at the huge size of his arolium. Yet Morasseggar could not dare oppose him, attentive as he had been from the inception of his novel function that his inseminator considered simply the harshest methods applicable for coping with him. Plus so he legged-it before his inseminator, halting when his inseminator halted plus running forward ditto when his inseminator produced any form of animation. Like this they circulated the chamber a few durations without much final occurring, certainly the entire procedure did not even appear like a chase since it was effected so gradually. Plus so Morasseggar did not move rapidly, for he worried that his inseminator could seize as a bit of deviant evilness any venture of his across the floor. For sure, he might not continue this method for long, for as his inseminator made many animations per movement he had only to effect a limited set of actions. He was previously starting to feel gasping, just as in his previous operation his expiration had not been ultra-good. As he was lurching all along, attempting to condense his vigour on legging-it, barely maintaining his eyes wide; in his bewildered status not even considering of any other course than merely forward motion; plus having nearly overlooked that all directions were available to him – abruptly an object flippantly thrown fell near to the rear of him plus span in front of him. It was a sclerotized vermiform larva; a second hardened maggot ensued instantly; Morasseggar halted in panic; there was no purpose in running, for his inseminator was resolute on attacking him. He had armed each raptorial tarsi plus was catapulting maggot after maggot, devoid of finding very effective trajectory for the moment. The petite sallow maggots span around the ground as if mesmerised plus ricocheted into each other. A maggot flung without excessive energy scraped Morasseggar's back plus bounced off undamagingly. Yet one more ensuing instantly hit just on his back plus embedded inside the pink skin; Morasseggar wished to pull himself onward, as though this disquieting, unbelievable hurt might be left to the rear of him; but he sensed as if he were pinned to the co-ordinate plus compressed himself out in a total unhinging of all his faculties. With his final cognisant glance he spectated the obstruction to his cell being ripped asunder plus his eratogyne rushing out in front of a rasping sister-nymph, in her spiracle plate, for her breathing pores on her thoracic segment had slackened to allow her absorb more oxygen plus recuperate from her collapse, he witnessed his ergatogyne hastening at his inseminator, defoliating discarded exuvial layers one by one behind her upon the ground, tripping over her layers directly to his inseminator plus grappling him, in total symbiosis – but at this point Morasseggar's vision started to go on the blink – with her prolegs clutching around his inseminator's shaft as she pleaded for her spawn's operation. The grave hurt applied to Morasseggar, which rendered him inoperative for a great period – the maggot continued to embed in his anatomy as an evident aide memoire as no insect dared to do away with it – appeared to have forced even his inseminator recall that Morasseggar belonged to the colony, in spite of his current unlucky plus nauseating form, plus should not to be handled as an adversary, that, opposite, brood responsibility demanded the containment of hatred plus the implementation of tolerance, nil but tolerance. Plus while his hurt had made damage, maybe always, his ability of motion, plus for the period being it took long, long periods to walk across his cell like an ancient cripple – there was little cause now of walking around – yet in his own estimation he was adequately remunerated for this deterioration of health by the fact that in the direction of dusk the cell's obstruction to the antechamber, which he would observe fixedly for great periods previously, was now constantly withdrawn, so that reclining in the gloom of his cell, blind to the brood, he might detect them all around the glow-worm plus eavesdrop their vibrating stridulation, by common approval as it were, ultra-dissimilar from his earlier bugging. Truthful, their transmissions were deficient of the vigorous nature of previous durations, which he had always recalled with a peculiar languor in the temporary nests where he had been customary to pause from scavenging, fatigued out, on humid nesting. They were now chiefly ultra-quiet. Shortly after feeding his inseminator might decrease activity; his ergatogyne plus sister-nymphs might pulse each other quiet; his ergatogyne, poised near the glow-worm, secreted wood-pulp from her construction gland; his sister-nymphs, attended to labour in the copularium. Some durations his inseminator awoke, plus as if almost oblivious that he had been dormant throbbed to his ergatogyne: 'What a bunch of palp you're producing at the moment!' plus instantly dropped off ditto, as the insects exchanged a weary vibration. With a sort of obstinacy his inseminator persevered in maintaining his spent soldier caste exoskeleton on his frame even inside the hive; his exuvia lay in vain on the floor plus he lay dormant plus completely armoured where he sat, as if he were prepared for activity at any time plus even present merely at the service of his leader. As a consequence, his livery, which was scavenged to begin with, started to appear grimy, regardless of all the affectionate attentions of the ergatogyne plus sister-nymphs to maintain it spotless, plus Morasseggar frequently exhausted entire dusks looking at the numerous disfigurements on the sclerite plates, polished by dermal glands keeping the exoskeleton in a nice condition, in which the mature insect lay dormant in severe discomposure plus yet relatively serenely. As the ambient temperature dropped in the chamber his ergatogyne attempted to stir his inseminator with soft stridulations plus to convince him into his own cell, for laying there he might lose too much body temperature. Yet with the obstinacy that had gripped him in maturity he constantly persisted on inactivity, and merely through the maximum of triggering might he finally scuttle into his own cell. Nevertheless tenaciously Morasseggar's eratogyne plus sister-nymphs maintained pressure with soft vibrations, he might continue gradually trembling his capitulum for a good period, maintaining metabolic inactivity, plus declined to raise his abdomen from the floor. The eratogyne nipped at his scutum, fluttering nectar-nothings in his auditory membrane, the sister-nymphs abandoned their work in the copularium to their eratogyne's assistance, but Morasseggar's inseminator was not to be triggered. He might only droop down flat on the floor and threaten total thermal transfer. Not before the insects levered him up by the proximal joins at his appendages did he actively peer at them, one by one, habitually with the vibration: 'Here is my function. This is the tranquillity plus calm of my maturity.' Plus propped upon the brood he might lever himself up, with trouble, as though a colossal encumbrance to himself, endure them to escort him as far as his cell's obstruction plus then gesticulate them off plus continue solitary, as the eratogyne deserted her mastication plus the sister-nymphs their maternity labour in orderliness to pursue after him plus assist him beyond. Who might discover duration, inside this weary plus fatigued brood, to fret about Morasseggar surplus than was completely necessary? The hive was depleted more plus more; the dulotic workers found themselves expelled; a giant exoskeletal parasite with pruinose bristles orbiting her capitulum entered in each sunrise plus dusk to feed on the accumulated detritus; all else was completed by Morasseggar's eratogyne, as well as huge mounds of palp. Even assorted brood bits and pieces, which his ergatogyne plus sister-nymphs horded, had to be executed, as Morasseggar found one dusk from eaves-dropping them all rattling to the effect. Yet what they seeped for most was the detail that they might depart the hive which was presently much too cavernous for their immediate conditions, yet they might not suppose of any methods to move Morasseggar. But Morasseggar noticed lucidly that deliberation for him was not the primary problem inhibiting the ejection, for they might have simply moved him by force of numbers; what actually forced them from migrating to another hive was instead their own total despondency plus the conviction that they had been selected for a calamity such as had certainly not occurred to any other colony. They satisfied the universal burdens of impoverished insects, the inseminator scavenged scraps, the ergatogyne gave her vigour to the dulotic vacuum while the sister-nymphs cooperated in the eusocial cultivation of colony pupa, but in excess of these tasks they had no more energy. Plus the gash in Morasseggar's back started to plague him anew. Once when his eratogyne plus sister-nymphs, following shifting his inseminator into his quarters, returned, abandoned their labour, moved intimate to each other plus poised clypeus by clypeus; when his eratogyne, feeling at his cell, rasped: 'repair that opening now, naiad,' plus he was put into shade ditto, as in the adjacent cell the insects intermingled their secretions or maybe poised inactive. Morasseggar barely slept at all nocturnal or by daylight. He was commonly plagued by the thought that next duration the obstruction was removed he might seize the brood's matters in hand ditto as he previously did; once again, afterwards this elongated period, there occurred in his thinking the apparition of the queen plus the nastusus, the scavengers plus the pubertal insects, the ordinance-drone who was so imperceptive, the dulotic cohorts enslaved on raiding expeditions– they all became visible, along with foreign arthropoda or insects he had almost overlooked, yet instead of assisting him plus his brood they were all distant plus he was happy as they disappeared. On other periods he might not appear disposed to vex about his brood, he was merely absorbed with anger at the method they were abandoning him, plus while he had little lucid impression of what he could want to feed on he might form tactics for finding into the edibles chamber to seize the edibles that were taking into account all his owing, even if he were not famished. His sister-nymphs no further effected consideration to deliver him what could particularly satisfy him, but at sunrise plus at noon, prior to departure, hastily shoved inside his cell with ambivalent tarsi any edible that was vacant, plus in the dusk removed it ditto with one brush of the pecten, neglectful of whether it had been simply nibbled, or – as most common to occur – left unharmed. The maintenance of his cell, which a sister-nymph undertook in the dusk, might not have been more hurriedly carried out. Smudges of filth smeared along the cell walls, here plus there accumulated mounds of soil plus waste. Early on Morasseggar used to position himself in a peculiarly disgusting place as his sister-nymphs entered, to point the finger at them with it, so to say. But he might have crouched there for ever without obtaining any adaption; they might detect the detritus as well as he did, but they had merely produced their wits to renounce it unaided. Plus yet, with an irritation that was novel to them, which appeared anyway to have plagued the total brood, they covetously protected their right to police Morasseggar's cell. His eratogyne once committed his cell to a systematic cleansing, accomplished merely by measure of ejaculating water from her frontal rostrum – all this damp for sure irritated Morasseggar plus he reclined spread-eagle, moody plus still below the exuvia – however, she was properly disciplined for it. Barely had one of his sister-nymphs perceived the modified feature of his cell that dusk than she hurried in raised anger into the antechamber plus, in spite of the entreatingly surrendered antennae of her eratogyne, ruptured into a tempest of defensive bile, as her progenitors – her inseminator had without doubt been frightened from dormancy – peered on initially in powerless astonishment; they, too, started to enter into activity; the inseminator rebuked the ergatogyne on his anterior for not reserving the maintenance of Morasseggar's cell to a sister-nymph; rattled at the sister-nymph on his posterior that never ever was she in particular to be sanctioned to maintain Morasseggar's cell alone; as the ergatogyne tried to drag the inseminator into his cell, because he was beside himself with aggression; the sister-nymph, trembling with vibration, then hammered upon the floor with her claws; plus Morasseggar murmured noisily with anger since not a single insect considered repairing the obstruction to release him such a display plus so much racket. Still, even though the sister-nymphs, fatigued by their labour, had become exhausted in maintaining Morasseggar as they did previously, there was little requirement for his eratogyne's interference or for Morasseggar's becoming derelict at all. The hemimetabola was there. This mature insect, whose muscular exoskeletal casing had permitted her to endure the most horrible an elongated operation might tender, by no means withdrew from Morasseggar. Devoid of inquisitiveness she had on one occasion by luck released the blockage of his cell plus at the vision of Morasseggar, who, seized by exposure, started to run to plus fro despite no such insect was pursuing him, simply remained poised with her pedipalps retracted. From that point she under never neglected to unblock his obstruction a bit for a period, sunrise plus sunset, to take a peek at him. Firstly she even used to beckon him to her with buzz-words which seemingly she mistook to be pleasant, such as: 'Come on, then, you dirty old man!' or 'Have a gander at the dirty old man, then!' To such addresses Morasseggar produced no reply, but remained still where he stood, as if the obstruction had not been unblocked. Rather than being authorized to bother him so stupidly as the fancy grabbed her, she might instead have been told to cleanse his cell, that hemimetabola! One time, early one sunrise – torrential drizzle was battering on the hive, maybe a symptom that temperate times were on the way – Morasseggar was so infuriated when she started talking to him ditto that he ran toward her, as if to assault her, however unhurriedly plus unconvincingly. Yet the insect rather than indicating fear simply readied her pedipalps elevated up and poised with her gaping hypognathous; it was lucid that she intended to strike Morasseggar's head. 'So you're not approaching any closer?' she rasped, as Morasseggar rotated away ditto pronto. Morasseggar was soon feeding barely nil-by-mouth. Just as he happened to bypass the edibles put out for him did he snatch a little of something and put it in his mouth as a distraction, left it there for a while plus normally vomited it out ditto. Initially he considered it was vexation over the condition of his cell that inhibited his appetite, yet he quickly adapted to the numerous alterations in his cell. It had become a routine in the brood to shove objects into his cell that there was no space for elsewhere, plus there were many of these currently, since other proximate cells were occupied by new insect inhabitants. These severe insects– all of them with setaceous antennae, as Morasseggar once saw through a fissure in the blockage – had a fervour for method, not simply in their own cells, since they were new components of the hive, engrossed in all its schedules, specially in the mess. Surplus matter, not to mention filthy matter they would not tolerate. In addition, they had conveyed with them nearly all of the secretions they required. For this rationale countless objects could be got rid of yet not be completely disposed of what's more. All these things established their entrance into Morasseggar's cell. The feeding detritus similarly plus the scavenging detritus. Everything not required for the tick was merely thrown into Morasseggar's cell by the hemimetabola, who did anything in a rush; luckily Morasseggar noticed the thing prior, plus the claw that gripped it. Maybe she planned to seize the objects away again as duration plus chance afforded, or to gather them pending discarding them all in a pile outside, yet in detail they rested where she transpired to exit them, apart from when Morasseggar shoved his path through the debris plus budged it a bit, primarily from need, because he had not cell enough to walk in, but afterwards with escalating pleasure, though following such expeditions, being melancholic plus fatigued to mortality, he might lay still for ages. Plus as the insects commonly fed in the hive in the communal chamber, the obstruction onto the chamber now remained closed often, but Morasseggar resigned himself quite simply to the closing of the blockage, for commonly enough on sunsets when it was dilated he had ignored it totally plus reclined in the shadowy crook of his cell, slightly disregarded by the brood. Yet one time the hemimetabola allowed the blockage dilate a bit plus it remained exposed even when the insects arrived for feeding plus a glow-worm was radiant. They placed themselves at the peak of the chamber where previously Morasseggar plus his insemi-nator plus ergatogyne had consumed their prey, outspread their pedipalps plus sharpened their mandibles. Instantly his ergatogyne became visible in the former obstruction portal with a sac of flesh plus near to the rear of her his sister-nymph with a larva of a moth. The edibles wriggled with nerves. The insects preyed above the edibles placed in front of them as though to inspect prior to consuming, in truth the insect in the hub, who appeared to assert entitlement over the others, tore a segment of flesh, clearly to determine if it were immature or might be expelled from the chamber. He displayed contentment, plus Morasseggar's ergatogyne plus sister-nymph, who had been observing nervously, expired unreservedly plus began to vacillate. The brood captured its proteins in the mess. However, Morasseggar's inseminator arrived into the chamber prior to disappearing inside the mess plus with a drawn out retraction, capitulum lowered, produced a reverb tone. The insects became erect plus vibrated their chelicerae. They consumed their edibles loudly. It appeared incredible to Morasseggar that amongst the numerous sounds arriving into the cell he might forever differentiate the resonance of palping maxilla, as though this were an indication to Morasseggar that an insect required chelicera fangs, to feed, plus that with fangless maws even of the optimum form an insect might do zilch. 'I'm sufficiently famished,' whispered Morasseggar miserably to himself, 'yet not for that type of edible. How these insects are gorging themselves, plus here am I tortured by malnourishment!' During that dusk – plus throughout the totality of his duration in the hive Morasseggar could not recall ever having eavesdropped such vehement stridulation over edibles. The insects had previously completed their feast, the hub insect had secreted from its sebaceous gland for the other insects to palp, plus currently they were setting to work performing secondary mastication. As attractive stridulations vibrated their auditory membranes, raised upon their appendages, plus went on tip-tip to the antechamber portal where they waited clustered in sync. Their animations might have been eavesdropped elsewhere, for Morasseggar's inseminator rasped: 'is the signal alarming you, insect brethren? It can be halted immediately.' 'To the polar opposite,' rattled a drone, 'might not the nymphs arrive plus placed in this cell, near us, where it is ultra-extra-expedient plus snug-as-a-bug?' 'Oh for sure,' fluttered Morasseggar's inseminator, as though he were originating the ritual sounds himself. The insect drones returned into the chamber plus paused. Currently Morasseggar's inseminator returned with the sister-nymphs. His sister-nymphs silently effused conditions preparing to begin colony vibration; his progenitors, who had certainly not been required to billet proximate cells before so had an inflated under-standing of the civility due to cleptoparasitic visitors, dared not endeavour to relax their poise; his inseminator propped up the blockage, lebaellum thrust below his integument; yet his ergatogyne was presented a position by one of the insects plus, since she was poised just at the point the drone offered, squat downwards in a spot adjacent. Morasseggar's sister-nymphs started to quiver; the inseminator plus ergatogyne, commencing which-ever position, fixedly observed the ritual animations of their abdomen. Morasseggar, engrossed by the oscilla-tions, gambled to shift a bit until his head was truly out-side his cell and inside the chamber. He sensed little astonishment at his mounting absence of concern for the others; there had been a duration when he delighted himself on being concerned. Plus yet right on this juncture he had ultra-cause than before to conceal him-self, as indebted to the quantity of dirt which encrusted dense in his cell plus puffed into the atmosphere at the smallest animation, he, also, was dusted with dirt; fuzz plus pubes plus left-overs of edibles snagged him, attached to his legs plus draped from his flank; his ambivalence to all was much too encompassing to cause him to squat on his posterior plus chafe himself sanitary on the floor, as he had effected a few durations before. Plus despite his state, no guilt discouraged him from forwarding a bit over the floor of the chamber. For sure, no insect was conscious of him. The intimate brood was utterly rapt in pheromonal activity; the encroaching insects, though, who positioned themselves, mandibles primed, greatly too near to the active females so as to receive the attractors – which might have upset the sister-nymphs – had rapidly withdrawn, half-vacillating with cowering capituli, plus remained there as his inseminator twitched an apprehensive feeler toward them. Certainly, they were displaying it more than palpable that they had been under whelmed in the anticipation of scenting active behavioural chemicals, that they had had ultra-adequate supply plus merely out of weak resistance endured a prolonged friction of their harmony. From the method they maintained secreting brown liquid from their sebaceous glands and smelt it through their labellum plus hypopharynx one might deduce their agitation. Plus yet Morasseggar's sister-nymphs were emitting so attractively. Their cephalus propped to the side, absorbedly plus ambivalently their compound eyes pursuing the thoracic animations of each other. Morasseggar stepped a bit forward plus kneeled and bent his head down to the floor so that it could be likely for his eyes to encounter his sister-nymphs. Was he really a human, when pheromonal behaviour had such an impression on him? He sensed as though the passage were dilating in front of him to the mysterious sustenance he desired. He was resolute to shove onward until he arrived at his sister-nymphs, to tag at their apical area plus so let them understand that they were to enter inside his own cell, for no insect out here was partial to their ritual as he might be partial to it. He might certainly not release them from his cell, as a minimum, not so further as he survived; his terrifying visage might become, primarily, functional to him; he might observe at the obstruction of his cell plus gob at trespassers; yet his sister-nymphs might require little restriction, they might remain with him of their own volition; they might repose next to him under the exuvial epidermis, lower their auditory membranes to him plus listen to him divulge that he had the solid intent of forming a fission colony, and even a claustral foundation, plus that, but for his calamity, before now – surely elongated before now? – he might have broadcast it to all neglecting any isolated protest. Following this admission his sister-nymphs might be so affected that they might seep, plus Morasseggar might then elevate himself up plus kiss them on the paraglossa. 'Inseminator!' rattled the hub insect, plus antennated, devoid of concern for massacring the nymph's trans-mission, at Morasseggar, now stalking unhurriedly onwards. The stridulation dropped dead, the hub insect primarily rasped to the brood with a tremor of the capitulum plus then peered at Morasseggar ditto. Substitute to herding Morasseggar out, his inseminator instead thought it ultra-vital to start by pacifying the insects, though they were not yet irritated plus in fact found Morasseggar more compelling than the nymph ritual. He rushed at them plus, multiplied his appendage area, attempting to impel them return inside their own cell plus simultaneously to obstruct their view of Morasseggar. They instantly started to be actually a bit vexed, one might not determine if so because of the mature insect's conduct since it had only emerged on them inadvertently that they possessed such a resident as Morasseggar. They stipulated details of his inseminator, they brandished their distally clavated antennae like him, jerked agitatedly at their bristles, plus only with disinclination withdrew to their cells. In the interim Morasseggar's sister-nymphs, who poised there as if misplaced when their dance was so unexpectedly ceased, became animated again, drew themselves symbiotically after pausing for a bit nerve-racked plus lynched plus gaping at the scene, started crawling past their eratogyne, who was set combating for oxygen, plus scuttling inside the insect's cells where they were instantly being steered by their inseminator ultra-fast. One might detect the domestic secretions and comforts hasty below the nymph's drone-worker crochets, preparing the cells in proper regulation. Prior to, the insects had arrived at their cells where the nymphs had completed assembling the comforts plus crept outwards. The more mature insect appeared even more to be totally obsessed by his obstinate monadic singularity that he was failing to remember all the value he might display to the brood. He maintained forcing them forward plus shifting them until in the portal of one cell the hub insect stamped his arolium pad noisily on the ground plus so conveyed himself to an arrest. 'I implore to broadcast,' transmitted the insect, raising one feeler plus feeling toward Morasseggar's eratogyne plus sister-nymph, 'that since such filthy circumstances operate in this brood' – here his labellum tip retched upon the ground with ardent terseness – 'I offer you notification on the blemish. Logically I refuse you protein remittance, for the dormancy spent here, inversely, we may chew over bringing forcible engagement and hostile reparation, founded on accusation – trust me – that can be simply prone to the swarm.' He stopped plus peered directly forward, as though he anticipated more. In detail the other insects instantly hurried into the pause: 'Plus we, legion, offer warning on the blemish.' On that he mawed the blockage open and disappeared. Morasseggar's inseminator, probing with his antennae, scurried plus dropped onto the floor; it appeared as though he might unfold himself there for a normal sunset diapause, yet the noticeable twitching of his capitulum, which were involuntary, displayed that he was distant from dormancy. Morasseggar had merely remained silently all the duration on the point where the insects had observed him. Displeasure at the collapse of his scheme, maybe plus the feebleness occurring from excess starvation, made it unlikely for animation. He worried, with a just quantity of conviction, that at any instant the broad apprehension would release itself in a collective assault on him, plus he sat in anticipation. He did not respond even to the sound produced by his ergatogyne's vacillating prolegs which emitted a reverberating shrill. 'My valued progenitors,' rasped his sister-nymphs, tapping the floor by way of prologue, 'matters can't continue like this. Maybe you do not notice that, but we do. We refuse to pronounce our sibling's moniker in the attendance of this monster, plus so all we demand is: we should attempt to dispose of it. We have attempted its cultivation, plus to ignore it as far as is arthropodly possible, plus we do not consider any insect might scold us in the least.' 'They are ultra-than just,' vibrated Morasseggar's inseminator to himself. His ergatogyne, who was remaining suffocated for loss of inhalation, started to splutter vacantly into her mandibles with an extreme pattern in her compound eyes. His sister-nymphs hurried to her plus clutched her capitulum. His inseminator's neurons appeared to have abandoned their imprecision at the sister-nymph's stridulation, he poised ultra-erect, clawing his armour sclerite plates that sat amid feeding debris on the floor from the insect's feast plus from duration to duration gazed at the inanimate form of Morasseggar. 'We should attempt to dispose of it,' his sister-nymphs pulsed out loud to their inseminator, as their eratogyne was spluttering too loud to absorb their vibrations, 'it might be the killing of all of us, we might detect that arriving.

When a swarm has to scavenge as tough as we do, all of us, a swarm cannot suffer this perpetual anguish in the hive to add to it. As a minimum we cannot suffer it further.' Plus they erupted into such fervent vacillation that secretions splashed on their eratogyne's clypeus, which she lapped automatically. 'My valued,' rattled the mature bug compassionately, plus with clear understanding, 'yet what can we accomplish?' Morasseggar's sister-nymphs simply rubbed their feelers to display their feeling of helplessness that had instantly surmounted them throughout their convulsions, in distinction to their previous poise. 'If he might comprehend us,' ground their inseminator, not whole curiously; the sister-nymphs, still discharging, violently gesticulated an antennae to display how unimaginable that would be. 'If he might comprehend us,' pulsed the mature bug, shielding his ommatidia to reflect on the nymph's estimation that comprehension was unlikely, 'then maybe we could arrive at an inquiline contract with him. Yet how it is –' 'He should depart,' shook Morasseggar's sister-nymph, 'this is the final solution, inseminator. You should simply attempt to dispose of the notion that here is Morasseggar. The presumption supposed so far is the source of all our dilemma. Yet how can this be Morasseggar? If here were Morasseggar, he definitely would have comprehended that arthropods cannot function with such homo sapiens, plus he'd have departed of his own volition. Then we might not have him, yet we'd be capable to continue functioning plus store his pheromone in credit. As is, this human plagues us, annoys our colony, clearly desires the total hive to itself plus might have us all rest in the soil. Only notice, inseminator,' the nymphs rattle in unanimity, 'it's doing it ditto!' Plus in an admission of alarm that was entirely unintelligible to Morasseggar they even abandoned their ergatogyne, actually leaping away from her as though they might prefer to forfeit their ergatogyne than remain so close to Morasseggar, plus gathered at the back of their inseminator, who also elevated upwards, being merely disturbed by their anxiety, plus almost unclenched his pedipalps outwards as though to defend them. But Morasseggar had not a least ambition of scaring any insect, even least his sister-nymphs. He had only started to rotate around to limp back to his cell, yet it was definitely a worrying manoeuvre to observe, since due to his crippled circumstance he might not implement the tricky revolving actions, apart from by raising his head high plus placing one foot against the floor over plus over again. He lingered plus glanced around. His nice purpose appeared to have been noticed; the panic had merely been temporary. Now they were all observing him in dismal quiet. His ergatogyne rested flat, her prolegs awkwardly folded plus compressed together, her compound optics nearly inactive for utter fatigue; his inseminator plus his sister-nymphs were clustered proximately, some of his sister-nymphs scaffolding the mature bug's poise. Maybe I can continue revolving around, thought Morasseggar, plus started his attempt ditto. He might not force himself from gasping with the endeavour, plus had to stop now plus then to seize a lungful of air. Nor did any of the insects trouble him, he was left completely to himself. When he had finished the manoeuvre he started immediately to limp back. He was astonished at the expanse dividing him from his cell plus could not comprehend how in his pallid condition he had coped to achieve the identical excursion a moment ago, nearly without mentioning it. Bent on walking as rapid as likely, he scarcely observed that not an isolated vibration, nor a quiver from his brood, impeded his advance. Only as he was by now in the threshold of his cell did he return his head around, not fully, for his neck muscles were becoming sore, but adequate to detect that nil had altered to the rear apart from that his sister-nymphs had risen. His final glimpse glanced on his ergatogyne, who was now almost overwhelmed by dormancy. Barely was he clearly within his cell when the obstruction was quickly shoved closed and new wax cerumen used to glue it shut. The unexpected sound to his posterior frightened him such that his legs collapsed below him. It was his sister-nymphs who had displayed such alacrity. They had been poised prepared plus had produced a nimble pounce forward, Morasseggar had not even eavesdropped them impending, plus they rasped 'Eventually!' to their progenitors as they secreted the cerumen in the gaps. 'What hence?' said Morasseggar to himself, peering around in the gloom. Soon he found that he was presently incapable of moving a limb. This did not stagger him, instead it appeared abnormal that he might ever really have been capable to walk on these two legs. Otherwise he felt moderately relaxed. Factually, his total anatomy was throbbing, but it appeared that the hurt was steadily decreasing plus might ultimately bypass altogether. The putrid maggot in his back plus the swollen eruption circling it, all swathed with debris, now barely concerned him. He considered his brood with compassion plus affection. The verdict that he should evaporate was one he supposed even ultra-fervently than his sister-nymphs – if that were at all possible. In this condition of expression-less reflection he lingered serenely. The initial increase of solar particles in the atmosphere exterior to his little vent permeated his awareness on one occasion more. Then his head descended to the floor unaided plus from his nostrils expired the final slight exit of air. When the hemimetabola appeared early on next sunrise – what divided by her force or her impetuosity she entered the hive so noisily, despite how regularly she had been implored to the opposite, no insect in the brood could maintain any calm aestivation in the course of her presence – she perceived naught uncustomary as she stole her habitula glancing into Morasseggar's cell. She considered he was laying down still deliberately, feigning bad humour; she accredited him with all forms of human acumen. As she possessed raptorially set pedipals she attempted to prickle him up with them from the threshold. When that also made no response she deemed aggravated plus jabbed at him a bit rigorously, plus only where she had shoved him over the floor neglecting any friction was her deliberation triggered. It did not take further to ascertain the reality of the trouble, plus her manifold gaped, she emitted a shrill, yet did not squander much duration to rip open first the inseminator's plus eratogyne's cells plus rasp inside the blackness at optimum stridulation: 'Just peer at this, it's deceased; it's laying here expired plus finished!' The inseminator plus ergatogyne startled inside their quarters plus before they apprehended the character of the hemimetabola's declaration had a bit of complexity in surmounting the trauma of it. But when they exited their cells swiftly, one on either side; in this confusion they crossed the threshold of Morasseggar's cell. In the interim the obstructions to the cells all around the antechamber became dilated, too, where nymphs nested during dormancy; the nymphs were all wholly decent as though they had not been at rest, which appeared to be established by the dimness of their antennae. 'Deceased?' rasped ergatogyne, peering inquisitively at the hemimetabola, though she might have inspected for herself. 'I might articulate so,' vibrated the hemimetabola, proving her words by pushing Morasseggar's carcass further along with her appendages. The ergatogyne produced a gesture as though to interrupt her, but curbed it. 'Right,' fluttered the inseminator, 'Praise be to

DDT.' He shivered, plus the insects duplicated his pattern. The nymphs whose compound eyes under no circumstances left the carcass, pulsed: 'Just feel how emaciated he was. It's such a long duration since he's consumed something. The edibles exited again just as they entered.' To be sure, Morasseggar's corpse was totally bony plus dehydrated, as might only now be noticed as it was no longer moving or crouching plus nothing stopped the swarm from observing intimately at it. 'Come inside next to us, for a bit,' gently rubbed the ergatogyne to the sister-nymphs with a trembling tone, plus the nymphs, not devoid of peering backwards at the carcass, pursued their progenitors into their quarters. The hemimetabola reset the obstruction plus tore the vent airy. Though it was very premature in the sunrise a peculiar gentleness was traceable in the clean atmosphere. The insect residents surfaced from their cells plus were stunned to detect no edibles; they had been overlooked. 'Where are our edibles?' rattled the hub resident spitefully to the hemimetabola. Yet she placed her claw to her mandible rapidly, devoid of a vibration, specified by signs that they might enter Morasseggar's cell. They acquiesced plus remained, their crochets embedded in the envelop of their fairly dilapidated integuments, circling Morasseggar's carcass in the cell where it was currently totally luminous. At this point the wax obstruction of the inseminator's cell gaped plus the inseminator become visible in his soldier-drone garb, supported by the ergatogyne and nymphs on each flank. They all appeared a bit agitated; the nymphs covered their genas under their inseminator's pleuron. 'Exit the hive immediately!' buzzed the inseminator, plus his distally swollen antennae directed to the exit devoid of extricating himself from the nymphs. 'What do you insinuate by that?' vacillated the hub insect, siezed a bit aback, with a frail denticulate. The other insects rendered their pedipalps geniculate behind them plus maintained rubbing them together, as if expectant of a first-rate battle in which they were sure to come out the conquerors. 'I indicate right what I stridulate,' buzzed the inseminator plus moved forward in an undiluted path with his brood towards the insect. He stayed his position primarily silently, sight deflected at the floor as though his attention were forming an adapted pattern in his capitulum. 'Then allow us exit, by any measure,' he pulsed, plus peered upwards at the inseminator as though an unexpected rush of meekness he were anticipating some transformed endorsement for this proposal. The inseminator simply indicated agreement for a moment once or twice with potent compound stare. Upon which the insect actually did depart with extended tread into the tunnel, his social group had entirely ceased rubbing their appendages for some moments plus now set off scuttling after him as if terrified that the inseminator could arrive into the exit tunnel prior to them plus incise them from their sovereign. In the tunnel they scavenged some consolation protein plus cowered quietly plus exited the hive. With a mistrust which verified reasonably groundless the inseminator plus the nymphs pursued them to the tunnel-mouth; perching over its aperture lip they observed the insects little by little disappearing downwards, diminishing from vision at the tunnel's bend, plus when an established colony scavenger met them plus crossed them in the tunnel arriving righteously with a chrysalis gripped in his mandibles, the inseminator plus the nymphs abandoned their position as though a weight had been taken from them. They settled on submitting to dormancy plus taking a local expedition; they had not only warranted such a interval from labour, but physiologically required it. Plus so they sat down and tapped out their reprove from work; While they were vacillating, the hemimetabola entered in to pulse her departure, as her sunrises duties were terminated. Primarily they merely tremoureil devoid of direct contact, yet as she maintained hovering there they eyed her impatiently. 'So?' rubbed the inseminator. The hemimetabola poised gaping in the threshold as though she maintained fine data to communicate to the brood but intended not to transmit a bit of it if not correctly triggered. The small clavate feather erect upon her on her capitulum, which had aggravated the inseminator from the time when she was colonised, was signalling promiscuously in every bearing. 'So, what is it next?' vibrated the ergatogyne, who needed ultra-esteem from the hemimetabola than the others. 'Oh,' fluttered the hemimetabola, vibrating so pleasantly that she might not instantly resume, 'simply this, you do not have to worry about what method to dispose of the entity in that cell. It's been attended to already.' The ergatogyne plus nymphs bent over as though engrossed; the inseminator, who could detect that she was keen to start reciting it all molecularly, halted her with a critical claw. But as she was not permitted to recite her account, she recalled the massive rush she was in, being clearly intensely angry: 'Goodbye, all,' she vibrated, whirling off violently, plus exited with a fearsome shatter of cerumen. 'She will be granted autonomy henceforth' rasped the inseminator, but nothing from his ergatogyne nor nymphs did he obtain any response, for the hemimetabola appeared to have devastated ditto the tranquillity they had almost accomplished. They emerged, grasping the brood rigid. The inseminator observed them silently for a bit. Then he vibrated out loud: 'Come too, instantly. Allow the previous be previous. Plus you could have some deliberation for me.' The insects conformed instantly, accelerated to him, plus embraced him. Then they exited the hive collectively, which was extra than they had maintained for ages, plus journeyed into the nature beyond the hive. The new expedition was overflowing with humid sunbeams. Moving contentedly they surveyed their forecast, plus it seemed on near scrutiny that these were not all negative, for the missions they had acquired, which hitherto they had for no reason shared, were all worthy plus likely to escort to enhanced matters anon on. The best instant advance in status might for sure occur from such migration and forming another hive; they wished to seize a more efficient but also superior positioned plus ultra-effortlessly managed hive than the dwelling they had now abandoned, which Morasseggar had chosen. As they were hence communicating, it dawned on both the inseminator plus the ergatogyne, symbiotically, while they happened to be alert to their nymph's rising exuberance, that despite all the distress of fresh effects, which had caused their genas pallid, they had blossomed into robust naiads with perfect form. They became silenced plus automatically swapped signals of total harmony, having arrived at the synthesis that it might presently be duration to acquire excellent inseminators for them. Plus it was as a verification of their adapted reflexes plus first-rate drive that at the termination of their expedition their nymphs pounced to their claws plus tensed their muscular exoskeletons.

FROZEN TEARS
PRESENTED BY JOHN RUSSELL

AUTHORS' INDEX

What follows is an extremely subjective selection
of texts, the majority of which have been extracted
from the journal *Curtains*, published by Paul Buck
throughout the 1970's. *Curtains* represents for me a
great act of intellectual generosity, a profound
contribution, somehow unimaginable in this age of
'literature'. The bibliographies reproduced here
have changed in my perception from concrete
information to concrete image; a picture of the
energies collecting at that time. As Paul rightly
said to me recently, "we were right to build our
own libraries".

Dedicated to Jim Russell (1933–2002)

Thanks

John Russell would like to thank Ruth Blacksell,
Becky Russell, Janice Hart, Katharine Heap,
Raymund Brinkmann, Peter Lloyd Lewis, David
Burrows at ARTicle Press and Martin McGeown
& Andrew Wheatley at The Cabinet Gallery.

Graham Ramsay would like to thank Kieron Corless.

Esther Planas's *Thee* is dedicated to Marc, Pedro
and Ivan Z.

Edited by John Russell
Cover design: John Russell
Page design and layout: Ruth Blacksell

Published by ARTicle Press
Birmingham Institute of Art & Design
University of Central England
Margaret Street
Birmingham B3 3BX
UK

UCE
Birmingham

THE LONDON
INSTITUTE **LONDON COLLEGE OF PRINTING**
CAMBERWELL COLLEGE OF ARTS CENTRAL
SAINT MARTINS COLLEGE OF ART AND DESIGN
CHELSEA COLLEGE OF ART AND DESIGN
LONDON COLLEGE OF FASHION